The Madness of Gods

BOOKS BY R.S. MOULE

THE ERLAND SAGA

The Fury of Kings

The Hunger of Empires

The Madness of Gods

R.S. MOULE

SECOND SKY

Published by Second Sky in 2024

An imprint of Storyfire Ltd.
Carmelite House
50 Victoria Embankment
London EC4Y 0DZ

www.secondskybooks.com

ISBN: 978-1-83525-593-3
eBook ISBN: 978-1-83525-592-6

For Tinks. My wife said I couldn't dedicate a book to our cat, but it turns out she was wrong.

The Ulvatian Imperium
over the Bleak Hills
Whitew
Irith
Pale River
Lordsferry
Violet Hall
Gwynæthwood
Halord's Bridge
Fortlands
Little Rive
Permouth
Cursed Bridge

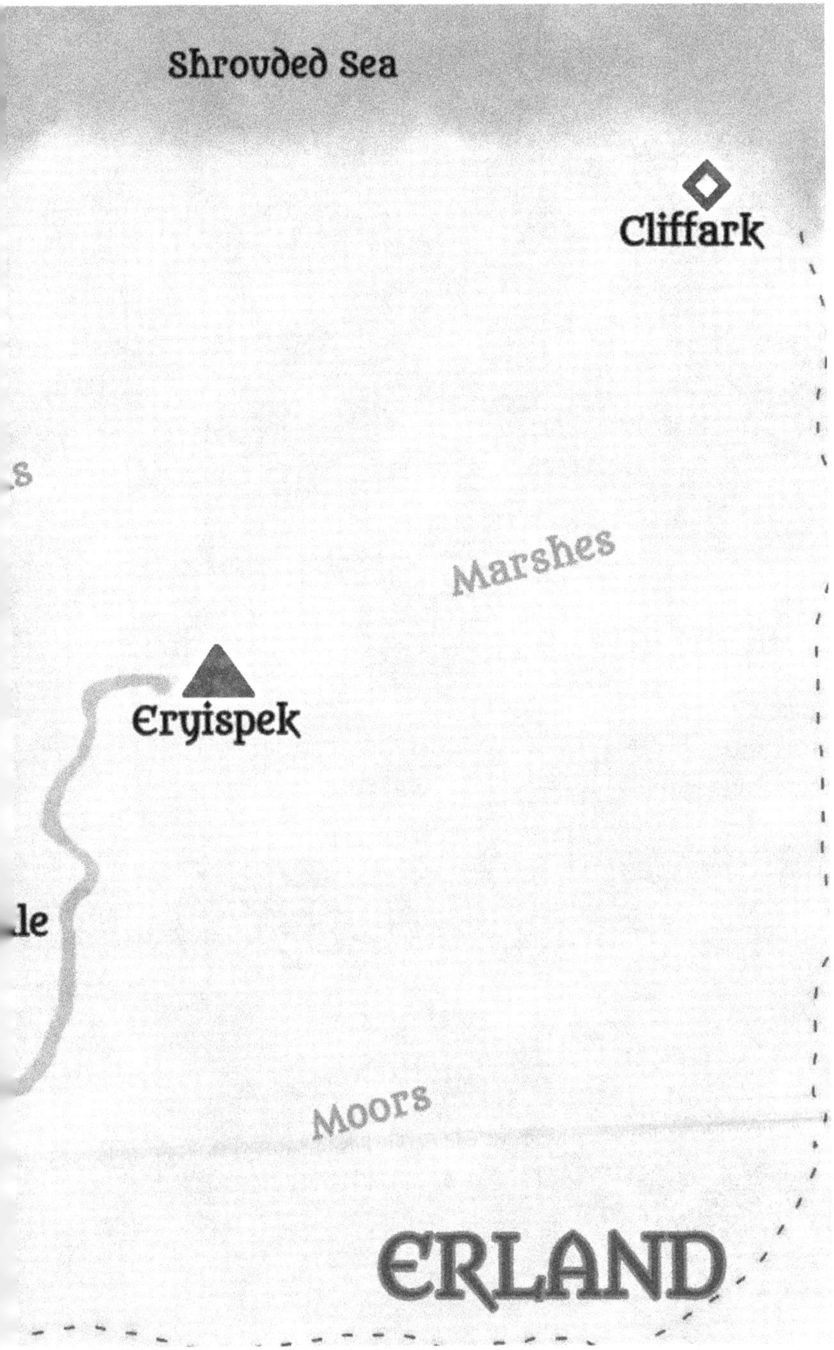

Shrovded Sea

Cliffark

s

Marshes

Eryispek

le

Moors

ERLAND

THE RULING FAMILIES OF ERLAND, THEIR ALLIES, AND THEIR FOES AT THE END OF THE HUNGER OF EMPIRES

* denotes a point-of-view character

† denotes the character is deceased

THE GODS ON THE MOUNTAIN

Eryi, trapped atop Eryispek, the magus who sacrificed himself to imprison Vulgatypha

Vulgatypha, trapped within Eryispek, the last of the Norhai, an ancient race of gods

EAST ERLAND

The Sangreals

King **Hessian Sangreal †**, murdered in his solar by Tansa of Cliffark

Queen **Elyana Sangreal †**, Hessian's first wife, dead seventeen years

And their children:

Prince **Jarhick Sangreal †**, slain in war against the Thrumb

Princess **Tarvana Sangreal**, wife to Lord Ulric Balyard

Princess ***Helana Sangreal**, imprisoned by Hu'ra of the Thrumb

Queen ***Ciera Istlewick**, Hessian's second wife, last seen fleeing Piperskeep and the forces of Ulric Balyard

And her companions:

Her infant son, **Andrick Sangreal**, *de jure* King of East Erland

Laphor, a veteran *hymerika* in her service

Burik, a *hymerika* in her service, a son of Naeem Bannhold

Arrik, a *hymerika* in her service, a younger son of Naeem Bannhold

Haisie, a young servant

Lord **Ulric Balyard**, husband to Tarvana Sangreal, *de facto* ruler of East Erland

The family of Andrick Barrelbreaker

Lord **Andrick Barrelbreaker †**, Hessian's half-brother and *balhymeri*, slain by Strovac Sigac

Lady **Viratia Brithwell**, Andrick's widow, last seen deep in the heart of the Mountain of Eryispek negotiating with Vulgatypha to save her daughter

And her companions:

Naeem, formerly Andrick's second-in-command

Delara, a magus and wisewoman of the Lutum tribe, whereabouts unknown

Sister **Aimya** of the Brides of Eryi, sent to warn Ciera Istlewick of the threat of the gods

Lord Andrick and Lady Viratia's children:

Errian Andrickson, the *balhymeri* of East Erland, allied with Lord Ulric Balyard, commanding the *Hymeriker* in the defence of Merivale

***Orsian Andrickson**, last seen fighting the forces of Ulric Balyard to allow Ciera Istlewick's escape

***Pherri Andrickdohtor**, apprentice magus, last seen battling Eryi atop the Mountain of Eryispek, fled to another world

Theodric †, magus and advisor to Hessian, mentor to Pherri, died of wounds received battling Eryi

The Ulvatian Imperium

Drast Fulkiro †, senator, commander of the Imperial invasion of Erland, slain by Krupal von Belkarez

Krupal von Belkarez, a magus summoned from another world

Strovac Sigac, warrior, commander of the Wild Brigade, a traitor to Erland, killer of Andrick Barrel-breaker

Alcantra, aide to Kzar **Saffia Murino**, last seen being restrained by Krupal and Strovac

Kvarm Murino, merchant, missing and presumed dead, last seen being magicked out of existence by Krupal

Hrogo, Kvarm's enslaved magus, missing and presumed dead, last seen being magicked out of existence by Krupal

WEST ERLAND

Lord ***Rymond Prindian**, rebel against Hessian and briefly King of West Erland, last seen fleeing the Imperial occupation of Irith

Breta Prindian, Rymond's mother, imprisoned by the Imperium

Adfric †, Rymond's master-at-arms and companion, slain by the Imperium

Captain-General **Gruenla**, leader of the Cylirien mercenaries, allied with Rymond

Brant, a scout, allied with Rymond

Residents of Cliffark

***Tansa**, a thief, last seen fleeing Piperskeep after assassinating Hessian

And her companions:

Tam †, brother of Tansa, lover of Ciera Istlewick, executed at Hessian's command

Cag †, their friend, dead from a poisoned wound suffered in the Imperium's siege of Merivale

Maud, Tansa's landlady, resident of Pauper's Hole

Pitt and **Esma**, young orphans last seen in Piperskeep

Lord **Per Istlewick**, ruler of Cliffark, father of Ciera Istlewick

Lady **Irena Istlewick,** mother of Ciera Istlewick

Abner, first mate of the *Jackdaw*, a sunken ship

The Thrumb

Chieftain **Ba'an**, leader of the Thrumb

And his children:

Ba'il †, slain by Jarhick Sangreal

Hu'ra, last seen defeating his father, taking the capital Thrumbalto, and imprisoning Helana Sangreal

Ti'en, ally to Hu'ra, false friend to Helana, killer of Jarhick Sangreal

Na'mu, Helana's friend

She'ab, a shaman

Da'ri †, tutor to Pherri, murdered by a crowd after Errian Andrickson failed to intervene

PROLOGUE

The night air was sharp with frost, so cold Delara could feel the ice seeping through her paper-thin skin into her bones. Through dancing snowflakes, the steep moonlit slope of Eryispek stretched out before her into the night, while overhead the low clouds hung close like smoke over a failing fire. The Mountain's snowy whiteness spread in every direction, so vast and endless that it almost made her feel dizzy. Delara pressed her staff to the snow and levered herself onwards. The joints of her ancient frame ached, but the icy temperature had placed her beyond pain; for three days now, she had not been able to feel her feet, and she was sure if she removed her boots she would find her toes blue with frostbite.

This was how a Lutum's life was supposed to end; they climbed until they could climb no more, and gave themselves to the Mountain. As they came of age, so they died.

And I am the last of them.

Delara harboured no illusions about that now. She had not known the fate of her tribe until she had seen Gelick Whitedoe, marching with his army of dead duplicates. And Gelick too was dead; nothing remained of the boy in that dark entity that hid behind his eyes.

A great fool, though no less foolish than me. Even at Delara's age, it was no easy thing to admit your own mistakes. So many long, slow decades looking up to the Mountain's endless peak and sensing the well of power that lurked there while another hummed beneath your feet, yet telling yourself that all that remained of the gods was the Mountain itself, the pillar of the ancient departed Norhai.

It had taken the rage of Vulgatypha, the last Norha, when Delara had been unable to stop Pherri learning magic, to lift the shroud from her eyes. Her folly and failure had begun the avalanche of events that led them to the day Gelick Whitedoe had claimed Pherri on behalf of his master, Eryi.

You tried to stop it, she reminded herself. *It is not your fault that reckless wizard did not heed you.* But she had not tried hard enough. Vulgatypha had sought help from the Adrari, and they too had failed. Pherri was with Eryi, her fate unknown.

Delara would die, but first she meant to see this Eryi. See him, and stop him if she could. One last desperate act of the magic she had spent her life despising, for the sake of the world. This man-god might be ancient, but Delara did not count her experience for naught. She had lived almost every day of her seventy-odd years on the Mountain's eastern slope, watching each morning the rising red dawn melt away the mists, gazing up at the great grey storm clouds rotating overhead, feeling the slight chill of the lazy flurries of snow that melted in the midday warmth, then as the sun passed overhead and fell beyond the endless peak withdrawing to her single-room hut to shiver under her blankets.

And with the night had come the dreams.

Delara had never troubled to try and understand her visions, what the magi of the flatlands called *prophika.* It was this gift of foresight that had led Delara's family to force her into a marriage against her will in the hopes of her bearing a child, a boy blessed with the same gift who might one day rise to be chieftain of the Lutums. She had resented the dreams, trying to push them from her memory like she had all those nights of her vile husband grunting away on top of her. To seek to understand them would have been to admit that they might mean something beyond her misery.

Yet for all that, she could still recall them to this day. Twisting twin shadows within prisons of ice; purple thunderbolts flashing against the night sky; a doe with a pair of human eyes; a chamber, empty save for an ever-blazing flame that burnt without fuel. It was as though her subconscious had recognised their significance, even as Delara fought against her own memory with every fibre of her being.

And suppose I had seen their meaning, what would I have done? Delara cackled, and it turned into a cough as a rush of cold night air penetrated her lungs. It had taken decades for the truth to reveal itself, for her to learn of Vulgatypha, the last Norha, and Eryi, the ancient magus who had sacrificed himself to bind her within the Mountain.

But it was not too late. She could practically feel the crushing weight of her own mortality, could feel it in the creak of her joints and the tremble of her gnarled blue fists that gripped her staff. If she could save Pherri and prevent Eryi escaping the Mountain, it would be a life well-spent.

Pherri. Delara felt a moment of guilt, then crushed it. If the girl was dead, her end belonged to her mother and the wizard. Even when Viratia had learnt of her daughter's capture, she had sought to blame Delara. It had been Delara who tried to save the girl. As the widow of Andrick Barrelbreaker had made her plans to travel with the Adrari to Vulgatypha, Delara had set out on her own, eschewing a meeting with the last Norha so that she might face Eryi. Face him, and stop him.

Delara pressed on, upwards, squinting through the cold

moonlight to keep her feet on the treacherous snow. The high winds that had troubled them all their way up the western slope had quietened, but snow still tumbled in earnest, covering Delara's hooded cloak and soaking through her clothes. Her lungs burnt in the thin air, and more than once she stopped to rest against her staff for minutes at a time.

The first blanket of cloud came from nowhere, and its bite took Delara's breath away, like being plunged into an icy pond. The bitter air rattled in her chest, and one of her legs almost buckled before she steadied herself against her staff, trembling with exertion as she levered herself up from a knee.

You can lie down and die later. Walk, damn you, you useless old nag. Delara spat out a blob of thick mucus into the snow, and forced herself on.

She felt the dead things before she saw them. A malignant presence on the air, like the stench of rot.

Delara lifted her bowed head. Like a curtain across the sky, the clouds had parted, and the moon's high silver glow revealed a sight that had she not already been frozen to her bones would have made her blood run cold.

She had seen the dead Gelicks before. Lower and more pitiful than the dumbest of beasts, with their bovine eyes, shuffling gaits, and horrific injuries, from missing arms to caved-in skulls to broken legs. An endless procession of them watched her from a snowy ridge, as patient as cattle for the slaughter. The true Gelick was there also, though with his vacant gaze all that separated him from the rest was the intactness of his body. Blood might yet flow in his veins, but that bold, stupid boy had been reduced to the level of the dead.

Below them, a figure strode towards Delara. He wore no cloak against the cold, his hair hung from his head in six plaits, and he crossed the snow like a proud lord striding the length of his hall. His face was unlined, and unremarkable.

None of that would have unsettled Delara, had it not been

for his eyes. He was still fifty feet away from her, but they seemed to swim and expand in her vision, with pinprick pupils and irises of blue so pale they were almost white. As the distance between them closed, she felt the mastery rolling off him in waves, a power that was to her own as the sea was to a stream.

He raised a bare arm in greeting, and Delara saw his skin was a motley of ashen white and angry pink, like curdled cream that had somehow been set aflame. In places, it seemed to be weeping watery blood. The face she had thought unremarkable was in truth featureless, a blank mask of sickly ivory that shone wanly under the moonlight.

'You are too late,' he greeted her, stopping twenty feet away. 'The girl is gone.' His voice crackled like burning vellum.

Delara felt a brief probe of *inflika* against her consciousness, little more than a cat pawing at a ball of yarn, and willed it aside. She would not allow this Eryi, whoever and whatever he was, to play with her. 'What have you done with her? Where is she?'

'Dead. Stumbling blindly through other worlds.' He shrugged. It was an awkward gesture, as though he could not quite get his body to obey him. 'It makes no matter. She served her purpose. I have a body, and I am free. Your talent is small, but if you serve me well, I will let you live. Magus blood is too rare to spill without reason.'

'That body looks slightly ill-fitting.' Delara pushed herself up on her staff, willing her hands not to tremble. She nodded to the pinkish blood fleeing down Eryi's wrist, staining the snow. 'I'm not sure it likes you.'

An angry sneer for a moment marred Eryi's expressionless visage. 'A minor inconvenience.' He wiped a hand down his arm. 'Vessels of flesh can be fickle. Perhaps, in time, you might help me take another.'

Delara covered her face as a swift burst of *phisika* gusted a vast cloud of snow towards her, and when it cleared Eryi had halved the distance between them. She flinched a step back, nearly dropping her staff, and took in his appearance again, watching him warily. This could not have been what he intended.

'Pherri fought you,' she said. 'Do not try to tell me you meant to end up like this. You'll be lucky if that body gets you down the Mountain without falling apart.'

Eryi's face flashed with fury again, and Delara tensed, ready for another burst of magic. The snow had lessened, but the damp clouds pressed in around her, leaving droplets of moisture to freeze on her face. 'I have waited over a thousand years,' he said. 'After so long, even this imperfect form is like music upon my soul. When I descend, all the world shall rush to my alliance – the Imperials shall be mine, my Thrumb descendants will march, your Lutums have already joined me' – he gestured up the slope towards the Gelicks – 'in a manner of speaking, and when the Erlanders see the alternative, what choice will they have but to join me also? There is none with the strength to oppose me.'

'Save Vulgatypha.'

'*I care not for Vulgatypha.*' The man-god's voice cracked like the sound of a thousand whips, for a moment brightening the night sky with a burst of white heat. 'She can rot beneath the ice.' He bared his teeth. 'If she opposes me, I will kill her. The world will belong to the magi again. It will belong to me.' His voice was as sharp as a newly whetted knife. 'If she is so powerful, why is it I who is free? I—'

Above the clouds, a pillar of flame burst from Eryispek's summit, splitting the black night in two. A great blast of noise echoed against the atmosphere and down the Mountain like a breaking wave, forcing Delara to press her hands to her ears. The sky began to rain soot and sulphur, and a shadow passed across the moon, dimming the world to darkness. Delara heard screaming, not of pain, but fear, the sort of fear that could drive a man to madness.

From the inferno, a single figure rose. She flew on wings of fire, hair streaming through the night like a burning storm, threads of purple lightning crackling against the sky.

'Impossible,' gasped Eryi. 'She—'

The figure descended in a fiery hailstorm, falling upon Eryi's army of Gelicks in a shower of flames. Within seconds, every one of them was ablaze. The dead men tore at their smouldering rags, crying wordlessly in terror to the callous night as their lifeless skin blistered and split. Like a thousand candles the flames consumed them, as they cavorted like demons, spilling across the mountainside in their dance of death.

The fiery figure floated in the air, and the flames that surrounded her began to dim, revealing a spectral silhouette with red-hot eyes. There was something familiar about her, and as Delara gazed at her, she knew. Her mouth fell open in wonder. *By the Mountain.* Vulgatypha, the last of the Norhai, had returned, and for all her divinity she wore a form that Delara knew well.

The face of Lady Viratia Brithwell gazed down at them, lips twisting to reveal a furious maw of pointed teeth, the last of the flames still rippling against her ghostly features.

Just feet away from Delara, Eryi stared, the plume of fire climbing into the sky and the dancing, burning silhouettes of his allies reflecting in his milk-blue eyes. No trace of the certainty he had shown mere moments before remained behind his glassy gaze. His mouth was slack, and his pores wept with blood.

Strangely, he began to laugh, and the mad sound seemed to echo off the sky. The figure watched him, her blazing eyes boring into him like burning arrows.

'Let us settle it here, Goddess.'

Without warning, the magus-god raised his hands, and in a

flash of *phisika* tore several tonnes of snow and rock from the Mountain and sent it hurtling into the sky.

Vulgatypha snarled and raised a hand. Her palm sizzled with purple lightning, and Delara felt the wave of *phisika* with which she sought to reverse Eryi's assault. But the tempest unleashed by the magus flew on, upwards, in a twisting sheet of a million tiny pieces. The Norha's red eyes grew wide, and her mouth twisted from fury to horror. A cry of triumph escaped Eryi's lips, but before the storm could reach Vulgatypha she flew into the sky, rising above the smouldering summit, higher and higher, until she was no more than a pinprick of pale light against the stars.

'Coward!' Eryi screeched after her, shaking his fist to the heavens. 'Come back and face me!'

But Vulgatypha did not return. Eryi's storm fell back to earth, flecks of ice evaporating against the flames that engulfed the writhing army of dead Gelicks.

He turned back to Delara. 'She is weak,' he rasped. His body was weeping blood worse than ever; there were bare patches of skin on his arms and face, revealing the bone and veins beneath. 'In the goddess's desperation to escape, she has taken the body of an ungifted mortal. She cannot hope to oppose me; her power is diluted, and I sense too much of Pherri's mother in her.' His pale lips stretched in a cadaverous smile. 'She is weak. That is why she flees.'

Delara gestured to Eryi's fresh wounds. 'Seems she's not the only one to embrace mortality.'

Eryi's smile fell slightly. 'This body is mine, taken from another realm. Not the one I hoped for, but I am no stranger to struggle. It was necessary to escape the Mountain. Were I still bound to my own form, she would have destroyed me.' He scratched at a lesion on his forearm, making the bleeding even worse. 'Whatever you may think of me, I assure you that if you truly knew her, you would fall to your knees and praise me as the world's saviour.'

'Bollocks,' spat Delara. 'Even if Vulgatypha's as bad as the Adrari told me, how could she be worse than you? You only want to rule the world, same as her, and trample over anyone who tries to stop you, folk like Pherri and Theodric and the Lutums.'

'You think *that* is her goal?' Eryi's laugh was like the breaking of ice. 'If you knew what she will do, what she would already have done if not for me—'

Now. Delara drew upon seven decades of unyielding will, and flung her staff towards him, pouring all her last reserves of strength into a blast of *phisika*. The frigid earth rumbled beneath her feet, the snow rippling outward in a maelstrom of white waves, and her staff shot towards Eryi like an arrow, aiming for his head.

Eryi's malformed face twisted in surprise, but Delara's staff exploded still yards apart from him, scattering splinters of beechwood to the night. She screamed as shards of wood flew towards her like a storm of bees, and when she flung up her hands her skin was sliced to ribbons on their sharp edges. One flew past her defences, and her scream lengthened to an animalistic wail as it pierced her eyeball, popping it like a grape in a fountain of blood.

Eryi's punch struck her in the sternum, and all the air went out of Delara as she was flung backwards, landing hard against the snow several yards away. A hidden rock punched against her spine, and she felt something crack inside her. She lay in the snow, trying to will the air back into her lungs and force her legs to stand, but found herself coughing on the blood dripping from her ruined eyeball.

Through her one good eye, she looked up at Eryi standing over her, his foggy-blue orbs tinged with red rage.

'Did you think that would work?' he sneered. 'You pathetic

worm. Do you believe I, who chained the last of the Norhai and has watched the rise and fall of civilisations, would fall by such a cheap trick?' In a fit of petulance, he kicked snow into Delara's face.

Delara tried to laugh, but all that came out was a weak rasp, as she felt herself choking on her own blood. She could not feel her legs, but the snow beneath her was strangely warm, as if a furnace blazed beneath the ice. *Isn't this what they say happens before the end?* With withered, palsied hands, she forced herself onto her side, and coughed blood across the snow. She manoeuvred herself to look up towards the heights of Eryispek. A great river of lava was snaking its way down the slope, burning away the clouds and subliming the snow to blistering hot vapour. The Mountain steamed like water thrown over a furnace, and all the while the stream of fire weaved towards them, like some great reptile with rippling scales of orange and bright hot crimson.

Eryi gave her one last contemptuous look. He turned to run. Magic lent fleetness to his feet, and he outdistanced the flowing magma in a matter of seconds.

Delara fell back upon the rapidly melting snow, gazing up towards the sky. The stars and moon were little more than the flicker of cinders against the bright fire that still spewed from the Mountain. A stain of smoke was spreading across the night, covering the sky in ashes.

The gods are free, and the world will burn. Weakened and bitter as they were, there lurked within them enough power to reduce Erland and the world to ruin. Delara had tried to stop it, little as that effort had been worth, and she had failed. A final caustic laugh escaped her lips. She was glad she would not be alive to see it.

The flames blazed so hot that Delara never even felt them. Her body burnt to dust, and was swiftly swallowed by the surging river of fire.

CHAPTER 1

Laphor looked up at the tower, breathing hard, the flanks of his mount slick with sweat. 'We should rest here, Majesty,' he said between gasps. 'Might be they'll think they've lost us.'

From her horse, Ciera's eyes followed those of the veteran *hymerika*. The tower looked to be long abandoned. It was no taller than Piperskeep's gatehouse, a single lonely sentinel at the very edge of the moors, set on a damp incline overlooking the swamps that spread for endless miles to their north. Its crumbling walls were thick with moss and vines, stretched over the battlements like the fingers of some bog giant threatening to drag it down the hill into the stagnant waters.

Ciera shivered inside her thick cloak, releasing the reins for a moment to wipe her rain-slick gloves. It was no more than a drizzle, but it had barely stopped in two days. It had soaked through to her underclothes, now cold and clammy against her skin. At least the miserable conditions had made her little party harder to spot; had they been travelling by daylight or in fairer weather the squad of *hymerikai* who had picked up their trail would surely have caught them by now.

'We shouldn't stay here,' said Arrik, the youngest of Ciera's three warriors, not a year older than she was. He pointed north-east, towards the outline of a fortress silhouetted against the burgeoning twilight. It could be no more than a few miles away, deeper into the mire. 'That's Fenhold. Strovac Sigac's seat.'

Laphor turned towards the young *hymerika*, irritation plain in his drawn face, his eyes swollen with fatigue. 'He won't look for us here.' Tempers had been rising for weeks, and Ciera could tell Laphor was tired of the younger men questioning his decisions. 'Strovac will have turned north, ready to ambush us in the marshes; he'll know these lands better than any of us. No, we'll stay here for a few hours and decide what to do.'

'And what about the *hymerikai* behind us?' said Burik, Arrik's older brother. 'We'll stand a better chance of getting past Strovac in the dark.' His mouth was set in a stubborn line beneath a dark beard that grew wilder with every passing day. 'And if he finds us, all the better,' he added, his voice thick with bravado. Burik could not let any mention of Strovac Sigac pass without expressing a desire to cross swords with him.

Laphor barked a laugh that turned into a hacking cough. No one's health had been improved by their desperate flight across Erland, least of all his. 'Even assuming you got through his Wild Brigade,' he said once he had regained his breath, 'Strovac would slice your heart out and break his fast on it. Are you so eager to die, boy?'

'We should keep heading east,' said Arrik. 'Stick to the moors and—'

'Endless miles of open country!' snapped Laphor. 'Only question is who'll catch us first: the Wild Brigade or Balyard's pet *hymerikai*. Do you even know what's waiting for us if we keep heading that way?'

'The Alkenfolk,' said Arrik. 'If we can cross the Green River—'

'Spineless shepherds! You think even if we get that far a few crook-wielding whitebeards'll stop Strovac and the rest? Only reason the Ffriseans haven't killed them all years ago is that there's nothing worth killing them for.'

'Better than staying here,' retorted Burik. 'What's your plan, wait for daylight before we move? Might as well raise a standard and lead Strovac right to us.'

Laphor glared at the younger man, but said nothing. After a few moments, he turned away with a sigh, then ran a gloved hand down his face and through his frost-shot beard. 'Eryi's bollocks.' He leaned over his horse and spat into the sodden grass. 'We're caught between the horn and the bloody hook here, ain't we?' He gestured towards the tower. 'At least if they find us in there we might give ourselves a fighting chance.'

'It should be the queen's decision,' piped up Haisie from where she sat behind Ciera, her hands tangled up in the folds of Ciera's cloak. The servant girl looked up at her. 'What should we do, Majesty?'

Ciera turned and gave the girl a small smile, then lifted her head to consider the shadow of Fenhold in the distance. She repressed a shudder. Even when she was a child in Cliffark, the stories of Strovac's rule of Fenhold and the surrounding lands had reached them: screams in the night, and servants who disappeared into the marshes and were never seen again.

When their band had fled from Merivale, it had been only the *Hymeriker* who pursued them, men who not even a fortnight earlier had sworn loyalty to Ciera as Erland's queen. Only by Laphor's wiles had they escaped them, the old warrior leading them through the night and by day forcing them to rest in patches of woodland or amidst the ruins of abandoned settlements. This had sustained their escape for over a week, and after several days without sight of a *hymerika*, they had dared to think they might have outwitted them.

But then, Burik had sighted a man on a distant hill, and named him immediately by his size as Strovac Sigac, traitor to East Erland and ally of the Imperium, and with him several dozen of his Wild Brigade. Only hours later, they had spotted a group of red-garbed *hymerikai* within two hundred yards of them, and it was only by the luck of the Norhai they had not been spotted. That had been two days earlier, and Laphor was convinced that at least one of these groups had picked up their trail. They had for a time hoped the two might encounter one another and come to battle, leaving them with only one to worry about, but so far they had somehow avoided each other.

Both the Imperium and Lord Balyard were seeking Ciera now. Or, more precisely, they were seeking her son, with whom they might legitimise their ambitions to rule Erland. Ciera glanced to where King Andrick Sangreal rested, swaddled in the arms of Arrik. Not even four months old and already a fugitive. It had troubled her to give up her son to Arrik, but Laphor had reasoned that the babe would be safer with him; if they were discovered, they would expect the king to be riding with Ciera.

She looked around at her companions. Laphor, Burik, Arrik, and Haisie. All that remained of her kingdom. The rest of the few warriors still loyal to her had not been able to escape Piperskeep; there had been no time when Errian had freed Balyard, and the two men had together launched a brief counter-rebellion, naming Ciera as Hessian's murderer. Laphor had spirited her away through a hidden passage below the keep, barely beyond Balyard's clutches, and Burik and Arrik had just managed to escape with their lives, showing the sense to find Haisie and bring the girl with them as well.

Ciera pushed her soaked hair back from her eyes, and looked again to the tower. It was leaning slightly to one side, and there were gaps in the stonework through which she could see rain was falling. *A far cry from being Queen of East Erland and mother to the king.* On their flight from Piperskeep, Ciera had refused to despair, sure that in time she could rise again and take back her rightful place, but standing between the barren moors and bleak marshes before a tumbledown tower she felt as miserable as she ever had in her life. Just how was she to take back a kingdom with only three warriors, while West Erland was in rebellion and the Ulvatian Imperium brought death to her people?

'It doesn't look that bad,' said Haisie. Ciera could only admire the girl's resilience. 'The inside might be in a better state. Maybe we can get a fire going.'

Ciera forced herself to smile. She looked around her companions, taking in their exhausted faces, their damp, bedraggled garb. It would serve them all well to have a roof over their heads for a few hours, and it was surely safer than remaining in the open. 'We'll stop here. Fens or moors, we need to rest.'

As Ciera pressed her mount forward, she cast a look back to their north-west, towards Eryispek. The sky was covered in charcoal-grey dust, and, though the summit that had been believed endless was not visible beyond the clouds, she could see the fire smouldering in the heights, spewing flame and ashes into the air as it had been for days. At least its rage appeared to be lessening. Eryispek's eruption had come days earlier just as darkness was setting in, loud enough to set the ground quaking, stirring them from sleep with a thunder that Ciera had been sure must be a thousand *hymerikai* charging upon their hiding place. The explosion had engulfed the night, so furiously bright it was as if the heavens had been set aflame. Could there have been any worse omen for Erland than the Mountain burning? What did it mean?

'Don't be thinking about it,' grumbled Laphor. The old warrior had been more disquieted than any of them by it. 'Let's get inside so I don't have to look at it no more.'

They urged their mounts towards the tower's entrance, where Laphor dismounted. He turned the double doors' great ring handle, and put his shoulder to it with a grunt. The left door screeched open, scraping against the flagstones within.

The tower's single ground-floor room was a scene of devastation. Empty, dust-covered bottles littered the floor, wooden furniture had been overturned and set aflame, and the walls were daubed with what might have been blood. A single black iron chandelier rested in the middle of the room, no doubt too heavy for anyone to steal.

Laphor sniffed. 'Smells like my old mother-in-law's house, may Eryi take her – no one else would. Looks like whoever lived here took everything that wasn't nailed down when they fled.'

'Fleeing Strovac probably,' said Burik. 'I've heard tales of Fenhold that would give you sleepless nights.' He glanced at Haisie, who was looking at him with wide eyes. 'Just tales of course,' he added hastily, 'nothing to worry about.'

'You don't think there's a chance he comes back this way?' asked Arrik.

Laphor shook his head. 'If they've followed us this far they must reckon we're headed for Cliffark. He'll be waiting in the fens.' He pointed to the narrow staircase against the wall that ran up to the floor above. 'You two – take a look upstairs. See if there's a bed for the queen.' Burik and Arrik hurried to obey.

Once they were gone, Laphor began gathering debris for a fire. Ciera had found a chair, in which she now sat cradling Andrick. She had retrieved the only intact candle from the fallen chandelier, and its solitary flame broke the gloom with a circle of pale light. 'Is that what you think?' she asked. 'That we should make for Cliffark?' The thought of her hometown brought a warmth to Ciera's heart.

Laphor swept a few twigs and ruined parchments towards his growing pile. 'I did, but those marshes are treacherous at night and by day Strovac will hunt us down like deer. Might be Arrik's idea is the better one; head east and hope all of them reckon we'll head north.'

'What then?' Ciera knew nothing of the moors, nor the peaceable Alkenfolk who dwelt beyond the Green River.

'Change our names and hope Balyard and the rest never come looking for you.' He shrugged his powerful shoulders. 'Maybe you find a handsome shepherd to wed; one who doesn't mind taking on a woman with another man's child. When the boy's old enough, I can train him to use a sword, assuming I live that long.'

'Are there warriors among the Alkenfolk?'

Laphor grunted a laugh. 'Probably they kill a few wolves, but that's about it.'

Ciera was silent for several moments, staring into the light of her flickering candle. There was nothing but exile for her in the east, and between her and Cliffark nothing but enemies. 'I had hoped to raise an army,' she said slowly. 'Retake Merivale.'

Laphor paused his gathering of firewood to glance sideways at Ciera. 'You want my advice? Forget about Balyard and Merivale. They ain't worth your life, nor your lad's.'

'But I can't just forget about it!' Ciera felt the blood rush to her cheeks. In her arms Andrick stirred. 'Erland belongs to my son! What was the point in saving me if you meant to drag me into exile?'

Laphor puffed out his cheeks. 'Majesty, I'm not dragging you anywhere. But it seems to me Erland's not worth what it used to be. Balyard and Errian are glad now, because they think they've fought off the Imperium – little as Balyard had to do with it – but they won't be laughing when those of them over the river turn up, and how do you suppose anyone'll get fed this winter? The last one was lean, and because of the war it'll be another poor harvest. And I don't like the look of Eryispek either; I'm not sure what all that fire and smoke means, but I'd wager nothing good.

'I got you out of Piperskeep for the sake of you and the babe. If you'll permit me to speak bluntly, East Erland is already lost to you. Whether it be the Imperials, Balyard, or the West Erlanders who ends up with it, it won't be you.'

Ciera sat up straighter. 'Then we'll go to Cliffark. My father will give me the men I need to retake Merivale.'

'Your father's folk are merchants and sailors, not warriors. How many fighting men's he got – a couple of thousand? What difference is that going to make when faced with the walls of Merivale? Enough to risk your life?'

Ciera felt an anger rising in her breast. 'You swore an oath to the Blood,' she seethed. 'Just like all the *hymerikai*. My son is your *king*, *Erland's* king, and your proposal is that I abandon his birthright? That I give up?'

'Majesty, the king is a babe in arms, and you've seen what men's oaths can be worth, even the *hymerikai*. If he were even five years older it might be different, but men won't fight for a child that's not even been weaned. Erland's never had a boy king, thank the Norhai.'

The rage began to leak out of Ciera like ale from a broken barrel. She closed her eyes. *What if he's right?* Even if she made it to Cliffark, what then? There was no army there worthy of the name. And she could not ask her father to shelter her; it would bring the wrath of Ciera's enemies down upon him. Cliffark would still mean exile, if not among the Alkenfolk then in any land that would take her.

'I hope you'll forgive my plain-speaking, Majesty,' said Laphor, leaving his pile of makeshift firewood and picking up Ciera's candle. 'Just seems no sense in gilding it.'

Ciera sank back into her chair, cradling Andrick. 'There is nothing to forgive.' If Laphor did not tell her the truth, nobody would.

It cannot end like this. Ciera's father had charged her with bringing prosperity to Erland, reasoning that it was the only way to save the kingdom from eventual disaster. Ciera had never even been given the chance; she had gone from broodmare to prisoner to widow in the blink of an eye, with her only brief opportunity to lead being marred by a war not of her making.

If Hessian still lived, or I had given them his killer... What had possessed her to let Tansa escape? Although once Hessian was dead, it may have made no difference; Errian had barely let the king's corpse turn cold before he had betrayed Ciera.

Laphor was crouched to his pile of kindling, attempting to light it with the candle, but in the swampy air was struggling to get the damp pile of wood to take the flame. He turned to look at Ciera. 'Forget Erland. You should do what's best for the boy. And for yourself.' His voice wavered slightly. 'My wife's been dead ten years, never had any children. You're the closest thing to family I've got. Don't make me watch you die.'

Ciera blinked away the beginnings of tears. 'Laphor, I—'

'Forget it, forget I said anything,' croaked the old warrior. He adjusted his shoulders, straightening himself. 'I'm a sentimental fool. Just remember: it's only a crown you're giving up. Better that than watching the boy be dragged back to Balyard, or be sold to the Imperium by Strovac Sigac or whatever else he might do.'

She instinctively held Andrick more tightly. Nobody would take her son, not while she still drew breath.

But for as long as they remained in Erland, both their lives were in danger.

But what sort of life would Andrick have among the Alkenfolk? Ciera stared down at the scrunched face of her sleeping child, trying to imagine him growing to hold a shepherd's crook rather than a king's sword, while she raised a gaggle of children for a stranger with whom she did not even share a tongue. If they went east across the moors, there would be no other life for either of them. As much as she tried, she could not picture it.

And it was not only their own futures she would be giving up on, but the futures of all those who had stayed loyal to her.

Haisie, Ciera knew, would walk through fire or beyond the Green River for her and never look back. So would Laphor, Burik, and Arrik, even if it meant casting aside their *hymerika* chainmail and never seeing their homes or family again. Orsian had given up his freedom and his position to save Ciera from Balyard's clutches and get her to safety. He might be rotting in a Piperskeep dungeon now. What did the future hold for Orsian if Ciera abandoned him?

'We need to decide tonight,' said Laphor. He let out a small cry of triumph as a stick finally started to smoulder, and began blowing on it to encourage the burgeoning flames. 'The longer we stay here, the more likely it is one of them finds us.'

Ciera nodded, leaning forward to savour the low heat of the rising flames. 'I will not abandon my son's crown,' she said. She had faced down Hessian, Balyard, and the Imperium; she would not back down for fear of Strovac Sigac and his Wild Brigade, nor the *hymerikai* who had turned against her. 'We will cross the marshes, towards Cliffark.'

CHAPTER 2

The sunlight burning through her eyelids woke her. With tiny fists, she rubbed at her eyes. Her head felt as though it had been wrapped in coarse cloth, and her mouth tasted of sawdust and bright copper. She rolled over, spat out a globule of phlegm, and groaned into the soft ground.

The day was warm, and the wind through the long grass was little more than a whisper. That was not right though. The wind did not whisper here; it howled, bringing with it a torrent of ice and the grim touch of dead things.

Slowly, Pherri pushed herself to a sitting position, fighting the nausea that threatened to bring a flood of bile rising from her throat. She gagged on her own tongue, and a spasm of pain burst against her brain. Blood pounded round her head like an army on the march.

Eryi's teeth, when did I last drink something?

The oath that flew unbidden to her mind sparked Pherri's memory. A pair of impossibly pale eyes flashed before her vision, and she had to clap a hand to her mouth to stop herself crying out.

'*Don't think about him.*' Pherri spoke aloud, hoping the

sound of her own voice might quell the fear in her chest. Somewhere, a bird cawed as if in reply.

Through a fog of barely repressed terror, she forced herself to replay in her mind the last event she remembered, and how she had come to be here alone. The visions spun through her head like a runaway cartwheel: turning the tide as her brothers fought against overwhelming odds to save Merivale; being dragged back through time in another reality as Eryi searched for the body that would release him from his mountain prison; her desperate leap into this world to stop him from claiming it. Had it worked? She remembered his rage and his terror, his frantic grasping for her as the window between the worlds faded. He had failed – she lived, in this world if not in her own, and his ritual was incomplete.

And yet, somehow Pherri knew it had not been enough. Eryi was too powerful to be thwarted by such a trick. He was delayed, or diminished, but not defeated. Far from it.

I have to get back.

The grass Pherri found herself in was perhaps as high as her waist, and gingerly she came to her feet, trying to resist the sickness that threatened to overwhelm her. She lurched a step forward, and nearly fell as the earth wobbled under her feet. She pressed her hand to her forehead, grimacing at the headache pounding against the inside of her skull.

First, find water. And food. Then I'll figure out how I'm getting back.

Slowly, she surveyed her surroundings. The sky was a cloudless summer blue, and the sun shone brightly at the apex of its arc. The verdant grass sloped downward, suggesting she was on a hillside. To get her bearings, she surveyed the horizon in each direction, searching for Eryispek, but despite the clear day could not see it. Was that usual? Theodric had never explicitly said that other realities had the same geography, but Eryispek was surely immutable.

Theodric. Pherri felt her empty stomach heave again, and not only because she had watched her mentor die. Without Theodric and Delara, she was *alone*, and twelve-year-olds were not supposed to be alone. She had never set foot outside Violet Hall without an escort. Eryi had made no secret of his intent to sacrifice her, but at least he had given her sustenance and warmth. The weight of Pherri's situation seemed to press down on her windpipe, making it hard to breathe. The thought of having to obtain food for herself in this strange land was at least as daunting as battling Eryi.

Tears quivered on her lower eyelids. *Stop it, stupid*, she told herself fiercely. *You can't eat tears. You just need to find someone who'll help you, an adult.*

But not all adults were friendly. She remembered the three men who had caught her in the woods, what seemed like half a lifetime ago. Or, what if Eryi managed to follow her? Suddenly panicked, she whirled on the spot, almost expecting to see his grim visage and long slender form coming towards her through the long grass.

There was nobody there.

Furiously, she wiped her eyes. *Fear won't help you here. Help yourself.*

Tentatively, Pherri tried to reach out with *spectika*, searching for any sign of life, reasoning that even if Eryi knew or could discover where she was, he did not have the means to get to her.

She drew upon her will and focus and tried to release a sliver of energy.

Nothing happened. She may as well have attempted to exert *inflika* on the mind of a stone, and even in her weakened, sickened state, she felt none of the tiredness she ought to have felt from such an attempt.

You're exhausted, she reasoned. *Of course it won't work*. But what if it would not work at all? What if it was not possible to draw on magic except in your own world? She and Theodric had deduced that the source of magic was likely Eryispek, and this world did not appear to have an Eryispek.

If she was to find anyone to help her, she would have to walk, before her dehydration headache and the empty feeling in her belly worsened. Reasoning that any water was likely to be downhill, she walked that way, and judged by the path of the sun that she might be moving south-west.

Everywhere, the untamed grass rose as high as her torso. It rustled as she cleaved a path through it, disturbing the chirping crickets that leapt away from her and a field mouse that scurried across her path. Pherri was hungry enough to swipe a hand for the crickets, but they were too fast. Overhead, swifts with forked tails and long bowed wings curved across the sky, and in a few high chestnut trees, wood pigeons cooed their familiar cry.

Pherri diverted from her path to consider one of the lonely trees, and whether she might be able to climb it and seek out a few chestnuts or bird eggs to feast on, but the trunks were too wide for her small arms, and there were no low branches with which she might have pulled herself. She walked on, glancing longingly back at the nesting pigeons. They looked tastier by the moment.

The high sun beat down mercilessly, and after a time, Pherri felt her scalp beginning to burn through her thin blonde hair, adding to her burgeoning headache. She had lost her cloak, and there was nothing to shade her except the trees, but she could not stop to rest without food or water. The day's heat was enough to make her think wistfully of frigid Eryispek. Snow might be cold, but at least it could sustain you for a time.

She was relieved then when the grass began to thin, granting her a clearer view of where the slope was leading her. Below, the ground levelled, and no more than a few miles away Pherri glimpsed a shimmering lake on the edge of a large copse of trees, bright blue under the clear sky, sunlight dancing across it like a coterie of tiny fairies.

Her legs were beginning to ache, and she resisted the urge to break into a run, knowing that she was still perhaps over an hour's walk away. The inside of her mouth was so dry she could not even summon spit. She gritted her teeth, and forced herself to walk on, steady and certain, one foot in front of the other, trying not to guess how far she might still have to travel.

Many miles away, just short of the horizon, Pherri thought she saw a settlement, with a low stone wall and smoke curling from a slim tower. She could not think about that now though; without water she would never reach it. Eventually, the soft grass gave way to thick tangles of thistles and brambles, and Pherri eagerly picked at the small, unripe blackberries, still pink and sour rather than black and sweet, but as the flavour burst upon her tongue and their cool juice soothed her parched throat they tasted like the nectar of the Norhai.

When the lake was no more than a few hundred yards away, Pherri broke into an ungainly, stumbling run, almost tripping a few times before she collapsed at the water's edge among the dirt bank and the reeds, and began desperately spooning the clear, chill water into her mouth with her cupped hands. The exertion left her gasping for air, but she dunked her head beneath the surface to soothe her scorching scalp, and then finally cast off her filthy clothes and threw herself naked into the water.

After her long walk, the lake was pleasantly cool. Pherri waded out past the reeds, and her bare feet found the rough sand of the shallow bottom. She turned to look back the way she had come. The point on the hill where she had woken was some distance away, and Pherri felt a burst of pride and elation at how far she had walked. To have travelled so far by herself to find water felt almost as significant as the first time she had done magic, or thwarting Eryi. Part of her wanted to spend the whole afternoon in the water; if she needed food, she did not have to go far back up the hill to find the wild blackberries.

A rustling behind her on the far side of the lake broke Pherri's reverie and set her blood running cold with fear. Immediately conscious of her vulnerability, she turned slowly towards the sound, her heart thumping in her chest, praying to whatever nameless god the world had left that it was only an animal, perhaps a deer or a curious water-vole.

Between the bushes on the far bank, a man was leaning over the water gripping a large bowl. He stared at her, and by his wide eyes he was at least as frightened of Pherri as she was of him. He looked like nobody Pherri had ever seen, garbed in strange robes that hung in rags from his shoulders, with scarred skin the colour of walnut, a withered, wrinkled belly as if he had lost a lot of weight in a short time, and one shoulder that looked several inches higher than the other. There were broken shackles on his wrists and ankles, including one on his left foot with a chain dragging from it. He had been well-fed once, perhaps, but the hard lines around his mouth and fearful eyes suggested a lifetime of suffering.

Forcing herself not to be afraid, Pherri spoke first. 'Do you mind?' she said, summoning up her best impression of how her mother or Princess Helana might have addressed the man. 'I am trying to bathe.'

The man looked up in surprise, and one of his feet slipped in the mud. With a great splash he toppled head-first into the water.

Pherri swam quickly for the bank and hauled herself out, then immediately pulled on her clothes without bothering to dry herself. By the time she stood, the man was heaving himself out of the lake.

He struggled to his feet on the bank, his long, ragged robes dripping water. One of his legs dragged, and when he stood he did so at an angle, as if one limb was longer than the other or had an awkward bend to it. Pherri stayed on her side of the lake, sure she could outrun him if she had to.

'I'm sorry,' said the man, 'I didn't mean to sneak up on you.' He busied himself wringing water from his robes, not quite meeting Pherri's eye. 'Could you help me get my bowl?' He pointed to the centre of the lake, where the vessel he had been holding was now bobbing.

'What do you need a bowl for?' said Pherri. She felt slightly foolish now for initially fearing this man; there was something slightly pitiful about him, with his strange clothes and ruined body. 'Just spoon it out with your hands.'

'It's for my mas...' The man paused, irritation flashing across his face. 'For my friend.'

'Why couldn't he come himself?'

'He's not well.' The bowl was bobbing towards the man's side of the pond now, and he sank to his haunches ready to retrieve it.

'Where is he? Is there a settlement nearby?' Pherri hoped not all the people in this other world were as peculiar as this man. 'Do you know any magi?' she asked on a whim. She assumed that a fellow magus would have the best prospects of returning her to her own world.

The man's face brightened. 'Are you here seeking a magus?'

'I'm here... it doesn't matter why I'm here.' Pherri did not rate her prospects of getting this man to believe she had come here from another world; the sheer unlikelihood of it was why she needed a magus. 'Do you know one or not?'

'I am one. Or at least I was.'

Taking in the man's tattered clothing, Pherri doubted that very much. She was beginning to think he might be mad, or at least simple. '*You* are a magus?' He did look like he ate a lot though, or he used to, and Theodric had always said the most important part of being a magus was having enough food.

'I was before.'

'Before what?'

'Before I was sent here.'

Sent here? Pherri quickly put together the deductions in her head. Why would a native to this world be behaving so oddly, scooping water from a lake by himself with a crude wooden bowl and frightened by a twelve-year-old girl? She took a deep breath. 'Did you come here from another world? Like *shadika* in reverse?'

The man was positively beaming now, his manic smile threatening to escape the bounds of his face. 'You don't belong here either!' Pherri took several alarmed steps backwards as the man shuffled around the pond towards her. 'I knew I couldn't be the only one! I knew it, I knew it!'

He stopped before her, breathless, still grinning. 'Did Krupal send you here too? Why would he send a girl? Are you really a magus?'

'Yes,' said Pherri, indignant that he would doubt her. 'What's me being a girl got to do with it? I've never heard of Krupal. That's not important – if you're a magus, perhaps we can find a way back together.' Pherri supposed it was possible they had come here from different worlds, but in the face of the sheer coincidence that the first person she should encounter here would be a fellow magus magicked here from somewhere else she doubted it.

The man's smile faltered. 'Ah. Have you tried doing magic since you've got here?'

'Only briefly. I'm tired. I'm sure it will work later once I'm rested.' Pherri felt suddenly aware of the great hunger in her stomach that a few unripe blackberries had not been able to satisfy. 'Do you have any food?'

'Back at our camp. If you come with me, you are welcome to share it. My name is Hrogo, by the way.'

'I'll come with you then. My name's Pherri.' She found it odd that Hrogo did not seem particularly concerned with finding a way back to their own world. How could someone think about anything else while separated from their friends and family?

'This way,' he said, pointing to the trees as Pherri pulled herself up onto the bank. 'We can dry ourselves by the fire.'

Pherri kept herself a few steps behind Hrogo as they walked into the wood, not yet ready to trust him fully. In truth though, she was beginning to feel sorry for him, with his limping gait and sad eyes.

'Sorry,' she said, quickening her stride to catch up with him.

Hrogo looked at her strangely. 'Sorry?'

'For being rude, before. I'm just tired, and you seemed a bit scary. You aren't now though. You're just lost, like me.'

Hrogo gave a rueful smile. 'I think that's the first time anyone's ever said sorry to me.'

Pherri thought she saw tears in Hrogo's soft eyes. 'No one's ever said sorry to you before?' she asked. 'But you can't have been hiding in the woods that long. Surely before—'

'I was a slave,' said Hrogo. 'In the Imperium.'

Pherri was so surprised by this she almost tripped over her own feet. It did though explain a great deal about Hrogo. 'I didn't know they still had magi in the Imperium, nor that they were slaves.' Da'ri had told her all the magi of the Imperium were long dead.

'They don't. I am— *was* the only one. It is a sad tale, and one I would rather not dwell on. Come on, it's not far.'

A short walk later, they emerged into a small clearing within a ring of bushes, with an open window to the sky between the tight tree branches. A burnt-out fire sat at the centre, and beside it a thin man with hollowed-out cheeks lay on a coarse, rolled-out blanket. He was old, much older than Hrogo, wearing fine clothes soiled with dirt. He had a heavy brow and a hook nose, and a proud face that suggested he might once have been a man of consequence, but his eyes were vacant, staring up into the blue nothingness of the sky.

Pherri stopped. 'Is he... mad?'

'That's one word you might use.' Hrogo busied himself around the clearing, setting down his bowl to gather fresh firewood. 'Take a seat.'

Pherri was a little reluctant to approach the strange man, and took a place opposite, with the fire between them. 'Does he speak?'

'Sometimes I think he's trying to.' Hrogo dropped a pile of firewood and crouched down to begin arranging it into a cone. 'Though none of it of any sense.'

'Who is he? What happened to him?'

Hrogo paused for a moment. He looked at the man, with a curious expression on his face as if he was struggling to place him. 'I was a slave, and he was my master. Kvarm, his name was. He has been insensible ever since we arrived; I believe the stress of being sent between realities scrambled his wits.' Pherri could not tell if the look on Hrogo's face was of sadness or shame. 'For decades, I dreamt of killing him. He would deserve it.'

Pherri considered the old man. He looked up at her, but his eyes stared past her into nothing. 'How long have you been here?' she asked.

Hrogo hesitated, and fumbled the knife he was striking a flint against. 'A few months, maybe. I stopped counting after the first week. It's been difficult – I've never been able to catch anything to eat, so we live on berries and plants mostly. I wondered for a while if Krupal might drag me back, but I'm still here.'

Pherri did not understand why Hrogo would trouble to share food with the man who had enslaved him. Perhaps it was not only Kvarm who'd had his wits jumbled.

'How did you get here?' asked Hrogo, as the fire finally sparked into life. He took a seat on the ground next to Kvarm.

Pherri would sooner have discussed how they were going to get back, but she supposed it was Hrogo's turn to ask a question. 'I was on Eryispek because... It's a long story.'

Hrogo tossed her a branch of berries, considerably riper than those Pherri had wolfed down on her way here. 'I have nothing but time.'

So Pherri told him. She began with the day she had met Theodric, and ended with escaping Eryi, and left out nothing in between. Their realisation about Eryispek, Delara, the Lutums who had found them, Vulgatypha, the encounter with Eryi's undead servants, facing Eryi and turning the tide of battle for the Erlanders.

By the time she finished, the sun was hidden behind the trees, Kvarm had fallen asleep, and Hrogo's jaw was practically on the floor. 'That's... that's...'

'Quite a tale,' agreed Pherri. 'And it's why I need to get back. If I can't defeat Eryi...' *If I can't find my way home and defeat Eryi, Erland is doomed, and everyone in it.* She looked at Hrogo. 'Will you help me?'

Hrogo appeared to consider it. 'I'm not sure that I can. I can't do magic any more. You probably can't either. And I'm not sure I want to go back. There's nothing for me here, but it's still better than being a slave.' Fear flashed in his eyes. 'Or facing Krupal again. Ever since I was born, magic's only been a curse.' He glanced around the clearing. 'I may still be a cripple, but at least here I'm free.'

Pherri refused to believe she could no longer do magic. She just needed to get her strength up, and that required more than just wild berries. She had eaten through the entire branch Hrogo had given her while telling her tale and felt nowhere close to sated. 'So you're just going to hide here for the rest of your life spoon-feeding your befuddled master?' She tried to keep the scorn out of her voice. 'You do whatever you like, but I'm going home. Do you know where Eryispek is from here?' It was unsettling she had not yet been able to see it, but Pherri reasoned that as it was through Eryispek she had ended up here, she should be able to get back the same way. She must have got her bearings muddled, but this was certainly Erland; it could not be that hard to find Eryispek. If she could reach the Mountain, with its power she could reopen the way between worlds and find her way home.

'Oh yes, I've seen it.' Hrogo gave a strange smile, his squat teeth purpled with berry juice. 'Come with me, we'll find more food on the way.'

That was something at least. Hrogo rose quickly, and once he had checked Kvarm was still breathing set out the opposite way to that which they had entered the forest from; roughly south if Pherri was any judge.

At the edge of the woods, Hrogo pushed back the low-hanging branch of a cedar tree, and pointed to the southern horizon. 'Do you see it?'

There was a familiarity to the landscape: the way the plains rose and fell, the hills covered with pink heather, and the way the evening sun glinted off a stream that she was sure ran all the way to the Pale River. This was East Erland, and not so far from where Pherri had left her own version of it, close to where Eryispek ought to be.

Through the indigo gloom of evening, Pherri squinted, and on the southern horizon saw something that made her breath catch in her throat.

Beyond the Sorrowlands, half-hidden within swirling smog, a familiar shape appeared like a mirage, disappearing into cloud so thick that it was impossible to discern a summit. It was red sand, rather than ice, but there was no doubting it.

In this world, Eryispek lay hundreds of miles to the south.

CHAPTER 3

The cold air reeked of dank and ancient death. The darkness hung, pressing down on him like a great black canvas, so heavy upon his senses that it almost seemed to hum in his ears, a constant undercurrent to the faint *drip, drip, drip* of distant water, or something else.

Orsian moved to rest his head against the wall, setting his rusted manacles jangling. It was as cool and clammy as the rest of the dungeon, but at least it gave him some connection to the world above, where the same stone rose through the above-ground levels of Piperskeep. It was some small comfort, a reminder that he was still within the castle, not banished to a netherworld where the sun never rose.

He reached forward, fumbling blindly for his water bowl, and found it empty, as he had known it would be. Eagerly, he licked the last drops of moisture from its bottom, and then turned his neck to do the same against the damp wall. It was desperate, but his throat was parched, and knowing there was still water reassured him that he could survive, even if every soul in the keep was to forget about him.

You could have taken the easy route, he reminded himself,

pointless as it was to dwell on. He could at this moment have been preparing the defence of Merivale with Errian, had he not let his reckless sense of honour get in the way. It was what his father would have done though; he had sworn his oath, and that meant defending the rights of Andrick and Ciera. Errian and the rest might prevaricate that Ciera was not a Sangreal and the boy king could rule without Hessian's widow, but that was not how Orsian saw it – by what right did Lord Balyard and Errian claim rule over Erland instead of Ciera, the wife to one king and the mother to another?

Orsian shifted to lean sideways against the wall, seeking respite for his aching back and numb arse. *I could not abandon Ciera, not after I put her in this situation.*

Tansa. The guilty memory of her in Orsian's heart ached worse than any hunger pain or bruise left by Balyard's men. He ought to have known, to have guessed; Tansa had never spoken of how or by whose hand her brother had died, and Orsian had never thought to ask. *Fool.* Perhaps being confined to the dungeon was fair recompense; if not for his mistake, for his blind infatuation, Hessian might still be alive.

It always ends with death, he reflected bitterly, interlocking his fingers and crushing his fists tight together. He had fought as best he could, and always it seemed to be for nothing. His father had never told him how little could be solved with the strength of a man's sword arm. What worth was one sword, tangled in a web of the fury of kings and the hunger of empires? What worth was he?

Pherri thought I was worth saving. The memory of his sister's touch on his mind during their stand against the Imperials seemed almost as though it were from a dream. He could not have imagined it, but if he was right in that, where was Pherri? *Who* was she?

'Pherri?' he whispered her name into the darkness, willing and wishing to feel the brush of her presence against his senses. Dozens of times in his weeks of imprisonment he had breathed her name into the void, holding onto hope that he might hear his sister speak his name like a soft gust of wind in his ear. Again though, nothing stirred; only the oppressive, rippling darkness and the endless, taunting dripping of unseen water.

Orsian wondered how far down he was. It was said there were levels of Piperskeep so deep men could be left there until they were forgotten. There could be rooms down here packed with bodies, nameless skeletons still chained to the wall by their manacles. This might not even be the deepest level; there could be floors even lower than this one, left to rot and manned by vengeful ghosts.

At the cell's far end, a warm yellow glow blossomed, indicating to Orsian that someone was coming with his next meal. It might be breakfast or dinner; he had long lost track of the time of day – even before he had come down here the meaning of time had seemed diminished, amidst the defence of Piperskeep reduced to only two states: fighting and sleeping.

'Stew again, is it?' he called into the lessening darkness as the light swelled. He supposed he ought to be grateful he was getting fed at all. 'How about some wine to wash it down with?' Orsian laughed at his own pitiful jest. His voice sounded strange in his ears; older, like the creak of a gate in need of oiling.

Orsian had expected some nameless, grizzled guard, but when his visitor's high shadow came around the corner Errian stood before him. His brother looked tired, his long blond hair frayed and dull, with deep bags under his eyes. He bore a bowl of stew in one hand, and a tall jug in the other.

'You honour me with your presence, Brother,' Orsian rasped. 'I regret though that I'm not currently well-placed to receive visitors.'

'I did not come here to honour you.' Errian's expression

remained as inert as the dungeon walls. 'Nor to humour your weak jests.'

'So you're here to kill me then?' He had threatened to, when Orsian first returned to Merivale. 'Put a blade in my hand and you're welcome to try.' Orsian spoke with a bravado he did not feel; even before they had left him to rot in the dark, Errian had been the better swordsman.

Errian blinked. 'I came to speak with you, Brother.' He stepped forward and squatted a few paces away. From his cloak, he produced two cups, and then a jug from which he began pouring wine.

Orsian gave a dry laugh. 'First time for everything, I suppose. Since the day I was born, you've shown no interest in addressing one word my way unless it was to insult me.'

Errian crouched and pushed a cup of wine towards him, which Orsian grasped in two hands. 'Do you wish me to say I was a bad brother? I admit it. But I did not come here to relive childhood quarrels. We aren't boys any more, Orsian. You showed your worth on the walls of Merivale. If you feel I mistreated you—'

'Mistreated me?' Orsian paused with the cup halfway to his mouth. 'Do you recall how many beatings you gave me? It wasn't enough that you got to be Lord of Violet Hall after Father; you had to rub it in my face every fucking day of our lives and I was just expected—'

'Eryi's blood, Orsian, let it go. I told you – we're not children any more. I'm here to settle things, for good.' He paused, as if summoning the will to say what he had to. 'I want you back. We need you. I've persuaded Balyard – he'll allow it, if you make a public apology. It's a good deal, given I'm the only thing that's been stopping him hanging you since Ciera escaped.'

Orsian covered his surprise with a sip of wine. The grapes burst like sweet nectar upon his tongue. 'Am I meant to care what Balyard thinks?' His encounters with Hessian's son-in-law had been brief, and he could imagine the lengths Errian had gone to in order to appease him, but the thought of making an apology made him want to choke on his wine. 'He's a bloody traitor. You and him.'

A flicker of anger crossed Errian's face. 'It was necessary. We both saw at Whitewater what can happen when a commander dies. I am not saying the men lost heart at Hessian's death, quite the opposite, but we'd have had a rebellion on our hands if we allowed Ciera to remain in power. I did what I had to do; we can't have fighting within the walls and fighting without – I'd do it again. I didn't swear any oath to bloody Ciera Istlewick.'

Orsian knocked back half his wine in one go. 'And handing the crown over to Balyard was just as necessary, I assume? The Norhai know I've made mistakes, but I've got barely a thimbleful of your talent for folly. Remind me whose fault it was we were at Whitewater?'

'I've made greater mistakes than most, I'll admit – I'll carry Whitewater until my dying day – but it was not my folly that brought the king's murderess into Piperskeep. You know there are also some among the *Hymeriker* who'd see you hang? They were prepared to give you the benefit of the doubt over what your little slut did to Hessian, until you drew steel against your own brother *hymerikai* to let Ciera escape. Might be that I'm the only thing stopping them.'

Orsian downed the rest of his wine and held out his cup for more. He had not eaten recently, and he could already feel it going to his head, but in that moment he did not care. Errian was uncharacteristically stoic in the face of Orsian's defiance, he had to admit; he had thought the reminder of Whitewater was sure to at least earn himself a punch. '*The benefit of the doubt*? I'm the one who saved this bloody city, or have you forgotten?'

'You played your part,' Errian admitted, pouring Orsian another cup. 'I've told you that. But so did thousands of others, and that doesn't give them a free pass to commit any treachery they please. I'm looking to make peace with you, but I'm not going to kiss your feet for it.'

'Treachery? It was you who conspired with Ciera to remove Balyard in the first place! And when Hessian returned and found out what he'd done, he kept him locked up. If there's a traitor here, Brother, it's you, twice over.'

Errian let the insult wash over him. 'I acted in the best interests of Erland. No harm would have come to Ciera or the young king if she had just cooperated, but you had to overreact. They're in far more danger outside Merivale than within Piperskeep.'

Orsian snorted. 'Not with Balyard around. He'll sell us out to the Imperium first chance he gets.' Orsian had been in Cliffark during Balyard's short reign and missed Ciera's brief and bloody coup, but he had heard enough to know Erland was not safe in Balyard's hands, whatever Errian may think.

'He's an able administrator,' said Errian. 'Someone has to deal with such matters, and it can't be me. I have a war to win, and the Imperials are rallying. I came down here hoping you'd be willing to seek forgiveness and take your sword to the true enemy, but I can see you're not ready yet.' Errian made to stand. 'I'll leave you the wine; hopefully it inspires some sense in you.'

'Rallying?' When Orsian had been brought down here, the Imperium had been practically a spent force, pushed back beyond the city walls. The citizenry had been flooding back into Merivale to repopulate it. 'But we were winning.'

Errian came to his feet. 'Didn't you say we had been lucky? There's no sign of their commander, but there's an old man in a brown robe in charge now and they look to have stemmed the flood of desertions. They're as dangerous as they ever were.' He scratched his chin, as if weighing something up in his mind. 'Did you ever hear of Eryispek exploding?'

Orsian stared at him, confused by the sudden divergence. 'Exploding?'

'It's been spewing smoke for days now. Wouldn't be a concern, but the streets are full of maniacs preaching the end of days, and some folk even seem inclined to believe them. A few of the men are saying it's a sign from Eryi that our victory is at hand.' He shrugged complacently. 'Sure it's nothing. Was just interested.' Errian picked up the lamp. 'Anyway, I'll leave you to it, seeing as you'd obviously rather rot down here than give up your pathetic pride.' The indifference on his face was laced with contempt. 'If you change your mind, just tell whoever brings your food. I'll be waiting.'

Orsian tried to imagine Eryispek hurling out smoke, but the idea was impossible; the Mountain was only ice and snow, and endless, without a summit. That was where his mother and Pherri were though. Why would Eryispek now have begun erupting? Was it an omen? Were his sister and mother dead? Panic seized his heart. 'Errian, listen to me. If Eryispek—'

'There's no more to be said, Orsian.' Errian was already turning to leave. 'If you wish to see it for yourself, the deal's still there for you. Best accept it soon, before the voices clamouring for your execution get any louder.' He turned on his heel and left without a backward glance, plunging Orsian back into darkness as the lanternlight receded.

Orsian hunched over his wine. *Eryispek erupting.* He had drunk too much, and his head swam with it, but in his addled mind he knew that it was of more significance than Errian could see. Pherri had gone to the Mountain for a reason. What if there was some aspect to the chaos in Erland they had not realised? His thoughts drifted again to Pherri, the faint touch of her mind against his as she turned the tide of battle in their favour. He had put her intervention down to the bond they shared, but what if there was more to this war than East and West, than

Erland and the Imperium? Eryispek suddenly spewing fire could not be a coincidence.

'Errian!' Orsian called after him. 'Come back, Brother!'

The only reply he received was his own voice echoing off the far wall of his cell. Orsian waited for the sound of returning steps, but none came.

By Eryi, I need to get out of here.

CHAPTER 4

Helana woke, and immediately wished she hadn't. Her jaw was on fire where someone had struck her, and when she raised her hand to touch it she let out a gasp at its tenderness. Her head was pounding, fiery blood beating at the back of her eyes. The light was low and grey, but still it seemed too bright to look at, like needles spiking her already scrambled brain. She slammed her eyes shut, trying to make sense of her scattered memories.

She'ab had given her more casheef, and she had been herself, but also not, and then something else had happened, and now she was tied to a chair in a bare, wooden room, with an icy wind whistling through the open window. She shivered against her bonds. Someone had stripped her, leaving her only a thin shift that did nothing to protect her from the cold.

She tried to remember where she was – and who was She'ab again? It hurt to think. There had been a scribbled note, then a beating, and screaming and fires on the forest floor below.

The forest. She was in Thrumbalto; that much she remembered. At least, she hoped she was still there. Helana tried to shuffle her chair to the window, but someone had nailed it to the floor. She tensed against her bonds, but that only made her headache worse.

Slowly, she made sense of the visions twisting through her head. Her cousin Pherri was important – that was why the shaman She'ab had given Helana casheef – but Helana had not been able to find her. She had briefly watched the girl fight a battle of wills atop Eryispek before she disappeared into the void, and Helana had followed her. The scribbled note had been left for herself – a *different* Helana in another world – with instructions to find Pherri. The sheer strangeness of that idea made Helana's head ache anew. Would this other Helana make sense of it, or just believe she was losing her mind?

And then had come her return to Thrumbalto, dehydrated and insensible. *Ti'en*. She remembered now, fragmented memories rushing back to her. The girl Helana had thought was her friend had been in league with her older brother Hu'ra all along, spying and plotting for the day they would overthrow Chieftain Ba'an, their father. Helana clenched her trapped fists, recalling Ti'en's betrayal, and again threw herself uselessly against her bonds. The effort of it made the room spin, and she closed her eyes again at the nausea that rose in her gut. The aftereffects of the casheef still lingered.

Once her stomach calmed, Helana gave herself a moment to consider her surroundings. She was in one of the Thrumb's tree huts, smaller than those she was used to, bare save for the chair she was sitting on and another facing her a few feet away. Through the single open window, Helana could see no other trees, only grey sky. A cold drizzle was falling, splattering rhythmically against the roof.

Helana jammed her entwined feet against the floor, trying to free her chair from the nails that held it, but she might as well have been trying to kick over the Irmintree. In her weakened state, the effort of the attempt soon overwhelmed her, and this time Helana could not stop herself gagging and coughing up yellow bile over the side of the chair.

As her head cleared, Helana was beginning to realise just how much trouble she was in. This was not Erland, where captors might have regarded her as a valuable hostage. To Hu'ra, Ti'en, and their allies, she was just an unwelcome irritation, her presence a symptom of Ba'an's misrule.

If they wanted you dead, they would have killed you already, she reasoned. But what if they had something worse in mind for her? Some hideous vengeance for the Thrumb who had died the year before at the hands of Jarhick, her dead brother?

Helana's blood ran cold as she heard the creak of a floorboard beneath her, followed by a single set of steps on the stairs leading upwards. The Thrumb usually navigated the trees via lifts and pulleys; that stairs were required to reach Helana was a measure of how isolated her prison must be.

The door burst open, and Ti'en stood there, short and shapely, dressed in Thrumb forest garb with a short bow over her shoulder, her hair hanging in the six plaits of the Thrumb and a broad, hungry grin on her pretty face. 'Thought I heard you rattling about. You're awake then.'

Helana stared at her, imagining how it would feel to put an arrow between her captor's eyes.

'Looking at me like that won't help you.' Ti'en's lopsided sneer brimmed with mockery. 'Thought you might have managed to free yourself. Your brother would probably have been out by now, but then he was a warrior, not some useless, gullible princess.'

The memory struck Helana like a thunderbolt. *Ti'en killed Jarhick*. How had she forgotten that? The casheef or the confinement had turned her mind to mush. With fury rising in her blood, she snarled, and threw herself against her bonds, swearing that she would not quit until either the chair broke or she did, but still the chair refused to move, and the knots began to tighten around her wrists.

Ti'en only watched, her arms folded, one satisfied eyebrow raised, until finally Helana stopped, breathing hard, her head swimming, her wrists raw and her fingers numb with a lack of blood flow.

'Finished?' asked Ti'en. Helana was at least glad to see a patch of orange bruising around Ti'en's left eye where she had struck her in the immediate aftermath of her waking from the casheef dream. But how were the bruises fading already?

'How long was I out?' panted Helana.

'Five days. I was ready to let you die, but Hu'ra insisted we trickle water into your mouth a few times a day. You kept pissing yourself; that's why we had to change your clothes.' She shrugged. 'Don't reckon all the bonds are necessary really, but Hu'ra insisted. He's chieftain now. Thrumbalto is ours.'

A week earlier, the idea of Hu'ra being chieftain would have baffled Helana. Ba'an and She'ab had barely considered him a threat. 'Are Ba'an and She'ab alive?' They were the only allies she had.

'That doesn't concern you. Suppose we can thank them for bringing you here though. Hu'ra's been desperate for you to wake up; he's on his way now.'

Helana's head spun again as she tried to make sense of it. Hu'ra hated her – she had expected him to kill her and be done with it.

Before Helana could ask what Hu'ra wanted with her, she heard a heavy tread on the stairs, and behind Ti'en Hu'ra burst through the door. He was panting hard, with a wild, bloodshot look to his usually cold eyes and a sickly sheen to his skin. There was a change in him, Helana noted. He had always been full of sneers and mockery, but now his bright grin was fanatical. 'She's awake,' he observed, and by his black-stained teeth Helana could tell he had been using casheef. 'Ti'en, leave us.'

Ti'en departed with some reluctance, and Hu'ra took the seat opposite Helana, splaying his long limbs out as if to take command of the whole hut. His tongue ran momentarily across the top teeth, and Helana caught a flash of something small and black move within his mouth.

'Casheef, reduced to pellet form.' He peeled back his lips to show her, a tiny dark sphere caught in the bud of his tongue, and then shifted it to press it against his cheek. 'Slow release, so I stay in this world but see the truth of things.'

'That stuff is dangerous. But by all means keep taking it.'

'Casheef is my birthright, as is the knowledge it imparts.' With his tongue, Hu'ra moved the pellet from one cheek to the other. 'It was wrong of She'ab and my father to keep it from me.'

'It doesn't tell you anything. It's a whole load of shit.' A gust of wind howled through the window, and in her thin shift Helana shivered. 'All I saw was nonsense.'

Hu'ra arched an eyebrow. 'It has revealed much to me already. She'ab and my father deceived us for years.'

'Fine. So you can see other realities – what of it? Drown in them, fuck another version of yourself silly for all I care. Just let me go and I'll leave you to it.'

Hu'ra gave a cold smile. 'Oh, I think you know more than you are telling us. We know what She'ab told you, about our ancestor Er'yi who gave himself to the Mountain, and how we Thrumb were forced from our native lands.

'My people have cowered in the trees for too long. It is time we took back what is ours. I have seen worlds where the Thrumb covered the land, all the way from the Dry River to beyond the eastern horizon.'

'So you mean to invade Erland? You don't have the men.' Yet as she said it, Helana suspected that did not bother Hu'ra in the slightest. Before, he had been hot-headed, easy to predict, but this cool yet unhinged certainty was another matter entirely. Perhaps he was mad enough to try it.

'We have something better than numbers – we have Er'yi.' From somewhere on his person, Hu'ra produced a small casheef leaf, dull black etched with shining golden-orange veins, and twirled it around by the stem in front of his face, staring at it so hard he was almost cross-eyed. 'The Magus of the Mountain has *woken*.'

Hu'ra rose and stalked to the window, and Helana had to crane her neck to follow him. 'Do you see?' he demanded, pointing towards the horizon. 'The Mountain smoulders, a banner of fire unfurled across the sky. Eryi calls for allies.'

Helana squinted into the grey ether. *He is seeing things*, she told herself, but then the clouds seemed to part slightly, and against the skyline she saw it: the outline of Eryispek, and high above a trail of devilish smoke and crimson flames belching into the sky, spreading like a black stain of blood. A chill ran up her bare forearms, leaving goosebumps.

Hu'ra looked back at her, his eyes glowed with certainty. 'The Thrumb shall answer his call, and, when we do' – he raised his hands and tilted his face to the sky – 'when Er'yi is victorious, we shall stand at his right hand! The Thrumb shall be rewarded beyond any of his servants!' Hu'ra's pupils began to tremble, and he crumbled a corner of the leaf between his finger and thumb, bent forward to violently inhale it through his right nostril. He let out a gasp, and for several moments clasped a hand to his forehead, wincing. Then the pain seemed to cease, and when he looked up at Helana, his right eye was so bloodshot it looked almost burnt. 'He talks to me!' he cried. His eye was beginning to weep pink tears. 'As he spoke to my brother, so he now speaks to me. Our day will come again, and the final battle is at hand!'

Helana resisted the urge to spit her disgust in his face. He was practically frothing at the mouth, his pupils like rapturous moons.

Through his one good eye, Hu'ra squinted at her. 'Your

family don't even understand the true power of Sangreal blood.' He took a step forward, bending closer as if to keep Helana in focus. 'Through casheef, I have witnessed dozens of realities, and in every one, your people were kings, as every other pitiful creature spun around you like spokes about an axle. In your blood rests *possibility*, and there are few things more potent than possibility.'

His voice was different, harsher, as if someone else spoke their own words through Hu'ra. 'And what of it?' asked Helana, more bravely than she felt, wishing she could shunt her chair further away from him. He had leant forward so close that he was within a few handspans of her face. She wished it was not so unnerving. 'If you think to ransom me—'

Hu'ra laughed, a high shrill sound that seemed to set the whole tree vibrating. 'Nothing so mundane as that. Do you know how magic was first discovered? Through sacrifice, the spilling of blood, the extinguishing not only of someone's life, but their life to come, to alter the entire path of history. In time, some found they could manipulate that path without bloodletting – the first magi – but the power remains.' He clenched his fist. 'From here, I am powerless. Er'yi has freed himself. He rides for Merivale. The battle for existence will be fought in the shadow of Eryispek, hundreds of war-torn leagues from here. Even if we left today, we would be too late.' He smiled. 'This is where you, Helana Sangreal, come in.'

He's mad. The casheef has already turned him insensible. Helana let out an uncertain laugh, trying not to think of what Hu'ra might intend. 'Death is death. My soul may not rise to meet Eryi above the clouds, but it will do you little good either.'

'We will see.' Hu'ra began spinning the leaf again, clockwise and counter-clockwise, its veins flashing in the low sunlight through the window. 'This little leaf thins the walls that divide our reality from others just enough for us to glimpse beyond. It is not truly magic, I am told, only the shadow of the truth the light throws onto the forest floor. True magic requires sacrifice. Your sacrifice.'

Helana tried to still her rushing heart. *He is bluffing. He is only trying to scare me.* 'You're a damn fool, Hu'ra. You think if there were some mystery... some *power* to death, that someone wouldn't have already discovered it? Will you use a silver dagger and drink my blood from a cup made of your ancestor's skull?'

Hu'ra's lips stretched in a smile, displaying two rows of yellowed teeth stained casheef black. 'You may mock, but I see your fear. It is odd, wouldn't you say, how casheef gives us a glimpse of another world, but we have no way of seeing another part of our own world? Yet my visions tell me that it is a question of matter and energy, that if you have the key between two worlds the distance between them is considerably less than between two points on a map.

'You went to Merivale, when you last took casheef. What do you suppose would have happened if I'd killed you in this world while you were there?'

Helana felt a cold sweat break out on the back of her neck. What happened if your body failed while your spirit was elsewhere? Would you die in the other world, or be trapped there? 'Whatever it is, it will look like a fucking dinner invitation next to what I'll do to you when I get out of here.'

Hu'ra laughed again. 'I can only admire your defiance. I will tell you. When your death is close, your consciousness will be so desperate to reunite with your body that it will tear a hole in the fabric of existence to return. A gateway between here and Merivale. We will only need to step through it.'

It was Helana's turn to laugh. 'I knew casheef would turn you mad. I'm only surprised it happened this quickly. I grew up with Theodric, my father's magus, and nothing he did ever resembled whatever you're talking about.'

And yet... She'ab had told her that Eryi had been the most

powerful magus of his age, strong enough to bind Vulgatypha, the last of the Norhai. If he was free, the old rules might no longer apply. With Helana's death, Hu'ra might march an army of Thrumb immediately within the walls of Merivale.

Hu'ra snorted another speck of crushed casheef leaf, this time through his other nostril. He gasped, and now it was his left eye's turn to burst red with broken blood vessels and begin weeping. 'After all you have seen, do you truly find it so unlikely? Or does denial take the edge off your fear?' Hu'ra wiped his weeping eyes. 'I wish I could tell you that your death will be quick and painless, but who can know? Perhaps it will be excruciating. When I stand before Er'yi I will not forget your sacrifice.'

With a final chilling grin, he retreated to the door and left her. Helana listened to his footsteps receding down the staircase below.

The window was still open, and the gust that blew through was as keen and cold as a freshly honed blade, but Helana did not feel it. Her heartbeat thundered in her ears like the rising surf of the incoming tide.

She twisted her neck towards the window again, and saw nothing but the distant silhouette of Eryispek smoking beyond the clouds. She might be hundreds of feet in the air. The only way down from this prison was by Hu'ra's will. And there was nobody coming to save her.

It was hard to judge what she feared more: being forced back into another reality against her will, or the bleak uncertainty of death. She gave an empty laugh at her own selfishness. Eryispek had erupted, its snowy heights giving way to the fire that boiled from its depths. If Hu'ra told it true and Eryi was free, all of Erland was doomed.

CHAPTER 5

'You sure this is something you want to be getting involved with?' asked Maud, squinting up at Tansa with her shrewd green eyes as she hobbled after her through the red-brick catacombs of Pauper's Hole. 'Getting mixed up in this sort of thing is what killed my husband.'

'You didn't have to come,' said Tansa, never averting her gaze from the corridor. It was not the first time her landlady had tried to talk her out of this.

'Perhaps I want to stop you doing something stupid,' Maud croaked. 'And slow down, would you?'

'I just don't want to be late,' said Tansa.

Maud cackled. 'That's what they say about rebellions; they always start on time.'

Tansa had returned to Cliffark only days ahead of the news of Hessian's death, mere hours before the sky had begun smoking and raining ash from Eryispek down upon them. The city had already been in uproar over Lord Istlewick's plan to conscript citizens into an army that would march to Merivale's aid, and the eruption had only increased the chaos, an invitation for all manner of crazed preachers to begin hollering in the street about the end of days, bidding that all men must repent and throw themselves upon the mercy of this god or that god. If only they could agree on which one.

The city's agitation was almost palpable; a frantic, feverish carousel of competing factions and ideas. In every tavern and on every corner, men muttered darkly about the coming conscription. The Brides of Eryi had sought to chase some of the more radical proselytisers out of the city and almost started a full-scale riot. Two city guards had been found at the bottom of the path leading up to Cliffark Tower with their throats slit. Conscription on its own might not have been enough to stir people, but throw in a smoking mountain and a dead king and the city was a hornets' nest just waiting for someone to set it on fire.

Rebellion. Tansa smiled to herself. She hadn't heard anyone use the word yet, not until Maud, but the sly, ambitious smile of the young sailor who had thrust a pamphlet with a place and time into her hand had been implication enough.

Tansa was jerked back suddenly by Maud's grip on her wrist, who with a surprising strength pulled her to a stop. 'Look at me, girl. Don't think I don't know what that look on your face means. Remember, I've seen this sort of thing before. Don't go throwing your life away for those you've lost; their deaths ain't worth your life.'

Tansa wrenched her hand away. 'It ain't about them.'

'It about the living then? That fancy boy of yours break your heart?'

'Ain't about him neither.' Tansa glared down at the old woman, taking no notice of the tremble in her chest at the mention of Orsian. 'Not everything is about *pissing boys*, dead or alive.' Her life was simpler without any of them. Orsian was just as much a fool as Tam or Cag; he was probably already dead.

'If you say so. Just remember, I've fifty years on you. Not

saying it's made me wise, but it means I've seen a thing or two. And I can tell you this: you getting yourself killed in some rebellion won't fix anything.'

Tansa was growing tired of Maud's interrogation; she had already told the old woman she didn't have to come. 'One death can change a great deal,' she murmured. It was hard to think of lords and kings as special, once you had killed one of them. There were clearly at least some in Cliffark who might feel the same. 'We're going to be late,' she added, then turned on her heel and began striding away, forcing Maud to hurry to keep up.

Tansa was used to Maud's sneering now, but after the weeks she had spent returning to Cliffark and reflecting on all that had happened in the last year, she had come to one inescapable conclusion: killing Hessian was not enough. If Hessian had not killed Tam and Cag, it would have been someone else, like Lord Istlewick dragging them into his doomed forced march to save his daughter. Hessian had deserved to die for what he had done, but he was only one spoke in a great cavalcade of shit. The problem was a country that had not deemed the lives of Tam and Cag worth a jot, and valued hers likely even less.

Their path led them into a part of Pauper's Hole Tansa could not recall seeing before. The brickwork became cleaner, the air cooler and less foul even as the corridors narrowed. One led them straight into a wall, and Tansa was sure they must have taken a wrong turn until she spotted a set of winding stairs through a narrow alcove.

'This ain't really Pauper's,' grumbled Maud. 'Just some fancy prick's cellar. Nothing worth seeing ever happened in these parts, mark my words.'

Tansa ignored her, following the directions she had been given and trusting herself that she was not already hopelessly lost.

Just as Tansa was preparing to reluctantly admit defeat and

retrace her steps in search of a familiar waypoint, they found the iron-banded door her contact had promised her, eight-feet high and set in grand, lacquered oak. Maud was right: this was definitely no longer Pauper's Hole.

She took a deep breath and knocked twice. For a moment, nothing happened, but then a lock clicked on the other side and the door opened an inch. Tansa leant forward, expecting some hooded figure to peer out at her, and came face to face with a thin stiletto-style blade.

From the darkness within, she caught the flash of yellow teeth and a sneering, thick-lipped mouth. 'Password, or I'll skewer you like a rat.'

Maud cackled. 'You ever tried skewering a rat? Fast little buggers.'

The point of the blade shifted towards Maud. 'No one asked you, crone.'

'The password is Saemon,' said Tansa.

'And who was Saemon?'

Maud let out a snort. 'Every fuckhead alive knows who Saemon was; the boy who became Portes Stormcaller, the King of the Waves and the Husband to Fish or whatever it was he called himself. If this is your idea of security, you might as well give yourselves up to the city guard now.'

'Look, it's not my bloody password,' hissed the man. 'Come in then, before I change my mind.'

The door creaked open, and Tansa went in ahead of Maud, raising her lantern to reveal the doorkeeper, a sallow-skinned, overweight man wearing a blood-splattered apron.

'You're just in time,' he told them, gesturing towards another corridor dimly lit by several hanging lamps. 'We're about to start.'

Tansa let the man lead on, and they emerged in a low-ceilinged chamber that might once have been a storeroom, packed with full benches facing a low dais with a lectern on it and alive with the noise of half-a-hundred clamorous conversations. There was a tapped barrel of ale in the corner, and while Maud took a seat at the end of the row Tansa paid a boy for two mugs, then took a spot leaning against the wall beside Maud.

She surveyed the room. Nearly nine in ten of those present were men, who mostly fell into a few distinct camps, and seemed to have organised themselves as such. Harassed-looking merchants in clothes that had seen better days brushed shoulders with ink-fingered, pencil-thin junior clerks, who in turn rubbed elbows with long-haired, rough-hewn sailors, smelling of the sea and talking too loudly to one another. The women were of a more diverse cast; Tansa saw at least two brightly made-up whores – though whether they were there for work or business she could not say – several washerwomen, a few shabby girls who might have been guttersnipes like her, and a smattering of merchants, considerably better dressed than their male counterparts.

'Some revolution,' whispered Maud, taking Tansa's offered beer without saying thank you. 'You fancy this lot in a shield wall against the *Hymeriker*?'

Tansa did not reply. She had tried to tell Maud several times that the *hymerikai* were in no fit state to descend on Clif-fark, but a woman who had seen the devastation the king's men had made of the city when it rose under Portes Stormcaller seemed to have difficulty believing that.

An almost apologetic tapping of a mallet against the wooden lectern brought matters to order, though it took a long time for the hubbub to fall to silence. A thin youth with greasy blond hair wearing a pair of eyeglasses, a billowing tunic, and breeches that were too short for him replaced the mallet with a nervous smile, and retrieved from his pocket a small notebook.

'Righ-righto,' he said, looking out at his audience with the same nervous smile. 'If we could start—'

'What's that jewellery on your face, lad?' called out one of the sailors, drawing a series of guffaws from his fellows. Eyeglasses were rare; Tansa had only ever seen them on the faces of wealthy merchants.

The boy's lip twitched. 'N-no. I don't see well.'

'That's because you've got them things over your eyes!' called a second sailor, drawing an even louder round of laughter from his friends.

Conversations elsewhere in the room began to restart. Tansa sighed heavily. *All that secrecy for this?*

The man pushed his glasses back up his overlong nose and waited for the hubbub to calm, but that did not look like happening any time soon. Some people were turning around to speak to those behind them, and others had returned to the barrel in the corner for more ale.

The bespectacled man tried again. 'Right. If everyone has finished—'

'Who put you in charge?' demanded a burly, bald sailor, who had taken over barrel duties and was now distributing tankards to any person who required one, whether they paid or not. Tansa looked over at him and started as she realised it was Abner, the first mate of the now-sunken *Jackdaw*, who had once held a knife to her throat while kidnapping Orsian. Tansa lifted her tankard to her face, hoping he had not already recognised her.

'We organised this meeting,' said a second man peevishly, rising from his seat at the front. He had a similar bearing to the bespectacled man, but with the beginnings of a gut rolling over the top of his smart trousers. 'Now I don't know who you are, but—'

'I'm asking who you are, lad,' said Abner, his muscles bulging against his shirtsleeves. 'I stood with Portes Stormcaller seventeen years back; what's a skinny boy like you got to tell me of rebellion?'

It was the man at the lectern who spoke. 'We are students of Cliffark's new university. I've studied—'

'Istlewick's vanity monument!' declared one of the whores. 'I'm here because I'm tired of his taxes – he lets the merchants do as they please while I'm left paying near half my income to his coffers! It's like he's built himself a counting house in my cunt.'

'The merchants haven't got it so easy as that!' said an older man behind her in fine clothes that were stained and beginning to fray. 'Ruined me when he let that Imperial lord administrator set up his enclave, and now that he's gone Istlewick's sycophants have stepped into his shoes. A man can't make an honest living any more!'

'At least neither of you have to worry about being conscripted!' declared a clerk with an unfortunate mole covering most of one cheek.

The clamour that had been on the verge of dying down restarted in earnest, every man and woman keen to have their say while the two university students looked on, seemingly at a loss as to what to do.

Maud was grinning in delight. 'I should listen to you more, girl – better entertainment than the playhouse, this.'

'This lot should try living in Merivale,' said Tansa. 'They'd be far worse off then.'

'Folk love to moan about their lords. I never thought Istlewick was a bad sort – he's better than his father. A man couldn't walk down Market Road in those days without having his purse lifted.'

Tansa opened her mouth to disagree, and then closed it again. It was not about whether a lord was a good lord; it was the whole idea of lordship in the first place. Why should she or Tam or Cag or anyone rely on the mercy of a lord? There was seldom any mercy to be found.

The two students were finding it impossible to restore order, but they were saved by a sailor who seemed a little more sober than the rest and ascended the dais. He loudly slapped his hand three times upon the lectern, and then when that did not work drew his steel and rapped it against his tankard.

'You've all said your bit!' he told the crowd. 'But it's these boys who've summoned us here, and clear they've got some ideas they want to share with us. I reckon the least courtesy we can give them is a proper listen.' He slapped the bespectacled student on the back, who stumbled forward and had to catch himself on the lectern. 'On you go, lad.' The sailor surrendered the stage.

The student looked up brightly. 'My name's Ulbert,' he told them. 'I've been studying this book...'

Maud let out a low moan. 'Naught good ever came of staring at marks on parchment.'

'...from Cjarthia, on the Silent Sea. They used to have kings and lords there, but they got rid of them. They've not had titles for over fifty years.' He held up a leather-bound book slightly larger than his palm. 'It's by a man named Lhazan Pijick, and he theorised that the source of all injustice is authority, that it was only when men started organising themselves into kings and lords and peasants that some people ended up with less than others. That's what Istlewick's taxation is; him exercising his authority to keep the rest of us down and feather his own nest.'

'And you needed a book to tell you that?' cawed Maud. 'I bloody know that, and I can't even read.' There were titters of agreement from the crowd.

Ulbert scratched his head. 'Well I suppose... It's just worth understanding the theory, because that's how you know what your aims are. It's when people can't identify the power structures that are the source of oppression that you get crimes like robbery and murder; that's the poor pulling one another down when they'd be better placed dismantling the arrangements that put them in that position in the first place. That's what men like

Istlewick rely on.' Ulbert paused, seemingly slightly surprised his audience was still listening. His face brightened. 'And how do they do it?'

'With guards and soldiers!' cried a sailor.

Ulbert pushed his eyeglasses back up his nose. 'Yes, that's how lords exercise their authority, but how do they convince people that they have authority in the first place? If the entire citizenry of Cliffark rose, the guards would not be able to do a thing against them.' He raised the book again. 'Pijick tells us that it comes from religion. "*The best justification for a king on earth is a god in the clouds. To free the mortal mind from the tyranny of kings, it is necessary to slay the hypothesis of gods.*" The priests preach of Eryi's will and the divine feast that awaits the worthy above the clouds, and why? So that we will wear the yokes that the lords place around our necks.

'But we have seen the truth now!' Ulbert shook the book in his fist. 'Eryispek burns, and we see the truth. There is no god above the clouds; it is only a tale, a tale designed to keep us under their boot heel.'

Maud tutted. 'Shame, he was just beginning to make sense before he started going on about gods. Not sure what he's getting at now.'

'You've seen the fire in the sky,' said Tansa. 'You reckon a god lives up there?' She was warming to Ulbert. He was a bit long-winded, but he was coming close to articulating her own view; Hessian had been a man of flesh and blood just like any other – why else other than a clever deception would anyone accept him as their king?

'Theory is all well and good,' declared the sailor who had silenced the room for Ulbert, 'but I remember Stormcaller. Doesn't matter whether Hessian and Istlewick had a right to or not; it weren't gods that slew the rebels, it were the *Hymeriker*. No theory in your books is going to change that.'

Ulbert was nodding. He seemed to be getting into his stride

now. 'But Portes Stormcaller wanted to maintain the existing power structure; did he not call himself King of the Waves and claim that when lightning struck his ship from the gods he received power over the wind and rain? He only sought to replace one authority with another.'

There were angry murmurs from the sailors.

'I am not condemning him!' Ulbert added hastily. 'He was just as downtrodden as the rest of us.'

'And what are you proposing?' asked Abner, still standing by the ale barrel with his arms folded. 'Are we to make you our king, or are you just saying we kill the gods?'

'I am saying there is no place for kings and gods at all.' Over his eyeglasses, Ulbert fixed Abner with a look that was hard as flint. 'For as long as any man or woman toils under the weight of authority, for as long as lords claim that land is theirs through the accident of birth, there is no liberty for any of us. The only true freedom is freedom for all.'

'Bunch of stuff and nonsense,' muttered Maud. 'Who's paying for my rooms if I can't say who gets what bed?'

It was clear that many shared Maud's view. One of the merchants rose to leave, and the sailors had begun talking to one another again. Ulbert's steely gaze faltered as he realised he was losing his audience.

Abner kissed his teeth. 'Not sure I like this idea. I've as much hate for the lords as any man – was one of them that sent my captain's ship to the bottom of the harbour. But a ship must have a captain. Who'd be in charge in this new world you speak of?'

'You're missing the point,' said Tansa before Ulbert could reply, hoping against hope that Abner did not recognise her. 'The rest of us must struggle because the lords' theft of land and wealth gives us no choice, but without them, we are all free to decide who will lead us. A sailor is not prevented from following a captain if he chooses; it's about giving people the power to make that a real choice rather than a forced one.' Tansa flushed as she realised everyone was looking at her.

Ulbert was staring at her with his mouth open, then seemed to come to his senses. 'Er. Yes. Yes. To the extent such a thing is possible – man cannot free himself from the universal weight of existence that we all bear. Liberty is the right to obey the laws one recognises as such, and not—'

'Isn't that what we all want?' Tansa spoke over him, sensing her moment. Ulbert had articulated her suspicions in a manner she could never have, but his audience had not come here because they wanted theory; they wanted *action*. 'To be able to follow laws that we consider just, rather than because some lord in a tall tower tells us they are the law? By what right does Lord Istlewick tax you and conscript you? And what if Eryispek burning does mean something – that it's time for change?

'Fucking kings and lords have no more right to tell me what to do than *anyone here*. What made them kings and lords anyway? It's not their better judgement based on what I've seen.' She tipped her ale back and took a long sip. 'And if you think it's bad here, you should see Merivale, see how having the king ruling over them has worked out.'

'The king is dead!' declared one of the whores.

'You're bloody right he is! But what of the next king? We can hope for better, or we can seize what's better for ourselves. And let me tell you – the *Hymeriker* won't be coming to stop us, not with how matters stand in Merivale. Will anyone here tell me they don't reckon they could take a half-drunk city guard?'

'Slow, cowardly bastards,' declared a red-cheeked sailor, lifting his tankard as he swayed in his seat. Other mariners roared in agreement, and one of the whores drew a knife from within her skirt to shout over the rising voices about how she had already gutted one guard for refusing to pay her and she would be glad to do another.

Ulbert's control was disintegrating by the moment. He

pushed his glasses back up his nose and raised his small book again. 'Yes, yes, in time! But we should discuss our aims! How will we be organised? What will we ask Lord Istlewick for? How—'

'Ask him for?' shouted a sailor. 'We won't be asking, we'll be demanding!'

'You've given us our aims!' cried Tansa, stepping onto a bench. 'No laws, no lords, and no gods. I'll bloody drink to that. I'll fight for that.'

The crowd roared in agreement; even Ulbert's fellow university student was roaring along with them. Ulbert opened and closed his mouth a few times, then seemed to admit defeat and joined in.

'No laws, no lords, no gods!' called Tansa at the top of her lungs, as the room began to shake with the mob stomping their feet on the floor. She had lost sight of Maud, but she did not care. A room full of people felt as she did, and she had them in the palm of her hand. She felt giddy. Perhaps this was how Orsian felt leading men into battle. She cried out again: 'No laws, no lords, no gods!' as others began to take up the chant.

They were silenced by Abner seizing the lectern from Ulbert and banging it several times against the floor with a heavy brass ringing sound.

'That's all square and shipshape,' he shouted over the decreasing tumult. 'But we're barely a hundred. You thinking to take Cliffark with a hundred people? We need more – thousands more.'

'Leave that to me,' said Tansa. She had seen how crowds worked, how a small force could triumph over a larger one, how folk could be inspired to risk their lives for an idea. Orsian had shown her.

'Who put you in charge?' shouted a merchant.

Tansa laughed. 'No one did, and no one's in charge! I don't

care a flying fuck to be in charge; it's like Ulbert said, we're all free to follow who we please.'

'That's not quite what I said,' began Ulbert. 'There's no—'

Tansa ignored him, and began the chant again. 'No laws, no lords, no gods!' and the whole room sang with it, echoing off the brickwork. Tansa let the noise overwhelm her, imagining this small misfit band shaking the whole city.

Killing Hessian had been only the beginning. She would bring the whole rotten edifice down.

CHAPTER 6

Through the distant haze of heat and dust over the Sorrowlands, the mountain that was not Eryispek shimmered like a reflection in a dirty lake, appearing one moment and disappearing in the next. If only it had been growing larger.

Pherri's feet ached. And her knees, and her thighs, and her head also, sweltering under the unrelenting heat which seemed to be the norm in this Erland without the cooling presence of Eryispek. She had guiltily stolen a wide-brimmed hat from the low boundary wall of a farm to keep the worst of the sun off her.

Hrogo plodded along beside her with his shuffling gait. The other man, Kvarm, brought up the rear a few yards behind, keeping his dull eyes trained upon the ground, seemingly content to follow Hrogo wherever his former slave should lead him.

'Is this your life from now on?' she asked Hrogo, pausing to take a deep swig from her waterskin as the land fell away below them into a sheer valley, giving her blistering feet a moment of respite. 'Letting your old master follow you around like a lost lamb?'

'For as long as he lives, I suppose.' Hrogo sighed. 'I expect you're wondering why I don't kill him. Believe me, I ask myself the same thing every morning when I wake up beside him. I dreamt of it for years, always waiting for the right moment that never came.' He looked behind them where Kvarm was shambling to keep up. 'Just seems pointless now. He'd want me to kill him if he could see himself like this. Either that or I'm a coward.'

'A coward would kill him,' said Pherri. Though she was sure others might have suggested it. It might even have been a kindness. 'Suppose he gets better?'

'You should hope he doesn't. He'd be itching to take you back to Ulvatia and make a slave of you.'

The bitterness in Hrogo's voice convinced Pherri to change the subject. She looked towards the distant mountain. 'How many miles do you...?' She trailed off, realising her question was senseless. The answer could only disappoint her; there could still be a thousand miles or more to go before they reached the mountain. She let out a deep sigh and sank down onto the grass, letting her legs splay down the slope. 'I wish we had magic.'

Hrogo lowered himself down to join her, wincing slightly. 'What if we could find a magus from this world to send you back?'

'That's what I thought. But what if it didn't work?' said Pherri. 'How would he or we know that he was sending us to the right one? We might end up more lost than ever. And we'd need to find a magus first.' Somehow she knew that was not the solution. Every fibre of instinct was telling her to go to Eryispek.

She looked across the many miles separating her from it. In a sense, this was still her homeland, but the contrast of the strange and familiar left her with a powerful sense of unease. The landscape and wildlife were the same, but seeing the mountain against the southern horizon was as disconcerting as it would have been to see the sun in the night's sky. Even the light in this world seemed wrong; the slanted shadows slightly too crisp, the sunlit dew slightly too glistening. She had to force herself not to look at anything too closely, lest it unsettle her. 'Are you still determined to stay here?'

Hrogo shifted awkwardly. 'Back home, I was a slave. Here, nobody even knows my name, and I can't be forced to do magic for someone if I can't actually touch it.'

'So if I hadn't arrived, you'd have just stayed in the woods eating berries?'

'Maybe,' said Hrogo. 'Or maybe I'd have gone to find people eventually. I'm sure there's some work I could do for someone. Not many people speak both Ulvatian and Erlish.'

Pherri did not point out that Hrogo could have done that at any point since his arrival and had not, nor that they did not even know if the Imperium existed in this world. 'We'll go back together,' she told him. 'I'll find a place at Violet Hall for you. You could tutor me about the Imperium, I've always wanted—'

'I'd sooner never think about the Imperium again.' He let out a harsh laugh. 'Were you hoping to learn about the gilded marble palaces and the ingeniously crafted pipes that deliver water to every home? I know how they were built – with slaves. Or perhaps you would like to hear how I got these crooked legs and this twisted spine?'

Pherri bit her lip, cringing back slightly from the vehemence with which Hrogo spoke. 'Sorry,' she said. 'I only read about it in books before, and it sounded interesting. I thought...' She tailed off, realising how pathetic her excuses sounded.

Hrogo said nothing, just stared over the valley with a faraway look in his eyes.

Pherri had scarcely thought of her home, Violet Hall, in months. She missed it, with its bright sandstone walls and creeping purple flowers, and she missed the carefree days when the most difficult choice she had to make was what book to read. It seemed a lifetime ago, and in a sense it had been, before she had met Theodric and he had put into her head that she wanted to do magic.

If I had stayed, what then? she wondered. Eryi might have been thwarted with that simple decision. But that had been the point of all he had designed, she supposed. With Jarhick's death, he had caused Errian to kill Da'ri, driven Erland to civil war, and sent Pherri to Piperskeep to meet Theodric.

'We should keep walking,' said Hrogo, struggling to his feet. The sun had still not passed its highest point.

'You don't have to come with me,' said Pherri quietly. 'I didn't mean to suggest you could tutor me.'

'It was a kind thought.' Hrogo sighed. 'I just don't think I have a place, in this world or ours. Perhaps that is what makes me keep Kvarm alive. Without him, who am I?'

Pherri spared a look back for Hrogo's old master. He was standing patiently, with his hands clasped behind his back, blinking and smiling at them beatifically. 'Do you think there's anything of him left in there?' she asked. The journey between worlds had been almost too much for her own mind to bear; it was no wonder that the experience seemed to have shattered Kvarm's.

'If there is, he is furious.'

They walked on, dipping into the valley to refill their waterskins and drink from a slow-flowing stream, then taking the gentlest path they could find up the other side. Kvarm followed uncomplainingly.

'Do you know anything of our route once we reach the Sorrowlands?' asked Hrogo. 'Assuming it's the same as in our world.'

Pherri had little recollection from the books she had read. The Sorrowlands were mentioned only in passing; books of Erlish history tended to focus upon King Piper's taming of Erland and the glory of the Sangreal line, with mentions of events prior to that usually focused upon the nomadic

Meridival tribe's resilience in the southern wastes beyond the Sorrows. 'None,' she admitted. 'There are no maps. The ground is harsh black flint and bubbling tar pits, where nothing grows. The Sorrowmen are shorter than Erlanders, small enough to ride goats, and they feed on the rodents that live beneath the surface. They gave King Piper safe passage through their lands in return for his agreement he would not trouble or seek to conquer them.' If the tales of the Sorrowlands' bleakness were true, she doubted Piper would have had any desire to anyway. It was possible, she supposed, that the Sorrowlands in this world were different to that in their own, but considering the uninviting shadow on the horizon and the murky cloud that hung over it she doubted that.

'And you're sure you want to walk across it?' said Hrogo. 'To this mountain that may or may not be the answer? I still think we should find someone closer who might be able to help.'

'Who could help us, and how would we find them? We've not seen a soul in days.' It felt sometimes as though the people of this Erland – if it was even true to call it that – were deliberately avoiding them. Pherri looked up, and found that Hrogo was not listening, instead staring into the distance, a peculiar expression on his face. 'Wha—?' Pherri followed his gaze, and in the far-off grassland saw a plume of rising dust, churned up by several horses who had just come into view, silhouetted against the sky.

'We've seen someone now,' said Hrogo. By his tone, Pherri took that he was not so keen on contact with other people as he had been a moment before. The horsemen looked to be setting quite a pace, and heading straight in their direction. 'We should hide.'

Pherri could only agree. There did not look to be many, but there was something threatening about the distant figures she could not place her finger on. 'Back to the valley; we can hide in the bushes.'

In a hurry, they retraced their steps. Fortunately, Kvarm followed, and the three of them crouched down in the undergrowth near the slope's crest, watching the horsemen and hoping they would pass them by. Pherri's stomach churned rhythmically.

'They're coming straight for us,' hissed Hrogo, his eyes wide. 'What do we do?'

'Just stay down. Why would they be coming for us?'

But as the distance narrowed, Pherri was not so sure. The horses were close enough to count now, four of them, the lead rider's unbound dark hair streaming like a banner.

'We should run,' whispered Hrogo, more insistently.

'Run where? If they're coming for us it's too late anyway.' Pherri steeled her heart against her sense of foreboding. Through the branches, she kept her eyes fixed on the oncoming riders, so close now that Pherri could feel the thunder of their hooves through the earth.

As Pherri had feared, they slowed to a stop not far from the valley. A tall, slender woman dismounted from the lead horse, and a short-haired blond man garbed in mail descended from a second mount, red-faced and scowling. They both looked towards the bushes, and Pherri had to stifle a gasp as she recognised them. Unless she was very much mistaken, the two figures were her cousins – Prince Jarhick and Princess Helana.

Helana stood stationary, her head cocked to one side, but her lips moved slightly and then Jarhick was stalking towards their hiding place, his hand resting upon the silvered hilt that protruded from an ornate scabbard.

'Come out of there, in the name of your king!' he called. 'There's no point hiding; my sister's already seen you. I swear you'll answer for what you've done to her!'

Pherri looked across to Hrogo. He smiled ruefully. 'Guess this serves me right for wanting to see people.'

With the branches clawing at their skin, they pushed their

way out the bush and emerged to face Jarhick, Kvarm following behind them.

The prince recoiled slightly at the sight of them. 'Gods, what are you?' He spat on the ground, then reached for the wineskin at his belt. 'Beggars of some sort? What did you do to my sister?'

Pherri glanced sideways to Hrogo. 'We didn't do anything.'

Jarhick's face flushed with rage. 'Liar!' He stalked towards them, lifting his sword half-a-foot free of his scabbard. 'I am King Jarhyck, and I swear that if you do not confess what evil you've done to my sister I will cleave your heads from your bodies.'

King Jarhyck? He said his name peculiarly, as if there were a bone stuck in his throat. Since when was he the king? And what did he suppose they'd done to Helana? How could they have?

Faced with the sight of live steel, Hrogo appeared too frightened to speak, while Kvarm stood to one side of him, humming to himself as if he did not even see Jarhyck. Clearly neither of them were going to be any use. Against every instinct for self-preservation Pherri had, she took a step forward. 'I swear we didn't do anything to Helana. We're not even from here. What's wrong with her?'

Her words did little to calm Jarhyck. He turned to his two companions, two *hymerikai* still ahorse. 'You, throw me your bow. We'll see if you sing the same tune with an arrow in your foot.' The nearest of them retrieved a short hunting bow from his back and tossed it to his king.

'But we aren't doing anything! I swear. If—'

Pherri gasped with fear as a cold hand seized her own, and was shocked to realise it belonged to Helana. Jarhyck's sister had somehow sneaked up on them. She wore a benign expression not unlike that of Kvarm, her mouth slack and her eyes glassy and unfocused. Up close, her long dark hair was a tangled nest of knots, and there was a sickly, salty smell to her as if she had not bathed in weeks. Pherri did not know her cousin well, but the Helana in this world seemed very little like the one in her own. She smiled blankly and gripped Pherri's hand tighter, staring back at Jarhyck who was testing the bowstring.

'Halyana, get back from there, now!' Jarhyck pulled the string a few more times then raised the bow with an arrow laid against it, but before he could go any further, Halyana reached out to take Hrogo's hand as well and pulled him to her, then took a step forward to place herself between them both and Jarhyck.

'Halyana, get out of the way!' Pherri had hardly seen anyone as deranged as Jarhyck was acting, but Halyana made no move to obey. 'I asked you to lead me to the villains who did this to you, now by Piper's balls you'll let me do what needs to be done.' He raised the bow again. 'I swear, if you don't tell me what you've done to her I'll put an arrow right between your fucking eyes.'

With insistent strength, Halyana pushed Hrogo and Pherri further behind her. Then, she spoke, her voice soft as a dream. 'I sent myself a note from another world. It said to find Pherri. I found her. We have to help her.'

Jarhyck seemed so shocked to hear his sister speak that he fumbled the arrow and it spun from his fingers to land in the dirt. 'Piper's ghost...' His face was still flushed, but now when he spoke it was almost tender. 'What did you say, Halyana?'

'It's Pherri,' she said more insistently. 'We have to help her. It was in my note.' She was gripping Pherri's hand so tightly now that Pherri could feel her fingers turning numb.

Jarhyck looked at Halyana strangely, then squinted past her to look at Pherri. His throat bobbed, but he seemed to overcome whatever nausea was plaguing him and held his gaze fixed on her, confusion playing out behind his eyes. Then his face hardened again. 'This is part of your bewitchment, isn't it? Why are you disguised as my cousin? Why is Halyana saying Phyrrai's name so strangely? What is the meaning of this note?' From his sleeve, he produced a haphazardly rolled piece of parchment and flung it towards them. 'Answer me!'

The sound of Pherri's name being butchered was unusually disconcerting, as if somebody had thrown cold water over her that did not leave her wet, or a mischievous spirit had spoken to her on the wind. She picked up the scrap from where it had landed beside Halyana and read it: *Find Pherri. Not your Pherri. On Eryispek. Help her.*

Pherri gave an intake of breath. *Someone knows I'm here.* Tears sprang to her eyes. Who though? Someone from her own world? It seemed likely, if they said to find her on Eryispek.

'My name is Pherri,' she told him. She held the note up and paused. He would not believe it, but she had to try. 'We were sent here from another world. You have to help us.'

'I don't have to do a damn thing,' said Jarhyck, his face implacable. 'Now tell me the truth or I swear—'

'It's true!' insisted Pherri. 'I swear. I have cousins of my own in my own world. Jarhick and Helana.' She saw no reason to reveal to Jarhyck that the other version of him was dead. 'I was on Eryispek—'

'And what in blazes is Eryispek? *You* left the note – it's written right there!' Jarhyck pulled the bowstring back again with an arrow set to it, and Halyana shoved Pherri back behind her.

How am I to explain Eryispek? 'It's... Well, it's that.' Pherri pointed towards the shrouded mirage beyond the Sorrowlands. 'Only it's in Erland, near here. It's how I came to be here. Eryi...' She could not explain Eryi and the events on the Mountain to him. Halyana's reaction seemed to have convinced Jarhyck that she and Hrogo were not from this world, but that could change in a moment. 'We were all sent here, by magic. To return, I believe I need to get there.' She pointed again to the huge shadow beyond the horizon. 'Can you help? Do you have a name for that mountain?'

'That's Pipersmont,' called one of the *hymerikai*. 'Don't tell me you don't know Pipersmont?'

'*Silence*,' said Jarhyck. 'I'm sure they know perfectly well about Pipersmont.' His voice was flatter now, calmer, but still danger lurked within his dark eyes. 'But nevertheless, I will humour you.' He angled the bow away from them. 'Seeing as you are so insistent on your tale, I will let you prove it: cure my sister of her malady, and I will escort you to the edge of the Sorrowlands, provided you swear never to return to Erland again.'

Pherri's heart sank. 'I am no healer.'

'You speak of magic. Use it.'

Pherri shared a glance with Hrogo, and shrugged. There was no harm in trying it. She had healed people with magic in her own world.

When struggling before, she had reached to Eryispek to help her. Pherri squinted, trying to pull the distant outline of Pipersmont upon the horizon towards her, to make it vibrate before her eyes and the distant high winds roar in her ears. She tried to reach for it, to draw on it, not only to heal Halyana but to open the whole of this strange world to herself with *spectika*.

Nothing happened. The only wind was the soft breeze that rustled the grass. Any magic that lingered in this world remained as divided from her as the land from the sky.

Jarhyck gave a small, thin smile, as if it was the result he had been expecting. 'You have been found wanting, whoever you are.'

'There must be someone who can,' said Pherri, her words coming in a rush. 'Find a magus, I'm sure—'

'There is *no such thing* as *magic*.'

Without warning, Jarhyck turned the bow and released.

Pherri let out a gasp.

The arrow took Kvarm in the breast, right over the heart, and Hrogo let out a small scream. The slavemaster's face remained as inert as it had been in life. His body crumpled, first falling to his knees and then forward onto his face. Blood began soaking from his tattered tunic into the grass.

Jarhyck made a small noise of satisfaction. 'Maybe now you will take my warnings seriously.' He gestured to his men. 'Bind them. We'll take them back to Merivale.' He looked at Pherri with a wicked glint in his eye. 'Perhaps there we can discover who and what you are.'

CHAPTER 7

With a crash of wood on wood, the bar within the high inner gate of Fallback Lodge splintered, and then cracked down the middle into two pieces. The West Erlanders dropped their tree trunk-hewn ram and poured through the gate.

The resistance was over in a matter of minutes. Barely fifty Imperial soldiers held the yard, and the slaves threw down their weapons and prostrated themselves before the West Erlanders as gold-armoured legionnaires screamed at them to fight from behind high metal shields. One Erlander took an arrow in the shoulder – perhaps a death sentence, given the Imperial fondness for coating their tips in poison – but after that it was slaughter. Close to three hundred Erlanders rushed over the small shield wall and up the steps of the ramparts towards the despised crossbowmen, burying them under a cascade of falling swords even as they screamed for quarter.

'Let some of the legionnaires live!' cried Rymond, stepping through the ruined gate at the head of their small reserve, though he knew that such a command would fall on deaf ears while his men's blood was up. The yard was already a maelstrom of steel and blood, and he was no Andrick Barrelbreaker, capable of keeping his ragtag band of fighters in check through fear.

At his side, Gruenla placed a hand on Rymond's shoulder as if to stop him intervening, though he had intended nothing of the sort. 'I'll see to it.' The Cylirien mercenary-woman strode forward towards a legionnaire trapped against the corner of the stairs, who had dropped to a knee while ably holding off three of Gruenla's men.

Rymond let her go, forcing himself to watch the battle rather than her. Seeing little chance of an Imperial counter-attack he removed his helmet. Adfric would have admonished him for such foolishness, but the old master-at-arms was months dead now. He missed him though, him and his cool head, never more so than in situations like this when the steel sang and the blood ran hot.

'Drink, Lord?' said Brant, the youthful, rake-thin scout who had sneaked up on Fallback Lodge to estimate the Imperium numbers. He waved an open skin in front of Rymond, sloshing dregs of wine onto the ground.

Rymond hesitated. Life was nothing but never-ending temptations. 'No thank you, Brant.' He had sworn an oath – no drink would pass his lips until he once again held Irith Castle. Assuming he lived that long, and that the Imperials had not ransacked his wine cellar. 'I'll take a smokestick.' A man should be entitled to some vices.

He puffed away on the tabac as his men shoved the few Imperials still living towards the centre of the yard. Mostly they were slaves, armoured with tough leather jerkins and little else. The few surviving legionnaires were forced to their knees and their wrists bound. The weapons were piled to one side, to be fought over and distributed at a later time.

'That had better not be casheef,' said Gruenla, returning, sheathing her dagger and eyeing the rolled cylinder between Rymond's lips.

Rymond blew the smoke into her face by way of answer. 'Does it smell like casheef?'

Gruenla raised a dark eyebrow, reached into a pouch for one of her own, and lit it. 'Just so long as you keep it that way.'

'Why would I need casheef?' He smiled at her. 'I am drunk on your beauty and high on victory.'

Gruenla snorted. 'Do this a hundred more times and maybe we'll call it a victory. And leave my beauty out of it – don't think I'll be letting you slip into my bedroll tonight just because you've captured one fort.'

'Your bedroll is quite safe – tonight, I will sleep on a bed of feathers rather than on a mound of leaves.' He had not been to Fallback Lodge since he was a child, but he was hopeful of finding a bed, ideally one that had not been ruined by some filthy legionnaire sleeping in it. Not that Rymond was much cleaner presently. 'I call that a victory.' Rymond turned towards her with a half-smile. 'Sure you wouldn't care to join me?' His desire was finally beginning to recover as his body shed itself of the last vestiges of casheef. He and Gruenla had been lovers before; why not again? She was no beauty, her face too squat and her nose too long, but Rymond could not deny the strange allure of seeing a woman armoured in mail and leather.

Gruenla sucked in a breath of smoke through her teeth. 'Afraid a man loses his charm once you've seen him pissing, shitting, and vomiting all at the same time.'

'Don't remind me.'

The first few weeks after their moonlight escape from Irith had been some of the worst of Rymond's life. Fleeing from woodland to woodland, shaking from casheef withdrawals and usually half-delirious with it, sweating arrowheads. And those were the parts he remembered.

It had got easier since. Not easy, but easier. He dreamt of it sometimes, and would wake sweating and trembling, then rise to scour his trunk for some of the drug before he remembered that he was sleeping rough and his trunk was back in Irith.

Garwen, a grizzled, heavy-bearded veteran Rymond had placed in charge of the assault, strode from where he had been restraining a particularly troublesome legionnaire to stand before Rymond. 'Two dozen legionnaires and thirty-one slaves, by my count, my King. Two and twenty-nine still living.'

'And ours?'

'Five dead, eight wounded. Leaves three hundred and seventy-six fighting men.'

'Might the slaves join us?'

'For their freedom, though skinny and starved as they are only Eryi knows what use they'd be.' Garwen scratched at his beard. 'Arrow fodder if we ever march on Irith, I suppose.'

Rymond considered his force, looking back and forth across the yard. On the rampart steps, Erlanders and Cyliriens were already dicing over their shares of the spoils, while others stripped the bodies and threw stuff onto the pile. Occasionally a bout of pushing and shoving would break out over an accusation that someone had pocketed something. *Hard men, but even with ten times so many I could not take back Irith.*

A mere two dozen had ridden out with Rymond on his escape, but in the weeks since their numbers had been swelled by loyal, willing Erlanders with every village they rode through and every Imperial patrol they ambushed. Others had come from Irith, escaping the Imperial occupation to seek him out. Rymond had endeavoured to learn from Gruenla and her Cyliriens – they had fought this sort of war against the Imperials before. Now they had enough men, they could turn their focus from ambushing Imperial patrols to retaking the south of the country where the Imperial yoke did not fall so heavy, claiming more fortresses or persuading recalcitrant lords to join them. It might though be many months before he had any hope of retaking his throne, perhaps even years.

'Your lads better not stiff mine,' warned Gruenla, her gaze following Rymond's to the dicing men. 'It's been hard enough keeping them in line with no pay and living on plants.'

Rymond sighed. 'Garwen, go with Gruenla and make sure everything goes on the pile and that the Cyliriens are paid fairly. I'll forgo my share.' The men deserved it. 'And send some men to search the keep and dungeons; there might be prisoners.'

Rymond dismissed the rest with orders to fix the gate, scour the kitchens for something that might be turned into a hot meal, and all manner of other tasks. Then, he ascended to the battlements, alone.

Fallback Lodge had been built in stone, on the site of an old wooden hillfort, set atop a ridge that gave a wide view of a valley stretching to the Dry River that marked Erland's western border. Beyond, the ground rose again into the high forests of the Thrumb, dense with tall treetops that swayed together like fields of wheat. It was a stronghold of the old Fortlands, where the men of West Erland had built a line of fortifications back when the Thrumb had been a true threat rather than a weaker neighbour.

Rymond's walk led him all along the western side, up to the north and around to the east. Here, the ground was flat, to the horizon and beyond, stretching all the way to Irith far to the north-east. The battlements were also several feet lower to the ground, and even without the security of the western ridge there was no moat or drawbridge to provide additional protection. Fallback Lodge had never been designed to withstand an army coming from the east; one of the reasons the place had fallen so easily.

It had been to the Prindians' detriment seventeen years past, during the short-lived rebellion of Ranulf, Rymond's older brother. Andrick Barrelbreaker had crushed the West Erlanders like a grain caught between pestle and mortar. If Rymond closed his eyes, he could still see the man lashing out with his sword, finding flesh with every swing like some great hero of myth.

The Barrelbreaker would know what to do. Although Lord Andrick would never have found himself in this position in the first place, cast out of his home with his country under occupation. Even if he had, such was his legend, the Barrelbreaker would have found himself with four thousand men rather than four hundred.

Rymond ran his hand over a merlon, gazing out at the long leagues that led to Irith. 'I was never cut out for this,' he muttered. Gruenla was right – Fallback was only one fort, meaningless in the grand scheme of this war. How did even four hundred have faith in him? These were truly the best of West Erland, the brave few who had flocked to him only because his name was Prindian, and all he could offer them was defeat. If the Imperium caught wind that he had taken Fallback Lodge, they would descend upon the fortress and crush him.

The image of his mother flashed in his mind's eye, shoving him onto a horse. *'You must be a king, now more than ever,'* she had told him. *'Not just a king, but a leader. If you cannot free us from the Imperium, who will?'*

'Wars aren't won in a day, Lord.'

Rymond turned his head at the voice, and found Garwen walking up the stairs towards him.

'We found fourteen Erlanders locked up in the dungeon,' continued Garwen. 'Puts us nine men up for the day, plus any of those slaves we can make use of, and we took the castle. A decent effort.'

Rymond gave a thin smile. 'Why are you here, Garwen?'

'Giving you a report. And you've the look of a man who needs an encouraging word. My boys used to get the same look whenever their arrows missed the target.'

'I don't mean on the battlements. I mean *here*, fighting with me.'

'Ain't much of a choice the Imperials have given us. And I don't see any others anyone's likely to follow, not since all those great lords went over to the Imperials.' Garwen hacked a great glob of spit over the edge of the walls. 'Eryi-forsaken cunts. You're the only one who's shown a bit of backbone.'

Had he? Rymond wanted to believe it. 'The Imperials have thousands. We have four hundred.'

'*Almost* four hundred. As I said, wars aren't won in a day. You're a young man still. Whether it takes thirty days or thirty years, I want my country back. We all do.'

'And what if I'm the one who lost it?'

Garwen kissed his teeth. 'Not worth dwelling on. We'd not ruled ourselves since the last time the Imperials came calling. My grandda used to tell me that story like he was there, back when I was young and stupid enough to believe he might have been. You're the closest anyone's come in centuries to doing it.'

Rymond Prindian – the half-year king. Even if not for the Imperium, Rymond could not help thinking he would have found some other way to make a fool of himself. 'Were you with me at Whitewater?' Whitewater, his triumph and his shame, where the West Erlanders had won the day and paid with Rymond's honour when Strovac Sigac slew Andrick Barrel-breaker.

Garwen shook his grizzled head. 'Too old. I fought here though, back in the day, alongside your brother. Was one of the lucky few to survive, so went back to Irith and took up brewing. I was better at beer than fighting.'

'You must have fought well enough to survive that day.' Rymond had watched the slaughter. 'Are your boys with us?'

Garwen hesitated, staring out over the horizon, the soft wind pulling at his beard. 'My older lad Millas is, but Gathis died.' His voice was hoarse. 'Died the day the Imperials took Irith.'

'I'm sorry.'

'Is what it is. I joined up with your ma's rebellion, brief as it was, then when news reached me she'd got you out I came to find you. Tough woman, your ma.'

Rymond laughed. 'Tough and then some.' Even if it did take him thirty years to win back West Erland, he half-suspected his mother would still be there to tell him he had done it wrong. Assuming the Imperium had not killed her already.

Garwen held out a wineskin. 'I never met a problem a drink couldn't cure.'

Rymond raised a palm. 'No thank you. Sometimes I think that's where all my problems began.'

Garwen shrugged. 'Suit yourself.' He took a long draught and put the skin away.

Rymond's gaze flicked to the east. A grey stain of smoke laced with fiery red still lingered over the horizon like an angry birthmark. 'What do you suppose that means?' he asked. There were no previous accounts of Eryispek erupting.

Garwen's gaze followed Rymond's. 'Honestly, Majesty, I've been trying not to think about it. An ill omen, I imagine.'

An ill omen. Rymond stroked his chin. But was that for West Erland, East Erland, the Imperium, or all three? Perhaps he could find a priest who would tell folk it was Eryi's blessing for his cause.

They turned away from Eryispek as a bald Cylirien with heavy black brows wearing a motley collection of armour came striding up the stairs. 'The captain's been questioning one of the Imps,' he told Rymond. 'This one speaks Erlish – an interpreter, he says. You'll want to hear what he has to say.'

Rymond had a strong suspicion what Gruenla's questioning involved. 'Lead the way then.'

The man led him inside the keep, and down a set of steep stairs with no handrail on one side and a sheer drop into the darkness on the other. A dim glow from somewhere below lit the way, and the steps were so slick underfoot that Rymond was relieved he had refused all offers of a drink.

'Did you have to question him down here?'

The Cylirien turned and grinned a row of cracked teeth. 'Captain's orders.'

They reached the bottom, and Rymond followed the Cylirien around a few corners, to a flat-ceilinged cellar lit by a single torch. In the room's centre, Gruenla crouched on a stool, cleaning under her nails with a knife tip, regarding a chained legionnaire, a slender man with a shock of silver-blond hair. He had been stripped naked, and even in the cool damp of below ground a sheen of mustardy sweat decorated his body. Rymond supposed that being hung upside down could have that effect on a man. His feet had been stirruped into a pair of leather thongs that hung from the ceiling, leaving his head just an inch from the ground. Judging by the perspiration pouring off him and the pink glow to his head, the Cyliriens had wasted no time in putting him to the question.

'I once saw a man last a whole day upside down before he died,' Gruenla was saying as she moved from one nail to the next. 'Saw another man's heart give out after twenty minutes. How long do you reckon you've been like that now?'

'Who knows?' drawled the man. Despite being upside down, he appeared to be smiling slightly. 'I'm thoroughly enjoying myself. The brothels in Ulvatia that offered this sort of treatment were well beyond the contents of my purse.'

His jest fell on stony silence. Gruenla jabbed her knife at him. 'And do the brothels in Ulvatia chop men's balls off as well?'

'Possibly. Is that how the Cyliriens made you?'

Rymond was laughing as he stepped into the light, drawing Gruenla's eye to him. 'Good to see you making yourself at home.'

Gruenla's smile was blood-chilling. 'Wasn't sure at the time, but keeping some of them alive was a good idea. If I give the other one to the men maybe they'll stop belly-aching about getting paid.' She rose from her stool and prodded the man in the neck with the point of her boot. 'This one thinks he's a real wit. Tell the king what you told me, and it better match exactly.'

'Could I at least be put the right way up first?'

'Just answer the damn question.'

The man sighed. 'Fine. My name is Rucius. I'm a translator, serving in the fifth column of the Eternal Legion, commanded by—'

Rymond winced as Gruenla suddenly put the point of her knife to Rucius's exposed testicles. 'No one gives a flying fuck what your name is. Get to the bit we care about.'

This seemed to focus Rucius's mind. 'There's a bounty on your head. Five hundred gold medallions to the man who kills you, a thousand if you're alive.'

Rymond supposed that was to be expected after a month of ambushing Imperial patrols and hanging them on Gruenla's advice as a warning to others, although likely they would have wanted him back anyway. 'I could use a thousand medallions. Captain, could you step away from his balls, please?'

'Making you uncomfortable, is it?' Gruenla laughed wickedly. 'There's more.' She looked down at Rucius in expectation, not moving her knife.

'Another five thousand troops of the Eternal Legion are crossing the Bleak Hills.'

Rymond frowned. 'Is that Alcantra's doing?'

'I don't know; no one seems to know what's happened to her. But Senator Fulkiro's dead. Slain in the siege of Merivale.' The man winced, trying to stretch out his shoulders, slight panic beginning to show in his strained face. 'Could you let me down now, please? I promise I'm much more amusing the right way up.'

Rymond let out a long breath. *They would not send so many*

just for me. Not unless they had impossibly overestimated his strength. 'What happened at Merivale?'

'No one knows. All the reports are confused – heard one saying we hold the city and the keep's about to fall, then the next we'd been routed, and then another saying the siege holds but Fulkiro's dead and some Erlish lord has taken over.'

Rymond ran his fingers through his wiry beard. There was little satisfaction to be taken from the Imperium's struggles in East Erland. He wondered if Strovac Sigac had anything to do with it – the man collected betrayals like turds collected flies. 'Most peculiar. But I don't hear anything telling me we should let you down. What of my mother?'

'She lives,' said Rucius. Rymond felt a great deal more relief than he had expected. 'But maybe not for long. Word is that the new force is led by Legate Acques Bazar.' He swallowed. 'He's ruthless.'

Gruenla spat on the floor. 'That's the Imp whoreson killed my brother, five years back. Invited him and half-a-dozen other Cylirien leaders to peace talks and buried them alive.'

Rucius was nodding, or at least trying to. 'That's him. He'll use your mother to draw you in. He'll—'

Rymond had heard enough. 'Cut him down.'

Gruenla sighed. 'Fine. Just let us keep the other one.' She stepped away and signalled to the Cylirien holding the torch, who with no thought for ceremony roughly cut the translator's wrist bonds and tugged his feet from the ceiling apparatus. Rucius barely got his arms up in time to protect himself as he landed heavily on the flagstones.

'Get him some clothes,' Rymond told the Cyliriens as Rucius came awkwardly to his feet. 'And for Eryi's sake don't kill him.' Having a translator might prove useful.

The stairs were less treacherous going up, though several times Rymond found himself lost in thought and had to throw out a palm to the wall to stop himself slipping. *Another five thousand fresh Imperials, and me with four hundred.* And then there was his mother, and this new legate. Garwen had predicted that retaking Irith and West Erland might take a lifetime, but that assumed Rymond would survive that long.

In the yard, enormous pewter cauldrons had been hefted forth from the kitchens and fired, several barrels of ale had been tapped, and the men had cast aside their weapons. Cries of laughter filled the air, with the rattle of dice and the din of two men attempting to draw a tune from a damaged lute and a goatskin drum. Nobody had yet thought to locate any mugs, so instead the men were using for vessels whatever they had to hand – helmets, boots, and one man was even drinking from a legionnaire's steel glove.

Rymond watched, bemused. *At least they can forget for a time how hopeless our position is.* Reluctantly, he ascended the first few stairs up to the battlements and tapped his sword a few times against the wall for silence. It took a high-pitched whistle from Garwen to bring everyone to order.

Rymond began. 'Well fought, all of you. You have the rest of the evening to enjoy yourselves. We move south an hour after first light.'

This pronouncement inspired a round of protests. 'We've been kipping under bushes for weeks!' someone cried, and another man added, 'Why would we leave? We've got all we need right here!'

'Because if the Imperials catch us here we're finished!' Rymond tried to speak quickly, before anyone could interrupt. 'We are too few to hold it. We have two advantages: our knowledge of the land and the speed that comes from moving in small numbers. If we stay here, we lose both. We march south, to Oldfort.' There were small holdfasts all along the western border – by the time they cleared them all of Imperials they might have gained enough men to think about striking something larger, perhaps a target that would convince some of the lords of West Erland to seek an alliance with him.

Any protests Rymond had expected were drowned out by the low, mournful blast of a horn from the western wall, followed by another. Alarmed, Rymond raced up the stairs two at a time and rushed around the ramparts.

He met Brant coming the other way, the youth slightly pink in the cheeks. Rymond felt a sinking dread in his stomach. 'Imperials?'

'No, Majesty. A dozen Thrumb just ran out of the forest. They're heading this way.'

CHAPTER 8

From her mare, Ciera eyed the horizon, the purple dusk tinged to pink by the fire that spewed from Eryispek. It had slowed now, but still the Mountain's fury bloomed grey clouds that spread across the sky and coated the west in shadow.

The path north looked only slightly more welcoming. When she had last come this way, it had been from Cliffark to Merivale, and she had had a guard of forty *hymerikai* to guide her around the edge of the fens, with a cushioned carriage to retreat to when she tired of riding. The wettest, deepest marshes of East Erland stretched out before her like a portent of doom, bleak humours and pools of dark water disguised by long grass. But only a few miles away, the ground would begin to rise, and on a clear night they might see the glow of Cliffark reflected against the sky.

For days now they had picked their way through the swamp, the distant torches of the *Hymeriker* visible occasionally behind them through banks of fog. The autumn days were growing shorter and greyer, and the incessant rain granted Ciera and her followers cover. Dark hooded cloaks masked their band against the gloom. By night, they stumbled through the wetland as best they could, and by day they slumped to rest in the water-sodden grass.

They had seen nothing of the Wild Brigade, but somewhere ahead Ciera was sure Strovac Sigac waited for them. His band would be in the hills to the south of Cliffark, watching for lights rising from the fens, ready to fight the *Hymeriker* for them like two monstrous beasts scrapping over cornered prey.

And there were other dangers. One misstep, and a horse could be lamed, or topple into the depths. Or a person. There were guides who knew the wetlands as well as their own child's face, but all of her companions had grown up in Merivale and the surrounding plains. Regardless of the light of Eryispek and the bright full moon that illuminated the bogs' dark water, they were somehow hopelessly lost. Every route they found seemed to turn them back the way they had come.

Ciera raised a frustrated hand. 'Hold. We are riding in circles.' From the path ahead, faces turned towards her. 'We need to stop somewhere and get our bearings.'

At the head of their party, Laphor's brow creased. 'Begging your pardon, Majesty, but there's nowhere *to* stop. I've not seen a patch of land with enough room to swing a cat.'

Ciera rotated her head left, then right. Only pitiless bogs and long, damp grass stared back at her. A rank fog rose from the black depths, wrinkling her nostrils. She leaned to look down at the ground. Her mount's hoof had sunk several inches into the soaking ground. To their left and right, algae-covered water twinkled like fireflies under the moon. They were on a narrow causeway, with just a foot either side between them and dark pits of water that might descend forever.

'We need to keep moving,' said Laphor. 'What use is stopping? If we're still stuck here come dawn, we'll be easy pickings, if they don't see our torches first.' Despite the risks, none of them had been keen to stumble blindly into this part of the marshes without torchlight. They could only hope the fog shrouded them sufficiently.

'Let them come,' said Burik. 'I'd rather die with a sword in my hand than stumble into a watery grave. We might hold this causeway at both ends against a hundred men.'

Laphor looked at him in annoyance. 'Ever heard of archers? You think they're going to stand in a line and let us take them one by one? Don't be so fucking daft.' He blew out his cheeks. 'Piss and balls.' He raised a hand to massage his temples, and then lifted his torch into the gloom. Ciera and the rest strained their eyes, scouring the mist for any sight of something that might be solid ground.

Laphor snarled. 'Nothing.'

'I could go searching,' said Haisie. The servant girl rode with Laphor, between the *hymerika* and his horse's neck. She looked back to Ciera, her innocent eyes shining. 'I'm the lightest; I won't sink.'

'And what will you do if your foot gets stuck?' said Laphor. 'No, girl, it's too dangerous.'

Swaddled tightly against Ciera's torso, Andrick stirred. He grizzled, and pressed his fist against his bare gums. She stroked his cheek. 'Is it any less dangerous than stopping here?' Ciera asked Laphor. Beneath her, the mare snorted irritably, clearly troubled by the terrain. She looked to Haisie. Sometimes hard choices were required. 'Haisie, nobody is asking you to go, but if you're willing...'

The girl was already darting down the side of Laphor's saddle, landing with a squelch on the soft earth.

'I'll go with her,' said Arrik. The youngest *hymerika* rode at the rear of their party. He raised his torch, bathing them in its glow. 'I can light her way and follow her steps. If she goes off the path I'll be there to pull her out.'

And who will pull you out? Ciera thought. Just looking at the black water was near enough to set her teeth chattering.

With the autumn winds rising, if one of them went under they might not be able to get them warm again. They had no wood, and the ground was too damp for a fire in any case. 'Let them go,' she told Laphor. She did not relish the thought of Haisie wandering off into the dark, but if they did not find a way north soon the consequences would be worse, for all of them. Haisie had lived through Hessian's rage after Tam was found in Ciera's bed, a coup attempt, the Imperium assault on Piperskeep, and Ciera's escape; what harm could come to her in a bog?

A lot, in truth, but Ciera suspected Haisie was too young to know that. Getting lost in the fens might seem a trifle after all she had survived.

'Take a rope,' said Laphor, throwing one down as Arrik squeezed between his horse and the unnerving water, following Haisie. 'Tie it to her, but not to you. If you go in, you're on your own.'

Arrik grinned. 'My da used to say that if you decide to wade into shit, don't expect anyone else to fish you out. Never thought he meant it so literally.'

'You weren't there when Derik fell into the pigsty,' said Burik.

The dark and the creeping mists rising from the water did not lend themselves to laughter, and the two boys' jesting drew only weak smiles from Ciera and Laphor. She watched Arrik and Haisie go, illuminated for a time by the silvery moonlight before the fog closed around them and they were lost from view.

'How will they find their way back?' asked Burik. The mist was thickening, marooning their little island in a sea of white.

'Haisie has a good memory,' said Ciera, with more confidence than she felt.

After several minutes watching and waiting in silence, they decided to dismount and spare their horses before it became too dark to do it safely. The mist was beginning to hide them even from the light of the moon.

Ciera led her mare back towards an island of solid ground that barely had room for their four horses, when at her rear Burik gave an alarmed cry, followed by the sound of splashing water.

She turned, just as Laphor rushed forward to haul Burik from the swamp. As Burik came free, Laphor stepped back and slipped on the sodden ground, and they went down together in a heap, their heads coming up only inches short of a pool of water the other side. The torch slipped from Laphor's grip and tumbled into the water, plunging them into darkness.

'You Norhai-forsaken idiot!' hissed Laphor. He shoved Burik off him and rolled onto his back, holding his feet up in the air, his face stricken with pain. 'Damn ankle's gone!'

Ciera rushed over to him, watching her steps in the pale moonlight, and knelt in the mud, heedless of the mess it was making of her cloak. 'Let me look.' Still holding Andrick, she rolled back his trouser leg, prised his boot off as gently as she could, and winced. Laphor's ankle had swollen to the size of a fist, and the skin was already beginning to purple.

He reached up to push Ciera's hand aside, and with a grimace clasped the joint. 'Just a sprain. Bad one though. That ankle's never been right since the Battle of the Hill.' He beat his fist against the ground in frustration. 'If my fighting days weren't already behind me, they are now.'

'Sorry,' said Burik. Naeem's son had come to his feet and was sheepishly squeezing the water from his boots.

'Not your fault,' said Laphor, still wincing. 'I'm the one who led us into this Eryi-forsaken fucking swamp.'

'No, it's my fault,' said Ciera. 'I should never have suggested this. I'm sorry, Laphor.' His ankle looked hideous; the bruising was already beginning to spread up his shin and down his foot.

'You should put it in the water,' said Burik. 'The cold will bring the swelling down.'

Laphor grunted. 'Not the worst idea.'

Together, they helped Laphor move himself closer to the water, and he dipped his bare ankle in. He lay back on his elbows, while a sopping wet and shivering Burik gathered the horses.

Ciera sat down next to Laphor. The fog seemed to be soaking her clothes anyway; what was a bit more water? They stared north, watching for any sign of Arrik and Haisie.

'I'm sorry,' she said again.

Laphor chuckled. 'Of all the injuries I've taken in service to the Sangreals, this may be the stupidest. But don't blame yourself – blame me, or that damn buffoon over there.' He gestured towards where Burik had led the horses and was now removing his waterlogged breeches. 'Or blame Hessian – may Eryi take him – or the Imperium, or Strovac fucking Sigac for murdering Lord Andrick. But none of this was your fault.' With a wince, he removed his ankle from the water. 'This was a shit idea – I'll get frostbite before I get this swelling down.'

'Look!' came Burik's cry from behind them.

Ciera glanced up hurriedly. Through the heavy mist, a faint light was bobbing towards them. Her heart rose, and she leapt to her feet. 'Arrik, Haisie, we're here! Over here!' She began waving. 'Our torch has gone out!'

She listened, straining her ears against the wind for their reply. None came. The spectral glow continued along its path, swinging and nodding, casting yellow light that emerged from the mist at intervals like the sun trying to burn through heavy cloud.

'Over here!' Ciera tried again. 'We're—'

Laphor grabbed Ciera's leg. 'Hush, girl. That isn't a torch.'

Ciera looked again, and an icy dread crept up her spine.

The light was only a few feet off the ground, and it did not dance with the fervour of an unguarded flame, nor burn with the brightness of oil-treated wood. Even through the mist, she could see it was too dim to be the torch Arrik had carried with him.

Laphor hissed back towards the horses, 'Burik, get over here. Get that sword out.'

'I'm not wearing anything,' came Burik's whispered reply. 'Give me a moment.'

Ciera watched the light, spellbound. When she was young, her father had told her of the Bog Tinker, whose wispy light lured unwary travellers into the marshes, but even then she had not believed it. It was only a story, designed to scare children away from the fens.

And yet, her heart began to beat a little faster.

Half-dressed, Burik raced back to them as fast as he dared, now carrying his sword. His eyes followed the bobbing light, widening in horror as it turned. It was coming straight towards them now, over the marshes, a way Ciera was sure that no man of flesh and blood could travel. Burik's teeth were chattering, from cold or from fear.

Ciera swallowed. It was within thirty yards of them now. 'Show yourself!' she called to it. Her voice came out in a wheeze, the words swallowed by the marshland's grey loneliness.

The light came on, and as tendrils of mist parted, Ciera glimpsed a short figure in long white robes that fell to the ankle, and a flash of long, silvery hair.

'Ghost,' whispered Ciera, so rapt she was not even sure she had spoken. She held Andrick a little closer to her.

'Eryi save us,' breathed Burik.

The figure moved slowly, almost floating across the water. Ciera could feel her heartbeat against the back of her throat. Laphor forced himself up on one foot. The point of Burik's sword was shaking.

Ten yards away, the figure stopped.

'What do you want?' demanded Burik, his voice trembling. 'Who are you?'

'Be quiet,' said the figure. A woman's voice. 'All of you. Sound moves strangely in the marshes, but they'll see my light. And put your sword down.'

The figure came forward, and Ciera saw a pair of sandalled feet beneath the robe. Such was her relief she thought her heart might give out. Beside her, Burik lowered his sword.

The woman raised her lamp, and a girl no older than Ciera stared back at them. She was pretty, with a stub nose and slender eyebrows, and the hair Ciera had in the moonlight taken for silver was blonde.

Laphor collapsed back to the ground, clutching his chest. 'By the fucking Norhai,' he gasped. 'Almost killed by a bloody Bride of Eryi!'

He was right, Ciera realised. She should have known the moment she saw the robes, although she looked like no bride Ciera had ever seen, too young and pretty.

'I told you to be quiet!' hissed the girl. 'If they hear you're with me they'll know to follow the light.'

'Who will?' asked Ciera again. 'Are they close?'

'I'll explain all once we're out of here,' said the girl grimly. 'We'll make for Cliffark. I know the way. You'll have to leave the horses. Quickly now.'

'You think I'm going anywhere without a horse?' said Laphor, pointing to his bulbous ankle. 'You planning to carry me?'

'What about my brother?' said Burik. 'He's out there somewhere.'

'They already have your brother,' said the bride. No trace of sentiment escaped her lips. 'The girl got away though, which is better than I can say for the rest of us if we don't get moving. I don't know how close they are.'

'We've not heard anyone,' said Ciera. What if this was some trick of their pursuers? 'Why should we trust you?'

'By Er— By the piss of the gods, be quiet a moment and listen then. Ignore the wind and the water and *listen.*'

Ciera did as she was bid, trying to let the lapping stillness of the water, the rustle of the grass, and rush of the wind wash over her.

And she heard it. A murmuring of men's voices, the tread of boots over muddy ground, and the whisper of mail brushing against leather. The sounds were faint as moonrise, maybe hundreds of yards away, and yet in the dense fog seemed to be all around her. Ciera's eyes scanned back and forth, searching for the silhouette of armoured men against the mist. She saw nobody, but that did nothing to quell the dreadful beat of her heart. In her arms, Andrick stirred.

Laphor struggled to his feet, already pulling his sword slowly and silently from its sheath. 'Where are they?' he whispered.

'We came from the west,' said the bride. 'When I met the *Hymeriker* on the road and learnt their purpose, I offered to help them. Lady Viratia told me to find you. I know ways they don't, but we need to go now.'

'What do you know of Lady Viratia?' demanded Ciera.

'I went up the Mountain with her, but she sent me back. She told me... We don't have time for this – it won't matter what she told me if the *hymerikai* find us, and there are other men waiting for you on the rise we'll have to slip past. My name's Aimya.'

Ciera studied the girl, overcome with questions. Why had Viratia not returned herself? And what message could she possibly have for Ciera? 'How do we know we can trust you?'

Aimya's nostrils flared in frustration. 'Why would I lie? If I meant you harm, I could have led them straight to you.'

'She's right,' added Laphor. 'Whatever her reasons, I'll take my chances with a Bride of Eryi over the *hymerikai* or stumbling straight into Strovac Sigac's clutches.'

Ciera nodded. Laphor was right. 'Can you walk?'

Laphor grimaced. 'After a fashion.' He put his sword to the ground and treated it as a walking stick, hobbling with an awkward two-step and resting his weight on his good leg.

Ciera was reluctant to leave their horses, but there seemed little choice. Burik had at least tied them up so they could not wander into the swamps. The *hymerikai* would take them, and Ciera's band would have to see how far they could get on foot by morning.

They gathered close to Aimya. 'I'll hold my light low,' she told them. 'Follow the steps of the person in front of you. You first, Majesty.'

As they set out across the fens, the voices of the *hymerikai* were clearer than ever, and when Ciera looked behind them, a torchlight floated beyond the hazy curtain of mists, weaving towards them. They made east, dogging Sister Aimya's steps.

There was no hope they would have found the way by themselves. Murky water lapped against their feet, so close that inches to either side might have sent them plunging to the depths. Wet mud sucked at their boots. Their footsteps squelched so loudly that it seemed almost unthinkable the *hymerikai* would not hear them. Aimya's pace was slow, almost stately, like some grim ritual that must be observed to free them from the marshes.

They had travelled a few hundred yards when Aimya raised a hand to bring them to a halt. Ciera cast a look back, and felt a sense of relief that she could no longer see the hunting light of the *hymerikai*. 'We'll need to be careful here,' she murmured back to them. 'Keep your eyes on the ground and the steps of the person in front of you. One misstep and the water here can suck you under.' She looked to Ciera. 'Best give the prince to me from here.'

Reluctantly, Ciera passed Andrick into Aimya's arms, and the bride led them onward.

Ciera kept her eyes fixed on Aimya's steps, and yet she could not hide from the waters at the edge of her vision. Left and right, they stretched into the mist, rippling, oily blackness as menacing as any chasing *hymerika*, the dim light of Aimya's lamp rolling across it like fire rippling across forged steel. From the darkness, a wave of icy water gushed against Ciera's foot, and she gasped as her sole slipped, almost stumbling forward into Aimya before she felt Burik's strong hand grip the collar of her cloak to keep her upright.

When her foot reached ground that was on the solid side of wet, Ciera let out a gasp of relief. It was only then she realised she had been holding her breath. They had reached a small islet, just large enough for them all to stand on. She looked back, and was relieved to see Laphor bringing up their rear, still leaning on his sword and blowing like a blacksmith's bellows.

'Bastard ankle,' he grunted, between breaths. 'Swear there were times there I was walking on water.'

'The *hymerikai* won't be able to follow us,' said Aimya, peering into the mist ahead of them. 'Though if you hear a splash, you'll know they've tried. If we're swift, we might be in Cliffark by morning.'

'What about my brother?' said Burik.

'And what about Haisie?' Ciera was not ready to give the girl up to the swamps. 'We can't just leave her.'

'You already have,' said Aimya. 'And I didn't lead you out of there just to go wandering back in. Forget the girl.'

'How can you be so heartless?' asked Ciera. Such had been their haste to escape the *hymerikai* she had barely thought of Haisie wandering alone in the fens. Guilt flooded through her. 'She's nine years old!'

'It was you who let her walk off by herself, not me,' bit back

Aimya. 'And I didn't save you for the sake of some servant girl – the reason I'm here concerns all of Erland, maybe all the world.'

'Well you'll tell us now, otherwise we're not going a step further!'

Aimya laughed. 'Fine, but don't blame me if you don't believe it. You wondered why the Mountain's started puffing out smoke?'

'We have, along with probably everyone else in Erland,' said Laphor.

'Well, Eryi's real,' said Aimya. 'And so are— *were* the Norhai. I was most of the way down the Mountain when the summit exploded, and that means he's free, him and the last of the Norhai. Their war will make Erland's war with the Imperium look like two sisters scrapping over a doll. Lady Viratia sent me to warn you, so you could summon all the strength you can in the defence of Erland. When they last fought it nearly ended the world!'

Ciera stared at her, wondering if the girl was mad. She was used to the Brides of Eryi's stern-faced piety, but this was something else – the Brides regarded the Norhai as a heresy. 'And Lady Viratia sent you to tell me this?'

'I wouldn't have believed it either, until I saw what I saw up on Eryispek.' Sister Aimya's delicate face was deadly serious. 'And yes, she did. Swear on my life.'

'Even if it's true,' said Laphor, 'what do you suppose the queen's going to do about it? We're running away, in case you hadn't noticed.'

'Balls, I don't know! I didn't want to come to you, but Viratia said Hessian wouldn't believe me, and now it turns out he's dead anyway!' Aimya threw up her hands. 'Guess I just wanted someone to believe me, and Viratia hoped you would. But you're right; you're no bloody use anyway. I should have just let the *hymerikai* have you.'

Aimya turned away from then, just as Ciera saw faint tears

beginning to blossom in her eyes. Ciera had hardly noticed, with Aimya's cool competence at leading them from the quagmire, but she was struck by how young the girl actually was. Her belief in her tale was evident, and she did not bear the burden easily.

'You didn't believe in Eryi before,' said Ciera. 'Did you?'

Aimya sniffed. 'What? No. My dad was the alderman of our village, and after he caught me in the long grass with a tinker's boy he paid a travelling priest to take me to the Brides, with a generous donation. Never occurred to the prick to just pay me that to be chaste. So no, I never believed. I've never even read the holy texts, but the elder bride took me on pilgrimage to Eryispek because I'm good with a staff. She's dead now. Eryi got inside her head. I killed her to save us.'

Laphor let out a low whistle. 'Killing the elder bride. That's quite a confession.'

'I believe her,' said Burik. 'My dad always said there was something odd about Eryispek. Aside from it being endless, I mean.' He paused, his eyes questioning. 'Was my dad with you? His name's Naeem.'

'Yeah, he was,' said Aimya, wiping her eyes. 'Don't know what happened to him when the summit exploded. Don't know what happened to any of them. Might be they're all dead. But I *saw* Eryi. He's real, and he ain't friendly. I'll do whatever I can to stop him, and the other one, Vulgatypha.'

Laphor inhaled sharply, pressing his lips against his teeth. He looked at Ciera. 'This doesn't change anything, Majesty – not yet. We can debate the truth of the gods once we're safely inside your father's walls.'

As sincere as Aimya's belief evidently was, Ciera could not shake her scepticism. Her father had always dismissed the gods as a fable for the weak-minded, and that had rubbed off on her. Travelling up Eryispek, beset by icy winds and no food, people might see all sorts of strange things. And why had Viratia and the rest not come with her? Had Aimya's companions died, and perhaps the shock of it rendered her insensible? They would see whether she told the same tale after a hot meal and a rest in a warm bed.

'Laphor is right,' said Ciera. She glanced behind, back into the mist they had come from. Balyard's *Hymeriker* and the Wild Brigade were her foes; any gods could wait. And all they could do for Haisie and Arrik now was hope. 'We will speak of this again when we reach Cliffark.'

CHAPTER 9

As they rode south, the silhouette of Piperskeep rose from the plains like a black claw against the sky, the familiar sight of Merivale's walls beneath it.

The city and the castle in this world looked no different to those in Pherri's own, and it was apparent they also went by the same names. It was a meagre source of comfort, given she was arriving as a prisoner.

She and Hrogo were shackled in the back of a peasant's cart, commandeered by Jarhyck for half its true value. Twice a day, a paltry meal of stew and stale bread was brought to them by a *hymerika*, after which their bonds were released so they could make water. All Pherri's attempts to engage their captors in conversation were met with silence.

The distant outline of Pipersmont was becoming clearer by the day, and with it Pherri's frustration was growing. They would never be able to satisfy Jarhyck's multitude of questions as to where they had come from and what had happened to his sister, and every hour lost was another hour in which for Eryi to tighten his grip upon Pherri's own world.

It felt so far away now, being here, in a land that was a mirror of her own. Her only sense of there being a world other than this one was her own memory. What if there was no way back? And what if there was an Eryi in this world as well? She might escape Jarhyck and journey the hundreds of miles to Pipersmont only to find a second Eryi there waiting to snatch her and force her to do his bidding. Nevertheless, she could not escape the feeling that Pipersmont should be her destination, and that was all she had to guide her.

'It will do you no good to fret on what you cannot change,' said Hrogo, regarding Pherri from the other side of the cart. 'For years, I dreamt of killing Kvarm, and now they have even taken that from me.' The former slave had taken to their captivity with far more grace than Pherri, and it made her want to scream at him. When they had shackled him, he had borne it with the air of a man for whom this was just the latest in a long line of misfortunes.

'How do you know we can't change it unless we try?' said Pherri. She was not ready to give up yet, far from it.

Hrogo did not reply, just stared dolefully towards the horizon. Something seemed to have broken in him with Kvarm's death, and Pherri could not say whether it was because he was saddened by it or because it had not occurred at his hand.

Pherri looked away from him. *Coward.* Magic or no magic, Theodric would never have given up like Hrogo was.

Pherri sensed eyes on her from beside the cart, and turned to see Halyana riding next to them, smiling. Whatever troubled her, it had not disturbed her ability to ride a horse.

'Can you help us?' Pherri asked, for what felt like the hundredth time in a matter of days. She pointed towards Pipersmont. 'I want to go there.'

But Halyana only smiled slackly back at her, her eyes like two dull marbles.

'Halyana!' Jarhyck's voice from behind them split the silence like breaking glass. 'Get away from them!'

Halyana did nothing. She smiled serenely at Pherri and continued to ride alongside her.

The king gave an angry shout and steered his horse towards the cart. 'It is bad enough what you have done to my sister,' he yelled at Pherri. 'Must you also torment me by forcing her to trail after you like a desperate child? Release your hold on her and I swear I shall free you.'

'We have no such hold,' said Pherri flatly. It was perhaps the dozenth time he had made the same demand. 'If you could just let me—'

'Why would you want to go to the Sorrowlands?' he demanded. 'You condemn yourself with your own mouth. Did Grawl send you to infiltrate Piperskeep disguised as my cousin? What did you do to my sister?'

Pherri threw up her hands, rattling the chains that bound her to the cart. Jarhyck's accusations became more absurd by the day. 'We'd never even been near your sister until you turned up. Do you suppose the Sorrowmen are in the habit of sending twelve-year-old girls to do their spying? Why would they trouble Halyana and not you?'

Jarhyck snarled in frustration, then veered his horse away.

Pherri had heard much of Jarhyck's complaints against the Sorrowmen and their chief, Horned Grawl, who had been raiding the lands on Erland's southern border. This though was the first time he had thought to accuse her and Hrogo of somehow being their agents. She doubted he truly believed half of what he said; he was lashing out because he could do nothing to cure his sister.

In a way though, Pherri was glad of Jarhyck's accusations. The more she could learn about the goat-riders of the Sorrows and their chief for her journey south the better. But first she needed to escape.

An hour later, they came within Merivale's walls, the cart rolling across the drawbridge and beneath the murder holes of the King's Gate into the city streets. Jarhyck led their procession below his banner, while fresh *hymerikai* formed up around the cart as a crowd of curious citizens stood on their tiptoes and tried to peer past the mass of horsemen at the new arrivals.

Pherri had not known the Merivale of her own world well. Nevertheless, she scoured the way for anything that obviously differed. She found nothing, save that the citizens were lightly dressed for the time of year, without cloaks or furs, many with their sleeves rolled up. She would have liked to see if the Sanctuary of the Brides of Eryi was still there, or the Eryian Church, but they were in another part of the city, not visible from the Castle Road. The answer seemed obvious though: without the Mountain, there would be no target for the Eryian faith. Did that then prove there was no Eryi in this world? Or did that give her another reason to be fearful, with the possibility that he lurked in the shadows? But Jarhyck had said there was no such thing as magic in this world, and perhaps that meant there was no Eryi either.

Pherri's contemplation of that question lasted all the way to Piperskeep, with the same high curtain wall, the same gates, the same high tower, the same chime of the bells as they struck the hour. The King Piper of this world had clearly not diverged greatly from the Piper of her own world in designing his dynasty's seat of power.

They came to a stop in the yard, the cart's wheels squeaking to a halt within the shadow of the keep. Jarhyck was the first to dismount, leaping from his horse and tossing the reins to a groom.

'What do you want done with them, Majesty?' asked a *hymerika*.

Jarhyck scowled. 'I need answers from them before I leave

for the wedding of Ramond Prindian and Siera Istlewick. Take them to the dungeons. Hop will loosen their tongues.'

Pherri's veins flooded with cold terror. She had heard rumours of the horrors that lurked beneath Piperskeep. Orsian had once told her that the men who went down there never came out again.

'But, Majesty,' a young *hymerika* cried out in dismay, 'look at her!'

The glare Jarhyck gave the man could have melted stone. 'Just because she looks like my cousin does not make her so. Seeing as you're so concerned for her welfare, you can be the one to take them down. And if you ever question me again, I swear you can join them down there.'

'She's just a girl,' said Hrogo. The blood had drained from his face. 'Take me if you must, but I swear we don't—'

Hrogo was silenced by the butt of a *hymerika*'s spear driven into his gut, doubling him over. 'Out,' demanded the wielder. 'Both of you.'

Pherri took a deep breath. *You faced down a god*, she told herself, *you can handle a dungeon*. Even so, Pherri could not stop herself shaking, and as she stepped down from the cart she stumbled and almost fell before Halyana caught her. She took Pherri's hand in her own and squeezed.

'Thank you,' whispered Pherri. The warmth of Halyana's palm made her feel slightly less alone.

'Piper's ghost, Halyana, get away from her.' Jarhyck ushered two more *hymerikai* forward to drag Halyana reluctantly away and then seized his sister firmly by the arm. 'Now get them to the dungeon,' he commanded the *hymerikai*. 'And get me answers.' He turned and strode towards the main keep, pulling Halyana along with him.

'You heard the king!' declared a *hymerika*. 'Into the dungeon!' Several men moved forward to seize Pherri and Hrogo. Neither of them bothered to struggle.

The scene had attracted several onlookers. A few *hymerikai* had congregated in the doorway of the barracks, and several guards had stopped their rounds of the battlements to gaze down at them. 'Isn't that the Barrelbreaker's girl?' shouted one of them. 'What's she being taken to the dungeons for? When he returns from beating Portis Stormcaller back into the Shrouded Sea he'll rip you apart!'

'The Barrelbreaker's daughter is there, fool,' said a *hymerika*. He pointed up towards a higher level of the keep. 'This is an imposter. Some goat-rider woman probably; all the Sorrowfolk are short.'

Pherri followed his finger. Her eyes came to rest on a high balcony several floors up, and she could not prevent the gasp that escaped her lips. Her head began to spin, as if she was looking down into darkness from a great height and the abyss was staring back at her. It was like gazing into a mirror broken into a thousand fragments, each one showing her a different piece of herself at slightly the wrong angle.

Her own face stared down at her, utterly mesmerised. The girl's hair had been styled into a long plait that hung over one shoulder, and she was older than Pherri could recall herself being, but there was no doubting it. It was like seeing herself in a looking glass. Their eyes met, and the moment seemed to stretch out into eternity. Pherri's skin crawled with the awful strangeness of it; a sense of murderous loathing flooded her mind, even as another part of her wanted to embrace the girl and never let go.

'That's enough!' The butt of a *hymerika*'s spear in the small of her back almost sent Pherri sprawling. 'Move!'

Reluctantly, Pherri let herself be pushed and prodded towards the outer steps that spiralled down to the dungeons. As she stepped across the threshold, she could not resist craning her neck for a final look back towards the balcony.

The girl was gone.

The guards left Pherri and Hrogo in a dark cell several floors down. Their bonds were removed and replaced with manacles chained to the wall, so heavy Pherri could hardly lift them. Blinded by darkness, all she could sense was the smell of filth, the cold clammy air on her skin, and the ambient hum of the deep earth.

This is fine, she told herself, willing her heartbeat to steady as the gloom closed in around her. *Being on the Mountain with Eryi was worse than this.*

But Eryi had needed her alive. What did Jarhyck need her for? All he wanted from her was answers, answers she could not give him. And what then? He would take mindless vengeance on them; no amount of pleading would convince him of their innocence. The very weight of Piperskeep seemed to press down upon her resolve, crushing it.

Pherri felt angry, fearful tears welling behind her eyes, but she wiped them away. She had to be strong; there were people counting on her.

'We could try magic again,' said Hrogo. His voice came from the other side of the cell, echoing in the close confines. He did not sound convinced by the idea. 'Maybe if we try together it might work.'

So try they did, and nothing happened. Pherri had failed at magic before, but even then the power had always felt within her grasp if only she could find sufficient focus. This was different, like grasping in the dark for a candle that had appeared to you only in a dream.

'It's no good,' said Hrogo, after several moments of silence as each of them fumbled for some slender thread of magic.

Though unable to see him, Pherri could sense him slumping forward, defeated. 'For years, I hated magic, and now I would gladly chop off my arm to feel a sliver of it. Do you think all the worlds are so cruel as this?' He laughed bitterly. 'Chains and torture have always been my lot in life. I suppose having no magic was hardly going to improve matters.'

Pherri breathed deep, her heart still racing. *Keep calm*, she insisted to herself. Nobody would dare to torture children in her own world; torture was for the worst of the worst, rebels like Ranulf Prindian who had slain Hessian's first wife's family. They wouldn't, would they?

They waited in silence for what could have been either minutes or hours, every distant sound setting Pherri's hairs on end as she imagined Jarhyck's torturer coming to claim her. She calmed, after a time, but by then the cold of the air and the stone floor had begun to seep into her skin, setting her shivering. There were no blankets, and the manacles prevented her coming to her feet, so she was forced to endure it, the icy touch of the stone creeping through her clothes and into her legs and buttocks until they turned numb.

Keep calm, she said to herself again. She blinked back fearful tears. It could not end like this, imprisoned by strangers, separated from her friends by the length and breadth of a whole world. She could not have escaped Eryi only to end up trapped here. Mute Halyana would come for her, or someone, or...

Footsteps sounded from the corridor, and Pherri's blood turned to icy water. She let out a whimper, and the footsteps shuffled closer. The faint glow of a lamp began to rise in the doorway.

Someone was coming for them.

I should tell them to take Hrogo, she thought. It was a shameful idea, but in the blinding terror she could think of no other escape. Visions of implements of torture rolled across her mind's eye. She had read of such things, hot pincers and great weights that could crush you and—

The glow grew in the doorway. Two shadows flickered, one high and one short, then after less than a moment were gone again. Seconds later, they weaved back again, and Pherri swore she heard voices.

'This way... we can't...' The first voice was weary and reluctant. 'If we're...'

'...just trust me... find them...'

Pherri swore she recognised the voices. The shadows were already receding again. Before she even knew what she was doing, she whispered into the darkness, 'We're *here*. Help us.'

The shadows lengthened, then disappeared, before the torchlight began to brighten.

'...madness... in the dark...'

'...swear... this way...'

'*I'm in here*,' Pherri hissed, as loudly as she dared. '*Please*.'

The two figures rounded the corner, and for a moment Pherri was not sure whether to be terrified or overjoyed.

Her double stood in the doorway, but Pherri barely spared her a glance. Next to her, holding the torch, stood Da'ri.

Her former tutor had not aged a day. He was as lean as when she had last seen him, at the Lordsferry fair on the day he died, with the same dignified upright posture and six greying plaits hanging from his scalp.

'*Da'ri*,' Pherri breathed. Her chest fluttered with emotion. And yet, he was looking at her as if he did not know her – indifferent, almost disgusted.

The girl who was not Pherri beamed and looked up at her tutor. 'See? I said she'd know you.'

Da'ri was not smiling. 'That could mean anything.'

The girl was already moving towards Pherri, producing a key from somewhere. She smiled again, and Pherri felt a brief spasm of wanting to strike her. Was that really what she looked like?

'I'm Phyrrai,' said the girl.

'I'm Pherri,' said Pherri. 'This is strange.'

'I know. When I saw you from the balcony, I thought I wanted to kill you.' Phyrrai's fingers shook as she tried to slip the key into the lock, which unlike the chains themselves was rusted with age. After a few tries, she got it in, but then the key would not turn, clunking uselessly against the mechanism. 'Da'ri, can you help?'

Despite his evident reluctance, the Thrumb bent down and after a few tries was able to release the manacles.

Pherri rubbed at her wrists and stumbled to her feet on dead legs, leaning against the wall as the blood rushed back to them. 'Why did you come?' she asked.

'To help you, of course.' Phyrrai had taken a few steps back and was frowning at her. 'I... I think it's best if we don't look at each other too much.' Her body gave a slight shudder of unease.

'Agreed.' Pherri tore her eyes away, fighting against the bestial desire to throw herself at Phyrrai and tear her throat out. 'But why are you here?'

'You can explain it all to one another later,' said Da'ri. He had returned to the doorway, looking left and right as if guards might appear from the darkness at any moment. 'At present, I suggest—'

Suddenly, Da'ri recoiled with a scream, tripping over his own feet and falling backwards over Hrogo's outstretched legs. Pherri's own cry caught in her throat as the new arrival stepped into the light.

It was Halyana. One hand rested against the wall, while the fingers of the other wound their way through her tangled hair. A beatific smile rested on her face.

Da'ri scrambled to his feet, a blush of anger or embarrassment rising on his cheeks. 'By the Ancestors, she scared me half to death. I told you we had to leave her behind!'

'She still has a mind of her own in there somewhere,' said Phyrrai. She stepped forward to take Halyana's hand. 'And she has every right to come with us – she's the reason we're here.' Halyana beamed down at her, her guileless eyes like two saucers.

'You say that as if it's a good thing,' said Da'ri, dusting himself down. 'Let's just go before they find us. Jarhyck is suspicious enough of me already.'

Pherri pointed to Hrogo. 'Unlock him as well.'

Phyrrai hurried over to Hrogo and crouched beside him, and in a moment the keyhole clicked open. 'A thousand thank yous,' said Hrogo, wincing as he awkwardly pushed himself to his feet and shrugged off his manacles. However, the fetters Pherri had found him with remained, including the one around his ankle with the length of chain hanging from it. 'Now just kill me and make an end of it before they catch us.'

'Can we leave?' hissed Da'ri, ignoring Hrogo. His eyes were tight with worry. 'This is madness. I swear, if—'

'Who's there?'

The voice from the corridor stopped them all in their tracks. The shadow of a man appeared on the wall, growing larger as he approached. 'I can see your lamp!' he cried. 'The king will have your heads for this!' The shadow shifted as he withdrew a long knife.

Pherri was frozen to the spot, they all were. Her heart was thudding against the back of her throat.

The man rounded the corner.

With a snarl, Halyana leapt out of the shadows and fell upon him. The man's cry of alarm was cut short as she drove her own knife up through his throat. He fell to the floor, the lantern slipping from his fingers to shatter violently against the flagstones, a gaping wound flapping open where his larynx had been.

The rest of them watched in transfixed horror as Halyana looked left and right along the corridor. After a moment, she beckoned them all forward, still holding the knife.

Seeing little choice, Pherri followed, hoping that one of their three rescuers knew a way out.

CHAPTER 10

They met in the shadow of the Irmintree, as the forest dust danced in the shards of noon sunlight that penetrated the canopy above. Thrumb in green-and-purple forest garb leant against tree trunks or sat on overhead branches with their feet dangling over the edge, passing jugs of cider to one another. Hu'ra's loyalists were dotted through the clearing, wearing supple leather armour and holding long iron-tipped spears.

Helana stood in her bare feet on the dry mud of the forest floor, the trees wavering in her vision as if she were waking from a dream. Her throat itched like it was on fire, and her legs were trembling uncontrollably. For two days, the Thrumb had denied her both food and water. When she had sought sleep to escape the nightmare, they had thrown cold water over her and slapped her awake. She could have fallen to her knees with exhaustion. *He wants me weak*, she thought stubbornly. *He wants to humiliate me*. She longed to collapse to the ground and close her eyes, but her pride kept her upright.

Across the clearing, Hu'ra – Chieftain Hu'ra, he called himself now – sat upon a grand seat carved from the stump of a great oak. He looked calmer today, a superior smile stretched across his face, but Helana could see the pinkish, bloodshot tinge to his eyes from excessive casheef. Unlike his guards, he had changed from his armour into his forest greens, a leafy tunic that covered him from neck to knee. The surprise assault against his father Chieftain Ba'an had been brief, bloody, and absolute. His men surrounded him in a semi-circle, facing the centre of the clearing, each as youthful as their leader. Behind him, two boys held a stitched blanket of leaves over his head, shielding him from the sun.

Hu'ra raised his hand for silence, and the low chattering of the assembled Thrumb diminished until the only sound was the leaves rustling in the mellow wind, and to Helana her own laboured breathing, coming rough and ragged through her bone-dry throat.

'Bring them down!' cried Hu'ra. Above them, a winch began to creak, and a great wooden cage began its descent.

Helana felt the jab of a blunt spear in her side. She stumbled, nearly going over on her ankle, but she did not cry out.

'Pay attention,' said Ti'en. Though the Thrumb girl was behind her, Helana could sense the cruel smile on her lips. 'It will be you next. You'd have been hanged with the rest if it was up to me, but Hu'ra says he's got something special in mind.'

Helana glanced up at the Irmintree, to the rows of bodies that hung from its branches like rotting, misshapen fruit. Ba'an and his closest allies would be spared that indignance; Hu'ra had ordered that as a mark of respect to his father they would be beheaded.

The bright sunlight hurt her eyes, elevating her already pounding headache, and Helana quickly averted her gaze downwards. She tried to summon some saliva, but the little she had barely touched her aching throat, only making it worse.

Ti'en jabbed her again with the spear. 'Nothing to say, Princess?'

Helana felt too tired and disorientated to say anything. It

hurt to speak. With a flicker of defiance, she imagined punching Ti'en in the jaw, then stealing her spear and charging at Hu'ra.

The cage struck the ground in an eruption of dust and dirt, and was immediately surrounded by spear-wielding Thrumb, jabbing at their prisoners and encouraging them outside. A dozen or so naked old men came forth, their steps clumsy and their skin red from so many long hours in the sun above the branches.

Helana knew most of the men by sight, but it was Ba'an and She'ab she looked for. The chieftain's magnificent plaits had been shorn, and his naked body was a patchwork of bruises and untended wounds. In his armour, he had been fearsome, but unclothed, his title usurped, he had aged twenty years in a matter of days. He could barely stand, and two other prisoners moved to either side to support him as they were led before Hu'ra.

She'ab came last. His body was as tough and wiry as ever, and despite his nakedness he walked out proud as a king, meeting the gaze of every Thrumb he passed until they were forced to look away. His eyes found Helana, and he gave a wry smile. Helana did her best to meet it.

One man was desperate enough to make a run for it, summoning unexpected strength to shoulder aside the nearest spearman and making a dash for the trees. A sling whirled, then whirred, and a pair of stringed stones tangled around his legs and brought him crashing to the ground like a felled tree. Two guards immediately leapt on him as the others laughed, subduing him in a barrage of punches. He was dragged before Hu'ra with the rest and forced to his knees.

Hu'ra was smiling. 'Reassuring, to see one of you still has some spirit.' He looked down at his father, his lip curling in contempt. 'Where has yours gone, Father?' He laughed. 'Do you wish to beg for mercy?'

Ba'an raised his head, but when he tried to speak could only produce a whispery croak. He coughed, and it turned into a hacking fit. Helana could see where the angry red skin on his bare head was beginning to peel. Finally, he managed to say something: 'Whatever you think to do, my son, you will not profit from it. All She'ab and I did was for our people's own protection. You may kill me, but I beg you, do not do what I think you are planning. You don't understand...' His voice trailed off in another fit of coughing.

He speaks of me, Helana knew. She looked at the execution's block intended for Ba'an and the rest, a chunk of dark wood carved hastily for this specific purpose. There would be no such mercy for Helana. *He will drive me mad with casheef before he kills me.* She wondered if before the end she would see Merivale again, as Hu'ra hoped for. Perhaps by the time death came she would not feel it. She tried to summon anger, some resistance she might hold onto in a last act of defiance, but it seeped away, unable to overcome the maddening tiredness behind her eyes or the spasming ache of her empty stomach.

'Kill my father last,' said Hu'ra. A low, steady drumbeat began, and the first of the Thrumb was forced to his knees before the block.

Helana forced herself to watch as they were brought forward. None of them spoke, nor showed any desire to. One by one, each of them was dispatched by a single swift swing of an axe made from a long curved tree branch and tipped with a blade of polished steel. Each head was lifted high, dripping viscous blood and greeted by cheers.

Then it was She'ab's turn. The shaman came forward and knelt willingly in front of the block. He looked up, his sharp eyes finding Hu'ra, and called across the clearing. 'By root or branch, the poisoned tree rots everything it touches.'

Hu'ra scowled. 'It's you and my father who are the rot, shaman.' He gestured to the executioner, who pushed She'ab forward onto the block. The man stepped away, picked up his axe, and raised it high. The blade fell, its edge gleaming in the noon sun. Helana suppressed a scream, and She'ab's head dropped to the dirt.

The drums quickened, building to a crescendo.

Hu'ra flicked out a lazy finger. 'And my father.'

Ba'an found the strength to shove his guards aside, and willingly laid his head upon the block. Helana stared. In his leather armour, with the wolf pelt hung over his shoulders, he had seemed enormous, but reduced to rags and with his head shaved and sunburnt he was only a frail old man. Some Thrumb appeared disquieted, and averted their eyes, but most of those left were of Hu'ra's generation, watching avidly from the edge of the clearing or from their seats in the criss-crossing branches above.

Once more, the axe fell.

The drums ceased, and the Thrumb fell silent with them. The executioner raised Ba'an's head by an ear to the hushed crowd, and then threw it into the trees.

Hu'ra blinked, as if unsure what to do next. He flailed his hand at a fly dancing around his temple. 'The traitor is dead!' he declared after a moment. His words sounded hollow in the stunned silence. 'No more shall the Thrumb allow thieves to claim dominion over our ancestral lands. Today is a reckoning, a reckoning with those content to deny our birthright.' He seized a spear and thrust it into the air. 'Victory to the Thrumb!'

'Victory to the Thrumb!' The reply shook nesting birds into the sky from the high branches of the Irmintree. Behind her, Helana heard Ti'en echo the words with the rest.

Hu'ra's eyes fixed on Helana, as if remembering why she was there. He gestured towards the four Thrumb surrounding her. 'Tie her to the Irmintree.'

Something in his words drew from Helana a final burst of resistance. She knew her struggle was worthless, but she drew a hiss of pain from Ti'en as her elbow struck the Thrumb girl's eye socket. If there was a world beyond this one, she would go there knowing that she fought until the hopeless end. She tried to grab a spear from one of her assailants and took a kick to the crotch for her trouble. She stumbled, and Ti'en angrily swept her legs away. Helana hit the ground, and Ti'en grabbed her hair to pull her head back and placed a knife under her jaw.

'No!' Hu'ra was on his feet. 'She is not to be harmed!'

Ti'en scowled, but did as her brother said. Helana fought uselessly as they dragged her towards the Irmintree. They forced her back against its trunk. A long rope was drawn around her abdomen, pulling her tight to the bark. She struggled as bindings were looped around her wrists, and her hands forced over her head with daggers poked against the bulb of her armpits. The ropes were looped around the branches and pulled tight, stretching Helana up onto her tiptoes, her shift pulled up to expose her bare legs.

A few Thrumb whooped and hollered, but Hu'ra raised a hand for silence. Helana's heartbeat behind her eyes was thudding like a blacksmith's hammer upon a heated blade. Her legs were free at least, so she aimed a clumsy kick towards a guard making sure her bonds were secure, and was rewarded with a punch to the gut that if not for her bindings would have dropped her to the floor.

'Stop that!' Hu'ra's voice cracked like a whip. 'Away from her.'

He rose and began to approach across the clearing. His mouth twisted and gurned, and up close his dark eyes danced with casheef and madness. Helana could almost smell the drug seeping from his pores.

It seemed all of Helana's skin was now drenched in fetid sweat. She had never before known true fear, but now it threatened to overwhelm her. *This isn't real,* she told herself feverishly. *Someone will stop it. Hu'ra will realise this is madness.*

Perhaps he would give her the casheef and be satisfied, then she would wake up back in her cell atop the Irmintree.

Hu'ra reached behind his back for a silver-bladed dagger, and Helana's whole body tensed as he raised it to her torso.

The blade slashed from navel to neck, and the front of Helana's shift split, spilling her breasts into the sunlight. Two more swift shanks along the sleeve, and the garment fell away, leaving Helana naked, the bark rough as sand against her bare back.

Salty tears were rolling down her cheeks to her lips, and Helana ran her tongue out to capture the moisture. She gasped as the cool metal of Hu'ra's knife was laid against her jaw. He did not press hard, but nevertheless she felt blood begin to bead where it touched her skin. A warm tide of crimson began to pulse onto the blade.

'Kill her,' hissed Ti'en, standing slightly back, grasping her spear as if she still meant to run Helana through with it. 'Do it for Ba'il!'

Hu'ra did not reply. His eyes were fixed on Helana, and in her terror she found she could not tear her gaze away. He ran his tongue over his lips. He gave some signal for the rope binding her to the trunk to be cut, and Helana was hoisted into the air, her shoulder joints screaming. They held her just a few inches off the ground, low enough that Hu'ra could still look her in the eye.

'This is not to humiliate you,' he said in a soft whisper. His mouth writhed, turning his pellet of casheef lodged in his cheek over and over. 'The casheef will be most effective with nothing holding you to the earth.' He dipped the blade into a pouch at his waist, and scooped out several measures of powdered casheef leaf, black and orange dark upon the blade's silver, held fast by Helana's blood. He held it up to admire it, and pricked a finger upon the tip, squeezing out his own blood to mingle with Helana's. Still, he was not finished. Hu'ra reached behind her towards the Irmintree and broke off a piece of bark, which he laid flat upon his blade.

Hu'ra held it out towards her, just below her bottom lip. 'Open your mouth.'

The air had become so hot that Helana could barely breathe. She kept her mouth slammed shut, turning her head away from him.

Hu'ra's other hand reached up to seize her throat, and though she had not drunk anything in two days Helana felt a dribble of urine roll down her leg. Did none of the other Thrumb see this? How were they allowing this to happen? Hu'ra smiled, a black, toothless maw of doom. 'The Irmintree to hold you in this world, and our bloods mixed together to hold you to me. Your destination shall be where I will it.'

He squeezed on Helana's neck, until she was forced to let her mouth open. Hu'ra's hand on her neck tensed. 'Wider.'

There were black spots on Helana's vision when he forced the blade inside her mouth to wipe the concoction on her tongue. She gagged on the bark's bitterness, the casheef's strange sweetness, the ferric taste of blood. She tried to spit it out, but Hu'ra clamped her jaw shut. The mixture crackled as the casheef began to dissolve. There was so much of it, even powdered, maybe three or four times as much as she had taken before.

She kept her eyes on Hu'ra. He placed the silver blade against his own tongue. His face began to melt, his eyes dripping wax-like down his face, his grimacing mouth eddying and twisting like a deep lake of dark water.

Helana gasped as Thrumbalto dissolved around her, the world slipping away as if she were drowning. The ropes holding her aloft fell away, and Helana felt herself thrust upward, past the height of the Irmintree and into the infinite blue of the sky. All of Thrumb and Erland spread out below her, the Pale River a blue-white ribbon, and then she was spinning, circling towards Eryispek as the Mountain rose before her like a cool white knife. She was going to hit it.

Helana screamed, and then her feet touched the ground.

She opened her eyes. Her arms were free, and the twin agonies of thirst and exhaustion no longer troubled her. He body was her own again. The inside of a dark tent came into focus, lit by a single crackling brazier. The walls were garishly striped, rich cloth of red and black and yellow.

Helana froze.

She was not alone.

At a long table in the centre of the tent sat two men, a feast arrayed before them of cheese, bread, and a pile of carved pork still steaming with the fire's heat. Helana ducked behind a wooden trunk with brass edges, ensconcing herself in shadow.

In the dim light she could not make out the features of the two men, only their silhouettes. The man closest to her was piling food onto his plate, while at the far end of the table the other man leant back in his chair, regarding the food but seemingly content to leave it alone.

'You demand too much,' the first man was saying. His voice was harsh, fiery with repressed anger. 'I cannot control every aspect of this without at least some assistance. No magus could.'

'*I* could.' The second voice was smooth as still water, but it rippled with authority, as if no force in the world would dare to contradict him.

Eryi. The knowledge came to Helana unbidden. The same malevolent presence she had felt when she saw Pherri fighting atop the Mountain. Suddenly afraid, Helana retreated deeper into the shadows.

The first man had begun to wolf down food, but paused mid-bite to speak again. 'Then why don't you?' As her eyes adjusted, Helana could make out the shape of a coarse brown robe covering the man's shoulders, and a wild crown of long white hair.

'I have told you.' The man's shadow rippled vigorously against the wall. 'I must save my strength. This... imperfect body I find myself forced to use will not retain the energy. I must bring the last Norha to battle soon, before she can recover her full strength. She will not hide forever. If you cannot even achieve this small task, perhaps you are not the ally I hoped you would be.'

'What would you have me do?' demanded the first man. 'This Balyard will only give me one of them.' He refused to be cowed, but Helana sensed his wariness, brushing against the edge of fear. 'If your aim is to defeat the goddess, then why do you obsess over the castle and these boys? They are nothing to us – no magic to speak of. Their sister—'

'They are a means to an end.' There was part of Helana that wanted to see what Eryi looked like, but dread kept her rooted behind the trunk. The castle – they could only be speaking of Piperskeep. Hu'ra had succeeded in sending her to Merivale. 'We must be clever; we do not yet have the men for a direct confrontation, at least not until the Thrumb ceremony is complete – having true believers willing to give themselves to me could make all the difference. We will draw the goddess to us; her mortal form is her weakness.'

Helana was momentarily deafened by the blood flooding through her ears. Hu'ra truly had been communicating with Eryi. But how had he not sensed her? Any moment, she expected to feel Hu'ra's cold blade pierce her heart and her mind rushing back to her body, but it did not come.

Such was her terror that she missed the other man's reply. Eryi was speaking again, his voice sharp as a knife. 'Need I remind you that you swore to obey me?' The god's shadow writhed. 'Our goals make us natural allies, but do not suppose that makes us equal. Even magi do not make demands of gods.' For the space of a blink, a pair of impossibly pale eyes pulsed in his shadowed face, and Helana recoiled in a flash of fear.

'Remember: you have already let me down twice. I will not tolerate a third failure.'

The man in the robe had stopped eating. His shoulders tensed as if he was preparing to rise. 'I have already explained to you why I let the Imperial woman go. Magic and fear have addled her wits – we could not have used her. And Strovac will not fail us. The Sangreal child will be dealt with.' The man paused, seemingly debating whether to say something else. 'Although, I must again admit I do not understand your obsession with this family.'

The Sangreal child. Helana's ears picked up. *What* Sangreal child? Was this one of the boys they had spoken of earlier? Her mind sang with confusion; she could hear something far away – the faint gallop of horses and the *thwip* of arrows.

'The next time you have a question, just recall that I have seen things you have not.' Eryi's voice was beginning to crackle with fury. 'I have seen the fall of empires and the rise of the magi, the beginning and end of all existence, so if I consider something *important* you must accept that it is *important.* The Sangreal child has more significance than you can imagine. Nevertheless, the child can wait, for years if we must. If I am to defeat the goddess and claim Erland, our focus must be on the two within Piperskeep.' He paused. 'And know this, Krupal: once we have them, you will be forced to demonstrate your worth to me. I already have the perfect task in mind. We must hope you are up to it. Now, what of...'

His voice tailed away as the noises grew louder in Helana's ears. How had the two men not heard them? Beneath the galloping hooves came the melody of clashing steel.

The tent flickered, for a moment lightening to sunlight and bright foliage. Helana found herself staring once more at Hu'ra. He raised his knife, its tip glinting terribly in the brazier-light.

Helana screamed.

The scene flickered again, and the two men at the table

rushed to their feet. '*Who's there?*' Eryi's pale-eyed shadow began moving towards her, but he let out a curse as he stumbled on something.

The two scenes flashed back and forth, so fast that Helana could hardly keep up. Hu'ra was shouting: 'I am coming Lord Er'yi, I am coming!' With a snarl of desperation, he brought the blade down towards Helana, the tip intent upon the hollow where her neck met her torso.

It descended inevitably towards her, while across the divide Eryi crossed the tent towards her. *It can't end like this.* The hooves and steel Helana thought she had heard had faded to less than a whisper beyond the thundering of her own blood.

As his arm fell, the rope binding Helana's right arm to the branch snapped like a broken lute string. She howled as her whole weight tore at her left shoulder, but the sudden movement caused Hu'ra's knife to miss and scratch against the side of Helana's neck. Across the divide, Eryi screamed with fury. Helana's feet hit the ground, and overcome with a bestial desire to survive she brought her free right hand up to grab Hu'ra's wrist as he readied another strike. He was stronger though, with gravity on his side, and Helana could hardly see straight. The blade descended, slowly, inexorably, certainly towards her neck.

A spear burst through the back of Hu'ra's head and out of his mouth like a terrible steel tongue.

Blood cascaded into Helana's face, but she twisted Hu'ra's wrist away, as his grip on the knife weakened.

'*NOOOOOO!*' Eryi's scream could have rent the tent in two. The two scenes were flickering so fast that Helana had to slam her eyes shut. The light of the brazier was bright as the sun. The weight of Hu'ra's body fell on top of her. There were horses galloping across the clearing below the Irmintree, with Thrumb fleeing in terror before them.

Helana sensed the rushing feet of the pale-eyed shadow, but

the tent was dissolving around her as the blood pulsed out of Hu'ra's lifeless corpse.

The second rope binding Helana to the Irmintree snapped. She fell, straight into somebody's arms and the dirt of Thrumbalto.

The warmth of a man enveloped her. He had a familiar smell, like warm fires and scented smokesticks that no amount of dirt and hard living could wash away.

'Helana!' His voice was familiar too, like honey poured over silk.

She looked up into the branches of the Irmintree, blinking to bring the face floating over her into focus. The clash of steel and hurried steps assailed her, so loud it was hard to concentrate, and the face of Rymond Prindian came into focus.

Helana could have laughed, but instead she only coughed up a gummy concoction of bark, blood, and bile. 'Oh, balls.' Her voice was like a rusty hinge. 'Of all the fools in the world, did it have to be you?'

He laughed, cradling her to his chest, and the sound was like music to her soul.

CHAPTER 11

Orsian sensed the approach of men before the lamplight came into view. He woke, immediately alert. Trapped in his cell, the darkness was constant, and yet by the chill in the fetid air he thought it might be the middle of the night. With his head leaning against the wall he could almost feel the snores of the castle above. That meant whoever his visitors were, their purpose was not a friendly one.

'Errian?' he breathed into the blackness.

Three shapes appeared in the wide entranceway, two taller men flanking a stout figure in the middle carrying the lantern, their shadows long and sharp against the close walls. Momentarily blinded by the lamplight, Orsian caught a flash of ruddy cheeks and a pot belly in a too-small doublet as the central figure approached.

Balyard's kick to his ribs sent Orsian sideways, his chains clanking piercingly against the stone and drawing a dull grunt of pain.

'That's for before,' he hissed, as Orsian cradled his aching side. 'And the least you deserve after the trouble you've caused.'

Orsian just managed to twist out of the way as he sensed a

second kick coming, and Balyard cursed as his toe collided with the wall. Orsian quickly moved to wrap his chains around Balyard's leg then jerked on them hard, toppling the older man to the ground.

Before Orsian could do anything further, a *hymerika* rushed forward and threw a low punch that set Orsian's ears ringing. The blow thumped his head against the stone floor, then the *hymerika* crouched to clasp a hand over his mouth as the other found his neck.

'Try that again and I'll break your fucking nose,' said Tarwen, the tamest of Balyard's pet *hymerikai*, a rangy, black-bearded man with a heavy brow. 'You're coming with us, but no one said you had to have all your bones intact, so reckon you'll want to behave yourself.'

Orsian stared back at him with fire in his eyes, his head and cheek stinging, repressing the urge to strike back against Tarwen or jam his thumbs into his eyes, but after a moment's hesitation let his hands drop. Chained as he was there was no point in making a fight of this.

'Bastard broke my toe,' hissed Balyard, hopping on one leg as the two *hymerikai* hauled Orsian to his feet. They released him from his chains, then immediately produced a fresh pair of manacles and clasped Orsian's hands behind his back. 'I'd make you pay for that, but we've places to be. You're wanted.'

'Come on.' Tarwen pushed him in the back and Orsian was nearly sent stumbling. 'Bloody traitor.'

'Might say the same to you,' said Orsian over his shoulder as Tarwen and the other *hymerika* began marching him through the dungeons. 'Don't recall making Balyard my king being part of my *hymerika* oath.'

'Never swore to make that murdering whore bitch your king neither,' said the second *hymerika*, a man Orsian recalled as going by the name Cullen, 'but that didn't stop you.'

'Perhaps he thought she'd let him fuck her,' said Tarwen with a sneer. 'All she's good for. I bet half the castle—'

'That's enough,' said Balyard sharply. 'Keep him moving.'

They marched him so swiftly through the dungeon that Orsian was scarcely able to draw breath. Balyard's bobbing light led the way as the two *hymerikai* pressed him down a series of corridors, too fast for him to deduce where they were going, until they reached a staircase and began to climb. The sheer number of stairs was a sharp reminder to Orsian of how deep they had buried him. The muscles in his legs ached from disuse, but it seemed like barely a moment since he had left his cell when they ascended into the cool autumn air, with the warming smell of night fires on the breeze. They were beneath two high walls on either side, and Orsian craned his neck to see sparks of watchmen's braziers high on the battlements. The sky overhead was a dark slate, and a soft rain was falling.

'We are between the double curtain wall,' said Orsian. Disorientated by the darkness, he had expected to emerge somewhere inside Piperskeep.

Where they had emerged, Balyard was lowering a heavy iron grate back into place. 'Not all of the Sangreals' hidden passages are so secret as they might have thought.' He gestured towards the outer wall. 'This way.'

They led Orsian to a rotting wooden door. 'Where are you taking me?' he asked.

'You'll find out soon enough,' said Balyard.

Nowhere good, Orsian thought. Prisoners were not seized from the dungeons in secrecy for the sake of a friendly conversation. For a moment, he wondered if they might be intending to execute him, but that made little sense given where they were taking him. He glanced briefly at the hilt of Tarwen's sheathed sword, wishing that they had bound his hands at the front.

Within was another dark passage, low and dripping with condensation, and Tarwen shoved him onward. 'Move. And don't be looking at my sword again if you know what's good for you.'

'Does Errian know about this?'

Tarwen cuffed him round the temple. Orsian took a momentary stumble, and then turned angrily on his captor before coming up short as the *hymerika*'s dagger pressed against his neck.

'Your brother is not in charge,' said Balyard. 'Now walk on, before I tell Tarwen and Cullen to cut off your ear. Nothing was said of you being delivered in one piece.'

Tarwen's dark eyes danced with amusement in the flickering torchlight. 'It would be my pleasure.' The pressure of his knife on Orsian's windpipe intensified.

Orsian glared at him, and then at Balyard. He needed to remain calm; if at some point they removed his manacles he might get a chance. It was better to wait. Reluctantly, he stepped back from Tarwen.

'Walk on, Orsian,' said Balyard. 'You have nothing to gain by prolonging this.'

Orsian did not move. 'You're taking me to the Imperium.' It was not a question; there was no other reason they would be sneaking him out of the castle in the dead of night.

Balyard smirked. 'We all have a part to play in this war. Even a fallen *hymerika* is of some use.'

'And what part did you play exactly? Never saw you on Merivale's walls when the Imperials turned up.'

'We have no time for this. Move.'

Cullen shoved Orsian in the back, and reluctantly he walked on. He would get a chance – even at this time of night, Merivale would not be deserted, and there would be many who knew his face; if Orsian made enough noise once they were outside Piperskeep somebody would come to his aid. Balyard might find getting him out of the city far harder than he anticipated.

The passageway ran through the width of the wall, and at the other end a high iron latticed gate blocked their way. Balyard pushed past Orsian to fiddle at the keyhole, and with a shriek it opened, dislodging brown shards of rust.

'Move.' Tarwen shoved Orsian in the back and he stumbled through the gate.

Orsian had expected to see some familiar part of Merivale, but instead the city's moat rose up from beneath him like a beast from the watery depths. He let out a cry and fell clumsily sideways into the muddy earth to stop himself tumbling over the edge.

Behind him, Tarwen's laughter broke the night's stillness. 'Careful there.'

On the ground, Orsian spat out bits of grass and flecks of mud. Cullen hauled him back to his feet, while Balyard upbraided Tarwen. 'Stop that – we want him alive, not drowned at the bottom of the moat.'

They were on a strip of earth running between the wall and the moat, barely wide enough for a man to walk along. Orsian looked down into the trench, the miasma of filth making his eyes water. Memories of wading through the same sewage to reach the Imperials' tunnel were fresh in his mind's eye. His efforts had barely delayed the Imperials an hour. *So much death, for so little gain.* He was still struggling to get his bearings after so long underground, but by the curve of the wall and the moat, he judged they were on the western side.

'I suppose you thought we would emerge within the city,' said Balyard, coming to stand next to him, a smug smile on his face. 'Easier this way, I'm sure you'll agree.'

Orsian resisted the urge to spit in his face or to try to kick him into the moat. 'I knew you were a treasonous worm, Balyard, but selling me to the Imperium is low even for you.'

'I am only fixing the mess that you and your mad queen have created. Now move, and mind your step.'

It was a familiar path for Orsian; they soon passed the alcove through which he had entered on his return to the city, and kept walking.

Orsian flexed his shoulders, aching from the way his bonds kept his arms pinned back. 'Do you know how long this wall is, Balyard? Do you mean for us to walk all the way to the Ram's Gate?'

'Fortunately not,' said Balyard. Across the moat, a torch flared into life, and Tarwen placed a firm hand on Orsian's shoulder to bring him to a halt. 'There's our contact now.'

A long ladder was lowered towards them, crossing the whole span of the moat, like those Orsian had seen used during the battle for Merivale, and Tarwen shoved the point of his dagger into the base of his spine. 'I'm going to take your bonds off, and you're going to crawl across. Either that, or I can cripple you.' Tarwen pressed the blade into Orsian's skin, hard enough that he could feel warm blood beginning to trickle down into his breeches.

'Threats stop being so threatening when you have to keep making them. Take my bonds off and see what happens.'

Tarwen tensed as if to press the blade in further, but before he could a low voice hissed from the darkness across the moat. 'Take his manacles off. *Now*.'

Orsian would have expected an angry retort from Tarwen, but the *hymerika* simply shrugged. 'Very well.' Dazedly, he produced a small key, and it clicked in the lock as a moment later the manacles fell to the ground.

Big mistake, Tarwen. Orsian whirled on the spot, elbowing aside the dagger as with his other hand he reached for the older man's sword hilt. Orsian's whole body seemed to come alive as he grasped it, an excited tingle of fire spreading from his fingertips all the way to his shoulder; he had forgotten how good that sweet, supple leather could feel.

Barely an inch of steel showed from the scabbard when the

voice spoke again. It came from across the moat, and yet it seemed to arrive from everywhere at once, not only in Orsian's ears but pounding inside his head. *'You don't need a blade. Put it back.'*

Orsian hesitated. But he *did* need a blade. Swords were strength – why would he not want one? The voice did seem to make a compelling case though. But if he did not take the blade, Tarwen would hit him and then he would be forced across the moat. The sword shrieked as he pulled it free another inch.

'You are among friends, your fellow hymerikai. Give your father back his sword.'

The words were like black ice through Orsian's veins. *My father is dead.* But he looked up, straight into the dark, hooded eyes of his own father, his mouth stern beneath his thick black beard.

Andrick Barrelbreaker lived.

Clumsily, Orsian let his hand fall away from the hilt, and it slipped back into its scabbard. His limbs felt strange and slow, as if moving through treacle. 'Father,' he whispered.

'Good. Now cross the moat.'

Orsian looked up again, and Tarwen's cold face with its spade-shaped beard stared down at him. How had he ever mistaken this man for his father? There were similarities, but Tarwen was over a decade younger, and slimmer, with none of his father's—

'Cross the moat. It is safe here. Your sister is waiting for you.'

Pherri. He glanced across and there she was, spear-thin beneath a haystack of blonde hair, her pale skin glowing in the trembling torchlight.

Orsian's mouth fell open. *Pherri.* Wordlessly, he fell to his knees, and grasped the first rung of the prone ladder. He did not question it after that, crawling as fast as he could, blind to the danger of the deep moat below.

On the other side, he leapt to his feet, but firm hands seized him, and he struggled helplessly as legionnaires in gleaming plate armour clicked a new set of manacles over his wrists. He looked around frantically, but Pherri was not there. Half-a-dozen legionnaires stared curiously, and a white-bearded man in a hooded brown robe smiled at him, but the small blonde girl was nowhere to be found.

Orsian shook his head violently, trying to dispel the confusion that seemed to have come over him. What had he been thinking? Of course Pherri was not here. It was as though a hand had clamped around his brain, manoeuvring him at will; he was acting as senselessly as if he were in a dream. He looked around again, and his eyes met those of the bearded man in the robe.

A single word rose in Orsian's mind.

Magus.

The man smiled a row of gleaming teeth, then winked at him. Orsian averted his eyes, his heart suddenly pounding. Balyard, Tarwen, and Cullen had begun to move across the ladder as if nothing had happened.

Orsian looked up at the walls of Merivale, willing someone to realise what was going on, but he saw no watchman's lantern through the light-falling rain. The legionnaires' torches flickered softly, and occasionally Orsian could not help his gaze being drawn to the magus, huddled within his robe. The influence on Orsian's mind had ended as suddenly as it had begun, and to the eye there was nothing unusual about the man; he could have strode up the Castle Road without anyone batting an eye.

Balyard and the *hymerikai* reached the other side. Balyard looked around, ignoring Orsian entirely. 'You have him,' he said. 'Now where is the king?'

The king? Orsian had been certain that Cicra must have escaped. It had surely been weeks ago that she fled Piperskeep.

The magus stepped forward with a smile. 'I have the girl and her child.' He gestured behind him. 'Bring her.'

Two legionnaires stepped forward into the torchlight, a slender young woman clutched between them. Orsian caught sight of her brunette curls and the bundle in her arms and his breath caught in his throat, until the torchlight slipped across them. Relief flooded through him. This woman was older than Ciera, and not half so beautiful, plain with a weak pointed chin and a high curved forehead. Then he saw the bundle she carried and almost laughed; where there ought to have been a child there was a swaddled marrow, bulbous and green. He kept quiet; he would let Balyard see what his folly had brought them. *The man has doomed us all.* Orsian swore he would take at least one of the Imperials with him, manacled or not.

The woman stepped forward, and Balyard raised his torch to examine her and the bundle. His lips curled in a sneer. 'Majesty. I do hope your little escape was worth it. Perhaps now you have learnt the value of obedience.'

A laugh escaped Orsian's lips. 'Eryi's balls, Balyard, at least look at the horse you are being sold before they kill us.'

Balyard gave Orsian a strange, glazed look. 'I don't know what you're talking about.' He took the swaddled marrow from the woman's arms, and fell to a knee. 'We are your loyal subjects, my Queen. I swear to rule justly in your son's name.'

Orsian stared at him, and suddenly a wave of realisation hit him. *The magus.* He looked to the white-bearded man, who was staring intently at Balyard and the two *hymerikai*.

Orsian shouted a warning. 'Balyard, use your eyes! For Eryi's sake, *look*!'

He expected one of the Imperials to strike him, but no rebuke came, and Balyard ignored him. 'Thank you, Lord,' said Balyard, handing the marrow back to the girl who was not Ciera, 'for this show of good faith.'

The magus waved his hand. 'A trifle. A pleasure dealing with you, Lord Balyard.'

Orsian could only stare in incredulity as Balyard departed. One *hymerika* lifted the girl while the other took the bundle, and together they picked their way back over the ladder with Balyard bringing up the rear.

'I'll tell you nothing,' Orsian told the magus, though deep in his gut dread lurked like an assassin. If the man could make him think his father and his sister were there, what else could he make him believe?

The magus's low chuckle sent a shiver down Orsian's neck. 'What makes you think you could tell us something worth knowing?'

The moon flashed from behind the cloud, and in its cold glow Orsian saw Balyard and the rest reach the other side of the moat. A legionnaire called across to him: 'Is your king well? He's not made a sound.'

The legionnaire lifted his torch higher to illuminate Balyard's distant face as he peeled back the swaddling. He blinked, and his expression turned in an instant, from self-satisfaction to confusion to rage. He stared down at the marrow, and when he seized it the Imperials could no longer contain their laughter as the swaddling fell away to reveal the striped green vegetable within.

'What is the meaning of this?' demanded Balyard, his puce face turning red with fury. He hurled the marrow across the moat where it struck the edge and split apart. 'What is this... this... sorcery, this trickery? I came to you in good faith—'

'You inspected the goods,' the magus called back, his voice soft as velvet. 'We know food in Piperskeep is running low and that you might appreciate a gift. Evidently not. Buyer beware, as they say.'

Balyard seethed. 'Now just look here—'

The magus's head tilted slightly, and four legionnaires

stepped from the darkness, each bearing a crossbow. They fired together, a single sharp whisper followed by the thud of four bolts striking Balyard and his companions, punching through layers of leather and mail.

The girl fell first, toppling into the moat with the quarrel through her torso. Cullen followed her, as Tarwen stumbled backwards and slumped against the wall, blood already seeping between his fingers. Balyard stared back at the magus, shock and agony written in his open mouth and the wide whites of his eyes. A quarrel was embedded in his neck. He tried to speak, and blood poured from his mouth. He tumbled forward and pitched into the moat, face first into the grimy water.

The magus was smiling. '"*Demonstrate my worth*", is it?' he whispered to himself, as if Orsian was not there. 'My *inflika* is implacable, as you will learn soon enough.'

The magus turned away into the darkness. Strange hands took Orsian by the shoulders and ushered him forward. They were gentler than Tarwen and Cullen had been at least.

There were horses waiting not far away, and Orsian found himself flung up onto the rump of one and bound to its haunches. He hoped they were not going far – tying a man to a horse like this was a good way to suffocate him. He shifted to make himself as comfortable as he could, and then looked up to find the brown-robed magus standing close by. His presence made Orsian recoil slightly; he did not want to be anywhere close to this man if he could help it. The compelling suggestion that if he crossed the moat he would find his sister lingered in his mind like a heavy fog.

The magus regarded Orsian peculiarly. His white brows were thick as gorse, and his face craggy with wrinkles, but there was an ageless quality to the stillness of his gaze as if he did not wholly belong to this world. 'Orsian Andrickson,' he said levelly. 'When my master sent me to collect you, I expected someone impressive, but I see only a savage child, no different to every other ungifted brat in this accursed land.'

'I suppose appearances can be deceiving. You must be a magus, but I see only an old man wearing a shit-stained horse blanket.'

The magus's face was as still as old stone. 'You are in the presence of Krupal the Great.' His voice pulsed with repressed fury. 'If you had a man's sense, you would fear me.'

'I'm not sure you get to choose your own nickname, Krupal Shitcloak.' It was foolish to so address a man who could probably turn his mind to pulp, but Orsian was past caring. It felt as if his life had been falling apart from the moment Tansa had murdered Hessian, and being placed in the care of a man who could reach inside his mind with an icy hand was just the latest in a long series of gradually worsening misfortunes.

'We will speak again at camp,' said Krupal. 'It will be dawn soon; it would not do to keep my master waiting. I suggest that if you value your sanity, you learn to address us both with more respect. The age of the magi is rising; soon all men will learn their true place in the order of things.'

Krupal mounted, and Orsian felt his horse being led south by a mounted legionnaire, as several others surrounded him. The rain had stopped, and the night was still. Orsian pricked his ears to try and catch anything they might be saying to each other. Even the smallest tidbit of information could prove invaluable.

He caught snatches of murmured conversation between the legionnaires riding behind him, and tried to piece together what they were saying from the smattering of Ulvatian he had learnt as a child. '...scares me... find out in Ulvatia...'

'They won't,' another of them hissed in reply. 'Ulvatian law doesn't... wants to use a magus...'

'...not right... what he was like before... Never leaves...'

'Quiet,' hissed a third man. 'He'll hear you.'

Orsian felt no closer to understanding why the Imperials would want him, but he sensed the legionnaires' fear, in their words and in the nervous glances several of them kept flashing towards Krupal.

He is a man worth fearing. Orsian imagined what a magus of Krupal's power might do to a man who displeased him, and a shudder flashed up his spine. He had spoken also of a master, and that was perhaps even more unnerving.

And yet, perhaps this was a chance to gain answers. A magus might know what had happened to Pherri, and why Eryispek was burning. In the sky, he could see faint flames billowing behind a bank of cloud. Orsian would learn all he could, and once he knew how best he could serve Erland and his sister, he would find a way to escape.

CHAPTER 12

It was seventhday, when many of Cliffark's workers were granted leave from their work, and despite the drizzling rain that threatened worse to come, the streets were heaving. It was approaching noon, and the atmosphere was almost akin to that of a festival, the air filled with drunken laughter. There was a hard edge to it though – a mixture of curiosity, fear, and anger that Tansa could never recall sensing in the city before. Nevertheless, she had expected it. To some extent, she was relying on it.

The word had come down from Cliffark Tower that this was the day Lord Istlewick would send his representatives into the city for the first ever conscription raffle. No man of fighting age was exempt, though those with the required means could pay a fee to be excluded. There was hardly a soul in Cliffark who thought it right that the young men of the city should go to their deaths for the sake of distant Merivale.

Tansa and her band allowed themselves to be swept along in the tide of people. Around them was the whole variety of Cliffark: hooting apprentice boys, emboldened by their numbers, jostling one another and calling out to any pretty girls who caught their eye; rosy-faced alewives, selling bottles and smokesticks from carts dragged by lanky sons and sullen daughters; richly garbed merchants, now with many fewer jewelled rings on their fingers thanks to Lord Istlewick's taxation.

'Decent crowd,' said Abner. The veteran mariner walked beside Tansa at her right hand. They had met several times now, and while he seemed a shrewd man he still seemed not to have realised that she was the same girl who had scuttled his ship only a few months earlier. If not for his endorsement of her plan, Tansa doubted she would have been able to rely on so many sailors. The mariners cared little for politics, but Istlewick's levying of a four-tenths tax on the goods of any ship at anchor had got them riled up, even before Istlewick's thugs had begun trawling the taverns and arresting men for drunkenness with the punishment of immediate conscription. 'How many d'you reckon will join us?'

'They all will,' she replied.

'How can you know?' asked Kirrian, a struggling young merchant whose fine velvet clothes Tansa was sure must have been bought on credit. He entwined his fingers nervously. 'You surely can't expect this lot to stand up to armed men?'

'Just trust me. You ever been in a riot?'

Tansa had seen before how quickly a crowd could turn, and the folk of Cliffark were ripe for it. She could see it in the hard eyes of the young men and the tight jaws of every woman old enough to have sired a son. They were dry tinder; all they needed was a spark.

Around three dozen others walked with them, a patchwork of sailors, washerwomen, merchants, seamstresses, tradesmen, whores, and students, united by a common cry: *No laws, no lords, no gods*. Ulbert and his fellow scholars brought up the rear, passing a bottle between themselves and looking about the crowd as if they were not quite sure what they were doing there. In truth, Tansa was not sure either; their movement had long outgrown Ulbert's games of theory and rhetoric. A cackling Maud, who had stayed in Pauper's today, had told her that the boy was in love with her, but that if Tansa wanted to take him to her bed she should get him to wash the ink off his fingers first. Tansa had no intention of doing anything of the sort, with anyone, least of all Ulbert. With Orsian, she had forgotten for a time who she was, and it had taken seeing Hessian again to wake herself up. Love could do that, she knew now. Orsian was a good man, but just like Ulbert he could never understand the world Tansa had come from. It was better for both of them this way.

She had wondered, at first, how it had come to pass that she should be the leader of Cliffark's nascent rebellion. Not only was she young, but she was also a woman, and more specifically the wrong kind of woman: the sort who merchants and tradesmen would decry as a thieving blight on good folk just trying to make an honest living, and who to the sailors should be beneath their notice, neither as lively nor as amusing as the painted whores they favoured.

There were though two reasons they tolerated it that she could deduce. Firstly, beneath the heavy heel of the lords of Erland they would all be crushed alike; perhaps the rest of them understood that as well as she did. Secondly, she had a plan, and the rest of them didn't have a clue. Tansa had prepared for the day with the meticulousness of Orsian preparing for battle; she owed him for teaching her the value of that at least. As he had commanded his several hundred guildsmen at Merivale, she now had several hundred of her own men, and today she had made sure that every one of them had a role to play.

A company of sailors was ready to seize control of the harbour and prevent any ships carrying news along the coast, and there were townsmen at every gate out of the city to prevent anybody leaving by land. The key though was the conscription raffle in Market Square; if the crowd did not rise with them then the rest would count for nothing. They would likely never have a better opportunity. Tansa had seen how quickly riots could happen, but what if they were too soon, or folk would not truly care unless they or a loved one were drafted? Cliffarkers had a natural independent streak. And she would not pretend she was a charismatic leader akin to the storied Portes Stormcaller, who it was said had the power to call down lightning upon his foes and turn the weather to his will. Alternatively, it only took one thing to go wrong, and even if everything else went right it would all count for little.

The mob swelled further as they neared Market Square, crowding around them. Tansa stayed close to Abner's knot of sailors, hoping the rest would have the sense to keep them in view and follow. The square was already beginning to fill up. Children were swarming over the central fountain seeking a better vantage point. At the far end, a wooden stage had been hastily erected in front of the guards' barracks, with a line of armoured men stretched in front of it facing the mass of people. Atop the stage, a single herald in a blue tunic stood next to a vast drum that Tansa assumed contained the name of every man of the right age who had given their name in the last census. More fool them if they had; Tansa had never appeared in any census.

'That's Lord Istlewick's household guard,' said Ulbert in a loud whisper, eyeing the line of mail-clad soldiers arrayed behind their shields etched with Istlewick's sea eagle banner. Tansa eyed their long, wickedly tipped spears, raised upright to the sky. Orsian had told her once that a spear was the right weapon to control a crowd, perfect for guards outnumbered by a mass of unarmed people.

'Soft cunts,' sneered a sailor. 'Hiding behind all that armour.

At least the city guard meet you man to man.' Like many of the sailors, he clutched a skin of liquor in his fist, dousing their band in a miasma of alcoholic fumes.

There were four city guardsmen behind the stage at the entrance to the barracks, a high arched double door, but otherwise defence of the herald looked to have been given wholly over to Lord Istlewick's own guard. Ciera frowned, thinking. It was unfortunate on one hand – these men were better trained than the city guard, and their presence indicated that they were expecting trouble – but on the other hand they did not know the people of Cliffark as the city guard did. They would be younger, prouder men, more likely to overreact rather than defuse a situation as an experienced city guardsman might.

'We need to get closer,' Tansa shouted over the din of the crowd. Abner's sailors and a few burly townsmen led the charge, shouldering people out of the way and making a beeline for the front. Angry curses followed them, but nobody was bold enough to challenge such a mass of people.

As they made their way through the throng, Tansa scanned the rooftops surrounding the square. They were well hidden, but she thought she caught a flash of movement to both sides of the barracks. Just as she had hoped. There were two streets leading into the square behind the stage, in the left and right corners, both guarded by a quartet of city guardsmen she had not noticed before. That was a complication, but not unexpected.

The crowd was thicker nearer the stage, but that did not dissuade the sailors clearing their path. One man was brave enough to confront them, but Abner threw a forearm into his face and sent him sprawling. After that, nobody dared complain, and soon they were right at the front, one line away from where the crowd was pressed up against the soldiers' shields.

Ulbert appeared at her elbow. 'Would you like some wine, Tansa?' He eagerly held out a bottle.

Tansa did want some wine. Her throat was parched, and the density of the mob was an unwelcome memory of the day she had been unable to save Tam from the hangman's noose. As it had then, the crowd's simmering rage hung over the square like a haze, so palpable that she might have cut it with a knife. This time though, it would be different: their anger was directed towards their lord, not men unjustly condemned.

The herald stepped out from behind the barrel and walked across the stage, drawing a chorus of boos so loud it was as if the whole city had crammed their way into the square. He stepped to the front of the stage, raised a palm, and waited. Something in his bearing seemed to settle the crowd. A deathly silence fell. The few who continued to cry out were quietened by their neighbours. The several thousand watching him were evidently curious enough to listen.

'Gentlefolk of Cliffark!' cried the herald. He was spear-slender, yet his deep voice was so thunderous they might have heard him in the harbour. 'I come before you today in strange circumstances. You will know of the foreign army that has invaded our king's lands, and of our own lord's efforts to save this country from ruin. Lord Istlewick regrets deeply the hardship these measures require of you. His only wish is to do what's right.'

'For us to throw down our lives for his daughter more like!' came a cry from further back. Tansa turned and craned her neck, but she could not see who had spoken. The guardsmen ahead of them tensed.

'This war is judgement upon the Sangreals!' cried an old man close to them huddled within a threadbare robe. 'See how the Mountain thunders and smokes – the Elements have judged them and found them wanting!'

The man might have attracted agreement with his first

comment, but few Cliffarkers were god-fearing folk. 'Shut the fuck up!' someone called in reply, and gave the man a shove.

'As you know!' continued the herald. 'Every man drafted today will be paid a wage equivalent to eight-tenths of his current earnings, to be paid to his family in the event of his death, with a *further* eight-tenths to be paid at the conclusion of hostilities.'

'Gold for dead sons!' cried a woman. 'We don't want your war!'

Shouts of agreement followed, but the herald merely smiled and raised a palm. 'Any man failing to appear at muster will be taken into the care of the city guard and shall be paid at a rate of only four-tenths. Over the next two days, we shall determine who among you is to march to Merivale. Only men between the ages of fourteen and forty are eligible, and any man who volunteers before their name is chosen from this barrel behind me shall be paid at the full rate of their current earnings.'

The crowd was so hostile that Tansa wondered if her plan was even necessary. The difficult part would not be getting them to riot, but ensuring events after that went to plan. Without direction, the mob could turn on itself. The herald stepped towards the barrel to begin, and Tansa tensed. That was the signal.

The herald reached inside, grasping for a name. A cry went up from the rooftops, and a dozen young boys raised their heads over the edge and each hurled a handful of mud and shit down towards the row of guards.

Snarls of disgust echoed along the line, while the crowd hooted and hollered. The throws had been well-aimed, and several guards now had brown muck dripping down their helmets onto their faces or staining their gambesons.

Before any of them could react, a second volley followed, this one striking a few unfortunate guards who had turned in search of their assailants. It was too much for some of them; a dozen or more broke from the line and raced for the streets in search of stairs leading to the rooves.

'You're a bit dirty there, friend,' hollered a sailor to the guard nearest him as the man wiped the sludge from his eyes. 'Have something to wash it off with!' He sloshed the dregs of the tankard of ale he was holding into the man's face. The sailors laughed wildly, but had to pull back quickly as the man lowered his spear and jabbed it towards them.

'Not yet,' hissed Tansa. The guard wiped his face with his gloved hand. He looked furious enough to pursue the sailor, but doing so would mean leaving the safety of the line. Just as Tansa had hoped, the attack had roused the guards' tempers. They were on edge, looking to one another for guidance as the crowd grew more agitated.

The herald continued as if nothing had happened. He withdrew from the barrel a small scrap of furled parchment and unrolled it. 'Dillon Maynard, of Bluewater Street, twenty-seven years old!'

Murmurs of discontent spread through the crowd. 'Not yet,' whispered Tansa. She could feel the men around her growing restless. She seized Abner's liquor-skin and took an eye-watering swig.

The herald continued. The next name was pulled out. 'Gusant Pemble, of Thread Alley, fourteen years old!'

'Fourteen? Have a heart, herald!' a large man in a butcher's apron nearby cried. Others were shouting as well. The guards' spears were beginning to dip, sensing trouble, as they nervously looked to one another for guidance.

They were unlikely to get a better time than now. 'Go,' said Tansa. 'Go,' she said again, looking around, searching for her followers.

'Come on, lads!' Abner downed the last of his skin and stepped forward to come face to face with the guard who had been riled earlier. He was perhaps no older than Tansa. 'You beardless little bitch. Think that spear makes you a man?'

'Step back!' A white-haired guard captain striding behind the line stopped to confront Abner. 'Step back, all of you!' Other sailors were stepping forward, shoving at the guards' shields, attacking their manhood and the morality of their mothers. 'Guards, stand firm!'

Abner hocked up saliva and spat it in an arc towards the captain. It fell short, but the point was made. 'That's what I think of you! Come out from behind that line of shields and we'll see how tough you are!'

'Stand firm!' called the man again, but a red flush was creeping up his cheeks beneath his whiskers.

Abner laughed. 'Fuck that.' He took a step forward. The guard tried to push him back with his shield but Abner was too vast to move. He flipped the man's helmet off and rammed a vicious headbutt into his face. The guard's nose broke with a sickening crunch and he went down, the spear toppling after him.

That was too much for the guard captain. 'Shove and spears!' he called along the line. 'Shove and spears!'

'Back!' cried Tansa. Moving in a single well-trained motion, the guardsmen drove forward several steps with their shields, forcing the sailors into a swift retreat. Then the spears came down, like a whole forest toppling at once, sending the crowd back several steps as they cried out in fear. The herald was still speaking, but nobody was paying much attention, the crowd's fear giving way swiftly to anger.

'Forward spears!' cried the captain, and the guards once more moved as one, thrusting out with their weapons and sending the crowd hastening back.

This time, away to Tansa's left, one man in the crowd was too slow. The spear took him in his unprotected gut, and when the guard pulled back he dragged half the man's guts with him.

The captain craned his neck to shout out again, but this time his voice was drowned out by the swell of anger from the crowd. As the guards stepped forward again, some of the crowd surged to meet them while those at the front cried out in fear and tried to retreat as the spears came for them. Some dodged or ducked, but others were not so lucky, impaled on spears and slipping to the ground with blood or guts spilling from their middles.

'You're killing us!' cried a woman. All around Tansa, men were furiously shaking their fists. 'For the love of Eryi, stop!'

The captain was looking uncertainly along the line of dying citizens. It had been seventeen years since Cliffark had seen combat, and faced with the sight before him he seemed no more sure what to do than his guards were. They stared open-mouthed at the carnage they had created, spears and shields suddenly wavering.

Hesitation was their mistake. As one, the crowd seemed to sense weakness, and poured forward.

Tansa sensed the moment, but Abner got there before her. 'Come on then!' he cried. With both hands, he grabbed a spear and wrenched it from the guard's grasp. He flung it aside and fell upon the man, tearing his shield away and striking him with a barrage of fists and elbows. He was the first, but all through the crowd others were following suit, pulling the spears away and falling upon the outnumbered guards. One by one, they were dragged to the ground by the weight of the several hundred Cliffarkers, to be ripped limb from limb or left with their skulls caved in.

Tansa hung back, standing on tiptoes amidst the surging crowd and looking for the next part of her plan. The more numerous city guard would soon be pouring from the barracks to restore order with their own brand of indiscriminate violence. She caught a glimpse at the left entrance to the square behind the stage where a mass of townsmen were falling upon the guards' position, swiftly overwhelming them with their superiority of numbers. From the other side, some had already reached the barracks and just beyond the stage Tansa could see them laying into the four guards outside the entrance. Before a single man could escape the barracks, the double door was chained and barred. Some guards were lying on the ground, dead or wounded, others were already fleeing.

Meanwhile, the clash of the crowd against the massed ranks of armed men was chaos. Several citizens were down, the wounded struggling to be heard over the swirling tumult. The guards were retreating, fending off the mob with their spears, but every few seconds another would fall, outnumbered four or five to one and taken to the ground, their helmets wrenched off and their heads beaten to a pulp beneath a barrage of fists.

Amidst the turmoil, Tansa continued to hang back, watching. The air churned with the scents of blood and the fury of the crowd; Cliffarkers were still charging forward, emboldened by the ease with which the battle had swung in their favour.

But to Tansa, it was not enough to be an instigator; she had to be a leader, and that meant being seen. She needed to show them what she was capable of. Nobody else in Cliffark, perhaps nobody else in the world, had slain a king.

Drawing on instinct and speed honed in the city's backstreets, Tansa weaved her way through the melee, making for the stage, stopping to drag the shortsword of a fallen guard from its scabbard. The herald had stopped reading names, but seemed to have no sense of the danger he was in until he saw Tansa coming. He raised his hands just as she pulled back the blade.

One thrust to the side of his neck, and it was done. She withdrew her sword in a gush of crimson, blood pouring from the artery like a river through a breached dam. As the herald fell, Tansa seized his tunic and lowered him to the ground. She knelt at his side, letting the pooling blood stain her knees, dipping her arms in it and letting it soak her sleeves. Better they saw her drenched in it, as if she had been at the front leading the charge.

Tansa knew she ought to feel repulsed at what she was doing, but in the heat and noise of the riot it seemed ordinary, almost expected. She was not immune to the heady, vicious joy of letting the crowd take you.

It was harder than she expected, to remove the head of a corpse. The blade was designed for thrusting, not the heavy work of a longsword, and by the time she had cut through the muscle and sinew binding the herald's head to his torso she was panting with the effort. The last of the guards had been backed up against the wall of the barracks now; they would be dealt with soon enough.

Tansa seized the head by the hair, and came to her feet, thrusting out the sword in one direction and the head in the other. The exposed neck dripped with gore, and the herald's blood had spread across the stage, dripping through the slats.

She pulled back her head, channelling all her rage and regret, and the howl that came pouring from her throat tore at her vocal cords, part animal and part performance. They had to see her, to respect her.

'People of Cliffark!' She was far from so loud as the herald, but with the crowd's surge forward there were many who would hear her, and those further back could not fail to recognise the decapitated head that hung from her left hand. The guards were dead, and many of the crowd were milling around the stage as if uncertain what to do next. She thought she could hear the pounding of fists against the inside of the barracks door, but ignored it. 'Today is a day of reckoning! A reckoning with Lord Istlewick, who asks us to starve and serve, to behave as thralls against every natural instinct! Cliffark is meant to be a free city – I say we make it so!'

The crowd howled, and Tansa's lips spread into a wild

smile, her teeth stained red where the herald's blood had gushed into her face.

'For too long we have allowed Lord Istlewick to ride roughshod over our rights, to gift the wealth of the city to his Imperial friends while our own folk work their fingers to the bone!'

This was met with a resounding roar. The lord administrator of the Imperial enclave may have been gone, but he remained a target of hatred. Tansa pressed on.

'But Lord Istlewick is merely a symptom.' Tansa paused, letting a confused quiet ripple through the crowd. 'It is the *system* that is at fault, a system that since Erland was formed places us at the mercy of lords and kings who steal wealth from us with one hand while squeezing blood from us with the other!' Tansa had never paid a penny in tax, but she had seen both Tam and Cag fall to the whims and wants of lords. 'And when we refuse, they threaten us with unjust laws and false gods.' This was not wholly true; Lord Istlewick was no believer as far as she was aware, but the rise of fanatics since Eryispek had erupted had made the city a more dangerous place, even to those who were devout themselves or at least respected other citizens' religions. 'Well, I have three demands for Lord Istlewick: no laws, no lords, and no gods!' She paused. 'Who is with me?'

The crowd bellowed their approval, faces twisted with righteous fury, even those towards the rear who could not possibly have heard her roaring along with their fellows.

'Then follow me to Cliffark Tower! You have seen today what Lord Istlewick thinks of you: demanding our blood for a war that we want no part of and sending his butchers to kill us when we refuse. Today, I say we show Lord Istlewick what we think of him.' Tansa dropped the head, and toppled the herald's barrel, releasing a tide of furled pieces of parchment across the blood-soaked stage. 'No laws, no lords, no gods!'

'No laws, no lords, no gods!' The crowd took up the chant as if it were a nursery rhyme of a shared childhood. *'No laws, no lords, no gods!'*

Tansa thrust the sword to the air. Overhead, seagulls and crows flew in a swirl, watching the chaos below through hungry eyes. 'To Istlewick's tower, then! For Cliffark and the people!'

CHAPTER 13

They climbed out of the marshes just as the glow of a new dawn was rising, and from atop the last hill before the sea, the city of Cliffark spread out before them. The four of them stopped, breathing deeply with both exhaustion and relief.

Ciera raised her hand against the blinding light of the early sun dancing off the water. She raised her nose to the scents of salt, fish, and ale that wafted up from the city on the sea breeze. Cawing seagulls danced overhead, and in the bay sleek caravels and fat-bottomed cogs bobbed on the white surf. From where she stood, the city did not seem greatly changed. Her father's school looked to have been finished, a high sandstone building in the east of the city that towered over even the spiralling white towers of the Imperial enclave in the west and the shining marble of the Temple to the Elements in Market Square. There were perhaps fewer boats in the bay. Otherwise Cliffark looked just as it had the previous summer, when she had last gazed upon the city as Andrick Barrelbreaker escorted her to Merivale.

Cliffark may not have changed, but I have. How had that been little over a year ago, with all she had been through since?

She looked down at Andrick, swaddled in her arms. 'That is your birthright, little one,' she whispered softly.

Her eyes moved from the coastal vale and scanned the cliff on which they stood, towards the high, precipitous causeway that led to the lonely light of Cliffark Tower, her father's castle. It was barely a fraction the size of Piperskeep, but from the bluff it loomed over the city like a vigilant guardsman. The window of her father's solar glowed dimly, as if Lord Per Istlewick had fallen asleep over his reading and let the fire burn low.

He and Ciera's mother had sent a short letter of congratulations and a set of illustrated books as a gift for Andrick in the wake of her son's birth, but otherwise she had not heard from them since her departure. Ciera was uncertain what kind of welcome awaited her; her mother would be cruel regardless, but her father's reaction was less certain. Had word of Hessian's death reached them? Would they blame Ciera?

'You ready, Majesty?' said Laphor. The old warrior was leaning over on his sword to keep the weight off his ankle, breathing heavily. 'I'd rather keep moving before my old joints seize up.'

'We headed there?' Aimya pointed to the tower at the end of the causeway. The bride had given them her full tale on the journey, every element of it harder to believe than the last.

Ciera nodded, reluctantly. She was more apprehensive than she was prepared to admit. Her father had never been a martial man; she did not relish bringing trouble to his doorstep. 'Just give me a moment.'

'I'm not sure we have a moment,' said Aimya. 'Unless you want our pursuers to catch us? They have horses, remember?'

There had been no sight nor sound of the *Hymeriker* since Aimya had led them out of the worst of the swamps, and with the girl's guidance they had managed to avoid the Wild Brigade as well. Nevertheless, Ciera accepted the rebuke and led them towards the causeway.

It was no surprise the ancient lords of Cliffark had chosen such a place for their seat, divided from the main coastline by such a narrow strip of land and from the city by a steep winding path. Ciera had never appreciated it before, but the unpredictable winds and sheer drop onto the rocks either side would have made for a treacherous approach for any advancing army. Their pursuers would not find retrieving her from Cliffark Tower easy.

They were halfway across when the first arrow flew from the walls, landing just five feet ahead of Ciera.

'Get down!' Laphor threw himself in front of her just as Ciera flung herself to the ground, turning her back to shield Andrick.

The bowman must have found his range, because there came the thud of something against Laphor's shield.

'What are you doing?' demanded Laphor, lifting his head over his shield and calling up to the battlements. There had not even been a warning. 'We've got Queen Ciera Istlewick here!'

'Stay back!' came a panicked voice in reply. 'Our orders are to shoot anyone crossing the causeway on sight!'

'It's your lord's daughter, idiot! What do you reckon he'll say then if you put an arrow in her? I suggest you go and find him!'

'Lord and Lady Istlewick left orders not to be disturbed.' Figuring the archer had stopped shooting, Ciera adjusted herself to get a proper look at him. The speaker had dipped his bow, but the man next to him was still aiming with his bowstring half drawn back. Behind Ciera, Burik was shielding himself and Aimya. 'Who are you anyway? Some pisshead from the town on a scouting mission?'

'Go home and sleep it off!' called the second man.

Laphor bristled. 'I am Laphor, of the *Hymeriker*. Now put down those bows before I shove them so hard down your gobs you'll spend the next week shitting wood!'

The first man laughed. '*Hymerika*, are you? Bollocks, you're just someone's old drunk dad. Now piss off before I put this arrow through your eye.' He raised his bow again.

'Laphor,' said Ciera, before he could escalate the matter further. There was fear in these men. Clearly something strange had happened, but she could worry about that once they were inside the walls. 'Cover Andrick and let me try.' She did not know what had got her father's guards so spooked, but shouting at them across the causeway was not going to solve it.

Laphor backed off, keeping his shield up, and knelt in front of Ciera. 'Just lay the boy on the ground; I'll keep him covered. Sure you know what you're doing?'

Not particularly. But if Ciera could not handle two guards of her own childhood home, what hope did she have against her enemies? Trying to project confidence, she placed Andrick on the ground and stepped out from behind Laphor's shield.

She walked slowly towards the gate.

'Stay back! Won't tell you again!' Perhaps something of Laphor's words had got through to the two guards, because they seemed reluctant to shoot again.

Ciera raised her palms and kept walking. 'I swear to you, I am Ciera Istlewick. Is my father well? I have his grandson here.'

The second guard's bow dropped an inch. She was within twenty yards of them now, close enough to see they were barely older than her. 'She does look a bit like Lord Istlewick's daughter,' he said to his fellow. He lowered his bow, letting the string go loose. 'Remember?'

'All right, all right!' The first guard reluctantly let his aim drop. 'You can approach, but your friends best stay where they are.'

'I need my son as well,' Ciera called back.

'Eryi's bollocks, bring your bleedin' son then! But be quick about it.'

Ciera retrieved Andrick and stood, smoothing her skirts out.

She would have liked to wash first, and check herself in a looking glass, but she would make do. Her father would not care how she looked, but her mother certainly would.

'If you could get us in there as well, quick as possible, I'd appreciate it,' grumbled Laphor, rising from behind his shield but not putting it away. He looked to the sky, where grey clouds were beginning to blow in from over the water. 'Looks like rain, and I don't want to be stuck out here if any of our friends show up.'

'I'll speak to my father. You'll be inside soon.' Though, if his guards were rattled, Lord Istlewick might be even more so. Something must have put the fear of the Norhai into him if he was ordering his men to shoot anybody who even approached the keep.

The portcullis creaked up, and Ciera stood before the heavy double doors as they opened inwards, then immediately closed behind her as she stepped into the yard. Nobody came to meet her, and even for early in the morning the area was strangely deserted.

She looked up towards the battlements, and found the two guards peering down at her open-mouthed. 'It's her!' said one to the other. He removed his helmet and went to a knee as the other scrambled to do the same. 'Lady, I'm sorry. Lord Istlewick—'

Ciera cut across him. 'Just let my companions in, or it will be *you* who gets left outside to have arrows launched at you. Where is my father?'

The guard wiped his brow. 'A thousand apologies. You'll find him in his study.'

'Thank you. And if I come back and find my friends still outside you will regret it. I suggest that one of you goes to find them some food.' She strode towards the keep.

Ciera did not stop as she wound her way up the many stairs that led to the upper reaches of Cliffark Tower. A few guards looked at her strangely, but none stopped her. Those at the bottom of the stairs leading to her father's solar recognised her, and smiled as they stepped out of her way.

At the top of the spiral stairs, she emerged into her father's study, a dim, circular room with books and scrolls covering every available shelf. A window on the north wall gave a broad view over the town and the bay below. At a central table lit by a single candle sat Lord Per Istlewick. He had fallen asleep, surrounded by open books and stacks of parchment, his bald pate resting on a page scrawled with ink, a quill still gripped in his right hand.

'Father?' Ciera padded forward.

Lord Istlewick mumbled something but did not rouse. A trail of drool from his open mouth was threatening to roll down onto his page.

Ciera selected the table's heaviest tome and closed it with a clap.

'Ah!' Lord Istlewick jolted awake. He blinked at her blearily, a smudge of ink staining his cheek. He rubbed at his eyes. 'Ciera?'

Ciera stared back at him, fighting back tears. 'I'm home, Father.' He seemed older now than he had a year ago; his final strands of hair had finally receded and disappeared, and the flesh on his face hung heavily, as if he had recently lost a great deal of weight.

Woken by the noise, Andrick stirred unhappily, but did not cry out. Lord Istlewick looked at him, and his sleepy eyes seemed to brighten. 'Is that...?'

Ciera smiled. 'Father, meet Andrick, King of Erland.'

Smiling, her father replaced his quill and struggled to his feet. He gripped the cane leaning against the table, and closed the gap to embrace Ciera, kissing her on the cheek. He gazed down at Andrick, and twenty years of tension seemed to loosen in his face.

'Your grandson.'

There were tears on his cheeks, rolling down his face and streaking the stains of ink. He sniffed. 'I never thought I'd see the day. After all that has happened, after all that could yet happen...' He paused, frowned, and looked back at Ciera. 'You said "king". The rumours...'

'Are true. Hessian is dead.'

Lord Istlewick's cane tremored in his hand. 'I had hoped... hoped... It is not important now, I suppose. Has Merivale fallen?'

Ciera had no idea how to explain all that had occurred, but was saved from doing so by a call from the stairs. 'Per! Per! Are you asleep again? You'll never believe what one of the guards just told me!'

Ciera took a deep breath, steeling herself against what was to come. Her mother.

'Irena!' Her father hobbled towards the stairs. 'Come up, Ciera's here!'

As the footsteps below grew closer, Ciera positioned herself on the other side of the table. The one upside to becoming Hessian's bride had been escaping her mother. *I am a queen now; she does not get to tell me what to do.* She had faced down great lords intent on deposing her, and yet somehow the voice of her mother made her feel as if she was twelve years old again, about to be sent to bed for overeating. Her father appeared just as worried, retaking his seat as if in supplication.

Lady Irena appeared in the doorway, her hawkish eyes taking in the scene before her. Despite her forty-something years, she seemed untroubled by the climb. She was of a height with Ciera, with the same heart-shaped face and chestnut curls, though hers were now streaked with steely grey.

Her shrewd green eyes regarded Ciera carefully, the faint crow's feet around them tightening as she took in Ciera's shabby state and the bundle in her arms. Ciera resisted the urge to smooth out her dress; stained as it was with sweat and marsh water it would make no difference.

'Well, at least you're alive.' Her mother spoke as if Ciera would have died just to spite her. 'And I suppose you're here because your husband is dead and Merivale has fallen.'

'Yes, he's dead.' Ciera's words came out in a squeak, and she raised her voice. 'Your grandson, Andrick, is the king now. When I left, Lord Balyard held Merivale. The Imperium were beaten back, but they still surrounded the city. Balyard turned the *Hymeriker* against me; I had to flee.'

'I was going to raise an army for you,' said her father. 'Five thousand men. I have the proclamation somewhere here...' He began scrabbling through the sheets of parchment that littered the table.

'An army?' Hope rose in Ciera's heart. Her parents had not abandoned her to her fate; with five thousand men she could challenge Balyard and Errian. She only regretted her father had not acted more quickly.

Her mother gave a mocking laugh. 'Your father believes wars can be won with papers and proclamations. He tried to bolster his forces by conscripting men from Cliffark and levying a tax on businesses to pay for mercenaries.' She gave her husband a hard look. 'That was only the beginning of our problems.'

'When can they leave?' asked Ciera, too full of hope to heed her mother's words. 'Or are they already marching?' That would explain why the castle was deserted. 'With your five thousand—'

'There is no five thousand men!' barked her mother. 'Thanks to your father's mad decrees the citizens have revolted. Cliffark is occupied; it's taken all the soldiers we have to hold the cliff path. If enough of the rebels come around the long way to block the causeway, we will be trapped from both sides. I have suggested fleeing, but your father refuses to listen.'

Ciera slumped into a chair, hope seeping out of her like wine from a broken barrel. 'But can't you beat the rebels back? You have soldiers, you have money, you could—'

'Do you suppose we haven't tried?' said her mother. She stared at Ciera. 'Is it true you killed Hessian? Will you bring the *Hymeriker* down on us as well?'

Lord Istlewick spoke. 'Irena...'

'We have to know, Per. We cannot stay here and wait for the *Hymeriker* to lay siege to our walls.' Her eyes never left Ciera. 'And by your daughter's face, I suggest she has something to tell us.'

Ciera swallowed. *She is only your mother. She can't hurt you, not really.* Quickly, she told them of how Hessian had died, her brief attempt to rule on behalf of her son, and that she might have led both the *Hymeriker* and the Wild Brigade to their door.

By the time she had finished, her father's head was in his hands, and her mother was staring at her as if taking a vindictive pleasure in Ciera's confession. 'Well,' she said. 'I thought marriage might change you, but you're still the same childish, selfish thing you were when you left, aren't you? You never, *never*, think about the consequences of your actions. Ever since you were a girl—'

'I am not a girl any more, Mother.' Ciera came to her feet. A hundred memories of her mother's treatment of her rushed through her head, all the many times she had been too afraid to challenge her, to fight back. It would never happen again; she had come too far to be spoken to like that. 'And marriage *did* change me, and not for the better. You have no idea what I went through to keep myself and my son safe, so don't you dare stand there and tell me this is my fault.' Years of pent-up anger surged from Ciera's heart. 'You sold me to Hessian, and I made the best I could of it! I am your *queen*, the mother of your king, so for once in your life you will speak to me with respect!'

When Ciera had finished, her mother's mouth was as tight as a miser's purse. She waited for the inevitable rebuke, steeling herself against the slap that might follow. But after eye contact of several breaths, it was Ciera's mother who looked away. 'Don't shout, Ciera,' she said softly. 'You're upsetting the child.' She was right; Andrick was beginning to stir in Ciera's arms. His eyes flickered open, and Irena's face softened slightly. 'Could I... hold him?'

Ciera's blood was racing, ready for the argument she had been sure was coming, but her mother's calm request stopped her in her tracks. 'What?' Her father was looking at Andrick as well, a blissful smile etched upon his face. The babe grizzled and waved a tiny fist in the air. 'Well, yes, I suppose...'

Irena swept upon Ciera so fast that she suspected her mother would have taken Andrick from her whether she agreed to it or not. Ciera could not recall her ever looking as she did when she took Andrick in her arms – she had never made any secret over her disappointment at only having a daughter. By giving her mother a grandson, Ciera might finally have silenced her. Lord Istlewick rose to join her, looking just as happy.

'Such a handsome little fellow,' said Irena. 'Takes after his grandfather.'

The tears were pouring openly down Lord Istlewick's cheeks now. 'I was beginning to wonder what a man in my position had left to live for,' he said. 'Now I know.'

Feeling not even a fraction of their joy, but content to let them enjoy one blissful moment amidst a sea of trouble, Ciera turned her back to them and moved to the north window. Her parents could not help her; given her mother's talk of fleeing it appeared they were prepared to give up on Cliffark entirely. The odds seemed to rise against her and Andrick by the minute.

The last time she had stood at this window, her father had been telling her of his plans for the future, how Ciera could use her new position to bring Cliffark's prosperity to all of Erland.

A great deal could change in a year. From here, she had a clearer view of the city than she had on her approach, almost top-down. Atop the highest buildings, the old banner of the dead rebel pirate Portes Stormcaller flew, a purple lightning bolt against a white sky over a blue sea. Barricades had been erected at every gate, and at the base of the cliff path almost directly below, her father's soldiers had retreated, leaving behind dozens of dead on both sides. The insurgents had for the time being given up on their attempt to storm the cliff, and looked to be reinforcing their barricade with barrels and an assortment of furniture.

'They are giving you the chance to leave,' murmured Ciera as her father came to join her. Cliffark Tower relied on the city and the sea for food; there was little to be hunted in the marshes.

'They are,' said her father gravely. 'I thought to fight them at first, but too many of my men have died. If I ask them to attack the barricades again they will turn against me as well.' He sighed. 'There will be no Andrick Barrelbreaker appearing to save me this time. It's only pride that has stopped me negotiating with the rebels for safe passage on a ship out of Erland. Perhaps it is time, if you will come with me.'

'Father, last year you described Cliffark as your life's work. Are you truly ready to give up on it so easily?' Ciera's breast burnt with fury at the city's ingratitude. *My father brought them wealth the likes of which Erland had never seen, and this is how they repay him.*

Lord Istlewick smiled sadly. 'I am afraid I see little choice in the matter. Sometimes I fear the smoke pouring from Eryispek is a portent of Erland's doom.'

Ciera remembered Sister Aimya's tale. *Eryi, Vulgatypha, and a war that will tear the sky in two.* It was not like her father though to be superstitious. 'You don't mean that.'

'With all that has occurred the last year, isn't there part of you that wonders?'

I cannot afford to wonder, thought Ciera. *I must fight my battles as they come.*

There came the sound of hobbling feet below. All of them turned in alarm towards the stairs, just as Laphor appeared, panting as if he had run all the way from the causeway. He rested against the doorframe, gasping and grimacing at the pain in his ankle.

'Laphor!' Ciera was at least glad he had been allowed inside. 'What's happened?'

'Strovac Sigac... at the gate... come now...'

He turned back, and Ciera raced after him, not even waiting to see if her parents were following. She overtook Laphor on the stairs and rushed through the keep.

Burik and Aimya had joined the two guards on the battlements over the gates. Ciera raced up the stairs to join them, her chest burning as Laphor hurried after her breathing like a blacksmith's bellows.

She reached the ramparts. Across the causeway, several hundred men were arrayed, all ahorse, each one looking meaner and more dangerous than the last. One of them had dismounted, and Ciera knew him by his reputation: Strovac Sigac, by far the largest man she had ever seen. His long blond hair wafted in the breeze, and even at this distance his cold smile drove a needle of fear into Ciera's heart. A man knelt at his feet, his wrists bound behind his back, a wooden block set in front of him. Through a mess of blood and bruises, Ciera recognised Arrik's stout, proud face. He kept his head held high, and his eyes sparkled with defiance.

Burik's face, however, was twisted in anguish. 'Just give me the bow,' he was telling a guard. 'I can hit him.'

Reluctantly, the guard handed over the weapon. Burik set an arrow, pulled back the string, and aimed high.

The arrow flew harmlessly over the edge of the causeway, caught by the blustery wind, and the Wild Brigade howled with laughter.

Strovac laughed along with them, though his mirth never reached his eyes. 'One day, Burik, you and your brothers will learn to stay out of my way. Until then, I'll keep killing you.' He glanced down at Arrik. 'Bet this one got his hopes up when we came riding out of the mist last night and massacred the *Hymeriker*.'

'Let him go!' shouted Ciera. 'He's nothing to you.'

'No, but he's something to you, and it's you and your son that I want.' Strovac pulled back his lips in a rictus grin. 'Other men might offer his life in exchange for your surrender, but I can't say I see the point; we both know he's not worth it. Better to show you I'm to be taken seriously.'

Strovac slid his sword from his scabbard. Arrik tried to shout something, but Strovac placed his foot on his back and pushed him down to the block. 'Never seen the point of last words either. Who gives a fuck what some dead cunt has to say?' He smirked. 'If you stay still, I'll make this easy. If I miss, I'll let you die slow.'

A weak cough of a laugh rose from Arrik's throat. 'A clean death? You've grown soft, Sigac.' He stretched his neck out. 'Hurry up then, you shitspawn son of a whore.'

Ciera could not bring herself to tear her eyes away. Beside her, Burik tensed, his tight knuckles white against the parapet.

Strovac's sword flashed, and fell.

The blade thunked against the lump of wood. For a moment, Ciera thought he might have missed, until Arrik's head slid from his neck. It rolled twice, and stopped, his empty gaze staring up at the sky. The Wild Brigade cheered, and with a grin, Strovac prodded it with his boot.

'Reckon we can dispense with burning it,' he said. 'Even less point now than before.' He took a mighty swing with his boot and sent the head sailing off high into the air and over the edge of the causeway. Next, he hauled up the corpse, and heaved it over the other edge. Ciera was too stunned to cry. Burik had not moved or made a sound, but his face had turned pale as chalk.

'What now then, Strovac?' bellowed Laphor. 'What did that little display gain any of us? If it's to be battle, then get on with it.'

Ciera glanced to either side at her father's guardsmen, each of them open-mouthed, staring wide-eyed at the several hundred-strong Wild Brigade. *If they charge, the gate will not hold them.* Their only escape would be down the cliff path, into the waiting arms of Cliffark's rebels.

Strovac pointed his sword towards Laphor and looked beady-eyed along its edge. His lips twisted in contempt. 'I don't think the queen will let it come to that.' He turned back towards the Wild Brigade. 'Bring the girl.'

A black-bearded warrior strode forward, and Ciera's nails dug into her hand so hard that she swore she could feel blood welling in her palm. He held his bundle out before him by an ankle, like a hunter presenting game for the pot. A blindfold covered Haisie's eyes, and her blonde hair was scattered and unbound, left to brush against the dirt.

The Wild Brigader held her up, giving those on the battlements a good look. 'She says she knows you,' said Strovac. He ran the tip of his sword down Haisie's face, delicate as a needle, and laughed as she screamed and clawed at it. 'Loyal to a fault this one. It's funny, the things people can get attached to, even servants.' Strovac Sigac's cut-throat eyes fixed upon Ciera. 'My boys are itching to storm your shitheap of a castle – they're even making bets on how quickly it would fall – but I've decided to disappoint them and make this easy for you: surrender yourself and the boy to me by morning, or I'll make you watch your little friend here suffer.'

CHAPTER 14

They rode south into the grey night, with Merivale and the towers of Piperskeep just a shadow against the sky behind them.

Pherri had been given her own horse, but she was out of practice and struggled to keep pace with Phyrrai, who rode ahead of her on a sleek silver palfrey that could have been a twin to Pherri's own. Silent Halyana led them, as if she knew the way Pherri wanted to go. Hrogo brought up the rear, mounted atop a plodding shire horse that bore him with placid indifference. Its soft temperament was likely the only thing keeping him ahorse; it was clear Hrogo was no rider.

'How long until they come after us?' Pherri called to Phyrrai over the rushing wind.

'They might already be giving chase,' said Da'ri grimly. He slowed his horse to a trot, gesturing for Phyrrai to do the same and riding closer to Pherri. Ahead, Halyana slowed as well. 'We should spare the horses; we might need their speed later.' He looked backward to where Hrogo was still struggling to control his mount, and dropped his voice. 'Hopefully they will catch him and be content.'

'We might have more time than you think,' said Phyrrai. 'I

slipped some powdered drowshroom into the evening meal. It might be morning before anyone realises we've gone.'

'Gods, Phyrrai...' Da'ri looked to the sky and let out a deep breath. 'Well, after this I suppose I could never have returned to Merivale anyway. Poisoning the whole castle... You might have signed the order for my execution.'

It was so strange to Pherri, to hear her tutor's voice again, chiding somebody who was her and yet was not. Her eyes flicked to Phyrrai, and she had to suppress a shiver. 'You could return to Thrumb?' she suggested. 'Da'ri in my world was planning to return to Thrumb before— before he... didn't.' This was complicated enough without telling this Da'ri that her Da'ri was dead. It was strange that he should have the same name and yet Halyana and Phyrrai did not, but the Thrumb kept the middle part of their name for themselves; perhaps those differed.

Da'ri gave an unhappy grunt. 'I doubt my cousin Ba'an would risk incurring Jarhyck's wrath, not while his daughter is married to Arrian.' He looked again to Phyrrai. 'I'm serious, Phyrrai; what possessed you? Don't tell me you believe in this *other world*? You have no evidence.'

Phyrrai hesitated, chewing her lip in a manner so familiar to Pherri that she found herself doing it as well. They looked at one another and smiled shyly, before Pherri had to look away as a wave of violent rage surged against her senses.

'I dreamt of her,' said Phyrrai simply. 'After we found Halyana's note. I saw a creepy man with pale eyes and a woman made of fire who looked a bit like my mother fighting atop an endless mountain of ice. The sky was aflame, and the earth was shaking, being ripped apart like parchment. She' – Phyrrai looked at Pherri – 'stopped them.' She shrugged, and looked away again, chewing her lip. 'That's all I remember.'

'How did I stop them?' asked Pherri. Perhaps her shadowtwin held the key to defeating Eryi and Vulgatypha.

'I told you, I don't remember.'

'You broke her out because you had a *dream*?' Da'ri pressed a hand to his temples and ran his fingers and thumb across his eyes. 'Dreams don't mean anything!'

'My dreams do!' said Pherri. 'It's called *prophika*; it's when dreams tell you things that haven't happened yet.'

She had never been able to speak to Da'ri of magic in her own world – it had been his demise that led her to Theodric, by Eryi's design – but Pherri was sure he would have believed her; the letter back to Thrumb Da'ri had never sent proved he knew something of the Mountain. His neat handwriting swam before her eyes: *They are waking.*

But this world's Da'ri was shaking his head. 'Every Thrumb child has dreamt of doing magic, of having visions, as the texts of our ancestors claim they could, thousands of years ago. All they see is nonsense, no matter how much casheef they consume. I tried it myself when I was young and foolish. I came to accept it: dreams are not prophecies.'

He sighed. 'But regrettably, I also had a dream. I saw Phyrrai, or someone I thought was Phyrrai, standing on Pipersmont. A void opened beneath her feet, and she disappeared. I told myself to drink less before bed and did my best to forget about it.'

'It was a void into my world!' exclaimed Pherri. 'Like how I got here.'

'How did you get here?' said Phyrrai. She glanced towards Pherri. 'What happened?'

'I...' Pherri's hands tightened on her reins. She had come so close to disaster against Eryi; it was only instinct and that she had no choice that had saved her life and thwarted him in his plan to retrieve a body that might free him from his prison, or so she hoped. She had forced herself not to think about it, to focus on the here and now of how she might return. 'I fought him,' she whispered. Tears welled in her eyes at the memory. She had been so cold, so scared, even if she had never really admitted it to herself. 'I fought Eryi. He's a god, of sorts, the man that you saw in your dream. I had to escape into this world to save myself.'

'So what I saw in my dream happened,' said Phyrrai. Her eyes widened in horror. 'Does that mean your world has ended?'

Pherri shook her head. 'No, at least not yet. He failed, but now I'm trapped here. Our world is like yours though.' She looked up at Da'ri. 'I knew I had to reach Pipersmont to get home. Your dream proves it. And if that's not enough to show I'm who I say I am, just *look* at me.'

Da'ri looked back and forth, from Pherri to Phyrrai, as if searching for some difference between them other than the neat plait of Phyrrai's hair and Pherri's windblown haystack. Pherri did not need a mirror to know he would not; she felt the impossible likeness every time they so much as glanced at one another; she swore even their hearts were beating in time with one another.

'And how else do you explain what Halyana wrote?' added Phyrrai triumphantly. '*Find Pherri. On Eryispek.* She knew Pherri was coming!'

Da'ri snorted. 'It makes no more sense than anything Halyana has done since that note was found. She is not well, Phyrrai.' He glanced towards Halyana, who had slowed her mount to ride alongside them, her guileless face pale under the moonlight. 'Sorry, Princess,' he said to her. 'If you were in your right mind, you would agree with me.' He released a reluctant sigh. 'But as much as I wish to deny Pherri's story and your dream, I cannot. What I thought was only a dream has stayed with me for weeks, and when I see the two of you together now it is as if two Phyrrais stare back at me. Though it offends every rational bone in my body, I must admit that your tale might be true.'

Hrogo had finally been able to get his horse under control, and had managed to match their pace. He was slumped over his horse's neck, and breathless from the exertion of riding. 'Where are we going?' he asked.

Da'ri ignored him. With soft eyes he looked again from Pherri to Phyrrai. He paused, straightening his thin frame in the saddle. 'It is too much coincidence, and I will not abandon Phyrrai to face this trial alone. Pherri... is it your wish to go to Pipersmont?'

Pherri scanned the southern horizon. The black wilderness of the Sorrowlands was just visible against the night sky. All who rode within sight of it described a desolate hinterland of lifeless rock where not even weeds grew. In the night's gloom, the phantom-like Pipersmont could be seen only in her mind's eye. It was impossible to know how far away it might be; it could be one hundred miles or one thousand. All Pherri knew was that it was her best hope, likely her only hope, of ever returning to her Erland.

It must be there for a reason, she told herself. Where else would she recover the secrets of her magic? She reached for her will, just to be sure, straining against the weight of the ether, searching for just the slenderest sliver of it.

It was gone, like trying to catch the shadow of smoke between her fingers. This world contained not even the barest memory of magic, or at least none she could find.

She raised a finger, pointing to what she hoped was Pipersmont's silhouette against the dark horizon. 'I have to get home, to save my family.' *To save everyone*. 'So yes, that's where we're going.'

'It will be hard,' said Da'ri. 'There are many leagues between here and Pipersmont. And Jarhyck will not give up on you, not while he believes you are responsible for Halyana's ailment. That she has fled with you will only strengthen his certainty. Should we escape him and the *Hymeriker*, we must then cross the Sorrows, and face the mysteries of that bleak land and the Sorrowfolk who dwell there. But if that is your and Phyrrai's desire, then that is where we shall go.'

They rode through the night, alternating between a trot and a canter to rest their horses. Halyana set a confident pace, and the rest of them did their best to keep up. They had not even been riding for an hour when Pherri began to yawn, and felt her eyelids starting to droop. To keep herself awake, she positioned herself next to Phyrrai, hoping the edgy nausea of being so close would keep her sufficiently tense to remain awake. It worked – Pherri only had to come within a few yards before a jitteriness settled in her stomach. It was deeply unpleasant, but she no longer felt tired.

'It's horrid, isn't it?' said Phyrrai, after several minutes of silence. Neither dared turn to look at one another. 'It's like I've eaten something strange. I want to reach out and hold your hand, but if I touch you, I'm scared I won't be able to stop myself killing you.'

Pherri shuddered. Phyrrai had put into words exactly how she felt. 'I was going to say the same thing.'

'Is your world like ours?'

'Almost the same.' Pherri pointed to where Pipersmont was beginning to take shape as the first whisper of dawn threatened the horizon. 'That should be in Erland and covered in ice. It's where magic comes from.'

'What will happen if you don't go back?'

A shiver ran up Pherri's spine. Her eyes remained fixed on the distant mountain. *What if there's an Eryi there as well? What if I wake him and doom this world too?* 'The gods are going to war. The last time they fought they say it nearly split the sky in two, nearly ended the world.' Her own words threatened to drown Pherri in despair. Because even if she made it back to her Erland, what if that was not enough? How could she hope to stop both Eryi and Vulgatypha?

'Would they end my world too?'

Pherri had spent hours thinking about that question in the cart on the way to Merivale. When everything else was so much the same, it was strange to think this world's fate would be any different, but this was a land without magic, seemingly without Eryi and Vulgatypha. 'I don't think so,' she said hesitantly. 'There are other realities as well, *other* other ones, I mean, and it's possible sometimes to draw things from them, but I think they all have their own gods, or maybe none at all. I hope so anyway.'

They rode in silence for a time, as the grassy plains of Erland began to brighten around them. With the rising sun came birdsong, and a faint warmth that made Pherri realise how cold she had become. A white-bearded shepherd on a nearby hill surrounded by ewes stopped to stare at them from beneath his wide-brimmed hat. A few hundred yards away to their right, Pherri could make out a hamlet, half-a-dozen squat hovels surrounding a tumbledown tower.

'If each reality has its own gods,' said Phyrrai, so suddenly that Pherri nearly jumped out of her skin, who made them?'

'The world, or the gods?'

'Both.'

Pherri thought, fighting against her tiredness and her desire to contemplate simpler matters, like how they might cross the hostile Sorrowlands with no food and no warriors. It was said the Norhai had made her world. Had other Norhai made other worlds? And who had made the Norhai? 'I don't know,' she admitted. 'I used to think I wanted to know everything. Now I wish I could go back to Violet Hall and hide, and never learn what magic was.'

Phyrrai chewed her lip, and once again Pherri found herself doing the same. 'I wish I had magic,' said Phyrrai, her voice half a whisper. 'You're lucky, or you would be if not for this. I am barely allowed to leave Violet Hall; the only reason I was at Piperskeep was because my parents are helping Jarhyck establish his rule. They're just waiting for the day I'm old enough to marry me off to some lord or other.'

'It was the same for me,' said Pherri. 'I always felt I could fight against what others wanted for me, even if I wasn't always sure how. But what I'm fighting now... how do I fight a god?' *And if Phyrrai's dream was* prophika, *how do I fight two of them?*

'You beat him once,' said Phyrrai. 'You'll beat him again.'

CHAPTER 15

They approached the great yellow-red-black tent, and the legionnaires shoved Orsian through the entrance flap then fled, as if they could not bear to be close to it any longer than they had to. They had at least unbound his hands, and Orsian stumbled before grabbing the edge of the long table at the centre to steady himself.

He whirled, ready to throw himself at whoever came through after him, but Krupal was quicker. '*Sit*,' said the magus, and Orsian felt his legs drawing him towards the far end of the table. He had felt able to fight the compulsion before, but now Krupal's will was like a vice grip around his limbs. A chair slid out of its own accord, and Orsian's legs forced him down into it.

Orsian's eyes darted around the room for a weapon, and found nothing. The tent was dimly lit by a single low brazier in the corner, crackling softly, and the table was bare save for a flagon of wine. There were several locked trunks, and a large bed that did not look to have been slept in, but nothing he might defend himself with. The air smelt of cinnamon, imbued strangely with a slight undercurrent of decay.

Orsian started as a low laughter filled the room. 'You should not waste your energy on such pitiful tricks.' At the sound, Orsian's head whipped to the other end of the table. The man sitting there had somehow escaped his interest. Orsian would have sworn he had not been there a moment before. The Imperial commander, Senator Drast Fulkiro, regarded him with a pair of dark green eyes set over a beak-like nose, his head shaved to the skin. There had been rumours he had died, but Orsian recognised him from their parley before the Imperials had first taken Merivale. 'Perhaps think of that before you complain you need more food.'

'And when did you last maintain *inflika* over so many?' demanded Krupal indignantly, folding his arms across his chest.

'The energy used in *inflika* is negligible, as you know,' replied Fulkiro. 'The girl would have had no difficulty. If you are struggling, perhaps your mastery is not all you claim it to be.'

'You know it is not so simple,' said Krupal. 'Not with so many, when I am expected to control their movements as well as their minds. Only the finest magi of the Imperium—'

'Enough.' Fulkiro did not even look at Krupal, his eyes fixed on Orsian. 'I have provided you enough food. The rest is up to you. The magi of my age could have done what I have asked you to do after a week of hunger.'

The senator seemed paler than when Orsian had last seen him, his eyes rimmed with red, and as he stood to reach for the flagon on the table his hand tremored. He looked at it, frowning, and replaced it. 'Help yourself to wine, Orsian. A welcome comfort after your captivity, I am sure.'

'Heard you were dead,' said Orsian. He did not reach for the flagon.

'War is rife with rumours.' Fulkiro smiled. 'I was most troubled to learn of your imprisonment; a poor way to repay your bravery in battle. The legionnaires whisper that it was as if you had the assistance of some divine force on your side.' He chuckled heartily.

Orsian said nothing.

'Well, now you have him,' said Krupal, scowling, clearly smarting from Fulkiro's insults. 'Just as you asked for. Do you just mean to sit here drinking wine and blowing smoke up the boy's arse, or do you actually have some use for him?'

Irritation flashed across Drast's features. As he turned to look at Krupal, Orsian swore there was something odd about the dim shadow he cast against the rear of the tent, as if the light bent around the edges of his body. 'Krupal – leave us. I have had all the use from you this evening I require.'

An angry flush blossomed beneath Krupal's white beard. 'You told me—'

'Whatever you think I told you is not important. *Leave*.'

For a moment, it looked as if Krupal was going to argue, but with a last look of loathing he turned and strode quickly from the tent. Orsian could barely understand it – Krupal could likely have turned the senator's mind to suet if he desired.

Fulkiro laughed, a high-pitched trill that set his shadow dancing and sent a sense of unease flooding through Orsian's veins. Just who was he? *What* was he? He had not seemed a man to fear when they had met before, but he had cowed Krupal as easily as if he were a beaten dog.

The senator quietened. 'The problem with Krupal is that he has never had to deal with anyone more powerful than him; he fluctuates between obedience and loathing like a tempestuous child. To think he believes I will share power once we are finished. Krupal will try to usurp me before then, of course. When I demonstrated the force of my magic, he was most eager for an alliance, but now he sees my patience and mistakes it for weakness. He has too much faith in his meagre power.' He leant forward, his gaze pinning Orsian to the chair like a cat's eyes upon a rodent. 'You're wondering who I am, aren't you?'

Orsian was suddenly conscious of how dry his mouth was. Though still only a low brazier burnt, the tent suddenly felt stifling, and the scent of rot was becoming overpowering. A bead of sweat formed on Orsian's temple, and he stretched for the flagon and poured himself a cup.

'Good,' said Fulkiro. His voice was different to last time as well, rumbling so deeply that Orsian could feel it through the table. 'We can now speak like civilised people.' There were cups in reaching distance, but he made no move to take any wine himself. 'I have questions, and if you will not give me answers, I will take them from you.'

Orsian tried to hold his hand steady as he grasped his cup. The dungeon had sapped his strength. His stomach rumbled. He took a slow, steady sip and laid it down. He spoke, trying to sound calm. 'I'm not sure what you think I know. I've been in a dungeon for weeks.' He realised suddenly that in the several minutes since he had sat down, Fulkiro had not blinked. He watched the Imperial's face, and when he spoke his mouth seemed to barely move.

'Where is Pherri?'

Orsian swallowed. What did Pherri have to do with this? 'I've not seen her in months. Not since I left Merivale with my father.' He paused. 'You are not Drast Fulkiro.'

'Is that so?' The man's lips stretched to a wolfish grin. 'It seems you are smarter than the average legionnaire.' His skin began to ripple, the shadow on the wall twisting madly. 'As you wish. Let us do away with the pretence.'

Fulkiro rose from the table, and his body began to change before Orsian's eyes, his limbs stretching and twisting, his features waning, softening. His shadow writhed as the brazier-light flickered back and forth like in a sudden wind.

A creature whose face was a smooth, featureless mask stood in his place, with hair styled in six long plaits hanging about his brow. His clothes were torn, and everywhere Orsian looked his pale skin was a motley of weeping burns and scars shedding pink, watery blood. In some places, the skin had rotted away entirely, revealing the sinew and bone beneath. The smell of it filled his nostrils. Orsian forced his eyes to meet the creature's stare, and immediately recoiled. Where once Drast Fulkiro's hooded eyes had regarded him was a pair of blue orbs, so pale they were almost white.

The thing smiled, showing a set of small, razor-pointed teeth. 'And now you see. I hope soon Drast Fulkiro will be dead for good.' The thing's voice seemed to echo between the tent walls. 'I will ask you again – where is Pherri?'

'I told you—'

'I know you spoke to her.' His voice cracked like a whip. 'I assure you, you do not want to disappoint me.'

'Who are you?'

'I am the difference between life and oblivion. The bright line between truth and endless darkness. The final guard who held the gate when all hope for mankind had fled. I am *Eryi*.'

In ordinary circumstances, Orsian might have laughed. But all the horrors of the last year had been scant compared to the terror he felt under the presence of the thing before him. A burgeoning malevolence rolled from it in waves, reducing Orsian's existence to the pitiless pair of white-blue orbs staring through him across the table and pinning him to his seat, swelling like two rising moons until they were all Orsian could see.

He had never believed in the gods, not really. Part of him still refused to trust his own instincts, swearing a rational explanation for the thing that had worn Drast Fulkiro's body like a coat of mail and shed it just as easily. He had felt Pherri's magic, but this was something else entirely: something ancient, unbound by any sense of shared humanity.

'I believe you,' said Orsian.

Eryi gave a slow, satisfied blink. 'Rare foresight for an ungifted. No wonder your sister thinks so highly of you. So I will ask you again – where is Pherri?'

There was no sense in lying to him. Orsian could feel the tendrils of Eryi's power clawing at his consciousness. *He already knows*. 'The last time I felt her was weeks ago. She guided my sword and won the battle for us.' The rest had put it down to the skill and fury of the *Hymeriker*, but Orsian knew otherwise. He had felt Pherri's touch on his mind as surely as if she had grasped his sword arm. 'Then she was gone.'

'And she has never come back to you since? Not once in your imprisonment?'

'Never.'

Eryi's eyes narrowed. 'I do believe you are telling the truth. And so I will make it plain for you. Your sister has passed through the space between worlds into another reality. I had hoped she might find her way back, but it is time I faced facts: she is gone. I must make do without her.' His scarred, pale hands gripped the back of his chair. 'With Pherri gone and the Thrumb lost to me, *you* must help me. I must have Piperskeep if I am to defeat the goddess. There is no other choice except death, for all of us.'

Orsian's heart was hammering in his chest. He had trained with sword and shield his whole life, until his palms blistered, but no amount of drilling in the practice yard could have prepared him to stand against what he faced now. In the rising glow of the brazier, shadows danced against the tent like spectres in some morbid play. He reached for his wine, trying to still his trembling fingers. 'What do you need Piperskeep for?' More importantly, what did Eryi need *him* for? Orsian was unsure of the Thrumb's significance; their lands beyond the Dry River were hundreds of miles away.

'There is power in the blood of the Sangreals. The same

strength that drove King Piper from the endless wastes runs in your veins, and in Pherri's. The Sangreals may have forgotten, but Piper forged Piperskeep with magic, and his power has seeped deep into the mortar. Power calls to power. The Sangreal blood is the key to defeating the goddess.'

Orsian forced himself to watch Eryi's strange, featureless face, searching for the truth of his words, but his blank visage gave away nothing. 'The goddess...' He took a sip of wine to steady himself. 'Am I supposed to know who that is?'

The glower Eryi gave him could have sliced through mail. 'She is the ruin of the world, the death of existence. And she is coming. Vulgatypha. *The last Norha.*'

Orsian could not help the shiver that ran down his spine. The Norhai were a myth, the idols of the old religion that worshipped the Mountain as a symbol of their power on earth. But if Eryi was real... He looked again at the god's shifting shadow then into the depths of his pale eyes. Could it be true?

But even if it was, Pherri had thwarted this creature; he would not betray her by helping him now. Orsian spoke slowly, carefully, forcing himself to meet Eryi's eye. 'And why can't you get inside Piperskeep yourself? The Imperials almost managed it; for you it ought to be easy.'

'I must preserve my strength. So must Krupal. But I need to act swiftly. I cannot predict when the goddess will regain her strength, nor how and when she will attack. And while I could turn its defenders to dust, the fortress has... *protections* against those without Sangreal blood who would seek to claim it. With the Thrumb on my side, I could have thrown thousands against the gates, and still it might not have been enough. I have lived too long to believe it is coincidence that when the Imperium was on the verge of victory, three with the blood of Piper in their veins conspired to thwart them. Sometimes possibilities are certainties, events threaded into the very fabric of existence.'

Eryi flexed his long fingers. 'You shall claim it for me, willingly or not.'

Orsian hesitated. He had felt enough of Pherri's terror when she had guided the sword arms of the Erlanders that he knew she would not want him to trust Eryi. Of that he was sure. 'Pherri is clever enough to find her own way back. Then she may help you if she chooses to.'

'"Clever" will not be enough when the goddess arrives. Heed my words, Orsian, or I swear you shall regret it.' Eryi flicked a finger, and against the wall a shadow of Tansa appeared. Before Orsian's eyes, she turned to look at him, her desperate face weeping blood, cascading down the tent like warm rain. 'I have seen your heart, Orsian. Do not make me hurt her.'

The god's gaze on him was like the weight of the sky. Orsian swallowed, and steeled himself for whatever fate his answer would bring. Tansa would be hundreds of miles away – Eryi said he was preserving his power, and nothing Orsian had seen suggested that the god could touch her. *I might have stayed in Cliffark with her, remained Ranulf and let the rest of the world burn.* It would have meant giving up everything, but at least they would have been together. The thought was like being stabbed in the gut. That brief time in Cliffark had been one of the happiest of Orsian's life.

'My answer's no,' said Orsian, steeling himself. 'I don't believe you. I know my sister, and whatever you say, I know she would not want me to help you.'

I'm dead anyway. Orsian leapt from his chair and made to run towards Eryi, ready to clamp his hands around his throat.

He made it barely two yards before a blast of force sent him flying against the table, toppling it as his hip struck painfully against the edge. The flagon burst upon the carpet in an explosion of wine. Orsian bit his tongue as he rolled to his feet, before invisible bindings seized him in a vice-like grip, so tight he could not even struggle.

With long, spider-like steps, Eryi approached. His unblinking pale eyes betrayed no emotion, as if he had only been waiting for Orsian to try something. 'The famed stubbornness of the Sangreals.' His ruined face grew into a pointed, grimacing smile. 'I suppose then we must take the hard and painful path. So be it.'

CHAPTER 16

They assembled in Lord Istlewick's solar, just as night began to fall. All the lamps had been lit, and the papers and ledgers strewn across the table put away. A spitting rain beat rhythmically against the roof. Out at sea, a brewing storm flashed with lightning, reflecting in the black water before seconds later the thunder would roll across the bay to echo against the keep.

There were seven of them. Ciera took the seat at one end of the table, opposite her father, with Burik and Laphor to either side of her. Also present were Sister Aimya, Ciera's mother, and Jerem, the youthful captain of her father's guard, a handsome, beardless man with golden blond hair sheared short.

As they assumed their seats, Ciera took it upon herself to seize control immediately. 'We need to be prepared for the Wild Brigade's attack. Laphor counts slightly over six hundred of them; can we match that sort of force?'

'I have three hundred still in my household guard,' said Lord Istlewick hopefully.

'And we have the high ground,' said Jerem. 'Three hundred within the walls can hold six hundred without comfortably. And first they must cross the causeway.'

Laphor took a loud slurp of beer and chuckled. 'Have any of your three hundred even seen a battle? Your soft boys won't hold the Wild Brigade for the time it takes me to take a shit.'

Jerem bristled, his brow knitting hotly as if he were considering asking Laphor to prove it at the point of a sword. 'My lads are brave. Don't mistake them for yourself, fleeing Merivale. They are ready to give their lives defending our lord.'

'I am hoping that won't be necessary, Jerem,' said Lord Istlewick, resting a hand on his captain's shoulder. 'Perhaps we can come to terms with this Strovac Sigac.'

Burik fixed Lord Istlewick with a stare. 'I'd say he made his terms quite clear when he lopped my brother's head off.'

'Strovac can't be trusted even if you could,' said Laphor. 'He is no mindless brute; he's proved his cunning enough times. You couldn't build a pyre big enough to burn all those he's knifed in the back.' He stroked his grizzled beard. 'We've got maybe twelve hours till he strikes. Maybe that's enough time to whip your guards into fighting shape where they might stand a chance.'

'And what then?' said Aimya, speaking for the first time. 'That would mean abandoning the cliff path to the Cliffarkers. Even if we held the gate, you'd only change who you were surrendering the castle to.'

'I'll challenge Strovac to single combat,' said Burik, glaring around the table as if daring someone to contradict him. 'One battle and one death to decide our fates.'

Laphor trilled his lips dismissively. 'You want to get us all killed? He could beat you holding a blunt knife. The Barrelbreaker could have defeated Strovac in a fair fight, or Lord Errian might have a chance on a good day... but you? Not a bloody prayer.'

'That's three of my brothers he's killed now.' Burik gave Laphor a hard stare. 'I mean to see him answer for it.'

'Has it escaped you that this is about Cliffark and my

daughter, not your petty male nonsense?' interjected Ciera's mother. 'Feel free to throw your life away on his blade if it pleases you, but it will solve nothing. There are other ways to defeat a man like that.'

Ciera watched them, listening as her mother's remark sparked another round of comments and counter-comments. Having made her point, her mother also seemed content to sit back and watch, while her father was so slumped in his chair that Ciera wondered if he was following the conversation at all.

She rolled their situation around her head. Both their routes out of Cliffark Tower were blocked, and they could not hope to defeat one foe without falling to the other. She could see no way out, other than to give Strovac Sigac what he wanted: her and Andrick. It was to her relief that nobody had suggested it.

Unless... The beginnings of an idea sparked in Ciera's head. If they could come to terms with the Cliffarkers, and also find a way to defeat Strovac Sigac... She smiled slightly to herself. *It might just work, if the gods favour us.* Though given Aimya's claims, who knew what they could rely on the gods for?

Just as Laphor, Burik, and Jerem looked to be on the verge of coming to blows, Ciera repeatedly slammed her palm on the table for silence.

'I have a suggestion,' she said, once all of them had fallen quiet. 'We give Strovac Sigac what he wants.'

'What he wants?' demanded Laphor. 'Majesty, do not make the mistake of thinking you can get Sigac to treat you honourably; too many good men have made that mistake.'

'If the man's reputation is true,' said Lady Istlewick, 'he will throw your son onto the rocks and give you to his men.'

Ciera raised an eyebrow. 'Did you not just say there were other ways to defeat a man? We will give him what he wants, for a price.'

On too little sleep, Ciera stepped out of Cliffark Tower's gate onto the causeway. It was dawn, when Strovac Sigac had promised his attack would come, but they had raised the white flag of parley over the gate and a stained, tattered banner that might once have been the same colour had risen above the Wild Brigade. Strovac Sigac was ready to talk.

Unless it is a ruse. Ciera's heartbeat came a little faster. She had been awake half the night persuading Laphor and the rest that this was the only way. Her fingers reached for the pouch her mother had given her. 'Widowsbane,' Lady Istlewick had told her. 'Should he break faith and seize you, just a pinch of that and it will be over.'

Strovac Sigac strode forward to meet her, so large that the causeway seemed almost to shake with every step. He was smiling, but his beady eyes were cold as the autumn sea. Ciera held his gaze, forcing down her fear. She had survived Hessian, and Balyard; Strovac was just another monster.

He stopped several feet away, a wormish smirk on his face. 'I asked for you and your son. I will not settle for half my due.'

Ciera took a deep breath. 'I came to offer you terms.'

'I told you my terms.'

'I propose a slight variation. To protect my position.'

'Your protection does not concern me. Fetch your son, and you and I shall leave your family in peace.'

Ciera resisted the urge to look away. *If he snatches me now, it is over.* She touched the vial of widowsbane hidden inside her sleeve. 'I have heard rumours about you, Strovac Sigac.'

'Rumours follow men like me.'

'The rumour I heard is that you are Hessian's son.' It was an old tale, but she had heard it shortly after the news that Strovac had gone over to the Prindians.

His nostrils flared, a rising fury marring his sneering pride. Ciera's breath caught in her throat as for a moment she thought he might reach out and strike her.

'Is it true?' she asked, willing her voice not to shake.

Strovac's eyes flashed. 'Yes, it's fucking true. Was obvious when I was born I wasn't my mother's husband's get. He was barely bigger than you; you think men my size grow on trees? What's it to you?'

If he sees through me I am done for. 'Do you want to be king?'

'I am Hessian's oldest son.' Ciera could almost feel the hot rage rolling off him. 'Why should it matter who my mother was? I should have been his heir from the day I was born. Instead he and his brother scorned me, banished me to the fens except when they needed a dumb brute to smash some skulls.' His face twisted. 'Well, I showed Andrick, and from what I hear you dealt with Hessian.'

Ciera kept her face blank, trying to appear as innocent as possible. 'You want to marry me, don't you?'

'What? Why would I need to marry you? The wizard has already promised me the crown.'

'To shore up your claim, of course,' Ciera replied, as if it was the most obvious solution in the world. 'You think your magus' – she could recall no word of a magus among the Imperial force; who was Strovac working with now? – 'will be around to help you forever? Marrying Hessian's queen gives you legitimacy, and places his son in your power.' The suggestion made Ciera's stomach churn; Strovac would dispose of Andrick and never think twice on it.

A crack appeared in Strovac's mask of contempt. He frowned uncertainly. 'Your son is a problem. How do I know you would not plot to kill me and ensure his succession?'

Ciera steeled herself. This was the most dangerous part of her deceit. 'Andrick is not Hessian's son.'

Her pronouncement earnt barely a flicker from Strovac. Perhaps a slight twitch of an eyebrow. A shout rose from the massed warriors at the end of the causeway – 'Come on

Strovac, just fuck her already!' – followed by gales of braying laughter.

Strovac ignored them. 'Why would you admit something like that to me?'

'To show he is no threat to you. The crown is yours, but like it or not you need me.'

The big warrior's pauses were becoming longer, more thoughtful. Ciera could practically hear the wheels of his mind turning. Unless she was mistaken, she almost had him. 'So what do you propose we do with him?'

'Just as you are Hessian's heir, Andrick is my father's. When my father passes and my son comes of age, he will rule here in Cliffark. And for Erland, I will give you sons, to rule after you are gone. You already know I'm fertile.'

Strovac's smirk stretched so far that his lips threatened to disappear. 'So if I spare your son, you will marry me and come willingly to my bed?' He looked up at the watchers on the battlements. 'Do the cowards up there fear me so?'

It was Ciera's turn to smirk. 'Do not think it so simple. I will marry you if you reclaim Cliffark. My father's men lack the ferocity to turn back the rebels. Deal with them, and you shall have my hand.'

His smirk disappeared. A sudden gust of wind raised the hairs on Ciera's arms, and Strovac's eyes turned hard as two pieces of flint. 'And why should I not just take you now? Who would stop me?'

Ciera's blood ran cold, but she had been ready for this. 'If you mean to rule Erland, men must see you are as good as your word. How will men support you if they cannot trust you?'

Strovac grimaced, his mouth set as if he was chewing a wasp, and Ciera saw the remark had found her target. Another shout rose from the men behind him, and he ignored it. 'So I destroy your father's enemies, and you will rule as my queen. Fine. It is no hardship to me; it has been too long now since my

Wild Brigade had a proper fight. A few thousand townsmen armed with knives and cleavers will suit them. Once they're vanquished though, I want the city for a day before I hand it back to your father.'

'Done,' said Ciera. 'And I want the girl, as a show of good faith.'

Strovac laughed, a high, cruel sound that echoed back off the battlements. 'Done.' He turned and whistled to his men. 'Bring the girl!'

There was some shuffling and arguing among the Wild Brigade, but one of them dragged Haisie forward, undid her blindfold, and shoved her down the causeway. There was a thin scar below her eye where Strovac had used his blade on her. When she saw Ciera she burst into tears, running half the length of the causeway to throw herself into Ciera's arms, sobbing.

'How touching,' sneered Strovac. 'Do you wish me to attack the rebels now, future wife?'

'I would suggest at dawn tomorrow,' said Ciera. 'While they are sleeping off their hangovers.'

Strovac's cold smile faltered. 'You would delay me a day?'

'I will require the rest of the day and tonight to ready Cliffark Tower for our wedding. Once the rebels are vanquished, I am yours to wed as you please.'

Strovac grunted. 'Fine. Dawn tomorrow then. Prepare well, wife.' He cast an appraising eye up and down Ciera's body, making her feel for a moment as if her dress were made of the thinnest silk. 'We will need the largest bed your father has.'

He turned on his heel and stomped back towards his men. Ciera took Haisie's hand and walked back towards Cliffark Tower, taking deep, calming breaths. Her negotiation with Strovac had bought them the time they needed. She squeezed Haisie's hand. 'Are you well?'

Haisie nodded, still tearful. 'They were cruel. They said

they would...' The rest of Haisie's words were lost beneath her struggle to hold back her sobs. 'I... I...'

Ciera crouched down to look Haisie in the eye, forcing a smile to stop herself wincing at the angry scar Strovac had left on her cheek. 'It's okay, Haisie. You're safe. We can cry once we're back inside, but until then I need you to walk slowly, as if you're not scared of them. Can you do that for me?'

Haisie nodded, wiping her cheeks. 'Yes.'

'Come on then.'

The walk felt like a mile, but finally the gates squeaked open for them, and they were back within the safety of Cliffark Tower. Ciera sank to her knees with her back against the door, as Haisie sobbed into her shoulder.

Laphor had been watching from the battlements, and raced down to meet them. 'What happened?' he asked. 'Did he—?' The rest followed behind him, including Andrick in the arms of Ciera's mother.

Ciera nodded as Haisie continued to sob. 'He agreed.'

'You tricked him! Eryi's balls, I can't believe it worked.' Laphor pulled Ciera to her feet and shocked Ciera by embracing her. 'Well done, Majesty. I was shitting myself up there, I thought... never mind what I thought. You were right!'

'So what now?' asked Lady Istlewick, stepping forward. Ciera reached for Andrick, but her mother ignored her. 'Do you still mean to speak with the rebels?'

Ciera nodded. 'As soon as I can.'

Some hours later, after a breakfast washed down with a calming mug of strong ale and a rest, Ciera found herself departing Cliffark Tower again. This time though, it was through the small, single gate in the north wall, leading to the steep and winding track that ran down towards the town.

In the end, once she had explained what Strovac had agreed to, even Ciera's mother had been congratulatory. She had bought them an additional day, for the price of a promise that she had no intention of keeping. She would sooner have returned to Hessian's bed than share one with Strovac Sigac, with his callous sneers and reptilian eyes.

Now, all she had to do was bring the rebels over to their side. *If I can pay Strovac Sigac in promises, then why should this be any different?* And Ciera was open to reform – changing how the city was run had been one of her primary goals in Merivale. If the rebels' demands were reasonable, they might be able to reach common ground. Notionally, this was the easier task.

She had even been able to bring Laphor with her this time. He had though removed the red mark of the *Hymeriker* from his mail; it would have made him no friends in Cliffark, where folk still remembered the fall of Portes Stormcaller at the hands of Andrick Barrelbreaker.

The entrance to Cliffark was a gap in the city's claywork walls fifteen yards across. When Ciera was a girl, it had always been guarded by four of her father's men. Today though, a blockade of planks, barrels, and spiked staves stood in their place, forming a barrier half again as tall as Ciera. Broken glass littered the ground, forcing Ciera to watch her step carefully. Over the barricade, rebel faces peered down at her, their bodies hidden behind the wall to protect them from archers. Among them she saw boys barely into their teens, stout-faced men in their middle years, and even a smattering of women.

Next to her, Laphor inhaled uneasily through his teeth. 'If this is the best they can do, the Wild Brigade will cut straight through them.'

'That's why we're here, isn't it?' said Ciera. 'To make sure that doesn't happen.'

She stopped a few yards away from the base of the barrier, looking up expectantly at the faces staring down at her. Word had been sent that Lord Istlewick wished to negotiate and would be sending an envoy, but Ciera doubted any of the rebels had expected their lord's only child.

A greasy-haired sailor holding a spear scrambled further up the barricade to squint down at her. 'You're the daughter, ain't you?'

Ciera nodded. 'I am here on behalf of my father, Lord Istlewick.'

A confused murmur passed along the defenders. 'Why would he send her?' cried a woman. 'Got to be a trap of some sort.'

'A trap?' came an incredulous reply from an older man, teetering atop the barricade. 'Some trap; the girl probably weighs about six stone soaking wet.' He leered down at her, showing ugly gums and too few teeth. 'What's a little thing like that going to do, pretty us to death?'

Next to her, Ciera felt Laphor bristle.

The sailor shrugged. 'The boss said to send Lord Istlewick's envoy straight to her, so that's what we'll do.'

Ciera's ears pricked up at that. The rebel leader was a woman. She pictured a hard-bitten landlady with crooked teeth, half-mad from strong drink.

'You'll have to climb up,' said the sailor. 'If you can.'

Ciera looked at Laphor. 'I can boost you up,' he said. 'Provided you're still sure about this.'

It was hardly the most dignified entry into Cliffark, but with Laphor's help Ciera made it atop the barricade, hauled up at the other end by the strong grip of the sailor. Laphor climbed up after her unsteadily, grimacing tightly at the pain in his slowly improving ankle.

'You're to hand over any weapons,' said the sailor once they were on the ground again, eyeing Laphor's sword.

With some reluctance, Laphor unbuckled his scabbard.

'Look after it, or we'll have words.' He held it out for the man to take.

Ciera looked around. The street had been taken over by something akin to a war camp. Dozens of spears rested against a wall, and a huge pig was rotating over a crackling fire pit. Some rebels sat, passing jugs of drink between themselves, while others threw dice against the corner of a building or played cards around a barrel. The atmosphere was joyous, the air filled with laughter, shouting, and the clashing of toasts. Any sense of social division seemed to have dissipated, apprentice boys and alewives rubbing shoulders with moneyed merchants and sailors still smelling of the sea.

Ciera eyed them all. *Rebellion certainly makes for strange alliances.*

The sailor whistled at her. 'You coming? Or just going to stand there gawking?'

Ciera and Laphor followed the man deeper into the city. He led them towards one of the wealthier districts. There were some signs of looting – ripped clothing discarded in the street; broken windows; doors torn from their hinges – but the city appeared mostly intact. Not at all what Ciera had suspected.

Twenty minutes later, they stopped outside a wall of wrought-iron bars topped with golden spikes, enclosing a vast complex of overgrown but verdant gardens and a three-storey villa of gleaming whitewash. Elegant towers soared from a roof of red tiles, and despite the autumn chill the hedges of many-hued flowers were bright and vibrant.

'This is the Imperial enclave,' said Ciera.

The sailor grinned. 'Been abandoned ever since the lord administrator left. We thought it was time someone put it to better use.'

He lifted the bar and opened the gate with a creak. A weaving path of clean white gravel led them to a high arched double door bordered by a pair of twisting, elegant pillars.

'The council is waiting for you,' said the sailor. He knocked twice, and the two sides swept open together.

It took Ciera's eyes a moment to adjust to the glow within. It seemed as if every candle the Imperial lord administrator had owned must have been collected and used to illuminate the long entrance hall. Three-pronged candle-holders ran along the walls, their light reflecting off the sheer white walls and marbled floor. The room's elegance was slightly offset by the pair of dogs scrapping over a chicken carcass in the corner, and the bored-looking men in ugly leather armour clutching spears. A tasselled red carpet down the centre of the room showed the way to a long table at the far end, at which a motley collection of people sat, four men and three women.

They all looked intriguing in their own ways, but it was the woman sitting at the middle of the table who drew Ciera's eye.

She looked up at their entry, and for a heartbeat Ciera was sure she must be mistaken. Short-cropped hair that was beginning to grow out, and a lean, pretty face with a smattering of freckles across her cheeks and nose.

It can't be, she thought. But there was no doubting it. And, why not? Ciera had already been a witness to her ruthlessness.

The woman came to her feet. With two fingers, Tansa of Cliffark beckoned Ciera forward.

CHAPTER 17

Tansa watched Ciera stride towards them, trying to hide her delight that the Queen of Erland should be forced to come to her like a supplicant. *We're both back in Cliffark where we began, though perhaps this time she finds the city a little less to her liking.*

After the riot at the conscription, the city had fallen to them in a matter of hours. The harbour and every route out of the city were closed. The city guard had been trapped in their barracks and left there starving for three days until they were forced to negotiate. In return for their lives, they had handed over the contents of their armoury.

It had not, however, all gone as Tansa had desired. There had been some burning and looting, and while that had since been put a stop to most of the perpetrators had escaped. There had also been an outbreak of opportunistic rapes, but there had been such a stirring of outrage that the offenders had been swiftly seized, and those not beaten to death by the mob were currently decorating the city's clock tower, castrated and locked in high cages too tight for them to even raise their arms against the onslaught of carrion birds feeding on their flesh. No laws did not mean no consequences; it meant justice based on the will of the many, not the whims of one man.

More pressing now was their failure to take Cliffark Tower. By the time the mob had reached the path, the remaining members of Lord Istlewick's household guard had been ready, and well-armed with the slope to their advantage had repelled the Cliffarkers' greater numbers. Instead, Tansa and the rebels had focused their efforts on securing the city, raising high barricades at every gate. It was said that had been Stormcaller's mistake – failing to protect Cliffark against the *Hymeriker*'s inevitable assault.

'What do you suppose she wants?' growled Abner as Ciera approached down the long hall of the Imperial enclave's manor. The former first mate of the *Jackdaw* was part of the newly constituted city council.

'Prettier than I recall,' said Hesten, a red-cheeked, heavy-gutted man never seen without a tankard of ale in his fist. He had been Cliffark's mayor – a ceremonial position there purely to fulfil any functions that Lord Istlewick could not be troubled with – and such was his popularity among the rich and poor alike it had seemed wise to include him. 'Looks like my first wife before she married me!' He laughed heartily at his own joke.

'Weak ankles,' croaked Maud, scrutinising Ciera through her heavy-lidded eyes. 'Though I suppose there's not much to her. Can't see her hauling a barrel or pushing a cart. One strong breeze and she'd be in the harbour.' Maud might have seemed a strange choice, but she said she would represent Pauper's Hole and nobody there seemed bothered enough to object. More importantly, Tansa still owed her several weeks' rent.

Rounding out the council was Marrec, the leader of the merchants' guild that was a reluctant participant in the rebellion – Tansa thought it better to keep him close to stop the town's wealthiest merchants betraying them and going over to Lord Istlewick, and she could drag his inclusion out as long as circumstances required; Hevetia, the chain-smoking owner of a disreputable inn called the Siren's Storm where Tansa had once hidden from the lord administrator's private guards; and a taciturn, unsmiling blacksmith named Alliver who Tansa suspected had been chosen from among the city's tradesmen only to either keep him out of their way or to intentionally rile the council. The students had also wanted a place, but the rest of them had become so heartily sick of their prattling that the suggestion had been unanimously rejected.

Ciera strode towards them as proudly as if she had assembled them here herself, her single *hymerika* advancing with her just a few steps behind. While Tansa might have imagined her as a supplicant, that was clearly not how Ciera saw herself. *Her exile has not changed her.* Tansa looked to her left and right at the other members of the council. She could see the subtle signs of deference already, the way that Marrec bowed his head and how Hesten was mopping at his brow and rearranging his wine-stained tunic. *If I give her half a chance, she will charm or trick them all into agreeing with her.* 'Just let me do the talking,' she whispered around the table.

As Ciera paused before them, a vision of Tam's lolling tongue and swollen neck flashed before Tansa's eyes. She was filled with a sense of loathing. The queen may not have passed the sentence, but Ciera was nearly as much to blame for her brother's death as Hessian. She had bewitched him, and Tam had been the one to face the consequences. Tansa supposed that Ciera might think that allowing her to escape Piperskeep made them even, or perhaps that Tansa even *owed her*, but not to her mind. Far from it.

'Ciera Istlewick,' said Tansa. She searched for a flicker of irritation at the absence of her title, but was disappointed not to see one. 'How can this council help you?'

'I am here to negotiate.' She looked from one end of the

table to the other, meeting every person's eye. 'On behalf of my father, and my son, the king.'

Tansa nodded. 'Very well.' She sat back in her chair, waiting.

Ciera appeared nonplussed, a slight crease in her brow marring her otherwise perfect face. 'What are your demands?'

'I'd say the question is what are your requests,' replied Tansa. She was already enjoying this more than she would care to admit. 'We hold the city, and we are prepared to allow your father to leave whenever he chooses. What demands could we possibly have?'

At her left hand, Maud let out a cackle. 'Eryi's bones, girl – no need to lay it on so thick. One whiff of power and you're speaking as if you're the bloody kzar of the Imperium.'

Before Tansa could respond, Hesten addressed Ciera, first giving her what Tansa supposed he thought of as his most disarming smile. 'I regret that you must come before us in such straitened circumstances, Majesty. I, and I believe all of this council, wish to express our condolences for the recent events in Merivale.' He wiped a non-existent tear from his eye. 'However, I am sure you must understand that we serve the people of Cliffark. Our demands are simple: an end to your father's conscription.'

'And no new taxes,' added Marrec.

'No lord either,' said Hevetia. 'We don't need a lord; we know what our city needs. We'd pay taxes to Merivale at a reduced rate though, in return for your blessing.'

'She doesn't even hold Merivale!' Tansa exclaimed. 'We don't need to pay taxes anywhere.'

'You've never paid nothing anyway,' put in Maud. Tansa detected the slight smiles of agreement that passed round the table, deepening her annoyance. They weren't meant to be undermining her like this – Ciera had hardly spoken a word and they were already falling over themselves to get in her good graces.

'And we want this council empowered with all the powers of your father,' added Abner. 'Seems only right that the folk who live in a place are the ones who make the decisions.'

Ciera smiled at him, and then at Hesten who had asked for an end to conscription. 'I am grateful for your words of condolence, although I regret I did not catch your name.'

'Hesten, Majesty,' said Hesten, almost tripping over his tongue in his haste to reply. 'I am— was the mayor here.'

This led to them going round the table and all introducing themselves, as if they were presenting themselves before Ciera rather than the other way around. Tansa tried her best to hide it, but she was seething. *Put a pretty girl with a title before them and they forget all the reasons we had to do this.* Well, she would salvage something from this, and then she would think about replacing the council with one that had some backbone.

Introductions complete, Ciera blessed them all with another smile. 'So, no conscription.' She held out four fingers and placed her other index finger against the first. 'I am sure my father can see the error in that – agreed.' She continued to go through all her fingers in turn as she addressed their points, cleverly discouraging any interruptions. 'On your second demand, I cannot give away my father's seat, so what I propose is this: my father continues as Lord of Cliffark until he dies or chooses to abdicate. Thereafter, you may pay your taxes to Merivale. I am content for a council to rule Cliffark with my blessing, and for it to have all the powers of a lord, but half the members should be appointed by Piperskeep.' She smiled again. 'That's my counterproposal.'

'Your second point is worthless,' said Tansa, immediately seeing what Ciera intended and leaning forward eagerly. 'When your father dies, your son will be Lord of Cliffark and also the King of Erland; the city will pay taxes directly to him regardless under the current system. You offer us nothing.'

'But you have a guarantee he will not appoint someone else as lord to serve in his stead,' said Ciera.

There were murmurs of agreement around the table. From everyone, even Maud who Tansa had thought would be the most hostile to Ciera. 'And supposing we agree to this,' said Maud, squinting at her, 'what do you want from us?'

Ciera's slight smile told Tansa that this was exactly the question she had hoped for. 'If I am to enforce this agreement, my son must be in his rightful place as king. As you are aware, I am currently on the run from those who seek to deny his crown. If we unite against our mutual enemies and defeat them, we can make an agreement as to Cliffark's status that will stand for the rest of time.'

'*Mutual enemies?*' Tansa could feel the blood rushing to her face. 'Don't shit in our pot and call it seasoning, Majesty – those are *your* enemies. We help you defeat your enemies and you'll give us what we already have? What sort of deal is that?'

Ciera's expression did not change, but Tansa could feel her sense of triumph. She could have punched her. 'They are your enemies as well,' said Ciera. 'Strovac Sigac has come to Cliffark, and once he has dealt with me and my father, he will turn on you. You may think yourself free now, but how long do you suppose it will be before the Imperium or Ulric Balyard turn their attention to Cliffark? The character and diligence of this city is renowned; they will not be content to sit by and let you rise alone.' She folded her arms. 'Face it: you need the protection of Merivale.'

The council members were already exchanging worried glances. 'Strovac Sigac,' muttered Abner. 'There's a man with as black a reputation as any pirate to ever sail the Silent Sea. How many men does he bring?'

'The girl's right,' said Maud. 'Most of you were alive to see what happened to Portes Stormcaller; think what would have been if he could have made a deal with the king in Merivale?'

Tansa watched Ciera through narrowed eyes. *I see you, Ciera Istlewick.* A feeling of helpless fury flooded her. The Queen of Erland had come into her home and turned everything upside down to suit herself. She looked from councillor to councillor, but she saw it was already too late. Marrec would have taken any opportunity to strike a deal with the lords. She had charmed Hesten and Abner. Hevetia and Maud did not know Ciera's ways as Tansa did. Only Alliver was showing any degree of scepticism, and he would not help Tansa's cause at all.

'He brings six hundred men,' Ciera told Abner. 'Sigac's reputation is well-earnt; his Wild Brigade are among the finest killers in the world, and they have come to take my son's life.' For a moment, the mask broke, and Tansa thought she was finally seeing a moment of sincerity. 'He believes he has made a deal with me: I will be his bride if he will retake this city for me.' She looked around the table beseechingly. 'I did this only to buy time so that I could come to you. I am here *begging* for your help. This city has given much to me and my family; ride with me against Strovac Sigac and the thieves of Merivale, and I swear you shall have what I have offered.'

'We can take six hundred men,' said Abner, as if the matter were already decided. And, as Tansa looked around the table, she could see that it was. 'It's a hard bargain, being asked to join a war we've already said isn't our fight, but I don't see how else we'll free ourselves. I doubt Strovac Sigac or the Imperium or this Lord Balyard would be ready to negotiate with us.'

After that, it was all over bar the shouting. Tansa seethed in silence as every other member of the council agreed to the queen's proposal. There was much discussion of a plan to defeat Strovac Sigac's Wild Brigade, but Tansa was hardly listening. She kept her gaze fixed on Ciera.

'You have my eternal gratitude,' Ciera told them. 'I must

now depart to Cliffark Tower to prepare for our battle. First though, I propose a toast.'

Hesten had probably never moved so fast in his life, such was his haste in which to seize a jug of wine and serve them each a cup. The seven of them stood to join Ciera Istlewick, before they all pressed their cups together and downed them. All except Tansa. She replaced hers on the table, undrunk. *You will give us everything you have agreed to and more, Ciera Istlewick.* Tansa would make sure of it.

CHAPTER 18

The rhythm of the cart as it trundled down the sloping forest was almost soothing, like a lullaby. Helana's head bounced gently against a soft pillow of piled clothing, and she rolled over and returned to sleep, throwing her arm over her head to cover her eyes against the warm yellow sun and her ear from the birdsong and the steady tread of men.

Someone above her laughed. 'I can see you're awake. Come on, Hel'na; it's been two days!'

Shielding her eyes, Helana looked up blearily, straight into the beaming face of Na'mu, brother to Ti'en and Hu'ra and one-time hunting companion of Helana. His moustache was a little untidy, but otherwise he looked as he had before, gangly with fair skin dotted with endless freckles.

'Na'mu? What are you doing here? Where have you been?' She could not recall seeing him in the aftermath of Hu'ra's uprising.

The Thrumb youth laughed again. 'Oh, just saving your life! How did you think Ry found you?'

Rubbing her face, Helana forced herself to sit upright, the motion of the cart suddenly no longer soothing but sickening.

Rymond. Not a dream then, obviously. She was grateful, but why had it had to be him who saved her? '"Ry" is it? Sounds like you two are the best of friends.'

'After Hu'ra took Thrumbalto, me and some friends managed to escape while the guards were drunk,' Na'mu continued. 'We fled into Erland, and fortunately straight into Ry and his West Erlanders! Once I was able to convince him that we weren't an invasion and told him you were in danger he ordered his men to march into Thrumb to save you! Hu'ra's dead, and Ti'en and the rest of his followers have been locked away at the top of the Irmintree. The elders have formed a council to rule things while they work out who the next chieftain is.' A frown crossed his expression for the first time, as if remembering all those who had died.

Na'mu was putting on a brave face, given that his father had been executed. 'Thank you,' said Helana. 'I owe you my life.' Not only that, Na'mu had thwarted Hu'ra's plan to join Eryi, but explaining that would require more strength than Helana could muster at that moment. 'Could you stop the cart? I'll walk.'

Na'mu brought the pair of harnessed mules to a halt, and Helana climbed down at the back. Her legs trembled slightly, but Na'mu let her lean on him for support.

With Na'mu's help, Helana took a few faltering steps to get her feet under her, following the mass of Erlanders who were making their way through the trees. Down the slope, she spied the arid gravel streambed that marked the line of the Dry River, the border between Erland and Thrumb. Beyond that, the ground levelled out into the open grassland of West Erland.

'Are you coming too?' she asked Na'mu. She had never expected to be so relieved to see Erland again.

'Not beyond the Dry River. Another few hundred yards and I'll leave you.' Na'mu paused. 'It was good knowing you,

Hel'na. Perhaps one day, once things are settled again, you can visit.'

The clatter of hooves behind them caused Helana to turn, and she found herself looking up at Rymond Prindian. He had grown a beard, and his handsome face was darker than when she had last seen him, when she had fled from his army as it returned to West Erland. Rather than his usual fine velvets, he was dressed for war, in mail and leather, with a sword hanging at his side. She could admit it suited him. He seemed older too, and not so bloodless, the softness of his cheeks carved away into a sharp jawline. Had it only been last winter that he had kissed her as he lay bleeding from a boar wound in his leg? The memory hardly seemed to belong to her.

'You're awake,' he said.

'Evidently,' she replied. She looked his mount up and down, a fine white mare as fair as her rider. 'Any chance I could have a horse instead of being rolled in a cart like an invalid?'

Rymond's lip twitched. 'Some thanks for rescuing you. I have no mounts to spare, and regrettably you have been an invalid. Whatever they gave you knocked you out for two days. For the first few hours I wasn't sure if you were going to make it, even after I stopped that madman gutting you.'

You don't know the half of it. Helana swallowed. 'Thank you.'

'Those might be the first grateful words that ever crossed your lips.'

'Don't get used to it.'

A part of Helana wanted to pick up their quarrel from when they had last met, with her uncle's decapitated head mounted atop a spear and the laughter of Strovac Sigac ringing in her ears. But what would be the point? She had felt the presence of true evil, and it had been endlessly worse than Strovac Sigac.

'We'll talk more tonight,' said Rymond. He looked down at

her, smiling strangely. 'You look well, all things considered. I'm glad you're safe.' He rode away towards the Dry River, a herd of riders streaming after him.

With Rymond gone, Helana trudged along with Na'mu, struggling to keep pace with the other Erlanders travelling on foot. 'Did you see what was happening—' She struggled to find the words. 'Did you see what Hu'ra was doing?'

Na'mu nodded, suddenly sombre. 'Yes, I saw. I'm sorry, I never suspected Ti'en, nor that Hu'ra would take it that far. His followers who survived were all out of their minds on casheef; they said by killing you he wanted to open a route to Merivale, that Er'yi had told him to do it.' He shuddered. 'Apparently my brother Ba'il began acting strangely too, last year before he died. I hope madness doesn't run in the family.'

'It wasn't madness,' Helana said quietly. 'Well, it was, but it wasn't. I *saw* him, I saw Eryi.'

Na'mu eyed her sideways, a doubtful look on his face. 'You weren't in your right mind. Hu'ra loaded you up with so much casheef you almost died. Whatever you saw, it wasn't real.'

'What about before?' bit back Helana. 'You heard what She'ab told me, about finding my cousin through casheef visions to stop Eryi. You seemed ready enough to believe it then.'

'And that was my mistake,' said Na'mu. 'I'm sorry he's dead, but She'ab was as mad as Hu'ra. Casheef doesn't show the truth or let you talk to gods or anything like that.' Helana looked up at him, and almost recoiled at the fury in his face. 'It *stole* two of my brothers, and my father, and every other Thrumb who's died at the hands of another.'

Na'mu was resolutely not looking at her, keeping his eyes fixed on the Dry River, his face as stern and serious as his father's. It seemed to suit him far more than the laughing fool he had pretended to be when Helana woke. That had been the old Na'mu.

If he needed to believe that casheef was to blame, she would let him. The Thrumb had seen enough misery.

'You don't actually want me to visit Thrumb someday,' said Helana. 'Do you?'

Na'mu hesitated. 'I think it would be for the best that you didn't. Every time Erland gets involved with affairs in Thrumb it seems to end in tragedy. We need to be left on our own for a while. The council and King Rymond have agreed a peace.'

Helana could understand that.

They walked as far as the Dry River together, where Na'mu pulled Helana into a tight embrace.

'Thanks for saving my life,' she whispered into his shoulder.

'Sorry for not realising what Ti'en was up to,' he replied. 'I hope we meet again one day. In a few lifetimes, perhaps.'

Helana laughed, and Na'mu pulled away smiling. It seemed genuine, even if slightly forced. 'Goodbye, Helana.'

'Goodbye, Na'mu.'

He turned, and Helana watched him as far as the trees. It was barely autumn, yet their green and purple leaves were already fading to orange and brown. He looked back, waved, and ducked beneath a branch to disappear up the slope.

'You coming, Sangreal?'

Helana turned at Rymond's cry. He had already crossed the Dry River, riding alongside a plain, dark-haired woman garbed in battered leather armour. It seemed much had happened in West Erland while she had been away: based on what she had overheard from the West Erlanders walking beside her, Rymond was now fighting to retake his kingdom from an invasion by the Imperium.

But what did the fate of West Erland and defeating the Imperials matter, next to what Helana had seen in the tent? She'ab had been right – Eryi was the true foe. Helana shuddered at the memory of his pale eyes. And if he was free, the

Norha Vulgatypha might not be far behind. She had to warn Erland.

Rymond watched as Helana trudged down into the dry gorge and up the other side. She was different to when he had last seen her, more guarded, with a brittle quality to her usual boldness. No surprise, after all she had been through.

'So that's the girl we galloped across the country to save,' said Gruenla. 'Pretty thing. Hardly worth giving up a kingdom for though.'

Rymond ground his teeth. He was growing tired of Gruenla needling him over his decision. 'West Erland is still here, is it not? My prospects are hardly worse than when I left.' He had not been prepared to let Helana die.

'Still here, with five thousand more Imperials in it, maybe more. What are you planning to do if we get back to Fallback Lodge and find it occupied by Imperials?'

'Take it back, I suppose.'

Gruenla snorted. 'That easy, is it? I swear you've learnt nothing. Acques Bazar's the new legate and he's an experienced commander, not some pampered senator like Drast Fulkiro; you need to start taking this more seriously. I didn't free you so we could go gallivanting off to save a princess.'

'What do you care? You're here for the money.'

'Yes, and I won't get paid unless you retake Irith. Your mother offered me a tidy sum to get your arse back on that ugly throne, but unlike Garwen my men and I aren't prepared to wait thirty years for that to happen.'

'Garwen doesn't mean that literally.' Although maybe he had; the veteran soldier had an old man's patience.

'Neither do I. Take a look at my men – do they look like they're in this for the long haul?'

Rymond glanced to either side of himself at the knots of mounted Cyliriens, easily noticeable among the Erlanders by their mismatched armour and darker features. They looked tired and ill-tempered, and there was a nasty bark to their occasional burst of laughter. They looked like men and women who had been at war too long.

'They don't seem too happy.' That was a problem – if the Cyliriens left it would rob him of a third of his force.

'That's putting it mildly. The only thing keeping them satisfied was being able to kill Imperials. I'm guessing you won't be paying them for letting you play the gallant prince.'

'They'll get paid when we retake Irith.'

Gruenla grunted a laugh at this. 'And that's the nub of it, isn't it? How exactly are you going to do that?'

Rymond did not know. He had hoped to make an alliance with the Thrumb again, but the forest-dwellers had their own challenges, and said they'd had a belly full of Erlander problems already. 'More men will come.'

'Farmers and swineherds will not retake Irith. Best think of something, because right now the only thing keeping my boys here is that we might get the chance to cross blades with Acques Bazar.'

Before Rymond could reply, Gruenla pushed her horse to a trot and wheeled off to speak with a group of her Cyliriens.

Rymond rubbed his tight jaw. Ideally, he would have been able to call on the loyalty of his sworn lords to assemble an army, but after he had stood up before the people of Cliffark and declared he had given West Erland over to the Imperium those men were not willing to support him. Every overture he had made to a lord had been rebuffed.

By Eryi, I wish Adfric was here. He might have offered solutions, whereas all Gruenla gave him was problems. He tightened his grip on the reins. *I lost Irith; I will take it back.*

Even in his own head, the words sounded hollow.

He rode a few miles in silence, his ragtag band of Erlanders and Cyliriens spread out haphazardly around him, those without horses plodding along at the rear. He knew he ought to make an effort to place them in formation, like Andrick Barrelbreaker might have done, but in that moment it was hard to care about such things. They might not even listen to him.

Rymond turned at the sound of beating hooves behind him, and was surprised to see Helana, ahorse and gaining on him. She slowed to a walk alongside him, a smug expression on her face.

'Your health seems to improve with each passing mile,' said Rymond. She was as beautiful as he recalled, her hair black as midnight, her green eyes deep enough to drown in. 'Where did you get a horse from?'

'Won it in a race against one of your men, Millas.'

Rymond recalled him; Millas was Garwen's son. 'What did you wager?'

'Nothing I was ever in danger of losing.'

Rymond smiled. He was relieved to see her well; he would never reveal to her the horror he had felt when he had arrived in Thrumbalto to see her stretched out ready to be butchered. Even afterwards there had been hours when he had thought she might not survive whatever the Thrumb usurper Hu'ra had done to her. 'Helana… what happened in Thrumb… if you need…' Rymond faltered over his words. 'What I mean to say is – you are under no obligation to remain with me. If you wish to return to Merivale, I will not stop you.'

'Is there news of Merivale? All I hear from the men is rumours, and none of them seem able to agree. I have had no news since the day I was forced to flee.'

Rymond remembered it well the day his army had returned to West Erland with Andrick Barrelbreaker's head. 'Helana, I'm sorry, I didn't—'

She raised a hand to silence him. 'Spare it. It's done, and

nothing you can say will change it. Just tell me what you know of Merivale and East Erland.'

Rymond swigged from his waterskin, and tried to tell her as plainly as he could. 'Queen Ciera gave birth to a son, and shortly after that the Imperials attacked. I understand Merivale fought them off...' He paused, swallowed. 'But your father is dead.'

Something that might have been grief flickered across Helana's face, but only for a moment. 'How?'

'I do not know.'

Helana's face remained as still and unreadable as ancient oak. Rymond knew what it was like to have a complicated relationship with one's parent, but for Helana it was likely even more so. There was affection between him and his mother, in a manner of speaking, but between Helana and Hessian he sensed only antagonism. He spoke again, 'If you need—'

'I don't need anything.' Helana looked away and quickly wiped her eye. 'Just tired.' When she next looked at him, all he detected was resolve. 'I am returning to Merivale. And you're coming with me.'

In surprise, Rymond let out a laugh. 'I am slightly busy trying to reclaim my kingdom, as you might have noticed.'

A strange shadow passed over Helana's face. 'Do you believe in Eryi?'

Rymond knew what she was going to tell him. 'We interrogated some of the Thrumb.' He tried to speak carefully; he did not want to upset her. 'I know what Hu'ra thought he was doing, how he dosed you with casheef hoping to ally himself with Eryi. If ingesting it is anything like smoking it, you would have seen all sorts of things; he put a load of ideas in your head, and you saw what you expected to. The man was mad, all of them said so.' Rymond cringed; he had put it a little more forcefully than he intended.

'No, what I saw was real. I saw Eryi. He was in a tent

outside Merivale. He's cruel, evil, we have to stop him.' Rymond found himself staring into Helana's eyes as she pleaded with him. 'I know how casheef works; She'ab taught me. Everything I saw was true.'

'I am familiar with casheef.' Rymond's fingers tremored at the memory of his lightless bedroom, with visions playing out on the ceiling like shadow puppets. 'I wouldn't trust a thing you saw. Give it time; I know how strange it can make you feel. In a few days you'll barely even remember it.'

Helana's face hardened. 'Hu'ra might have been mad, but I'm not. I *know* whether something is real or not, Rymond, and whether it's taking place in our world or in another. This was real, and if he's free there's worse to come.'

'Helana, the whole reason I lost Irith is because I didn't understand what casheef was doing to me! That stuff doesn't give you cosmic insights or let you see beyond the veil or whatever; it gets its claws into you and strips everything away until there's nothing left.' Rymond swallowed. 'A lot of good men died because I didn't understand what I was doing. I can't abandon West Erland to go chasing a pipe dream about a god coming to life.'

'Fine.' The look Helana gave him was somewhere in between hitting him and bursting into tears. 'Don't believe me then. I'll go to Merivale myself. You can stay here and try and get your crown back, for all the good it will do you. Coward.'

Before Rymond could reply, Helana spun her horse and galloped away. A few Erlanders turned to watch her pass, and then looked to Rymond as if wondering what they might have quarrelled about, or why the man they had taken as their king had troubled himself to rescue her.

Rymond let out a long sigh, resisting the urge to call after her. He ran a frustrated hand through his hair.

It is not that I don't believe her, it's that I don't trust casheef. If she stayed, he was sure she would come to her senses in a few days, once the drug had worn off. And if she left... there would be nothing he could do; he had already risked enough for Helana Sangreal.

Evening found them in the depths of Gwynæthwood, the ancient woodland where it was said that Algareth, the first King of West Erland, had won the heart of a wood-nymph. Rymond's retinue made camp in a clearing close to the wood's centre, in the midst of the evergreens with a clear navy sky overhead. A handful of fires were spread across the glade, and more glowed within the woods, where those not among Rymond's immediate circle had bedded down for the night.

Helana considered the cards in her hand, though she was barely seeing them. She was hardly paying attention, and was thus losing badly, but the sums were so small as to be beneath her notice, and in any case payment was contingent upon her opponents' survival in the battles to come.

She ran her finger along one of her cards, the lord of swords, imagining that the lord was Hu'ra about to bury his blade in her chest. That part she recalled vividly, but the events she had witnessed in the tent were already beginning to fray at the edges, just as Rymond had predicted. She hated that her own mind was proving him right.

It was real, she swore to herself. *You saw him.* She had felt him, sensed his otherness, the unfeeling malice rolling off him like noxious fumes. If Eryi was left unfettered, it would mean ill consequences for Erland. She could not allow Rymond's strange relationship with casheef to make her doubt her own sanity. It would have been easier not to believe, but she knew what she had seen.

Her thoughts had focused on that in the hours since they spoke, rather than on her father. It was better that he was dead, and she hated herself for the moment of weakness in which grief had touched her. Yet, the two things were not wholly separable. Eryi had spoken of a Sangreal child – could that be Hessian's son, her brother?

She forced herself to the simpler matter in hand. The triumph pot was represented by a collection of mismatched tokens placed on a tree stump, and the players sitting around it were no less diverse. Brant, a scout of around Helana's age, sat to her left, and to her right was Gruenla, the mercenary captain of the Cyliriens. Opposite her sat Garwen, a stout, bearded West Erlander in his middle years with a shock of white hair atop a heavy forehead. He was the father of Millas, the young Erlander whom Helana had won her horse from, who was also present. Garwen had now barred his son from placing any further wagers, except playing triumph for low stakes.

'...son of Algareth son of Alfreth he was, petty king of Pennyfort,' Garwen was telling them. 'Algareth the Elder had died the winter past, and at sixteen years old Algareth the Younger was in some difficulty. He—'

'And was that more or less difficult than getting you to make a bet?' asked Gruenla. 'Stop stalling, old man.'

Garwen chuckled. 'Well, if we're going to sit playing cards in the Gwynæthwood, don't it make sense to tell you the history of the place? Now, Pennyfort was surrounded on all sides; Oldfort to the north, Blackfort to the south, and Kilyansfort to the east, all larger and with many more warriors, and all demanding homage.

'Algareth came to these woods to escape the demands of his new kingdom. Whichever one of his foes he chose to do homage to, the other two would make war on Pennyfort. His father's kingdom was doomed, and he knew it.

'Lost in his thoughts, Algareth wandered where his foot led him, right to the edge of a clearing. This clearing, as it happens, a perfect ring of peacefulness under the sky.'

Gruenla snorted. 'And what did he find there, a man hoping to win at cards by talking the other players to death?'

Laughter flooded the clearing, for it was not only those around the tree stump who were listening to Garwen, and Helana laughed along with them. It felt good to play a simple game of triumph again and to hear a man's fireside story, like sneaking into the Piperskeep barracks as she had as a girl.

Garwen was grinning also. 'Close! At the centre of the glade on a tree stump – this stump, some say – sat a young woman, the fairest woman Algareth had ever seen. She was slender as a willow, with auburn hair that hung to her waist, and she wore a dress made of leaves sewn with spider silk. In her hands she clutched a harp, and the melodies she played made the grass dance and the raindrops sparkle.

'The rain fell thick and fierce, but Algareth stepped into the clearing, barely feeling the ground beneath his feet. She stood to meet him, and he was surprised to realise that she was of a height with him, with long limbs that moved with easy grace.

'And she said to him these words. She said—'

'"You are the first Man to find me here," she said. "How did you hear my harp?"'

The five of them looked up, and found Rymond looking over them, garbed in a heavy cloak of wool against the evening's chill. Helana noticed that unlike the rest of the camp he appeared to have a flagon of weak beer in his hand, rather than a cup of wine or rough spirits.

'You know the story, Lord?' asked Garwen.

'Of course. My nurse told it to me in the cradle. She said Algareth was the first Prindian. If he existed of course.'

'Of course he existed!' exclaimed Garwen. 'He was my ancestor as well; my family toiled the Fortlands for hundreds of years before I went to Irith to make something of myself!'

Rymond grinned, his teeth gleaming white before the bright firelight. 'Even if he did live, he was no ancestor of mine.

Versions of the same tale predates the Prindian ancestors' arrival in Erland by several centuries.'

Garwen made a dismissive noise. 'Fine, but I'll finish my story even so.' He glanced up at Rymond. 'Unless you'd like to finish it, Lord?'

'As long as *someone* finishes it,' said Gruenla with a roll of her eyes. 'Kingdoms have risen and fallen in the time it takes Garwen to make a bid.'

Rymond took up Garwen's offer. '"I do not believe I did," said Algareth. "I walked and I arrived here, as if my feet had grown a mind of their own."

'"You are Algareth, the Unifier," she told him, and all the while her fingers continued to strum at her harp.

'"They called my father Algareth the Unyielding," said Algareth, "for he held our kingdom for forty years against three greater powers who threatened Pennyfort's destruction. I have not heard of Algareth the Unifier, and I am yet to be named. Algareth the Last, perhaps."

'Her eyes shimmered, and her dress of leaves appeared to dance with a mind of its own. "I am Gwynæth of the Woods, and you are Algareth the Unifier. One day, you will rule over all the lands from the hills in the west to the river in the east, and I shall be your queen."'

Helana had heard similar stories before – it was not only West Erland's Gwynæthwood that was the setting for a tale involving an ancient lord coming into his kingdom by meeting a woodnymph – but it had been told well. She was clearly not the only one to think so, for other card games around other fires had fallen silent to listen to Rymond finish the tale.

He was no longer the boy she had fled from half-a-year ago. She had never thought to see him sleeping in a field and sharing peasants' tales with the likes of Garwen and Brant, but if war with East Erland had not changed him, losing his kingdom to the Imperials certainly had. For a moment she almost forgot to feel angry with him for refusing to ride to Merivale.

Rymond shrugged, and took a sip of his beer. 'Just a story of course.'

'Every story has a grain of truth to it,' said Garwen. 'Perhaps, hundreds of years from now, there'll be folk around a fire telling the tale of how King Rymond of West Erland plotted to retake his kingdom, in the Gwynæthwood, with a woodnymph whispering in his ear.'

Those assembled laughed, and Helana and Rymond shared a warm glance, their earlier quarrel briefly forgotten. For a pampered lord who barely knew one end of a sword from the other he was hard to hate, even if he could not bring himself to believe her.

'We all finished with story time?' said Gruenla. 'Get on with it Garwen.'

The white-haired Erlander kissed his teeth and placed his cards on the stump face down. 'I fold.'

The eruption of laughter from Helana, Brant, Rymond, and everyone else who had been listening drowned out the string of Cylirien curses that spewed from Gruenla's mouth. Helana doubled over to the dew-sprinkled grass, utterly unable to contain herself.

As the laughter died down, Helana righted herself, wiping her eyes. Rymond had walked off, still chortling away.

Helana threw her cards down opposite Garwen's. 'I fold as well.' She had barely finished her sentence before Gruenla began sweeping up the pot. 'I'm out the next hand.' There was no point Helana continuing to play; she could not concentrate.

'I'll take the lady's place, if you'll allow me.'

They turned to the new arrival. It was Rucius, who Rymond had introduced to Helana as an Imperial defector. He smirked confidently, as if hoping to disarm them with his undoubted handsomeness. He looked at Gruenla. 'Cards are more my style than torture, though by that pile of coins in front of you it seems you're good at both.'

Gruenla glared at him. 'You're free to play, but not with me. Doesn't smell so good around here all of a sudden.' She gathered up her winnings and left in a hurry.

Rucius sat down with a shrug. 'I do believe she's warming to me.'

'What did you do that for?' exclaimed Millas, whose coin pile was looking quite diminished. 'I wanted to win some of that back!'

Garwen snorted. 'Lad, you should thank him for stopping her taking the rest of you.'

Rymond retreated to sit apart from the rest of camp in the shadow of a tree, warming his hands around his tiny fire. In the woods behind him, fallen leaves rustled as a rodent scurried by, and from further afield came the hideous screeching of mating foxes. A shadow passed overhead, perhaps an owl taking wing to hunt.

His thoughts lingered on the last evening he spent in the Gwynæthwood, when he and Adfric had waited for the arrival of Strovac Sigac, fretting over whether he meant to join them or kill them. It might have been the former, but in the end Strovac Sigac had been more responsible than anyone for Rymond's downfall, first killing Andrick Barrelbreaker and then siding with the Imperials. Rymond smiled ruefully to himself. He had thought of Algareth that night as well.

The only other person more responsible than Strovac for this situation, Rymond knew, was himself.

He prodded at his fire with a stick, sending out a shower of sparks. Strovac Sigac had been a mistake, but one of many. Rymond had surrounded himself with advisors – his mother,

Gruenla, Strovac, the lords Storaut and Darlton – and sought to make compromises with all of them. Without experience of governance, or warfare, or making alliances, he had relied on them, and it had led him to disaster.

If I had taken more responsibility for myself, I would never have fallen to casheef. He had been a king in name only, and even that reluctantly. If he could remove the Imperium, he would have to do better. The West Erland kings of old had been men to fear; men who had demanded loyalty rather than bargaining for it, with great achievements to their names like the outlawing of thraldom and defeating the Sorrowmen.

If Rymond was to succeed, he needed to exercise his authority as they had. His attempts at ruling so far had shamed his lineage. Never again would he allow others, like his mother, to rule West Erland for him. Kings might have advisors, but the ultimate fate of Rymond's kingdom rested with himself. When he retook his throne, he would remember that.

His musings were interrupted by the sudden pounding of hooves through the woods, and the rattle of mail and the shriek of weapons being drawn as men roused themselves. Rymond leapt to his feet, seizing his sword from its place against the tree.

A pair of horses rode into the clearing, bearing two golden-armoured Imperial legionnaires, one waving a white flag of parlay over his shoulder. 'We're looking for Rymond Prindian,' said the other, a hard-faced veteran unconcernedly scanning the glade and the collection of armed Erlanders before him. 'We've a message from the supreme legate, Acques Bazar.'

'And another from his mother,' added the second man, a faint sneer detectable on his face in the light of the glade's torches.

Rymond took a step forward. 'I am King Rymond Prindian.'

The Imperial's eyes flicked to him impassively. 'The Eternal Legion has retaken Fallback Lodge, and all other fortresses are closed to you.' He looked around the clearing. 'You are outnumbered by more than twenty to one, not including your own lords who have already given us their support. For all your spilling of Imperial blood, you must know your cause is doomed.

'However, the supreme legate is prepared to be merciful. You may present yourself before the gates of Irith by the dawn of this day a week hence, and he shall allow you to go into honourable exile. Otherwise, for every hour you delay, a thousand of your people will die.' The Imperial paused to retrieve something from a saddlebag. 'Your mother's to die first.' He tossed the object to Rymond, who caught it between two hands, a delicately carved wooden box with a simple brass clasp. 'The supreme legate hopes this will prove his sincerity.'

With a curious look to the legionnaire, Rymond opened it.

Within was a woman's finger, a ring of Prindian green still sitting below the lower knuckle, and a lock of familiar copper hair.

CHAPTER 19

Phyrrai estimated that her dosing of Piperskeep's evening meal might give them a twelve-hour head start on their pursuers. It was, according to Da'ri, three days' hard riding to reach Erland's southern border and the beginning of the Sorrowlands. They would need to do it in three and a half to stay ahead of pursuit, and if their hunters were Jarhyck and his *hymerikai* with spare mounts and dogs able to pick up their scent then even that might not be enough. With Hrogo in tow their prospects of outpacing them were bleak, but Pherri refused to countenance leaving him behind.

The advantage they had was several hundred square miles of open plains. They forded the Little River after a few brief hours of rest just before dawn on the second day, and then returned the other way to follow the northern bank westward, and crossed at a different spot a half-day's ride away. It cost them their head start, but Da'ri's view was that it was a worthwhile gamble to disguise their trail. They altered their course towards the south-west, aiming for the Cursed Bridge that spanned the Pale River, though Da'ri and Phyrrai claimed never to have heard of it.

'I only wish there were a bridge,' said Da'ri. 'We will follow the Pale River's eastern bank. We can trail it south through the Sorrowlands towards the source. That way we'll have water at least.'

'What if Jarhyck comes to the same thought?' said Phyrrai.

'I am more concerned by the prospect of encountering the Sorrowfolk. They are bolder since the king's death. They were hardly heard of in Erland before now, but now it seems every week news of a fresh raid reaches us. Once we enter their lands, it may be a question of when they find us, rather than if.'

For much of the second day, once they were far enough away to feel something close to safe, Pherri scanned the countryside, looking for differences and similarities to her own Erland. She gave up when she realised how little she knew of this part of the country; even if there were common landmarks, she would not spot them. Instead, her contemplation switched between looking back, readying herself for the sight of a dust cloud rising from their pursuers on the horizon, and gazing towards Pipersmont, trying to gauge its distance. Its silhouette against the southern sky seemed not to have changed at all.

Phyrrai had brought a pack of dried meat and cheese for the journey, but between their fellowship of five it ran out partway through the second day. They had enough oats for the horses at least.

As evening fell, Hrogo cantered clumsily up to their lead group to breathlessly inform them that Halyana had disappeared.

'Perhaps she's split off in the hope of covering our tracks?' Phyrrai suggested.

'Or she might have got lost,' said Da'ri. 'Either way, we can't stop.' Without time to delay, they rode on.

Halyana returned as night was falling, plucking the remains of a duck she had skewered with an arrow. Another hung from her saddle harness. She wore a guileless smile, as if she was proud of herself but not quite sure why. They stopped for little over an hour, long enough to roast the brace of ducks over a fire until their meat was pink rather than raw. Pherri thanked Halyana with the rest, and when she gripped her hand the older girl squeezed back. Something remained of her at least. Pherri wanted to believe the princess had taken to heart the contents of the mysterious letter telling her to help Pherri.

They rode on by starlight and moonshine under a sky slowly darkening from purple to black, chilled by a biting northerly wind that brought with it the sulphurous stench of the Sorrows, like rotten eggs or stagnant water. Pherri felt a little more tired with every stride, the sleeplessness of their first night and the brief rest of the second beginning to catch up with her. To her right, Phyrrai's eyelids were beginning to droop also.

When Da'ri had to act quickly to stop Phyrrai slipping from her saddle, he finally brought their band to a stop. 'Three hours' rest, no more,' he told them. 'No point setting a watch; if they find us it will be too late anyway.' They hobbled their horses, though the beasts were as exhausted as their riders, and huddled together under their cloaks.

They woke when the dawn of the third day was a red promise against the eastern sky. 'Looks like rain,' said Da'ri, looking up at the grey clouds rolling slowly westward as he stiffly vaulted onto his horse. The air was sweet and muggy. 'Would suit us; might cover our tracks. We could make the Sorrows by late tonight.'

They rode on, and the rain came just an hour later, great fat beads that ran from Pherri's hair and down her clothes, soaking her to the skin. It was warm at least, so humid that it felt at times as if their horses were having to swim through the air. Patches of showers followed them through the morning and into the afternoon. The Sorrowlands were close enough to discern now, a desolate mass of dark, stony crags, sharp against the grey sky. Forked lightning flashed over them at intervals, sending out booming thunder, like a herald welcoming them to their doom. To their south-west, Pherri could just make out the rush of the White Falls, where water cascaded from a high precipice to form the Pale River.

'Aim for the falls!' cried Da'ri. As if on cue, the clouds above burst, and the rain came thicker, plummeting in a great flood that hid the falls from Pherri's view behind a torrent of water.

'There are riders!' called Hrogo over the deluge and the earth-churning rumble of their horses' hooves. 'To our left!'

Pherri turned in her saddle, and sure enough she saw them, half-a-dozen distant horsemen on a hill, silhouetted against the grim sky. As she watched, they spurred into a thundering gallop, riding straight for them.

'There are more!' screeched Phyrrai. 'North-west!'

Pherri's head whipped the other way. Another six, following the line of the Pale River, on a course to intercept them before they could reach the falls.

Da'ri urged them on, Pherri riding alongside Phyrrai as Halyana pulled ahead and Hrogo began to fall behind. She could already tell though that it was hopeless; they were still miles from the Sorrows, and the horsemen were unrelenting. She looked left and saw the first group of pursuers had closed the gap to a few hundred yards. The rain slowed for a moment, and they were close enough for Pherri to see the red blotch on their mail marking them as *hymerikai*.

As they approached the Sorrowlands and the grass began to give way to fine gravel and black dirt, the twelve horsemen overtook them. They fanned out to surround them, corralling them up the slope into a half-moon wall of bright mail and horseflesh to block them from escaping Erland. The White Falls were just a hundred yards away, close enough to hear the rush of plummeting water. The sun had reappeared, illuminating the Sorrows' steepening cliffs of black flint and the stony trails that ran between them.

At the centre of the *hymerikai* rode Jarhyck, his blond hair flying free, his face stern and determined. Pherri crowded closer to Phyrrai, all discomfort of the other's presence forgotten. Their mounts were panting frantically, their coats slick with sweat. Da'ri stopped alongside them, standing in his stirrups, while Halyana rode her horse defiantly left and right between them and her brother's men. Fifty yards back, Hrogo's horse had refused to take another step, forcing him to dismount and lead the beast on foot. Jarhyck waited in silence, as if expecting them to prostrate themselves before him in search of his forgiveness.

'We could run for it?' said Phyrrai. 'What have we got to lose?'

'They would not dare harm you... or Halyana,' said Da'ri. He was bent over his horse's neck, breathing heavily. 'The rest of us... perhaps our lives are forfeit anyway.'

'Do not trouble to dismount, tutor.' Jarhyck urged his horse forward to meet them, followed by the *hymerikai*. 'We will be heading straight back to Merivale for your execution. Was it you who poisoned the whole castle?'

'It was me,' said Phyrrai. 'Majesty, you don't understand—'

'Silence!' The king's voice cracked like a whip. 'It is not your place, cousin, to tell me what I do and do not understand. I will be giving you over to your father to discipline; he has allowed you a free rein for too long. This Thrumb will be your last tutor, I assure you of that.' His hard eyes flicked to Pherri and Hrogo. 'I don't know who you are, nor what magic has given you the appearance of my cousin and allowed you to hoodwink her, but we will find out. I suggest you appreciate the scenery on our way home; it will be the last sky you ever see.'

Hrogo let out a low moan.

Pherri felt a strange sense of calm. It could not end like this, left to die in a Piperskeep dungeon by a dead man. It *would not* end like this; there was too much at stake, she had come too far. Perhaps her exhaustion had driven her to madness, but she began to laugh at the absurdity of the situation, and once she started, she could not stop, even once she was doubled over on her horse with her abdomen aching.

'Why are you laughing?' demanded Jarhyck. 'What's so—'

Something in the air whistled, followed by a shrill whir as something thumped against a *hymerika*'s head and he tumbled from his horse. A single ululating cry came from the Sorrowlands, where atop a crag stood a squat man with a vast nest of hair, spinning his slingshot for another go. He released, and a second stone thudded off a horse's rump. It whinnied, and reared up on its hind legs as its rider struggled to control it.

Jarhyck whirled angrily. 'Get him!'

As the *hymerikai* turned, a thunderous noise rose from the Sorrows. Several more slingshotters appeared against the sky, just as hundreds of riders poured from a dozen different paths, down the slope and into Erland in a cacophony of hooves. Their ululating war cry filled the air, so loud there could have been thousands of them and not only hundreds.

'Protect the king!' cried a *hymerika*. They rode to form a circle around Jarhyck as the invaders galloped towards them.

Pherri could hardly believe that the Sorrowlands could contain such a horde of men. She was so spellbound watching them that she even forgot to feel afraid. Their mounts were considerably smaller than the *hymerikai*'s warhorses, and as they came closer she realised they were not horses but large goats, with tridents of long horns protruding from their heads.

'Retreat, you fools!' cried Da'ri. 'There are too many!'

The *hymerikai* did not listen. 'We'll fight our way free!' yelled Jarhyck. The goat-riders had not made to attack, but were instead circling their two parties as more and more of them streamed from the hills. More missiles flew, but the *hymerikai* had donned their helmets and the stones dinged off them. There were more riders every way Pherri looked. One carried a ragged flag showing a crude goat's head on a white background, and the rest bore an assortment of axes and mauls topped with forbidding black flint. They shook them in their fists as they came on, still wailing their war cry.

'What do we do?' asked Phyrrai, looking to Da'ri.

'Wait till they attack the *hymerikai*.' The tutor's voice was calm, though by his wide eyes he was no less panicked than the rest of them. The Sorrowmen outnumbered the *hymerikai* perhaps twenty to one, but they seemed reluctant to engage, perhaps due to the Erlanders' taller mounts and superior arms. 'That might give us an opening to escape.'

Pherri watched them, studying the Sorrowmen. Their hair was long and wild, their dark, bearded faces squat and broad and smeared with paint, and they appeared to be shorter than the Erlanders, perhaps barely taller than Pherri herself.

'They're slowing,' said Phyrrai. Pherri's heart was hammering, and she was sure her double's must also be.

The goat-riders were indeed slowing, until as one they stopped, and their war cry and the beat of their cloven hooves fell silent. They faced inward, eyeing the two groups of Erlanders, as if deciding which of them they would eat first.

The one with the banner broke the circle, riding to within fifteen yards of where the *hymerikai* faced them with longswords drawn and shields raised. Jarhyck's horse snorted and tramped the earth, as if preparing to charge.

The bannerman's mouth stretched to a graveyard of blackened teeth. He spoke from his throat, in a guttural approximation of Erlish. 'Chief Horned Grawl is come to speak.'

Another man broke from the circle. His goat was a head taller than the rest, with a fourth and fifth horn sprouting from behind its ears, but the mount was less remarkable than the rider. In each fist, Horned Grawl held a double-headed axe. His dark face was a tapestry of criss-crossing white scars, beneath a pair of eyes black as coal, and unlike the other Sorrowmen his head had been shaved, displaying how he had got his name:

from his scalp grew two horns half-a-foot in length, filed to sharp points.

He stopped beneath his banner, and raised an axe towards the *hymerikai*. 'You are King Jarhyck?' He spoke Erlish slightly better than his herald.

'I am,' said Jarhyck, urging his mount forward ahead of his warriors to face the chief. 'You are in my lands, savage.'

Grawl's face registered nothing. 'To the strong the land belongs. Ours to take.' He ran his axes together in a piercing shriek. 'You ours to take also, I think.' He scanned from the *hymerikai* to where Pherri and the rest stood, and gestured with one axe towards the second gathering. 'Good thrall look to them these have.' He gestured back towards the *hymerikai*. 'Poor slaves warriors make.' Grawl began to beat his axeheads together in a steady rhythm and the Sorrowmen joined him, slapping their weapons against their palms. Their force began to circle again, swiftly picking up speed, raising their howling, yapping war cry once more to the sky in a hellish racket. As they accelerated to a gallop, Grawl cried something in his own language, lifting his weapons to the air and crossing his wrists.

'Wedge!' cried Jarhyck, raising his sword high. The *hymerikai* formed up behind him, fanning out to form a narrow point, lifting their blades to join their king's.

The Sorrowmen kept circling, and Jarhyck brought his sword down. 'Forward!'

The Erlanders charged, and as if they had been waiting for their moment the savages descended upon them from every direction.

The *hymerikai* careered into the goat-riders, trampling over the men's smaller mounts in a tumult of distressed bleating and furious shrieks. Swords flashed downward, hacking a path for them and sending dead Sorrowlanders falling from their squat steeds. A goat-rider stood and leapt from his mount straight onto the point of Jarhyck's sword, as dozens of others crowded in around the Erlanders, slowing their charge to a crawl.

At first, it looked to Pherri as if Jarhyck might win free. He and his *hymerikai* fought ferociously, seemingly finding flesh with every swing of their swords, the Sorrowmen's short, crude weapons never able to get past the horses' crushing hooves and the sharp steel of the Erlanders.

Then one *hymerika* fell under the sheer weight of the goat-riders' numbers, and another's horse went down with its guts spilling from the long axe wound that had been left in its belly. More followed, as hundreds of Sorrowmen flocked to them, dispatching fallen warriors in a maelstrom of hacking weapons.

Jarhyck was the last, turning his mount in a wild circle in a desperate attempt to escape the mass of goat-riders. Horned Grawl had seemed content to watch the carnage, but then urged his mount forward at a gallop, and standing on its back launched himself atop Jarhyck's horse via the rump, directly behind the king. One arm wrapped around the shoulder of Jarhyck's sword arm, and with his other hand Grawl placed the sharp edge of an axe under his neck.

The Erland king struggled to free himself, steering his horse with his legs and dropping his shield to try and throw Grawl off with his other hand, but the chieftain held firm. He squeezed his thighs and the stallion bucked and kicked as it turned, forcing the Sorrowmen back and felling two with heavy hoof-blows to the skull. Jarhyck fought on, dropping his head and twisting it this way and that to stop Grawl getting a firm contact on his throat with the axe.

Pherri watched open-mouthed, staring at the churning mass of mud and screaming Sorrowmen. Even with his men dead and surrounded by hundreds of foes it looked as if Jarhyck might escape, until a Sorrowmen's maul crashed heavily down between the eyes of his horse, shattering its skull and killing it in an instant. The beast's legs collapsed beneath its weight, tumbling Jarhyck and Grawl into the dirt where the Erlander was set upon by a dozen howling goat-riders, leaping from their mounts to fall upon their foe.

'We should have run,' whispered Phyrrai to Pherri.

'Too late,' said Da'ri grimly. He gestured sideways, to where a collection of thickset Sorrowmen were approaching on foot, threateningly twirling their slingshots.

Horned Grawl rose triumphantly from the mass of Sorrowmen, waving Jarhyck's sword like a flag and laughing in a creaking, croaking rattle.

Still struggling, Jarhyck was dragged to his feet. There was blood pouring from over one eye, and his mail was caked in mud. No less than eight Sorrowmen held him, grinning their black teeth and laughing ominously along with their leader. In addition to the dozen *hymerikai*, thirty or more Sorrowmen lay dead. Riderless goats had already begun to feed upon them, tearing at their faces with pointed teeth.

Jarhyck's eyes blazed. 'By Piper's ghost I swear you'll answer for this! You killed my men!'

Grawl placed the point of the sword under Jarhyck's chin. 'You next, unless behave. Now negotiate.' He said something in his own language to the men who held Jarhyck. One of them forced a sack over his head, as more advanced with thick ropes to bind his arms and legs.

The chief turned to Pherri and her companions. He studied them carefully, and when his eye passed over Pherri she forced herself to hold his gaze. 'Friends of king. You also come.' His stare fell upon Da'ri, and lingered there, as if his curiosity was piqued. He turned to one of his warriors and muttered something to him. The goat-rider's eyes flicked to Da'ri. He shrugged, and produced a slingshot which he began to whirl around his head.

Pherri felt as if she saw the event before it happened, as if history were echoing back on itself. The Sorrowman acted so fast that she never had a chance to cry out. His slingshot spun to a sudden halt, and the stone whistled piercingly through the air to strike Da'ri with a hard thud between the eyes.

There was no blood, but Da'ri's eyes rolled back in their sockets. His body crumpled forward, and as his hands came loose on his reins he slipped wordlessly from his horse and folded to a heap. He groaned, and tried to rise, but he could not seem to get his limbs to work properly, scrabbling ineffectually for purchase in the dark, damp earth.

Grawl said something else to the slingshotter, and the man urged his mount forward, his maul humming through the air in place of the slingshot.

As he swung the weapon towards Da'ri's head, Pherri heard herself screaming, until she realised it was Phyrrai. It was a familiar sound, and Pherri was suddenly transported to the day her own Da'ri had been pulled apart by the mob at Lordsferry's summer fair, the day that had been the stone to begin the avalanche that had led her to now.

The maul came down, Phyrrai's scream reached a screeching, horrified crescendo, and its black flint head blew apart Da'ri's skull in an eruption of blood and bone.

CHAPTER 20

The bleak dawn found Ciera in her father's solar, staring through the west window towards a spot a few hundred yards along the cliff, at the main path that twisted down the bluff into Cliffark. If she stepped to the north side, she could eye the narrow track that ran down to the city from Cliffark Tower. It was close to deserted. Just enough guards remained that if Strovac Sigac was to look over the cliff, he was unlikely to be troubled. The bulk of her father's soldiers waited in the shadow of the keep's main gate, awaiting Ciera's word.

She was relatively pleased with the outcome of her negotiation with Cliffark's rebels. Upon her father's death, Cliffark would by royal proclamation be granted rights which no settlement had been granted in living memory. The city would be governed by a council of leading citizens, with reduced taxes paid directly to Merivale. That could though be years from now, by which time circumstances might have changed. Ciera yearned for reform as much as the Cliffarkers, but she had always seen herself as being the agent of change, and it would not please her if Cliffark were treated differently to the rest of Erland.

In return, Ciera had an army. Not one either experienced or well-trained, but she hoped enough would follow her from Cliffark to be of use. There were minor lords between here and Merivale she hoped to persuade to join her, and having several thousand in support might make all the difference.

It would not matter though if they did not succeed today. Ciera gripped the windowsill, watching the tower's shadow sharpen as the sun behind her rose. If the citizens failed, they could wave their hard-won rights goodbye. Ciera stood to lose more though: a marriage to Strovac Sigac would mean the loss of her freedom, her son, and eventually her life. Whatever happened, she could not allow that to come to pass.

Atop the cliff, above the main path, the several hundred Wild Brigaders were forming up. Burly men with filthy beards passed wineskins between themselves, rubbing their thumbs over the hilts of their swords and laughing feverishly. Their faces bore the unthinking expressions of men who knew no doubt in their head, for whom this would just be another exercise in slaughter, akin to those carried out half-a-hundred times before.

A series of creaks came from the stairs. Laphor appeared, and came to join Ciera at the window, still limping slightly on his heavily strapped ankle. 'The men await your signal, Majesty.' He cast his eyes over the Wild Brigade and winced. 'Lot of hard men there who know their business. You still think the Cliffarkers will stand against the likes of them?'

They would have to. Ciera pressed her fingers into her palm. 'They stand a better chance than we would.'

'Not if we run.'

I will not run. Even if they lose.

Laphor's eyes scanned back and forth. 'I don't see Strovac down there.'

Ciera's gaze followed his. He was right; Strovac stood a

head taller than most men, yet he was nowhere to be seen. She frowned. 'Perhaps they are waiting for him to join them,' she said uncertainly. Strovac Sigac ought to have been in the first line, leading his men.

At the table behind them, Ciera's mother snorted. 'Or perhaps he's decided they don't need him to fight a rabble.' She began to pour herself a cup of wine from the flagon on the table. 'Folk like these rebels are cowards at heart; they'll turn and run at the first sight of steel.'

'If they are cowards, what does that make your guards who surrendered the city?' asked Ciera, not turning away from the window. She refused to be needled by her mother, not today with so much at stake.

'What indeed? They are still apparently brave enough that you're willing to place your faith in them. Come midday, Strovac Sigac will be within our walls.'

'We must believe in Ciera, my dear.' Glancing back, Ciera saw her father place a calming hand on his wife's shoulder. 'The keep would have fallen to the Wild Brigade yesterday if not for her.'

Ciera felt a warmth of gratitude rise in her chest. Her father had faith in her at least, even if her mother never had.

A cry from Laphor interrupted the sensation. 'They're on the move!'

Ciera looked up, and the many-legged beast of the Wild Brigade began slithering down the path towards the city. Her heart tightened in her chest. *If this fails, I am doomed.* The Wild Brigade wrenched their swords free from their scabbards, and their pace quickened as they reached the downward slope.

'Should we raise the signals?'

Burik's voice from the north window shook Ciera to her senses. Such was her focus upon the advancing warriors she had nearly forgotten. 'Yes, both of you.'

Together, Burik to the north and Aimya at the south window overlooking the yard unfurled ragged flags of bright red, and frantically waved them for several seconds. Far below them, Ciera caught the sound of the main gate creaking open, and she rushed to Aimya's window as the few hundred remaining warriors of Cliffark Tower streamed out of the keep and along the causeway, then veered right towards the way the Wild Brigade had gone.

Next, Ciera raced to the north window. As she had hoped, only a handful of Cliffarkers remained on the barricades, and from the west of the city came the din of a trumpet. She winced, hoping that the Wild Brigade had not heard the alarm.

Her hope was that as Strovac Sigac's band engaged the Cliffarkers – and unless the citizens surprised her, that would be slaughter – her father's household guard would come down the path behind them and take them in the rear, trapping them. Laphor had assured her that not even a trained, armed force could prevail when trapped between two foes. But even just watching from a tower, Ciera's heart was in her mouth. Imagining what the fighting would be like for those on the ground filled her heart with horror and thrill in equal measure. She stretched her neck, trying to see past the bluff, imagining she could hear the song of steel at the Cliffarkers' other barricade.

'They're still a few minutes away,' Laphor reassured her.

Ciera nodded. *But where is Strovac Sigac?* For a hopeful moment, she wondered if perhaps a disgruntled Wild Brigader had killed him in his sleep.

'Can you see anything?' asked her father. He was sitting at the table, his hands clenched and trembling.

'Nothing,' said Ciera.

For several minutes, she watched the Cliffarkers assembling on the barricades, while the heavy tread of the Wild Brigade and the shake of their mail faded in and out of earshot as they weaved down the path. Her father's soldiers were hidden from view now; they would be following the cliff path after the Wild Brigade, ready to trap them against the rebels' blockade.

'There!'

Laphor was pointing from the west window, and Ciera ran back to join him just in time to see the Wild Brigade break against the barrier, as the citizens jeered and hurled stones which deflected off their mail and clattered off their helmets. Those at the front began throwing themselves against the barrier, attempting to scale it while the Cliffarkers continued to pelt them with missiles. A Wild Brigader fell backwards screaming as a pot of sizzling water was poured down over him, and another toppled with an eating knife shoved through his eye. Many though had ignored the barricade and were scaling the stone walls where the resistance was not so fierce.

'It's pulling the citizens away from the barricade,' said Laphor. 'Watch.'

There were several hundred Cliffarkers milling around within the walls, enough to outnumber the Wild Brigade many times over, but in a matter of moments Ciera saw the benefit of the warriors' experience. Some of those on the barrier scaled the walls in an attempt to push the climbing warriors back, and were dragged from the walls for their troubles. Gaps were appearing where Cliffarkers were moving to the walls, and reinforcements from the rear were too few and too slow, with many obviously unwilling to engage the warriors. The first Wild Brigader scaled the barricade just as several more summited the wall, and with a flash of his sword sent two sailors toppling. He gave a blood-curdling howl, and Ciera swore she saw the rebels physically cringe back.

Burik and Aimya had joined them at the west window. 'Our men need to hurry,' Burik murmured. 'They won't hold much longer.'

The words had hardly left his mouth when the few hundred of Cliffark Tower broke upon the Wild Brigade's rear like a wave. Cries of surprise and the splintering of shields reached them on the wind, and suddenly the Wild Brigade were on the turn, earning the rebels much needed respite. With their fellows suddenly occupied, those who had mounted the barricade found themselves beset by a mass of emboldened Cliffarkers, and either leapt into the twisting mass of steel and flesh beneath them or were overwhelmed by the press of rebels. One found himself seized between two burly sailors and thrown inside the blockade to be set upon by a forest of knives, as another atop the wall was dragged onto his back with a muscular bicep wrapped around his neck strangling the life from him.

'Are they winning?' asked Aimya.

'For now,' growled Laphor. 'It may not last.' He pointed into the swirling maelstrom of armour, and Ciera could see he spoke truly. The element of surprise had given the Istlewick soldiers only a brief window of advantage; already the Wild Brigade looked to be gaining the upper hand.

'Those sailors need to get themselves together.' Burik cupped his hands to his mouth and bellowed, 'Fight, you lazy whoresons! Fight!'

'Still no Strovac,' muttered Laphor. He looked to Aimya, still watching at the south window. 'Any more Wild Brigade that way?'

The sister shook her head. 'None.'

Laphor tugged at his beard. 'I don't like this at all. Where is the bastard?' He looked to Ciera's parents. Lord Istlewick was running his fingers over each other, while Ciera's mother had moved to stand at the north window where she was slowly sipping her wine. 'Are there any guards left in the keep?'

Lord Istlewick looked up, blinking his eyes as if rising from slumber. The stress of the past day had aged him further; he looked to have not slept a wink. 'N-no. We sent them all.'

'At your suggestion,' added Lady Istlewick, turning to look sharply at Ciera. 'There is a token force holding our cliff path, but you said no others could be spared.'

Horror dawned in Ciera's mind, just as they heard the rapid tread of boots on the stairs, like a staccato drum summoning the condemned to the gallows.

Laphor wrenched his sword free and hobbled to the door on the north side. With fire in his eyes, he looked to the shaking Lord Istlewick. 'Hope you're able to lock this.'

Ciera's mother swept up her skirts and hurried across the room to a bookshelf, producing a long brass key. 'Here.' As the sound of climbing feet grew louder, she tossed the key to Laphor, who plunged it into the lock and turned it with a click.

Then, Lady Istlewick hurried over to Ciera and seized her by the shoulders. 'Ciera, do you still have the widowsbane?'

Ciera nodded, suddenly too overcome with fear to speak.

'Give it to me.'

With shaking fingers, Ciera reached into her sleeve and produced the pouch of poison her mother had given her before she met with Strovac Sigac. With practised efficiency, her mother opened it and poured most of it into a second pouch, then pressed the first pouch back into Ciera's hands. 'There's still enough. Use it only if you absolutely must.' In a rare sign of affection, she squeezed Ciera's hand, then poured some into her cup before racing to the flagon on the table.

A heavy shoulder barrelled into wood only seconds later, with enough force to rattle the hinges and send several volumes from the shelves plummeting to the floor. Ciera's father rose with a gasp to recover them, as Laphor swung the bar down over the door.

A second impact followed, a kick direct to the keyhole that sent the wrought-iron handle clattering to the floor.

Laphor and Burik stood shoulder to shoulder, ready. 'All of you get against the south wall!' said Laphor. Ciera hurried to obey him, as Aimya slipped past her, seizing her staff from where it leant against a bookshelf. Ciera's father had seized a weapon also, a fire poker which he held in one shaking hand, steadying himself against the table with the other.

'Don't be ridiculous, Per!' said Lady Istlewick, as she hustled Ciera towards the south wall to stand in front of Andrick's cot, where he was mercifully still asleep. 'Get back!'

Per Istlewick did not move.

The door shook again with the impact of Strovac's boot. It was splintering at the hinge and around the lock now, and the bar was beginning to buckle.

The door broke apart in a burst of splinters, and swung open to reveal Strovac Sigac. His smile contained all the humour of a skull's grimace. He stepped over the threshold, naked blade in hand, and together Laphor and Burik rushed him.

Strovac's left hand flicked up, and a cloud of dirt flew at Burik's face, and the young *hymerika* pulled up, shielding his eyes. Laphor's sword flashed towards Strovac, and the larger man's own blade deflected the strike with contemptuous ease, knocking Laphor's two-handed swipe aside and flicking the tip up into his face. Laphor flinched back, and the sword point split his chin in a flash of crimson.

Strovac did not give his foes a moment. Burik had recovered, but his thrust was wild, and with practised grace Strovac sidestepped it and shoved Burik face first into the doorframe.

Laphor had steadied himself, and Ciera saw the opportunity just as he did. Strovac was turning away from Burik, but too slowly, and Ciera tensed in anticipation as Laphor's sword fell towards Strovac's head.

The battle between the Wild Brigade and the Cliffarkers did not matter now. Her heart was beating fit to burst.

Laphor roared in triumph.

Strovac spun on a heel, and his thrust was through Laphor's neck in the blink of an eye. As he fell, Ciera swore she saw his gaze flick towards her, almost as if in apology.

Strovac dragged his blade free, and wiped it on a curtain. 'Shame. Could have been quite the fight thirty years ago. Warriors should not live so long.' Burik was rising dazedly, pulling himself up by the doorframe, but as he made it to his feet Strovac turned and flung him down the spiral stairs.

He had clearly not given Sister Aimya even a moment's notice. With two quick steps the diminutive priestess closed the gap between them, and aimed her staff towards the giant's head.

It struck home with a heavy thud, hard enough that Ciera was sure it would have sent an ordinary man to his knees. But Strovac was already on the turn. Aimya pulled back for a second strike, and Strovac's hand came out whip-fast. It caught the staff a forearm's breadth from his head, and he scornfully pulled it from Aimya's grasp and drove his boot into her chest to send her sprawling against a bookshelf, sending volumes tumbling down on her.

Strovac touched his temple, wincing. 'Always hated the bloody Brides.' He threw the staff out of the window, and turned towards Ciera, his mouth stretched in a rictus smile. 'Knew you'd play me false, so I sneaked over your walls last night and told my men to go ahead without me. Bet your guards won't feel too clever when they get back and find you all butchered.'

'Your warriors are dying,' said Ciera, her voice quivering. 'Look out of the window.' On the floor, Laphor's corpse was flooding the study with blood.

'If any of them die to a bunch of pirates and washerwomen or those pitiful cowards I saw rushing out of your main gate then I'm better off without them. Fewer men means more plunder for the rest, and a king must be open-handed.' His hungry eyes looked past Ciera to Andrick's crib. 'And kings don't need hand-me-down queens or rival claimants still at the teat either. If you value the lives of you and your brat, it's past time you started begging. Step away from the crib, girl.'

He'll kill me anyway. Ciera stayed where she was, though her legs were shaking.

Strovac shoved his sword back into its sheath. 'So be it. It's more fun when they fight.'

He stepped towards Ciera, and Lord Istlewick moved across his path. The fire poker was still clenched in his trembling fist. 'Stay back.' He raised the poker to prod Strovac in the chest. 'Leave this place.'

'No, Father.' Ciera's voice came out in a squeak. 'Run.'

'Hush, Ciera.' Lord Istlewick prodded Strovac in the chest again. 'I'm warning you.'

Strovac raised an eyebrow. 'I've never really understood the value some men place in courage, but in this case it amuses me. I'll make you a deal: strike me with that poker again before I kill you, and I'll turn around and never come back.'

Ciera screamed. Lord Istlewick swung the poker, and Strovac kicked him so hard between the legs that it lifted him off the ground. He collapsed to the floor, his eyes wide and his lips gulping like a fish. He groaned, and vomit pulsed from his mouth across the floor.

Strovac's laugh was high and terrible. He bent to pick up the poker, and from behind him came the whisper of feet across the floor.

Aimya leapt and threw her arms around his neck, scrabbling with her hands for Strovac's eye sockets. A finger gouged deep into one, and the sound Strovac made was like nothing human. He squealed like a spit pig as he threw Aimya against a shelf, and the whole thing toppled down on her.

'Fucking bitch!' Strovac roared, holding a hand to his eye.

His finger came away bloody. He looked towards where Aimya had fallen, blinding fury in his undamaged eye. 'I'll deal with you once I'm done with these.'

He grabbed the poker and drove it down into Per Istlewick's back. He wore no armour, and it tore through his padded tunic as if it were made of suet.

A second scream ripped through Ciera's throat. Behind her, Andrick woke and added his wails to hers. Strovac stomped once on Lord Istlewick's head, caving in his skull, and strode towards Ciera. Her feet were frozen to the floor, and a flood of tears blinded her eyes. All she could do was spread herself, covering Andrick's crib. She prepared herself to beg; she would have dropped to her knees, but that would have meant exposing the crib. *Take me, leave him, please.*

He was three steps away when Ciera's mother stepped across Strovac's path. 'Lord Strovac, you have made your point.' Ciera had been so scared she had almost forgotten her mother was there. How did she sound so calm? Her eyes never even glanced to her husband's body. 'Perhaps we can negotiate. A strong king should also be merciful.'

Strovac's eyes remained fixed on Ciera, but he paused. 'All that I want, I can take. What could you possibly offer me?'

'Just as was agreed with my daughter before. She will lend legitimacy to your claim. I told her that her plan was folly. If you are merciful, I swear she will be a loyal wife. Her son can stay here as Lord of Cliffark. By the time he comes of age he will think of you as his beloved stepfather.'

'Mother—' Ciera began.

'For once in your life be quiet.' Her voice was like a slap. 'I am trying to save your life, you fool.' She held out her cup towards Strovac. 'Perhaps a cup of wine while you consider the proposal, Majesty?'

Strovac blinked down at her, and slowly took the cup. His

left hand fingered the hilt of his sword. 'Your plea for mercy has moved me, Lady Istlewick.' His good eye glittered like a black beetle. He raised the cup. 'A toast then, to my new kingdom and bride?'

Ciera stared. Part of her wanted to cry out a warning to her mother, but as Strovac lifted the cup towards his mouth she held her tongue, trying to still the hopeful beating of her heart lest Strovac hear it. He watched Lady Istlewick over the rim of his wine, his hand slowing as it approached his lips.

He paused, and quick as lightning seized Irena Istlewick by the neck, then tipped her head back to pour the entire cup down her throat.

'NO!' Ciera flinched forward, but it was already too late.

The veins in her mother's neck swelled like blood blisters, and the skin began to purple to a bruise. Her mouth gulped, her tongue lolled like a fat worm, and her throat bobbed, panting for a breath that never came. She sank to her knees. Her eyes locked with Ciera's, and instead of terror Ciera saw only resignation.

Through her tears, Ciera forced herself to watch. She would have fallen to her knees and clutched her mother's hand, but that would have meant moving aside from the crib. She never tore her eyes away, not until her mother's hands and helplessly jerking legs fell still.

With a toe, Strovac prodded Lady Istlewick's corpse aside. 'Poison,' he said contemptuously. 'Trust a woman.' He laughed. Behind Ciera, Andrick was still wailing. 'Nothing worth crying about yet, you little bastard.' He looked about the room, taking in the corpses of Laphor and her parents and Aimya's lifeless body. 'Such fine friends you have, to find so many willing to die for you.' Ciera willed Burik to wake on the stairs below, but there came no hurried tread of feet.

Strovac's eyes fell upon the flagon of wine on the table, and he claimed a cup. He lifted the container, sniffed, and grimaced.

'I'd have to be bloody stupid.' Strovac replaced it and seized a fresh one from a shelf. 'I'm damn thirsty though.' He began to pour. 'Long time to hide in your yard for.' He grinned. 'Well worth it though.' He took a long draught, and advanced towards Ciera. 'This would be a good time to beg for your life.'

Ciera backed up to the crib and gripped the edge with both hands. 'Please...' she whispered. She sobbed, hardly able to get the words out. 'My son...'

Strovac was shaking his head. 'Pitiful.' He tipped the cup back and drank again, long and deep. 'I've seen better—'

He paused suddenly, and his hand rushed to his throat. 'I've seen better—' He coughed, and a vein swelled in his throat. His eyes widened in sudden horror. '*No*,' he gasped. His hand fumbled for his sword.

Before she knew what she was doing, Ciera rushed forward and leapt up to jam her finger into Strovac's one good eye. He howled like a beast caught in a trap, and with his left hand he backhanded her across the face and sent her sprawling. Strovac's face and neck were swelling, turning purple. He tried for his sword again, but soon his fingernails scrabbled at his windpipe, tearing the skin to bloodied shreds. Blood was trickling from his neck, veins swelling as if they might burst.

He stared at Ciera through bloodshot eyes, and in them she saw fear.

Strovac lasted longer than her mother had. It felt to Ciera as if he was half an hour dying, though it may have only been half a minute. By the time he sank to his knees, his hands were covered in blood to their wrists, his neck flayed open to reveal his windpipe. By then, the light in his eyes had gone out, and he collapsed forward, face first onto the stone.

When it was over, Ciera crawled to her mother's corpse, her face now a swollen purple melon.

'You thought of everything,' she whispered. Irena Istlewick's hand still grasped the empty pouch of widowsbane.

Ciera had not even seen her put any in the second flagon. 'How could you know?' In the distance, she thought she could hear the cries of celebrating Cliffarkers, but, as Ciera looked around at the bodies of her friends and family, all she knew was loss. They had died for her. She cradled her mother's head in her hands and wept.

CHAPTER 21

They gave Orsian his own tent, coloured in the verdant purple of the Imperium, with a straw mattress, a trunk that doubled as a table, and little else save a few pieces of armour scattered in a corner. He suspected the tent had once belonged to a captain of the Eternal Legion, now dead.

One of the two legionnaires escorting him said something in Ulvatian to the other as they shoved him inside, and the Imperials laughed together. They left him alone, taking guard positions outside.

Orsian slumped onto the bed, his head swimming with exhaustion, drunkenness, hunger, and dread. The wine taken on an empty stomach had done little to quell his fear at the thing that wore Drast Fulkiro's face. A slave appeared with fresh clothes and a plate of food. They said nothing, keeping their head bowed and never looking at him.

The food was simple fare; doughy bread, hard cheese, and a reddish, gamey meat that he suspected might be horse. He wolfed it all down nevertheless, savouring the relief of his gnawing hunger as it hit his stomach. Next, he threw off the sweat-stinking rags he had been wearing since being sent to the dungeon, and stuck his head out of the tent flap to call for water. The slave reappeared quarter-of-an-hour later bearing a small tub of cold water and a thin cloth. Orsian made do, washing himself as best he could and drying himself on the tent wall.

The garments they had given him might also have belonged to the dead legionnaire, leather trousers that cuffed at the ankle and a loose shirt of simple linen. There were no shoes. He donned the clothes, and lay down on the mattress.

He rubbed at the rough fuzz of his washed beard. A tent was at least better than a dungeon cell. He might steal a horse and be gone by morning. If Eryi thought Orsian would cooperate, he would be waiting until his Mountain home fell to dust. Whatever was asked of him, whatever magic they threw at him, he would fight them. He owed that to Pherri, wherever she was.

He had envisaged staying awake into the night, waiting until the guards fell asleep and making his escape. But, between the soft mattress, the fresh clothes against his skin, and a full belly of meat, bread, and wine, he soon found he could not keep his eyes open. Orsian drifted into an exhausted sleep, his dreams a maelstrom of unnerving pale eyes, of Pherri's voice calling for him, and Balyard's shocked face as he toppled into the moat with an arrow protruding from his neck.

It was still dark when he woke, as if he had barely closed his eyes. Before his vision adjusted, Orsian thought for a moment he was back in the dungeon. A pot of steaming tea had been left on the chest for him. His throat was aching, so he forced himself up and poured a cup. He realised he had not checked the chest, so he set the cup aside and tried the lid. It did not budge.

'Did you think we would leave you in a tent with a chest full of weapons?' Krupal stood in the entrance, watching him.

Orsian picked up his cup and sat down on the mattress. 'Why is it still night?'

Krupal gave a bark of laughter. 'It is evening the next day.'

Orsian stared at him. The slant of the shadows at Krupal's back told the same story. He had slept through the entire day. He sniffed the tea, suddenly suspicious, his mind whirring.

'We thought we would let you rest,' said Krupal, taking a step inside the tent. 'It is time.'

'Time for what? I told Eryi, I won't do it.'

'I am afraid you don't get a choice.' The magus lifted an index finger towards the chest. The lock clicked, and it swung open. Within was golden plate armour, a legionnaire helmet with its absurd purple headdress, and the purple cape that marked this as the uniform of a captain of the Eternal Legion. 'This is for you. If you are going to lead the assault on Piperskeep, you had best look the part.'

Orsian stared down at it. 'Have you gone mad?' His bravado was an attempt to hide his fear. He had felt Eryi's power; he might resist the will of a magus, but he could not defeat it.

'*Get him to put the armour on.*' Eryi's voice rose from nowhere, and the air in the tent seemed to shudder with the force of it. The cup in Orsian's hand tremored.

Krupal blinked. '*You are a legionnaire. Put the armour on.*' Orsian readied himself to resist, but the magus's voice was inside his head within the space of a breath.

Every muscle and sinew of Orsian's body strained to obey. He was a legionnaire; the voice had said so. He rose, and his legs jerked towards the chest. The urge was part of him, spreading out from his torso through his limbs.

And yet, his own small voice struggled against the compulsion. *I am not. That is not my armour.* His hands reached for the open chest even so, a hot sweat forming on his forearms.

'*The armour,*' the magus's voice insisted.

Orsian could not stop himself. His hands brushed the

smooth steel plate. He forced his eyes away, towards Krupal. The magus was rapt with concentration, and Orsian could see a sheen of sweat forming on his forehead. By the base of the chest, the vessel of tea was still steaming. With a scream, Orsian wrenched his hand away from the armour, and pressed his palm against the pot.

The shriek that burst from his lips as his skin scalded forced Krupal from his mind. Orsian's consciousness and body crashed into one another like two shield walls, and he collapsed to the floor, his ears ringing discordantly.

Somewhere far away, Eryi was laughing, and Krupal was spitting in frustration. '*Inflika* is temperamental! I had him yesterday! We shouldn't have fed him; if he were still hungry—'

'*I am tired of you blaming everyone else for your own failings.*' Eryi's mirth was short-lived. His voice seemed to slice through the air, forcing Krupal back a step towards the tent flap. '*I swear all those years stuck underground have addled your wits. Now, watch.*'

Krupal's face was like thunder, and for a moment Orsian dared to think the two magi might come to blows, but then Eryi's pale, pupilless eyes rose in Orsian's vision, and he slipped inside Orsian's mind like a host of hungry rats.

'*Stand up.*'

This time, Orsian could not resist. He found himself obeying, his limbs moving of their own accord. A sudden, heavy weight of cold steel fell upon his skull, a helmet so heavy that his neck had to strain to hold his head upright. He looked down only moments later, and found himself garbed head to heel in golden Imperial armour, with a cuirass over his shoulders covering a wool tunic, steel-and-leather armguards, and armoured strips falling from his waist to cover his lower body. He staggered under the weight of it all, almost falling to a knee. It was heavier than mail, and he was weakened from his time in the dungeon.

'I have broken him for you,' sneered Eryi. Krupal flushed. *'Try to keep hold of him this time.'*

Orsian felt the pressure against his mind briefly lift, and he knew a moment of freedom before Krupal was inside his head again, and this time Orsian was powerless to resist. Though Krupal had not spoken a word, a silent sensation of knowing what he had to do swept through him, not so much a command as an urging. Orsian strode from the tent, the plate armour as much a part of him as his own arm.

They swept upon the walls of Merivale under cover of darkness, like wraiths rising from the shadow of their funeral pyres. Across the putrid moat, the barbican of the rebuilt Ram's Gate flickered under cloud-dappled moonlight. The legionnaires considered it for a moment, then moved northward up the western wall.

They were a dozen, and Orsian led them. He guided them far out of sight of the battlements, until the torches of patrolling watchmen were little more than distant rushlights. When they came within sight of a section of wall shrouded in darkness, Orsian stopped them with a raised fist, and they turned back towards the city.

They carried two ladders among them, and when there came no cry of alarm from the battlements they laid the first of these across the width of the moat. Orsian was the first to cross. Standing in the narrow mud strip below the wall, he took the other ladder and laid it against the stonework.

He scaled the ramparts. All along the walkway, the night's silence reigned. With the Imperials thought to be almost beaten, standards among the guardians of Merivale must have slipped. The nearest patrol was hundreds of yards away, too far in the darkness to realise that a dozen men had scaled the wall.

A voice penetrated his daze, a voice he knew, harsh and unyielding in his ears. *'What are you waiting for? Get them moving!'*

A second voice barked a riposte. *'Do not rush me, unless you want to do this yourself!'*

Orsian vaguely recalled the men to whom the bickering voices belonged, but then that spark of memory burnt out, and he lost the thread of why he would care. Up the hill loomed the towers of a high, foreboding fortress, and it was to there that Orsian's eyes wandered. That was their purpose.

Once they were all atop the battlements, they set off back towards the Ram's Gate. Below, the city slept, the night given over to the stray dogs who crept through the alleys and the cats who prowled the sloping rooves of the back-to-back dwellings. To the twelve legionnaires, none even raised an ear.

The first patrol of the Merivale Watch they encountered fell to Orsian's blade, swept from the sheath and across the pair's pale throats before either could cry out a warning. They tumbled their corpses over the edge and into the moat, a brief splash into shallow water.

There was something strange about the scene Orsian could not quite place his finger on. A shattered memory, of standing alongside these fearful pink faces against a common foe. He shook it from his mind.

At the second patrol, Orsian hesitated. As a man bearing a torch turned towards him, Orsian's sword licked out towards his neck, and a twitch of muscle caused him to pull up short. The watchman stepped back, his mouth already opening to call others to his aid.

A voice echoed in his head. *'Damn you, Krupal!'*

This time, a familiar scene flickered at the edge of Orsian's vision, a tent's gloomy interior, and an old man hunched over a table, tearing at a vast plate of pork and root vegetables, his face tight and his eyes half-closed in concentration. Despite the meal in front of him, he seemed to grow gaunter by the moment, fresh lines appearing on his face as flesh melted away.

Back atop the battlements, Orsian watched a legionnaire slip past him, and cut off the man's cry with a slash across his face. Coming to his senses, Orsian seized the gravely wounded guardsman with the legionnaire and together they tumbled him head-first into the moat.

They hurried on towards the Ram's Gate.

'*Get that gate open, now.*'

'*Patience,*' the second voice was tense. Orsian could almost feel Krupal's exhausted hunger in his own stomach.

This is wrong. The thought sent a lance of pain through Orsian's skull. There was no time to think; they were almost at the Ram's Gate; they would have to fight. That was what he lived for.

The battlements here bustled with soldiers and archers, but Orsian paid them no mind. As the first cries of 'Imperials! Imperials inside the walls!' rose from the assembled men, Orsian leapt from the high ramparts. A whisper at the back of his mind told him this was foolish, but he landed softly on the cobbles and immediately he was on the move again. He rushed up the stairs into the gatehouse.

Within the windowless room, a single soldier sat dozing beside the drawbridge winch. He woke, just in time to see Orsian's blade pierce his neck. Orsian kicked the dying man aside.

In the wake of the Ram's Gate's destruction a month earlier, so far only the drawbridge had been rebuilt. The mechanisms for the portcullis and the inner and outer gates lay useless, so Orsian ignored them and threw his weight against the winch for the drawbridge. It spun into life, the chain clinking as it rapidly unwound, and after a few seconds there came an enormous thud from outside as the bridge landed against the far edge of the moat. A moment later, Orsian heard a roar, and several hundred Imperial feet pounding on the wooden slats.

Orsian raced back down the stairs and emerged into chaos. A massed Imperial shield wall had formed in the archway. Panicked Erlanders were rushing down from the battlements straight into the ranks of legionnaires who swiftly dispatched them. He leapt down the last few stairs and by some impulse shoved his way to the front, taking up the vast rectangular shield of a fallen legionnaire and stepping into the first rank, locking it into place with the others.

High above Piperskeep, a lone bell was ringing. Orsian could feel the city waking around them; more Erlanders would soon follow. 'Forward!' he cried, and the shield wall moved as one, a walking fortress bristling with swords and spears.

The Eternal Legion advanced as if controlled by a single mind, and Orsian allowed himself to be swept along in the tide. It felt so familiar, so right, to be leading men into battle again. He pressed down the strange unease that rippled through his skin, wishing only to lose himself in the press of his brothers against his shoulder and the comforting weight of a sword in his hand.

They fought clear of the gateway, and spread their shield wall out to span the whole street. In twos and threes, men in the red livery of the Merivale Watch rushed them with their blades raised, their faces contorted in ear-splitting curses. Orsian barely heard them, and when one came near him he lashed out with his sword, taking a chunk out of the man's jaw and sending him spinning to the ground.

'Forward!' he yelled again, as his fellows took up the cry. 'To the Castle Road! To Piperskeep!' The words felt familiar on his tongue. What was Piperskeep to him? He could not recall. All that mattered was the battle to come, and the safety of the men at his left and right.

Unopposed, they accelerated to a run, making for the Castle

Road. The tolling bell seemed to become louder, more desperate. Cloth-garbed peasants ran from them like terrified rodents, but Orsian and his brothers ignored them. The true foe was to come; a battle Orsian had fought before, in the hot, closed confines trapped between the two great gates of Piperskeep, an unyielding corridor of horror and red death.

An agitated frisson ran up Orsian's spine. He had been a defender then; he had held a different sword, an ugly, heavier lump of metal, and his shield had been round and built from iron-rimmed wood. A red mark had been daubed on his mail, just like the sworn brothers who fought alongside him.

'*No, Orsian.*' He gasped and almost fell to his knees at the bright burst of pain that broke behind his eyes. '*Do not think. FIGHT.*'

Fight. Yes, he had always fought. But why did this feel so different? Battle was blood and fury, passion and beating steel. But most all it was fear, the fear that rose in your guts and threatened to overwhelm your senses. Fear not only for yourself, but fear for your cause, for your friends. His father had said that fear kept a man alive. Fear was good.

So where was it?

They seemed to have traversed the Castle Road in the blink of an eye. Piperskeep rose above them like the great stone guardian of the Mountain belching smoke that loomed in the distance. A fierce mass of armed men was rushing to meet them, wearing mail and holding round shields as Orsian once had.

And still he felt no fear. He felt nothing at all, only the vague sense that this was wrong. He looked down at his sword, left and right at the blank faces alongside him. What were they here for again? The castle? The shield felt heavy on his arm, his face hot with sweat under the absurd helmet he wore. He had the sudden urge to take it off.

And then the battle was joined, and Orsian forgot to feel anything at all.

The *Hymeriker* shield wall crashed into them like a many-limbed beast of wood, metal, and sweat-stained leather. The Legion slipped back a step on the sloping cobbles, as swords clashed in a high song against their bright shields, leaving dents and rattling them against one another in the hands of the legionnaires. Orsian struggled to hold his own shield steady, keeping his face low and pressed against it as spears dashed forward in search of flesh and short swords swept for exposed ankles. The two walls strained against one another, trying to push the other back. With the slope on their side, the *hymerikai* were winning.

'Hold it together, Krupal!'

The tent flashed again in Orsian's vision. Krupal, gaunt as a scarecrow, forcing down bread and hunks of cheese. Eryi standing over him, his pale eyes glittering with avarice.

Orsian risked a look above his rim as an arrow clanged off his helmet. A tall blond warrior screamed in his face, his mouth a curdled mass of bloodstained teeth. The warrior roared again, and spat a pink globule of spit and blood against Orsian's nose guard as he drove forward, his sword pecking at Orsian's shield in search of weakness.

Orsian roared back at him, flicking the rim of his shield up towards the man's face as he lashed out below with his sword to graze off the links of the warrior's mail. The air was filled with cries of pain and fury and the metallic scent of freshly drawn blood. For Orsian, the world narrowed to the scene in front of him, the press of his cheek against his shield and the weight of his opponent. A sword clanged off his helmet from a man to his right, and Orsian lashed out over his shield, driving the point of his own blade into the man's armpit.

It was a grave error. The movement set Orsian off-balance, and the man opposite him lashed out at his feet. Orsian stumbled, and when his opponent shoved forward he fell towards the uneven cobbles. His feet slid forward, and in the press of bodies got tangled with the blond *hymerika*, pulling the warrior down on top of him.

The fall might have saved Orsian's life. At that moment, the Imperial line broke, and the *Hymeriker* drove forward, crowing as they came on in a furious rush of steel. Only the protection of the man atop him stopped Orsian being trampled.

'*You have failed, Krupal!*' Eryi's voice burst painfully against the inside of Orsian's skull, followed by an incandescent anger that set red flames dancing in his fading eyesight. '*I will do it myself.*'

The strange foe snarled in his face again, and Orsian snarled back at him. His left arm was trapped beneath his shield, but his right was free, and he released his sword to grab a dagger from his belt and thrust it towards his opponent's head. The man's left hand came up in a flash to grab Orsian's, squeezing and turning the blade back towards him. Orsian tried to push back, but the *hymerika* was stronger. Inch by inch the point came towards Orsian's eye.

'Die, Imperial bastard!'

The sound of his enemy's voice stirred something in Orsian. *Errian?* The sense of wrongness was so shocking that he almost ceased his resistance. He did not belong here, on this side, in this armour. He was a—

Errian roared, the wide whites of his eyes shining with bloodlust. '*DIE!*'

Orsian tried to say his brother's name, but his tongue felt suddenly too big for his mouth. The only sound he could produce was something in Ulvatian he did not understand.

He strained with every ounce of strength he had, the muscles in his arm and shoulder burning, but Errian was too powerful. His older brother had freed his right hand and was grasping to take a grip on Orsian's neck. He tried ineffectually to push him away with his shield, but his left arm was trapped fast against his torso.

Orsian howled and redoubled his efforts. By the sound at the edge of his senses, the battle had moved on, leaving him and Errian locked together on the ground. For a moment, he thought he saw a flicker of recognition, Errian's blue eyes blinking in confusion, before they paled and his grip tightened around Orsian's hand. The dagger shook in their fists.

Orsian could not explain what had happened; how had he ever believed he was an Imperial? It could not end like this, dying beneath a brother who did not even recognise him. He tried to speak again, just as Errian's fingers found Orsian's throat, and all that came out was a strangled squawk. He tried to summon saliva to spit in his brother's eye, but his mouth was dry as old bone. When that failed, he fought to release the knife to deal with Errian's hand around his neck, but his brother's grip around his fingers held firm.

Then, something seemed to change in the air around Orsian. The sky brightened to a vivid blue, and his brother's grip upon him loosened. Errian stared down at him in confusion. 'Orsian?'

Before Orsian could reply, the Eternal Legion swept over them in a tide of *Hymeriker* blood. Through his delirium, their blades seemed to rise and fall in perfect unison, as if individual limbs of a single mind. The *hymerikai* were retreating. Orsian pushed Errian off him, and looked up to see their desperate rearguard forced back all the way to Piperskeep's half-repaired outer gate. The legionnaires kept coming, and soon the *hymerikai* were away, falling back within the curtain wall even as the Eternal Legion plunged through the gate after them.

Something dragged Errian off Orsian, then threw him aside, and finally Orsian could breathe again. He gulped down air, and looked up into Eryi's pale, pitiless gaze. Again, he wore the appearance of Drast Fulkiro, but, as the first strands of dawn sunlight found them, Orsian squinted against the stinging sweat in his eyes, and perceived the warped, scarred body beneath the glamour.

'And finally, Piperskeep is mine.' The magus's smile could have flayed skin from bone. 'As are both of you. It is a pleasure to meet you, Lord Errian.'

CHAPTER 22

Beads of sweat ran from Helana's forehead. She raised her left arm to wipe her eyes, and in a second Gruenla was on her. The mercenary woman stepped into range and aimed her blunted blade for Helana's midriff, and Helana dropped her shield barely in time to knock the blow aside. She stepped away, circling as the mercenary captain pursued her, the blade in her right hand moving like a snake ready to strike.

'If you must wipe your brow, do it with your sword arm. The shield blocks your eyes.' Gruenla lunged in again, and with a feint managed to evade Helana's shield. Helana brought her blade across in an awkward block, and flicked the point towards Gruenla's forearm, but the Cylirien woman was too quick. Her foot flicked out and swept Helana's leg from under her.

Helana landed heavily on her hip with a grunt. She tried to bring her shield up to cover herself, but Gruenla's blade got there first, a cold curve of blunt steel against Helana's neck.

She looked up at the grinning Cylirien. Behind her, the stars were beginning to come out. 'At least you kept hold of your sword this time,' said Gruenla. She held out a hand and helped Helana to her feet.

Helana left her sword and shield on the ground. She stood with one hand on the back of her head and the other rubbing her tender hip bone, taking deep breaths of the brisk evening air.

'I'm getting better, I think,' she said. The two women's friendship had blossomed over their fiercely competitive games of triumph. It had been Gruenla's idea to train Helana to fight – after they had run out of men willing to lose their coin to them at cards – and she had eagerly accepted. Years of hunting with spear and bow had not prevented Hu'ra imprisoning her; Helana intended never to be helpless again.

'Yes,' said Gruenla. 'There are ten-year-old Cyliriens you might beat.' She took a swig from her waterskin. 'One more before we return to camp?'

They were practising in a dell next to a stream, open to the sky but surrounded by foliage to spare Helana the embarrassment of being soundly defeated in front of curious eyes. She nodded, and took a drink from her own skin. 'Fine. Five gold says I get a hit on you this time.'

She didn't – Gruenla ended their bout with a firm strike to Helana's shoulder that she knew would bruise even through the leather armour she wore – but she was getting closer.

'You need to improve your footwork,' Gruenla told her as they walked the few minutes back to camp, passing a skin of wine back and forth. She looked down at Helana's legs. 'You have weak calves.'

Helana laughed. She could always rely on Gruenla to speak plainly; something to value in a friend. Although she had thought the same about Ti'en. 'I'll see what I can do. Thanks for teaching me.' She looked sideways to measure Gruenla's reaction to her next question. 'If you don't mind me asking, why are you still here?'

'To get paid and fight the Imperials,' said Gruenla instantly.

'But you aren't getting paid.' Rymond's treasury was in

Irith; she doubted the Prindians had a stash of coins in every bit of West Erland woodland.

'We will if he wins.'

That was true, Helana had to admit, but it did not make victory for Rymond any more likely. The delivery of his mother's finger had changed the atmosphere in the camp; everyone knew that the king could not wait until his position strengthened to take the fight to the Imperials. Their numbers had swelled to six hundred now, with seemingly more Erlanders finding him every day, and the addition of the shirtless, shaggy Ffriseans led by their chieftain, Arka, who had joined their camp the day before. They had gone over to the Imperials when Irith fell, but had now returned to Rymond's banner, complaining of Imperial mistreatment and a failure to recognise their worth.

But he could not retake Irith with only six hundred men. 'Do you think he has a plan?' asked Helana.

Gruenla shrugged. 'He's cleverer than he looks sometimes. Not just a pretty face.'

Helana hoped Gruenla was right. Every day, she thought of leaving for Merivale to face whatever awaited her there. Sometimes though, she dreamt of the presence she had felt in that tent, and woke up startled and shaking. It was not loyalty or gratitude that kept her beside Rymond, but the fear of going to Merivale alone.

Their campsite was divided into sections spread through the forest at hundred-yard intervals, with roving sentries patrolling their flanks. Rymond's main camp was at the centre, marked by a tall wooden pole with a helmet balanced on top in place of a Prindian flag. They all slept in the open, under whatever shelters they could fashion from twigs and discarded clothes. A single cookfire was belching smoke, while a vast cauldron bubbled over it.

Rymond was standing nearby, deep in discussion with

Brant and Rucius, the captured Imperial translator. Both men had been away for several days, and it showed in their travel-stained cloaks and their tired eyes. Rymond's face too was drawn, with a tense, glum aspect to it. He caressed his jaw as he listened to whatever Brant was telling him.

'What's the news?' called Helana.

He looked round at her. 'We have no hope of retaking Fall-back Lodge. Brant says a whole company of Imperials are garrisoned there, over a thousand men.' He clenched his fist around a roll of parchment. 'I had hoped it might fall easily and we could use it as a base. It changes nothing though: we must retake Irith.'

They had been moving north ever since the Imperial messengers had found them in the Gwynæthwood, so Helana had suspected Rymond's plan. She could not see though how he hoped to achieve it. 'With six hundred men? What happened to patience?'

'My mother's finger in a box happened.' Rymond looked away from her. 'A thousand dead West Erlanders for every hour I'm late happened.' His mouth was set in a hard line, and Helana saw not a trace of indecision in him. 'I have no choice.'

'They're bluffing,' said Helana. 'It would be madness; they'd lose the support—'

'Acques Bazar does not bluff,' said Gruenla, looking at Helana with hard eyes. 'I saw him bring men to him in Cylirien the same way. He keeps his promises.'

'She's right,' said Rucius. 'I went to Irith. Every legionnaire I spoke to said the same thing: they're building a huge platform outside the castle, and Bazar's got the smiths forging heavy axes that can take a man's head off with one swing.' The translator's mouth quirked. 'Cleaner for them than being hanged, I suppose.'

'And Alcantra's as unyielding as Bazar is,' said Rymond. He pushed a strand of unkempt hair off his brow and looked to

Rucius. 'You've done well. Have some food and wine and then feel free to get some rest.'

'I was beginning to think you'd never ask,' said Rucius. He departed towards the cookfire.

'You do have a plan then?' asked Helana.

Rymond flashed a handsome smile. 'All in good time.' He clapped Brant on the shoulder. 'I am afraid I must ask you to leave again, Brant. Ride north. Drink in the taverns and learn what men are saying. Some lords might be wavering in their support for the Imperium; perhaps Darlton or Storaut has come back west. Find as many supportive ears as you can, and tell them I'm making for Irith, then wait for us in the woodland west of the city. There are fresh supplies already in your saddlebags.'

If Brant was at all irritated at being commanded to leave again, he hid it well. 'Aye, Majesty.' He departed swiftly, rushing to a horse tied up against the tree line.

'That's your grand plan then?' said Helana. 'Hope one of your lords takes pity on you and decides to double-cross the Imperials? Seems a bit optimistic.' Perhaps she really would be better to make for Merivale.

'Actually, no. I'm going to surrender.'

Rymond had been ready for the perplexed looks they were giving him. He made them wait though, summoning a small inner circle to him shortly after their evening meal had been served. They had little ale or wine to spare, and so he required all those attending him drink nothing but water, gathered from a nearby spring. He sat on a tree stump, surrounded by Gruenla, Garwen, Helana, Rucius, and Arka of the Ffriseans. Another new arrival was Urwen Storaut, a narrow-faced youth of around Rymond's age, the grandson of the elderly Lord

Storaut, now believed dead. He spoke with verve of his desire to restore Rymond to his throne, though he had brought only two warriors with him.

'This Acques Bazar has tipped his hand by telling us by when I must present myself at the gate,' Rymond told them. 'Whether or not I turn up, he'll execute my mother first.' He swallowed the lump in his throat; there was nothing he could do for her unless this plan worked. 'He'll want a spectacle, to show the West Erlanders that Prindian power is truly broken. They'll be sending word across all the nearby towns and villages – "Come to Irith and see Breta Prindian die."

'That means they'll have the city gates open so people can come and watch. We can get men inside the walls. People will be bringing goods to sell as well; we can get a cart of something, and hide weapons underneath. We might get hundreds of armed Erlanders in there.'

'Don't you think they'll have thought of this?' said Helana. 'Why are you so sure they'll go through with this if you surrender yourself?'

Rymond grinned at her, hoping he sounded more confident than he felt. 'That's why it's not going to look like a surrender.' He nodded to Gruenla. 'The Cyliriens will bring me in. Say they're tired of not getting paid and they want to claim the reward.'

'Not just not getting paid,' added Gruenla. 'The poor leadership, the awful food, the smell of—'

'Yes, all that.' Rymond reached for a smokestick and paused to light it against the diminishing fire. 'Next, I'd wager that they'll still go through with the execution, and get me to watch, or even line me up for the headsman as well.'

Rymond paused, watching their faces. Helana looked doubtful. Arka and Gruenla were impassive, weighing his words as trained warriors, their arms crossed over their chests.

'So say that all goes to plan,' said Gruenla slowly. 'You've got men and weapons inside the walls, you're bound and ready to be executed. What then?'

Rymond's smile faltered, but he covered himself with a long pull of his smokestick. 'There's a limit to what we can plan for. I was thinking I would ask for a chance to address the crowd, and then give a rousing speech or something. When our men start pulling their weapons and attacking the Imperials hopefully the rest will follow.'

'What of the Ffriseans?' Arka slapped a meaty hand against his bare torso. 'We do not hide.'

'Be ready to assault the gate once the commotion starts,' said Rymond. 'Hopefully they'll still be open and they'll be pulling guards away towards the execution.'

Helana's face was a mask of disbelief. 'That... *That* is your plan?' Her eyes went to the sky. 'All you're doing is attacking Irith with six hundred men, some of them now disguised as peasants, but adding the extra step of you being captured and tied up for execution. That's not a plan, it's a death sentence.'

'I think it's a little more sophisticated than that,' said Rymond, though Helana's words had rather dampened his enthusiasm. 'There are thousands of West Erlanders who will rise with us.'

'Is it possible that you're slightly overestimating the value they place on your life?'

'Every true West Erlander is loyal to King Rymond,' said Urwen Storaut. 'The city will rise with us, Majesty, have no fear. I volunteer myself to drive the weapons cart.'

'Loyal like your grandfather was?' said Helana. 'He was a traitor twice over.'

Colour rose on Urwen's cheeks. 'Were you a man, I would make you defend those words with steel in hand.'

'We're not here to fight each other.' Rymond spoke over them before Helana could reply. He looked at Helana. She was somehow even more beautiful when she was indignant. 'I admit, it needs some work.' He shrugged. 'It's a starting point. We can refine it once I have Brant's report of matters in Irith. He'll hear things that Rucius didn't.'

'True enough,' said Rucius with a rueful smile. 'When I tried to enter an Erlander tavern in my legionnaire uniform they threatened to shove my bollocks up my bum. My curiosity lasted for about three seconds before I made a run for it.'

'This plan gets me within a blade's length of Bazar,' said Gruenla, hunger gleaming in her eyes. She fingered the hilt of her sword. 'That's reason enough for me to like it.'

Rymond nodded. Everyone except Helana seemed pleased enough with it, and she had been criticising every decision he made already; her focus was on getting him to ride to Merivale, not retaking Irith.

He toyed with explaining to her why it was so important. He had been the one to lose Irith, and he could not retake it without putting himself at risk. As a king, it was his responsibility to share the dangers his people faced; why should any man submit to his rule if he was not prepared to risk his own life for West Erland? The privileges of kingship and its responsibilities were inseparable. It was a shame that it had taken him relinquishing his kingdom to see that. There were thousands of lives at stake, and try as he might, Rymond could see no other way of saving them, not with so little time and so few men.

'That's settled then,' he said. 'We ride north tomorrow and hope the Imperials don't catch us before we get there.'

Helana was already turning away. 'You'll get every one of us killed.'

Later that evening, beneath a tree, Helana lay on her pillow of bunched clothing, fuming. *It's as if he thinks it's Thrumbalto all over again, that he can just waltz in and save the day.*

And she was powerless to prevent it. Nobody else seemed to recognise what a Norhai-cursed awful plan it was. That was another problem with not knowing how to use a sword – if she had been a man, a warrior trained from birth, Rymond would have given her concerns their due weight.

Helana rolled over on the cold ground and found a pair of boots staring back at her. She looked up and found Gruenla observing her.

The Cylirien woman thrust out a skin. 'Whisky,' she said. 'Last I've got. Thought we might share it.'

Helana rose to a sitting position, leaning her back against the tree. Gruenla sank to join her. 'Thanks.' The mercenary took the first swig and passed it to Helana, who followed suit and gasped as the sweet, powerful liquor hit her tongue. 'He just drives me mad. You would think being deposed would change a man, but he's the same as ever, thinking that he's untouchable and everything will just work out.'

Gruenla accepted the return of the skin. 'He rode through two days and nights to come to your rescue – I'd say he's changed. He's finally taking some responsibility. Taken him long enough.' She glanced sideways at Helana. 'It's not just that though.'

'No? What else?'

Gruenla dropped her voice. 'When we met, I thought he was just a good source of gold.' She grinned wickedly. 'But it turns out he's a decent fuck as well.'

The two of them fell into a fit of laughter, covering their mouths so as not to wake the camp. Helana was enjoying Gruenla's company more by the moment.

'I'm joking,' added Gruenla. 'He's terrible. Lazy. Too skinny.'

This set off another round of giggles, this time accompanied by irritated shouts as men rolled over in their bedrolls to call for them to be quiet.

'Seriously though,' said Gruenla, once they had got control of themselves, wiping her eye. 'He has changed. He never used to be a leader, but now everyone takes notice of him, even Arka. He's made mistakes, but I can see he's determined to put them right. You should have seen him when he was deep into casheef – well, actually it's for the best you didn't – I thought he was done for, but he's come back.'

Helana found herself agreeing. 'I never thought I'd see him so comfortable sleeping outdoors.' She paused. 'But how do I make him see that his plan's a festering pile of dung?' She looked at Gruenla, who passed Helana the skin. 'You can't actually think it will work, do you?'

Gruenla shrugged. 'Plans, maps, contracts... they all look good on parchment. But they don't mean much when someone sticks a knife up against your spine. It's not planning that wins you battles; it's people, some more than others. On parchment, East Erland wins the Battle of Whitewater while barely having to draw a blade, but kill Andrick Barrelbreaker and what happens? All that planning was for nothing.

'I had a brother, back in Cylirien. Talinn. Five years old than me. I worshipped him. He had a plan – there was an Imperial wagon convoy passing close to our village, too lightly defended. Him and his friends figured it out meticulously; attack by night, draw off the men guarding it with a distraction, then hit them with the main force and steal everything they could get their hands on. It couldn't fail.'

Gruenla's eyes had taken on a faraway look, brimming with regret. 'I was too young to help, but he let me be a lookout. What Talinn and his friends didn't know was that one of the wagons was full of huyar. An Imperial arrow missed Talinn and went in through its one tiny window. Whole thing exploded, and took my brother with it. No amount of planning can save you from one lucky shot.'

Helana handed Gruenla the whisky, who took it without

looking. 'I'm sorry,' said Helana. She hoped she sounded sympathetic, but her mind was racing. Rymond's plan was bad, but she could change that. All she needed to do was—

'You know Rucius, that Imperial translator?'

Gruenla looked at her sharply. 'Yeah, was up to me he'd be dead. What about him?'

'Do you know where he sleeps?'

Gruenla snorted. 'That story about my brother being blown to dust got your blood up or something?' She pointed through the trees. 'He sleeps through there. Likes to keep himself apart from us.' Her mouth curved in a smirk. 'Wise man. There are some of my lads still hoping we get the chance to skin him.'

Helana hurried to her feet. 'Thanks.' She paused awkwardly, looking down at Gruenla. 'I'm sorry. About your brother.'

Gruenla waved her away. 'Don't mention it. He died better than most. I hope his tale was useful.'

More useful than you know. Helana hurried off in search of Rucius. She had a hunch, something that might turn Rymond's pile-of-shit plan into a hoard of gold.

CHAPTER 23

Amidst the boundless black rock, on a high hill, the Sorrowmen's ring fort came into view like a birthmark against the bloodshot horizon. Together, the goat-riders raised their weapons to the air and in unison wailed to the sky, then urged their mounts forward to get their column moving again, snaking up a steep gravel track.

Pherri's goat gave a plaintive bleat and moved with the rest of them. The Erlanders had each been given their own mount, but of a smaller variety to those of the Sorrowmen, and without horns. Together, they rode between two columns of warriors, so close to them that Pherri's legs brushed against the rough goat hair breeches of the riders either side.

It had been several days' march from the border, at first following the Pale River until it disappeared underground to a hidden spring. The air stank of sulphur and goat excrement, and warmth rolled off the black earth like the heat of a sleeping giant. Here and there, a few small pits of tar bubbled forebodingly, and the Sorrowmen's tracks weaved across the landscape to avoid them.

Pherri had watched every inch of the landscape she could

as they rode, but after a while it had become senseless. The terrain dipped and rose, between sheer drops to valleys bristling with sharp rocks and jagged hills impossibly steep, but otherwise it never changed. There were no trees, no meadows, no wildlife. The Sorrowmen fed them on dried pieces of stringy goat meat that left Pherri's teeth aching, and served them horns of surprisingly sweet milk.

Pherri glanced back and forth along the column. Phyrrai and Helana rode ahead of her, and Hrogo behind. Bringing up the rear was Jarhyck, but rather than giving him a goat to ride the Sorrowmen had suspended him by his limbs on a frame of three lengths of wood, carried by a rotating collection of riders. A rag had been shoved in his mouth, and his long hair trailed in the dirt from his lolling head. If it was meant as a lesson to the rest of them not to attempt escape it was unnecessary; there was nowhere to go, and, though some had split off to take different routes, over a hundred Sorrowmen still rode with them.

But they were at least moving south. The shadow of Pipersmont still split the hazy sky of the distant horizon, larger now than when they had departed. An impossible journey still, but less impossible than before.

Keep your eyes open, Pherri told herself. The ideal would be if she could somehow make an ally of the Sorrowmen leader, Horned Grawl, always laughing, throwing back cup after cup of fermented goat's milk while he rode beside Jarhyck tormenting him in his broken Erlish. Otherwise, she would need to discover how far it was to Pipersmont, find appropriate provisions, and escape. Perhaps with time the Sorrowlanders would forget about her.

Ahead of her, Phyrrai's plait bounced with the motion of her steed, the line of her neck and shoulders so strangely familiar that it made Pherri light-headed. She had tried to comfort her after Da'ri's death, but Pherri's shadowtwin had been inconsolable. Pherri understood; she had been the same after her Da'ri had met his end at the hands and fists of the Lordsferry mob. Phyrrai's wails of grief though had drawn no sympathy from Grawl and the Sorrowlanders, and furious demands as to why they had felt the need to slay an unarmed man in his latter years had been met with silence.

Pherri wondered if the world had written that it would be that way. Perhaps in every existence, a man named Da'ri met a violent end far from home, and the Sorrowlanders were only stringed puppets recreating the same scene. But if that were true, what did it mean for her journey? Was she fated to return, or fated to remain here?

As they crested the steep track, Pherri began to appreciate the scale of the ring fort. It was as large perhaps as the outer wall of Violet Hall, formed from high stakes of white wood that had somehow been hammered into the hard earth. The whole structure was covered in goat hides, and as they got closer she saw by the exposed spikes of the palisade that the wood had been lacquered, most likely with the tar harvested from the pits they passed. More stout, squash-faced Sorrowmen stared down at them, until Horned Grawl called up something in their own language. Winches began to creak, and inch by inch a gate of wooden stakes rose.

As they passed beneath, the interior came into view. A second, smaller ring rose above them, separated from the main wall by thirty yards of bright green meadow that seemed to stretch all around the circumference. There were more goats than Pherri could count, some dozing beneath crude wooden shelters and others happily grazing on the grass, watched by skinny boys in sleeveless leather jerkins. Pherri could only imagine a spring of water rising from underground made such lushness possible, surrounded as they were by endless barren rock.

Horned Grawl gave a command, and the Sorrowmen began to disperse, dismounting and leading their goats towards the pasture. The gate dropped closed behind them, and the goat-rider chief raised his eyes to the parapet of the inner ring.

Pherri followed his gaze, and was surprised to see atop the battlements her first Sorrowwomen, a pair of them. They were dressed like their menfolk, and appeared to be of a similar stature, but were smooth-skinned where the men had beards.

Grawl shouted something to them. The women looked at each other, shrugged, and signalled to someone below. The inner ring's gate began to rise.

Pherri urged her goat forward until she was alongside Phyrrai, and they looked at one another with sad smiles. In the midst of Phyrrai's grief over Da'ri, the awkwardness between them had evaporated the last few days; they could look at one another and be close for short periods, and Pherri had even thought of reaching out a hand to her shadowtwin, but before too long the uneasy, violent urge to hurt her always returned.

'They're all leaving,' said Phyrrai, looking to the departing Sorrowmen. They had even released Jarhyck, and four men were guiding him stumbling towards a ramshackle hut.

Hrogo eyed the inner fort anxiously. 'What do you think they'll do to us in there?' He swallowed, and picked at his teeth to retrieve a string of goat gristle. 'I'll not be a slave again. They'll have to kill me first.' Being captured twice appeared to have knocked out of him whatever spirit he'd had when Pherri first arrived; now whenever he spoke it was usually to wish for his own death.

Clutching a horn of strong, sour-smelling milk, Grawl brought his mount forward to address them. The gate behind him finished its climb and stopped. 'In there, women. Safe, best place for you.' He slapped Hrogo's goat on the rump, and as it moved forward the mounts of Pherri, Phyrrai, and Halyana fell into step. The chieftain said something to the few remaining Sorrowmen, and all of them departed for the pasture, as the outer gate groaned shut behind them.

The four of them passed beneath the shadow of the inner gate, and several women ran forward to assist them from their mounts, and then ushered the goats back towards the outer meadow with shooing and slaps to the rump.

The four women were all garbed in goatskin, sleeveless vests and breeches cut off at the knee. Bright eyes peered out from cavernous sockets, set in bronzed faces beneath dark bird's-nest hair. They eyed the new arrivals curiously. One reached out to stroke Phyrrai's hair, who flinched back, drawing a hiss from the Sorrowwoman. Another stepped behind Hrogo, and began running her hands along his shoulders, murmuring to herself. The magus tried to push her away, but the woman continued to paw at him.

Someone gave a shrill whistle, and the Sorrowwomen retreated swiftly to a safe distance. Pherri turned towards the sound to see another woman striding towards them. She was taller than the others, and her goatskin vest was studded with mismatched coins. A necklace of bones and a diverse assortment of gold hung around her neck. She was strangely pretty, with full lips and high cheekbones sloping to a finely pointed chin. But Pherri's eyes were drawn to the woman's head, where, amidst a crown of shining chestnut hair, a pair of horns protruded just above her brow.

'Welcome to Ulsenfort!' she exclaimed, beaming at them. There was only the barest trace of an accent. 'Grawl sent word ahead. We've lodgings for all of you.' She pointed to Hrogo. 'You are on the south side; Arnha will show you.' The woman gestured to the one who had tried to touch Phyrrai's hair, who took Hrogo by the hand and led him away, his broken chain dragging in the dirt.

The magus turned back to them and shrugged unhappily. 'I'll find you later.'

Pherri had been so distracted she had not yet considered their surroundings. The inner fort was like a small village, with scattered, flat-roofed houses of dried mud, fenced paddocks filled with orderly rows of vegetable plants, and a larger circular pavilion at the centre. Every face Pherri saw was that of a woman, some tending the gardens, others washing clothes in buckets drawn from a nearby well, and all other manner of tasks. Outside one of the huts, there appeared to be a lesson in progress, an old Sorrowwoman hunched on a stool addressing a gaggle of young girls.

Do the men all live outside and all the women in here? Pherri wondered. It certainly looked that way. She refocused her attention on what the woman was saying to Phyrrai.

'Yes, a few of us speak Erlish. The men bring back books and scrolls sometimes and ask us to read them.' She spoke it perfectly, a jarring contrast to Grawl's halting attempts. 'I'm Hawla.' She extended a hand for the three of them to grasp.

Phyrrai did not offer her hand. She scowled up at Hawla. 'You killed my friend. I want to know why.'

Hawla's smile wavered. 'I apologise for your treatment at the hands of my brother-husband. Your friend... was he mounted at the time?'

Phyrrai nodded. 'Yes. On a horse.'

Hawla's face softened. 'I'm sorry. Among the Horned Folk, only the warriors ride. To them, your friend was theirs to kill. You three were spared because you are women, and I assume your other friend was on foot.'

Hrogo had been, Pherri recalled. It had likely saved his life. Da'ri would have been more useful though; he knew this world. Hrogo would be of no more help than Pherri herself.

'That's bollocks,' said Phyrrai fiercely. 'Da'ri wasn't a warrior. He wasn't even armed.'

Hawla placed a sympathetic hand on Phyrrai's shoulder. 'When a man's blood is up, there is no telling what harm he might do. It is the way of the world. I am glad that neither of you were hurt.'

'And what of the king?' asked Pherri. 'Will he be harmed?' She was not sure why she cared; it was Jarhyck's fault they were here.

'He is to be Grawl's guest. Tonight, they will drink and feast together, as no outsider has in living memory. My brother-husband does your king a great honour.'

Pherri very much doubted Jarhyck would see it that way after several days spent trussed up like a slaughtered pig, but she said nothing. Without him pursuing them they might have avoided the Sorrowlanders, and Da'ri would still be alive. If Jarhyck wanted to escape and starve to death making his way back to Erland she would not be the one to stop him.

'Come,' said Hawla. She grunted something in her own language to two of the other women. 'Your rooms are this way.'

The Sorrowwoman led them counter-clockwise around the wall, past more mud huts and small patches of what might have been carrots and turnips. The ground here was the same barren black rock as outside, but somehow the Sorrowwomen had cultivated growth. As they passed, women stopped from their tasks to stare.

Pherri glanced behind her. The two other women were dogging their steps, with blunt axes hanging from their belts. She eyed the walls up and down. Every stake was tightly packed between its neighbours, and on the ramparts thirty feet above them pairs of guardswomen stood sentry at intervals. The inner fort appeared impenetrable, and inescapable.

She fell into step with Phyrrai. 'Do you think they're up there to keep us in, or to keep something out?' she whispered.

'They're to keep the men out,' said Hawla, without missing a beat. 'The women rule from within while the men do our bidding outside. They are allowed within the goat ring, but no further.'

Pherri shared a glance with Phyrrai. So far, Hawla had been welcoming, but her words implied that the attacks against

Erland had been at her command. Had she ordered Grawl to kidnap them as well? Pherri dismissed the idea; Hawla would not have even known who they were.

They stopped in front of a hut. Hawla gestured towards Halyana. Sometimes the older girl was so silent that Phyrrai forgot she was there. 'You will sleep here, Princess.'

Pherri would have struggled to describe the expression on Halyana's face. It remained as guileless as ever, but there was a spark of defiance behind her eyes. She moved closer to Pherri. Hawla reached out for her, and Halyana hissed violently, slapping her hand away. The two guardswomen stepped forward, reaching for their axes.

'It's fine!' Pherri told her, placing herself in the way of the approaching women and touching a placating hand to Halyana's arm. 'We'll be fine, I promise.'

Halyana looked doubtful. Her eyes flickered between Pherri and the hut, while Hawla smiled and gestured towards the entrance. After a moment's hesitation, she briefly gripped Pherri and Phyrrai's hands and then with slow steps walked towards the tent.

'You are so kind to that poor girl,' said Hawla. 'She will be quite safe, I assure you. You will see her this evening.' She smiled, revealing two rows of small squat teeth. 'Now, come. There is someone I would like you to meet.' She placed a hand on each of the girls' shoulders and ushered them on.

As they approached the southern side of the fort, Hawla guided them up a set of creaking wooden stairs to the battlements. Here, Pipersmont looked closer than ever, and Pherri stepped to the parapet to stare at it, resting one hand on the crenelation. An advantage to the Sorrowlanders' short stature was that everything was much more suited to her size.

Phyrrai came to join her, and stared over the edge, down at the meadow filled with grazing goats and Sorrowmen sprawled on the grass supping on horns of fermented milk. A few curious eyes looked up at them.

'We could negotiate,' murmured Phyrrai, her eyes lifting towards Pipersmont in the distance. 'Maybe we can give them something in exchange for safe passage.'

'But we have nothing,' replied Pherri.

Hawla came to stand behind them. 'There will be time to admire the view later. It would not be polite to keep her waiting.'

Pherri had assumed that Hawla was the power within Ulsenfort, but perhaps she answered to somebody else. She steered them back along the battlements, towards a strange structure right at the southern end. It was set between the parapets, upon an unwalled balcony stretching out over the goat ring. A single length of wood protruded up from the battlements to give it form, with a huge sheet of leather stretched over it and pinned to the floor to form a tent shaped in a tall, narrow cone. It had one entrance, a single flap beating against itself in the high breeze. The interior glowed with orange firelight, and Pherri could almost see the air within dancing in the heat.

'You will enter one at a time,' said Hawla. 'Pherri of Erland, you will go first.'

'What is it for?' Pherri did not want to go in there. A spasm of fear ran up her spine. The confined space and the fire made her think of her imprisonment in Eryi's cave, only with clammy heat rather than unbearable cold. Even the leather walls looked to be weeping perspiration.

'You do not need to be afraid.' Hawla smiled down at her. 'Every woman of the Horned Folk enters the Sorrowseer's tent to learn something of the tribe's path. It is a great honour.'

Pherri swallowed. 'What will I see?'

'Only the Sorrowseer can answer that.'

Was the Sorrowseer some god of theirs? Pherri wished she

knew more of the Sorrowlanders, or the Horned Folk as they called themselves. They were barely mentioned in the books she had read, even in the tales of King Piper's arrival in Erland. But then, what was to say these Sorrowlanders were like those in her own world?

In her fear, she instinctively reached for Phyrrai's hand.

The shock of their palms touching was like a shower of sparks up Pherri's arm. They leapt away from each other with a gasp, and for a moment Pherri's vision swam with stars. She rubbed at her eyes, dizzy. Her hand was numb where Phyrrai had touched it.

Then, the shock faded. They looked at one another, and instead of rage Pherri felt a burst of elation. *My shadowtwin.* They stared at each other for several moments, marvelling at the perfect vision of themselves, almost overcome with affection.

Then it passed, and a wave of revulsion surged through Pherri. She looked away.

'I won't go anywhere,' said Phyrrai, also not looking at her. 'It will be fine.' But at the edge of her vision, Phyrrai could see her twin's doubt by the way she chewed her lip.

'It is rude to keep the Sorrowseer waiting.' Hawla's mouth was a hard line. 'She has been preparing a long time for this moment; do not disappoint her.' The two guardswomen took a step forward.

Preparing for what? Pherri breathed deep and pushed the hair back from her eyes. She stepped forward, held the flap open, and dipped her head beneath the entrance.

Inside, a wall of wet heat seemed to soak through her clothes in an instant, leaving a clammy layer upon her skin. The thick, steamy air was hard to breathe, filling her mouth and nostrils. In the centre, a single fire burnt without smoke and without wood, and instead of lighting the tent seemed to suck the brightness from it, bathing Pherri in darkness. Tentatively, she took a few steps towards it, to where a simple square stool waited for her. If anything, it was cooler nearer the blaze, with air that did not hurt her lungs to inhale.

Pherri sat down, looked into the flames, and almost fell off her seat.

From the other side, a floating face stared back at her. A woman with a long, narrow head rose over the fire. Her thick hair hung in graceful ringlets, black as midnight. A thin silken smock clung to her lithe frame. The flames rose with her, as if part of her. Her face was unlined and white as bone, but her brown eyes were deep with wisdom. Pherri would never have been able to guess how old she was.

Pherri swallowed, almost gagging on the thick air. 'You're not a Sorrowlander.'

The woman raised a fine dark eyebrow. 'Is that so? Are you so wise in our ways?' Her voice rose and fell like a lilting lullaby.

'I mean you don't look like them.'

'Not everything is as it first appears.' The woman's lips curled in an invisible smile. 'What do you suppose people see when they first see you?'

'I don't know what you mean.' Pherri's throat was dry. Huge beads of sweat were rolling down her face, past her neck, soaking into her clothes.

'I think you do.' The woman threw powder into the fire, and in the flames Pherri saw Eryispek. Her Eryispek, and her last desperate battle with Eryi atop the summit, their wills bending against one another like streams of light through broken glass. The fire flashed, and the image of Pherri blinked out of existence.

The woman was kneeling before the fire now, her long face floating above the flames. She spoke, her dark lips swelling like two blood-filled leeches. 'Do you even realise how unlikely you are, Pherri? How rare it is for one to cross the veil between worlds?'

Pherri stared at her. Her heart was pounding like a drum. 'Who *are* you?'

'Who are *you*?' The Sorrowseer's eyes danced in the heat like two great orbs. 'You do not belong here. You must return.' She waved her hand, and wavering shadows appeared in the fire. Orsian and Errian together, their blades raised against one another. Black smoke pouring from the summit of Eryispek. Eryi, looming over Piperskeep like a giant, his pale eyes hungry and searching.

Tears sprang to Pherri's eyes. 'Is that what's happening?' she asked. Her voice quivered uncontrollably.

'Many things are possible.' The shadows faded. The Sorrowseer smiled, straight teeth glowing silver in the firelight. 'But it is not they that should disturb you, but the threat yet unseen. There is another. She lurks at the edge of my dreams, watching, always waiting. You know of whom I speak.'

'*Vulgatypha.*' The goddess who Eryi had named the true threat.

'She must be stopped.' The Sorrowseer's eyes flashed. 'If she succeeds, a shadow will fall over every world, every different possibility, so bleak and so terrible that no light nor life will ever shine again. Every existence, reduced to a pinprick, reigned over by Vulgatypha.'

Pherri was rapt. '*Every* world? This one as well?'

'Left unchecked, she has that power.'

'What can I do?' asked Pherri.

'You must go back.'

'Yes.' Pherri could not stop the sob that rose in her throat. 'I know. Can you help me?'

'It is you who can help yourself.' The woman rose, and in a single swift motion swept away a leather curtain at the rear of the tent, revealing the distant shape of Pipersmont. Evening was falling, but the mountain was as clear and bright as a knife passed over flame.

Pherri wiped her eyes. 'Is that where I have to go?'

'Yes.' Once more the flames seemed to move with the Sorrowseer's voice. 'Only there, on the Eryispek that might have been, will you find the power to break through the veil that divides our world from yours.' Her eyes glittered, like starlight reflected in a dark well. 'But the veil is hard to pierce. Few have tried, even fewer have succeeded.' The woman paused. 'Have you deduced yet, what you must do?'

Pherri shook her head. 'I don't even know if I can get there.'

'There can be no victory without sacrifice. You must go there, and on the slopes of the ancient pillar of the Norhai slay the girl you might have been. You must kill Phyrrai, and open the way between the worlds. I have seen it. Only by returning to your own world can you hope to defeat Vulgatypha.'

CHAPTER 24

The endless column of people rolled over the cliffside hills. It stretched like a hungry snake, each day steadily eating away the miles. At the head, the mail of the warriors sparkled beneath the Istlewicks' sea eagle banner, followed by half-a-dozen smaller banners belonging to the minor lords and landowners who swore allegiance to Cliffark, and mixed in with them a few hundred Wild Brigaders, who had surrendered and defected rather than face the noose.

What followed behind was a confused throng of sailors, guardsmen, and townsmen. They wore no armour, armed with hatchets, knives, clubs, and cheap pirate steel for a lucky few, but more than made up for it with their noise, different groups howling along to three different songs to make the miles go swifter. Many were obviously in a celebratory mood; in return for their service to Ciera Istlewick and marching to Merivale, they would secure independence for the city of Cliffark, and they were evidently keen to crow about it.

At the very rear came the dregs of the march. Whores, perhaps eager to make their fortune from their short supply of competitors; boys considered too young to fight, orphans and escaped apprentices and everything in between; and then the baggage train, guarded by whichever men had drawn the short straw that day: a creaking procession of seemingly every cart and wagon that could be found in Cliffark.

From the very head of the march, Tansa turned and craned her neck to look back on the horde that followed them. It was more people than she had ever seen in one place – nearly six thousand, she had heard one Istlewick warrior say.

They had disguised her as Ciera's new maid. Tansa now wore an unwieldy long dress that she could barely walk or ride in, light jewellery the rattling of which was likely to drive her mad, and the warmest cloak she had ever owned, which would have been a pleasure if not for the presence of the Istlewick sea eagle over her breast marking her as if she were Ciera's property.

Ciera insisted that if Tansa was to join her at the head of the march to Merivale she needed to be disguised, for the sake of appearances and so that nobody would recognise her as Hessian's killer. As true as that might have been, it did not improve Tansa's mood. The rest of Cliffark's rebellion council who had joined the march seemed content to ride further back, but Tansa thought that idiocy – they could not allow Ciera to slither away based on a vague promise. They needed to keep her feet to the fire. Maud would have understood that, but the landlady had said she was much too old to join them. '*Never ridden a horse or been to Merivale, and it's too late to start now. I didn't live this long with that sort of foolishness,*' she had told Tansa.

Tansa glanced sideways. The queen sat straight as an arrow in the saddle, and despite the wind and the spitting rain looked no less perfectly groomed than usual, her chestnut hair flowing in lush curls beneath the hood of her cloak and her face seemingly impervious to the raindrops that were dripping from Tansa's hood and into her eyes.

Ciera did not look at her, but Tansa knew what she would be wondering: why was the girl still here?

Yes, Tansa thought, *I'm coming with you. I don't care how many clothes you force me to wear or how wet I get, until you give us the reforms we were promised, I am your shadow.*

Tansa sighed as the rain began to thicken, and with a resigned air pulled her hood forward and tightened her cloak about herself. The first time she had made this trek, she had been angry with Tam for forcing them to leave. The second, with Orsian. This time, it was Ciera Istlewick who vexed her. The journey to Merivale was never a happy one.

The thought of Orsian only increased Tansa's sense of melancholy, matching the bleak sky and the iron-grey waters that churned to their right. How had he fared since she fled? Did he hate her now? He was just as much a victim of the Sangreals as she was, even if he did not realise it. In another life, with different choices, they might have stayed in Cliffark, and he could have remained Ranulf and they could have lived with Maud in Pauper's Hole and laughed in her kitchen while drinking the old woman's horrid acidic wine. Instead... Tansa felt a guilty lump in her throat. He might be dead, slain by his own people for allowing Hessian's murderer into the keep.

She looked again to Ciera. Did the queen feel a fraction of the grief that Tansa did for all those she had lost? The tale was that her father, mother, and sworn protector had all been killed in the warrior Strovac Sigac's one-man assault on Cliffark Tower, and yet within a week she was riding at the head of an army, bound for war. If the dead troubled her, Ciera Istlewick did not show it. She was as icy cold as the Shrouded Sea.

'Tansa, if you have something to say to me, then say it.' Ciera's imperious tone shook Tansa to her senses. 'You watching me is making me nervous.'

Tansa itched to bite back at her, but held her tongue. *I was just wondering whether if I stabbed you in the heart I'd hit anything, Majesty.* She swore this servant role she was being forced to play was in part to humiliate her. She was a leader of the rebellion; she should have been able to ride where she pleased. In Cliffark, the advantage had been theirs, but the council had been tricked by Ciera into a deal that surrendered their power for little more than a promise. Ciera had sworn that reform would come, but now she held the reins on when that would be, and if she broke her word what could they do to stop her?

'I was just wondering when we might discuss the reforms again,' said Tansa. 'There's a lot we could thrash out, seeing how we're together so much.'

'There is no point discussing anything further until my son is restored to his crown,' said Ciera. She spoke with a practised air, as if she had rehearsed it. The young king was in a covered cart riding close by, swaddled in so many layers that Tansa thought it a wonder he could breathe. 'I promise you I am as passionate for reform as you are.'

Tansa doubted that very much. When Cliffark was free, she could finally put her feud with the Sangreals to bed, and perhaps tell herself that Tam and Cag's deaths had meant something. 'I'd like an idea of how long it will take once you're back in power. Just want to make sure I'm still alive when it happens.'

Ciera did not even look at her. 'I have many reforms in mind, of which Cliffark is one. I am interested in how *well* I can reorganise Erland, so that these changes can last long beyond the lifetimes of both of us, less so in how *quickly* I can do it.'

Tansa scowled. She did not care about whatever else Ciera had in mind for Erland. That could wait – the Cliffarkers were fulfilling their end of the bargain by joining her in an assault on Merivale, but the young queen had so far done nothing to show she was upholding hers.

Tansa was about to tell Ciera this, but she was interrupted

by the sight of two riders galloping towards them from the west. Immediately, she recognised Burik, a *hymerika* she knew from Merivale but who did not seem to recall her, and Sister Aimya, who was nursing a bandaged head. Several times, Tansa had heard Aimya making claims about what might await them as they neared Merivale – a tale of gods come down from Eryispek which Tansa had easily dismissed as nonsense. Everyone knew the Brides were half-mad. Tansa sensed that Ciera did not wholly trust the story either.

Ciera hailed them with a raised hand, and the pair brought their horses around to ride alongside them.

'What word from Lord Gurathet?' she asked Burik. The *hymerika*'s face was still heavily bruised from his fall down the stairs.

Tansa did not wholly understand for a moment – Orsian had told her Lord Gurathet had died in the siege of Merivale – until she realised Burik must mean one of his sons. The nobility set such store in ensuring their lands were passed on to their children; another reason she did not trust Ciera on Cliffark.

'He'd be glad to receive you at Hardhall,' replied Burik, 'though he says he can accommodate no more than fifty, and the rest are to stay at least five miles away.' His face hardened. 'Lord Madine is there too, discussing some land dispute. I wouldn't be surprised if he's already sent a man riding for Merivale to warn Balyard.'

'All the better that he's there,' said Ciera, undaunted. 'I mean for him to join us as well. I remember Hessian complaining that Madine didn't send enough men to Merivale – perhaps this time we might persuade him to be more generous.'

Burik frowned. 'Well, it won't be out of any sense of loyalty. The Barrelbreaker said once that if you asked to use Madine's privy he'd ask first what was in it for him. He didn't respond to our calls for aid against the Imperials either.'

Ciera gave a thin smile. 'No doubt he will say that our messengers failed to reach him. We will ride for Hardhall.' She turned behind her to where the captain of her father's guard rode, a clean-shaven blond man who always looked at Tansa as if sure she did not belong there, even if he could not figure out why. 'Jerem, keep the column moving. Watch for any riders heading to Merivale, and deal with them. I will return by morning.'

'I should stay with you, Majesty,' said Jerem. 'We don't know if we can trust these men.'

'If I do not return tomorrow, feel free to assault Hardhall.'

Sister Aimya spoke up suddenly, her words coming in a rush as if she had been reluctantly holding them back. 'Majesty, while you move against Balyard, we have no idea what Eryi and Vulgatypha are doing. We should ride to Merivale and make common cause with Lord Balyard.' Her voice strained with sincerity. 'If I tell him what I saw on the Mountain, he might listen.'

'He won't,' said Burik. 'But we should send riders towards Eryispek. Maybe by now my father and Lady Viratia have come down.' He looked to Ciera. 'They might confirm what Aimya's told us.'

Tansa considered telling the *hymerika* that if he thought anyone up on the Mountain had survived its summit erupting, he'd taken too many swords to the helmet, but Ciera spoke first. 'Aimya, I have not forgotten what you told me, but what would you have us do? Scour the country for these two gods that nobody else has seen? Perhaps eventually they will reveal themselves, but until then I must fight the foe in front of me, not the one that might be hiding in the shadows.'

Aimya glowered silently. It was perhaps the first thing Tansa agreed with Ciera on; once people accepted all-powerful gods existed it was not such a stretch to believing in all-powerful lords.

But, like Aimya, Tansa had learnt where the queen's priorities lay, and it was neither the bride's war against the gods nor the deal she had made with the rebellion. Tansa was very interested to see what she was prepared to offer these two lords for their allegiance, and she suspected it would be far more than she had granted the people of Cliffark.

Hardhall sat on a high bluff, close enough to the water that they could hear the waves roaring against the cliff as they approached. It was a stout, broad fortress forged in grey granite, patches of it coated in tree-green moss, surrounded by a low wall that a particularly agile horse might have been able to hurdle. A patchwork of dwellings on their way to becoming a town sat in its shadow, some built in stone but many more of straw and mud with steep thatched rooves. Tansa could see at least one inn, a windmill turning briskly in the coastal wind, and several granaries, but it was a bleak place, of dark, damp grass and dreary skies. The sort of place that made one glad to be from Cliffark.

'I didn't expect Gurathet to come from a place like this,' muttered Ciera as they approached.

'The Gurathets like strong wine and good steel,' said Burik. 'They keep their people fed, just about, but they've little interest in doing much more than that.'

There were eighteen of them, including the boy king and a nursemaid Ciera had found in Cliffark. Tansa had insisted on coming, and their company was rounded out by Sister Aimya and a dozen guardsmen.

They passed the gate, and curious eyes followed them as they ascended the gentle hill towards Hardhall, as if they were watching merpeople who had climbed up to them from the cliffs below. Mostly they were women – Tansa had seen the men toiling the fields outside the walls, bringing in a paltry-looking harvest.

A flag showing a black spear on a yellow field fluttered insistently from Hardhall's single tower, and as they approached a sole, sad bell began to toll, marking the middle of the day, but the weather was so grim it felt almost evening.

At the double doors to Hardhall, two lords waited for them, flanked by a half-dozen spears. The younger of them Tansa would have guessed was closer to thirty than twenty, but with a spreading gut that stretched his mail uncomfortably tight and marked him immediately as the new Lord Gurathet. He was grinning heartily, with bright red cheeks that suggested he might be simple, drunk, merely friendly, or all three.

The man standing beside him looked to be only slightly older, but minuscule, and Tansa did not think that was only by comparison to Gurathet. A pair of wild black eyebrows blossomed from a squashed, shrunken face, over two shrewd eyes like a pair of apple pips. This man did not wear mail, but a long cloak of dark wool clasped at the waist with a golden medallion, which only seemed to make him appear smaller. Tansa doubted there was more than an inch in height between this man and the diminutive Sister Aimya.

Beside her, Aimya sniggered. 'He wants to be careful in this wind, he might blow away.'

Ciera jerked her head around and scowled. 'Keep your voice down. That's Lord Madine.'

As they came to a stop in front of the door, the larger man strode forward and before anyone could stop him he hauled Ciera from the saddle as if she was a sack of grain, then sank to a knee, heedless of the wet grass. 'Lord Mikol Gurathet, at your service, Majesty! You honour me with your presence.' His head swivelled towards the horse on which the nursemaid was cradling King Andrick. 'And this must be the king! There's been no king in these parts since King Esrik went to war against my great-uncle Hesten.' He laughed heartily. 'Hesten the Halfwit my grandfather called him! Never go to war against a Sangreal.'

Lord Madine slinked forward, clasping his hands behind his back. 'Come now, Mikol. They did not come here to stand in the rain and listen to stories about your mad relatives.' He smiled and bowed, immediately putting Tansa in mind of a rodent seeking the choicest piece of cheese. 'Let's get inside and hear what the queen has to offer us.'

'I am delighted to meet both of you.' Ciera extended her hand to each of them, but Tansa saw how her gaze lingered on Lord Madine. Despite his stature, it was clear Ciera believed he was the power here.

The main doors opened directly into Gurathet's hall. The interior was blindingly bright, with two roaring fires and countless candles lit against the cold and damp of the outside. The wooden floor was awash with a patchwork of furs and fleeces, and at the far end of the hall past an empty bench a servant was turning a small pig over yet another fire. The air was crowded with thick smoke, strong enough to make Tansa's throat tickle and her eyes water.

Gurathet led them to a collection of chairs arranged around one of the fireplaces. He bid Ciera take the one nearest the heat, and seemed ready to assume the one beside her, until a slight but audible cough from Lord Madine caused him to think twice. Instead, Gurathet took a chair opposite, beside Madine.

Tansa would have been glad to get closer to the fire, but a look from Ciera told her to hang back. The chairs were not for servants. Burik and Aimya took the other seats, while Tansa lingered at the edge behind Ciera, silently seething at the injustice of it. She spied a knife with a gilded handle on a nearby table and stuffed it up her sleeve. If she could not trust the nobles, she could at least rob from them.

'Wine!' declared Gurathet. He clapped his pudgy hands together twice. 'Someone get on and serve it!' He was sweating slightly, either from the heat or from drunkenness – Tansa noted the two empty flagons on the table beside her.

The hall seemed strangely absent of servants. Ciera looked round. 'Tansa – wine for us all if you please.'

Tansa was sure she was not imagining the gleeful glint in Ciera's eye as she gave the instruction. *Bloody bitch.* There was no need for such pretence – neither Madine nor Gurathet would recognise her – it was purely to humiliate her. Nevertheless, she would play her role. She stepped forward, and poured wine for each of them, although Madine stopped her when his cup contained barely a thimbleful.

'I spotted your army in the distance this morning,' said Gurathet. 'Gave me quite a shock – had me wondering where my brothers had got so many men. I knew they wanted me gone, I just never realised how badly!' He laughed again, a little too loudly, slapping meatily at his thigh. When nobody else laughed, his face fell and he began to speak more sombrely. 'Not that my bloody brothers will stop me coming to Merivale with you.'

'I did not realise your brothers were causing you such trouble,' said Ciera.

Gurathet waved a hand carelessly. 'My father had too many sons and not enough land for all of us. I've dealt with them now, with Madine's help.

'Anyway.' He cleared his throat. 'My father was always a loyal friend to the Sangreals, and I mean to be the same. Lord Balyard or the Imperium, it makes no difference to me, I'll smash them just as I smashed my brothers.'

He was fumbling for the sword at his waist as if to demonstrate this when Madine put a hand on his shoulder. 'Lord.' His voice rustled like soft velvet cloth. 'If we are to march to Merivale, perhaps you should see to provisioning and arming your troops. I am sure the queen wishes us to be on the move as soon as possible, and it would inspire the men to have you giving them commands directly.'

Gurathet looked at Madine askance as if preparing to disagree. His face flushed a shade redder, but then he said, 'Right, yes. Good idea, Madine.' He rose abruptly, sloshing his wine. His eyes lingered on Ciera, and he bowed clumsily before adding, 'If you need anything while you're at Hardhall, Majesty, just come and find me.'

He hurried off, leaving the rest of them alone with Lord Madine. He let them sit in silence for a moment, the only sounds the crackle of the fire and Gurathet's heavy retreating steps.

Madine smiled over the top of his wine. 'He's very enthusiastic, is Lord Mikol. I've known him since we were boys. Such awful trouble he's having with his brothers.' He gave an exaggerated sigh.

'He's lucky to have you as an ally,' said Burik. 'My father always spoke very highly of you, Lord.'

Madine's mouth twitched. 'Oh, I doubt that. I am familiar with the terms in which martial men speak of me. A weakling and a weasel, a silver-stealing rat.' He leant back in his chair, a fire-tinged reflection dancing in his dark eyes. 'My father was a great warrior, just like yours, but he had no talent for lordship.' Tansa watched his gaze move to Ciera. 'I greatly admire *your* father, Majesty – he saw the potential of Cliffark, and in the space of fifteen years turned it into the envy of Erland.'

'My father has sadly passed,' said Ciera. 'But I am grateful for your kind words.'

'I am sorry to hear that.' Madine's voice was so flat he might have been speaking of the weather. 'But such a legacy. My wife is pregnant with our first. I hope one day to leave behind a legacy that is just as impressive.'

Tansa looked at the flagon, wondering if anyone would

object if she poured her own cup. There was a tension in the room; Madine was building to something, but Tansa could not yet see what. She watched Ciera, who was leaning slightly forward towards Madine, her brow furrowed.

'Alas, Lord Gurathet will have no such legacy,' said Madine. He took a tiny sip of wine. 'He has borrowed heavily from me to defend against the incursions of his brothers – his father took all the true fighting men with him when he became *balhymeri*, and, for all his bluster, Mikol is no warrior. Within a decade, all the land you can see from Hardhall will be mine, unless a sea serpent made of gold washes up on one of his beaches.' He paused meaningfully. 'So, Majesty, understand this: Mikol Gurathet by himself is as much use to the cause of you and your son as a sword made of straw. He will jump the way I tell him to jump.'

Ciera took a slow sip of wine. 'As you say. And I assume you set your own worth considerably higher.'

A small smile flashed across Madine's lips. 'I would say so. My lands along the coast are modest, but I have chosen my enterprises carefully. I have eight hundred warriors under my banner.'

'You never sent them to Hessian though,' interjected Burik. 'Where were they when we went to fight the Prindians?'

'A man could not bargain with Hessian,' said Madine. He did not even glance at Burik, his eyes fixed on Ciera. 'Too wild and too changeable. But if you are anything like your father, you will see the advantage of a mutual benefit.'

'Very well,' said Ciera. 'And what is it you want in return for your support?'

'My wants are modest,' Madine purred. He set his wine aside, undrunk. 'Firstly, neither you nor your son will interfere with my dealings on this length of coast between the lands belonging to Cliffark and those in the west belonging to the Darltons.'

Ciera blinked. 'Done.'

'Secondly, my taxes to Merivale are to be halved.'

'I can reduce them to seven-tenths.'

A brief pause. 'Agreed.'

Tansa watched, enraptured. Ciera was giving Madine exactly what he wanted; in Cliffark she had pulled at every single thread until their deal was a bare shadow of what they had originally sought.

Madine was ticking off his demands on his fingers. 'Finally,' he said, 'I lose too many peasants to Cliffark. They flee, and by the time someone realises they're gone they've already lost themselves in that maze of alleys, and only Eryi knows what happens to them there.' His face was wracked with apparent concern. 'It's not in their best interests – the city eats them up and spits them out. The men end up in debt and out at sea, and the women...' He grimaced. 'It is not for polite company. This land needs tighter controls on where the commonfolk may or may not sell their labour. Yes, I get their land back, but what use is that with no one to work it?' Madine shook his head. 'I'm always glad to look after them when they return, but really it would be better if they did not go in the first place.'

The gaze that Tansa turned on Madine could have blown his shrivelled head apart like a squashed prune, but through the heat and smoke of the hall he paid her no attention. *What he's proposing is practically thraldom.* Thraldom had been outlawed in Erland for centuries; she had expected Ciera to be more generous in her dealings with lords than she had been to the folk of Cliffark, but she could not possibly agree to that. That would not only be turning her back on reform, it would be rolling back rights that Erlanders had held for hundreds of years.

Ciera paused for several moments. Her face was so still it was as if she had stopped breathing. Yet, when she spoke, her voice betrayed nothing. 'In your lands only,' she said, 'and after twenty years of labour, your peasants must be free to leave.'

'Twenty-five, and I may use my own men to track down any absconders, even in Cliffark.'

'Done.'

CHAPTER 25

Orsian woke stripped to his underclothes, his skin frigid against the icy cobbles. Manacles locked him to the wall, and they rattled heavily as he was able to push himself to a sitting position, hugging his knees to his chest. He shivered uncontrollably, the hairs on his skin like a forest of spears.

He looked around himself, blinking against the gloom, wondering if he had ever left Piperskeep's dungeon at all or if that had been a vivid dream. But this cell was different to before, smaller, with a locked door containing a small open window covered by a wrought-iron crossbar. By the dim light, this cell was several floors above the previous one.

'Finally, you're awake. More's the pity. If not for these chains I'd have strangled you in your sleep.'

Errian's mocking voice broke the silent darkness. Orsian looked up, and saw his brother silhouetted in grey against the dark stone. He was as naked as Orsian, tied to the opposite wall beside the door.

'What are we doing here?' he croaked.

Errian coughed up a bitter laugh. 'I'm here because you betrayed us. Though looks as if your new friends weren't so keen on you as you thought.' He glowered at Orsian with murderous intent. 'What happened? Did some dungeon guard free you and you wormed your way out through the tunnels straight to the Imperium?'

'What?' Orsian's mind was moving too slowly. His head felt like it was made of sawdust. Recollections of events since leaving his old cell slipped through his memory like water. 'No... Balyard took me.' An image of Balyard's puce face in the darkness sparked Orsian's memory. 'He sold me to the Imperium!'

'And then what, you just decided you'd fight for them?' Errian clenched his fists and rattled at his chains, his eyes bulging. Orsian could tell that he would at that moment have gladly beaten him to a bloody pulp. 'Bollocks, traitor.'

'It's true! How else do you think I'd have got out?'

'Then why fight for them? You think being angry with me and Balyard gives you the right to betray Erland? After all we've fought for?'

Orsian's head was pounding. He pressed his fingers against his temples. 'I didn't...' Visions tumbled through his head, grating against his mind like fingernails on slate. A darkened tent and a man's false face flickering in the dim light. Climbing the walls and opening the gate, carving a bloody swathe from the Ram's Gate to Piperskeep, the terror of the shield wall and Errian's mad, blood-soaked face hovering above him as they fought in the dirt.

'I...' He put a hand on the wall for support. 'I did not know my own mind. The magus did something to me. He was inside my head.' He realised as he spoke how unconvincing that must sound; Errian knew nothing of any magus, nor of Eryi. 'Did you see the man, right after we fought, when the Legion broke through the gate?'

'I saw Drast Fulkiro stopping me from killing you.' Errian's disbelief was unmoved. 'Is he a magus now?'

'Errian, *think*! You know I would never betray Erland. And how would I have escaped the dungeon unless Balyard took me out? How do you think the Legion got inside the walls or took Piperskeep with so few men? There are two of them, the magus, Krupal, and—' Orsian paused, knowing what he was about to say would give his tale even less credence. '*Eryi*. Drast Fulkiro died, you heard that just as I did. That wasn't him, that was Eryi.'

A sliver of doubt appeared in Errian's face. 'They got inside your head and made you fight for the Imperium?'

'Yes. Though I barely remember it. Just pieces.'

Errian paused. 'And is that how I ended up here?' He slumped back against the wall, letting his chains go loose. 'I remember now. I tried to take his head off and my sword shattered in my hand. They told me to walk in here and I just did it.' Realisation dawned on his face, and then the fury surged back like a rising tide. 'By...' Errian twisted and lashed out at the door with his bare sole. 'Damn them all!' The door bounced against its hinges, and he kicked it again.

'Errian, stop!' Relief flooded through Orsian that his brother believed him. 'We need to find a way out of here.' Orsian could feel his mind clearing by the moment. 'He's got a plan for us, he told me; we need a way out.'

Errian was still raging, padding back and forth within the lengths of his chains like a caged beast. 'That's how they defeated us, magic. The Legion fought—'

'Yes, just as I said, and just as we defeated them when they nearly took Piperskeep the first time.' Quickly, Orsian told Errian of what he had experienced in the battle for Merivale, when he had felt Pherri's presence flooding through the *Hymeriker* and coordinating them to push back the Imperium.

By the time he finished, Errian had slumped to his haunches. He threw back his head and laughed. 'I guess it fits. Suppose I always underestimated her. Can she help us?'

'No, she's… she's away somewhere, I'm not sure.'

Errian came to his feet. 'Guess we're on our own then, until we can free the others.' He looked to the door, as if by sheer desire he might see through it and find where they were keeping the other *hymerikai*. 'How are we getting out of here?'

'Try pressing the bricks,' said Orsian, already turning towards his own wall to do the same. 'Maybe there's a passage out somewhere.' Piperskeep was a warren of passages; he would not have put it past the Sangreals of old to have a dungeon cell with a hidden exit.

They tried every brick they could reach, without success.

'How about the door?' suggested Errian. 'I can reach it.'

He aimed several more kicks at it, but it hardly moved. The wood was inches thick with solid hinges and the lock was beyond his reach.

Errian sank back, defeated. Orsian was still feeling about the cell, trying every inch for a section of brick that might suddenly rotate in his hand.

'What do you think he wants us for?' asked Errian.

Orsian stopped. 'I'm not sure. Something to do with Pherri? Eryi asked me about her. Maybe he thinks he can call her back with us. But there's another thing. He spoke of a goddess, Vulgatypha. He seemed to think there was something significant about Piperskeep, something that would help him defeat her. If—'

He was interrupted by the click of a key in the lock, and together the brothers turned towards the door. It opened in a glow of firelight, revealing two Imperial legionnaires each bearing a torch. Six more came behind them, and together they trooped into the cell.

Errian grinned madly. 'Eight on two, is it? Let me out of these chains and I'll show you how a *hymerika* dies. Come on, you Imperial sons of shit.'

Wordlessly, the legionnaires spread out. Three held each of

them tightly while a fourth undid the manacles, then a simple tunic and trousers were dragged onto their frames. Errian struggled, but Orsian remained still and allowed them to dress him.

'Save your strength,' Orsian told him. They were to be taken out of the cell, and if a chance to escape presented itself they needed to be ready.

Once they were garbed, the eight legionnaires escorted them out, four to a man. The walls were damp and green with mould, ominous even bathed in the yellow light of the Imperial torches. He and Errian had not been given shoes, and their bare feet slapped against the stone, echoing along the corridor.

Orsian looked left and right. They passed cells like their own, and he tried to steal a glimpse through the windows, wondering if they held members of the *Hymeriker*. If they could somehow seize the key, and hold off the Imperials long enough to open one of the doors, if they had not troubled to use the manacles—

A legionnaire shoved Orsian forward. 'Come on, faster.'

The legionnaires pushed them up the stairs, and Orsian hissed as his bare foot slid on the slick steps and his knee collided painfully with the edge. A legionnaire hauled him to his feet and forced him on.

As they ascended, Orsian blinked against the light, the glow of sconces becoming warmer with each step. When they reached the ground floor their guards turned them towards the great hall.

Orsian's eyes scanned the corridors as they passed, searching for something that might give them an opportunity to free themselves. He sensed Errian doing the same, but there was nothing. The keep seemed to be deserted, every passage and staircase as silent as the dead. It was as if every guard and servant of Piperskeep had fled during the night.

The carved double doors of the hall swung open as they approached, and the legionnaires forced them inside.

At the far end of the hall, atop the dais, Eryi waited for them. He had shed the face of Drast Fulkiro, revealing his own smooth, expressionless visage, his wide ice-pale eyes seeming to look everywhere at once. The walls were lined with armoured, blank-faced legionnaires, four-deep, their spears held upright towards the ceiling, their purple plumes standing in rows like a field of poison wheat. The room that ought to have been filled with the commotion of hundreds of *hymerikai* was still and silent, as if smothered with an unseen blanket of mist. Orsian's eyes roamed the rows of faces, searching for any recognition.

'I hope you don't mind witnesses, Orsian. It does me good to see men's faces again after so many centuries alone.' Eryi's voice seemed barely more than a breath of wind in his ear, and yet somehow filled the whole room. He glanced to Errian. 'And Errian. I am glad to meet you at last. I owe you more than you can possibly imagine.'

Errian faced him with his chin held high. Without warning, he began to struggle again against the grip of his guards, momentarily freeing an arm and punching one in the face before two more stepped forward to help their comrades. 'And I owe you a sword in the belly,' he snarled as they forced him to his knees. 'Where are my men?'

Eryi's laughter was like breaking ice. 'Such mindless defiance.' He gestured to his left. 'I kept your men safe for you.'

Together, Orsian and Errian looked to where Eryi was pointing, where Krupal stood off to the side at the edge of the dais. The magus's beard had become stringy and unkempt, covering a face that was a ruin of crags and liver spots. His robe half-drowned him, his once ample frame reduced to skin and bone. His eyes were heavily hooded, dull and lifeless.

But his appearance was far less shocking than the scene behind him.

Dozens of *hymerikai*, supine on their backs, still wearing their armour. They lay so still they might have been dead, but their chests still rose and fell with breath, and their staring eyes were bright with life. The closest to them lay at Krupal's feet, collapsed over the edge of the dais so that Orsian could not see his face. His hair had turned brittle, and his collarbone was sharp against grey skin. He looked like a man starved for weeks, driven to the edge of death.

Orsian was momentarily stunned into silence by the horror of it – he recognised some of these men – while Errian cursed and made to stride towards Eryi before being grasped by a pair of legionnaires. 'What are you doing to them?'

Eryi's mouth twisted. 'Putting them to use. Krupal lacks the necessary fortitude to eat enough to retain control' – he gestured around the hall at the silently assembled soldiers – 'so we have made other arrangements. With the life force of your *hymerikai*.' His eyes flicked down to the prone warrior. 'I think that one might be dead.'

Wordlessly, two legionnaires stepped forward and threw the man aside. A second struggling *hymerika* was dragged forward before Krupal. The magus dipped a hand to touch him and almost immediately their bodies started to change, the *hymerika*'s skin beginning to fade from his bones and his long hair turning to brittle strands of dust, as Krupal's hue began to brighten and his beard thickened.

Eryi stepped forward on the dais, his six plaits twisting like a nest of snakes. 'We have hundreds more in the dungeon. For you two though, I have a higher purpose.' He waved his hand towards the hall's ceiling, and a vision of the smoking summit of Eryispek appeared above them. 'In another life, we might have been allies, but alas the hour grows late.' His gaze flicked over their heads towards Krupal. 'As we discussed.'

Krupal waved a hand, and a team of legionnaires detached themselves from the walls. Four pairs of armoured hands seized Orsian and pulled him towards one side of the hall as Errian was dragged screaming and cursing to the other. The Eternal

Legion closed in, forming a square of bright shields the width of the dais, with Orsian in one corner and Errian in the other.

A pair of swords had appeared in Eryi's hand. He tossed one towards Orsian, and it spun through the air like a sycamore seed in an updraught. On instinct, Orsian reached for the leather hilt. The blade's weight sent a thrill through him as he turned it over in his hand.

Across the floor, Errian was still struggling, spitting and snarling at the four men who held him. A pair of circular wooden shields daubed with the red mark of the *Hymeriker* were thrown to the floor in front of them.

More legionnaires had moved to form a line in front of the dais. Orsian looked up at Eryi. He felt the weight of the blade in his hand, measuring the yards and realising he had no hope of reaching him before being overwhelmed by Imperials. 'Do you expect us to fight?' He tried to keep his voice level. 'We won't do it.' Though the way Errian was raging to get to Krupal and the *hymerikai* he might have been willing to fight anyone.

Eryi's face was a grim white mask. 'Have you ever wondered what happened to your mother? No, I don't want to spoil it for you. When one of you slays the other, here, where the blood of the Sangreals runs through the mortar as it runs through your veins, I shall summon the goddess to me.' His eyes widened, pale and impossibly bright. 'There is power in this keep. I saw it rise. I have seen it fall and rise and fall again a thousand times.' Eryi's dark power seemed to surge in him like a flash flood. 'King Piper did not raise this fortress with the strength of men alone; there is magic in this pile of stones, for those with the wit to see it.' He paused, and an ominous stillness filled the hall. 'And there is power in blood, and no more so than in the blood of the Sangreals. She must be defeated, before it becomes too late. If you knew her intentions, you would understand.'

Across the width of the square of legionnaires, Orsian met

his brother's eyes. Errian had finally stopped struggling, but was glowering at Eryi with undisguised hatred. Orsian had no idea what Eryi was talking about, but who could understand the whims of a god? Whether truly a god or not, the man was mad. 'And I suppose we're just meant to do as you command? I may not like my brother, but if you want him dead you can kill him yourself.'

Eryi's lips twisted in a smile that never reached his cold eyes. 'Observe.'

The magus passed his hand across the air in front of him, and from the ether a window formed, with shapeless grey shadows writhing within. Orsian squinted, and the figures sharpened as the window expanded, until above Eryi it filled a whole side of the hall.

From a world of darkness and shadow, the face of Andrick Barrelbreaker loomed above them, in profile, his head supported by a mountain of cushions. He was aged, his hair and beard both turned completely to white, with eyes that had once been as hard as shards of onyx now seemingly on the brink of tears. His face was drawn and strained with deep wrinkles. Two wizened, weakened hands gripped something, and yet were unable to stop themselves shaking.

Orsian could only stare. His father, as he might have been thirty or forty years from now. And then he spoke, and as the ghostly vision widened, Orsian saw to whom.

'Errian,' his father whispered, his voice somehow at once both heavy and feeble. 'I know you will serve King Jarhick well. My *balhymeri*.' He blinked, and with a final rasping breath Andrick Barrelbreaker passed from the world.

Orsian's gaze flicked to Errian. There were tears in his brother's eyes, but they were tears of renewed, righteous rage. His nostrils flared like a bull in heat, his breath blowing furnace hot.

'Andrick Barrelbreaker!' boomed Eryi. 'As he might have

been. He might have lived another thirty years, to watch his sons grow to manhood, to see his oldest son become *balhymeri*. He would have been so proud.'

'Errian,' said Orsian. 'Our father would not have wished to die like that. He would have sooner died on an axe blade than in a soft bed, with his strength ebbing away and his eyes failing. I grieve him every day, but he would never have wanted that.'

Errian looked up, his eyes as cold and black as a moonless winter night. His words came so quiet that Orsian almost did not hear them: 'You let him die. You caused all of this.'

Eryi threw the second sword into the air. With a snarl, Errian seized it from its flight, and charged towards Orsian.

CHAPTER 26

Helana waited at the edge of the woods, shifting anxiously from foot to foot against the pre-dawn chill, trampling the dew-glazed grass. To the east and across the plains, the stout walls of Irith loomed, legionnaires crawling the battlements like gold-armoured ants. The city's fortifications were not so high or thick as those of Merivale, but they were imposing enough. The western gate was still closed.

Rucius was late. Helana paced. *Bloody Imperial. Should never have trusted him.* He was probably still inside the city walls, drinking on her coin, laughing with his Imperial friends that the Erlanders had been foolish enough to let him go, again. She had hoped the promise of land and a lordship in East Erland would be enough to sway him, but evidently not.

Several more minutes passed. At the front of the cart, hidden slightly in the shadow of the trees, Helana could not fail to notice the uneasy glance that passed between Garwen and his son, Millas. *If he doesn't return soon, I'll have to go back and confess my folly to Rymond.* At least then he would be forced to set aside his hare-brained scheme, unless he decided to take his chances even if Rucius was currently spreading the tale all over the Imperial barracks.

'He'll come back,' said Garwen. The iron-haired veteran was leaning against a tree beside the cart. 'Did before, didn't he?'

'We can still get into the city,' said Millas, 'should be easy.' He indicated the several stacked barrels of ale behind him on the rear of the cart. 'What do we need Rucius for?'

Helana did not reply. She had not told the two men her plan. She had persuaded them to come with her in exchange for Helana returning Millas's gambled horse, but she doubted they would have been so keen had they known what she had in mind.

More time passed. The glow of the rising dawn now bathed the plains in soft sunlight, stretching the shadow of Irith's walls across the grass. Helana kept pacing. *Just a bit longer*. Then she would return to camp and admit to Rymond and Gruenla what she had done. The mercenary captain might drown her in one of the ale barrels. Helana counted the seconds.

'There!'

Millas stood up in the cart, pointing north-east towards a single rider galloping towards them, his legionnaire's armour flashing with sparks of reflected sunlight. He raised an arm in greeting, and as the horseman came into focus Helana recognised Rucius's silver-blond hair.

He pulled up a few yards from her and dismounted in a rush. 'I found it!' he exclaimed breathlessly, hurrying towards Helana. 'Took me half the night to get a man from the thirty-eighth division drunk enough, but he let it slip just before he passed out!' He took a moment to catch his breath, standing back with his hands on his hips. 'I've already been to look; it's right where he told me it would be.'

Helana let out the exhale it felt like she had been holding in for hours. 'Thank the Norhai.' She looked to Garwen and

Millas. 'Go with Rucius. Meet me back here as soon as you can. I'll go back to camp and tell Rymond.' Once she'd told him he might finally be prepared to give up on his absurd scheme.

She turned to rush back into the woods, but Garwen's voice stopped her. 'Hold on!' he cried. 'You've not even told us what it is we're collecting!'

'Rucius will tell you once you're there.' She did not want the two Erlanders growing fearful and backing out. 'Go.'

With only a little grumbling from Garwen, the three men were on their way, and Helana hastened back to camp, a few hundred yards away.

Preparations were already in full swing. The weapons had been split between three carts, hidden beneath layers of cabbages, wool, and corn. To give them their best chance, each would enter the city by a different gate. Two trusted men were preparing to set off with the cabbages cart. The rest were arranging themselves to look like peasants come to the city for the day, setting aside their armour and donning their filthiest cloaks and most threadbare tunics. The Ffriseans were sitting by themselves looking discontented, too conspicuous to be included with the men who would seek to enter Irith. The fires had been doused, and all the makeshift shelters torn down; whatever the outcome of the day, none of them would be returning here.

Helana looked around frantically. There was no sign of Rymond. 'Where's the king?' she asked a man busying himself with ensuring the wool was properly covering the swords.

The man looked up at her. 'He's already gone. Him and the Cyliriens left a quarter-hour ago.'

Oh, Eryi's balls. She was already too late. Without even thanking him, Helana turned to race back the way she had come, before halting and heading for the Ffriseans.

Chieftain Arka was sitting cross-legged among his men, frowning in concentration as he polished his great wooden staff with an oiled rag. He did not look up at Helana until she was standing almost directly on top of him.

'Arka, I need you, but we have to hurry.'

The chieftain looked up at her, his thick brows angled in puzzlement. 'Rymond say we wait here until time to attack gates.'

'No, change of plan. Hurry!'

The giant Ffrisean came to his feet maddeningly slowly, like a bent tree unfolding itself. 'Fine. We go.'

Helana raced back towards where she had left Rucius, trusting Arka to follow her.

A few hundred yards from Irith, Rymond was at that moment being manhandled towards its southern gate by Gruenla and a gaggle of Cyliriens. His hands had been bound in front of him, and every few steps he stumbled as a Cylirien prodded him in the back to make their ruse look genuine.

He felt as glum as if he were truly their prisoner. With every step closer they came to Irith, the reliability of a plan that in the relative safety of the woodland had seemed a gallant act of sacrifice and daring that was sure to win the hearts of his subjects seemed to diminish. What had he been thinking? Helana was right – this was madness. He had not even been able to say farewell to her that morning; she had disappeared, perhaps fleeing to Merivale alone when she realised he was genuinely going through with this.

Gruenla was walking on his right with a tight grip on Rymond's shoulder. 'I was thinking,' she said, smiling slightly. 'Wouldn't it be funny if we just took the reward money and left?'

'Don't even jest about it,' said Rymond. 'I am regretting this foolishness more with every step. And don't smile; what if a guard sees you?'

'You think jailers don't laugh with their captives?' Unexpectedly, Gruenla shoved him on the shoulder, which would have sent Rymond to the ground had she not been quick to grasp his arm. The Cyliriens sniggered to one another. 'If you can't stop being so damn serious I might let you fall next time. If this is my last day, I mean to live it with a smile on my face. We're coming in with you, what could go wrong?'

'Ho!' A cry from the battlements stopped them in their tracks, a hundred yards or so from the gate. 'Who goes there?' The speaker was an Imperial soldier, his tell-tale purple plume vivid against the brightening sky.

Gruenla raised a hand and shouted something back in what Rymond could only assume was Ulvatian.

'What did you say?'

'That I've got a lunatic here who reckons he's Rymond Prindian.'

The guard had turned away, and looked to be in deep discussion with someone behind him. After several moments, he turned back to them and called again across the grass, 'Drop your weapons where you are, and bring him another fifty yards forward! Someone will come down to you.'

Rymond looked to Gruenla. They had not been prepared for the possibility the Cyliriens would have to disarm.

She shrugged. 'Six of us weren't going to take on the whole Eternal Legion by ourselves. We'll find weapons on the other side. You still sure about this?'

Rymond nodded reluctantly. It was too late to back out now. His mouth was suddenly as dry as ashes. 'Best do as he says before I change my mind.'

The Cyliriens disarmed, and the seven of them walked forward to within fifty yards of the gate. One side of the double doors creaked open, and three Imperials rode out. The two in the rear were legionnaires, but the man who led them wore no helmet to cover his bald pate, and his golden breastplate was decorated with swirls of purple enamel.

He pulled up before them, a flint-eyed, full-jawed man with slightly protruding ears and a forehead rutted with deep furrows. His mouth was set so firmly that Rymond doubted he could have smiled even if he was of a mind to. He sensed immediately that this must be Acques Bazar. Beside him, he felt Gruenla and the Cyliriens tense.

Bazar's steely gaze fixed on Rymond. 'I knew you would come.' His eyes twinkled as if on the verge of amusement. 'Glad I saved myself the trouble of rounding up thousands of Erlanders to kill in your place. Though it appears I misjudged you; you have been such a thorn in our side these past months that I expected you would be brave enough to hand yourself in.' He cast an eye over the Cyliriens. 'You want the reward then?'

The way Gruenla was looking at Bazar could have poisoned a barrel of fish. 'That's why we're here.'

The supreme legate made a noise in his throat and produced from the rump of his horse a heavy burlap bag rattling with coins. He held it up. 'Hand him over and I'll throw it to you.'

'We thought we might escort him inside the city,' said Gruenla. 'My men and I have a taste for Imperial gold. For—'

Bazar's laughter was like a hinge in need of oiling. 'No. The Imperium has no need of Cylirien mongrels. To catch a rat, send a rat, but I'll not have your sort in my city.' His hand came to rest on the curved golden pommel of his sword. 'Hand him over and get out of here.'

Well, so much for planning, Rymond thought. He was not even inside the city, and the whole thing was already crumbling. He could not even look at Gruenla and try to work out what she was thinking; that would give their ruse away.

'How do I know all the gold is there?' said Gruenla. 'I'll need to count it first. I can't do that out here.'

'You can give us the prisoner and take the gold, or I can keep the gold and take the prisoner along with your lives.' Bazar gave some imperceptible signal to his guards, who drew their swords with a shriek of steel. 'Your choice.'

The Cyliriens bristled, teeming with repressed fury, but Rymond knew they had already lost. They had twice Bazar's number, but the Imperials were armed and ahorse. All the Cyliriens' weapons had been discarded in the grass fifty yards away. They might still have some knives hidden about themselves, but they would do little.

Gruenla gave a stiff nod. 'The first one then.' She shoved Rymond forward.

'Wise choice.' Bazar threw the bag to Gruenla. He looked down at Rymond. 'To the gate. Your mother is waiting for you.'

'How is she?'

'Spirited.'

Rymond was surprised not to see Alcantra with Bazar. He felt sure she would have enjoyed his downfall. 'Where is Alcantra?'

'Missed her, did you? Alcantra is indisposed.'

Rymond went ahead of the three Imperials. As they headed towards the gate, he cast a look back. The Cyliriens were just standing there, watching him go. He had wondered if they might rush for their weapons and attempt to make a fight of it, but they would never have made it.

It's fine, he told himself, as a panicked sweat broke out at the back of his neck. Entering without the Cyliriens was just a minor hiccup. This would save the thousands that Bazar had sworn to execute. Once enough of his own men were within the walls, they would save him, and when the people of Irith rose with them, they would outnumber the Eternal Legion ten times over or more.

Approaching the gate, Rymond caught the smells and sounds of the city, as familiar to him as his own face in the mirror. It was barely past dawn, but already he heard the roll of a cart over the cobbles and the cries of its owner announcing the best roasted chestnuts in the city. Their warm, rich scent mingled with the earthy haze of woodsmoke, morning cookfires already blazing into life. He smiled. This was still his city, and he would take it back, with or without the Cyliriens.

'Stop.' A legionnaire jabbed Rymond in the back with his boot, and he came to a halt before the gates.

He looked over his shoulder towards Bazar. 'Are we going in?'

'Not yet,' said Bazar. Rymond could hear heavy wheels rolling towards the gate.

Two horses stepped out, pulling a four-wheeled flatbed cart carrying a high, narrow cage forged in steel. With a sinking feeling, Rymond realised it must be intended for him.

'It would not do to have you walk in a free man,' said Bazar. 'And it's no bones to me, but if you want your people to remember you well, I suggest you face the axe like a man, not pissing and pleading like some damn Cylirien.'

'It is the axe then?' said Rymond. He tried to sound calm, but his heart was beating like a blacksmith's hammer. 'That's a relief, I was expecting the noose.'

'A relief.' Bazar's lip quirked, almost threatening a smile, but when he spoke his voice was stiff as iron. 'Rymond Prindian, mere months ago, you stood in front of this very city and swore your fealty, declaring the kingdom of West Erland to be a territory of the Ulvatian Imperium. You are guilty of treason, rebellion, and the murder of the kzar's soldiers. For these crimes, your limbs shall be divided from your body, with one to be sent to every corner of West Erland. Your wounds shall be closed, and the rest of you hung from the walls of Irith Castle until you are dead. May Parmé go gently on you.'

By the end of Bazar's sentence, Rymond was hardly listening, hot blood thrashing in his ears like a river of fire, his gossamer-light legs on the verge of giving way beneath him. He forced down a dry swallow, and lifted his head high as the legionnaires led him to the cage. *Hold it together*, he told himself. *They are coming for you.*

On the other side of Irith, Helana was approaching the city's north gate with Garwen and Millas. They had all changed into peasant garb, with the two men at the front driving the horse and Helana sitting at the rear with the barrels, dressed in a plain roughspun skirt and a coarse blouse. Rucius had gone ahead of them, still in his legionnaire's uniform.

They joined the queue of wagons and people in front of the gate. Behind them came the cart of cabbages with swords hidden underneath. She recognised the man driving from camp, but he had not looked twice at Helana, so she was satisfied that her disguise was a good one.

Helana twisted her neck to look towards the gate. It was taking forever; the sentries were questioning everyone. As she watched, a man was dragged from his cart while several legionnaires pulled apart his cargo, ripping open every single sack and scattering vegetables onto the ground. The vendor and his wife could only watch, dismay plain on their faces.

Garwen dismounted from the front and walked round to the rear. 'We'll never get through here, Princess. We should leave while we can.'

'If we run they'll know something's up,' hissed Helana. 'And if you don't want to get caught, don't call me "Princess".' She paused. She did not feel good about what they would have to do. 'Just stick with the plan. Rucius hasn't failed us yet.'

Garwen blew out his cheeks, and glanced to the wagon

behind them, but said nothing. 'All right, but this had better work.'

Slowly, the line crept forward. Helana began to fret they had left it too late; what if the executions began before they got there? The carts going to the west and south gate might already be inside, unless they had been caught. By the time there was only one wagon ahead of them, her heart was thudding fit to burst, and her skin was glazed with a layer of sweat.

The wagon ahead was ushered through, and then it was their turn. Three legionnaires approached, one towards Garwen at the front and two coming around to the rear. Helana saw Rucius, standing apart, leaning against a gate post. She caught his eye, and he pushed himself away from the wall.

'Your own ale?' asked a legionnaire, leaning into the cart and sniffing at the barrels.

Helana nodded. 'My father brews it,' she said, indicating towards where Garwen was speaking with the lead sentry with his head bowed. She suppressed a wince as she realised she had not disguised her accent. Hopefully the Imperials were too unfamiliar with Erlish dialects to notice.

The two legionnaires began inspecting the nearest barrels until they were joined by Garwen and the third sentry. Garwen's forehead was drenched in sweat, which he was wiping away with his sleeve.

'We'll open them all.' The lead Imperial pointed to the one nearest Helana. 'Start with that one.'

Garwen blew out his cheeks. 'All right. I'll have to get my lad to do it; I'm not as young as I was.' He called forward to Millas. 'Boy, get back here!'

Helana stepped aside to stand as Millas appeared with hammer and chisel in hand. He climbed into the cart and began removing the rings with practised efficiency and rhythmic strikes to the chisel.

The youngest legionnaire tasted the contents of the first

barrel, made a face, then said something in Ulvatian that made the other two laugh. As each lid came off, the Imperials inspected the contents carefully, first sniffing and then cupping their hands in for a drink, then shrugged. Soon enough, Millas was wrenching the lid of the fourth barrel. Helana was growing tense, and she could feel the nervous heat emanating from Garwen. Where was Rucius?

'Hey!' A loud shout came from the cart behind, and everyone's head turned.

Rucius was standing beside it, holding a sword aloft. He shouted something in Ulvatian, then threw the sword down and reached into the cart for another. The two Erlanders manning the cart looked at one another and started running.

The legionnaires searching Helana's cart reacted immediately. The two in the flatbed leapt down and gave chase, while Rucius continued to pull more swords from beneath the cabbages.

The captain's eyes were wide as Imperial medallions. He gave Garwen a cursory glance. 'Go.' He hurried towards the cabbages.

'Quickly!' hissed Garwen. 'Before they change their mind.' Helana rushed with him to the front, leaving Millas in the back. Garwen whipped the horse's reins and the cart began to roll forward, drawing a cry from Millas as ale sloshed over the side of one of the barrels.

The cart trundled beneath the gate arch onto the cobbles, and Garwen wiped the sweat from his head, now absolutely dripping. 'Eryi's balls, thought we were done for.' He spared a glance back through the gate to where the two Erlanders had been caught and forced to the ground. 'Don't feel good about that though. What if none of the other carts get through?'

Helana did not want to think about it, nor what the legionnaires might do to the two men they had just sacrificed. 'It doesn't matter. This is more important.'

Garwen grimaced. 'How do you know? You've still not even decided what we're going to do with it! Where are we even going?'

Helana looked around the streets of Irith. She had been here once before, but none of the surroundings looked familiar. The north side was Irith's Old Quarter, a quieter area of high houses and airy gardens. They fell in behind a slow-moving wagon stacked with silks, and the merchant driving it glanced back and gave their cart a disdainful look up and down. A man walking alongside them called out: 'Good sir! Wench! A mug of your finest ale!'

Helana ignored him and took a deep breath. 'Just follow the flow of people,' she told Garwen. She looked to the south-east, to the high hill of Irith Castle. She raised her arm and pointed. 'That's where they'll take him. We need to hurry.'

With his hands gripping the bars of his cage, Rymond watched the castle of his birth grow closer with each rotation of the wagon's wheels. The crowd thickened, all of them moving the same way, but the citizens of Irith kept their distance, mindful of the spears and irritable tempers of the horse-backed legionnaires arranged around the cage. Bazar rode behind, surrounded by his own guards and attendants. Sometimes, Rymond watched his captor instead; Acques Bazar scanned constantly over the crowd, raising his nose to the air as if he might scent unrest before it happened.

Rymond eyed the citizens also. They seemed cowed, the few who met his gaze staring back with dull, uncomprehending eyes. It was possible they did not recognise him; he was haggard, filthy, and bearded, whereas King Rymond had always appeared to them clean and closely shaven, in rich green silks and velvets. The worse thought was that they did recognise him, and did not care, and who could blame them? When the city had last seen him he had been out of his mind on casheef, proclaiming that he was giving his kingdom over to the Imperium. If he were executed, some of them might cheer it.

A lone voice from the mass shook Rymond from his reverie: 'Hail King Ry!'

A few half-hearted echoes rose from the indistinct murmur of the crowd, but Bazar was swift to put an end to it. 'Who said that?' he demanded, standing up in his stirrups and scanning the crowd hawkishly. 'Five golden medallions to whoever brings me the man who said that!'

The murmuring ceased, but nobody cried out to reveal the culprit. The crowd's air was one of apathy, as if they cared neither for the fate of Rymond nor the man who shouted, but equally would not trouble themselves to condemn them. Rymond allowed himself a smile. He could work with apathy; he had worked with his own for most of his life.

The throng became even denser as they approached the gentle incline leading to the castle. Shield-bearing legionnaires stood on both sides, funnelling the crowd towards the castle. Rymond hoped his mother was flattered that so many were turning out to watch her die.

Acques Bazar, however, had evidently lost patience. 'Forward!' he demanded. 'Clear a path!'

The cavalrymen hurried to obey. Expertly, they formed themselves into a wedge, and with a cry increased their pace to a fast canter that beat out a staccato rhythm on the cobbles. The man on the bench ahead of Rymond cracked his whip, and the two horses dragging the cart increased their pace. Erlanders leapt out of the way to avoid the mass of horseflesh, crying out in terror as they tumbled into one another or went down beneath the pounding hooves. The road was wide, but still some were forced into the soldiers lining the way, who set to pushing them back with their shields and lashing out with armoured fists.

Rymond had seen enough. He turned to the rear of the cage and called to Bazar: 'That's enough! People will die!'

Bazar gave no indication he had heard him, just spurred his mount on in the wake of the cavalry wedge, and within moments they had made a clear path up to the castle, Erlanders falling back to either side. As he looked back, Rymond saw some holding crimson-sodden cloths to their heads, while others had failed to rise. The air was filled with the wailing of children and the angry protests of men as legionnaires continued beating them back.

And before Rymond had a chance to object again, the column of Imperials had left them behind. The legionnaires' horses slowed, and the crowd thinned and moved aside.

Rymond stared back in disbelief. Had it been like this when he was in his room, hallucinating while his people suffered? He had never realised, hardly even wondered. His fists tightened against the bars of the cage. He had condemned them to this.

He was so incensed that he hardly noticed the cart had stopped beside the castle's outer wall, not until Supreme Legate Bazar pulled his horse up alongside the cage.

'Most touching,' he said serenely. 'I do believe you actually care. Perhaps you are not what I was led to believe.' Absently, Bazar drew his knife and held it to his eye, polishing its already shining face with a scrap of cloth. 'It is all for nothing, you know. You may rage and you may plead, but you will die, the same as your countrymen. This is a weak city, in a weak land, full of sloth and vice, and you, Rymond, are a man made in its image.' He spoke without feeling, as if reading a report of a subordinate. 'Some are simply born to be slaves.'

He cast an arm along the wall. Slightly aside from the main gate, they had erected a podium, occupied only by an axe leaning against a block. Thousands of legionnaires three-men deep stretched all the way along the wall, dividing the structure from the watching mass of Erlanders. The battlements were crowded also, with crossbow-wielding legionnaires spaced only feet apart.

'Such a turnout, for such a death,' continued Bazar. 'Do you understand why you need to die, as ineffective a ruler as you were? No? Allow me to explain: a people is its symbols, and the Prindians are a symbol of West Erland. The mistake the Sangreals made hundreds of years ago – the mistake Alcantra made – was allowing the Prindians to survive. While you live, Erland will forever be West and East, as long as the people can look up and see something that separates you from them. They eat the same food, speak the same language, worship the same gods, and yet you fight one another like cats in a sack. The Prindians are memory, and for as long as West Erland has that, they can never truly be enslaved.' He had finished polishing his knife, and finally replaced it in its sheath. 'We do not need to eradicate a people to take their land; we only need to make them forget who they are. Starting by removing you.'

'A people is more than its symbols,' Rymond croaked. He would have gladly surrendered his title in exchange for a cup of wine. 'This has been West Erland for hundreds of years.' He had never truly thought about how remarkable it was that its people – *his* people – still endured. Something Garwen had told him echoed in his ears: '*Whether it takes thirty days or thirty years, I want our country back*.' For as long as there were men like Garwen, West Erland would survive. Rymond had never before thought of kingship as a duty to do right by such men, those willing to give their lives for his kingdom, but perhaps imminent dismemberment had a way of revealing the truth. 'Kill me if you must, but you will never erase that.'

'We shall see.' Bazar turned away. 'Enough talk. Would you like to see your mother?'

Rymond followed the man's gaze towards the main gate.

The portcullis rose, and a cage not unlike Rymond's own emerged.

Her dress was an emerald mosaic of shimmering silks and lush velvets, cinched at the waist and fanning out so far at the bottom that it took over the cage. Her hair flowed like a shifting cascade of fire-tinged gold, and her fingers, neck, ears all dripped in jewellery. Even as a prisoner, Breta Prindian stood with the pride of a queen.

'Do not worry,' said Bazar. 'We'll give your mother a clean death. Then it's your turn.'

CHAPTER 27

On a bed made from stitched animal skins stretched over a frame of bones, Pherri tossed and turned through the night. It was the first time she had slept in a bed since she had last been at the Piperskeep of her own world, so many months ago, and despite the plainness of the furnishings it ought to have felt like the height of luxury. The words of the Sorrowseer though had unbalanced her. Her dreams were a maelstrom of butchery. A knife shaking in her fists as she stood over Phyrrai's sleeping frame, that when she tried to resist plunging it into her shadowtwin's heart turned into a snake, and the reptile wrapped itself around Pherri's arms and crawled to her neck to crush against her windpipe, and then the dream shattered into fragments and other versions of herself were standing over yet more shadowtwins, some killing and some being killed, an endless chain of mirrors reflecting back all the infinite possibilities.

Pherri forced herself awake, and sat up in bed with sweat pouring off her in sheets. Her skin was aflame, her eyes were red and swollen, and her head felt as if she had drunk several flagons of wine. She rushed to the chamber pot and vomited, her vision swimming with dancing black spots. She groaned, and vomited again. At the bottom of the pot among the bile and the half-digested goat were stringy streaks of blood.

Phyrrai's warm hand appeared on her back. 'Don't,' Pherri gasped. The sensation of her shadowtwin's skin on her own only made it worse. She fell to her hands and knees, and crawled back to the bed, taking deep desperate breaths. 'Water,' she gasped.

She heard Phyrrai's bare feet slapping against the floor, then the creak of the door and a bang as it slammed shut. Pherri lay with her eyes closed and her head against the bed, groaning and gasping, the acidic taste of bile in her throat, silent tears flooding down her cheeks. Every inch of her body felt as if it were on fire and screaming.

Phyrrai returned with a bucket of water, which Pherri took several hungry gulps of before pouring half of what remained over her head. She set the bucket aside and sat up with her back against the bed, savouring the cooling liquid as it ran down her back and chest and soaked into the coarse nightgown Hawla had given her.

'Thanks,' she murmured, once she no longer felt like her organs were trying to break out of her skin. Pherri rubbed her eyes and looked up at Phyrrai. Her shadowtwin was pale with worry.

'What is it?' whispered Phyrrai. 'Are you ill?'

Pherri shook her head. 'Slept badly. Strange dreams.' She remembered her nightmare again and shuddered. 'The Sorrowseer...' Pherri paused; she could hardly tell Phyrrai that the Sorrowseer had said Pherri must murder her. 'It was just... unsettling.' She ran her hands over her face and through her soaking hair, and forced herself to smile. Shakily she pushed herself up to sit on the bed. She looked at Phyrrai again. Unlike Pherri, her shadowtwin seemed to be in the best of health, if still slightly shocked at what she had woken up to. 'Did she... What did she say to you?'

Phyrrai frowned. 'Just that I had to help you.' She scowled. 'I don't trust her though – they killed Da'ri. And I'm helping you anyway, not because she told me to.' Phyrrai reached out a hand to Pherri, and then seemed to change her mind. 'What can I do?'

'Nothing, I'm fine, honestly. Probably just some bad goat. Please don't tell anyone I was sick.' The blood was troubling, but she did not want anyone asking questions about what the Sorrowseer had said to her.

Pherri looked around their hut. She had been too tired the night before to take it in properly. It was circular, with rough, unsanded floorboards, identical twin beds, a heavy stone chamber pot, and a single square window covered with flimsy gauze that allowed in just enough light to see by. By the brightness outside it was already morning. Pherri stretched up her arms and yawned. She felt exhausted, but she had no choice but to get up and face the day; she needed to learn more about what the Sorrowseer had told her, and then she had to escape. The Sorrowseer had as good as confirmed that she should go to Pipersmont, so for now she would focus on that and ignore the darker half of her vision.

'Do you think we'll be fed?' she asked Phyrrai.

'We should go and look. And we need to make sure Halyana is well.'

'And Hrogo.' Neither of them mentioned Jarhyck.

'We should let them think we're cooperating,' said Phyrrai, dropping her voice. 'Make them think we trust them while we work out how we're getting out of here.'

'Agreed,' said Pherri. She doubted though that Phyrrai would be so keen for them to continue travelling together if she knew what the Sorrowseer had said to Pherri.

Together they dressed, replacing their Sorrowland nightgowns with the hardy travelling clothes that had got them this far, trying to ignore their smell. They might have asked the

Sorrowlanders to wash them, but neither was willing to trust their captors – hosts, Hawla might have claimed – with their clothing.

They had dressed and were ready to leave when there was a double knock at the door and Hawla entered, bearing two steaming cups. Her horns brushed against the ceiling. She smiled. 'Good morning. Did you sleep well?'

'Very well, thank you.' The words tumbled out of Pherri's mouth before Phyrrai could contradict her. 'And thank you for your generous treatment.'

'It is the least we can do.' Hawla handed them each a wooden cup. 'The Sorrowseer was most intrigued by you. She's asked that you both attend her again today, together.'

Pherri suppressed a shiver at the memory of the Sorrowseer's stifling tent. Her head was still a little woozy, but the fragrant steam rising from her cup stirred her senses, and when she took a sip it tasted of cloves and nutmeg, though she doubted the Sorrowlanders had access to such things.

'We would be honoured,' said Phyrrai, though Pherri could tell she did not mean it.

Hawla smiled again. 'You must be hungry.' She held the door open for them. 'Come.'

Pherri stepped outside, and was struck again by the foreignness of their surroundings. The black ground was rough and uneven, like rock pools left when the tide had gone out, and the stakes of the ring fort were so pale it was as if the wood had been bleached. Even the sun seemed different here, bright with an orange glow that penetrated the low bank of cloud hanging over them.

Hawla led them past the women already at their work, tending gardens and pulling water from the well, to an open central pavilion, where surrounded by three long tables several spits were being roasted over a low burning fire pit. As they approached, Pherri saw that the creatures being roasted were snakes and lizards. Phyrrai gave a sharp intake of breath.

'We are not blessed with varied livestock,' said Hawla, as if reading their minds. 'And sometimes we grow tired of eating goat.'

At the end of one of the long tables, Hrogo was sitting with Halyana, who noticed them and waved.

'Go to your friends,' said Hawla. 'I will bring you food.'

She departed, and Pherri and Phyrrai joined them at the table.

Pherri still did not feel well, and by the look of Hrogo neither did he. His face was drawn, with dim eyes and a tense, tired frown, and he looked to be shivering slightly. Halyana appeared to have slept well, though the girl was mute as ever.

'What's the matter?' asked Pherri, sitting down beside Hrogo as Phyrrai slid in at the end beside Halyana. 'Did you sleep badly?'

Hrogo was hunched over his trencher, picking at a length of thin, charred snake with a blunt knife. 'Terribly,' he grunted. 'They've had to put guards on my door to stop the women disturbing me.' He did not seem pleased by the prospect. 'And I've been ill this morning.' His eyes slid sideways to where Hawla was preparing a serving for Pherri and Phyrrai. 'Where have they put you?' he asked, keeping his voice to a whisper.

'Together in one of the huts,' said Phyrrai. She gestured towards where they had come from.

'What do you think of them? Of her?'

Pherri chewed her lip doubtfully. 'I'm not sure.' Her eyes slid towards a group of Sorrowwomen eating at the other end of the table. 'They seem nice enough. Different to the men.' She glanced along the table towards Phyrrai. 'I think we should be patient, for now.' She took another sip of Hawla's tea, hoping it might clear her still aching head.

Like Phyrrai, she did not want to trust them. That would

mean trusting the sickening prophecy of the Sorrowseer. But nobody else had offered her a solution for returning to her own world. And the Sorrowseer knew who Vulgatypha was. As horrifying as it was, what if the Sorrowseer was right? She looked up at Phyrrai. Could she do it? The fate of existence might depend on it.

Phyrrai's attention was elsewhere, listening to the chatter of conversation between the Sorrowwomen at the other end of the long table. A few of the syllables seemed familiar, even in their guttural tones, but Pherri could not understand any of the words. 'It's a bit like Ancient Meridivalian,' murmured Phyrrai to herself. 'Because they're so isolated here I suppose the language hasn't changed much.'

'How do you know Ancient Meridivalian?' asked Pherri.

Phyrrai looked at her. 'Da'ri taught me.' She seemed startled by the question. 'Did your Da'ri teach you any?'

Pherri was saved from having to tell Phyrrai that he hadn't by Hawla's reappearance. The chieftainess placed down trenchers of charred, stringy reptile before them. 'After breakfast, you may return to your huts and rest,' she told them. 'The Sorrowseer wishes to speak to you at noon.'

Hrogo glanced up. 'To who? All of us?'

'Only Pherri and Phyrrai. I have arranged for you to be introduced to the ways of our goat-riders. There are some younger boys who speak Erlish to a passable standard.'

Hrogo cringed, looking even more pained than before. 'Must I? I don't feel well.'

He did not look well either. As he spoke, Pherri realised his nose had begun to trickle blood, which turned her own uneasy stomach. 'Hrogo, your—' Pherri raised an illustrative finger to her nostril, and when she took it away it came with a smear of crimson on it. Frowning, she touched her nose again, and more appeared. 'I'm bleeding.' She felt suddenly as if her head was too heavy, that she could no longer support its weight. Her stomach heaved, and more bile rose in her throat. She tried to swallow it with a sip of still steaming tea and almost gagged.

Hrogo touched his own nose, and when he saw the blood on his finger paled even further. 'Oh no.' He tried to rise from the table, but somehow got his feet tangled in his ankle chain, then toppled backward off the bench with a yelp.

'It's probably the strange food,' said Hawla, unperturbedly, gesturing to a pair of Sorrowwomen who hurried to Hrogo's aid. 'Or the change in climate. Take him back to his hut.'

Hrogo half-walked, half-stumbled away, the two Sorrowwomen supporting him. Pherri watched him go, wondering if he too had been woken by violent vomiting and an awful headache. She touched her nose again, and found the blood was still flowing. Hawla's explanation made no sense; the weather was mild, and Pherri had not even touched her food.

Say nothing. She looked up at Hawla. 'Most likely. I'm sure we'll get used to it.' Pherri took a small bite of snake, and though it felt like her stomach was about to escape from her mouth managed to force it down. It was important she kept her strength up.

Halyana was tugging at Phyrrai's sleeve, pointing across the fort to the gate. Phyrrai appeared confused for a moment until she realised what Halyana wanted. 'How is King Jarhyck?'

Hawla smiled thinly, her narrow eyes flashing dangerously. 'Your cousin is well cared for. Do not concern yourself.' She looked to Pherri and Phyrrai. 'I will meet you both at noon.'

Pherri was relieved when Hawla had departed. Her nose would not stop running, and she swore she could feel her blood vessels pressing against the inside of her skin. Her stomach rumbled, but she was too fearful of what might happen to try any more of her breakfast. She let out a breath of pain and felt a fresh splatter of warm blood splash from her nose and down her face.

Phyrrai hurried around the table to help her rise from the

bench. Pherri felt so weak that she was able to ignore the frisson of discomfort that ran up her spine at her twin's touch. 'Back to the hut?' asked Phyrrai, her brow creased in concern.

Pherri's eyes were filling with tears. 'Please,' she gasped.

Leaning on Phyrrai, she hobbled back to the hut, ignoring the pointed stares of the Sorrowwomen and the stalking steps of two guards following fifteen paces behind them. Pherri collapsed over the threshold, and with her last vestige of strength threw herself onto her bed and let sleep take her.

When Pherri woke, Hawla was sitting over her, spooning a cold fluid into her mouth. It tasted slightly of sulphur, but she managed to resist her initial nausea and keep it down. Phyrrai hung back by the wall, worry etched on her face.

'You are a calmer patient than the man,' murmured Hawla, putting down the spoon and helping to manoeuvre Pherri to a sitting position against the head of the bed.

Pherri opened her mouth to speak, but was immediately distracted. There was someone else in the hut with them. She edged a look around Hawla towards the entrance.

The Sorrowseer was sitting against the door. In the light of day, Pherri realised that what she had taken as a face was actually a mask, a pale, glossy approximation of a young woman, with pouting bright red lips, dark brows, and a sleek nose. How had she ever thought that was the Sorrowseer's actual face? The darkness of her tent and the lateness of the hour had been playing tricks on her.

'When I heard you were taken ill, I thought it best if I came to you.' Her voice was a soft and soothing melody.

Pherri blinked back at her, struggling to keep her head raised under the weight of her exhaustion. 'Why do you wear a mask?'

The mask remained still, but Pherri swore she saw amusement in the curl of its mouth and in the bright, dark irises that danced in the holes cut for the eyes. 'The sad affliction of vanity. I am old, and the years in my face shame me.'

'The Sorrowseer grew up with my grandmother's grandmother,' said Hawla. 'The years have given her wisdom.'

There was something reassuring about learning that the Sorrowseer was flesh and blood, even with the uncanny mask, and not some apparition of the heat of the tent. If the Sorrowseer was human, that meant she was fallible, and perhaps she was wrong that Pherri would have to kill her twin.

'Do you have a true name?' said Phyrrai, leaning against the side of the hut. 'We can't just keep calling you "Sorrowseer".'

The eyes behind the mask blinked slowly. 'Names are strange things. Much store is placed in them, and yet, when you stare into the eyes of someone who is as much *you* as yourself yet has a different name, they seem like fragile, impermanent things, do they not? Pherri could be Phyrrai and Phyrrai Pherri, yet even such a small change would cause you great distress.'

Pherri met Phyrrai's eye, wondering how it would feel to be her. Her shadowtwin's smile was thin, but Pherri could feel the affection in it. They had been through a lot together, and despite for a time being unable to bear to look at or touch one another had fallen into an easy camaraderie. It was unsettling though, like your reflection staring back from the mirror and talking to you. Yet no matter their similarities, they were different people.

'I hardly see what that has to do with you not having a name,' said Phyrrai, folding her arms aggressively across her chest. Pherri wondered if her previous experience with the Sorrowseer had been more troubling than she let on.

'Do you know what's wrong with me?' said Pherri. The Sorrowseer knew about Vulgatypha; she might know more as well.

'Do not worry, Pherri,' said Hawla, stroking Pherri's sweat-sodden hair back with her strong, long-nailed hands. 'The Sorrowseer has told me. We are going to help you.'

'You were never meant to be here, Pherri.' The Sorrowseer's mask stirred again, the long forehead appearing to crease in a frown, until Pherri blinked and realised it had not moved. 'This is your body reacting to this unfamiliar world, and realising it cannot sustain itself. The paths of the sun and moon are different, though you might never even realise it. The flickering of a fire, the way the trees and the grass dance in the breeze, the uncanny flip of a coin... It is too much for the body and mind to bear. I cannot tell how long you have, but I can tell you this: you must find a way to return to your own world and defeat Vulgatypha soon. Otherwise, you will die, and all of existence will fall.'

CHAPTER 28

'How many is that?' said Millas as he handed down the final sword from the other cart. 'Two hundred?'

'Near enough,' said Garwen, grimly eyeing the barrels on the back of their own cart. He looked to Helana, who was standing lookout for any patrolling legionnaires. 'How many were you expecting?'

They had encountered the one other wagon to successfully enter Irith when their way to the castle had been blocked by the throng of people going the same way. Some quick thinking by Garwen had led them here, a wide muddy alley in the New Quarter between an abandoned brewery and a locked inn.

'There were five hundred of us trying to enter the city,' said Helana glumly. Where had the rest gone? They did not have enough swords for them all anyway, with one cart they had left trapped at the gate and the other missing, presumably also having failed to gain entry.

There were still a dozen men milling about as if waiting for someone to start issuing orders. 'What's in them?' said one of them, indicating towards the barrels.

'Don't worry about those,' said Helana. The fewer people

knew the better. 'Just get up to the castle before you miss everything.'

'Aren't you coming?'

'It's pointless anyway,' said another man. 'You said yourself we've less than two hundred inside the walls; how are two hundred going to fight the Legion?'

'There's a plan, don't worry,' Helana assured him. *My plan.* Though the best she could say of it was that was better than Rymond's. Before he had headed for the castle, Urwen Storaut had told them the Imperials had turned the Cyliriens away and Rymond had entered the city alone. 'There'll be reinforcements when the time comes.' *Maybe.* Otherwise there were going to be a lot of dead Erlanders in an hour or so. 'Now, get up to the castle. All of you.'

'We'll be right behind you,' Millas assured them. 'Just waiting for any stragglers.'

The men did not look best pleased about being kept in the dark, but grudgingly they left, and disappeared at the corner of the alley heading in the direction of Irith Castle.

At the alley mouth, Helana looked down the street. It was deserted; the New Quarter did not bustle to life until noon at the earliest.

'*Psst.*'

Helana whirled on the spot and came nose to nose with Rucius.

'Eryi's balls,' she hissed. 'Scared me half to death!'

'We're running out of time,' said the Imperial, uncharacteristically serious. 'Acques Bazar considers the day wasted if he hasn't executed someone within two hours of sun-up.' He looked to the cart of barrels. 'Get it open, but for Urmé's sake be careful.'

They cleared the wagon's rear of all the barrels, except one. Together, Millas and Rucius gingerly slid the remaining barrel to the rear and lowered it to the mud. Garwen helped from the ground, then once it was safely down pulled back as far as he could, while Millas began working to remove the bands and get the lid off. As the top came free, the alley filled with a strong, earthy scent of charcoal and sulphur, and the four of them crowded over the barrel to look.

'Well,' said Garwen, looking at that moment as if he would rather have been anywhere else. 'That's huyar then.'

Inside, the barrel was packed with wet straw, but a bulbous clay pot with a thin stem was visible just beneath the top layer. With exaggerated care, Rucius lifted it free and held it up away from them.

'Hold it by the base,' he told them, stepping away and placing it down carefully at the far end of the alley. 'You don't want to risk dropping it.'

'It needs a flame, doesn't it?' said Helana. That had been her understanding at least.

'Maybe once, but huyar is temperamental, and it's travelled all the way across the Bleak Hills. That's why they were keeping it so far from the city.' Rucius's mouth shifted doubtfully. 'And why I wouldn't have given one to that Ffrisean barbarian.'

'Arka was delighted with it. How many do we have left?'

'Three.'

'Only three!' Helana stared at Rucius in disbelief. 'How are we—'

The Imperial shushed her insistently. '*Don't shout so near it,*' he hissed. 'Three is dangerous enough. Urmé's wounds, just one is dangerous. Any more in there and one bad bump could have blown you back to Thrumbalto.'

'You didn't bloody tell us that when we were loading it up,' said Garwen, taking another step away from the barrel.

They were wasting time. Helana reached her hands in and began removing another layer of sodden straw, then looked at

Millas and Garwen. 'One for me, one for Rucius, and one for either of you.'

'Now hold on,' said Millas, taking a step back towards his father. 'You never said we'd have to carry it!'

Garwen clapped him on the back. 'I reckon it might be time to grow a pair, lad,' he said, taking a step forward. 'We'll take one each. Helana's a lot more valuable than the two of us.'

Helana gripped the next pot down and drew it free. She looked down at the thin stem that was stoppered with a cork, and then held it up to her ear. It even *sounded* dangerous; the pot had an ominous hum to it, like a seashell carved from obsidian.

They carefully lifted the last one out, and then Rucius intervened, placed them all at different corners of the alley. 'It has a multiplier effect,' he explained. 'Three times as much is nine times as dangerous.'

'You seem to know a lot about it for a translator,' said Garwen, eyeing the pots nervously.

'I know enough to be afraid of it.'

'Take yours to where the Imperials are barracked,' Helana said to Rucius. There were thousands of legionnaires in the city, and not all of them could be up at Irith Castle. She pointed to Garwen and Millas. 'You two are coming with me. We'll take the horses.'

She could only hope they were not too late.

Atop Irith Castle's low hill, Rymond held himself steady as the door to his cage was finally flung open and two legionnaires dragged him out. He did not struggle, but that did not stop them throwing him to the ground like a side of meat.

'You could have just asked nicely,' he said, as they hauled him to his feet by his bound arms.

Divided from them by several hundred legionnaires, the crowd had swelled down the hill and all the way across the breadth of the castle, as far as the southern outer wall that marked the edge of the vast square. The air was buzzing, the atmosphere one of hostile curiosity at the spectacle the Imperials were preparing. Rymond scanned the crowd for familiar faces, but picking out individuals proved impossible.

A legionnaire grabbed him. 'Walk, *King*.' His fellows laughed, and Rymond was shoved towards the platform, where a black-garbed headsman was now waiting, working through a series of exaggerated stretches.

'I had not realised executions could be such strenuous work,' said Rymond, talking just to quell his fear. But even if his captors understood him, they were not listening. What were the words of a condemned man worth?

He found that he was strangely calm, though it was not because of any great belief in his plan. Disaster had seemed inevitable the moment the Cyliriens were forced to give him up, and who knew how many of his followers were actually inside the city? They might continue the plan without him, but he could be missing all four of his limbs by then.

It was the absurdity of it that soothed him, he supposed. A year ago, he had feared Hessian would slay him in his bed, but now Hessian was dead, and Rymond was somehow a king himself, about to be tortured and slain in full view of his subjects by a foreign power because he had willingly surrendered. It was not an end anyone was likely to sing of.

The guards brought him to a stop at the foot of the stairs, and Rymond found himself alongside his mother, her hands bound behind her back like his. Up close, he could see the toll of imprisonment; her usually exquisite copper hair was spotted with strands of grey, and she looked tired, her face etched with slight lines he could not recall being there before.

Breta Prindian looked him up and down, taking in his

unkempt beard, rough skin, and dirtied peasant's clothes. She sniffed. 'Did you crawl here through pig shit?'

'Felt like it. Nice to see you as well, Mother.' He tried to bend down to kiss her cheek, but a legionnaire grabbed him by the back of the hair to wrench him back.

'I had been wondering what happened to you. It's a relief to see you alive, even if you do need a bath.' She leant as close to Rymond as she could dare and dropped her voice. 'I hope you have a plan?'

Rymond repressed a wince. He was glad he did not have to explain it. 'Of sorts.'

His mother's reply was interrupted by Acques Bazar mounting the steps and raising his hand to the crowd for silence. His purple cape danced in the gentle breeze, and his tough leather boots rapped patiently against the wooden platform. When the crowd did not quieten, he signalled to the row of legionnaires in front of him, who began to beat frantically against their shields to gain the crowd's attention, and the murmuring dropped a notch.

'This blowhard again,' muttered Rymond's mother. 'Perhaps he means to talk us to death. You know Alcantra's back? The woman's quite mad – Bazar's locked her away somewhere to avoid embarrassment.'

'People of Irith!' Bazar began. The crowd fell in volume again as folk strained to listen. 'I am glad to see so many of you here today, to witness the moment you finally become free citizens of the glorious empire of the Ulvatian Imperium! The age of kings and queens in Erland is at an end. From today, no longer shall you bow and scrape to those who put themselves above you; every person here shall be free to choose their own path.'

'A free choice between slavery and death,' muttered Breta. 'He does not even believe this rubbish himself.'

Rymond had seen the state of the town; he doubted there

were many of the crowd foolish enough to take Bazar at his word. So why were they staring in silence? Why were they not shouting him down and throwing things? His eyes roved along the row of legionnaires dividing the crowd from the castle, who had lowered their spears towards the mob, and then across the rows of uncomprehending expressions facing them. *They are afraid*, Rymond realised. Those with the spirit to fight had risen with his mother and been put down, or fled to join him. Those left had no stomach for it.

At least not at the moment. He, Rymond Prindian, had sold these people out for the comforting oblivion of the casheef leaf; was it any wonder they would not rise for him? If he could address them, perhaps he could find the words to conquer their fear and send them screaming towards the armed legionnaires. If he could rile even a fraction of the crowd to violence, the rest would follow. He scanned the mass of people again for familiar faces, men who had fought with him and come today bearing swords, but he found none of them.

Acques Bazar was still droning on. 'There can be no new age without the closing of the old! Today, we extinguish the Prindian line, and give rise to the free people of Erland!'

Bazar rose to a crescendo and stopped, as if expecting a wall of noise to greet his words. A smattering of confused applause swiftly petered out. Rymond saw Bazar frown, say something to the headsman, then return down the stairs.

'Your people have a sheep's wits,' he told Rymond as he reached the ground.

'Might I address them?' asked Rymond. 'I should like to say goodbye.'

Bazar's lip curled dismissively. 'Your last request? Very well. But if you say anything that displeases me, the headsman will take your limbs inch by inch.' He looked to a legionnaire standing by. 'Take her up. Just a beheading for this one.'

Two legionnaires were already moving to seize Breta.

Rymond looked at Bazar in panic. He had not prepared for this. 'Actually, I was hoping I might go first.'

'Make a mother watch her son die? Even I'm not that cruel. I knew you were a coward, Prindian.'

Rymond's reached his bound hands out towards his mother, but he was shoved aside as the soldiers strong-armed her up the steps.

'Mother...'

She gave no sign she had even heard him. Breta Prindian climbed the steps with her head raised high, her hair flashing in the low sun, and the hush that fell over the crowd could have been cut with a knife. Too late, Rymond shouldered aside one of his guards and tried to run forward ahead of her, but a legionnaire's punch to the gut sent him to his knees.

'No!' He stared up at the platform, his eyes streaming with pain. The legionnaires had released his mother, and she was gliding towards the headsman with practised grace as if this were a grand meal, watched by a gaggle of eager lords instead of a sullen crowd, as if the air smelt of candles, perfume, and roasting meat instead of filth and fear.

Rymond struggled to his feet, and a guard grasped him from behind, forcing him to watch.

Breta Prindian knelt, and lowered her head towards the block. A legionnaire stepped forward to brush her hair away from her neck. She looked up to say something to the headsman, who gave a gruff laugh. He took up his axe, five feet of carved oak topped with a huge single head, wickedly sharp. He ran his finger down the blade, grunted. He stepped forward, lifted the axe over his head, and a gasp went through the crowd like a gust of wind.

No. Rymond looked around for Bazar. 'Stop this, please!'

The axe whistled towards Breta Prindian's neck, and Rymond screamed as something like fire burst against his eyes.

Helana, Garwen, and Millas abandoned their horses at the foot of the hill, and weaved their way up through the crowd. The pots of huyar were wrapped in pieces of torn cloth, bundled tight against Garwen and Millas's torsos with both hands to stop them falling or being jarred by the crowd.

They might have found the going easier closer to the edges, but Helana did not want to draw the curiosity of the guards who lined the road. Instead, they ducked and dived through the thickest part of the crowd, Helana leading the way and expecting the others to follow. She stood taller than most of the throng, and used this to her advantage, aiming for where there were others trying to move ahead of the pace as well. A few people she passed shouted after her in complaint, but Helana kept moving.

The crowd was still swelling uphill, with nobody coming the other way. That was good news – it meant Rymond must still be alive. They were nearing the castle now. A broad-backed man stepped across Helana's path, drawing a cry of frustration before she weaved past him, then looked behind to make sure Garwen and Millas were following.

Helana struggled forward and right, making for the city's southern wall that jutted from the castle's outer bailey. The view here was poor, but the crowd was thinner. Helana could only just see the platform in front of the gate. Some people had even sat down in the muddy grass, or were leaning against the wall, curious about the spectacle rather than eager to see it.

Garwen reached her, breathing hard and clutching his pot, with Millas following close behind. 'Well, what now?' said Garwen.

Helana glanced towards the wall, twenty-feet high in ragged grey stone. On the other side was twenty yards of open ground ending in Irith's outer wall. And on the other side of that, she hoped there was a small army of Ffriseans, ready to blow their own pot of huyar and storm through the breach. Were they ready? There was only one way to find out.

She pulled out a length of cord that Rucius had called a fuse, several yards long and smelling of firewood. 'We'll stack the pots against the wall, light the fuse, then run as if the wood-nymphs are chasing us.' She looked back towards the podium, where some Imperial was droning on, but they were too far away to make out the words.

'What about all these people?' said Millas.

'If they've got any sense they'll start running as well.'

'Do we know how far we need to get?' asked Garwen.

Helana bit down her irritation. 'I don't know. Rucius said it's temperamental.' She wished she had asked precisely *how* temperamental; a sudden vision of a single pot taking out half the city blazed across her mind's eye. She reached out to take a jar from Millas. 'We'll just run as fast and far as we can before it goes off.'

Garwen blew out his cheeks. 'Have I mentioned I don't like this?' He looked towards the crowd, most of whom wore the downtrodden faces of the conquered. 'You think a few extra warriors rushing through a hole in the wall is going to stir this lot to violence? I've seen more fight in a blackmaster's wagon.'

Helana's eyes though were not on the crowd. On the stage, the headsman was standing at the edge nearest them caressing his axe, as a woman crowned with a mane of copper hair ascended the far stairs. Helana's gasp seemed to run through the whole crowd.

Her grip on the pot of huyar momentarily tightened, and she felt the substance growl under her palm. The last time Helana had seen Breta Prindian, she had been fleeing from her. Even bound for death she seemed indomitable, striding towards the block like a commander meeting his opponent on the battlefield.

Helana's mouth was at once too wet and too dry. She wiped it with the back of her hand. Breta Prindian had schemed to arrange the murder of Helana's uncle. Watching Andrick Barrelbreaker's mutilated head dance against the blue sky, Helana's hand had itched to deliver justice with her own blade. Yet now, watching the executioner caress his axe as Breta Prindian laid her head upon the block, she felt a strange, cold certainty that her death could not be allowed to pass. Too much had changed since then. By what right did the Imperials condemn Breta Prindian to death? She had to live, live and face what she had done.

Garwen was watching her. 'Helana?'

She thrust the fuse into his hands. 'Just use one. Lay it right there.' She pointed to a section of wall with just a few people milling around it; the stonework looked to be sagging slightly. Garwen took the fuse, and clutching the second pot Helana ran for the platform, ignoring the two men's confused cries.

Towards the front and centre, the crowd was thickest of all. Helana instead hurried directly towards the line of legionnaires, then moved left, cutting through whatever gaps she could find. The headsman was moving towards Breta, his axe raised high. Several times the press was so tight that Helana thought the pot might be wrenched from her grasp, but she clung on. A man shoved her and Helana nearly tripped, but caught herself on a woman's long tunic. The woman shrieked, then someone pushed her from behind, and Helana fell awkwardly, twisting to land on her rump rather than the huyar.

She hurried to her feet, with a shock realising that she had been thrust right into the gap between the crowd and the line of spear-wielding soldiers. She met the eye of the nearest one, who was staring at Helana, his mouth wide open in horror.

She looked down, and realised the cloth covering the clay pot had fallen away.

'Huyar!' the legionnaire cried. 'Huyar!' He looked along the line, a row of faces just like his, seemingly unsure whether to attack Helana or flee from her.

Helana looked for the platform, still thirty or forty yards away. The headsman's terrible axe flashed high. Unthinkingly, Helana launched the huyar with all her might towards the castle gate.

It spun through the air. Every legionnaire turned to watch, their faces frozen in masks of terror. The missile tumbled in time with the fall of the axe. Events seemed to slow, some soldiers fleeing on legs that moved as if through treacle while others scrambled forward to grasp Helana. The people of Irith only stared, wide-eyed and open-mouthed.

Helana watched it too. It arced over the stage and towards the castle gate. The firm hand of a legionnaire grasped her. The axe was within a forearm span of Breta Prindian's neck.

And then the world exploded.

A roar of fire and tumbling stone burst against Helana's eardrums. The earth rumbled, and the air turned to steam as a great gust of blistering wind threw her to the ground. Helana caught a glimpse as a flying piece of wall decapitated the headsman. A legionnaire fell on top of her, a flash of masonry missing him by inches.

Helana could hardly get her wits straight. The man was screaming in her face, but she could not hear him over the shrieking hum in her ears. Something hard and heavy was trapping her legs below the knee, and the bulk of the legionnaire was stopping her reaching for the dagger sheathed in her belt.

His fist struck hard against her face, scrambling her senses further. She tried to knee him in the groin, but couldn't move with the weight on her lower leg. She kicked it off and tried again, but the legionnaire twisted out of the way and punched her a second time. The humming was fading, and Helana began to hear the screams, and then a second explosion that set her ears ringing again, immediately followed by a third.

The man drew back his fist for another punch, but then went limp as a huge piece of stonework fell from the heavens and thudded onto his back, killing him instantly. The blow drove the wind out of Helana, and as more masonry fell around her like great hailstones she threw her arms over her head, hoping the dead man's armour would protect her.

When she was sure the barrage of falling limestone had stopped, Helana threw the man off, kicked away the length of wood that was trapping her legs, and managed to roll over and up onto her feet.

She realised immediately how lucky she had been. The lump of stone that had slain the man had been the size of a boar, and other smaller chunks littered the ground around her.

But that was to say nothing of the chaos further afield. The huyar had not just blown apart the gatehouse entrance to Irith Castle, it had brought half the outer wall down, and several hundred legionnaires with it. Only rubble remained, a huge jumble of shattered stone peppered with maimed Imperials. Where the platform had stood was now a mass of broken, twisted timber, like someone had ripped open a corpse and perversely pulled the ribs this way and that. Legionnaires and citizens stumbled around in a daze, holding their heads, limping, shouting incomprehensibly at the chaos. Some were still on the ground, either too shocked to rise or crushed beneath the stone missiles Helana had unleashed on them.

A roar from the southern wall turned Helana around. The great stone barrier was even more devastated than the castle. In the madness, she had forgotten that the second explosion must have been Garwen and Millas, and the third Arka breaching the outer battlements. A great hole more than thirty yards wide had been smashed into the wall, and even through her shattered senses and the desire to fall to the ground and never rise again, triumph rose in Helana, as several hundred Cyliriens and

Ffriseans began pouring through the gap, sweeping over the confused legionnaires like a tide.

Urgh. Rymond's ears were ringing so hard it hurt. He was on the ground, though he did not recall how he got there. His tunic was ripped all down the front, and he had somehow lost one of his boots. Both his palms were grazed where he had used his bound hands down to break his fall.

Wincing, he tried to come to his feet and overbalanced, throwing out his arms against a huge hunk of stone and crying out as its jagged edge ripped against his skin.

He manoeuvred himself to rest his rear against it, and sat back, putting his hands to the back of his head and taking deep calming breaths.

Around him, the Imperials appeared to have forgotten about him entirely. Legionnaires were rushing towards the south wall, and through bleary eyes Rymond swore he saw Gruenla and Arka at the head of an army, engaging the stunned Imperials and forcing them back. Hundreds of legionnaires lay dead, either fallen from the castle's outer wall or crushed by masonry. The line of soldiers dividing the ruined platform from the crowd had disintegrated. The West Erlanders seemed nearly as dazed as Rymond and the guards – the crowd looked as though it had been flattened by a charge of zebrephants – but some were coming to their feet with swords in hand. They found their fellows, and these small groups snowballed to a larger force which charged towards the remaining Imperials.

The ringing in Rymond's ears was beginning to quieten now, replaced with the shrill clashing of steel and the cries of battle. He did not understand where Arka and Gruenla had come from, but they looked to be getting the best of it.

And more Erlanders were running to engage them as well.

Most were unarmed, but seemed to take heart from the bravery of their fellows, and having been further from the blast had retrieved their wits faster than the beleaguered Imperials.

Rymond rubbed at his face and cleared away a coating of dust. The front of the castle – his castle – had been destroyed, as had a large chunk of the southern wall. *Whoever is responsible for this is getting a lordship.* It put his own feeble plan to shame; left to his own devices he had been about to get himself killed.

Mother. The thought broke through the haze like sunshine through fog. The stage was a mass of broken timber. Rymond could appreciate how lucky he had been to avoid serious injury – he had been blown perhaps twenty yards from the stage and yet all he had to show for it was bruises; his limbs were all still attached to him and nothing was broken. There were Imperials with jagged lengths of wood sticking out of them and others lying crushed. The headsman's headless corpse lay several feet away from the stage, but Breta Prindian was nowhere to be seen.

Mother. On dead legs, Rymond hobbled across the mass of corpses and broken stone towards the ruins of the platform.

He was halfway there when an arm reached up and dragged him to the ground. Rymond landed with a grunt as all the air was knocked out of him, and in an instant Acques Bazar was on him, pinning him to the ground and throwing his hands around Rymond's neck. The supreme legate's bald head was bathed in blood, like a terrifying red skull, grimacing two rows of stark white teeth, and Rymond gasped for breath as he bore down upon his throat.

'What did you do?' Bazar released his grip with one hand to punch Rymond across the face. Rymond spluttered down air before both fists were tight around his neck again. He returned the blow, but Bazar barely seemed to notice. Rymond instead scrabbled to jab his fingers into Bazar's eyes, but the legate twisted and bit down on his hand.

Rymond hardly felt it. There were already black spots dancing in his eyes, and the din of battle was fading to the edges, drowned out by the hot beat of blood in Rymond's head as his life ebbed away under Bazar's vice-like grip around his windpipe.

Even through his panicked last moments Rymond could have laughed at the ridiculousness of it. *Through all the odds, I might have won, and yet I am going to die.* His bowels loosened, and he felt a strange sense of acceptance come over him. Bazar's bloodstained visage was almost a comfort; it would be over soon.

The legate gave a snarl of triumph. He threw back his head and laughed, all gravity forgotten.

A bright length of metal flashed in Rymond's dimming vision, and the top of Bazar's skull disappeared in a wash of blood. The legate's wild eyes widened in shock, and a second blow caught him flat across the cheek. His corpse toppled from Rymond, and his grip on Rymond's neck fell away with it.

Rymond's throat opened, and he began coughing and sucking down desperate breaths of sweet air. He tried to come to his feet, but his body would not obey him. He rolled to the side, wheezing, the sounds of ringing steel and desperate men returning to his ears.

'I've never held one of these before.'

The familiar voice brought Rymond's face up, staring at his saviour. Silhouetted against the blue sky stood his mother, leaning on her newly acquired sword like a stick. Her hair was in disarray, caked in gore, her dress was a torn and bloody mess, and one of her eyes was swollen shut and purple, but she was alive.

'Mother,' wheezed Rymond through his ruined throat. It hurt to speak. 'You're—'

'Alive?' She laughed, and it sounded to Rymond as if the

sound came from a thousand miles away. 'So are you, despite your best efforts. Can you walk?'

Rymond tried to rise, but none of his limbs would do what he wanted. Every inch of him ached, whatever bravado that had driven him to his feet fading by the moment. He lay there in the dirt, surrounded by the ruins of Irith Castle's wall, as all around him the legionnaires fell under the weight of the West Erlanders. Unless he was mistaken, he thought he might be winning.

CHAPTER 29

Orsian raised his shield just in time to meet Errian's ferocious overhand strike, the blade clanging against the iron rim and buying Orsian time to take a hurried pace back. A second blow followed, just as powerful as the first, and its impact against the centre of his shield shook Orsian's arm to the shoulder, sending chips of wood flying. He made an attack of his own, a clumsy, off-balance sideswipe that Errian deflected easily, but it gave Orsian a chance to put more distance between himself and his brother, backing away towards the wall of metal shields.

'Errian—'

His attempt to call for calm was broken by Errian's rapid advance, ending in a breakneck flurry of blows that Orsian deflected with a combination of sword and shield. He had no chance to get in a strike of his own, and allowed Errian on, and then as their dance reached the barrier of legionnaires Orsian spun away and pushed his brother into them with his shield.

He backed off again with rapid steps, seeking to put as many yards as possible between them. 'Errian, stop! This is madness!'

His brother's reply was a wild snarl, shaking with hatred.

On bare feet, he thundered forward to ram into Orsian with his shield. Orsian crouched low and took the blow full on his own shield, nearly falling back with the impact, then dodged his head to the side as Errian's blade flicked over the rim like a serpent's tongue.

Orsian backed away again, peering at his brother over his guard. Errian followed, his breathing feverish, his eyes blazing like twin night fires. 'Stop running, Brother! Fight me! Fight, you coward!'

'I will not.' Orsian thought of throwing his sword aside, but that would have been insanity. 'Errian, you are free to hate me, but I did not kill Father. Look around you – I am not your enemy!'

Errian continued stalking towards him. Orsian was beginning to run out of room; Errian had backed him into a corner where two sides of shield-bearing Imperials met. Orsian tried to dart away to the right, but his brother closed the angle, forcing him deeper into the corner. Errian leapt into range, and when Orsian stepped back he reversed straight into the cold steel of a legionnaire's shield. As Errian's next blow fell, Orsian ducked and aimed a stab towards his lower leg, but the rim of his brother's shield was too quick, and Orsian nearly lost his sword as it clanged sharply against the stone floor.

He retreated again awkwardly, straight into another legionnaire at the other side of the corner. Errian's blade flashed towards Orsian fast as fire, but the Imperial's intervention saved him; the man shoved Orsian forward, and he stumbled straight into Errian. The blow scraped harmlessly against the Imperial's high shield and Orsian and Errian fell in a tangle with Orsian's shield trapped between them.

As they fell, Orsian freed his left hand from his shield, and when he landed atop his brother drove an opportunistic jab into Errian's jaw. Errian grunted, but recovered quickly, bringing his long legs up and kicking Orsian aside. Orsian landed, and was saved only by his instincts, pushing up with both hands and leaping to his feet as Errian's blade clashed against the stone where Orsian's head had been a moment before.

He had lost his shield now. Errian kicked it aside into the mass of the Eternal Legion. Eryi's high laughter rang in Orsian's ears like discordant bells.

Errian came on, grinning wildly, a trickle of crimson trailing from his lip where Orsian had struck him. 'First blood to you, Brother.' He reached up to wipe it with the back of his sword hand. 'And it's all you shall have of me.'

Without his shield, Orsian knew he was outmatched. Errian's reach was longer, and Orsian had seen him fight upon the walls of Piperskeep; his brother was still better than him. Now though, Errian seemed to be advancing more cautiously, allowing Orsian time to get his breath.

'Enough of this!' cried Eryi. He was still atop the dais, behind and over Errian's left shoulder. The air crackled around him, as if the sheer potency of the moment was lending him power. 'I have seen your death, Orsian Andrickson. Krupal, finish it!'

'Yes, Master!' A croaking voice came from behind Orsian, and he turned his head slightly to see Krupal squeezed into line between two Imperial soldiers, the only animated face amidst a sea of blank expressions. He still clung to a *hymerika,* though the prisoner was fading, little more than dying grey skin stretched over a skull, his unseeing eyes like marbles lost deep in gaping sockets.

The glance backward saved Orsian's life. Four Imperial spears thrust for him at once, and he twisted out of the way of one and then rolled under two more.

But at the same moment, Errian charged. Orsian sprang to his feet, bringing his sword up, but Errian beat it aside with his own and drove his shield's iron rim up into Orsian's jaw.

A wave of pain exploded across his face. He felt himself

falling, but the moment slowed as if in a dream, each millisecond magnified to the length of an age, the scream of every nerve rising to a crescendo. *Just hold onto your sword.* He gripped it as if it were his own child. He looked up, expecting to see Errian twisting his blade back, ready to bury it in Orsian's undefended torso.

But Errian was not looking at him. His body was moving towards Orsian, his face twisted in triumph, but his eyes were looking past him into the wall of legionnaires.

Time accelerated, and Orsian's back struck the ground heavily, driving the breath from him. He tried to bring his sword up, but Errian's foot trapped his wrist against the floor. His brother stood over him, the cold point of his blade pressed to Orsian's throat.

Their eyes met, and for an imperceptible moment, Orsian saw his brother wink, the shadow of a smile touching the edge of his lips.

'*Do it. KILL HIM.*' Eryi's voice cracked with hunger. Past Errian, Orsian saw him raising his hands to the sky as if in prayer. 'Do you feel it, *Goddess*? Your son is *dying*.'

Errian smirked. He drew his blade back, the tip aimed for Orsian's throat.

Orsian kept his eyes wide open. He would make Errian meet his gaze as he murdered him, let it haunt him all the rest of his days. *End it then, Brother. End it and doom us all.*

But Errian's blade never fell.

Errian leapt over Orsian towards Krupal, and before the magus could even raise a hand wrenched his sword across his throat in a fountain of blood.

As Krupal fell, before Orsian could rise Eryi's scream abruptly pinned him to the floor. The noise was so sharp and screeching that it seemed to rend the air in two, splitting grains of ether and leaving a pungent, burning scent in its wake, like a lightning strike tearing the night apart. It went on and on, for so long Orsian was sure it would bring Piperskeep crashing down around them.

Finally it ceased, fading to echoes bouncing off the high ceiling. Krupal's corpse lay on the flagstones, seeping blood. The hall stirred into motion as his hold over the *hymerikai* and the legionnaires slipped away with his life, like a congregation rising as a priest finished his final blessing, and suddenly the room was filled with the whispers of Imperials, their eyes dancing in confusion from their spears to the magus's blood-gushing corpse.

'Men of the *Hymeriker*!' Errian's voice filled the hall. 'Kill the Imperials!'

A stunned silence fell, shortly followed by the war cries of East Erland warriors. They were unarmed, outnumbered, yet rose from their fugue state to heedlessly leap upon their Imperial captors, crushing those nearest to them under weight of numbers and wrenching spears from their grasp and swords from their scabbards. The corner of the hall they had risen from became a storm of steel, sundered flesh, and cries of pain and triumph. The Imperials barely raised a weapon in their defence, and those nearest to Orsian were looking around with weary eyes, rubbing their faces or letting their mouths fall open in bewilderment as if they did not know where they were. The Erlanders had come to their senses faster than the legionnaires, perhaps from having spent less time under Krupal's sorcery.

Orsian looked about himself, realising he had somehow come to his feet, sword in hand. One of the more alert legionnaires rushed him, and Orsian slashed away the head of the man's spear before driving his blade up under his chin and out through his forehead. He heard movement behind him, so yanked it free and turned, ready to bring it to bear once more.

It was Errian. His brother embraced him, and then swiftly shoved him away. His eyes were bright with battle fervour. 'You knew, didn't you?'

'I had no idea!' Orsian pushed his brother in the chest. 'I thought you were going to kill me!'

'I nearly did.' Errian's grin was a rictus of madness. He looked away towards Eryi, and Orsian lashed out with his sword to sweep aside the thrust of a rushing Imperial and bury his blade in the man's throat. They were coming to their senses now, but the *hymerikai* had already gained the upper hand, taking shields from slain Imperials and forming a wall as their enemies struggled to organise themselves. 'Think we can take him?' Eryi was still standing on the dais, gazing on in horror as Krupal's puppet army fell apart.

Orsian wiped his sword on his breeches. 'Time to find out.'

The brothers fanned out, and leapt atop the dais, Errian to Eryi's left and Orsian to his right. They charged towards him, with a bellowing war cry that tore Orsian's throat to ribbons.

Their swords fell towards Eryi together, and shattered in a shower of metal.

The impact sent Orsian flying backwards, the shards of his broken sword ripping apart his clothes and tearing at his skin. He cried out and covered his eyes, Eryi's high laughter ringing once more in his ears, the steel splinters swirling around him like a storm of bitter, deadly ice.

'*FOOLS!*' Eryi's voice was everywhere all at once; in his head, twisting through the air with the remnants of the sword, rolling off the walls, falling from the ceiling and bringing cracked pieces of masonry with it. A chunk of mortared stone landed next to Orsian's head, as a dozen more fragments fell around him, punching huge dents in the dais. He tried to rise, but the spinning metal and plummeting rocks forced him down.

Eryi was standing with his hands raised, conducting a silent orchestra of destruction, oblivious to the battle continuing between the Legion and the *Hymeriker*. Past him, Orsian saw Errian trying to rise, beating back the debris with his shield until a stone the size of a fist struck him in the temple and sent him sprawling.

'It will not be in vain.' Eryi waved his hands, swirling the storm to a blizzard around the three of them, so fast and thick that Orsian could barely see. He forced himself to his feet, his cry of determination ripping at his vocal cords. Orsian flung his broken blade towards Eryi, but it went spinning away with the rest of the debris. The maelstrom was ripping Eryi apart as well, flaying the already weeping wounds he bore, filling the air with streams of blood. 'If I must kill you both, so be it.' The shards swirled tighter and tighter, spinning a high staff of shining steel in Eryi's fist, an ugly edifice of broken edges and jagged metal. 'Where are you, *Goddess*? *Coward!*'

Beyond the tempest, Orsian saw Errian was treading towards Eryi. He was covering his head with his shield, accepting the cuts the shards of metal left on his forearms as the ceiling continued to rain rubble down on his head. Each step seemed an effort of will, muscles in his thighs straining beneath his shredded breeches. Doggedly he ate away the yards, until he stood at Eryi's back. With a desperate snarl, he raised the shield to bring its rim down on Eryi's head—

The staff twirled in Eryi's hands, and he spun to bury it in Errian's torso.

Errian's mouth fell open in surprise, and the shield slipped from his fingers, clattering to the floor. His shocked gaze found Orsian, and for one last time the brothers looked one another in the eye. For a moment, it almost looked as if Errian was going to say something, perhaps an apology, an appeal to be remembered fondly, a message for any of their family who still lived, a last demand for vengeance, a razor-tongued insult, some favourite memory of a time he had beaten his brother to a pulp.

Orsian would never know. With a ghostly shriek, the staff came free, and Errian's body crumpled to the ground.

Orsian howled, with an anguish he had never before

believed was possible. He threw himself against the storm that held him in place with renewed fury, his eyes blinded with tears and blood, his shirt hanging off him in rags, his bare skin streaked with cuts.

Eryi turned, his face a mess of weeping injuries. He was breathing heavily, and the storm seemed to slow around him. He smiled, and it was like staring into the maw of death itself.

'Your mother is coming, Orsian,' he hissed. 'But too late.'

Around them, the hall seemed to fall very still, the battle between the *Hymeriker* and the Legion fading to a thin whisper of metal beating against metal. The air thickened, like the last breath of heat before the rising storm. The earth began to shake, more stonework raining from the ceiling as if some buried giant had seized the foundations of Piperskeep and was shaking them in his monstrous fists.

A rush of wind swept down the length of the hall, and the double doors leapt off their hinges, sending two groups of legionnaires flying into their fellows.

A woman stood in the entrance, so tall that her head brushed the top of the arched doorway. Her naked flesh shone like the face of the moon, her hair was a golden storm, and her face was equal parts beautiful and terrible, a masterwork of strokes and angles, a sculptor's dream given life.

But as he stared down the hall towards the woman, amidst Eryi's storm of shards of stone, Orsian paid these truths no mind. He saw her red eyes, brighter than the hottest fire; an uncanny, impossible resemblance to his own mother; and that her mesmerising face was twisted with unquenchable rage.

Eryi's tempest began to quicken again, and he brought it closer, forming a shield around himself and allowing Orsian some respite. The magus's lips stretched to a mocking smile. 'I said you would come, Goddess. The earthly flesh you have taken for yourself could not resist its child's call.' He bent to seize Errian's corpse by the hair, yanking his dead face up so the goddess could see it. 'Your son is *dead*!'

Vulgatypha leant back and from her maw of a mouth unleashed a shriek that would have shattered the teeth of any mortal woman. She glided down the hall towards the dais, the men falling back in terror from the shimmering aura that weaved around her like a tide of invisible ribbons.

Orsian found himself rooted to the spot, staring up into the goddess's face. From one moment to the next the resemblance to his mother ebbed and flowed, Vulgatypha's face moving in the space of an instant from the mournful, vengeful fury that could have belonged to Viratia Brithwell to a cold hunger for dominion that could only belong to a god. Light and power swelled around her like a blazing sun, so bright that Orsian had to shield his eyes and both legionnaires and *hymerikai* were falling back in terror.

Eryi was smiling maniacally, conflict with Orsian forgotten, his storm swirling so fast now that it was no more than a blur. 'She comes, Orsian!' His voice hungered for it.

As the goddess approached, she seemed to shrink before Orsian's eyes, the height and the elegant limbs shortening and the radiance dimming to a brilliant glow. She opened her mouth and two voices speaking as one seemed to rise from her throat. 'We will hurt you for this, magus.'

Vulgatypha raised a hand, and without warning Eryi hurled his spinning maelstrom at her.

The explosion rocked Orsian off his feet and halfway across the dais to within a hand's breadth of the wall. He sat up, spitting out flecks of fallen ceiling.

A vast hole had appeared in the stone floor, and the front half of the dais had been reduced to rubble. For a moment, Orsian thought Eryi's magic must have triumphed, until he saw them.

They were within yards of each other, on the dais, close to where Orsian had been standing. Vulgatypha held Eryi's swirling storm squeezed between two huge hands held an arm's length apart, a vast mass of stone and steel spinning impossibly fast in the closed space. Her face was fixed in a rictus of concentration, eyes like red-hot sparks and sharp teeth bared like two rows of honed blades. Eryi stood just feet apart from her, his face spellbound, his own hands extended towards the storm as if to hold it away from him. Still his wounds wept, and the blood spun from his flesh to join the maelstrom as he strived to hold the goddess back. Her bare feet clawed at the floor, coming on inch by inch as Eryi's feet slid against the dais, forcing him backwards. The warring *hymerikai* and legionnaires had stopped; every face was turned towards the dais, rapt in wonder.

She is stronger, Orsian realised, struggling to his feet. He could almost feel the waves of magic bursting from Eryi as he sought to pin Vulgatypha back. Flesh was sloughing from him as if he were on fire, blood running so hot that it seemed to evaporate as it fled from his body.

'*Your strength is failing, magus.*' Vulgatypha's voice was like a crack of thunder. Another powerful step forward, the storm spinning so fast that Orsian could smell the air burning.

With a frustrated cry, Eryi leapt backwards, using the force of the storm to propel himself towards Orsian. Before Orsian could react, the magus seized him around the throat from behind, the bone of Eryi's emaciated forearm pressed up against his neck. Orsian fought, kicking and biting at his captor, but the magus held firm, magic lending strength to his ruined flesh.

'*Stop or I'll kill him*,' he shrieked desperately. 'I know you're in there, Viratia. I see you!'

The storm still spun, but a flicker of something that might have been doubt trembled in Vulgatypha's features. The mouth softened; the red eyes dimmed slightly, becoming a little more human; two fat tears rolled down her sheer porcelain cheekbones. In the face of a goddess, Orsian's mother appeared, wracked with grief, longing, terror.

Then Orsian blinked, and Vulgatypha's fearsome red eyes stared back at him. With a blood-curdling snarl, she launched the storm upward, right over his and Eryi's heads.

The ceiling exploded, and a hail of brick and broken timber thundered down, crushing everyone in the hall beneath half the weight of Piperskeep. Orsian felt a breath of wind rush past his face, and then everything went dark.

CHAPTER 30

For Ciera, the long journey to Merivale passed in a fug of grief and recrimination, eased only by knowing she had not revealed her woe to anyone. It was ever-present, all-consuming in a way that meant she barely felt the ache of so many weeks ahorse.

She had burnt the bodies of both her parents over the gate to Cliffark Tower, then tossed their ashes to the air, so that a little of them might come to rest on the well-trodden path to their home, or make a bed between the cobbles of the keep's courtyard, or be swept out over the town that her father had been so proud of. Afterwards, she had retreated to her father's study, weeping softly as she scrutinised his ledgers. He had once said to her that in the event of his death, she would find all she needed to know in that study. To Ciera, it was as if a little of him lived on in the ordered rows and columns annotated with his tight, neat script, and as the small hours crawled around the grief finally overcame her, great wracking sobs and plump tears that began to stain the pages until she pushed the books away from her. She had slept in his study, her head cradled by an open book, just like her father. Far from faultless, but a good man.

But within sight of the rest of the castle, she had never shed a tear. To be a queen was to have control, even over oneself.

It was perhaps her mother that was the more painful memory, coming as it did with the realisation that Ciera had never truly known her. Had all those years of censure and disapproval been for this, for the day that Ciera would have to find her own path? Perhaps Ciera's grandmother had been just the same, and it was that severity which had imbued Irena Istlewick with the fearless cunning to slay Strovac Sigac, who had sent so many countless men to their deaths and wielded his blade with such skill and ferocity that folk had thought him unbeatable. She had been a remarkable woman, and it was a dragging weight against Ciera's heart that she had never realised until the end.

'Lord Madine's men look like they can handle themselves,' said Burik from beside her, breaking Ciera's bleak reverie. 'Well, they frighten me at least.'

Ciera glanced behind her, to the eight hundred men riding under Lord Madine's banner, showing a leaping silver fish on a pink background. He had not journeyed with them himself, citing weak lungs and an easily upset stomach, and though Ciera did not believe him she had been glad to see the back of him. His force was a mix of his own men and ink-skinned Cjarthian mercenaries, who armoured like Erlanders but shaved their whole heads every morning to better display the swirling tattoos that covered their scalps and faces. There were many other bands of warriors garnered from the succession of minor lords whose land they had crossed on their journey, but few drew the eye like the Cjarthians. They had seven thousand men now, near enough, just over half of them Cliffark rebels and the rest warriors.

'Who do you reckon would win,' Burik went on, 'a hundred of them or a hundred Wild Brigaders?' The last remnants of Strovac Sigac's band rode further back in the column, giving a mean eye to anyone who dared to come too close.

Ciera closed her eyes and let out a quiet sigh. Riding beside her, Burik struggled to repress the impulse to fill any silence for the sake of it. Perhaps a result of having lost so many brothers, including Derik, his twin. Ciera was almost minded to tell him to direct his wonderings to Aimya instead – she had seen how the pretty, young bride looked at Burik – but she doubted he would obey her; since Laphor's death Burik had hardly let Ciera out of his sight. He was an able warrior, but he was no replacement for the older man's steadiness. Ciera touched the pouch of ashes she carried around her neck. Without Laphor, she would never have made it this far. She would never have escaped Piperskeep. In all their time travelling together, she had never thought to ask Laphor what she should do with his remains in the event of his death. She would scatter them in the yard at Piperskeep, outside the barracks.

Laphor would have come up with some other way of dealing with Lord Madine. All Ciera had managed to do was give him what he wanted. It had seemed unimportant at the time, merely a matter of words, but Madine had required her to sign her name to a document confirming their agreement. That did not prevent her withdrawing later, but it would be a tale Madine could spread far and wide to discredit her.

His demand to use his own men to track fleeing peasants in Cliffark was worthless – Cliffark was a maze, even to those who knew the city – but Ciera could see how the deal had lowered her in the eyes of Tansa, and the girl had been suspicious enough of her as it was.

I will prove myself by my deeds when I am queen again, not by the promises I make to get there. Then, Tansa and the rest would see that she was a woman of her word, as long as holding to a bargain was for the good of Erland and the rule of her son. Her reforms would raise all of Erland together.

'Majesty?' said Burik.

Sister Aimya saved Ciera from having to reply. 'I'd say we're within ten miles of Merivale.' The young bride still sometimes tried to engage folk in discussing what she claimed to have seen on Eryispek, but it fell on deaf ears. Trying to guess what would meet them in Merivale was uncertainty enough. Aimya pointed towards the skyline. 'If I squint, I can just see the flag over Piperskeep.'

Ciera turned to her sharply. 'What colour?' Sangreal crimson would mean Balyard still ruled, assuming he was still maintaining his pretence that he did so in the name of her son, but a streaming purple banner would mean the Imperium had finally taken the castle. That had not seemed likely when she left, but fortunes could change swiftly in war.

Aimya narrowed her eyes and leant towards the horizon. 'Red, I think. Hard to tell in this light.' The grey rains of autumn had followed them all the way from the coast.

Ciera said nothing, unsure if that was a good or a bad sign. But after months on the run, after so many nights falling asleep not knowing whether she would be woken by the dawn or a pursuing foe, to be returning to Merivale felt like a miracle from the gods. She hoped Balyard looked from his balcony at her approaching host and trembled.

'Queen Ciera!'

She turned at the sound of her name and the heavy rhythm of horseshoes. Mikol Gurathet was riding up the edge of the column, on a horse that would have better suited a considerably smaller man.

He pulled up, panting, and brought his mount into step with them. 'The men are saying that we are approaching the capital.' He raised his helmet to wipe at his brow. 'I beg the honour of leading your foreguard – I am dying to cross swords with an Imperial and avenge my father.'

Ciera shared a glance with Burik. She had assured Madine

she would keep the rash Gurathet out of harm's way, a concern she presumed arose from Madine's desire to gain his land rather than any affection he held for the other man. Nevertheless, Ciera had a mind to thwart Madine, at least in this.

Burik merely shrugged, so Ciera decided to grant Gurathet's wish. 'Take fifty men of your choosing. Engage if you must, but your priority is to learn what you can and return. Just their numbers, how the siege is progressing. If the Imperials are gone, wait for me.' Some might have counselled caution, but there would be no hiding an army of this size for long. Better to lay their cards down and see how Balyard reacted.

Mikol Gurathet gave an eager grin. 'I won't let you down, Majesty.' He tipped his helmet to her then glanced towards Burik. 'Fancy joining me, Burik? Might not be any of them left by the time you get there otherwise.'

Burik replied immediately. 'My place is with Queen Ciera.'

'As you please! Next time you see me I'll be up to my neck in Imperial blood.' With a jubilant laugh, Gurathet swung his poor horse around and headed back along the line recruiting.

Burik stared after him. 'If it comes to battle, I'll give you even odds that sack of lard shits down his leg.'

'I'm just glad to see warriors taking orders from a woman,' said Aimya. 'Reminds me of Lady Viratia.'

By the glowing tones in which Aimya spoke of Andrick's widow, Ciera was beginning to wonder if Aimya also thought that she was a god. At Aimya's behest, she had sent more riders towards Eryispek as they rode south, but all the word they brought back was of a silent land coated in black ash, with no sign of survivors, gods, or anything else.

Gurathet swiftly gathered his fifty, and together Ciera's party watched them stream towards the horizon. Ciera's eyes were not so sharp as Aimya's, but she thought she could see a red smear against the skyline that might be a Sangreal banner.

As their column continued to eat away at the miles, Ciera

looked about herself, taking in the strangeness of her companions. Tansa and Jerem rode behind her, Jerem carrying Ciera's own Sangreal banner, and Haisie was there also, riding a docile pony alongside the tall, covered wagon containing Andrick and his nursemaid. Ciera would have liked her son to ride up with her, but the risks were too great – all it took was one stumble, or one man with a grudge and a good bow arm, and Ciera's world and all her hopes would be torn apart. A dozen of Jerem's men surrounded the wagon, each handpicked by him and interviewed by Ciera to confirm she was content for them to guard her son.

Her companions were all so young, too young. It made Ciera wish all the more that Laphor still lived. Jerem was in his middle-twenties, and yet he was the oldest of them. So much age and experience had been lost to the war – Andrick and Hessian both dead; Viratia and Theodric both missing. When all the wars were over, it would be for Erland's youth to forge a country in their own image. The thought made a thrill shiver through Ciera's fingers. It would be her life's work.

First though, they needed to win, against whatever faced them here. Ciera pushed herself upright in the saddle. When the people of Merivale looked out at the arriving army, they needed to see a queen. She reached into her saddlebag and produced a jagged, ugly crown of dull bronze that had been forged for her in a rush by a smith at Hardhall and placed it on her head, then tapped her heels against her mount's flanks to bring it to a trot. The column stirred behind her as every man followed her lead, adding a spark of delight to the muddle of elation and fear that coursed through her veins. Those on foot would not be able to keep pace, but Ciera could not contain her impatience. Finally, she was returning to Merivale, for vengeance against those who had made her run.

Over the next hour, the city walls swelled into view, and when they were within a few miles they found the first traces of the Imperial camp. Tents, sodden with rain and collapsed into the dirt. Discarded weapons shining in the worn earth like the silver edges of sunlight against the dark clouds that watched from overhead. The vast striped carcasses of zebrephants, flesh picked clean by scavengers, plates of steel no one had troubled to remove tilted against mountains of bare bones.

'Not sorry to see the back of those,' muttered Burik as the column passed one of them, scattering strutting crows to the sky.

Ciera did not reply. They had seemed such magnificent, beautiful creatures when she watched from atop Piperskeep as their handlers exercised them every morning. Yet there had always been a doleful cast to their wrinkled faces and strange long snouts, and when night fell and the air filled with their mournful trumpeting Ciera had often felt the overwhelming urge to weep. She felt the same way now, watching their corpses, wondering where they had come from and whether their grief had been true or merely the mindless hooting of monsters. She wondered also if the last of them had made the same noises as they watched their fellows die, before they too finally succumbed to hunger.

'Suppose they couldn't keep them fed,' said Tansa. 'Hope they killed them quick instead of letting them suffer.'

Ciera hoped so too.

The ruins of the Imperial camp were deserted, and the consideration of what that might mean pulled Ciera back from agonising over dead war beasts. There were no corpses and no fire pits where the Erlanders might have piled the Imperial dead. That could only mean they had fled or had died within the walls.

The one structure still standing was the Imperial command tent, the ludicrous, striped behemoth that to those within Merivale had been a source of fascination during the Imperial assault. Burik steered his mount towards it; the entrance was so high that even mounted he did not have to duck to enter.

He returned moments later, his mouth downturned in distaste. 'Drast Fulkiro's stinking corpse,' he declared. 'Not a mark on him. Poison, probably.'

They rode on, closing in on the city. A strange stillness seemed to coat Merivale, as if even the buildings slept. There were watchmen on the wall, a few of whom called out to them, but Ciera ignored them. Someone would recognise her, and then some creature of Balyard's would have to bring terms. A succession of eyes followed them, red-garbed men of the Merivale Watch striding along the walls to keep pace with them, some mouths falling open in wonder at the tail of men she dragged behind. This close, there was no mistaking it: the banner over Piperskeep was red, a cruel mockery of what Balyard had stolen from her.

Along the wall's south side, they found Gurathet and his fifty waiting patiently outside the King's Gate. The drawbridge was up, but the battlements were a bustle of activity, more men arriving seemingly every second to stare down and call out questions.

'I did just as you said, Majesty,' said Gurathet. His jowls wobbled proudly. 'Waited here and not even drawn my sword. No Imperials, more's the pity.'

'What would you do otherwise?' scoffed Burik. 'Take the King's Gate with fifty men?'

The words had hardly left Burik's lips when with a clunking groan the drawbridge began to lower. Ciera sat a little straighter and urged her horse forward. She looked to the wagon and gave a command: 'Secure the king!' Already, the wagon driver was whipping his horses to turn. At her rear, Ciera could feel the tension in her men creeping deeper with every inch the bridge fell. Metal chimed as men loosened the swords from their scabbards and set their feet in their stirrups, ready for battle.

The drawbridge touched down on the grass, and behind it the high, iron-banded double doors of the King's Gate began to creak open. Ciera's grip tightened on her reins, ready to wheel and flee to make way for the warriors behind her. Burik and Jerem had come forward to flank her, hands ready on their sword hilts. She held her breath.

A solitary rider appeared, and Ciera felt every person behind her let out a long, relieving breath. A familiar midnight-black stallion stepped across the threshold, letting out an impatient snort and pawing at the earth.

The messenger was mailed but wore no helmet, revealing a crown of blonde hair tied up in a knot. The horse tried to rush forward, and with a cry of 'Valour, easy!' the rider tugged back on the reins and slowed it to a reluctant trot, its hooves drumming on the dark wood of the drawbridge.

It was only once Ciera heard the voice that she realised it was a woman. She was tall, handsome rather than pretty, and rode with a poise that few warriors could have matched. While a man might have sought to tame the black beast beneath her with brute power, she tempered her strength with an easy, long-limbed grace, like a solitary, circling she-wolf.

'Lady Gough?' Burik was staring at her in disbelief. 'You're with Balyard now?'

'Burik.' Lady Gough nodded to him, a slight smile on her lips. 'I did not expect to see you again. You could call me Yriella again, if you prefer.'

Ciera recalled that a woman, a lord's widow, had commanded men and ridden alongside Lady Viratia when she had taken command of the *Hymeriker*. Was this some taunt of Balyard's, telling her that he did not object to women wielding power, only her?

'What message does Balyard send?' Ciera called to Lady Gough. 'Do you bring terms?'

Yriella Gough brought Valour forward until only a few yards separated them. Ciera's horse skittered nervously sideways. 'We found Balyard face down in the moat with an arrow through his neck,' said Yriella. 'But Lady Viratia will be glad to receive you up at Piperskeep. Welcome back to Merivale, Queen Ciera.'

There was no question of all Ciera's seven thousand entering Merivale, so she left Jerem in charge with instructions to prepare camp and scavenge what they could from what remained of the Imperials. There was some grumbling, but Ciera knew it would be unwise to bring so many armed men into a city still barely recovering from the Imperial assault, particularly when there was no love lost between the *Hymeriker* and the few surviving men of the Wild Brigade.

In truth though, she gave the orders in a haze of bewilderment. Of all the scenarios in Merivale she had considered, that both the Imperium and Balyard might have been ousted by Lady Viratia Brithwell had not been one of them.

Riding up the Castle Road, with Andrick in her arms and Burik, Haisie, and Sister Aimya at her heels – Tansa had agreed to remain outside the city for now, in case an observant *hymerika* recognised her – Ciera listened as Yriella Gough shared her story.

'My men and I were raiding against the Imperial camp for weeks,' she told them. 'There weren't enough of us to break past them and reach Merivale, so we did what we could, burning their tents or getting them to pursue us and then ambushing them with a larger force. Kept at it even after they took the city. Then after they fell back there seemed to be less of them every day – we caught plenty of their slaves who'd deserted – so we thought we'd keep at it until they retreated.' Yriella exhaled ruefully. 'Bit of a mystery what happened to allow them to rally and take Piperskeep; even the *hymerikai* who fought don't seem able to explain it, or what happened next.' She shrugged, smiling. 'You'll have to get the full tale from Lady Viratia.'

'Has she mentioned my father at all?' asked Burik. 'He was with her on Eryispek.'

'I was there with her, before,' added Aimya. 'Has she said anything of what happened up there? After I left? I found Queen Ciera, just as she told me to. When did she return?' She spoke feverishly, almost tripping over her own tongue in her haste.

'You'll both have to ask her yourself,' said Yriella. 'She's been too busy to talk really – fixing the hall where the ceiling fell in, clearing out the bodies, putting men to work to ensure everyone's fed. Honestly, if not for her I'm not sure there'd be a Merivale left at this point.'

Eager as she was to learn more of what had transpired, Ciera forced herself to be patient. What mattered was that Piperskeep would be hers again, without a single sword being drawn, and by what Yriella was saying she would have to work hard to live up to the standards of leadership being set by Viratia Brithwell.

She studied the sights of the Castle Road. The Imperium's occupation of the city had been brief but also bloody, coming off the back of a period of famine arising from the war with the Prindians, and the evidence for these twin hardships was everywhere. Abandoned, looted homes with their doors half-hanging off; hollow-eyed, half-dressed children begging silently for food as their procession went by; the stomach-churning smell from pits of burning corpses.

They passed a crowd congregating at the entrance to a side street, surrounding a gaunt, bearded man in a ragged tunic that fell past his knees who appeared to be preaching. 'Repent!' he cried in a croaking voice, raising his arms outstretched to the sky. 'Eryi's priests and whores sell you falsehoods and grow fat, safe within their gilded holds, while leaving us to *starve*! Cast the blindness from your eyes and embrace the wisdom of the Norhai! Only by...'

The man's voice tailed off as they rode away, but Ciera could not resist turning in her saddle for a longer look. It was rare to hear the old religion being proclaimed on the streets of Merivale.

'The eruption's brought all the crackpots out,' said Yriella. 'Thought they might have calmed down by now, but seems like more are appearing every day.'

'It was the same in Cliffark,' said Ciera.

A few people waved to her, and one family who seemed to be getting by better than most came close enough to see that Ciera was clutching Andrick and turned away shouting, 'A king! The king has returned!' Many more though saw the bronze crown on Ciera's brow and turned away with sullen eyes. There would be much to do in Merivale to regain people's trust in the strength of Piperskeep; all it had brought them in the last year was misery.

The outer gate to Piperskeep was already open for them. Signs of the Imperials' brief success were visible, sections of broken wood which had been nailed over with panels and a new bar set inside the gatehouse ready to be slammed down and barricade the door if the need arose.

As they rode into the shadow of Piperskeep, Ciera tensed as a company of *hymerikai* came down the passage towards them, remembering the last time she had seen so many they had been chasing her at Balyard's command. Each of them gave Lady Gough a short nod, and then stopped in their tracks as they recognised Ciera. For a moment, they seemed unsure, but then one by one bowed to her and Andrick, then rode on, each of them clasping wrists warmly with Burik as they passed, enmity evidently forgotten.

'Lady Viratia told them that as the king's mother, your place is here,' said Yriella.

'And will they obey me?' asked Ciera. It was surely too much to hope for.

Yriella's brow crinkled. 'Best to talk that over with Lady Viratia. The command of the *Hymeriker*'s a bit uncertain with Lord Errian being dead.'

'Dead?' Burik's eyes almost bulged out of his skull. 'He can't be dead.'

'Pulled him out of the rubble myself,' said Yriella. She lowered her voice. 'Lady Viratia's asked that he not be mentioned in her presence though, too upsetting, especially with Orsian missing. Says she'll grieve for him properly once the war is won.'

Burik fell silent, his grip on the reins loosening. His eyes went blank, and his face slackened as if suddenly numb. He gulped wordlessly, until Haisie handed him a cloth and he waved it away. Then his mouth tightened again, and the only trace of grief was a moist twinkle in his eyes. He swallowed. 'If he is dead, then he is dead. May Eryi take him.'

'What do you mean, Orsian's missing?' demanded Ciera. She would shed no tears for Errian, but surely Orsian could not be dead as well, not after what he had done for her. 'And what war if the Imperium's defeated?'

'She means the war of the gods,' Aimya whispered under her breath.

'He's just missing,' replied Yriella simply. 'Last anyone remembers seeing of him was in the dungeon, but they've sent men down to every level – never found him. Not among the rubble either.' She quickened Valour's pace, forcing the rest of them to follow before they could ask more questions.

The yard was a hive of activity, so full of mailed men that

Ciera almost wondered if they were under attack. It was packed with *hymerikai*; sparring with blades, practising shield walls, and six fresh men mounting their horses at the inner wall's gate.

The man leading the force looked towards them as they rode into the yard. 'Burik!' he exclaimed. 'Eryi's balls, is it good to see you.' His fellows behind echoed him, calling out greetings.

Burik edged his horse towards him and clasped the man's wrist, grinning. 'Drayen – good to see you. You heading down to the city?'

Drayen grimaced. 'That's it. Grunt work. Lady Viratia's got us organising the city's restoration. Said it's the best use we can make of ourselves right now – hearts and minds, wants the commonfolk to love her.'

While Burik was greeting his fellows, Ciera dismounted and gazed up at the towering fortress, a colossus of sheer granite and spiralling turrets. It had not changed, but then it never did. Suddenly though, she noticed that a whole section of ground-floor tiles was missing, with just the top of a single stunted, crumbling pillar visible where before had been the roof of the keep's great hall.

Yriella came to stand next to her. 'Yes, that's the hall. Or it was.'

Ciera's mouth was hanging open. 'What happened?' She was amazed the keep was still standing.

'The Imperium happened. Lady Viratia will fix it though – we've already got most of the rubble cleared away.'

Ciera felt that Yriella was ascribing a little too much power to Lady Viratia – bringing in enough fresh stone through the keep to rebuild the hall might take years. 'Where is she?'

'In the solar.'

Ciera gave a dark laugh. Of course. It seemed that anyone who sought to rule Piperskeep could not resist the pull of the tower solar, from where one could look out of the window and see endless miles of their dominion.

Inside the keep, the rest of which appeared unscathed, Ciera let Yriella lead her up the familiar stairs to Hessian's tower. The others followed her eagerly; she could feel Aimya and Burik's impatience to reach Lady Viratia.

The door at the top of the stairs was already open, revealing the solar aglow with flames, every wall sconce burning brightly and candles lining every spare surface. At the table where so often Hessian had been found hunched, tendrils of smoke morphed and curled, obscuring the features of the woman standing behind it.

Viratia Brithwell wore a long dark dress, standing among the flickering candles like the black priestess of some forgotten faith. In her middle years, she wore the easy beauty of the nobility in the golden gleam of her hair and the waspishness of her waist. Her face shone brightly in the firelight, belying her years in the smoothness of her skin and the brightness of her cheeks, yet her blue eyes glinted with a wisdom beyond their years. Her mouth was a straight line, as if someone had made a jest and she had declined to laugh.

Their eyes met, and Ciera drew an intake of breath. A shrewd gaze fixed her in place, as if Viratia was measuring and weighing her with eyes.

'Welcome.' Viratia's voice seemed to ring with gratitude at their presence. Her smile was like a beam of sunlight, capturing them in its glow. In Ciera's arms, Andrick stirred in his sleep and grimaced. 'Queen Ciera Istlewick, mother to King Andrick. Piperskeep is yours.'

CHAPTER 31

The sky was black and violent red, like burning pitch. The fire rolled over the clouds and the cold sunlight, until all the world was cloaked in shadow. On the horizon, Eryispek thundered, endless flames pouring from it in a spiralling tornado of powerful heat. On the plains of Erland, two armies clashed, painting the ground with blood and shaken earth, alive with the clamour of combat as men fell from their horses, skewered by spears or trampled beneath the ceaseless churn of battle.

It was impossible to tell whether either side was winning. Pherri wanted to scream at them: '*Look at the sky!*' but they would never hear her. The sky was raining grey ash, coating the battlefield in cinders, but the warriors never turned from their task, from the constant rattling of swords and the shattering of shields.

The ground rumbled, and as it reached a feverish, quaking crescendo the fighting finally stopped. The combatants turned in confusion. Even the sky was shaking, and the rain of embers had become a tempest.

A beautiful shining light exploded from the plains, throwing men backwards. It rose into the sky, a woman fifty-feet tall with crimson eyes bright and terrible as fiery dawn. Men fell to their knees, shielding their gaze against the impossible incandescence. It burnt Pherri's eyes to look at her, but she knew this was really a dream, a vision from beyond the vast, impenetrable veil that separated the worlds. Nothing she saw her could hurt her, not really.

The brightness faded, and Pherri's heart she swore nearly stopped. The figure wore her mother's face, but her smile was one Pherri had never seen her mother bear. Her lips were so thin as to be non-existent, the teeth small and pointed amidst a cavernous black mouth. Her eyes shone, and her hair writhed in the air like a pit of snakes. She was naked, her body so perfect and white it was as though she had been carved from alabaster. Men on their knees gazed in stunned wonder, their mouths hanging open, their weapons dropping from dead fingers.

'SERVE ME.' The voice filled the battlefield. Even the raining ash seemed to fall back from her, curving around her irresistible power. 'THIS WORLD IS *MINE.*'

Pherri woke, breathless, her skin coated in sweat, her head pounding like the beating of drums. She rose, rushed to the chamber pot, and vomited, then reached for an urn of water placed beside her bed and tipped half of it down her gullet before coming back for more. Her throat blazed like someone had poured liquid fire down it.

Phyrrai rushed to her, handing Pherri a cloth of goat fur to wipe her sweat-soaked skin. She ran it down her face, and it came away stained red. Her nose was bleeding again. She fell to her knees, panting with her hands set against the bed frame.

'It's getting worse,' she gasped. Every move she made sent agony through her. It would ebb through the day, she knew, but the pain would never go away entirely, and night would mean more fitful sleep and overwhelming dreams and then another morning of vomiting and shaking. She looked down at her trembling fingers; the skin around her nails was beginning to blacken, tingling as if submerged in icy water. She whimpered at the new symptom; her whole body seemed to be falling apart.

Phyrrai rubbed her back. 'Hawla and the Sorrowseer will be here soon. Perhaps you can finally leave.'

'I hope so.' Pherri let out a low moan and placed her forehead against the cool floorboards. It was not just her at least; Hrogo's symptoms were much the same. Phyrrai and Halyana were both fine, which supported what the Sorrowseer had said, that their ailment was a result of being in an unfamiliar world.

It took her a moment to realise that Phyrrai had said 'you'.

Pherri looked up at her through tear-stained eyes. 'What do you mean, "*you* can finally leave"?'

Phyrrai hesitated. She ran a hand through her braid. 'Well... I was wondering if you still needed me. I'm not sure I can do this. I thought I might... go home.'

'Go home how?'

'Erland is closer than Pipersmont,' replied Phyrrai. She sank down onto the bed, and Pherri realised she seemed to be on the brink of tears. 'It's just... I don't think there's anything more I can do for you, and... Da'ri's dead because of me. He was the useful one, him and Halyana; I can't do anything.' Her eyes brimmed. 'I want to go home.'

As the words left her lips, she burst into tears, and now it was Pherri's turn to comfort Phyrrai. Their deep unease at each other's touch had ceased to trouble them, and so Pherri pulled herself up onto the bed and embraced Phyrrai while she sobbed into her shoulder.

If the Sorrowseer was right, all that would save her was reaching the distant mountain, and there killing Phyrrai. Pherri gritted her teeth. *I can't do it. I won't.* But her dream, some vestige of the *prophika* she had used in her own world, only proved to her that she had to return. Otherwise her world would fall, if not at the hand of Eryi then at the hand of

Vulgatypha, and then finally every other world including this one.

So she *did* need Phyrrai. *No*. She would find some other way – she had to.

But... what if she did not?

'I do need you,' Pherri whispered as her twin continued to sob. 'I can't go on with just Hrogo and Helana. If it weren't for you, I'd still be in the dungeon.'

Immediately, she was wracked with guilt. *I don't want Phyrrai to die*, she told herself. But in that case, why wasn't she telling her what the Sorrowseer had said?

Because then she would be even more unwilling to go with you.

Whether there was another way, she had to reach Pipersmont, and so far a plan to do that had eluded them. Hawla had spoken with Grawl, but the chieftain was reportedly adamant that he would not give up his prisoners. If a deal could be struck with Jarhyck to grant the Sorrowmen land in Erland's south, he apparently saw the rest of them as valuable hostages for the agreement being fulfilled. Their attempts to reach the mountain in the southern wastes were of no interest to him.

By the time Hawla and the Sorrowseer arrived, Phyrrai had calmed herself, and the worst effects of Pherri's illness had receded. She was sitting up in bed with a cool cloth on her forehead. Wordlessly, Hawla administered a cup of steaming, fragrant tea, which Pherri held to her nose and took deep breaths of.

'We have a plan,' croaked the Sorrowseer from behind her strange mask.

'You leave tonight,' said Hawla. 'It is a full moon, when we allow the men to enter the compound for the length of the moon's rise and fall. Only the young boys will be left to tend the goats, so there will be fewer eyes on you.'

'You must come to my tent an hour after moonrise,' said the

Sorrowseer. 'We will cast a rope from the inner to the outer wall, directly over their heads, and pray to the Great Buck that none of them look up. We will have to be quick.'

'You're coming with us?' said Phyrrai.

The Sorrowseer nodded. 'Pherri may need me if you are to reach the mountain. There are many miles between here and there; we must keep your strength up.'

'Can you tell how far it is?' said Pherri. She had stood upon the walls and stared south several times, but found the distance impossible to judge. 'Do you know the way?'

'We will need to be quick,' said the Sorrowseer, ignoring her questions. 'Only you two and the man.'

'We can't just leave Halyana here,' said Phyrrai. 'How's she meant to look after herself?'

'The girl's wits are addled,' barked the Sorrowseer. Her mask seemed to flash into a scowl, but Pherri was used to the illusion now, even if she did not understand it. 'She won't survive either way. How do you suppose she's going to get back to Erland? Be thankful I'm willing to bring Hrogo, as much as he'll slow us down.'

'And how do you suppose I will get back to Erland?' said Phyrrai. It seemed Pherri's intervention had already persuaded her to go with them. 'We came this way to help Pherri; we can work out how to get back later. Halyana can hunt; she's useful.'

She doesn't expect Phyrrai to return, realised Pherri, looking at the Sorrowseer's blank mask. Was she so sure that Pherri would kill her shadowtwin to return to her own world? The idea that the Sorrowseer might be thinking that made Pherri fear she might vomit again.

'We aren't leaving without her,' said Phyrrai, folding her arms over her chest. 'Or Jarhyck.'

Hawla laughed. 'You've more chance of persuading Grawl to give you his favourite goat than getting him to release the

Erlish king. The other two I will leave in the hands of the Sorrowseer, but him – never.'

'Fine – the girl came come.' The Sorrowseer's reluctance was plain by the gravel in her voice and the set of her jaw. 'But if she falls behind, she will be left behind.'

'There'll be goats waiting for you outside,' said Hawla. 'One of my sons will arrange it. He'll do anything I ask provided it upsets Grawl.' She paused, and looked from Pherri to Phyrrai. 'Just know that if you are caught, I will deny all knowledge. I will be able to save the Sorrowseer, but your lives will be forfeit. Grawl will suspect you are fleeing to raise an army in Erland to free the king. It will mean your deaths.'

Pherri swallowed. She would die anyway if they did not reach Pipersmont, her body slowly failing, her dreams becoming more vivid and the flow of blood from her nose becoming a torrent. If Grawl caught her it would only mean a quick death rather than a slow one. She looked at Phyrrai. 'Are you sure you want to do this?'

Phyrrai came to her bedside and squeezed her hand, without any of the crushing discomfort Pherri would have felt weeks ago. 'I swore to help you, didn't I? Nothing has changed, Sister. I will stay with you for as long as you need me.'

It felt a long day, waiting for the moon to rise. The sense of excitement within the inner fort at the prospect of the men's arrival seemed to grow throughout the morning, the Sorrowwomen moving with an extra spring in their step as they went about their daily tasks. As the afternoon drew in, many turned to the task of preparing for the men's arrival, setting out tables crowded with empty horns and urns of fermented goat's milk. Some were even decorating themselves in anticipation, daubing black tar paint under their cheeks and donning extravagant horned headdresses.

Pherri felt none of this, only a mixture of hope and fear that settled in her stomach and did not leave her through the day, even as her sickness faded and she was able to rise from bed, eat a few bites of goat meat, and walk by herself.

What do Hawla and the Sorrowseer gain from helping us? she wondered in quieter moments. The Sorrowseer seemed to know much, and she was grateful for the strange woman's help, but there were too many unanswered questions for Pherri to wholly trust her. She swore the woman knew more of Pipersmont than she was letting on. And what was that mask hiding? Even Hawla said she had never seen her face.

'We don't have a choice,' Phyrrai told her, when Pherri dared to speak these concerns aloud. 'I don't trust them either, but where does that leave us? We'll only stay trapped here with them.' Pherri reluctantly accepted the point, and they did not speak again of it.

They gathered Hrogo and Halyana to them, at a deserted section of the fort's wall, and told them in low whispers of their plan to escape. Hrogo accepted the plan without question, nodding weakly along with them as he struggled against the same illness that plagued Pherri. Halyana as ever was mute, but there was a keen understanding in her sharp eyes as Pherri and Phyrrai told them all to be ready to meet at the Sorrowseer's tent once the festivities began.

When the moon rose, Pherri was still atop the wall, listening to the excited babbling from the women within and the men without. The gate groaned open, and with a great cheer the Sorrowmen poured in. She watched as Grawl took Hawla in his arms to kiss her long and passionately, then seized a horn of milk as they retired to her hut. Other couples broke off in much the same manner, while the younger men and women congregated around the tables, knocking back goat's milk in the torchlight while three great drums beat on in the background. As they rose to a crescendo, the Sorrowlanders would dance, and then as they began to fall again would return to their drinks, gathering in small groups and speaking quickly in their native tongue, laughing uproariously at things Pherri did not understand.

'If the boys standing guard drink half so much as them, we ought to have no trouble,' said Phyrrai. 'Hawla told me she sent them each two flagons of fermented milk.'

Pherri wished she shared her shadowtwin's optimism. The dread in her stomach was not just the lingering effects of this day's bout of illness. If they failed, Grawl would take them, and there would be no more comfortable beds and being woken with cups of tea.

The revelry was still in its early stages when they walked along the parapet to the Sorrowseer's tent on its platform sticking over the southern end of the fort. With a look over their shoulders and along the walkway to be sure they were not seen, Pherri and Phyrrai stepped through the entrance.

The Sorrowseer was again sitting on the other side of her fire, the flames reflecting in her sheer white mask. Hrogo was already present, and Halyana ducked in behind them. Her gaze fell upon the Sorrowseer and immediately her eyes grew wide. She gave an alarmed hiss, took a step back, then seemed to change her mind, and threw herself across the tent.

Only Hrogo's quick thinking stopped Halyana reaching the Sorrowseer. He threw out a leg, and Halyana went sprawling. In an instant she was on her feet again, trying to make a rush for the Sorrowseer, but Hrogo grabbed her from behind and held her tight, crushing her arms against her torso. Halyana struggled and spat and hissed like a trapped wildcat, heedless of the blood trickling from her mouth.

The Sorrowseer rose. 'I told you she should not be coming!' She sounded genuinely shaken. 'I told you, the girl is mad!'

'She's never done anything like this before!' Phyrrai rushed forward to where Hrogo was still struggling to hold Halyana back and reached up to take her face in her hands, whispering calming words and forcing the older girl to meet her eye. Slowly, Halyana calmed, and cautiously Hrogo and Phyrrai guided her back to the edge of the tent, as far from the Sorrowseer as they could.

'Just stay there, Halyana,' Phyrrai told her, grasping her hand and holding the girl's eye. 'No one's going to hurt you, understand?'

Halyana's eyes flicked to the Sorrowseer, her teeth bared and radiating hatred, but slowly she nodded, and when Phyrrai pulled away she stayed where she was, staring into nothingness, as if she had forgotten the Sorrowseer was there at all.

Pherri looked from Halyana to the Sorrowseer and back again. What did that mean? Halyana had hardly reacted to anything their whole journey here, never mind with violence.

'Well,' said the Sorrowseer, speaking in clipped tones. 'Unless you are ready to agree we leave her behind, I suggest we proceed.'

She strode to the back of the tent, and peeled back the canvas to the night. The horizon was dark, but Pipersmont glowed like a rusted knife under the silvery moonlight. Across the divide of the goat field, the bleached wood walls of the outer fort also shone, though in the darkness it took Pherri a moment to spot the coarse length of rope that ran taut from the tent to the outer wall.

'That thing?' exclaimed Hrogo in dismay, hobbling forward on his twisted legs. 'How are we all supposed to cross that?'

'Keep your voice down,' hissed the Sorrowseer. 'There are boys minding the goats right below us.'

Pherri peered over the edge, and saw them. Thirty feet below, they sat in pairs, passing horns of milk back and forth and surrounded by sleeping goats. Some of the boys looked to be nodding off already as well. 'Go quickly and go quietly,' said the Sorrowseer. 'Just watch and do what I do. Come one at a time.'

Without hesitation, the Sorrowseer grasped the rope and swung herself down, wrapping her legs in their goat hide breeches around it and locking her ankles together. Gripping the rope between her two strong hands, she began pulling herself along, the rasp of her feet against the cord barely audible over the ambience of the night. Pherri's mouth fell open in disbelief. Hawla had said the Sorrowseer had known her great-great-grandmother. It should not have been possible.

Hrogo looked visibly anxious. 'Someone else should go next.'

Halyana was still withdrawn at the back of the tent. Pherri looked to Phyrrai, knowing it had to be one of them. Pherri could still feel the faint aftereffects of that morning's sickness.

Phyrrai nodded. 'I'll go next.'

The Sorrowseer reached the other side. With more surprising strength, she twisted her body round and hauled herself up onto the deserted walkway. She stood there serenely, waiting. Her mask had not even been knocked askew.

Phyrrai was already lowering herself onto the rope. She did as the Sorrowseer had, clinging on with her stick-thin arms and locking her legs. A gasp escaped her lips as one of her hands slipped. Pherri gasped with her – she was surely going to fall – but then she managed to get her hand back on and lock her fingers. Slowly, Phyrrai began edging her way along the rope, eventually falling into a steady rhythm.

She began to slow as she reached the other end, tiring, but just as it looked as if her grip was about to come loose the Sorrowseer threw out a hand and pulled her to safety.

'Are we sure that's an old woman behind that mask?' murmured Hrogo. 'How old do you think she actually is?'

Pherri could not help wondering the same. What was the Sorrowseer hiding?

There was no time to think about that now though – it was her turn. She tried to do as Phyrrai did, and managed to cling on.

Crossing the gap between the two walls was even harder than it looked. The thirty or so yards had seemed barely anything when she had crossed between the gates below, but now it seemed like a chasm. Her shoulders burnt, and she could feel blisters forming on her palms from the coarse rope. She forced herself on, one hand at a time, and kept her eyes closed, refusing to look towards the vast distance still to go or how far she would fall if her grip slipped.

Time seemed to stretch, each reach of her arm taking longer and hurting more than the last. Pherri gritted her teeth, and felt a fresh trail of blood begin to trickle from her nose. She craned her head back further to stem the flow, praying no blood would land on any of the boys below.

When the Sorrowseer's hand grasped her arm, Pherri nearly let go in surprise. Together, Phyrrai and the Sorrowseer pulled her onto the walkway, and Pherri lay back on the wood, breathing deeply.

'There are fires to the north,' whispered Phyrrai excitedly, pointing. 'They're moving!'

'Quiet!' hissed the Sorrowseer.

Vaguely aware that Halyana was clambering out onto the rope behind her, Pherri looked the way Phyrrai was indicating, towards the north and Erland. There were indeed fires, torches meandering over the rugged black rocks of the Sorrows, unmistakably heading for Ulsenfort. She gaped, the torchglow revealing mailed men on horseback – they were Erlanders, perhaps the *hymerikai*.

She turned on the Sorrowseer. 'You knew! That's why it had to be tonight!'

'Be silent!' The Sorrowseer took Pherri by surprise and seized her throat, not roughly but not gently either. 'Do you want to get caught?'

Pherri pulled away, rubbing her neck. Halyana was steadily making her way across. When the Erlanders attacked, it would be the perfect opportunity to escape, but they had to hurry, before the alarm sounded and the walls swarmed with Sorrowmen. The *hymerikai* were already making their way up the hill towards the fort.

Pherri watched with her heart in her mouth. Halyana was making swift progress, and Hrogo was waiting eagerly on the other side to begin his crossing.

'You could go back with them,' Pherri hissed to Phyrrai, watching the oncoming *hymerikai*. 'You and Halyana.' *Save yourself*, she thought. *Save yourself from what I might have to do.*

And then the first fire arrows began to fly.

The Erlanders announced themselves with a thunderous war cry. 'JARHYCK! KING! JARHYCK! KING!' Something began to pound against the eastern gate off to Pherri's left as flaming projectiles arced like shooting stars over the walls, and in seconds the young goatherds were awake. Flames were already dancing across patches of grass, and the air was suddenly filled with the alarmed cries of men and the bleating of goats.

'We need to go!' shouted the Sorrowseer over the din. There were flames licking up the eastern wall now. 'Leave them!'

Halyana was only halfway across, but in the panic Hrogo leapt onto the rope, and the cord creaked with the strain. His slave chain swung wildly through the air as he began an ungainly shuffle across. Halyana looked back and quickened her pace. Pherri watched in horror; the rope was already beginning to fray.

Then, everything seemed to happen all at once. With a

thunderous crack, the eastern gate burst open; a young goatherd looked up and cried out as he saw the escapees; the inner gate slammed open and furious Sorrowmen began to pour into the outer ring; then finally the rope *snapped*.

It ruptured in the middle, and Halyana plummeted towards the ground as Hrogo lost his grasp on his own splitting end of rope and fell heavily onto the grass below, landing on his back. Halyana was luckier; she held on as her end swung towards the outer wall, and leapt clear just before impact. She landed lithely on her feet and immediately looked around, rushing to where Hrogo was still lying on his back wheezing.

'Just leave them!' said the Sorrowseer again. 'They're as good as dead down there.'

Pherri and Phyrrai did not reply. They stared north as the two forces, *hymerikai* and Sorrowmen, crashed into each other in a great cacophony of steel, blood, and flesh. The *hymerikai* were outnumbered, but they were the aggressors, the more battle-ready, and they were able to force the Sorrowmen back towards the inner gate, fanning out on their horses and riding down their foe. The Sorrowmen were fighting furiously to reach their goats, but they were penned in. A few brave boys from the fields tried to flank them, and were swiftly dispatched with downward thrusts of sword and spear from the *hymerikai*.

'What's she doing?' Phyrrai was pointing down towards Halyana. She was supporting Hrogo under one arm and together they were hobbling towards the shattered eastern gate, but as Pherri watched Halyana diverted towards a ramshackle hut, little more than a lean-to below the inner wall. The door was locked, so Halyana seized a discarded axe and began hacking away at the lock, eventually reducing it to smithereens.

Halyana leapt back as the prisoner within kicked his way free, and there in the doorway stood Jarhyck, half-naked, covered in a patchwork of bruises, bellowing his fury. He was barely fifty yards from the battle, and a cry went up from a *hymerika* at the sight of him and soon half-a-dozen of them had broken off from the main assault and were riding towards their king.

'Look!' It was Phyrrai's turn to point this time, to their left, westward. A force of Sorrowmen perhaps a hundred-strong had left the inner fort by a different gate and claimed their goats. They rode hard towards Jarhyck and the *hymerikai*, their axes raised in their fists and a guttural, ululating war cry bursting from their lips. Horned Grawl was at the front, his face frozen in a howl of battle lust.

'You should go,' hissed Pherri to Phyrrai again. 'Get to Jarhyck and go!'

'No.' Phyrrai turned to her, her eyes tight with determination. 'I told you, I'm not leaving you.' She grasped Pherri's hand.

A strong bony hand seized Pherri's shoulder. 'We need to leave!' The Sorrowseer's terrifying mask stared down at her, its expression full of fear and fury. 'They're safe, look!'

It was true. Pherri followed her pointing finger, and saw Halyana and Hrogo dodging the edges of the melee to escape via the eastern gate. The battle was more even now; the *Hymeriker* had lost the element of surprise and were now fighting on two fronts, the Sorrowmen from the inner gate and those who had flanked them from the south. The fires the Erlanders' arrows had lit were beginning to spread though; the Sorrowlanders needed water or their whole stronghold would go up in flames.

The Sorrowseer's grip tightened on Pherri's shoulder, and she steered her to the palisaded edge of the southern wall and thrust another rope into her hands. 'Climb down. This isn't our fight.'

Whatever else the Sorrowseer might be, she was right. Pherri took the rope and scrambled over the edge, the sounds of battle and burning ringing in her ears.

CHAPTER 32

The room stank of old sweat, smokestick ash, and unwashed sheets. There were no windows, and the only lights came from the lamp Rymond held before him as he stepped over the threshold and the orange glow of the single occupant's smokestick. It reminded Rymond of the room the Imperials had left him in to rot, which he had turned into his private casheef den, surrounded by burnt-out ends and his own filth.

The woman who had plotted to arrange that looked rather different now. Alcantra's fingers around the smokestick had been bitten down the cuticle, and trembled slightly as she raised it to her lips. Her blonde hair was growing out in greasy strands plastered to her gaunt face, and her skin had turned sallow and lifeless.

It was easy to see why Acques Bazar had left her here.

A fortnight had passed since the successful recapture of Irith, and Rymond felt as though he had barely had time to catch his breath. There had been a ceremony in the hall to reinvest Rymond with his crown and to pay tribute to all those who had fallen in reclaiming it; clearing away the rubble of the outer bailey and main gate had begun; all of Rymond's lords had been summoned to Irith; he had addressed the city and his return had been the cause of much rejoicing; the final legionnaires in the city had either surrendered or been beaten to death by the mob; and he had dealt with a hundred practical matters that needed his attention ranging from where his men would sleep to the disposal of the hundreds of corpses being picked out of the wreckage. It had only been the day before that someone had thought to tell him Alcantra had been found in a low chamber half-hidden beneath a set of stairs.

She looked up at him with a weak smile, and blew out a haze of smoke. To Rymond's relief he detected no hint of casheef. 'You've returned.'

'So have you,' he replied. There was nowhere to sit, so he remained standing by the door. 'Do you get many visitors?'

Alcantra shook her head. 'Bazar forbade it.' She laughed, a creaking, throaty sound that belonged to a much older woman. 'Said I'd lost my mind. Left me here with my tabac and not enough food.' She took a drag on her smokestick. 'Heard you killed him.'

'My mother killed him.'

Alcantra paused. 'Are you here to kill me as well?'

It was something Rymond had thought on. Nobody would have faulted him for it; Alcantra was perhaps the main reason he had lost his crown in the first place. It was she who had got him hooked on casheef, and then plotted with Dom and Strovac to betray him. But looking at Alcantra now, it seemed a petty revenge. The woman sitting before him was barely a shadow of the one who had schemed against him. 'That depends. Tell me of Merivale.'

She croaked out another laugh. 'We were winning. Would have won, if not for Drast Fulkiro.' Alcantra looked away, towards a cold fireplace littered with embers. 'Krupal killed him though. A magus. Parmé only knows where he came from.' She paused to take another long drag on her smokestick. 'I was lucky enough to escape, and when I tried to warn Bazar that a magus was on the loose he locked me away in here. Said the magi were all dead, and I was making excuses for my failure.' Her mouth bent in a bitter smile. 'Shame he never found out the truth for himself, but I suppose I can live with him being dead.'

Rymond knew there were still magi. It was said that Hessian's magus, Theodric, had ears everywhere. Folk still spoke of him in hushed, fearful tones, though the man had not been seen in half-a-year. He had never though heard of Krupal; perhaps he was the second man Helana had seen in the casheef vision he had dismissed as a hallucination. 'Helana Sangreal urges me to march to Merivale,' he said. 'She tells a tale similar to yours.' He saw no reason to tell Alcantra of Helana's claim that the god Eryi was there also; either she would not believe him, or the news would only unbalance her further.

Alcantra looked up at him with deep, haunted eyes. For several seconds, she was perfectly still, the last whisker of her smokestick burning down to her fingers. 'Stay away,' she said finally. Her voice was a fearful rasp. 'Tumble the bridges into the river, and never think of East Erland again. What he can do is *unnatural*.'

Before Rymond could reply, a knock came from behind him, and Alcantra dropped her smokestick with a yelp. The door scraped open, revealing Rymond's mother.

'Several of your lords await you in the antechamber,' she told him, not even looking at Alcantra. 'I suggest that would be a better use of your time.'

Rymond nodded. He could not afford to keep such men waiting – not if he meant to keep his crown this time. That his mother had come to fetch him rather than sending a servant indicated she felt the same. He looked to Alcantra and smiled apologetically. 'We shall speak again.'

But Alcantra did not seem to hear him. She was hunched

over her lap, already rolling another smokestick between her trembling fingers.

Rymond exited with his mother, and together they walked towards the hall, at the other end of the castle. The wall sconces were lit and the floor had been recently swept, which was no small feat given the number of servants who had disappeared during the Imperial occupation.

'You know the girl is quite mad,' said Breta. 'They made me share a room with her for a time. Perhaps they hoped I would tire of her and kill her – give them another reason to execute me.'

'Given you were prisoners together I would have thought you might have more sympathy.' His mother had taken a day's rest after her liberation and then immediately began inserting herself into every aspect of Rymond's burgeoning rule. The tale that she had slain Acques Bazar and saved Rymond's life had spread through the castle like wildfire.

'Sympathy? I lost my finger, not my wits.' She held up her left hand, proudly displaying the stump where her third digit had been. 'And surely you're not overcome with understanding for her?'

Rymond put a finger to his temple. He could feel a headache coming on. 'I am merely interested in what she has to say of East Erland. You don't believe her, presumably?'

Breta raised an eyebrow. 'I am told there was a man named Krupal with the Imperial force in East Erland who may have been a magus, but I have had no word from there though since a report that the Imperials had taken Piperskeep. That may have changed by now – a messenger reached me this morning with word that Ciera Istlewick is leading a force from Cliffark to retake Merivale. If the Imperials are as weak as they say, they are finished.'

Rymond nodded, thinking. 'Perhaps we should not concern ourselves with East Erland for the time being.' He had promised

Helana he would go, but his first duties were to restore Irith and reach favourable terms with the lords he had abandoned to fight the Imperium by themselves. If Ciera Istlewick had the strength to deal with whoever assailed Merivale, then he need not trouble himself. There might be a rogue magus on the loose in East Erland, but no spy of his mother's had mentioned Eryi rising to life from the Mountain.

'I have already told those who matter that we will ride for Merivale within the fortnight.'

His mother's revelation stopped Rymond in his tracks. He turned to stare at her. 'Why—'

'I would have thought the answer obvious,' she replied, interrupting him.

Rymond ran an aggravated hand through his recently trimmed beard. *It never ends.* 'You think our time has come to seize the whole of Erland.'

His mother raised an eyebrow. 'Or Merivale at least. The East Erlanders and the Imperium will have bled the city to ruin these past months. All you must do is reach out and take it, and the rest of East Erland will fall at your feet.'

'And what of Helana's tale?' Helana remained as adamant as ever of what she had seen during the Thrumb's casheef-addled execution ceremony. That at least gave Rymond cause to entertain the possibility of Eryi's involvement.

His mother snorted. 'Next you will be believing in wood-nymphs. Hessian was half-mad; why should his daughter not be as well? All we will find in East Erland is two beaten armies, and the *hymerikai* fighting for either that fool Balyard or a child still on the tit. They will beg you to take the crown.'

'We have enough to do here in Irith,' said Rymond. Even just repairing the destruction caused by the huyar seemed an improbable task. 'And it might take months for us to put together an army with the strength to conquer Merivale.'

'Precisely why I altered the missives summoning your lords. You have commanded them to bring their full strength here.'

That was too much for Rymond. 'You had no right!' He dropped his voice to an undertone, conscious they were speaking in an open corridor. 'My authority with them hangs by a thread already, if it exists at all, and now you're telling them to come here in force! I'll be lucky if they don't use those men to drag me out of the city and hang me!'

'And that is why you must give them no opportunity to question your authority.' His mother seized him by the arm. 'Remember: you are their *king*. Act like it, and they will follow. Where were they while I languished in a cell and you were out there fighting? Answer me that. By the end of their audience with you, they should be counting themselves fortunate they still have their heads.'

It was an interesting supposition. Rymond rolled it around in his mind. He had been so preoccupied with his own responsibility for the Imperial presence in West Erland he had not considered whether his lords ought to have done more. It had been easy for them to roll over when the word was sent out that Rymond Prindian, half-mad on casheef and locked in a filthy dark chamber, had granted West Erland to the Imperium. Why had none of them fought as he had?

He tried to recall which of his lords had arrived in the city already. He knew Urwen Storaut, grandson of the old Lord Storaut. The slender young lord had joined Rymond's camp weeks ago and proven his strength and skill in the capture of Irith, but most of the Storaut strength was lost to him, gone to East Erland with their dead lord and never returned. The rest were also young men – lords Clymore, Peregryn, Chagres. Rymond supposed that suited him: there were no veterans who would naturally expect deference from their youthful king. The lands of these three were modest, and close to Irith, comprising a few hundred hectares and simple stone holdfasts, earnt by their forefathers for deeds long forgotten.

Rymond had to conclude that his mother was right. Such men should be eager to prove themselves worthy of their overlord. They were no threat to him. He would greet them as a single-minded king, demanding their allegiance and being clear in what he expected of them. There was word that the heir to Lord Rudge Darlton – another dead in service to the Imperials, not long after the inheritance of his own title – had arrived in the city, but he would likely be another young man. He would fall into line with the rest, eager to prove he was not a traitor like his father.

'You must present yourself as a king worthy of the name,' continued his mother. 'If you can do that, Merivale will be yours.'

Rymond took the easy decision to send his mother away before he met his lords – it would be harder to command their respect if they thought Breta Prindian pulled his strings.

As he entered the antechamber though, Rymond was surprised to discover that only one man was present, and not one he was familiar with. A handsome stranger sat at the head of the table, with hard dark green eyes and a beard trimmed short revealing an anvil-like jaw. Rymond would have placed him in his thirties, for there was no trace of grey in his coal-black hair drawn back in a tail, and he stood from the table to reveal a lean, tapered torso, no doubt honed from many hours at sword and in the saddle.

'Majesty,' the man greeted him. He stepped forward to seize Rymond in a tight grip of his forearm. He was tall as well, overtopping Rymond by several fingers. 'Lord Rostar Darlton, at your service.' He kept his face stern, unsmiling. 'The other lords agreed that I would represent them, so that we would speak with one voice.'

Rymond could easily see how the younger lords might have been cowed by Rostar Darlton. His voice was deep and gritty, and he was garbed for war, in full mail with a sword at his belt, making Rymond feel slightly foolish in his well-tailored court clothes of green linen and velvet decorated with threads of gold and silver, which fortunately had not been pilfered by the Imperials. 'Well met, Lord,' Rymond replied, hastily freeing himself from the lord's grip, wracking his brain as to how this man could be related to the overproud and portly Lord Rudge Darlton. 'I regret—'

'I'm his youngest brother,' said Darlton, retaking his seat where he had already poured himself a cup of wine. 'I assume that's what you were going to ask. I doubt you recall me – I've been away from Erland.'

Rymond hastily took his own seat. A servant stepped forward to serve him, but Rymond waved him away from the flagon of wine and regretfully served himself a mug of weak ale. 'It was. I had thought there was a son—'

'My nephew, Tamas,' interrupted Darlton. Rymond got the sense that Rostar Darlton was a man who did not hold much store in rank and custom. His voice took on a bitter note. 'Dead, him and the rest. He was twelve.'

'You have my condolences,' said Rymond. 'There has been much suffering in West Erland the last year. It is my aim to bring that to an end.'

'Don't you want to know how he died?' shot back Darlton. 'I suspect my brother thought that if he fought alongside the Imperials they would leave him alone, but this Acques Bazar had other ideas.' He glowered at Rymond, his black brows furrowed. 'They turned up at Whitewater Motte two months ago. Tamas had too few to hold the castle against them, but he was a fierce little beast, as hard-headed as my brother. He tried to make a stand, and when the Imperials took the bailey, they butchered everyone, all my brother's family.' He took a long slug of wine, keeping his eyes fixed on Rymond.

'I hope to see every Imperial brought to justice,' replied Rymond quickly. He had begun to sweat slightly under Rostar Darlton's hard gaze. 'You'll have seen the Imperials we slew here. There are more in the dungeon. If the killers of your family are among them—'

'They're not among them, because I killed those whoresons myself.' Darlton leant forward towards Rymond. 'I've been away the last two years, fighting in Cylirien – a younger son must find his glory where he can. I landed back in Whitewater a month ago, and when I heard what had happened, I rowed two dozen men to the Motte under cover of darkness. There's a secret way up from below the cliff. Only my family knew of it, so the Imperials set no guards.' His swelling pupils had turned his green eyes to pitiless pools of darkness. 'We butchered hundreds of them in their beds and stuck their corpses up on the cliffs as a warning, as my forebears did in days of old.

'There's nothing special about my story. Near every man in the country knows someone dead at the Imperials' hand. Lucky in some ways, I suppose; better than being made a slave and sent back to Ulvatia.

'But the other lords and I are agreed. It's not only the Imperials responsible for this. My nephew's death is on your hands as much as theirs, because you gave up and handed your rule over to them without a fight.'

Rymond tried to cover his expression with a sip of beer, but it went down the wrong way and he ended up spluttering. He thought fearfully of Rostar Darlton's sword hanging from his belt, just out of sight below the table. *The man is mad; only a madman would be so desperate for violence that they would go to Cylirien.* 'I also took back everything they stole from me,' he forced himself to say. His voice sounded thin and unconvincing next to Darlton's. 'Nobody has killed more of the Eternal Legion than I.' If he counted those crushed by the wall and Helana's huyar that was certainly true.

'And I suppose you think that should mean something.' Darlton snorted. 'Well, this isn't about the rights and wrongs of what's been done, it's about what's to come. When a man who I would charitably regard as a *weak, drug-addled, indolent, mummy's boy coward* proclaims himself my king and summons me to Irith with all my strength, that gets my blood up. By what *right* do *you*, who caused the slaughter of all my kin, summon *me*?' He was standing now, his hands planted on the table as he leant forward over Rymond, his dark eyes glittering with barely repressed fury. 'Nevertheless.' His voice fell a notch. 'Here I am, with what strength I have – two hundred who returned with me in Cylirien and five hundred mustered from Whitewater town. Only question now is what I do with them. The other lords I've spoken to are all wondering the same thing.' He paused. 'So let me tell you what we want: fair recompense from the Prindian treasury for ills suffered.' From inside his mail, he produced several rolls of parchment, and threw them down on the table. 'Accounts of losses suffered due to the Imperial occupation, valued in gold.'

Rymond held Darlton's gaze, though by the time the lord finished speaking blood was coursing through him like a raging tide. There were Prindian kings of old who would have sent men to the dungeon for speaking to them like that, and part of him wanted to do just the same.

But the threat could not have been clearer. If he did not grant what his lords considered justice, then this reign would be just as ill-fated as the last one. There were still many lords left to arrive, but Rymond doubted he could rely on them to uphold his rights as king.

Darlton had sat back down, coolly sipping his wine as if he were sitting on his balcony watching the sunset. If Rymond sought to coerce or bully the man he would only make himself look foolish.

He unrolled one of the parchments, and as he read down the inventory of losses his eyes widened like cartwheels. The sums involved were staggering. He could likely pay some of them off in land, especially now Strovac Sigac's claim on the Fortlands was forfeit – wherever he happened to be now – but if every one of his lords made similar claims it would bankrupt him. His treasury was already much diminished by what the Imperials had stolen from him.

Rymond tried not to let his panic show. He had little choice but to accept Darlton's demands, but he needed to soften the blow, regain some control of the situation.

'And if we reach agreement in principle,' he said slowly. Rostar Darlton looked up at him. 'Then you will all follow me to Merivale?'

Darlton's mouth quirked. Evidently he knew he had won. 'If that is what our king commands.'

'Then I offer you this.' Rymond reached forward to pour himself a cup of wine – he needed it; he might never be able to afford to drink the like again. 'I will pay half these sums, in land where agreement can be reached, with credit to be given for whatever plunder you take when we conquer Merivale.'

Darlton raised an eyebrow. The man seemed calmer for having told Rymond exactly what he thought of him, though no less dangerous. 'Make it seven-tenths, and I will endorse the offer to my fellow nobles, and while I can't speak for those yet to arrive, I will recommend to them that their losses be determined on the same basis.'

'Six-tenths,' said Rymond stubbornly. 'And I'll pay you your sum in full today. But only you.'

Darlton's gaze flashed at him darkly. '*Seven*-tenths, with half of that to be paid immediately to all.' He leant forward conspiratorially and whispered: 'Don't think you can connive your way out of this, *Majesty*. It's for my fellow lords I'm making this deal, not myself. If it were up to me, after what you've brought on West Erland, you'd be up on the tallest tower hanging from a gibbet.'

Rymond swallowed. He could afford seven-tenths. It might mean delaying paying the Cyliriens, but that could not be helped. His life and kingship were on the line here – it was a choice between becoming king of all Erland and being dragged from his throne with a noose around his neck. 'Very well,' he said, his voice cracking slightly. He would keep Rostar Darlton close, and hope an opportunity to remove the man presented itself. 'We have a deal.'

CHAPTER 33

Something in Viratia's presence seemed to strike them momentarily dumb. For Ciera, it was like looking into a mirror and seeing the woman she wanted to be staring back at her. It was easy to see why men had followed her to war. The Barrel-breaker's widow wore her beauty like a coat of mail, and something in the archness of her smile made Ciera instinctively want her approval, as if Viratia held a wisdom beyond what men could offer.

It was Burik who broke the spell, by falling to his knees with tears rolling down his cheeks. 'I thought you were dead,' he gasped. 'My father—'

'Your father saved my life,' said Viratia. Her smile fell away, and she closed her eyes with a heavy breath. 'I am so sorry, Burik. Your father was as loyal to me as any man could have been, and it cost him dearly.'

Without warning, Andrick woke in Ciera's arms, before his mouth yawned open and he began wailing as if he meant to shake the tower to its foundations.

'That's quite a battle cry on him!' yelled Yriella over the din.

He had been peaceful only seconds earlier; Ciera wondered

if so many strangers and their new surroundings had unsettled him. 'His nurse is downstairs,' she cried. Andrick was howling so loudly that Ciera's ears were already ringing.

Yriella stepped forward and scooped up the babe before Ciera could object. 'I'll take him down,' she said. 'Does me good to be reminded of the favour my dead husbands did me never getting me with child.'

'Thank you,' said Ciera. Lady Gough seemed a safe pair of hands, and she wanted to be able to speak to Viratia without having to contend with her son's screaming. Yriella stepped away and made for the door, and Andrick began to quieten almost immediately, as if there had been something in the solar that disturbed him.

'What happened up there?' demanded Aimya once Yriella had departed. Her face was tight, as if Viratia had somehow tricked her by appearing alive. 'I did everything you asked, and it made me a laughingstock! I told people what happened on Eryispek and they looked at me like I was mad, while you just swanned back into Piperskeep and—'

'I'm sorry, Aimya,' said Viratia. She entwined her hands in front of her as if in penance. 'I did what I thought was best at the time. I swear I will explain.' She gestured towards the table. 'Sit, and I promise I shall tell you everything I can.'

Burik rose from his knees and wiped away his tears. 'May Eryi take my father. I would hear how he died.' He walked to the table and took a seat.

Ciera joined him. She was mainly curious to learn what had happened in Merivale, but she owed Burik enough to first hear about Naeem's death. Aimya hesitated, but then with a reluctant scowl came to join them.

Viratia served them each a cup of wine from a flagon, then looked to Aimya. 'You have told Burik of Eryispek?'

Aimya was still scowling, and had crossed her arms across her chest. 'I told everyone. I found Queen Ciera in the marshes and told her what you said to tell her: that the gods were coming and we had to be ready.'

Viratia nodded. She looked to Ciera and Burik. 'Everything she told you of what happened is true.' With soft eyes, her gaze flitted back to Aimya. 'After Aimya left us, Naeem and I went seeking Vulgatypha, the last Norha. The Adrari led us higher up the Mountain. I had never believed anywhere could be so cold, but it was the only way we could find Vulgatypha. I hoped she might be able to help us free Pherri from Eryi's clutches.' She looked away, swirling her wine, seemingly lost in thought. Her face was a mask, as if she sought to hide her grief.

'We were too late. Eryi freed himself, and my daughter was gone. A week after we left the Adrari village, we found them.' Viratia's sad eyes glowed with reflected candlelight. 'Eryi and Vulgatypha, raging at one another atop the Mountain's summit. I would sooner live through a hundred battles than witness such monstrousness again, so please forgive me for not dwelling on it. At one point I believed the sky was going to swallow me up, and at the time I would have welcomed it.

'Eryi won, and with Vulgatypha's end the Mountain's peak sundered in two, revealing the inferno that burns within. But he was weakened, and when he declared himself the lord of existence, Naeem stepped forward, and with his sword drove that monster who killed my daughter back into the fiery crater.' She paused to wipe her eye. 'He was like a god himself that night. I doubt even my husband could have stood against him. Alas, he fell with Eryi, and that was when the Mountain exploded.

'The blast threw me down the slope for miles. I tumbled through the air on gusts of blistering wind so hot that I swore they would kill me before the landing did, but I survived, and by some final miracle of the gods I landed in a snowdrift, far enough from the peak that I was able to escape the fires that chased me. What became of the Adrari who led me, I don't know.'

Ciera listened in rapture, and when Viratia paused she realised that her throat had become so dry she could hardly swallow. She took a restoring sip of wine.

Viratia continued, her eyes soft with empathy. 'Aimya, had I known when you left us what would happen, I would have sent you to safety, not across the country in search of Ciera. I am sorry.'

Aimya was watching Viratia curiously, but she nodded as if she understood. 'You have nothing to apologise for, Lady. I'm just glad the gods won't trouble us.' She gave a thin smile. 'Suppose the world thinking I'm mad is a small price to pay for that. I'm sorry about your daughter.'

Viratia reached across the table and took Aimya's hand in hers. 'If you want, I will stand up in front of everyone and tell them you told the truth. And if anyone calls you mad, they'll have me to answer to.'

Aimya pulled her hand away. 'It's fine, honestly.' She looked to her side. 'You all right, Burik?'

Burik was staring down at the table. He wiped his eyes, sniffed, and took a long glug of wine. 'At least someone's death meant something,' he said hoarsely. 'And at least I know now. Guess I'll have to be the one to tell my mum this time.' He gave a small, dark laugh. 'I'll go now, if you'll permit me.'

Ciera placed a hand on Burik's shoulder. 'Of course.' There was no more to say. After all Burik's losses and all his family had given, she could find no words of comfort that would be enough.

Without a word to any of them, Burik rose and left, heading for the tower stairs as if he were not quite sure where he was going.

'And what happened then?' asked Aimya. 'How did you get back to Piperskeep?'

'I walked,' said Viratia simply. 'It was hard – no horse, no food, no companions – but I had nowhere else to go. I barely escaped ahead of the fire still pouring from Eryispek, and I don't believe any of the Adrari were so lucky. Even the ones at Fisherton might have died in the night when the lava came. It took weeks, living on berries and acorn paste. I'd lost my boots as well, so I was barefoot.' She grimaced. 'Then I arrived back and saw a purple Imperial banner flying atop Piperskeep. That was quite a shock, but I found a way back into the city and someone told me what had happened: the Imperium managed to surprise us and fight their way up to Piperskeep before anyone could muster a proper defence.

'I knew what I had to do. Andrick had told me of some of the secret ways into Merivale, so I took one that led me to the dungeon. Many of the *hymerikai* had already been killed, but I managed to free those left.'

'And you took back the castle?' asked Aimya. 'Unarmed?'

'How many legionnaires were left?' said Ciera. 'Was it you who dropped the great hall on them?'

For the first time, Viratia laughed. 'No, they did that themselves. Some madness of the magus they had with them brought the ceiling down on them. There were a few left, but the slaves and conscripts all threw down their weapons when they saw the *Hymeriker* coming for them.' She paused, suddenly sober. 'There were *hymerikai* in there too, including Errian. We never found any survivors.'

At the mention of her son, something strange happened to Viratia's face. A candle flickered and almost went out, and for the breath of a blink, Ciera swore she saw Viratia with floods of tears streaming down her face, her eyes rimmed red, fingernails tearing at her face in unspeakable grief. Then the flame settled, and once again Viratia was an embodiment of poise and calm.

Ciera rubbed her eyes. *Just some trick of the light.* She suddenly felt very tired. She looked forward to sleeping on a mattress again.

'But how do you know what happened in the hall?' asked Aimya. 'Were you there when it happened?'

'We found it like that,' said Viratia. 'I can only guess, really. Some of the *hymerikai* heard the ceiling collapse from their dungeon cells and said it might have been huyar, but no one's sure.'

'I'm sorry for your loss,' said Ciera, having to stop herself saying '*may Eryi take him*'. Errian had betrayed her, but before that he had been her champion when nobody else would stand for her. 'Errian was one of the bravest men I knew. The city would have fallen long before that if not for him.'

Viratia's face was still, as if her quiet dignity in the face of sorrow was a rock she could cling to. 'Sometimes I feared he was destined to die young. I can only do what I can to honour his memory, and that of the rest of my family.'

She had not spoken of Orsian, but Ciera decided to spare Viratia the further misery. Perhaps she had already given him up for dead to spare herself the heartache.

'We must look to the present and the future,' Viratia continued. 'I have done what I can to rebuild the city in your absence, but it is a relief to have you back, Majesty.' Her eyes met Ciera's. 'Because even with the gods gone and the Imperium defeated, there is one more threat to face.

'Ever since Piperskeep, I have had strange dreams. At first, I thought them trauma, or some symptom of spending so long on the Mountain, but then they showed me how I would free the *Hymeriker*. They are not dreams, they are *visions*, and this past week, I have had only one, every time I place my head on the pillow.'

She paused, and met Ciera's eyes with a hard, heavy stare. 'The Prindians are marching, Majesty, and they are closer than you would believe, perhaps only days away. I am afraid there is one battle still left to win.'

CHAPTER 34

The air was the same temperature as his skin, such that Orsian could not tell where his body ended and everything else began. He was not even sure there was air in such a place as this. His lungs moved, his heart continued to beat, but it felt like an illusion, as if he were merely a puppet imbued with the artifice of life.

'Where are we?' he asked, staring at the nothingness. For that was all there was. They seemed to have stepped outside existence, divided by two murky windows from twin visions of Eryispek, one where it thundered with jets of flame and one where it merely smoked.

'We are between the worlds,' said Eryi, and though his voice was the only sound it seemed less than a whisper, like the half-remembered delusion of a dream. 'Where she cannot reach me. That is where this feeble excuse for a body came from.' He was more a soul than a corporeal being here – both of them were – but Orsian grasped that he was speaking of the smoking world, a blazing peak of smog beneath a black ash sky. 'We have left our own world without passing over into the other. I did not know such a thing was possible, but I have always dared to tread in places that lesser men considered to be madness.'

Eryi's dazed voice betrayed no emotion, and Orsian too found he could not even summon the anger he ought to have felt. Errian was gone. Dead, with so much left unsaid between them, so many more years of rivalry and reconciliation, striving for understanding of one another and always falling short. His mother... Even here, beyond existence, that was almost too painful to recall. He had seen her, trapped and bound to the monstrous goddess who wore her flesh like a lacquered mask. He wanted to scream, to beat his fists at the unfairness of it all, but the memories and emotions slipped away from him as if he were clutching for a puff of smoke. All that remained was the eerie calmness of being nowhere, being here, where blood did not pump and grass did not grow and his heart did not seem to truly feel anything.

'Shall I show you why I have to stop her?' asked Eryi. 'You are all so quick to resist what you don't understand, but here I can show you what Vulgatypha means for the world.'

A vision rose in the empty ether.

The sky was a curtain of ash. The sun a cold pewter coin, its warmth less than a memory. The clouds rained dust and rock, spewing foul vapours that filled a man's lungs and could not be coughed out. Great rivers of magma flowed down the mountain, like red eels burning all they touched. Trapped men screamed silently to the sky, their cries deafened by the rumbling of the great fire above them, the only source of heat in a world turned grey.

Against all sense, a man climbed, his skin and clothes so coated in soot that he was unrecognisable. Through blackened wastes he crawled, low to the billowing smoke that threatened to smother him.

'Er'yi!' a voice cried out above him. A dark silhouette

perched on a rocky outcropping, his arms raised wide to the torrent of lava that wound its way towards them.

'Another of my people,' said Eryi to Orsian. 'Watch.'

'Ir'vo.' The Er'yi of the vision dragged himself forward, and Orsian felt him adding his own will to Ir'vo's as he fought to hold back the fiery tide. Gasping, he pulled himself onto the outcropping. 'Run, help the others. They have lent their strength to mine – I must face her alone.'

Ir'vo turned towards Er'yi, and in the space of a blink his eyes flashed from green to a furious blood-red. A blade of black onyx in his fist thrust towards Er'yi, but the magus caught the other man's wrist, twisted, and buried it in Ir'vo's heart.

The man stared up at Er'yi, his soot-stained face draining of colour, his eyes green once more. 'Brother?' he gasped.

Er'yi blinked away tears. 'I am sorry, Brother.' As the light left Ir'vo's gaze, Er'yi laid him down to be swallowed by the lava, and climbed on.

'She was always cunning,' said Eryi to Orsian. 'We knew, by then. So many times, she turned magus against magus, picking off the most powerful of us one by one, laying the way for her final act.'

Over Eryispek, the sky was breaking, bone-white fractures splintering the heavens as ash rained and purple lightning forked. It shattered, and Orsian found himself staring into an endless void, blacker than night and more final than death. It hummed, and though he was not sure if he still had a body Orsian felt himself vibrating from his head to his toes.

A familiar shadow made of fire rose at the summit. A woman as tall as the sky, so terrible that Orsian swore his eyes would drip from their sockets, and so beautiful that he could not tear his gaze away.

'*You come too late, magus.*' Vulgatypha's voice was like the shriek of a blade; it echoed against the heavens and rattled the world from Eryispek to the lands of ice and back again. Overhead, the sky was shaking. '*Surrender, and I will make it quick. You will never even know what you lost.*'

Against all the horror of the end of the world, Er'yi stood alone. His will was as unyielding as cold iron, his focus sharper than the most carefully honed blade. He spoke, and Orsian felt Eryi mouthing along with the words of his ancient self beside him. 'If all must end, let it be said that it ended with a battle cry of resistance, and not a sob of fear. Remember my name, Vulgatypha. I am Er'yi, and I will not go quietly.' With a howl of fury, the magus threw himself into the sky towards Vulgatypha.

The vision began to fade. 'I will spare you the battle itself,' said Eryi. 'For three days, the goddess and I fought atop the Mountain, the brethren who lent their strength to mine failing or dying one by one. I won, and the world was saved.'

'But this time you lost,' said Orsian. He did not seek to goad. It was simply an expression of fact. 'You fled from her.'

'So it appears,' said Eryi. Orsian felt his perception shift back the way they had come, where the crater atop Eryispek continue to belch lazy smoke that as it rose mingled with the air and disappeared. 'Did you see her? Your mother?'

Orsian could not recall who Eryi was speaking of. 'If you have lost, you could let me go.' Perhaps then he would remember things.

'You don't recall.' Eryi sighed. 'Did you not recognise the form the goddess wore? That was your mother.'

Orsian did remember a mother. He might have just been thinking of her. He clung to that thought, refusing to let it escape. There had been a face, one that resembled his mother's but with every shred of tenderness and compassion flayed from it, a merciless, magisterial power that had stolen his mother's likeness. A single tear rolled down his cheek, though he could recall what that was supposed to mean. 'That was not my mother.'

'A strong resemblance at least,' said Eryi. Orsian imagined that if they had been having this conversation somewhere else, his lips would have spread into a cold smile. 'I have not lost, because I know what she is going to do. The last Norha is a devious beast. She will bring the Prindians to Merivale, and from there she will manipulate the two sides to a final battle. When she reveals herself, they shall be too weak to resist her, and she will channel their sacrifice for her unspeakable aims. But she still does not understand what she has done to herself. Vulgatypha could have ended both of us, yet the part of your mother that remains gave us the chance to escape.

'I could have taken any vessel, but something of its old nature will always linger, with humans particularly. That is why I worked so hard to retrieve an imitation of my own body, broken and battered thing that it is.

'It is that which will be her undoing. I will admit, I erred in killing your brother. That unleashed your mother's *rage*, and to rage the goddess is no stranger. What I require is your mother's mercy, and now I have seen it. In Vulgatypha's impatience, she has handed me the very tools I need for her final destruction. And you, of course, will help me. We have only to wait.'

It all meant so little to Orsian. He tried to recall his life, some reason to care which of Vulgatypha and Eryi would triumph, and every memory he might have conjured disappeared into the infinity of intangible ether that surrounded him.

There was one name that did flash in his consciousness though. It was so close it was at the tip of his tongue, an image of the person to whom it belonged flickering at the edge of his vision.

Pherri. *Pherri*. Pherri would save them all.

If only he could recall who Pherri was.

CHAPTER 35

Helana let a breath out, and released the arrow. She felt a moment's tension, and then came the satisfying thump of it striking the middle of the wicker target. She smiled. Right where she had aimed it.

There was a smattering of applause as men practising their swordplay or receiving instruction in how to form a shield wall turned to admire the shot. Helana tried not to look too content with herself – she knew how good she was with a bow. More pleasing than her aim was that no man objected to a woman practising with a weapon, especially so close to them. Even men who were strangers to her would give her respectful nods as she passed them in the yard, presumably because it seemed everyone knew they had Helana's huyar to thank for retaking Irith. Aside from the occasional ribald joke, she was left alone. That was all she had ever wanted – to be free to do as she pleased, without expectations arising from her sex and high birth.

But as she looked across the yard, Helana felt a pang of regret. As much as she might wish to be left alone and forget who she was, that was not a choice she could make, and perhaps would never be. She had helped place Rymond back on his throne, and now she had to deal with the consequences. These men were training for war, a war that would take them to the doorstep of Helana's home, and somehow she had ended up on the wrong side.

She would soon need to find a way to correct that.

'My turn,' said Millas. The stout, square youth stepped forward, set himself, and readied his arrow.

He held the bow steady, and had a strong and smooth release, but his arrow struck the target right at the edge, a whole two feet to the left of Helana's.

The men nearby had obviously been watching Millas's shot as well, because they immediately burst into laughter. 'You can sit the next battle out,' cried a man wearing the blue and pink colours of Lord Darlton. 'We'll take the girl instead!'

This led to a further round of laughter, while Millas flushed with embarrassment. 'That's not even a proper bow!' he declared hotly, referring to the short hunting bow Helana had favoured ever since being given one in Thrumbalto. 'That's never going to punch through leather!'

'Neither will you if you miss,' said Garwen, Millas's father. He was standing to the side, clutching a foaming mug of ale in his good hand. His other arm was tied up in a sling, his shoulder having been dislocated by a piece of rubble blown from the wall.

'You might hit the man next to your target though,' said Rucius, leaning insouciantly against the wall, cleaning his nails with a small knife. On the advice of everyone, the translator had finally removed his legionnaire armour and replaced it with a nondescript leather tunic. Irith was no longer a safe place for Imperials. 'At least if you aim for the same man as Helana it's not an arrow wasted.'

Millas scowled. 'Why are you here, Rucius? You don't even use a bow.'

Rucius let out an exaggerated sigh. 'Unfortunately, you three are the closest I have to friends here. It seems even out of my uniform your countrymen remain immune to my charms.'

Helana had noticed the dark looks Rucius seemed to attract. 'They wouldn't be so quick to judge if they knew what you'd done for us,' she said, glowering across the vast open yard of Irith Castle – it seemed as if every inch of it was occupied by men practising with swords or bows, from the central keep all the way to the ruins of the outer wall. 'You've probably killed more Imperials than all of them combined.' Of where the legionnaires had been barracked in Irith's town, only a pile of rubble remained, blown to bits by Rucius's huyar.

'What will you do now?' asked Garwen. 'Sure you don't want an ale?'

'Doesn't agree with his delicate Ulvatian stomach,' said Millas, grinning.

Rucius smiled wincingly. 'You are not far wrong in truth. I may never touch your foul Erlish swill again for as long as I live.' They had spent nearly a whole week drunk after their victory, rolling from tavern to tavern or indulging themselves in wine from Rymond's cellar. Helana had thought herself no stranger to hard drinking, but a few days carousing with soldiers had put her right on that, and when Garwen had finally put her to bed she had woken the next day in a puddle of her own vomit. Rucius had fared no better, being thrown into a pigpen by Millas after falling asleep at the table. Rucius sighed again. 'The wine is the only thing I shall miss about Ulvatia.'

'You'll stay here then?' said Millas. He was holding his bow up and frowning at it, as if there might be a kink in it that had thrown his arrow off course.

'Well, I can hardly go back.' Rucius stroked a hand along his chin and through his hair, as if debating something. 'My mother was from Erland. She taught me the language.'

'In Ulvatia?' asked Helana. 'How did that happen?'

'She was a slave.'

Helana grimaced. Slave raids on Erland's northern coast were uncommon, but not unheard of. 'Sorry.'

Rucius waved a hand. 'Don't mention it. Gave the other Ulvatians a reason to hate me, and gave me a reason to come here. I'll stay here as long as King Rymond will tolerate me.'

'There he is now,' said Garwen. He raised his mug in the direction of the keep where Rymond had just emerged, surrounded by a multitude of lords. Helana recognised the tall, dark features of Rostar Darlton deep in conversation with Rymond, the comparatively scrawny Urwen Storaut walking behind them, and Lord Clymore, a minor lord with a bulky frame and stained mail whose lands were only a half-day's ride away, plus half-a-dozen others she might have met at one time or another.

'No time for the likes of us now,' said Garwen dourly.

There was some truth in that – Rymond's life as an outlaw had broken down barriers just as surely as his return as king had put them back up again. 'He remembers you fondly,' said Helana. 'Only last night he regaled the table with the tale of how Fallback Lodge was taken.' Every evening, Helana joined Rymond and his lords at the top table in the hall, though she tended to make her excuses and leave early. Urwen Storaut was pleasant enough, if a little earnest, and Rostar Darlton was handsome for an old man and very charming, but most of the rest of them were as dull as Lord Clymore's mail.

'So I'll be invited to the wedding, then?' said Garwen, a smile creeping up his face.

This drew an appreciative laugh from Millas, but Helana turned on Garwen scowling, a hot rage rushing to her face. 'I'm not marrying him, for the last fucking time.' She jabbed an arrow at him. 'I'm not marrying anyone!'

Garwen was laughing now, which only made Helana crosser. 'Just a joke, Princess. Just a joke.'

'Don't call me that!' Helana turned away from him and put another arrow to her bow. It was typical, she had won this bloody castle and even Garwen who had seen her do it still seemed to think of her as little more than a broodmare. No matter how good she was with a bow, some things would stay the same. It was maddening.

She might though have been angrier with Rymond than she was with Garwen. In the weeks since they had retaken Irith, she had hardly seen him for how busy he was, except at dinner. She had expected a little more gratitude for saving his and his mother's life. It annoyed her more that she cared.

In her temper, she released the arrow too quickly, and it struck low on the target.

Rucius made a face. 'Hit him in the balls. Were you imagining Garwen or Rymond?'

'I'm sorry, Helana,' said Garwen. 'You're right – it's not for me to joke about.'

'It's the worst-kept secret in the castle,' put in Millas. 'Surely my dad's not the first person to joke about it?'

Helana turned away and laid another arrow to her bow. 'No,' she said quietly to herself. 'Not the worst-kept secret.'

She could have forgiven Rymond for being busy, but not for seemingly thinking her a fool. He had saved her from the Thrumb, and nearly thrown his life away on the cause of West Erland, but he was still his mother's son.

Helana knew Rymond did not believe what she had seen in Thrumbalto, regardless of his promise that when he had won back Irith they would go to Merivale. Truthfully, it felt so long ago now that she was beginning to doubt it herself – Eryispek no longer smoked, and nobody had arrived from East Erland spreading tales of a vicious god preparing to take over the country. And yet, he had still not come to her for an honest conversation as to why he had gathered such a mass of men to Irith.

There were so many now that the castle and the city could

not support them all; the plains outside the city were covered in enough tents that it had almost become a small town in and of itself.

And Helana knew why, and it was nothing to do with fulfilling an oath to her. Rymond was preparing to assault Merivale. She was tired of the pretence – did he honestly think she would believe he had summoned all these lords here based on her vision, or did he simply not care what she thought? She hoped it was the latter.

Helana's reverie was interrupted by a cry from Garwen, and she turned to see Gruenla stomping towards them.

The mercenary captain's face was crimson with rage. 'That bloody cheat!' she thundered, grabbing a wineskin from Garwen's fist before he could offer it to her and pouring it straight into her mouth. 'I knew he'd do this!' She threw down the empty skin, drew her sword, and shoved Rucius out of the way to begin hacking at the spare target he had been leaning on.

The air was soon filled with Gruenla's curses and the last gasps of the swiftly disintegrating target. Rucius, Garwen, and Millas all looked at each other. 'Maybe I could try the Erlish wine again, actually,' said Rucius. 'I'd quite like to be away before she turns that sword on me.'

'Sounds a decent idea seeing as she just polished off mine,' said Garwen. He looked to Helana. 'Coming?'

'You're three useless cowards,' she told them. 'I'll stay with Gruenla.'

Garwen shrugged. 'I didn't learn much from being married, but I learnt to stay out of the way of a woman who's that angry and holding a sword.'

The men departed towards the keep in search of wine and ale, and Helana watched Gruenla hack the target to splinters.

It did not take long. Once there was nothing left to attack, Gruenla dropped her sword into the grass and slumped down after it.

'Feeling better?' asked Helana. She sat down next to her and thrust out a spare skin she had been hiding from the men, which Gruenla grasped from her.

'Nearly,' said Gruenla. She took a long swig.

'Rymond?' asked Helana.

'How did you know?'

'Seemed the most obvious candidate.'

'The bloody cheat,' hissed Gruenla again. She turned to Helana, fire still burning in her eyes. 'Did you know he was going to do this?'

'Whatever it was, definitely not,' said Helana hastily. 'What's he done?'

'Says he can't pay us until we've taken Merivale.' Gruenla spat on the ground and took another slug from the skin. 'That was never the deal. How's he expect me to sell that to my men? I'll be lucky if they don't skin me alive. I don't even want to go to Merivale – I want to take our gold and go home. Suddenly because he's a king again he thinks he can swindle us!'

Helana supposed that meant Rymond was planning to use Piperskeep's treasury to pay off his debts. It was hard to disagree with Gruenla's assessment of the situation. 'Bloody cheat,' she agreed. 'Though at least he's admitted that he's planning to take Merivale.'

Gruenla hacked up a laugh. 'Only the whole bloody castle knows. Does he reckon you don't talk to people?' She looked sideways at Helana. 'We should go see him together. Might not get us what we want, but it'll make us feel better.'

Helana did not reply, instead thinking quickly. 'I might know a way you can get your gold.'

Gruenla looked at her sharply. 'Know where the Prindians hide their coin?'

'No – I'll pay you. All you have to do is fight for me instead.'

'You been dragging a wagon of gold around with you I've missed?'

'No, but I know where my father kept his.'

Gruenla's mouth quirked. 'Go on.'

Helana took a deep breath. She was playing with fire now. 'Word is that there's another force marching on Merivale, several thousand strong. Ciera Istlewick, my stepmother. There'll be a battle, and when the time comes, I want you fighting for me. If we win, I'll pay you all that Rymond owes you.'

The mercenary captain gave a low whistle. 'Fight for your stepmother? Hardly seems worth it. There's a few hundred of us left, not enough to turn a battle.'

'Depends if they expect you're not on their side.'

Gruenla's eyebrows shot up. She considered a few seconds and let out a wicked laugh. 'You're a cold bitch, Helana Sangreal. Sure you're not mistaking me for Strovac Sigac?'

'You're Captain-General Gruenla. There's no mistaking you for anyone.'

Gruenla gave an appreciative chuckle. 'I do like flattery, but not as much as I like gold.' She paused, her mouth settling into a hard line. 'And not as much as I like showing treacherous fucking weasels who they're messing with. I'll make Rymond Prindian regret the day he double-crossed me.'

Helana smiled, the knot of concern in her stomach shrinking to nothing as she realised she had correctly judged Gruenla. *Two can play at your game, Rymond Prindian.* West Erland's returning king was about to get a sharp lesson in underestimating the Sangreals.

They only had to wait a few days before the Prindian host was ready to move out. Helana rode with the veterans of Rymond's resistance, Garwen on one side and Rucius on the other. Gruenla and the Cyliriens were slightly ahead of them, just behind the Prindians, Rymond freshly groomed and noble as a king should be, sitting atop a sleek white charger with his crown, bright mail, and lustrous emerald cloak shining. Overhead, a huge Prindian banner rippled against the slate-grey sky of a chill pre-dawn. His mother rode beside him, her hair flowing in the wind like a molten river.

Helana watched them. By rank, she might have claimed a place alongside them, but she preferred to be among those she considered friends. Rymond had still not spoken to her, but at least he had not stopped her from riding with them, perhaps mindful of the promise he had given her. As horrific as the prospect was, Helana still half-hoped she was right that a confrontation with the merciless god Eryi awaited them. At least then Rymond would have to admit she had been right, and she would not have to watch him go into battle for the crown of Erland against her baby half-brother.

She looked back at the rest of the Prindian host. There were many thousands more than Rymond had commanded in his capture of Irith, but still far fewer than the twenty thousand who had once ridden to war against Hessian Sangreal and Andrick Barrelbreaker. More banners flew, belonging to the dozen or so lords who had answered Rymond's summons. Some Irith townsmen had come to lend their numbers, many armed with little more than cudgels and knives, and a few hundred Imperials who had decided to take their chances in Rymond's war party rather than his dungeon.

'How far to Merivale?' asked Rucius. 'I did everything I could to avoid going there; crossing the Bleak Hills was more than enough.'

Helana considered. 'For this many, perhaps three weeks. Depends on the weather.'

Rucius made a face. 'To think we were assured that Erland was a small country.'

Ahead of them, Rymond drew his sword and lifted it

shining into the air. The assembled army fell silent, awaiting the command to march. Helana steeled herself. She was finally going home.

She watched as Rymond inhaled deeply so that his voice might carry the length of their force. 'FOR—'

The words caught in his throat, as ahead of him, the air began to ripple. First slowly, like reflections in a lake on the cusp of freezing, and then fast and then all at once, as if the very ether were being torn by a thousand different sword strokes. The grass and the sky disappeared behind a huge undulating window, expanding until it was perhaps fifty yards across, revealing in its depths a huge dark fortress looming over a walled city.

Merivale. Helana recognised it immediately. Her mouth fell open in wonder. It continued to grow and sharpen, until it was as if they were standing just a few hundred yards from the city.

'Cock of Eryi,' swore Garwen. 'I never...' Like everyone else, he appeared to be lost for words. Thousands stared, marvelling. Some began murmuring prayers, while others leapt from their horses and began prostrating themselves with their heads against the cold earth.

A memory stirred in Helana. *This is what Hu'ra spoke of. He meant to open a way for the Thrumb to travel to Merivale.* She looked ahead to Rymond and Breta, who by the tilt of their heads were not speaking, just gazing in wonder with the rest of them.

Without a word to her stunned companions, Helana urged her horse forward and cantered up the line to join them.

Rymond barely seemed to notice her until she was right on top of him. He turned and gawped at her. 'Is this magic?' His voice came out like a confused child's. 'Is this what you spoke of, before?'

Helana swallowed. 'It may be. I think Hu'ra hoped to use

something similar for the Thrumb to reach Merivale. He thought my death would open the way.'

Rymond shook himself to his senses. 'It seems someone is just as keen for us to reach Merivale.'

'It might be a trap,' said Helana.

'Perhaps Hessian's wizard has returned,' said Breta. Even her unflappable calm seemed to have been ruffled. 'We should move cautiously.'

'Or something worse,' said Rymond, and Helana could tell he was thinking of the vision she had shared with him; Eryi and his companion, outside Merivale, discussing their conflict with the goddess and the fate of Erland. A frisson of fearful certainty ran up her spine. This gateway might prove the truth of it. But did it also mean Eryi *wanted* them to come to Merivale? Trying to recall what he had said in the tent made Helana's mind feel sluggish, like she was wading through sludge in search of the memory.

A voice came from the other side of Rymond. 'I'll go, Majesty.' Helana craned her neck round him and saw Brant, Rymond's scout.

Rymond grinned ruefully. 'Does any journey frighten you, Brant? Very well. Ride through, come back, then tell me what you've seen. If you survive, I will make you a lord.'

Brant needed no more encouragement than that. He spurred his bay mare forward with a cry that was equal parts bravado and fear. The door in the air stood close enough to cover the whole landscape of West Erland that would otherwise have spread out before them. Brant's horse whinnied in protest, but he dug his heels in and urged it forward, driving it to a gallop as he closed upon the threshold.

He entered in a ripple of eerie blue, and then was gone, as if he had passed beyond a curtain.

There were gasps of consternation from what seemed like every man present. Rymond's face had turned to chalk, and

Helana swore she saw even Breta Prindian murmuring words of prayer to some deity or other.

In a matter of seconds, Brant reappeared. There were more gasps, first of relief and then alarm. The rear end of Brant's horse remained beyond the veil, giving the odd impression that Brant was riding a mount that had been cauterised at the rump.

'It's real!' he yelled, laughing manically. 'I saw it, Merivale, as real as you are!'

Rymond swallowed, and reached up to his neck to adjust his cloak. 'I'll go next,' he said, in a voice dry as a parched field.

'We will *all* go,' corrected his mother.

Rymond nodded, swallowed, and once again raised his sword in the air. At a cautious walk, the ten thousand-strong host approached the shimmering gateway.

Helana rode alongside them, her mouth dry as old bones. What did it mean? She suspected they would discover on the other side, though she doubted if anyone present would like the answer.

CHAPTER 36

They traipsed across the Sorrowlands, leaving Ulsenfort burning behind them. As night faded to a crimson and gold dawn, it remained visible, a single smudge of fire against the northern horizon.

'Suppose they never got a chance to put it out,' said Phyrrai, staring back at it. Its smoke had followed them, bathing the world in grey and covering the foul airs of the Sorrowlands with a cloying woody smell.

'Ulsenfort is no more,' said the Sorrowseer. 'Your king has no use for it, so he has burnt it to the ground, together with many of the Horned Folk. Those who survive will travel to build a new one.'

'Did you know that would happen?' asked Hrogo. The magus was behind them, wheezing and struggling to keep pace, the chain he had dragged on his ankle all the way from Erland scraping against the rough terrain. Pherri supposed there had never been a convenient moment to have it removed. 'That the Erlanders would come?'

'Perhaps,' admitted the Sorrowseer. 'Our journey is more important.'

'Then I am grateful; they would not have been kind to me.' A darkness flashed across Hrogo's face; Pherri supposed that even with their ailment, this was preferable for Hrogo to the Piperskeep dungeon or his old life as a slave. 'But if you knew, why didn't you stop them?'

'I could not. That Grawl would be defeated by the Erlanders was inevitable. I could no more have stopped it than I could halt the path of the sun. I would be dead, and all of you would be returning to Erland.'

Pherri could not avoid being troubled by the Sorrowseer's answer. *But if you knew it was going to happen, why not warn someone?* How much did the Sorrowseer truly see? When she had told Pherri she must kill Phyrrai, had that been an instruction or a prophecy?

'It's better this way,' said Phyrrai. 'Means none of them will follow us.'

They walked through the rest of the day, until Pherri began to fall asleep standing up and nearly collapsed several times. They found shelter in the mouth of a cave built into a high, sheer mound of rock, at the edge of a fissure that plummeted into the earth. Pherri peered down and sniffed at the rising sulphurous vapour. An inky red drop slipped from her nose and down into the depths.

Her symptoms seemed to have lessened in the feverish rush of their escape, but so many hours later they were beginning to return. Hrogo though seemed fine, tucking into his dried goat meat with abandon as they all sat around a small fire. Pherri's eyes flickered between the flames and Pipersmont's silhouette in the distance, but when the sun fell and the temperature began to drop she could no longer keep her eyes open. She slipped into sleep.

After another disturbed night of visions, Pherri woke the next morning to the smell of goat roasting over a fire, marred by the acrid reek of something else. She hurried out from underneath her sweat-stained cloak, then stumbled to the edge of the cave and vomited. She did not have to look to know there would be blood in it. The nausea was part of her routine now; at least it did not seem to be as debilitating as it had been in Ulsenfort. The black rot of her fingers though had crept beyond her nails and was halfway to her middle finger joint; every day Pherri's digits seemed to have a little less feeling.

Outside, the Sorrowseer had set alight a tar pit, and was turning the goat over it. Pherri wiped her bleary eyes against the fumes, wishing they could have had a few more hours of rest. The others slept on, but Pherri wrapped her cloak around herself against the morning chill and went to join her. She accepted the Sorrowseer's offer of a carved slice and ate it, barely tasting the sweet flesh.

'I heard you telling Phyrrai to leave,' said the Sorrowseer, her tone sharp with accusation.

The ice in the Sorrowseer's voice made Pherri pull her cloak more tightly around herself. 'And?' She lowered her voice, and cast a furtive glance back towards the cave. 'You don't really expect me to kill her, do you? There has to be another way.'

'I do.' The Sorrowseer's tone was as unyielding as the ground on which they stood. 'If you do not return, the chaos of Vulgatypha that will soon engulf your world will spread to others. She has the power to bring all reality collapsing in on itself. Every sun will go out, every love will fade, every life will be extinguished as if it never existed at all. The Norhai lust for power is unquenchable. She will burn everything to rise on a throne of the ashes.' The Sorrowseer's gaze narrowed. 'Unless you stop her.' The Sorrowseer carved another hunk of goat and handed it to Pherri. 'And stop her you must.'

Pherri stared at her through the smoke and accepted the meat. *It is too much.* She doubted she could defeat Eryi; what was she to do against Vulgatypha? 'Why are you so sure? How do you know?'

The flames' reflection danced in the Sorrowseer's pale mask. It occurred to Pherri that she had never seen her eat. Would she remove her mask to do so? 'Reality is like a tree. Branches sprout from the trunk, and each branch grows its own branches, and so on. When I see the future and there is a divergence, I see the creation of a new world. But they are all the same tree. A branch may end, but it can also burn, and with it the whole tree.' She carved another slice of meat. 'I have seen this world burning with the rest. That is what Vulgatypha seeks; an ending to everything, and another world rising in her image, only for her.'

Pherri sat, chewing, silently pondering the Sorrowseer's words. Theodric had told her of *prophika*, the rare gift that allowed Pherri to sometimes see visions of future events, but he had said nothing of gaining insight into events in other worlds. Did it work differently here? In this world without magic, did that somehow make the Sorrowseer's *prophika* more effective?

Before Pherri could ask further questions, the others began to stir. Hrogo and Phyrrai came to the cavemouth. Halyana was awake also, but kept her distance, pressing herself against the back wall of the small cavern. The Sorrowseer looked up at her, and Halyana bared her teeth and hissed like a cornered animal.

'It would have been kinder to leave her,' said the Sorrowseer. 'She could have returned with her brother.'

It was true, yet Halyana had chosen to remain with them. Pherri frowned. Was it the Sorrowseer's strange appearance that frightened Halyana, or something else?

Pherri moved to join Halyana at the rear of the cave, bearing some extra meat for her. The older girl took it from her and ate it slowly, her eyes never leaving the Sorrowseer.

'What is she to you?' whispered Pherri. 'Why do you hate her? Are you afraid?'

But Halyana of course said nothing. She only stared towards the entrance, her face taut with hatred.

The Sorrowseer estimated a ten-day march to the southern wastes. Not for the first time, she added that they would be quicker if they left Halyana behind, but that suggestion fell on deaf ears. Halyana was the hardiest of all of them, often striking out ahead of them and only returning to them in the evening, sometimes with a small, black-scaled lizard to be eaten as a change from goat. She kept her distance from the Sorrowseer, but still Pherri would sometimes see Halyana eyeing her with revulsion.

Pherri had expected Hrogo to struggle, but despite his awkward gait he kept pace with the rest of them ably. If their shared ailment troubled him, he hid it well; Pherri never saw him have a nosebleed, and his nights and mornings seemed free of her fever and nausea. As far as she knew, the Sorrowseer had not spoken to him of how they would return; she could only assume it was his faith that they would find answers on Pipersmont that kept him going.

Pherri's own symptoms usually disappeared while they walked, only returning to plague her when they stopped for the evening, with nosebleeds, aching limbs, and the jumbled, feverish dreams she had come to dread. The sickness often left her too weak to speak with her companions, not that there was much conversation to be had, but the main disappointment was she could not ask further questions of the Sorrowseer. Instead, she had to leave that task to Phyrrai.

The Sorrowseer refused to speak while they walked, insistent she had to be focused on finding their way, to avoid the fissures, tar pits, and rockslides that could doom them. Sometimes, this meant scrabbling up steep slopes with their hands, even when there looked to be an easier, more even path only yards away from them. At the top, the Sorrowseer always paused to point out the impassable obstruction they had managed to avoid below.

Food became scarce as their supply of goat ran low, which reduced conversation even further, each of them trapped in a private struggle against hunger and the treacherous black flint.

But on the fifth day, as they crossed a particularly flat expanse of rock, Phyrrai fell into step with Pherri, with the Sorrowseer ten yards ahead. 'We should walk off the path slightly,' she murmured. 'We've not seen a fissure or a tar pit all day.'

They had walked in silence for so long that it took Pherri several seconds to register that someone had spoken to her. She glanced to Phyrrai and gave a small nod, and with their eyes on the Sorrowseer they veered off the track they had been following into rougher terrain.

'She says we're almost halfway,' breathed Phyrrai, once they were far enough away that they could not be overheard.

Pherri looked towards the horizon. Pipersmont towered over them now, like a huge cliff face that hung from the sky, all red sand and churning dust with its higher reaches lost behind a cloak of swirling cloud.

Phyrrai dropped her voice further, and cast an uneasy glance towards where the Sorrowseer walked the path perhaps twenty-five yards ahead and to their right. 'What do you make of her?'

Pherri chewed her lip. 'She has done her best to help us. I just want to reach Pipersmont.' That was what she hoped for, and yet she also hoped it never came. Every day, they came a step closer to a decision Pherri dreaded. The thought of killing Phyrrai was like a rusty knife to her heart. But could she face the alternative, watching existence burn to save her shadowtwin? What was the death of one person next to that?

Phyrrai's eyes were still fixed on the Sorrowseer. 'Have you noticed she never eats or drinks anything?'

'I assume she does it after we're asleep so she can take her mask off.'

Phyrrai shook her head. 'That doesn't make any sense.' She barely moved her lips, so Pherri had to strain to hear her. 'If she's so old, how in Piper's name did she cross the rope so easily? She never goes to make water either.'

'Again, what if she just goes after we're asleep?' Pherri tried to think of an explanation for the Sorrowseer's startling strength, but her mind was full of fog. She closed her eyes and shook her head, and felt a spot of warm blood drip from her nostril. 'It's not our business. Maybe she's just strong?'

'She doesn't move like an old woman either,' insisted Phyrrai. 'And if she's one of them, how's she so much taller than the other Sorrowfolk?'

Pherri could hardly deny the strangeness of the Sorrowseer. She had been too preoccupied with her illness and reaching Pipersmont to think on it. Sometimes it felt as if her mind was beginning to succumb to her affliction as well. 'I don't know,' she admitted. 'But if she gets us to Pipersmont what does it matter?'

'But why does she want to come with us? And why abandon her people? There's something she's not telling us, I'm sure of it.' Phyrrai paused. 'What did she tell you that first night?'

Pherri's throat bobbed. *To kill you.* 'That to return to my own world I have to reach Pipersmont.' That was true.

'There's more to it. There's something in it for her, I'm sure of it.'

Pherri was beginning to feel weak. A second drop of blood slipped from her nose. Her limbs were starting to feel as if they were made of soft, heavy wool. 'Maybe, but I can't think about this now.' She wiped away the blood, but as she did so her foot caught a lump of rock. She grabbed for Phyrrai's shoulder to stop herself, but cried out as her knee struck the ground.

Away to their right, the Sorrowseer turned at the sound and

cried out in alarm. 'Get back to the path! There could be hidden tar pits over there! Get back!'

Wincing, Pherri hauled herself to her feet. Her knee was grazed and bloody where she had fallen. 'I know it's strange,' she told Phyrrai. 'But I think we have to trust her. Who knows if we can get to Pipersmont without her?'

'That's the thing,' whispered Phyrrai, as they made their way back to the main group. 'I don't trust her. Not in the least. What if Halyana has the right of it?'

'Who knows what Halyana's thinking? Maybe she's just scared of the mask? I need to reach Pipersmont, and that means trusting the Sorrowseer.'

But Pherri did not want to trust the Sorrowseer. She glanced sideways at Phyrrai. They had barely spoken in recent days, and yet sometimes it was as if they shared one mind. Phyrrai would hand Pherri a cut of meat just seconds before Pherri reached for one herself, or they would find their steps following one another perfectly, even stumbling on the same uneven patch of rock. Killing Phyrrai would be like killing a part of herself.

And yet, she could not shake the feeling that there must be truth in what the Sorrowseer had told her. *Magic demands sacrifice.* Only through death had Eryi been able to pull his army of undead Gelicks from other worlds, and only through dooming Pherri had he hoped to retrieve an earthly body for himself. She recalled Eryi's own words: '*Where there is sacrifice, there is change, and the gaps between realities move, inch by inch.*'

But could Pherri summon the strength to do it?

On the tenth day, they reached the end of the Sorrows, starving, sore, and exhausted. A vista of red sand stretched before them, every bit as desolate as the bleak land they had come from. Pherri wavered on the spot, fighting to keep her feet. Hrogo fell to his knees, resting his head on the earth and taking deep panting breaths. Even tireless Halyana looked to be on the verge of collapse.

The sky overhead was bright blue, but the sun was obscured by a mist of flying sand. With a fierce southerly wind came a sudden storm of red dust, forcing them to cover their mouths with their hands or strips of cloth until it passed.

'The wastes,' croaked the Sorrowseer. 'The homeland of the Meridivals.'

Phyrrai coughed sand out of her mouth and took a drink of water sourced from an underground stream. 'I can see why they left.'

'It did not always look so,' said the Sorrowseer. 'Millennia ago, this desert was as verdant as the plains of Erland.'

Pherri caught Phyrrai's eye, and she knew what her shadowtwin was thinking: how did the Sorrowseer know of the Erlish plains and the history of the wastes?

'How does your magic work?' asked Pherri suddenly. It was the first time in days they had stopped without her being wracked with chills and nosebleeds. 'How does yours work when mine doesn't?'

The Sorrowseer turned, and an irritated sneer flashed on the mask. Pherri had given up trying to pretend to herself she was seeing something: it was no mere mask. 'Because I am of this world, and you are not. Magic here is rare. All I have is visions.'

Pherri had seen enough to doubt that. She gazed into the distance, towards Pipersmont, a towering curtain that covered half the sky. This close, it looked nothing like Eryispek. It was steeper, surrounded by soft, rolling dunes instead of foothills, and formed from the same sand as the surrounding desert. 'Do you expect us to climb that?' she asked.

'There are other ways to enter,' said the Sorrowseer. 'Now come. We should be there in half a day, certainly by evening.' She pointed to a gap in the rocks where the steady trickle of an underground river could be heard. 'Drink your water and refill from there. It may not feel hot now, but it will once we enter the sand.'

She was not wrong. They felt the heat more as soon as they descended the gravel-strewn incline that marked the edge of the Sorrowlands. They left the sulphur-tinged winds behind, facing instead the heat of the rising sun and its reflection from the sand, so bright that Pherri had to cover her eyes with her hand.

There was no cooling respite when the breeze blew down in the wastes. It threw hot sand into their faces, and soon they and their clothing were covered in red grime. The ground shifted beneath their feet, sucking at their boots; just a few paces were enough for them to realise this terrain was even tougher than that of the Sorrowlands. They formed into a line, the Sorrowseer leading the way while the rest of them struggled to follow her footsteps, where the crushed sand provided a more stable footing.

It became even harder when the dunes began to rise. Here, one awkward step could send a person sliding back down the slope. At times, they were forced to crawl on their hands and knees, going slowly so as not to kick sand into the face of the person behind. It was not possible to avoid entirely though; with every yard they travelled it seemed Pherri had to turn and spit out sand that Phyrrai had accidentally scooped into her face. Behind her, Pherri could hear Hrogo spluttering and wheezing.

But the Sorrowseer never stopped. The wastes seemed to further invigorate her already ceaseless energy, as she scaled every dune like a goat-rider and barked at the rest of them to hurry while they tried to catch up. They kept up the punishing pace for hours, barely pausing to take a breath or a drink of water. Pherri's stomach rumbled, but they were down to the very last of their goat meat, and the wilds seemed bare of life except buzzing insects that flitted in and out of the sand. A few times she thought she saw the shape of a rodent burrowing through the ground, and when they stopped atop one dune she swore she saw wild horses on a far-off hill against the blue horizon. She blinked, and they disappeared.

They crested the last sandbank, and the sheer slope of Pipersmont rose to meet them. It was not made from sand, as Pherri had thought, but from red clay, as dry and bare as the desert itself. They collapsed together into the shadow of a large rock, hiding from the sun and the flurries of dust.

Pherri sat next to Phyrrai, clutching her hand. Fat, exhausted tears were rolling down her face, and she licked the moisture into her mouth as they reached her lips. Halyana was leaning back against the rock with her eyes closed, and Hrogo's head was in his hands, groaning, his lips chafed and his eyes raw from tiredness.

'We must go on.' The Sorrowseer was standing over them, her mask bright with zeal. How did she even breathe wearing it? 'The entrance is on the eastern side. Come, quickly.'

Pherri poured the last few trickles of water into her mouth. Just from half a day in the sands she could feel her skin beginning to burn. Had Pipersmont been another day's walk or more she doubted they would have made it.

'I can't do it,' moaned Hrogo, stumbling to his feet. He was sweating profusely, as if their proximity to their goal had overwhelmed him. 'Please, no.'

'There is a stream inside the mountain,' said the Sorrowseer, paying him no heed. She threw them each a strip of dried goat meat. 'Quickly now.'

They were all too tired to ask what the hurry was.

It was another hour traversing the low edge of the mountain's slope, but finally they reached the entrance the Sorrowseer had spoken of. Within the rock face, an entranceway had been cut, bordered with red brick, high and wide enough for a man to squeeze through. The Sorrowseer ushered them inside.

They found themselves in a cool, dark chamber, carved from the very clay of Pipersmont. It was large and square, with stairs leading upward in three directions. Small pictures drawn in paint ran around the wall at mid-height, but it was too dark to make them out properly. The rough floor was bare, save what looked to be a monument at the room's centre, a crude marker of heavy red stone that had been somehow set into the clay ground.

The Sorrowseer hurried them along, striding towards the middle stairs. 'This way will take us to water. Come on.'

Hrogo wheezed out a rattling breath. 'Not yet, please.' He shuffled to the wall and collapsed against it. He began muttering to himself agitatedly.

Pherri pointed towards the marker. 'What's that?'

'Nothing to be concerned by,' barked the Sorrowseer. 'The stairs, quickly.'

But Phyrrai was already approaching the stone. 'There's writing on it,' she said, pointing. 'Look.'

Pherri followed behind her. Five lines of text had been etched on the marker, but though the letters were familiar, the language was not.

'It's Ancient Meridivalian,' said Phyrrai excitedly. 'Da'ri taught it to me. We've spent the last year reading it together.'

'Is it a grave?' said Pherri. She had heard some cultures buried their dead in the ground rather than burning them, like the people of the Imperium.

'No.' Phyrrai pointed to the first line. She frowned, thinking. 'This reads, I think, "*Here, Ker Piper defeated the last Norha, as it was prophesised.*"' Her eyes widened. 'Piper was here!'

'What about the rest of it?' said Pherri.

'It is merely a monument to his vanity,' said the Sorrowseer from where she stood on the stairs. There were shafts of light behind her, as if holes had been drilled into the clay to allow the sun in. 'We will find the place that will take Pherri back to her own world upstairs.'

'This bit is more complicated,' said Phyrrai, too engrossed to heed the Sorrowseer. 'It's a poem:

'Line of *kers* – that's a Meridivalian king – yet born to a nameless mother. As a youth gained... shall gain... glory in the summer of his... his... I think *seventeenth* year – they used a different counting system to us; it all rhymes in Ancient Meridivalian – amidst the breaking of... cups? Containers? Some sort of... barrel, perhaps... and rich blood spilling, shall steal from... no, *cheat* death and defeat the goddess. Yes – that's it! So, all together it would be something like—

'"*Born of the line of kings to a nameless mother*
As a youth shall gain glory in the summer of his seventeenth year
Amidst the breaking of barrels and rich blood spilling
Shall cheat death and defeat the goddess"'

Phyrrai beamed. 'That confirms it! It was prophesised that King Piper of the Meridivals would defeat the last of the Norhai, and he did, here! He and the Meridivals must have migrated to Erland afterwards – perhaps it was the Norha's death that turned this land into a desert.'

But Pherri was hardly listening. The Sorrowseer had said reality and time were like a tree, a single trunk but many branches. Would then that also be true of ancient prophecy? Because the first three lines of the poem did not just apply to Piper.

They applied to her father.

But her father was dead, and the last Norha of Pherri's own world was still alive.

Suddenly faint, Pherri collapsed to her knees.

Phyrrai tried to hold her up, but Pherri fell forward, face down in the dirt. 'Pherri! What's wrong?'

Warm tears rolled down Pherri's cheeks and spilt onto the ground. 'If that prophecy is true, even if I return to my own world and stop Eryi, we cannot stop Vulgatypha. That poem describes my father, and my father is already dead.'

CHAPTER 37

Ciera stood on the balcony of the solar, wrapped tight in her furs against the cold but still shivering. Faint fumes continued to emanate from Eryispek, but that had not changed the chill winds that blew from the Mountain and across the plains. Ideally, she would have been within the solar – Viratia had gladly given it over to her, and in the days since Ciera had begun redecorating it in her image, with soft chairs, piles of furs, and sweet incense that might drive away the ghost of Hessian – but the balcony was the one place within Piperskeep she could happily believe she and her companions would not be overheard.

Below, Merivale was alive with the lights of hundreds of fires burning against the night. Other than the Castle Road, the city was hardly changed from when Ciera had last looked down on it, the damage from the Imperials' brief recent occupation seemingly relatively minor. The Imperials on their second breach of the city walls appeared to have been solely focused on reaching and holding Piperskeep.

Burik and Sister Aimya leant over the balcony beside her, clutching cups of warmed spiced wine against the autumn chill.

They were not who Ciera would have chosen to take advice from, but they were two of the few people she could trust. Perhaps more importantly, they both knew Lady Viratia.

She could have danced into Piperskeep when the gates were thrown open for her. For Ciera, Lady Viratia's return had changed everything: Piperskeep was hers without a drop of blood being spilt; the *Hymeriker* followed Lady Viratia, so provided the two women remained united their loyalty no longer seemed to be in question.

And yet, with every moment spent in the company of Lady Viratia, Ciera could not shake her sense of unease. It should not have been so: Viratia was by all appearances and deeds Ciera's fierce ally. Nevertheless, she troubled Ciera. Her silences were a little too long, her words and gestures a little too forced, and more troubling was this prediction of a Prindian invasion, which so far it seemed nobody was able to prove the truth of.

'Anything from your scouts?' she asked Burik.

Burik frowned thoughtfully. 'Nothing yet. When they cross we'll know, whether it's at Halord's Bridge or Whitewater.'

'If they're coming at all,' said Aimya, standing at Ciera's other shoulder. Beneath a heavy woollen blanket that hung from her shoulders, she still wore the garb of an Eryian bride. Ciera had offered her other clothes, but despite her hostility towards her old order Aimya continued to wear the robes.

Burik flashed her a sharp look. 'What do you mean by that?'

Aimya looked at him as if she was about to say something, but then glanced away and took a sip of her wine. 'Nothing.'

'I would hear your thoughts, Aimya,' said Ciera. She dropped her voice. 'You knew Lady Viratia before. Do you doubt her?'

'Doubt her?' exclaimed Burik. 'After what she's done? How—'

Ciera turned to Burik and placed a finger to her lips. 'Burik,

I will hear from you, but I would hear what Aimya has to say first.'

Aimya ran her tongue over her teeth, staring out into the darkness. She stalled with another sip of wine. 'I'm different to how I was before, after what I saw up there.' Her eyes shifted towards the shadowy outline of Eryispek. 'Would be hard to stay the same, for anyone.'

'So you trust her,' said Burik.

'I wanted to.' Aimya pushed a loose strand of blonde hair back inside her hood. 'She sent me to warn you of Eryi and Vulgatypha, and I did that. But now—' She paused, sighing. 'I don't believe after what I saw that it can have been as simple as Naeem pushing Eryi into a crater. When he possessed Sister Velna, the elder bride, Naeem never even drew his sword.'

'My father wasn't a coward,' interrupted Burik. 'If Lady Viratia says—'

'That's not what I'm saying,' said Aimya, slapping her palm against the handrail. 'Eryi's servants defeated two magi to take Pherri, and then it took several of us together to take down Velna. Am I meant to believe your dad defeated Eryi himself by just grabbing him and falling down a hole? There's no chance he fell so easily.' Burik said nothing, so emboldened Aimya continued. 'And then she was the only one to survive and just wandered into Piperskeep and freed the *Hymeriker* while the Imperials brought a ceiling down on themselves? You know that doesn't make sense.'

'That's what the *Hymeriker* say happened as well,' said Burik.

'That doesn't make the story any less strange. And what about Orsian? She climbed up Eryispek when Pherri went missing. I don't know Orsian, but by all accounts he's alive somewhere. The Viratia I knew would have torn Merivale apart looking for him.'

'Orsian's a warrior. If he's alive, he can make his own way.

It's nothing like the situation with Pherri – we didn't have the Prindians coming to kill us then.'

'We don't know they are now.'

Their conversation had come full circle, and they both fell silent, gazing out over the darkness and sipping at their wine as if they were afraid they might say something they'd regret.

'So you don't trust her,' murmured Ciera.

Aimya gave a long sigh. 'I might, if she seemed the same as she was on the Mountain. You could tell she was wracked with worry about her daughter, but she was always friendly, asking me about my life, helping me when I... It doesn't matter – she's practically a different person now. She's never even asked how I am.'

Ciera could feel the anger rolling off Burik in waves. 'Well you might be different if one of your children was dead and the other two were missing,' he hissed towards Aimya, his teeth bared. 'You know what I think? I think you're just upset that you look a bit foolish. You've been running around telling everyone who'll listen about the danger of the gods, but Viratia and my father already dealt with it!'

'*I* look foolish?' Aimya looked at Burik and laughed. 'You and all the *hymerikai* are out in the city every day doing what exactly?' She gestured down towards Merivale. 'None of you know anything about repairing or rebuilding anything, and you can't fix that there's no food either. It's either that or you're drilling each other for a Prindian invasion that there's no evidence for! That all sounds pretty bloody foolish to me. And if the gods are dealt with, how do you explain what's going on in the city? When I went down there, I saw a different preacher on every corner, all extolling the wisdom of the Norhai and telling folk to turn away from Eryi.' She looked to Ciera. 'You ask me, Lady Viratia wants the *hymerikai* distracted, not asking questions about how they took back Piperskeep. I'm not calling her a liar, but there's something else going on here.'

'And what would you have me do?' asked Ciera.

Aimya hesitated. 'Do not trust her. Do not share your plans with her. Remove her influence over the *Hymeriker*.'

Sensing Burik was about to explode, Ciera laid a restraining hand on his shoulder. 'Thank you, both of you. I have heard enough. Now let me think, please.'

Ciera was more disquieted than she would have cared to admit by the vehemence of the disagreement between her closest companions. If not for Ciera's presence and the need for secrecy, it would likely have descended into a full-blown row.

She rubbed her chin with her thumb, staring down into her wine cup and swirling it, wishing the spinning liquid held some answer for her. It was impossible to disagree that Viratia had been acting strangely, but as Burik had said, was that any surprise? And the existence of the gods had already made little sense to Ciera's mind, so who was she to say that their end would be any more believable?

Most importantly though, Viratia was her ally, and it was because of her bravery and loyalty to Ciera as the mother of the new king that they held Piperskeep and were ready to withstand a West Erland assault, if ever it came. Also, it was only because of Viratia that she could be sure of the *Hymeriker*'s loyalty. She could not afford to jeopardise that, not now.

'I do not understand Lady Viratia's tale,' she said, making her decision. 'I'll admit that, but she has been a true friend to me. If the Prindians do appear, then we will be even deeper in her debt, and perhaps that would also prove the truth of her visions. If they do not come, all the better. We must wait and watch.'

Inside the keep, Tansa crept through the passages, keeping a hand on the frigid stone of the wall and the other holding aloft a lantern, half-closing her eyes in concentration as she mapped the keep in her head. Her only previous experience of the concealed burrows of Piperskeep had been escaping from Hessian's solar, but navigating the castle was not so hard, not if you knew where you were going, and not for someone who had grown up sneaking through the tunnels and alleys of Cliffark. The secrets of Merivale were no more complicated than those of Pauper's Hole, only bleaker. She clawed her way through dusty cobwebs, at one point disturbing a tortoiseshell cat bent over a piece of cheese that hissed at her before fleeing into the darkness.

In the days since their arrival, Tansa had spent most of the hours focused on avoiding anyone who might recognise her. It was unlikely – her hair was longer, and few would think to find Hessian's murderer serving as Ciera Istlewick's maid – but it was still a risk she would prefer to avoid.

The passages were good for hiding. They were also good for thieving. In the course of exploring, Tansa had amassed a growing collection of trinkets and baubles pilfered from otherwise locked rooms. Not enough that anyone would notice – silver cutlery, jewelled brooches, a miniature wood-carved king with tiny rubies for eyes – but enough to make a difference if she ever had to strike out on her own again.

There was another advantage to keeping to the hidden passages though: Tansa never had to remember. It seemed sometimes as if every inch of Piperskeep held some secret pain for her. Tam in the yard, strangled to death at the end of a rope. Cag, finally succumbing to the poison that his body had fought so hard against. Orsian. *Orsian.* Looking back, their love had been doomed from the moment they had returned here. Every time Tansa had tried to pull away from Piperskeep, Orsian had seemed to hold more tightly to it. He was the one person she would have been glad to see, but he was missing and it seemed as if nobody was troubled by this.

She had searched the dungeons alone, whispering his name, to no avail.

Perhaps it was her son that Lady Viratia wished to speak to her of. Tansa was not sure how she would know of their relationship, or could even know of Tansa's existence, but she could see no other reason that Orsian's mother would summon her.

As she neared the guest wing, Tansa slowed her footsteps, pacing the distance from where the corridor turned. As she had hoped, when she reached her destination, one cobwebbed wall sconce was crooked.

Tansa swallowed, and put her hand to it. The sconce was stiff, and as it turned the metal grated horribly against the stone, shrieking loud enough to wake the ghosts of Piperskeep. The wall clicked, and a narrow section slid open, flooding the passage with the glow of a fire. With a deep breath, Tansa stepped inside.

The room was generously proportioned. High-ceilinged, with a dressing table and a large bed, occupied by a plain mattress missing the pile of furs that was usually so common to the rooms of the nobility. An icy night breeze blew between two open windows. Tansa's eyes were drawn to the fire, and against it the dark silhouette of the back of a lone woman's head, staring into the flames.

Slowly, Lady Viratia turned to greet her. 'You received my note then?'

'Well I'm not here by accident,' said Tansa. She had hardly hesitated on receipt of the note. If she and Lady Viratia could find Orsian, perhaps he could then make Ciera honour their deal.

Lady Viratia made a noise that might have been a laugh. Her bright blue eyes found Tansa, and she was once again struck by this woman's beauty, as if she had stepped from a painting. There was little physical resemblance between her and Orsian, though perhaps they shared a similarly solemn bearing. 'Do you know why you are here?'

'Is it because of Orsian?'

At the mention of her son's name, Viratia's face tightened slightly, and one of her pupils seemed to dilate. Then she blinked, and it was gone, replaced again by a cool noble blankness. 'Orsian is missing. No...' Viratia paused, and smiled, her teeth shining like pearls. 'I wish to speak of Queen Ciera.'

That was a surprise. Perhaps the two noblewomen were not such close allies as they appeared. Though Tansa had not been invited to sit, she took a chair opposite Viratia, nearer the warmth of the fire. She looked again at the open windows and the bare bed. 'Do you not get cold when you sleep?'

'I find little time for sleep, sadly.' A half-smile flashed on Viratia's lips. 'Piperskeep is Ciera's son's by right. I am concerned, however, with her plans for Erland. Particularly as regards the agreement she has made with the city of Cliffark.'

Tansa's ears pricked up. 'What of it?'

'Do you trust her to keep her word?'

Tansa hesitated. Was this some trap? 'Shouldn't I?'

Viratia smiled. 'I suggest you be honest with me. Perhaps I can help. I understand there was some trouble on the way from Cliffark? A second deal that was perhaps not to your liking.'

'Not trouble exactly.' Tansa shifted in her chair, unable to get comfortable. 'There was...' She paused. Trusting Ciera was impossible after what she had seen between her and Lord Madine, but what made this woman any better? 'Why do I feel like you want me to tell you things you already know?'

Viratia frowned. 'You are suspicious.' Her hand moved to the table next to her and picked up a cup. Tansa could not recall it being there a moment earlier, and then to her surprise Viratia leant forward to offer it to her. 'It's no surprise, I suppose. Your experience of the nobility has not been pleasant, has it? Dishonesty, mistreatment, *death*?'

The question hung in the air. Tansa accepted the cup, and found it hot and filled to the brim with spiced wine. She took a sip, and the seasoning burst against her tongue. 'You're one of them though.'

'Yes, but there is a difference: I sincerely want what's best for Erland.' Viratia let out a doleful sigh. 'Sometimes I think the queen does too, and at others...' Viratia tailed off, and rose suddenly, and moved to stare out of the western window. 'You have heard that the Prindians will arrive soon?'

'I have heard the rumour.' Tansa knew little of the Prindians; Merivale was the closest she had come to the Pale River.

'They will.' Viratia spoke as if by saying it she could make it so. 'Do you know what Rymond Prindian thinks of Cliffark?'

Tansa snorted. 'About as much as I think of him. Merivale is far from Cliffark as it is, never mind Irith.'

Viratia smiled. She was so pale the firelight seemed to slide off her face, as though the flames were afraid of tarnishing her. 'And of the two of them, who do you think is more likely to give Cliffark the independence it deserves?'

Tansa pursed her lips, and stalled with another sip of hot wine. She knew when she was being manipulated, but she could see what Orsian's mother was getting at. 'Likely Rymond Prindian,' she said slowly. 'He has no blood claim to the city, and Irith is far to the west. Cliffark would be nothing to him as long as he received his taxes.'

'Indeed.' Viratia turned back towards Tansa, and as the firelight shifted across her features Tansa swore she saw two different expressions on her face. There was the satisfied smile, but behind it was a silent rictus of anguish, tears of torment running down flushed cheeks. Tansa blinked, and the illusion was gone. It had been only a trick of the light.

For reasons she could not explain, Tansa's heart was suddenly thundering. She felt something warm and wet above her mouth, and when she touched her finger to it, she found there was blood dripping from her nose. 'Are you saying we should try and ensure that Rymond Prindian wins? Why would you want that?'

Viratia's smile was razor-sharp. 'I only want what's best for Erland. All you must do is ensure that his and Ciera Istlewick's forces come to battle, and I will do the rest.'

High above Viratia and Tansa, Ciera too was looking to the west, and despite the icy cold found she could not tear herself away from the balcony. Sleep would not find her tonight. She had dismissed Burik and Aimya, and the two of them had departed separately, without speaking. Haisie had come to join her, carrying a pile of furs so large that it dwarfed her small frame. The two of them huddled together, each clutching a cup of hot spiced wine, Haisie resting her chin against the balustrade as they stared over Merivale and the plains beyond. The sky was beginning to brighten. Dawn would break soon; Ciera had wasted the whole night lost in contemplation.

'What do you think to Lady Viratia, Haisie?' she said. 'You may speak freely.'

Haisie looked up at her, startled. 'She's... She always seemed kind before, when she stayed in Piperskeep. Now...' Haisie's nose twitched. 'She seems cold. She scares me.'

Ciera nodded. 'She scares me too.'

The plains were quiet, yet Ciera could feel a strange charge in the air, like clouds on the cusp of a thunderstorm. The sky though was clear, the glow of a bright white crescent moon and stars like specks of dust painting the balcony in silvery light. Perhaps it was her unease with Lady Viratia, but there was a sense of agitation within Ciera that even a brisk wind and the stimulating herbs of the wine could not shift.

She sighed. *This is the price of power*. She would not sleep tonight; there was too much uncertainty. Lady Viratia – ally or enemy? The Prindians – would they come? Eryi and Vulgatypha – dead, alive, or merely myth? She had come to Merivale believing she would face an enemy she knew, yet the shape of the conflict to come remained as changeable as the weather.

I shall wait three days, she decided. Three days for some sight of the Prindians to reach them. If they did not come, she would refocus upon her reforms, starting with granting the Cliffarkers their independence. She might even dismiss Lord Madine's men and send him a missive renouncing their agreement. Perhaps then Tansa might be willing to trust her.

Then the real work could begin. Untilled fertile land would be given to anyone prepared to farm it, for a price that could be repaid in harvests. Never again would her people suffer for lack of food. Her tax reforms could be completed, removing individual levies based on the use of the king's property and replacing them with charges based on income. She might even open a school in Merivale, where children could learn to read and write and sum figures.

None of that of course would resolve the problem of Lady Viratia. The *Hymeriker*'s allegiance was still to the Barrelbreaker's widow, and that meant Ciera ruled only with Viratia's leave. She needed her own *balhymeri*, one loyal to her, someone the *hymerikai* would be sure to follow.

'It's cold, Majesty,' said Haisie, her teeth chattering.

Ciera looked down and saw the girl was shivering. 'Agreed. We should go inside and get the fire going.' She brushed Haisie's hair back from her forehead, and began to turn away from the balcony. Perhaps she could steal a few hours of rest before the day truly began.

Across the plains, a flash of pale blue light stopped Ciera in her tracks. It flashed for only a moment, several miles from the city, and then was gone. She stared after it, but no further flash followed.

'Did you see that, Haisie?'

The girl looked up at her. 'See what, Majesty?'

Ciera frowned. Perhaps she had imagined it. 'Nothing. Inside then.' She turned away.

The second flash was so bright that it illuminated the night. Ghostly blue light flared against the sky and moon and glazed the land west of Merivale. Ciera turned back, gripping the parapet as it flashed again, brighter and larger, the glow reflecting in her gaze so intensely that she had to shield her eyes against it.

It was expanding, stretching from a single light to a mass hundreds of yards in width, like some great spectre come to swallow Merivale. It seemed to hum, vibrating against Ciera's numb cheeks and warming them to a rosy red.

'What is that?' shrieked Haisie.

The light became so bright and the humming so deafening that two guards rushed from the solar onto the balcony. 'Eryi's balls!' cried one of them. 'What witchcraft—'

The light stopped glowing, and a great host of men and horses burst from it in a flood. They bore banners, illuminated in the night by the gateway's incandescence, casting long shadows up and down the city and the walls of Piperskeep. Silhouetted against the blazing light it seemed an army of ghosts, as dark and featureless as reflections in black water.

Still they came, thousands of them, horses and supply wagons and men stumbling over the impossible threshold into the heart of East Erland.

'What are they?' cried one of the guards. He had drawn his sword, seemingly not sure what else to do.

Ciera said nothing. She could barely contemplate what she saw, never mind speak of it.

As the last of the host passed beyond the barrier, the blue

faded, and beyond the gateway Ciera thought she could just make out a town and a stout castle in the distance. It began to shrink, dissolving in the night air, until within seconds it was as if the gateway had never stood there at all.

In its place stood a vast army, and by the light of the heavens Ciera could make out the standard that led their way. It was made of rich emerald cloth, drawing golden tassels behind it that flittered in the breeze like restless dragonflies. She had never set eyes on the silver-crowned figure beneath it, but she knew him.

Rymond Prindian had come to Merivale.

CHAPTER 38

Rymond woke as the first rays of the sun broached the walls of Merivale, bathing the interior of his pavilion in light tinged the green of its canvas. He yawned and looked about the tent. His servants had prepared it the night before, with the long table across the middle between the two tallest supporting poles and his trunks set around the edges.

Just to be sure the day before had not been a dream, he rose, wrapped his nightgown around himself, then stalked for the entrance. He stuck his head out and there it was: the great walled capital of Erland, stinking and ugly on the slope of a hill, the dark fortress of the Sangreals looming over it like an overbearing father.

'Majesty.' One of the two guards standing outside greeted him.

'We're really here then,' said Rymond, his eyes never leaving the city. A great gateway truly had appeared in the air and led them to Merivale. As far as he knew, every single man, beast, and personal effect was accounted for, other than one citizen of Irith who had reportedly sprained an ankle crossing the threshold and elected to return home.

Only a few guards were visible staring out at them from atop the battlements. It seemed strangely calm, for a city Helana had claimed was in imminent danger. The remains of the Imperial camp could be seen a few hundred yards east of their position; skeletal tent frames, latrine pits and shallow graves, the cindered remains of a towering mangonel. The turrets of Piperskeep seemed to reach towards the brightening sky like grasping fingers, many flying the blood-red banner of the Sangreals. He was told he had come to Merivale once before, as a child, but he did not recall it, and the place had taken on a mythic, nightmarish quality in his mind, like the den of a rapacious ogre.

But now Hessian was dead, and by the looks of it the city was no longer in need of saving from whatever foe Helana had hallucinated under the heady influence of casheef. It was his for the taking.

He sensed that the guard had said something to him. 'I'm sorry?'

'Said it looks peaceful, Majesty,' said the guard. 'You still expecting fighting?'

That depends on the Sangreals. Rymond did not know Ciera Istlewick. Helana had made her stepmother sound like a simpering maid, but there was little truth to that if she had recaptured Merivale from the Imperium. 'All I'll say is keep your blade sharp.'

There would never be a better time to take Merivale. He did not know how they had vanquished the Imperials, but it ought to have cost them dearly. Could they have the numbers to resist him? He thought of immediately ordering his forces to form up and assault the Ram's Gate, but doubt held him back. He had made the mistake of overconfidence against the Sangreals before. Andrick Barrelbreaker might be dead, but Rymond had not forgotten the lesson of their skirmish at Imberwych.

With a start, Rymond realised Lord Darlton was striding towards the tent from across the field, already clad in mail and with an ambitious gleam in his eye. Rymond had appointed the dark and uncompromising lord to lead his forces. Since their settlement, the man had become Rymond's fiercest champion, at least to his face, as if calling his king a '*weak, drug-addled, indolent, mummy's boy coward*' had been a figment of Rymond's imagination. He was not Adfric, and he would not inspire fear as Strovac Sigac might have – there was a rumour circulating that the man had died; Rymond hoped it was true – but he was suitably fierce and he had retaken Whitewater Motte well enough.

Darlton hailed his king with a raised hand. 'Majesty.' He thrust out his hand and seized Rymond's forearm, the lord's mail hard against the silk of Rymond's gown. 'I've given the command for our forces to ready themselves.' He pointed east, to where Rymond could see mailed men forming up into lines. 'Will you lead the assault?'

Rymond's heart almost dropped into the pit of his bowels. It was easy to be brave when you had no choice, but the thought of voluntarily leading an assault on the walls of Merivale filled him with cold dread. Darlton was looking at him expectantly, smirking slightly, expecting him to refuse. 'Have them stand down. I would assess the Sangreal forces first – we'll wait for them to call for parley.'

Darlton frowned. 'We have surprise on our side, but we lose a measure of it with every hour. Were it up to me we would have begun the assault last night.'

And probably stumbled into the moat in the dark. No doubt Darlton still thought him a coward, but Rymond's pride was not worth men's lives if battle could be avoided. 'If they are as weak as I believe, then they should seek terms.' He only hoped Ciera Istlewick was not as stubborn as his mother or Helana.

The thought of Helana Sangreal seemed to summon her, for

over Darlton's shoulder Rymond saw her striding towards him. She too was dressed for battle, in a ring mail leather jerkin with a sword belted at her waist. Whether she knew how to wield it was another matter, but at that moment she looked quite prepared to use it on Rymond. He wished he had got dressed before he stuck his head out of the tent.

'This lunatic has them forming up for battle,' she declared, while Darlton smiled sardonically beneath his beard. 'Don't tell me you mean to attack?'

'Your concerns about the gods appear unfounded,' said Rymond. 'Whatever you believe you saw in Thrumbalto, it's gone.'

She stared at him in incredulity. 'We've just travelled here through... I don't even know what to call it, through a *magic hole*, and you still doubt me? A gateway did not appear in the air by happenstance, Rymond.'

Rymond had decided not to dwell on it. *We are here now; never mind how we got here.* It was a question for once he was within Piperskeep. 'The future of Merivale rests in the hands of those who currently hold it. If they will surrender to me, none of them will be harmed.'

'Have you gone mad?' Helana grasped for Rymond as if to shake him by the collar, but Darlton was whip-fast and caught her before the guards could intervene. The lord pinned her arms to her sides and held her tightly as she struggled.

'What do you want done with her, Majesty?' He asked the question like a cook speaking of a sow to be served.

Rymond raised a hand for calm. 'No harm is to come to her.' He looked Helana square in the eye. 'I will do what I must, Helana. It is not personal. Do you suppose the country will prosper under the reign of some suckling newborn?'

'That's not the point!' she raged against Darlton's grip but the lord held firm. 'Do you think this is about who rules in

Merivale? *Something* wants this battle to happen, Rymond. Don't fall for this.'

'There will be no battle if Ciera Istlewick acts sensibly. However, in the circumstances, if you wish to join your family within the walls, I will not stop you. You are free to go.'

Helana had finally stopped struggling, and Rymond nodded to Darlton to release her. 'I'll stay,' she said. The hurt in her eyes came close to breaking Rymond's resolve. 'I'll stay in the hope I can talk sense into you. Those inside Merivale are not your enemy.'

'That is entirely a decision for them.'

With a nod to Darlton, Rymond withdrew inside his tent, tore off his gown and began dressing himself. He could have waited for a servant, but he wanted to lose himself in the ritual of ensuring he looked his best when the Sangreals' representatives arrived.

I owe her nothing, he reminded himself, thinking of Helana. *This is what must be done. Casheef visions are meaningless.*

So why did he feel so guilty?

Ciera ascended the battlements over the rebuilt Ram's Gate, flanked by Burik and Viratia. She had not summoned the Barrelbreaker's widow, but as Viratia was currently the apparent mistress of the *Hymeriker* she could hardly refuse her. There was still an unsettling undercurrent to Viratia's presence, something in her taut smiles and the way her eyes looked past Ciera that said she knew something she ought not to. Ciera could not deny though that she had been right about the arrival of the Prindians.

Through a magic gateway. That was even more unsettling than Viratia's presence, and Ciera could tell by the tight, pale faces of the watchmen eyeing the Prindian host that she was not the only one who thought so. The whole city was on edge; already, wild-eyed holy men were pouring into the streets to preach that this was an army of the dead or the vengeance of the Norhai come to drag them to their doom, and the Eryian priests and Brides of Eryi had sent frantic delegations to Piperskeep insisting that these charlatans be dealt with, as if these street preachers were somehow more important than the army at their gates.

The West Erlanders had made camp just beyond the ruins of the Imperial encampment, hundreds of tents and makeshift shelters arranged around two huge green marquees that Ciera assumed were the shelters of Rymond Prindian and his mother. It was already a hive of activity; there were men digging latrine ditches, seeing to the horses, roasting vast urns of stew over campfires, and some even forming up in lines for battle.

Ciera turned to Burik. 'How many?'

It was Viratia who answered. 'Ten thousand, more or less,' she said without feeling. 'Fresh from Irith.'

'How did you know?' asked Ciera. 'How could you? What even—' The memory of the blue light that had soaked over the entire city flashed in her mind. 'What *did* that? Do they have a magus?' She could not imagine even Theodric being capable of such a thing. Could magi move ten thousand men hundreds of miles?

'I told you – I dreamt it.' Viratia spoke as though to a child, as if Ciera had been a fool to ever doubt her. 'Since Eryispek I am blessed with visions.'

Ciera tried to glance at Burik, but he did not meet her eye. She could sense a worried tension among the wall's watchmen, but the half-dozen-strong ring of *hymerikai* escorting them appeared untroubled. Viratia's apparent clairvoyance had evidently strengthened their love for their patron.

'We should prepare to attack,' said Viratia. 'Before they have a chance to dig in.'

'And give up the walls?' said Burik, looking at her in surprise.

'Are you afraid, Burik?' asked a *hymerika* with a laugh. 'Forget their numbers, that rabble won't stand against a charge of the *Hymeriker*. We defeated the Imperium remember.'

Burik turned to glare at the man. 'The Imperials took the city, *twice*.'

'Maybe that's because we hid inside the walls!'

Ciera was shaking her head. Viratia might have been right about the Prindians, but it was hard to trust her. She would not send men to die for her until it was necessary. She would have to tread carefully disagreeing with Viratia though; the loyalty of the *Hymeriker* depended on her grace.

'In time, perhaps,' she said, keeping her eyes on the Prindian camp. A procession of servants was heading towards the largest tent bearing trays of food. 'First I would speak with them; perhaps some accommodation can be reached.' She turned to address the chief watchman, a greybeard whose name she recalled as Horath. 'Raise the flag of parley. Before we make any decisions, I would know the Prindian intention.'

'I'd say their intention is plain enough,' grumbled Burik. 'Some luck this city's had the last few months.'

'We shall prevail,' said Viratia. The iron certainty in her voice sent a chill up Ciera's neck. 'Have your parley, Majesty. The *Hymeriker* and I shall prepare for battle.'

Ciera wished she could take those words as a comfort.

Within a small tent of plain canvas, Helana sat opposite Gruenla, watching the Cylirien woman deal the cards.

'I don't know how you can play triumph at a time like this,' said Helana, taking up her hand. Gruenla inhaled on a smoke-stick. 'And since when do you smoke?'

The captain-general blew out the fumes. 'I always smoke before a battle. Always a risk it's the last chance I have. Tastes even better afterwards.' She considered her hand. 'As for playing triumph, this isn't my first orgy; battle is nine-tenths waiting and one-tenth fighting, and this is the best way to pass the waiting.' She looked up at Helana. 'Seeing as you're so distracted maybe I'll even beat you this time.'

Helana considered her hand and began arranging her cards into suits. 'I knew what he was plotting,' she said. 'But you'd think a fucking doorway opening in the air would make him think a bit harder.'

'That's kings for you,' said Gruenla, offering Helana a smokestick. 'Maybe he's taking it as a sign. If he won't change his mind for you, he won't change it for anyone.'

Helana took the tube, opened their lantern, lit it, and inhaled. Her eyes watered, but she resisted the urge to cough. She had not tried a smokestick since Jarhick was alive. 'He's a fucking arsehole,' she spat. 'Knew I couldn't trust him.'

Gruenla shrugged. 'So you keep saying. We playing or not?'

Helana studied her cards again, and pushed forward a few coins as an opening bid. She felt like a fool; Rymond's struggle to retake Irith had been nothing to her, but she had helped him anyway, and he was going to repay her by going to war on her home city. Helana had known it was coming, but she had held onto an irrational hope that in the end she might dissuade him. Perhaps she had thought Rymond a better man than he truly was. Or perhaps she could have found a better method of persuasion than yelling at him.

'Our deal still on?' Helana asked, as Gruenla matched Helana's bid.

Gruenla nodded. 'I'm your woman, Princess. Unless our esteemed majesty and his mother decide to pay me.' She dropped her voice. 'If it does come to battle, we're with you.'

The tread of approaching footsteps sounded from outside.

The flap of the tent was thrown open, and Chieftain Arka's ducked head appeared. 'Parley,' grunted the Ffrisean warlord. 'Rymond calls you.'

Helana rose with a resigned shrug. 'Wonder what he wants us there for.'

'To show off probably,' said Gruenla. She addressed Arka, 'Your Erlish is getting better.'

The Ffrisean bunched his shoulders. 'Some.'

Arka led them towards Rymond's grand tent, past rows of identical shelters and men who like Gruenla and Helana were doing what they could to pass the time: sharpening their weapons, passing skins around a fire, or throwing dice for future plunder.

They reached the marquee. Arka pulled back the flap.

'Guess it's time to find out who speaks for my infant half-brother,' muttered Helana to Gruenla. It was hard to believe she had a new sibling; perhaps that was why she scarcely thought of him.

The tent's interior was well-lit. Rolls of cloth had been pulled back from the outside to allow daylight in, and several lanterns were scattered around the room and at the middle of the table.

Helana's eyes ran across those assembled. On the far side sat Rymond and his mother, flanked by the coterie of lords that had formed around him in the days after the capture of Irith. He looked up at her with a small smile. 'I thought it best if we waited for you.' He next addressed those facing him and gestured towards Helana. 'May I present Princess Helana Sangreal. As you can see, she's been well looked after.'

Those sitting closest to Helana turned around. At the centre of them, she recognised her father's young widow, Ciera Istlewick, though they'd had little to do with one another between the wedding that had ended with Ciera's brief abduction and Helana's night flight from Merivale. They might be a similar age, but Helana had wanted nothing to do with the woman her father planned to use to replace Jarhick.

Nevertheless, Ciera rose and swept upon Helana, standing on her toes to kiss her on both cheeks, which Helana reluctantly returned. 'I'm so relieved you're alive. Are you well? Your father—'

'I know he's dead. If you're going to tell me he was worried for me, don't bother.' Helana could not tolerate the falseness; it had always been obvious that nobody in Merivale had missed her. She looked along the table at the rest of Ciera's delegation – two *hymerikai*, including Burik, who she recalled; a Bride of Eryi for some reason; and—

'Aunt Viratia?'

Helana's aunt smiled and came to her feet. 'My dearest niece.' She crossed the distance between them in a few quick steps and pulled Helana into a fierce hug.

Surprised as she was, Helana returned the embrace. She had admired her aunt from afar for her fierce spirit, but the two of them had never been close. Over Viratia's shoulder, Helana scanned the table again, wondering whether she had missed Orsian.

But her cousin was not there.

'Where is Orsian?' Helana asked as Viratia withdrew from their greeting. 'Still inside the city?' The Orsian she knew would have insisted on being here.

Viratia's smile faltered. 'Still missing, I'm afraid.'

Helana frowned. 'Is someone looking for him? And what of Pherri and Errian? Are they well?'

'Pherri is missing, and Errian sadly dead.' A single tear beaded in Viratia's eye, and just for a moment Helana felt as if she was seeing something Viratia did not wish her to see. Then Helana blinked, and the tear was gone. 'Errian fell in the defence of Merivale against the Imperials.'

On the other side of the table, Breta Prindian came to her

feet. 'Perhaps we could save your heartfelt reunion for another time? We are here to discuss Merivale's surrender after all.'

'Forgive me,' said Viratia. She turned to Breta Prindian wearing a cold smile. 'But nobody has spoken of surrender.'

Helana positioned herself away from the table, at the edge of the tent slightly shadowed by the bulk of Chieftain Arka, her head spinning.

She stared at her aunt. She could not claim to know Viratia well, but she knew enough: Lady Viratia Brithwell would not sit idly by while two of her children were missing, certainly not when the eldest of them was dead. Helana had seen growing up how her aunt was with her two boys. She had been as fiercely envious as only a child could be, railing against the unfairness that her mother should have died while her cousins' doted on them.

In different circumstances, Helana might have dismissed it as her aunt putting on a brave face in front of her enemies, but after seeing Eryi just a stone's throw from here and crossing Erland in the space of a blink she had no taste for convenient explanations.

A cold and certain terror spread all the way up Helana's spine from her tailbone to her neck. Whoever this woman was, it was not Viratia Brithwell.

'Well,' said Breta Prindian, scrutinising Ciera from across the table, 'you've certainly come a long way since I last saw you. I did wonder if you would survive Hessian, but in the end it was he who did not survive you. Widowhood suits you, Lady Ciera.'

Ciera held Breta's gaze but did not smile. When they had last seen one another, Breta had kidnapped her, and Ciera had been dragged unconscious from the Pale River before being locked away by Hessian for her own safety. 'You look well also,

Lady Prindian, but shall we turn to weightier matters?' Ciera had not come here for verbal sparring. It did not suit her to leave Merivale and come to the West Erland war camp; ideally, they would have come to her, but she did not want the Prindians seeing too closely the perilous state of the recently rebuilt Ram's Gate. Perhaps more importantly, she hoped to keep their numbers a secret.

Lady Prindian flashed a practised smile, as if Ciera had raised her bet and she was preparing to go all in. 'If that is what you wish. In that case though it will be a rather short meeting – our demands are straightforward.'

While Breta spoke, Ciera's eyes slid towards Helana, standing away from the table. Though the two of them had never had the opportunity to spend much time together, Ciera had hoped for some sort of recognition from her stepdaughter, perhaps a signal of where she stood in this matter. However, Helana did not meet her eye, and there was a glazed look to her as if she was troubled by something.

A long document was unfurled on the table, and Rymond Prindian briefly rose to place empty tankards at the corners to keep it flat. He might have been Ciera's husband if not for Hessian's intervention, and he was strikingly handsome, if slightly too pretty. The sheen of his golden hair and the smoothness of his cheeks suggested that he had spent more time arranging himself for this meeting than Ciera had. He wore a sleek velvet green cape over his mail, and on his head sat an elegantly wrought crown studded with dazzling emeralds that made Ciera feel slightly self-conscious of her own shabby bronze circlet. She could admit he looked more a king than Andrick did, currently in the charge of a team of nurses and six *hymerikai* whom she trusted.

Ciera looked down and realised the parchment was a document that she was evidently supposed to sign. She glanced at Rymond. 'What is this?'

He cleared his throat and took a sip of ale. Ciera had heard that Rymond Prindian favoured wine, in vast quantities, but it appeared she had been misinformed. 'A document under which you, on behalf of your son, give up any claim to the kingdom of Erland. In return you shall receive your weight in Imperial gold, in addition to an annual pension for both you and your son for the span of your lives, and swear never to set foot on Erlish soil again. Two hundred of my men are ready to escort you, your son, and any servants to Whitewater to take ship to anywhere you please.'

Ciera studied the document, trying to maintain her composure and to not fling it across the room. It showed how little the Prindians knew of her that they thought she might sign this. At every turn, people had told her to run. Not now, not ever.

'It is a kinder offer than I would have proposed,' said Breta Prindian. 'My son has always had a generous heart.'

'Do you suppose the line of succession can be set aside in exchange for gold?' asked Burik scathingly. 'The Prindians haven't ruled East Erland for three hundred years. If you think—'

Ciera placed a hand on his arm. 'I shall need time to consider this,' she said. How much did the Prindians know? If they thought Merivale's forces weakened from a battle with the Imperium, they would not know their true strength. In which case, Viratia's proposal for a surprise attack was an option. 'Might I take the document with me?'

Rymond began to speak. 'I think—'

'I think we were not born yesterday,' interrupted his mother. 'Do you suppose we shall give you the chance to strengthen your position while you um and aah over stepping aside?' She leant forward over the table, and to Ciera's surprise grabbed her wrist. 'It is a better deal than you and your son deserve. Even in Irith we have heard the whispers. The boy's father—'

'The boy's father was Hessian Sangreal.' Burik kicked his

chair back and came to his feet. 'A blind man could see it. Your lies will not serve you in this, Prindian.' He turned his blazing gaze on Rymond. 'I've seen enough of my brothers die on West Erland blades – we can settle this outside. You for the Prindians, me for the Sangreals.' Already, two Prindian guards were advancing towards Burik, but he stepped away from them with his hand ready on his sword hilt.

The new Lord Darlton was laughing silently, dark eyes glinting as he stared at Burik. He came patiently to his feet. 'Always thought the *Hymeriker* couldn't be all that, and you, boy, might be the proof of it. I'll stand for the Prindians.'

Rymond Prindian rushed to his feet so fast that his chair toppled backwards. 'Stop, both of you! I'll not sully these talks with violence.' He glared at Darlton, while Ciera turned to usher a furious Burik back to his seat. Viratia had not even moved. She was still sitting beside Ciera, regarding the Prindians with curious disinterest.

Rymond continued. 'Mother, I suggest whatever you were going to say does not need saying.' He tapped twice on the document. 'You may take it, Lady Ciera, but I will have your answer by dawn tomorrow. Otherwise, the outcome will be the same, but first your people will bleed for it, and you can go into exile with only your son and the clothes on your back. How do you suppose a woman like you will feed herself on the streets of a foreign city?'

'You are truly pathetic, Rymond Prindian.' A voice came from the shadows of the tent, dripping with disdain. It was Helana. Her face was a mask of revulsion. 'Even now, you're still a coward. Do you suppose your threats make you honourable? That letting my brother live makes you better for stealing his birthright?' Her lip curled. 'You disgust me.'

Rymond's throat bobbed up and down, and in that moment Ciera saw him for what he was: a scared boy, stuck between what he thought must be done and how far he was willing to go for it. 'I will not climb over dead children to take the crown,' he said, speaking slowly as if otherwise his voice might crack. 'But if there must be battle, let it be tomorrow. I will claim all of Erland as the Sangreals did, and my ancestors did before them. With blood and steel.' With careful movements, he set the tankards aside and rolled up the parchment. He handed it to Ciera. 'Your answer, by dawn.'

All through the talks, Helana kept her eyes fixed on her aunt, her agitation growing with every second. Viratia had remained seated throughout, not even responding to Burik or Helana's outbursts. At times Helana swore she even saw her smiling.

As the representatives of Merivale prepared to depart, Breta Prindian finally spoke of it. 'You have been unexpectedly quiet, Lady Brithwell. Are you well?'

Viratia looked up at her, smiling. 'Quite well, Lady Prindian. We shall see you tomorrow.'

Helana was relieved someone else had noticed, but Breta Prindian seemed to think nothing of it. She wanted to scream at them: '*That isn't my aunt!*' She did not even *move* like her, taking long clumsy strides as if she could hardly control her own legs. Viratia had always seemed to glide purposefully across the ground, as if by grace and will alone she could arrange all her eyes fell upon to her liking.

She thought of approaching Ciera and asking to speak alone, but the Merivalers were already leaving.

Helana was about to tell Rymond she had changed her mind and wanted to enter Merivale after all, but a thought stopped her. The woman pretending to be her aunt had seemed quite content with Helana and Burik's belligerent outbursts. Did she want the Prindians to attack?

What Helana needed was time. An anxious sweat rose

beneath her arms. *Time to work out what in the Norha's cunt is going on.* That meant one thing: speaking with Rymond. Rymond, who she had just named a coward in front of a tent full of people, who seemed as intent on battle as his mother.

Once the East Erlanders had departed, Rymond poured himself a large cup of wine. He scarcely drank wine now, except at moments of high tension, but he saw half the measure off in one gulp then leant back in his chair with his eyes closed.

'That was well done,' said his mother. 'If she is as shrewd as her father, she will take the deal.'

Rymond shook his head, his face still tilted up at the ceiling. 'She won't. She has come too far in this to retreat now.' He exhaled heavily and gestured to a servant for a smokestick. 'It will be battle. It must be, to prove I am a man of my word.' He coughed a bitter laugh. 'The things you would have me do for a kingdom.'

'Rymond,' said Helana, stepping forward to the edge of the table. 'Might we speak alone?'

Breta turned to Helana with a fierce glare. 'Do you suppose your outburst helped matters? How do you suppose your father would have reacted to being called a coward in front of his enemies?'

'But I am not Hessian,' said Rymond. He smiled to himself and murmured, 'At least I hope not.' He drew on his smokestick. 'Everybody out. Helana, make it quick.'

'Do not let her talk you into peace,' Rymond's mother told him, as the servants and guards hurried from the tent. She stood on her toes to kiss him on the cheek. 'You are a king now, and men see you as such. If you allow your will to break here, then all your deeds up till now will have been for nothing.'

Rymond squeezed his mother's hand. 'Do you suppose I

don't know that?' He had come too far to baulk now. To do so would mean his death, either at the hands of disgruntled lords or in many years' time when Andrick Sangreal came of age. This was an opportunity his ancestors could not have imagined in their most vivid dreams; he was encamped outside Merivale with ten thousand men, and he faced a Sangreal force already weary of war and led by a king still in swaddling.

Breta Prindian departed also, and Rymond was left alone with Helana.

'I'm sorry,' she said, taking a seat opposite him and reaching for the jug of watered ale. 'I should not have called you a coward.'

'Even though I am.' Rymond smiled. He knew himself well enough to know that it was true. 'You know the only time I ever felt brave was when I kissed you after that boar gored me?' It felt like a lifetime ago, when there had still been a chance he might walk away from the demands of his birth. 'But if you want to persuade me to peace, you know I can't do that. It's too late.'

'All I ask is that you wait.' There were fraught lines of tension around Helana's mouth. 'I know you want to ignore what I saw and that we crossed hundreds of miles through a window that appeared in the air, but I am begging you not to. Lady Viratia... I don't think she's who she says she is.'

Rymond struggled to make sense of that. 'I've met her before,' he told Helana, his brow furrowing. 'I know who she is.'

'But you don't!' exclaimed Helana. Rymond was struck by the genuine agitation in her voice; if this was a ruse, it was a strange one. 'She's—' Rymond watched as she struggled to find the words. 'Just give them, give me more time, please? I can prove it, I'm sure I can.'

Rymond took a sip of wine, rolling the idea around his head. 'I need a better reason than that,' he told her. 'If I delay—'

'Marriage. If you give me just one more day, I'll marry you.'

CHAPTER 39

Outside Rymond's tent, Ciera remounted her horse before she, Burik, Aimya, and Viratia raced the half-mile back to Merivale. Burik tried to say something to her, but with the flurry of thoughts circling Ciera's head she barely heard him.

I will not run again. Not for all the gold in the Prindian vault. Merivale was hers, her son's, and she had faced down too many threats to surrender it now.

If the Prindians knew anything of the mysterious gateway by which they had come to Merivale, they had hidden it well, but surely something was pulling their strings. Had one of the godly entities Aimya spoken of secretly taken up the Prindian cause?

She could sense Viratia riding at her flank, but Ciera studiously refused to look at her. How had she predicted the Prindian arrival? And what else did she know?

They slowed to cross the drawbridge, hooves beating on the heavy wood. A dozen watchmen stood guard over the gate as the portcullis rose. 'When you predicted the Prindians would come,' said Ciera, turning towards Viratia, 'did you know they would appear like that? How did they do it?'

Viratia shook her head once, her expression as unreadable as ever. 'My visions show only what they show. Probably they have a magus.'

The response could not have been less to Ciera's liking. She could not shake the feeling that Viratia was holding something back. But Ciera could not question her too closely, not if she wanted the loyalty of the *Hymeriker*.

She led them under the gatehouse back inside the city. 'We'll return to Piperskeep,' said Ciera. They might have stayed at the wall, but before they discussed a response to Rymond she needed to be closer to her son. Being apart from him filled her with anxiety, as if the Prindians might snatch him away and force him into exile without her. 'Burik, escort Lady Viratia back to the keep – I need to speak to the watchmen. Aimya, wait with me.'

'I should come with you,' said Burik.

'There are dozens of watchmen, I'll be quite safe.' Ciera threw her reins to a nearby *hymerika* and dismounted. 'Meet me in the solar, but first summon representatives from all our forces and the half-dozen most experienced *hymerikai*.' There was no time to waste.

'I am all the representation the *Hymeriker* requires,' said Viratia, smiling serenely, as if they had just returned from an afternoon of leisure rather than a fruitless negotiation. 'We will meet you there, Majesty.'

Ciera watched Burik and Viratia ride away into the maze of streets heading for the Castle Road, and once she was satisfied they were out of earshot took Aimya by the hand and led her under the nearby awning of a ruined inn, stinking of stale urine and with a ceiling of bare, blackened beams.

'Did you see anything strange in the Prindian camp?' she asked urgently. 'Anything that reminded you of the gods you saw?'

Aimya shook her head, frowning. 'Nothing. Does that mean

you believe me?'

'But you don't think they're gone?'

'No. I told you – Lady Viratia's tale makes no sense. I don't know why but I'm certain she's lying to us.'

Ciera's head was hurting. She needed Viratia; she could not hold the city without the *Hymeriker*. 'Did you see anything like that gateway on the Mountain?'

'Never.'

Ciera closed her eyes. If the gods did have a role in this, she wished they would show themselves. At least then the Prindians might have the sense to put aside their avarice for the Erlish crown, unless Rymond had already taken one of the gods as his patron. It would have been wiser to ask about the source of the Prindians' gateway at the negotiation. She longed for more time to investigate, but there was none to be had.

'What will you do?' asked Aimya.

'We'll return to Piperskeep,' said Ciera. She could not draw up a plan for the defence of Merivale based on the possibility that two gods might be tangled up in this conflict, not without revealing that she did not trust Viratia. 'But I want you to keep an eye on Lady Viratia.'

Back at the keep, Ciera and Aimya entered the solar to find it already packed with people. Viratia and Burik for the *Hymeriker*; Jerem and Abner for the Cliffarkers; Yoran for the Wild Brigade, a fierce black-bearded man with cold reptilian eyes; and half-a-dozen more representing the various other factions of Ciera's force. They were crowded round the small table, standing with Viratia taking a place at the head and clearly leading the discussion. To Ciera's slight surprise there was no sign of Tansa. She had hardly seen the Cliffark girl since they entered Piperskeep.

She looked up as Ciera and Aimya entered. 'We were discussing our plan of attack,' she said. 'We are assuming you do not wish to accept Rymond's offer.'

'Never,' said Ciera. East Erland was her son's by rights, and it remained her hope that one day he would rule over the West as well. She would never give up on that. 'Burik, what did you make of their force?'

Burik pursed his lips thoughtfully. 'They outnumber us, but not by much, and while they've got plenty of seasoned fighters the others will be little more than warm bodies to suck up the arrows. They'll dig trenches and look tough standing alongside their friends, but they won't hold against armoured men. If Prindian and those advising him have any sense, he'll temper them with his experienced warriors. That will dilute them as a force, but it will keep his numbers together.'

'We've got useless mouths of our own,' growled Yoran. 'Your Cliffarkers are mostly beardless boys with wits even duller than their blades.'

'They were still enough to beat your lot,' said Abner, folding his arms to show off his tattooed sleeves bursting with corded muscle. In reply, Yoran only sneered.

'Do we have enough to hold them outside the walls?' asked Ciera.

Burik pondered, one hand scratching his jaw. Abruptly, he began circling the room, pacing it as if the walls of the solar were the ramparts of Merivale. Ciera could not judge his strength as a commander, but there was nobody else she trusted. Jerem might have served, but the closest he had come to battle was routing the Wild Brigade from their rear.

'Maybe,' said Burik. 'I think so.' His uncertainty troubled Ciera – she found herself wishing that Orsian and Errian were with them.

'Holding back will only embolden the Prindians,' said Viratia scornfully. 'By giving us time, Prindian has sealed his own defeat.' The widow gave a cold smile. 'Their camp is poorly defended. They have no earthworks, no trenches, no high ground. We should hit them hard and fast while they sleep. If the *Hymeriker* move quickly and quietly, the Prindian numbers will count for nothing.'

Burik frowned. 'You want us to abandon our walls against a larger force?'

Viratia eyed him, her eyes like flint, her smile like two rows of blades. 'You followed me into West Erland, Burik. Do you suppose I know so little of war? It is the last thing they will suspect. Prindian is complacent.'

Yoran grinned at her hungrily. 'I like it. Sleeping men die easier.'

'They will only strengthen their position the longer they're left there,' put in Jerem. 'Had we known they were coming, we could have routed them last night. Every hour we delay loses us a possible advantage.'

Ciera watched Viratia. *What are you planning?* She had been right about the Prindians, but still Ciera could not shift her sense of unease. Did Viratia mean to enable their defeat? Or had all the treachery Ciera had faced made her overly suspicious rather than shrewd?

'What do you think, Burik?' she asked.

Burik was frowning, but slowly he began to nod. 'There is a postern gate at the King's Gate. We can send the *Hymeriker* and the Wild Brigade – one group going the long way round the walls to the north and the other group coming up from the south, hit them from both sides before the sun comes up. We have the rest waiting in reserve at the Ram's Gate.' He gave a grim smile. 'They'll never suspect it. It's like how Errian and Orsian dealt with the Imperials' mangonels.'

For a moment, Ciera thought she saw a flicker of doubt in Viratia's face at the mention of her son, as if somewhere beneath the façade she showed the world there was a second Viratia, a grieving widow and mother who could not bear to hear the names of her lost children. Then it was gone, like sunlight briefly appearing through a break in the clouds.

Ciera thought briefly of offering Viratia comfort, but seeing her steely expression she resisted. Perhaps that was how she had to deal with her grief – hiding it behind a cold determination to follow in her dead husband's footsteps and finish the Prindians. Ciera wondered if she had been too hasty to suspect Viratia of some duplicity; Burik knew her well enough, and he trusted her.

'That's settled then,' said Ciera. Her queenship and the reign of Andrick Sangreal would rise or fall upon the fates of a few hundred *hymerikai*, pouring into the grey pre-dawn. One final battle on the plains of East Erland, the weight of a whole country teetering on the edge of a blade. 'I will leave you to make the arrangements.' Ciera swallowed. She did not like what she was about to ask, but this was not the time for soft-heartedness. 'Aim straight for the tent of Rymond Prindian. If he should fall, West Erland will fall with him.'

Viratia gave a cold smile, the brief crack of tenderness Ciera had seen barely a memory, so fleeting that Ciera wondered if she had imagined it. 'Have no fear, Majesty,' she said. 'The *Hymeriker* will be ready. The fate of Erland shall be settled on the morrow.'

Night fell over Piperskeep, and found Tansa brooding, staring out of a rain-streaked window at the city, the West Erland camp a blur of light in the dark distance. The days were growing shorter. It would be winter soon; she could feel its icy fingers clawing at her through the gaps in the frame. Her last winter in Merivale had been as hard as any time in her life, beset with cold and hunger, and then, at the end, her brother's death.

Do you see me, Tam? she wondered. *Or do you watch Ciera Istlewick instead?* Not even death would have dulled her brother's longing for the Erland queen.

Ciera had given her Orsian's old room, perhaps thinking it a kindness, but Tansa could find no peace there. It was where Cag had died. She had come here instead, a small window alcove hidden in shadows, where the sconce light did not reach, hoping to avoid everyone.

Tansa scratched irritably at her armpit, where the itchy servant's dress Ciera forced her to wear pinched. *This is not for much longer*, she reminded herself. She could do as Lady Viratia asked, and then Ciera Istlewick would be gone, far away.

'Tansa?'

She whirled around, alarmed at the sound of her name, and breathed a sigh of relief to see two children, not *hymerikai* with their blades drawn.

Tansa could not resist the smile that spread over her face. 'Pitt and Esma. I am so glad to see you.' They were taller than she recalled, and dressed in the plain tunic and jerkin of kitchen servants.

The two barrelled towards her and almost knocked her sprawling with the force of their embrace, tripping over one another in their haste to tell her of all they had been doing.

'We work in the kitchen now,' Pitt was saying. 'I like it, even if—'

'Pitt keeps stealing food!' interjected Esma. 'If Pella catches him—'

'I'm the fastest,' continued Pitt. 'If they need something sent quick—'

'I'm better with the food. Pella says I could—'

'Tell me one at a time!' said Tansa, laughing. She lowered herself to the small bench below the window and let Esma jump up on her lap while Pitt sat beside her.

'Where's Ranulf?' said Pitt, meaning Orsian. Even in Piperskeep, he had stubbornly refused to call Orsian by his true name. 'He disappeared right after you. I asked a *hymerika* and he tried to hit me and chased me, but I escaped through the belltower.'

'Is he with you?' asked Esma hopefully.

Tansa smiled sadly. She had tried to deny it to herself, but Orsian had been a difficult memory to leave behind. Further searches of the dungeons had proved fruitless, and she could hardly reveal her identity by going around asking if anyone had seen him. 'I don't know where he is. No one seems to.'

A shadow fell across their alcove, and Tansa found herself staring up into the shrewd face of Lady Viratia. She smiled, and the stiffness of it turned Tansa's veins to ice. In her lap, she felt Esma freeze.

'Children.' Viratia did not even look at them. 'Leave us.'

Something about Viratia put the fear of the Norhai into Pitt and Esma. They leapt from the seat and raced off down the corridor before Tansa could even ask where she might see them again.

'We were just speaking of Orsian,' said Tansa. 'We were wondering—'

'No, I still do not know where he is,' said Viratia, as if nothing could have concerned her less. 'My son will return when he chooses.' She did not move to join Tansa in the alcove, only stood there, blocking out the light. Tansa could not help feeling afraid of this woman, with her icy smiles and strange, penetrating gazes, but they had the same aim: to prevent Ciera Istlewick's victory and keep Cliffark out of her perfectly trimmed clutches.

'It is time,' said Viratia. 'The *Hymeriker* will attack the Prindian camp before dawn. You are to go to Rymond Prindian and tell him to be ready.'

Tansa swallowed. This was her opportunity to finally

thwart Ciera Istlewick, so why did she feel so reluctant? 'I've been thinking,' she said. 'What if—'

Her heart skipped a beat as Viratia Brithwell suddenly loomed over her, her face a tight rictus of fury. Blood-red eyes and a mouth of tiny, serrated teeth flashed, and a small scream escaped Tansa's lips before Viratia's face returned to normal.

Tansa's heart was hammering. *Just a trick of the light.*

'*You will do it*,' said Viratia. 'Otherwise I will tell the *Hymeriker* who you are. And if you even think of trying to run away, I *will* know about it.' She smiled, and Tansa's breath caught in her throat. 'We had a deal, Tansa. You do not want to learn the consequences of betraying me.'

Tansa could only nod. She would do it. For in that moment, all she wanted was to be as far away from Viratia Brithwell as possible.

Rymond rolled over again, then threw off the furs and rose from his scratchy straw mattress. Regardless of how much he tossed and turned, sleep would not find him. Perhaps he had become too accustomed to sleeping under bushes.

Rubbing his stubbled jaw, he moved to the table and poured himself a cup of wine. Perhaps it would give him the clarity of thought needed to resolve the matters that kept swirling around his head.

I blame Helana for this. He was half-minded to send for her; it was she who had left him sleepless, so she ought to share in his misery.

He had hardly thought of marriage since she had escaped him before, and now on the eve of his triumph the question had raised its head again. He rubbed at the ache in his temple. It was not for love of him, he knew, but to preserve Merivale. Rymond did not know what to make of her insistence that the gods still had a part to play in this conflict; he had seen all sorts of things while under the influence of casheef but none of them had stayed with him as long as this obsession of Helana's.

Rymond sipped the cloying wine, the grapes bursting against his tongue. It was not the thought of marriage that kept him awake, but the doubt Helana had instilled in him: was that what he wanted?

It is not a question of want, but a question of need. In twenty years, he would be a man in his middle-age, with a gut and grey hairs sprinkled among the gold. East Erland would rise again, with Andrick Sangreal a man coming into his prime, and if he took after his lineage he would never be content to rule half a kingdom. Erland would not endure as two separate realms forever.

If he backed away from this, the only way to secure his future in West Erland was to marry Helana, and hope that ties of blood would stay the young Sangreal's hand. The alternative... Rymond's cup trembled in his grip. If Ciera Istlewick defied him, some day he might regret allowing her and her son to go into exile, if in the years to come there fell a day when the lords of East Erland tired of his rule. And if he began his kingship with such a display of mercy, some would see only weakness where a true king would have been ruthless. It was a bad choice. A harder king might have promised them death, or a slyer king sent a cold-eyed assassin after them across the water, but he was neither of those men.

Rymond hung his head, staring into the bottom of his cup. *I cannot do what must be done.* He needed more time. Decisions had been easier when he was trying to win back his kingdom, not rule it. He sank into a chair. He would send a message to Ciera Istlewick immediately, granting her two more days. That would give him time to get his head straight. His mother would fume and his lords would bluster, and there was every chance that they would still have to do battle eventually, but Rymond could not face it tomorrow.

Delay, prevaricate, defer. Rymond smiled as he took another sip of wine. He had not changed so much in the last year. Those had been his tactics when he had first learnt that Jarhick Sangreal was dead, and it had nearly earnt him the horrors of the Sangreal dungeons before he had realised that the storm of the succession crisis would sweep him up whether he wanted it or not.

Preparing to step out into the night, Rymond rose and turned towards the bed to claim his robe, but stopped when at the corner of his eye he glimpsed a ripple of shadow against the wall.

Rymond froze. The wise thing would be to shout for his guards, but all the saliva seemed to have fled from his throat. He kept one eye on the spot, at the same time moving towards his sword belt at the end of the bed.

His fingers had grasped his hilt, when the shadow *moved.* Rymond gripped his sword, and it shook in his hand as he brought it up ready to defend himself.

Somebody stood from behind one of his trunks.

Rymond's terror evaporated as the intruder stepped into the dull glow of the lantern on the table. The light revealed a young woman, with short hair and a flash of Sangreal red cloth peeking out beneath her dark cloak.

'Don't scream,' she hissed. 'I'm not here to hurt you.'

Rymond smiled. 'No. You are too pretty to be an assassin.' He kept his grip on the sword all the same; he recalled the rumour that Jarhick Sangreal had been slain by a woman in his own tent. 'Who are you?'

'I'm here to warn you.' She took a step forward. 'An hour before dawn, the *Hymeriker* will attack, half from the south and half from the north. They have orders to make directly for your tent and slay you in your sleep.'

Rymond cursed. *So much for more time.* The Sangreal taste for subterfuge had evidently passed to Hessian's widow. 'How do you know that? Who sent you?' Was there some ally in Merivale unaccounted for?

'Not important.' The girl was already retreating towards the trunk. 'You know what you need to. Don't follow me.'

She slipped into the shadows and disappeared, and Rymond rushed forward after her. But when he reached the trunk she was gone, with only a sliced hole in the canvas there to prove it had not been a dream.

'Majesty?'

Rymond turned abruptly to see a guard's head sticking through the tent flap. 'Were you speaking with someone?'

Rymond grimaced. Whoever she was, the spy's news had taken the decision out of his hands. It would be battle, and when he won he would decide what was to be done with Ciera Istlewick and her child. 'The *Hymeriker* will attack our camp before dawn,' he said.

The guard paused, clearly fighting the desire to ask what the source was for Rymond's apparent premonition. 'Should I alert Lord Darlton? Do you want the men woken?'

'Bring me Darlton, but do *not* wake anyone else.' Rymond's lips stretched to an unhappy smile. 'Not yet. I mean to give the East Erlanders a surprise of their own.'

Helana blearily opened her eyes and looked up at Gruenla shaking her awake.

'What's happening?' she asked. It took her a moment to remember where she was. The only light was a small lantern Gruenla had placed at the entrance. It was still dark outside. Helana reached for her skin of watered ale. It was nothing so grand as Rymond's shelter, just long enough for her to lie down in and with space for a travel sack to sit beside her, but it kept the damp and the worst of the cold out.

'By the Mother, it's like trying to wake the dead.' Gruenla rocked back on her heels while Helana rolled over and sat up to face her. 'Only a noble would sleep so peacefully.'

'What's happening?' Helana repeated. She tipped a measure of ale into her mouth. 'Is it morning?' The days were getting shorter.

Gruenla shook her head. 'Dawn's still a few hours away.' She shuffled back to give Helana more room while she pulled a fur about herself against the chill in the air. 'There's news – I came to wake you as soon as I heard.'

Hope rose in Helana's chest. 'Has Rymond granted them more time?' She thought for a moment her desperate offer had worked, but then realised Gruenla would not have woken her in the night to tell her that. 'No... he's planning to attack, isn't he? That—'

'Worse,' said Gruenla. 'Well, worse for you. Potentially lucrative for me.' The corners of her mouth spread to a flat grin. 'He's had word the East Erlanders will attack an hour before dawn. He means to lure them in and put an end to this.'

Helana's mouth fell open. 'No!' She bundled the fur around herself and made to move past Gruenla. 'He can't!'

Gruenla raised an arm to bar her path. 'He can, and he's going to. We don't need to act rashly. I'm on your side, remember?' She cocked an eyebrow. 'But my price has doubled.'

'Doubled?!' Gruenla's price had already been preposterous. 'Where am I meant to get that sort of coin?'

Gruenla shrugged, a slight smirk on her lips. 'We can settle it in instalments, or you can work for me to repay it. Assuming I'm still alive; maybe we'll all die if you're lucky. That's why the price has gone up: I'd expected a situation we could control, but this will be nasty, risky, close work, no hiding for anyone. The *Hymeriker* will be ahorse, so they'll likely have the best of it early on, but word is there's less than five hundred of them now. We'll be ready, and even if they've got others with them, we'll have them outnumbered. They'll be trapped – an easy victory.' She grinned. 'Or so Rymond thinks. My lads will hang back in their tents, then when I think it's time, I'll give the signal and we'll take the West Erlanders in the rear. Turn the whole battle just in time for the Sangreal reinforcements to show up.'

Helana's throat was bone dry. She forced down another glug of ale. Their campsite would be a bloody battlefield within a matter of hours. 'I should ride for Merivale,' she said. 'I don't want to be here when the *Hymeriker* arrive.' Or perhaps she should try and persuade Rymond... no, it was too late now, far too late. He would be locked away with his lords; he'd refuse to see her.

Gruenla's face hardened. 'Do you think you can just walk away from this? If you want my services, you'll bear the same risk as me and my men. I didn't teach you to use that sword for scratching your arse.'

Helana felt like she might throw up. She tried to cover it with another swallow of ale, but gagged and almost brought it back up again. 'I've had probably less than five hours of lessons,' she gasped. A feverish sweat had broken out across her forehead. *Battle*. 'If you think—'

Gruenla clapped her on the shoulder. 'Just stick close to me, and keep your shield up. Worst that happens is we die. The best that happens...' She flashed a broad grin. 'Best case is that we win and you owe me a whole caravan full of fucking gold. And I want it in Imperial medallions if possible. Fuck knows what your Erlish coins will be worth after this.'

Helana's head was swimming. She took another swig of her ale and found it empty. 'Gods, I need a real drink.' *Battle*. If that was what it took, she would have to bear it. She had survived worse, she thought, barely.

Nevertheless, she could not shake the nagging voice at the

back of her mind. *This is the gods' doing.* In the black gloom of her tent, she felt a fleeting memory of another dark tent, and a sinister, silhouetted figure speaking of a final battle against the enigmatic figure of the last Norha. Battle was imminent, and where would one be more likely to find a god than battle? All through the camp, men would be clasping their hands in prayer, as if through words alone the gods might grant their mercy and allow them to survive whatever was to come.

Helana knew otherwise. *The gods do not care.* She expected they would prove it, before the end.

Ciera ascended the battlements over the Ram's Gate. Her hair was tied back, and she wore a red surcoat over her dress in the style of the city's watchmen, so that from the West Erland camp she would appear to be just another guard patrolling the wall. To the west, the first whispers of rising sunlight were beginning to paint the low clouds in a reflected crimson glow.

Only Viratia and Aimya climbed with her. Burik had parted from them halfway down the Castle Road, riding on to the King's Gate with the remaining five hundred *hymerikai*. A symmetrical force of Wild Brigaders and Lord Madine's mercenaries had ridden from the Lesser Gate an hour earlier, taking the long way round the city to the north.

A thousand men, on whom the fate of the city and the Sangreal dynasty rested. Less than one-eighth of their force, now bolstered by the addition of the *Hymeriker* and the Merivalers fit to fight, but their finest warriors. Of those waiting in the city below, over half were Cliffarkers, unhorsed and undisciplined, armed with clubs, cudgels, and the tools of their trade. A rabble, with barely more business being on the battlefield than Ciera herself.

She had sent Andrick deep into the bowels of Piperskeep

with Haisie and a team of trusted servants, with a chain of messengers ready to tell them to flee along the escape tunnel should their plan fail. Burik had begged Ciera to go with them, but she knew she could not face it, waiting in the darkness and not knowing.

I will send men to their death today. The least I can do is share a small measure of the risk. As Ciera scaled the steps, she felt the icy touch of her dagger against her thigh. She did not usually go armed, but the weight of cool steel against her skin was a reminder that no matter what happened, there was a way out of this for her.

Perhaps I might charm Rymond into marriage, she thought as she took the last step. She smiled to herself. Little chance of that; he would see this assault as nothing short of treachery, an underhand trick after his benevolence in delaying his attack to give her a chance to surrender. If she lost, she was dead, but it would be at her own hand, and perhaps in the decades to come she would watch from above the clouds as her exiled son battled to reclaim his birthright. Death might even shed light on the existence and schemes of the gods. She glanced sideways, first to Viratia and then to Aimya, wondering which of them told the truth.

'Is something funny, Majesty?' said Aimya. Still she wore her robes, despite her insistence she was done with the old order.

'Nothing,' said Ciera. 'I'm just nervous.'

'All will be well,' said Viratia through a quiet smile. 'By the end of today, everything will be settled, for good or ill.'

Her words sent a shiver up Ciera's spine. Whatever horror Viratia Brithwell had seen on Eryispek, it had rendered her a different person. If they prevailed, Ciera hoped she would return to Violet Hall. It was hers, as far as Ciera was concerned. All Andrick Barrelbreaker's heirs were dead or missing.

They were at the parapet now, standing alongside Horath

and the men of the Merivale Watch, the city's final line of defence, even more depleted by the Imperium invasion than the *Hymeriker*. Half a mile away, the Prindian camp was as silent as the ashes of a funeral pyre, the grand tents of King Rymond and his mother towering over the rest. A few sentries dotted the perimeter, leaning on their spears as if they were the only things keeping them upright, and occasionally half-dressed men would appear from their tents to walk the short distance to the latrine trench, but otherwise all was quiet.

'Should there not be more men awake?' said Ciera.

'Rymond Prindian was always lazy,' said Viratia. 'It is no surprise. The *Hymeriker* will butcher him in his bed before he so much as reaches for a sword.'

No doubt she meant those words to be reassuring, but they sent the blood rushing to Ciera's ears like panicked men rushing to defend their lord. *This will echo down the ages. Ciera Istlewick, Butcher of Kings*. But it would have been naïve to think it could be otherwise. To hold power was to be without scruples. Lord Balyard had taught her that.

'Here they come, Majesty,' said Horath.

From south and north, a thousand warriors on horseback roared out of the plains. They had swung far clear of Merivale to come at the Prindian camp from both sides, and Ciera could not fault Burik's timing. The two halves closed the distance together, devouring the hundreds of yards in a sea of churned grass, the dirt soft from a night of rain. In the half-light, their features and the details of their armour were indistinct, bathed in shadow, as if they were the shades of the deceased returned to wreak vengeance upon those who had wronged them. They gave no war cry, but the thunder of their hooves was loud enough, growing more urgent with every yard. Spears were readied, primed to be thrust or thrown before the swords came free for the hot, close work of slaughter.

Ciera swallowed dryly. The Prindian sentries had neither

moved nor raised a cry, though the din of the approaching *hymerikai* was rising to a crescendo. 'Shouldn't they have seen them?' she asked. How could they not have? The *hymerikai* were within two hundred yards now, and the other half of their force only slightly further back.

'Fallen asleep,' said Viratia. Her eyes glittered with battle hunger. 'Watch.'

As they leapt the latrine ditches at the edge of the Prindian camp, the *hymerikai* could no longer contain themselves, and several hundred voices strained together in a cry of 'ERLAND!' It shattered the cold peace of pre-dawn, and the first sleeping sentry was dispatched by the thrust of a *hymerika*'s spear that took him through the neck.

Or it ought to have done. The spear found no resistance in the man's flesh, and burst through the other side in an eruption of straw. The *hymerika* was almost toppled from his horse in surprise at the lack of resistance, but released the spear and galloped on, seemingly none the wiser that he had just slain a scarecrow.

Ciera gasped, and Horath took the words out of her mouth: 'They're made of straw!'

There were others. The *hymerikai* galloped over them, destroying them with hooves and spear. Some realised immediately and slowed, but others rode on, their blood running too hot to see their foes were not made of flesh.

Ciera's heart was pounding like the hooves of the *hymerikai*. She wanted to shout out a warning, but they would never hear her at this distance. What Prindian trickery was this?

Still the warriors rode on, the Wild Brigade descending from the north to join the fray, some circling the camp and trampling over tents as others drove towards the centre from either side like the thrust of two swords. Small fires went up as flints were set to oil-soaked torches. Still no West Erland soldiers emerged, but Ciera swore she saw Burik leading the southern assault towards the grand tent of Rymond Prindian, a burning torch clutched high like a banner of fire, flames flickering at his gloved hand.

'No,' Ciera whispered. She reached out to clasp Aimya's hand. There should have been Prindian resistance by now. The *hymerikai* had only been in the camp a matter of seconds, but the West Erlanders ought to have—

A dozen torches arced spinning through the air, bathing Rymond's great emerald tent in a red glow. They landed on the roof, and the warriors slowed to watch as several blazes licked up and down and holes began to appear in the canopy. A split opened directly beneath a torch, and through the rising smoke and licking flames Ciera saw it plunge into the hole.

And then the tent exploded.

Ciera had to shield her eyes as a firestorm burst like an erupting sun, illuminating the sky and the land with scorching red light. The noise broke upon the walls of Merivale as if all the stones collapsed as one, and a hot wind flashed across Ciera's face like dragon's breath. Beside her, she heard Aimya and Horath scream, covering their eyes.

The light and noise faded to echoes, replaced by the screams of men and horses.

Ciera forced herself to watch. The blast had sent warriors and their mounts flying into their air, their twisted corpses now lying in a tangle amidst the ruins of smouldering tents. Others were bathed in flames, leaping from their shrieking horses and rolling in the dirt to douse themselves. Where the Prindian tent had stood there was only a crater, and a rain of ash and tattered cloth fell upon the battlefield through a mist of smoke like a flurry of sleet, as if the plains of Erland had been transported to the snowbound heights of Eryispek.

'Huyar,' breathed Horath. His face was pale with horror. 'Imperial incendiaries.'

Viratia's face though was alive, animated by a feverish longing. 'It's almost time,' she whispered to herself.

Ciera could only stare. The best of her force had been decimated. Those outside the blast radius had stopped to gape, struggling to control their distressed horses, as almost half their brethren lay dead or drenched in flame around the crater, their battle cries now turned to dumb silence.

Then a cry did go up. From the east and west sides of the camp tents flew open, and West Erland soldiers began pouring from them, more than Ciera would have believed they could hold. They were unmounted, but they swiftly formed up into lines and raced screaming towards the stunned *hymerikai*.

Through the smoke, Ciera thought she saw Burik, wheeling his horse around and casting off his burning shield. His sword came free of his scabbard and he raised it to the air. 'To me! To me!'

Some heeded the cry and rode to meet him, but others were not swift enough. The sea of West Erlanders fell upon them, and within seconds the Prindian camp became a swirling maelstrom of steel, horses, and flesh.

Helana had known the blast was coming, but the noise of it still forced her to cover her ears, and even through the canvas of the Cyliriens' low but large tent and surrounded by mercenaries she felt the heat of it on her skin like the warmth of the sun.

'Hold!' Beside Helana, Gruenla came to her feet, her sword ready at her side. 'We wait. Let them encircle the East Erlanders first.'

Helana did not want to wait. As the first shouts of the emerging West Erlanders rose, she felt a trickle of urine run down her thigh, but every second they delayed could mean another dead East Erlander. Her heart hammered with fear.

Gruenla had insisted that this was the way; wait until the engagement and then fall upon the Prindian rear.

Gruenla crouched down beside her as the first clashes of steel sounded. 'Scared?'

Helana was afraid if she spoke it would come out as a squeak, so she simply nodded. Her palms had started to sweat.

The Cylirien woman nodded, seemingly satisfied. 'Good. Hold onto that; it might keep you alive. No one's expecting you to actually do anything, so just keep your shield up and go for the easy targets. There'll be four men to keep you safe; if you die, I'll have to throw myself before the mercy of your queen for payment.'

Helana wanted to run, but if she stood she was sure her legs would buckle. *Pull yourself together*, she scolded herself. *It's nothing men haven't done thousands of times*. She looked around the sea of Cylirien faces, hoping to see somebody as frightened as her.

Gruenla gave a low chuckle. 'Don't worry, there's a few here as scared as you are. Doesn't sit well with some of them, turning on men they've fought alongside for a year, but they prefer it to being cheated out of what's ours.' The rattle of steel and the confused cries of embattled men were growing louder now, and just as Helana was about to ask if it was time, Gruenla pulled her sword free. 'Come on then!' she screamed, and the several hundred men crammed into the tent answered her cry in unison. 'For gold and glory!'

'GOLD AND GLORY!'

Somebody threw the tent flap back, and with a wordless cry of fear and fury the Cyliriens rushed into the plains. From a second tent, the other half of their force was also pouring out, and they formed a single torrent of men, bound for battle.

Helana kept her eyes focused on the back of the man in front, treading carefully and gripping her sword with white-knuckle tightness, fearful she might drop it. A thick smoke hung over the camp, and they hurtled past crushed tents and the bodies of West Erlanders who had been trampled to death within them before the explosion that marked the beginning of the ambush. At the front, a few steps ahead of Helana, she could see Gruenla, moving fluid as water and unswervingly towards the swinging swords and whirling horses that appeared beyond the smoke like a mirage.

Just survive. Survive. The word ran through her blood-rushed head like the mantra of a priest. Helana hefted her shield on her arm and ran towards the hellish cacophony of battle.

A *hymerika*'s sword thrust towards him from horseback, and Rymond barely got his shield up in time, the vibration springing up his shoulder and nearly sending him staggering back. With no time to think of honour, he plunged his sword into the horse's neck. The animal keened wildly, its eyes rolling in its head as blood rushed from the wound over Rymond's arm, and he freed his blade and leapt back as the beast's front legs gave way and it crumpled to the ground. The *hymerika* vaulted free, straight onto Rymond's blade. A gap at his neck opened and Rymond flashed the edge across it in a spray of crimson.

He breathed and stepped back. This *hymerika* had become separated from his brothers, and for what felt like the first time since the assault had begun Rymond found himself withdrawn from the clash of battle. He stepped up onto the dead horse and tried to survey the battlefield, but the huyar smoke hung so heavy it was as if a grey curtain of fog had been drawn across the air. As he had hoped, they had the bulk of the *Hymeriker* and their allies encircled around the ruins of his tent, without space in which they could bring their horses to the full advantage, but there were other patches of resistance where some of the East Erlanders had been too far from the centre. His standard was perhaps only fifteen yards ahead of him, but such was the crush of flesh it may as well have been fifty yards for all the sense he could make of the battle.

As Rymond looked about at the carnage, the young Lord Clymore forced his way through the crush, clutching his shoulder and grimacing. Blood was dripping from the sleeve of his armour, and he was favouring one leg.

Rymond called to him. 'Lord Clymore, report!'

Clymore stared up at him, the whites of his eyes large and bright as twin moons. 'It's a bloody slaughter, Majesty, on both sides. Hundreds dead, including half of mine! Our numbers will tell though.' He shifted his shoulder and gave a gasp of pain. 'I need to withdraw.'

'Go.' Rymond gestured him towards their rear, although there were more men pressing forward all the time, eager to cross blades with the *Hymeriker*.

The smoke had cleared slightly, giving Rymond a better view of the field. The trapped *hymerikai* had rallied, the Sangreal warriors fighting as if possessed, but his own men were giving as good as they got. Trapped as they were the East Erlanders had nothing to lose; they would fight to the last man. He watched as a mounted *hymerika* pressed on all sides whirled his horse around, dealing red death with his longsword before the press of men became too much and the horse fell, taking its rider down with it before he was dispatched in a flurry of West Erlander blades.

Rymond raised his sword to the air, pointing towards the slaughter. 'Onward!' he cried. 'Fight! For West Erland!'

A cheer went up from the men around him, and they pressed forward, tightening the noose around the *Hymeriker*. Further afield, other smaller skirmishes were still being fought, but most of the East Erlanders were trapped around the crater. Some of them might have already been pushed into it by the weight of numbers, but through the veil of smoke it was impossible to tell.

'Majesty!'

Rymond looked down and saw Brant calling up to him, his wide-eyed face drenched in blood. 'Brant! What—'

'The Cyliriens! They're—'

Whatever Brant had been about to say was drowned out by the cries of men and the rattle of steel. Not from the *Hymeriker*, but to the West Erlanders' rear. Rymond turned, almost losing his balance atop the dead horse, and what he saw filled his heart with dread.

The Cyliriens had plunged into the rear of their force, and were laying about with their swords. Such was the press of men they could hardly miss.

'Majesty!' Lord Clymore was suddenly back at his side, pointing east back towards the *Hymeriker*. 'Look!'

Such was the alarm in his voice that Rymond turned. Men were pouring from Merivale's western gate, a strange motley of mailed warriors and a rabble of hollering peasants, all shaking their makeshift weapons to the sky. They came at a shambling run, any discipline they'd ever had forgotten, more a stampeding herd than an army, and with a crazed howl the bravest of them clattered into the rear of the other side of the Prindian force.

'Eryi's balls!' cried Rymond. He had thought he might have the Sangreals outnumbered at least two to one, but now it was his force that was in danger of being surrounded and split into two, with the twin hammers of the Cyliriens and this fresh force crushing them against the anvil of the *Hymeriker*.

A riderless horse cantered past, fleeing from the chaos ahead, and Rymond instinctively grabbed its bridle and brought the beast to a reluctant halt. He leapt up into the saddle, and turned for a better view of the far side of the main battle where every second new soldiers from the city were arriving to throw themselves upon his men. They were ramshackle and undisciplined, but they had taken his force by surprise.

'We need to head them off!' he shouted to Clymore and Brant. If they could flank the new arrivals they might send them running back to Merivale before they could do any lasting damage. 'Men!' He raised his sword vertically to the air, his new mount dancing restlessly beneath him. 'With me!'

Clymore immediately began shoving at nearby men who until now had been moving forward towards the *Hymeriker*. 'You heard him! Follow your king!'

'What about the Cyliriens?' shouted Brant.

Rymond looked back at their rear. The fighting looked fierce, but there were only a few hundred Cyliriens; he needed to have faith that the men turning to face them would prevail. It was the Merivalers whose strength might turn the tide of this battle. 'Later!' he shouted. 'With me!'

Rymond dug his heels into the horse's flanks. It leapt forward, forcing men to dive out of the way as he furrowed a channel towards their northern flank, not looking back to see if anyone was following. Faces flashed by him in a blur, and in a matter of seconds he was free, tugging the horse around in a turn as those following on foot struggled to keep pace.

He pulled back on the reins, giving them a chance to catch up with him as the horse snorted against the bit. They were no more than fifty, perhaps too few, but the East Erlander counterattack was a disorganised rabble; one charge might send a thousand of them running back towards Merivale. 'With me!' he cried again, and drove his horse forward across the muddy ground as the rest tore after him in his wake.

Rymond felt his first small measure of fear when he was within thirty yards of the East Erlanders and the first few pale, confused faces turned towards him. He gritted his teeth and drove his mount on, thrusting his sword out before him, digging his heels into the horse's sides and leaning low over its neck to draw from it a last burst of speed. He must have outstripped his followers, but it was too late to turn back now.

The ground between them closed in the blink of an eye. With a wild yell of bloodlust, Rymond swung his blade in a downward arc to strike the first man across the face, and then they were all around him, so many foes that he could scarcely see which he struck and those he didn't. He was shouting wordlessly, swinging the warhorse around as it kicked out at the endless sea of faces. They fell back before him, and Rymond rode them down, never staying still for a moment. He was laughing now, tasting the splatter of other men's blood as it burst against his face. Some were running, or throwing themselves into the mud to escape him. A bald, bearish man with a shock of white whiskers stepped across his path, and Rymond pulled his sword back—

The man's hammer throw took the horse directly between the eyes, and suddenly Rymond's world was spinning. He saw grey clouds laced with the light of dawn, and then the dirt rushing up to meet him.

He landed on his left shoulder and rolled into the impact, feeling a white-hot spurt of pain as the joint almost popped from the socket. He staggered upright, and the momentum he took from the fall almost certainly saved his life, his assailant's vicious axe swing narrowly missing Rymond's collarbone.

The man's elbow struck Rymond instead, and Rymond heard him let out a hiss of pain at the impact of mail against his bare flesh. Somehow, Rymond had held onto his sword, and as he stepped past the man he drove his heels into the mud to stop himself and off-balance swung the blade in a backward arc.

The blow should have taken the man's head from his shoulders, but as the horse went down more East Erlanders had pressed in again. The tip of Rymond's sword dinged against an ugly, tarnished helmet, and the bald man's axe fell towards Rymond's wrist.

There was a flash of blinding pain, like a searing heat that spread all the way from his hand to his shoulder. The world seemed to pause, and for less than the blink of an eye all Rymond knew was agony, before it was tempered by his feverish madness for battle. His thrust had been deflected wide, so he brought his arm back to slice across the bald man's throat—

And watched as his sword tumbled to the mud, his severed hand falling with it.

My hand, he thought, and the stupidity of that sentiment struck him at the same time as a barrage of maddening, all-consuming agony. The reverse strike he had hoped would tear out the bald man's throat instead bathed him in the blood spewing from Rymond's severed wrist.

The last thing he saw as he fell was a flash of blinding white light, so bright he was sure it was Eryi coming to guide his spirit about the clouds.

Atop the battlements, for several minutes nobody spoke. Ciera could only watch in horror at the carnage she had unleashed on the world.

It ought to have been a slaughter, but for a time the *Hymeriker*, the Wild Brigade, and Madine's mercenaries had rallied, refusing to let themselves become bogged down under the weight of West Erland swords and instead keeping their horses moving, turning in whatever space they could find and using their mounted advantage. That had given Ciera a chance to send the rest, every single one of the seven thousand left under her command now running from the gate towards the battle, including her brave, untrained Cliffarkers. It might yet turn the tide, but it would not save the trapped *hymerikai*.

Their dead now were beyond counting. So many had been

slain or wounded by the blast of huyar, and with every second the odds worsened, the patch of land the *Hymeriker* had managed to hold growing smaller and smaller. Some horses were becoming tangled in the ruins of burnt-out tents, and as Ciera watched a *hymerika* had to leap clear of his horse as it slid down into the crater. The best warriors of East Erland were being butchered, man by man.

'By all the fucking gods,' whispered Aimya, her face as white as her robes.

'The rest might win through,' croaked Horath. 'They might open a way out for them.'

Ciera shook her head. 'It's too late.' She wiped her eyes as she watched a *hymerika* be pulled from his horse into a throng of waiting foes. A little way away from the main battle a handful of *hymerikai* had escaped the slaughter, and now charged against the massed West Erlanders, killing several before being beaten back. They turned and galloped towards them again, but Ciera could see they were too few to prevail. 'Those brave fools,' she breathed. *How did I let it come to this?* So many lives thrown away, on a plan with such little chance of success. She placed a hand on the parapet to steady herself. It seemed every second that another mounted man fell and the *Hymeriker*'s patch of battlefield became a little smaller. It had been Viratia's idea; by what madness—

Beside her, Aimya set out a sudden gasp. 'Look!'

She pointed towards the far side of the field, and Ciera squinted through the smoke towards where she was pointing. Several hundred men in mismatched armour were racing towards the West Erlanders. For a moment, Ciera's heart sank, sure these were reinforcements come to lead a death blow against the *Hymeriker*, but as her eyes adjusted to the fumes she realised their blades were drawn, and with a shared cry of fury these strangers turned their swords upon the Prindians' rear.

Ciera gripped the parapet so tight her knuckles turned

white. 'Who are they?' There were only a few hundred of them, but they had taken the West Erlanders completely by surprise. The massed ranks of the Prindians were struggling to turn against the new assault, and even closer to the *hymerikai* men's heads were turning towards the disturbance.

'Look like mercenaries!' said Horath. He looked to Ciera. 'Do we have mercenaries in their camp?'

Ciera shook her head dumbly. It had only been a matter of seconds, but the Prindian rear was starting to disintegrate, men either falling or trying to flee and collapsing into one another. This was likely where the weakest of their forces were, those too untrained or cowardly to be at the front against the *hymerikai*, and it was already becoming a bloodbath. The mercenaries had the advantage of surprise, and they acted as a unit, forming a shield wall and positioning themselves between ranks of tents to stop themselves being flanked.

A second later, the first line of the Sangreal reserve's chaotic charge crashed into the other side of the Prindian force encircling the *Hymeriker*. Cries of shock and terror reached Ciera on the smoke-tinged breeze. From both sides now, men were turning away from the *hymerikai* towards the source of their fellows' distress, and as the pressure on their position relented the men of East Erland took full advantage, turning their mounts as swiftly as the tight confines and the piled corpses would allow and charging upon the West Erlanders. It was now the Prindians who risked being surrounded, divided into two and with foes trapping them to both the east and west, with the *hymerikai* fighting for their lives in the middle of it all.

'We may yet win,' Ciera whispered to herself. *But at what cost?* A tear rolled down her cheek as the cries of the dead and dying seemed to rise a notch. The battle might be decided by whichever side had the last man standing. Her Cliffarkers were being slaughtered in their effort to relieve the *hymerikai*, and on the far side of the battle the same was happening to the

Prindian forces under the assault of the defecting mercenaries. The dead lay in their thousands, with thousands more yet to come.

Viratia moved forward to stand beside Ciera. In all the madness, Ciera had forgotten the woman was here. 'It is a beautiful thing, battle,' she said. Her voice seemed to come from a hundred miles away, and yet somehow Ciera felt its resonance deep within her skull. Overhead, the sky was darkening, and the first drop of cold rain fell on the back of her hand. 'The desperation, the sacrifice, the *death*...' Ciera looked to her, horrified, but realised that Viratia was not speaking to her at all. She seemed to have grown taller, and her red eyes were fixed upon the battlefield. 'When men despair, they look to their gods to save them. Little knowing that it is your own hubris, your own ceaseless lust for power that shall be your undoing. Those like you and Rymond Prindian, who seek to name yourselves kings and queens, and place yourself in the rightful place of the Norhai.'

Ciera flinched back from her. 'What are you talking about?'

'I am speaking of your end, *Majesty*. The end of the age of men, of kings and queens, and the dominion of the last Norha.' Viratia was growing larger, now somehow towering over Ciera by several feet. Ciera tried to retreat, fell backwards against the parapet, and nearly slipped to the ground. Viratia was *floating*, rising from the battlements as if lifted by strings. Thunder rolled, fat drops of rain were falling, and Ciera leapt back with a scream and fell as a bolt of purple lightning flashed from the sky and struck Viratia. It broke upon her head and out through her feet, flashing upon the ground and punching a house-sized crater in the earth. Viratia's whole body was for a moment translucent, revealing every bone as her eyes flashed a bloody, portentous crimson.

Ciera shuffled backwards on her hands. Horath and the guards were staring open-mouthed; some had even sunk to their knees, weeping or placing their foreheads against the stone in prayer. Aimya rushed forward and hurled a spear, but Viratia raised a hand and the weapon disintegrated in a burst of blinding flame.

'What are you?' whispered Ciera.

Viratia hung in the air, the sky crackling with fiery lightning behind her. Still she grew, now three or four times the height of a man. Her clothes had burnt away, and she floated naked in the air, her hair fanned out and writhing like a bed of worms. Her face was changing too, the face that had once belonged to Viratia Brithwell stretching, the brows lifting, the nose bridging and lengthening, the ears extending to sharp points, the lips becoming fuller and darkening to the black blood of a mortal wound.

Ciera looked upon the beautiful, terrible face of a goddess, and saw true, maddening power staring back at her through eyes like the blistering fires of a thousand suns. All her dreams for herself, Erland, and her son crumbled into dust and dirt. This was a true queen, imbued with divine power and a devastating hunger to bend men to her will.

Aimya rushed forward to throw another spear, but fell screaming as the weapon burst into flames in her grip.

The goddess's smile was chilling, as if every light on the face of the world was about to be plunged into darkness. The clouds flashed and crackled, and the cold rain came down like buckets poured from the heavens. 'I am Vulgatypha, and existence is mine. *Kneel.*'

Ciera could not have refused the command even if she wanted to. The rain was soaking through her clothes, and with a shivering she could not stop Ciera sank to her knees, as around her every man still standing did the same. Even Aimya followed, clutching her scorched hand.

Vulgatypha's lips parted to reveal a mouth of blinding silver teeth like vermeiled spear points. 'Now watch.'

The goddess spiralled into the sky, soaring towards the battlefield.

Helana's eyes stung with sweat and blood. She sensed movement beyond her shield, and blindly thrust her short sword past its rim and felt her blade deflect off a layer of mail. The flat of a blade beat clumsily against her briefly exposed arm, and she pulled back with a yelp of pain. Something struck at the centre of her shield, and though she could hardly feel her grip on it she managed to keep her guard up and together with those of the men alongside her.

She could not recall how she had ended up here. At first it had been bloody slaughter, like wolves among undefended sheep. Helana had slain two men herself, one with a well-placed thrust to the neck and a second who had in his fear run directly onto the point of her blade. In her own fright, Helana had plunged it deep into the boy's bowels and then made an end of it with a stab under his ribs into the heart as the life seeped from the boy's horrified eyes.

But then the West Erlanders had rallied, and somehow Helana had ended up at the front of the Cylirien wall, her existence reduced to the wood of her shield and the hot, heady, churning terror of battle.

'Forward!' someone cried, and with the rest Helana forced herself to move, her feet sinking into the wet, roiled earth. It had begun to rain, and she tilted her face to the sky in the hope the water would wash the gore from her eyes.

For all the horror, Helana could not help sensing that they were *winning*. It felt like forever since she had been able to glimpse the surviving *hymerikai*, but when she last had they had seemed to be rallying, driving the packed West Erland ranks backwards into the shields and blades of the Cyliriens.

'Ffriseans!' someone cried. Past her shield, Helana glimpsed a naked, hairy savage bearing down upon her, his bulk obscuring the sky, his huge log skewered with ugly nails about to fall upon her. In desperation, Helana thrust out her sword and felt a warm rush of blood surge over her gloved hand.

The Ffrisean collapsed, straight onto Helana, and the weight of his corpse toppled her backwards into the dirt. She felt her nose *break* as her shield smashed against her face, and she was pinned in the dirt, trapped beneath the weight of the Ffrisean and her own shield. Her right arm was pinned also, her sword flat against her stomach. Helana released it, and managed to free her hand, as the weight of battle moved past her.

Move or die. It was not so much a thought as an instinct. With a heave of strength she did not know she had Helana rolled the shield and the dead Ffrisean off her and scrambled to her hands and knees, coughing in the smoke and the dirt, gasping for breath. The air stank of burning and the iron scent of blood. Though it felt as if her legs might never work again, she forced herself to her feet, and fled, half running half stumbling, her own tears mingling in her eyes with the sweat and gore.

Helana got no more than ten yards and collapsed back to earth. With her bloodied hands she tried to push herself to her feet, and one fell upon the cold, clammy face of a corpse. She shrieked, rolled away, and came face to face with a second. Driven by terror, she lurched to her feet and nearly tripped over into the mass of bodies. Her only desire in that moment was to escape the pressing flesh of corpses and get as far from the bloody heat of battle as her numb legs would allow.

The rain continued to lash down, running in rivulets from Helana's sweat-drenched hair all the way to her underclothes. She had lost her helmet, and somehow managed to get turned around so she was facing towards the battle. The screams of the

Cyliriens and the West Erlanders they had turned against were like blades shrieking against her skull.

Above the throng, against the black clouds crackling with lightning, a great glow appeared in the sky. Before Helana's eyes it grew in luminescence, until she had to raise her hand to spare her gaze from it. It hummed like a swarm of bees, and the lightning flashing from the sky seemed drawn to it, striking upon the light in sparks of jagged purple fury. The clamour of battle dropped, men turning away from their foes and towards the glow, swaying on the spot from exhaustion, covering their eyes like Helana against the blazing light.

It dimmed, and Helana's mouth fell open. A naked woman hung in the sky, impossibly tall, her beautiful face stretched in a frightful rictus. Her eyes shone like unquenchable flames, as bright and deadly as huyar, but as her gaze fell upon Helana something made her think of Viratia, her weeping, horrified face flashing like a fitful dream behind Helana's eyes. Then she was gone, and all that remained was the terrible vision of a woman. Lightning flashed at her fingertips, her gleaming hair coiled around her bare breasts like a river of gold, and a wave of heat broke upon Helana's face as the air around the woman was burnt to nothing.

Norha. The word sparked in Helana's mind, as certain as the dawn that rose above the silhouette of Merivale. The woman spoke, and the whole earth and sky seemed to rumble at her words.

'*KNEEL.*' Her voice cracked like thunder, louder than all the mountains of the earth crumbling to dust, bursting the blood vessels of Helana's ears in a gust of hot animalistic pain. '*KNEEL BEFORE VULGATYPHA, AND BE WITNESS TO THE END OF THE WORLD.*'

And all across the plains of Erland, men trembled. Their weapons fell from frigid fingers, and their knees crumpled into the dirt before the irresistible will of a goddess.

CHAPTER 40

In the chamber at the base of Pipersmont, Pherri wept, pressing her forehead against the dusty red stone, staining it with her tears.

The whole weight of her journey seemed to hit her at once. All this way, fleeing from Eryi and crossing half the world, and it would not be enough. *We are too late.* All along, she had believed her return was the key to saving Erland, and yet it should have been her father. Her dead father.

'It may not mean anything,' said Phyrrai. She placed a hand on Pherri's shoulder. 'Who is to say prophecies are the same in every world? That they have to mean anything?'

'You don't understand,' whispered Pherri. She could not kill Phyrrai. Not knowing it would all be for nothing. Her nose had begun to bleed again. Exhaustion flooded through her. She sniffed. 'I can't do it. I never could, certainly not now. It's not worth the cost.'

'What isn't?' asked Phyrrai. 'You can tell me.'

Pherri wiped her nose. 'It doesn't matter.' She tried to get to her feet, and Phyrrai helped her up. She rubbed her eyes, focusing them again on the stone marker. Eryi had not been able to fully defeat Vulgatypha the way Piper had. Piper had defeated the last Norha in this world so soundly that magic had disappeared forever. What if her world was doomed to fall to Vulgatypha no matter what she did?

She looked to the Sorrowseer. 'Is it true?'

'I do not know,' said the Sorrowseer. 'Do not rely on dreams and prophecy when trying to make sense of the world. This one came true, but it just as easily might not have. Who is to say that only the one prophesised may do the deed, or that in every world the Norha will be defeated and never rise? Nothing is so clearly written.'

Phyrrai's hand was still resting on Pherri's shoulder, and as the Sorrowseer spoke Pherri felt her shadowtwin's grip tense.

'We should proceed to the heart of the mountain,' continued the Sorrowseer. 'I fear time is short, Pherri. You can die in this world, or take your chances in your own.'

Pherri dabbed at her bleeding nose with her sleeve, and let out a cry when she pulled it away. The blood had risen to a torrent, pouring from her nose like a crimson waterfall. Her legs cramped, and her head swam with sudden heat.

She would have fallen, but Phyrrai got both arms around her to hold her upright. 'What's happening to me?' Pherri whimpered.

'Quickly!' screeched the Sorrowseer. 'You are running out of time!'

Without warning, Hrogo pushed Phyrrai aside, swept Pherri up in his arms, and rushed to the top of the stairs with her.

'This way,' said the Sorrowseer, and gave Hrogo no time to rest before she began striding up the weaving stairs that had been carved into the core of Pipersmont.

Over Hrogo's shoulder, Pherri watched Phyrrai and Halyana struggle to keep pace. Blood was still gushing from her nose, and she could feel it rising in her gut as well. Hrogo's damaged body seemed not to trouble him, as if Pherri's sudden affliction had lent speed to his twisted legs. His chain dragged behind him, clunking against every stair.

The journey flashed by in glimpses for Pherri, overcome with fever. Endless stairs, walkways without edges, and below a vast endless nothingness. She felt Hrogo look down, and a gasp escaped his lips. They were staring into oblivion. Pherri let out a moan as the pit rose up towards her, threatening to devour her.

'This is the place,' said the Sorrowseer. Pherri had closed her eyes against a dizziness that made her eyes swirl in their sockets, but when Hrogo put her down she managed to get her feet underneath her, staggering against a wall to keep herself upright, taking deep wheezing breaths. She coughed and almost keeled over.

She lowered herself to sit against the wall. They were on a high outcropping, with shafts of light reaching down to them from hollows in the mountain rock. The whole interior of Pipersmont seemed to have been carved out. Above them was only the steep rock of the mountain's slope, and when Pherri dared to look over the edge she saw a warren of stairs and walkways, leading deeper into the abyss. The endless darkness throbbed before Pherri's eyes, humming so resonantly that she felt it echoing in her bones. A force seized her, beckoning her to throw herself into the void, but an instinctive terror drew Pherri back from the edge.

'What's down there?' she asked. Their companions staggered over the top of the stairs, and Hrogo collapsed into the dirt, breathing deeply.

'Passage to the world of the dead.' The Sorrowseer was standing at the far edge of the outcropping, beside a dense block of red clay as high as her waist and the width of two men. There was a new brightness in her grey eyes behind the cold features of the mask. She placed a gloved hand upon the altar. 'This is the heart of the mountain, the centre of the world, where the last Norha's powers were strongest. From here she ruled over everything. Men would journey across half the world to come seeking her blessing, or for her aid against their foes.' The mask stretched in a grimace. 'Before Piper. Before she fell.'

'The world of the dead?' said Pherri. Even Theodric had never spoken of such a thing. Did that mean the dead went somewhere? Every form of every person from every world?

The Sorrowseer ignored her question. 'If you are to return home, it must be now.' A slim silvery dagger had appeared in her hand, and she placed it on the altar. 'There is only one way. You know this.'

Pherri rose on shaky legs. Her nosebleed had stopped, and her head felt clearer by the moment. 'Will it work?'

'What do we do now?' said Phyrrai, approaching to stand beside Pherri. Halyana was with her, and both of them were panting. Hrogo had come to his feet, leaning against the wall for support.

The Sorrowseer's mask flashed a smile. 'Are you ready, Pherri?'

Pherri felt stronger by the moment, as if the ancient power of Pipersmont and the Norha who had dwelt here coursed through her veins. She looked at the dagger, and then to Phyrrai, her mind racing. *I have to try*, she told herself, thinking of the prophecy that in her world could never come true. *How do I know if I don't try?* She could see it in her mind – Phyrrai on the altar, and the silver blade in Pherri's grip dropping towards her heart. One death, that in her world would never mean anything; Phyrrai was only a possibility, someone she could have been.

And yet... Pherri stared at her shadowtwin, taking in every inch of her, the familiar angles of her face and the inquisitive blue eyes that she had seen in her looking glass so many times. Phyrrai had come with her all this way, based on no more than a dream, even though at the beginning they could hardly stand to look at one another. Now, when Pherri looked at Phyrrai, she only felt overcome with gratitude and admiration. Sometimes, it was as if they shared one mind. Phyrrai was looking at her curiously, as if she could see the choice Pherri faced and already knew which way she would fall.

Pherri turned to the Sorrowseer. 'No. I won't do it. There has to be another way.'

The Sorrowseer's masked face hardened. 'Disappointing, though I did suspect as much. So be it. Such a disappointment, after all I have told you – do you suppose I lie?' She paused. 'Now, Hrogo.'

Pherri shrieked as Hrogo seized her from behind. A leathery hand covered her mouth as the other gripped her by the waist and lifted her off the ground. She thrashed at him, elbows striking at his shoulders and her feet flying at his knees, but he was too strong. Writhing, she managed to sink her teeth into his hand, and Hrogo let out a scream.

Phyrrai was screaming as well. 'What are you doing? Stop it!' She leapt for Hrogo, but as he struggled to contain Pherri his elbow caught Phyrrai in the face and knocked her back. Pherri aimed a kick at his groin, drawing a pained grunt, but still he held firm.

The Sorrowseer's eyes were wide with anticipation. 'Good. Bring her. *Bring her*.'

'I'm sorry, Pherri,' wheezed Hrogo. She was still struggling, but her strength was failing fast. She caught a glimpse of tears on his cheeks. 'I have to.'

As they approached the edge, Hrogo turned them around so that Pherri was facing the stairs, and the Sorrowseer began lashing her to the altar with ropes that had materialised as if from nowhere. Towards the stairs, Phyrrai was rising in the dirt, her nose now bleeding freely where Hrogo had struck her.

Pherri struggled as the Sorrowseer tightened the bindings, but they coursed around her limbs and waist like squirming eels. One slithered over her neck, cutting off the scream that rose in her throat. Phyrrai rushed towards her, but Hrogo broke from the altar and lifted her into the air by the waist while Phyrrai kicked uselessly at thin air.

'Why?' she demanded, wretched tears staining her face. 'Why, Hrogo?'

'I'm sorry!' he cried. 'She made me a promise.' There were bright tears on his cheeks as well. 'My dreams... I saw it, I saw it all, every night.' He fell to his knees, dragging Phyrrai down with him.

The Sorrowseer cackled. 'Men are such predictable creatures. Tell them what I promised you, Hrogo.'

Shame spread across Hrogo's face. 'She promised... The Sorrowseer promised that if I helped her, she would save me. She showed me another world, one where the magi are free, where we are beloved. She said if I did as she asked, I could go there.' He hung his head. 'Forgive me, Pherri, I had to. I can't go back there, never. I just want to be left in peace, somewhere no one can hurt me.'

Pherri's nose was bleeding heavily again, her head a fog of fever. If not for the ropes holding her to the altar, she was sure she would have collapsed. 'I don't understand,' she said, her voice a pained and weakened whimper. 'You told me I had to stop Vulgatypha.'

The Sorrowseer opened her mouth to reply, but something flew at her in a blur of fury. She shrieked, and Pherri realised it was Halyana, scratching at the Sorrowseer's mask with her nails. The Sorrowseer tried to throw her off, but Halyana had her legs wrapped tight around her waist. Halyana's hands grasped for the disguise, the Sorrowseer shrieked and tried to grab her wrists, and her howl became shriller as a leather strap and part of the mask were torn away, just before the Sorrowseer twisted to hide her face.

The edge over the abyss was just a few feet away, and

Pherri realised what the Sorrowseer was going to do just as she thought Halyana did. The princess hissed and spat, fighting with all her might, but the Sorrowseer had taken a fierce grasp of her wrists. Halyana released the grip of her legs, but the Sorrowseer seemed to anticipate this and grabbed Halyana by the belt, while her other hand continued to restrain her wrists.

With impossible strength, the Sorrowseer hauled Halyana over her head and cast her into the abyss.

Pherri was not close enough to the edge to watch Halyana fall into oblivion. No howl broke from her lips, but Pherri imagined her round mouth of surprise as her body plummeted into the unknown darkness.

The Sorrowseer was breathing deeply, her chest rising and falling. 'Mad bitch,' she muttered.

'She knew what you were,' said Phyrrai in a soft voice.

The Sorrowseer did not turn to face them, but Pherri saw her body stiffen. She stood up straight, still staring down after Halyana, and laughed. 'I don't know what you mean. Hrogo, get on with it.'

Hrogo rose and left Phyrrai in the dirt, seized the knife that still lay on the altar, and thrust it into Phyrrai's hands. 'You have to kill her,' he said. 'If you won't do it willingly, I'll force you.' He moved to stand behind her, ready to grab her wrists if she refused.

Phyrrai looked down at the blade, a strange smile creeping across her face. 'What was the plan, Sorrowseer? Get Pherri to kill me to open the way between worlds? Is that what you told her?'

'I wouldn't have done it,' said Pherri. She struggled helplessly against her bonds, and tears sprang to her eyes as they tightened. 'She said it was the only way, but I swear I wouldn't have. I couldn't.'

Phyrrai was turning the blade over in her hand, watching the light from the high windows above ripple across it. 'I don't think that would have worked anyway,' she said calmly. 'In fact, I think the Sorrowseer is full of lies.'

Still the Sorrowseer had not turned to face them. 'A liar, am I? You think that *you*, some bastard's snot-nosed brat, know magic better than I?' she spat. 'Get on with it, Hrogo! Think of what I have promised you!'

Hrogo reached forward and grasped Phyrrai's hands, forcing her to take a tight grip on the knife, but Phyrrai hardly seemed to have noticed. She stared at the Sorrowseer, and then spoke. 'Show me your face, *Norha*.'

The word hung in the air like smoke. Pherri's mind raced. *Norha*. Phyrrai had said *Norha*.

Still the Sorrowseer did not turn. Her voice came in a dangerous whisper, like an assassin's blade in the dark. 'When did you realise?'

'You were never all you seemed, Sorrowseer,' said Phyrrai. 'We knew that. But when you knew this place, what else could you have been? It's a shame poor Halyana realised before I did.'

'Well, I suppose you are more intelligent than several generations of the Horned Folk.' The Sorrowseer cackled. 'I suspect Halyana's dalliance with the way between worlds gave her a glimpse of what I was, not that she had the wits to use it. Now, you both know as well, but it won't save you.'

'The poem said Piper defeated you,' said Pherri. Her head was still spinning. The altar was pressing painfully against her back, the ropes tightening every time she moved.

'He did,' said the Sorrowseer. 'But he should have killed me. We stood on this very platform, and when he opened the way and sought to throw me into the world of the dead, I begged him for my life. Riches, women, renown... I offered him all of them, and he turned them down. If you want to make a man proud, make him the subject of a prophecy.' She rasped a laugh. The mask was still half hanging off, but still Pherri could not get a clear view of her face. 'He could have been a king, but he dreamt of prophecy, and after that he could not leave me alone. As I lay here, dying, I offered him the only two things I could that he would listen to: a passage from these dying lands, and the retention of his magic. For if I died, magic would die with me. And with these things, I bought my life.'

Her tone changed, becoming more sinister. 'Unknown to him was that magic was lost to the world the moment he defeated me. He made the deal, and then in the next instant realised he had been tricked.' She spat over the edge into the abyss. 'Nevertheless, his honour demanded he keep his word, and I would keep mine.

'And so we crossed the Sorrows, and he met the Horned Folk, on the same hill where Ulsenfort stood.' Her head moved slightly, and Pherri almost glimpsed her face. 'It was there that he betrayed me. The one magic left to me was prophecy, and with his own fulfilled Piper had no use for that. In my weakened state, as vengeance for my trickery, he traded me to the Sorrowmen. And there I have stayed for three hundred years, long enough that every one of them forgot who I truly was. I became the *Sorrowseer*, hiding my nature behind a mask. Just enough magic remained to me that I was able to make you sick, to believe that somehow this world was rejecting you.' She laughed. 'Did you not see how conveniently your illness came and went? I feared giving too much away, but you never even considered it, almost as if you *wanted* to kill her to get home. The young do love to suffer. But when I heard you telling Phyrrai to leave it was obvious I needed an alternative.' She paused. 'Hrogo, force Phyrrai to plunge the knife into her chest. Make an end of this.'

But Hrogo did not move. 'So what do you gain from this?' he asked. 'Your magic?'

'All magic is sacrifice,' said the Sorrowseer. 'The giving of something in exchange for something taken from another world. Death is the greatest sacrifice of us.' She paused, and slowly began to turn. Pherri held her breath. 'The world of the dead is where my magic is,' said the Sorrowseer. 'Today, I shall retrieve it.' She turned, and revealed her face.

Pherri had to catch her scream in her throat. Hrogo let out a whimper, and Phyrrai's face turned white as cold moonlight.

Where one half of the mask had been torn away, a skull of crumbling bone was revealed, run through with a patchwork of veins and arteries, thrombosed blood flowing like black sludge. There was no eye in the exposed socket, and as Pherri stared a fat, blood-red worm oozed out of it, crawling down the skull and up through a broken nostril.

'For one shadowtwin to kill the other, here, at the centre of my power, will be a most powerful death indeed,' said the Sorrowseer. She smiled a dark toothless grin. 'Enough for me to open the world of the dead and reclaim my magic. Magic with which to re-establish my rightful dominion, to bring all the world under my spell. A queen, an empress, a *god*, as I was always destined to be.

'But why stop there?' She paused, seemingly relishing the horror on their faces. 'With your death, I will open *all* the worlds. And finally, I shall end what began millennia ago. My sisters will fall, and all of existence will be mine.'

'Your sisters?' said Pherri. Her voice was strained; one of the ropes was beginning to tighten around her throat. 'You mean—'

'The Norhai,' said the Sorrowseer. 'All of us, together again, as it was at the beginning.

'Our father made the world, and then he gave it to us, its guardians. I loved them once, but as the millennia crept by we grew too powerful, too vengeful, too jealous. In search of mastery over one another, we nearly tore the world apart. For that, our father split existence, and banished each of us to our own paltry reflection of it, dooming us to fall to the forces of men, trapping us with great mounds of rock, monuments to his own vanity.' She almost seemed to be choking on her own bitterness. 'Our punishment.'

'But they died,' said Pherri. 'The Norhai from my world are all dead, except Vulgatypha.'

The Sorrowseer laughed, an awful creaking sound that scraped painfully against Pherri's ears. 'Foolish girl, are you not listening? That is false, a myth dreamt up by men to explain what they cannot understand.

'I had not thought of Vulgatypha in centuries. I imagined that all my sisters had fallen to the same fate; betrayed and bested by men. Until I sensed a sliver of her power pass from her world into this, a power I had not known since the days of Piper. And with that, I felt her deep longing to fold existence back on itself, to end it all and start again. Perhaps all my sisters sensed it; perhaps Vulgatypha and I are two of many, and in every world a Norha thirsts to regain her power.

'At first, I accepted that she would succeed where I could never. In this world, my power was less than that of the lowest of the magi.' A deep light in her eye glinted hungrily. 'So, imagine my surprise when you, Pherri, fell into my lap. A girl such a threat to Vulgatypha that she devoted what limited power she had to try and stop you learning magic. A plan formed. I manoeuvred the Sorrowmen to seize you; they slew the Thrumb who might have seen what I was; I gave you just enough of the truth that you both came here willingly.'

She looked to each of them, her empty black eye socket staring out at them like the endless void below. 'Imagine Vulgatypha's rage when she realises. With one death, I will do what she sought to do with thousands. My sisters were never subtle. I shall end it all. There shall be one world, made in my image, removed from the uncertainty of time and chance, and all else shall perish. My sisters and all our father created will die, and he will tremble before the strength of the last Norha.'

A cold squall rushed up from the abyss, and Pherri would

have shivered had her bonds not been so impossibly tight. She could feel her fingers going dead, and, with the Sorrowseer's words, all hope disappearing. The end of the world, the end of all the worlds. Her heart wrenched with helplessness. *I was never going to get home.*

'Well, you've failed,' said Phyrrai. Pherri could not help being astounded at her bravery. 'Neither of us is killing the other.' Hrogo had backed away from the Sorrowseer in horror, realisation dawning in his face at the evil that he had been so close to committing. 'So, what now? Just let us leave?'

'Oh, no.' The Sorrowseer grinned her dead half-grin again. 'You disappoint me, Hrogo; I would have given you everything you wanted, but no matter.' The mask that so many times Pherri had seen move as if it were alive was now nothing but lifeless leather. 'It is less elegant, perhaps, but there is always another way.'

Without warning, more ropes snapped forward from the altar. Phyrrai shrieked as the cords seized her at the shoulders, ankles, and waist, trying uselessly to thrash her way free as they tightened around her. She hacked at one with the knife but a vine knocked it from her fingers and up into her face, slicing a bloody gash from jaw to forehead.

Phyrrai cried and pleaded as the ropes dragged her towards Pherri and the altar, but the Sorrowseer only laughed her death rattle. 'Do you remember you asked my name?' she said. 'My name was *Laguthina*, and it shall be again. Not just the *last* Norha, but *the* Norha, fated to reign over all!' The bonds began tightening Phyrrai to the altar alongside Pherri. Above, the sky crackled, and a bolt of blue forked lightning flashed from a wide opening in the mountain into the abyss, setting the air fizzing with sparks. The darkness flashed back, and for a moment Pherri could hardly breathe, its weight overwhelming her senses. She could feel it, the world of the dead calling to her, Laguthina's magic reaching out for its mistress.

'Do you see me, Piper?' Laguthina howled at the sky. More lightning struck, and great chunks of red rock began breaking away and plummeting into the void. Her mask had fallen away completely, leaving behind only her skull and slow-flowing veins. Another bolt flashed and struck her. She screamed as it burnt away her clothes, revealing a skeleton, held together only with the last vestiges of Laguthina's ancient magic. 'I told you, I told you! Prophecy is nothing next to the power of the Norhai!'

Beside Pherri, Phyrrai was still struggling, but she was faring no better than Pherri had. Their bonds constricted around them, as hard and sharp as steel, blood welling from fresh wounds and flowing down onto the altar.

Laguthina now held the knife. 'One stroke, to kill both of you. If such a sacrifice as that will not bring my magic back from the dead, nothing will.' She ran a boned finger down its length, and the dagger stretched into a sword. 'And then, I shall end it all.' She strode towards them. Plumes of shadow billowed in the steel like inky smoke, and as they writhed Pherri felt as if she was staring once more into the world of the dead, but now unable to tear her gaze from it.

In all the madness, she had forgotten about Hrogo. Though his eyes were still alive with fear, he had taken a few shuddering steps forward towards the altar.

Pherri willed herself to keep her gaze on Laguthina. The Norha was now so close she could smell her breath, the foul taste of raw dead flesh. There was a heart beneath her ribs, but it was black as night, thudding as it pumped its corruption around flesh that no longer existed.

'I shall be beautiful again,' said Laguthina. 'I shall reforge a single world, with a new race of men, men who shall travel for hundreds of miles to swear their allegiance, and they shall both love and fear me.' Pherri and Phyrrai gasped together as she drew the blade up with a piercing whistle through the air. Thunder cracked, lightning flashed, and the blade began to fall.

And Hrogo threw himself at Laguthina.

He hit her with his shoulder, and his sheer weight and the suddenness of the attack sent the Norha staggering. Hrogo stumbled with the impact, but got his feet under him and drove into her again, pushing her away from the altar and lurching towards the edge of the platform. She was only a few feet away. Hrogo steadied himself and charged.

Laguthina saw it coming.

At the last moment, she threw herself out of the way, leaving behind a lingering leg that caught Hrogo's ankle. He nearly stopped himself, but Laguthina aimed a shove at his back, and Pherri and Phyrrai screamed together as Hrogo flew over the edge.

The Sorrowseer rose to her full height, fury written on her skull face. 'Damn cripple fool. Did—'

Her eyes bulged as something pulled her face first to the ground. Pherri had to twist her neck to see – the broken chain Hrogo had left on his ankle had somehow got tangled up in Laguthina's foot. Over the edge, she could hear Hrogo screaming as he stared down into the void, while the Norha clawed at the ground to stop herself being dragged backwards.

Laguthina snarled, cried out, keened in fury, but she could get no grip on the dusty red stone. She screamed over and over, her bone fingertips being eroded by the slow, hot friction as she was dragged backwards by the weight of Hrogo. Her feet clawed at the ground, one constrained by the tangled chain, but it made no difference. Inch by inch, her skeletal form was hauled towards the edge. Her feet went over, and she looked up into Pherri's eyes. 'Please,' she begged. 'I'll give you—'

With one last, long scream, she flew over the edge.

In an instant, Pherri and Phyrrai's bonds loosened, fading like snow before the sun into dust that slipped over the edge into the abyss. On shaking limbs, drenched in sweat, they rushed to the edge. Pherri squinted into the darkness, sure she could still see them; two bodies, one of flesh and one of bone, joined at the foot, plummeting into the abyss.

Then they disappeared, and the blackness rushed up to meet them.

Pherri grabbed Phyrrai and leapt for safety behind the altar. They cowered there, a wild wind rushing in their ears and threatening to rip the skin from their bones. They sat together with their arms wrapped over their ears and eyes, too scared to look or listen to whatever was rising from the pit of darkness below Pipersmont.

It ceased, and against every instinct of self-preservation, Pherri rose from behind the altar. The Sorrowseer was gone, and she was trapped for eternity in this world; nothing could hurt her now.

She stared over the edge, and Merivale appeared before her, shimmering like a reflection in a lake. The black abyss was gone, replaced by a vision of Erland, as if she were watching it from the clouds. Her Erland. *My Erland.* She knew on instinct, as a child knows its mother.

Phyrrai rushed to join her. 'Is that—'

'My Erland,' breathed Pherri. She had stared into the face of death, but the sight seemed to inspire new life in her. She could see men rushing around like beetles, two groups of them, while a bright light shone over their heads, almost blinding to look at even through the veil.

'The Sorrowseer said death could open the way,' said Phyrrai. 'She just didn't know it would be hers.'

Merivale was many hundreds of feet below them. Pherri willed herself to be brave. She swallowed the swelling lump of fear at the back of her throat, and it settled in her gut. She reached out to grasp Phyrrai's hand, and looked into the eyes of her shadowtwin. Their faces were a mess of sweat, dust, and tears. There was blood flowing down their hands from where the bonds had bitten into their wrists, now mingling as they pressed their palms tightly against each other.

'Go now,' said Phyrrai. 'Before the world of the dead returns. We don't know how long the way will be open.'

Pherri tore her eyes away from her twin, and stared down again at the spectral vision of her home. *Even if the prophecy can't be fulfilled, I have to try.*

'Piper didn't complete his prophecy,' said Phyrrai, as if reading her mind. 'Hrogo did. If he can do it—'

'If he can do it, I can.' Pherri finished it for her, and turned to kiss her shadowtwin on the cheek. Back to Erland. Back to Eryi, and to Vulgatypha. She could only try. She looked into Phyrrai's tear-stained eyes. 'Will you be able to get home?'

'I don't know,' said Phyrrai. 'It doesn't matter. Just go. *Quickly*.'

Pherri could already see the vision receding at the edges. She had to go. Eryi and Vulgatypha were waiting for her. With a cry of fear, she leapt.

CHAPTER 41

'It is time, Orsian.'

The voice of the pale man penetrated Orsian's concentration. *That was my name once.* A thousand years ago, within the flap of a moth's wing. *Time is nothing.*

'Can we not stay here?' he heard himself say. He blinked, and the centuries rolled back like skin being shed from a snake as it devoured its own tail; civilisations rose and fell and rose again, before a blinding surge of light and heat burst against his eyes. A million goddesses withdrew, shrinking back into nothingness, and all was blackness, the vision of a million worlds just a twinkle in the eye of the nameless creator. A single, indifferent eye fell upon Orsian for the briefest fraction of a moment, and then was gone, like the merest ripple in an endless pool.

'*Orsian.*'

Orsian blinked. 'What was that?'

'A shadow of a memory. A reflection seen by a blind eye. Nothing.' Eryi gestured, and what to a boy named Orsian had been the present appeared beyond the veil. Thousands of corpses piled high before the gates of a walled city; broken, bloodied men kneeling in mud and gore; and above it all a single, shining malevolent light, the black-hearted goddess who Eryi meant to fight for the fate of existence.

'It is time to go back, Orsian.'

'Will it hurt?'

'I do not know. Come.'

A cold dead hand seized Orsian by the heart, and dragged him over the threshold, back to life.

Immediately Orsian's consciousness was thrust back into his body. He felt a mouth, feet, a beating heart, lungs... His strange form shuddered, gasping for air, choking on a void. *Breathe. Breathe!* His lungs spasmed into life, and he took down a gulp of air and gagged on the strange taste. He screamed as bile rose up his gullet, burning against freshly formed skin, and retched violently as every organ in his body came to life at once. Blood thundered through his veins, wind tore at his flesh, and reclaimed memories buzzed through his mind like a flight of dragonflies as everything came flooding back.

He opened his eyes, and a high scream ripped at his throat as he found himself plunging towards Merivale.

Eryi tumbled with him, laughing wildly, his grip upon Orsian tight as falcon's talons. 'Fear not, dear Orsian! We hurtle together towards our destinies!'

They were plummeting towards the highest tower of Piperskeep. Orsian closed his eyes, the air ripping at his skin like hair-thin blades as it hurtled past, readying himself for impact upon the unyielding stone, imagining his broken body tumbling down the roof and landing shattered upon the battlements. But as the castle rose up before them, they began to slow. Orsian opened his eyes, and Eryi soared like a gliding bird, bringing them to land upon the tower roof as softly as if it were made of down.

Orsian's relief was short-lived. Eryi jammed a dagger up against his throat, and a hot bead of blood ran from Orsian's neck along the steel. With unfamiliar limbs he wrenched furious at Eryi's grip, slamming an elbow into his torso, aiming a kick for his knee, but the magus held firm, the air resounding with his high hysterical laughter. His hold on Orsian's neck tightened like a noose, the blade pressing harder against Orsian's windpipe until his struggling ceased.

Below them, the light of the Norha still shone, bathing the kneeling masses in spectral whiteness, illuminating the hammering rain like dying fireflies. Even on the battlements, men had sunk to their knees, gazing in rapture as Vulgatypha's voice boomed against the sky.

'*BEHOLD YOUR QUEEN. GAZE UPON ME AND KNOW FEAR.*' Her banshee screams assailed Orsian's senses, churning his guts and stabbing at his skin like needles, and he felt the irresistible compulsion to *kneel* if only Eryi would let him. '*SURRENDER YOURSELF TO ME AND SERVE IN THE NEW WORLD, OR DEFY ME AND DIE IN AGONY.*' Above, fissures of crackling orange light were appearing in the sky, as if at any moment the heavens might collapse.

'*See what I am trying to stop,*' hissed Eryi. '*She will spare no one. I am their last hope.*'

'*Viratia.*' Eryi's cry was soft as a whisper, and yet Vulgatypha's huge head whipped around at the sound of it. Through the rain, Orsian could almost see his mother's features, Vulgatypha's eyes flickering from red to blue as they fixed upon the tower.

Then Orsian blinked, and only the fiery red remained. With a scream, she soared higher into the air and sped like an arrow towards them, her eyes like fire, her lips twisted in a murderous grimace.

Behind him, Orsian felt Eryi smile. 'You see. Look how she comes to save you.'

The goddess stopped thirty yards above them, her luminescence mingling with the warmth of the red rising dawn. The sky continued to fracture and crackle as bolts of purple lightning sizzled against the storm clouds.

Vulgatypha bared a row of sharp, silver teeth. '*KNEEL, MAGUS. KNEEL, AND DIE.*'

Her voice sent tiles tumbling from the tower, but Eryi's grip on Orsian never wavered. 'Never.' The blade pressed so tight against Orsian's neck he could not help the squeak that came from his mouth. 'Do you suppose I waited for a thousand years to let you end everything? Erland is *mine*.'

Vulgatypha howled her fury, and Orsian screamed as it shrilled through his ears. Below them, the kneeling masses had turned to watch, their battle a distant memory.

'*Viratia*,' said Eryi again. His voice slithered through the air like a winged snake. 'I know you're in there, Viratia. *Fight her*, or I will kill your only living child.'

Vulgatypha shrieked again. The sky thundered and lightning forked from the sky, sending more tiles plummeting to the battlements below. The rain was incessant, but the heat of Eryi's power seemed to burn it away before it landed, sizzling against an invisible cocoon he had spun. A bolt of lightning slashed through the air towards them, and exploded in a flash of fire.

'*Viratia*,' he said again, pouring the name into the sky like honey as he drew the blade an inch across Orsian's skin to bring forth a dribble of blood.

And this time, Vulgatypha hesitated. Her eyes flashed from fire to azure and back again. Tears poured from her eyes and turned to steam upon the blazing heat of her skin. Her limbs writhed, and as a woman's scream burst from her throat her face flashed, and Orsian's mother looked down at him.

It lasted less than a moment, before Vulgatypha and Viratia began tearing at their own shared skin, their fingernails sharp as razors, howling into the raging sky.

And all the while, Eryi laughed, as high and terrible as the wailing wind.

Tansa raced up the stairs to Hessian's solar, her lungs burning, her rain-wet soles almost slipping on the slick stone. She hurled herself through the door, and without stopping ran for the balcony. Above, she could hear the thunder, so close it was as if it was in the room with her, and with it the wild screams of Vulgatypha and the mad laughter of Eryi, a hellish cacophony that threatened to bring the whole castle crumbling down. She could feel the foundations shaking as the ground quaked with the twin powers of the goddess and the magus, as if at any moment the whole castle might be swallowed to the depths of the earth.

I did this, she thought as she put her hands against the tower wall and began her ascent, staring up into the endless beating rain. The stone was slick with it, but Tansa knew how to climb. *I might be a fool, but I can climb.* She had let herself be tricked by Vulgatypha, and her message to Rymond Prindian had killed thousands, opening the way for the goddess to rise on their despair and bring them under her will. A tile fell from the roof to shatter against the balcony, but Tansa kept climbing.

Don't look down. Tansa forced her face up into the rain. She might not be able to stop the gods from killing each other or dooming the world, but she could at least save Orsian from being torn apart. Seeing him at the mercy of the gods had brought it rushing back to her; Orsian was the only person left alive she loved, the only one who might see what she had attained for Cliffark and be *proud*, rather than consumed with trying to stop her. If she had to watch another person she loved die, it would all be for nothing.

In the sky, Vulgatypha thrashed against herself, her white-hot glow casting an eerie radiance against the rain-slick walls of the tower. Tansa kept climbing, her pounding heart drowned out by the rumbling beat of the rain.

She dragged herself over the balcony and paused, drawing her knife. Eryi and Orsian were barely ten yards away from her, but they were both intent upon Vulgatypha. The goddess's silvery skin had been torn to ribbons by her own hands, but her writhing was beginning to slow, and her eyes were a fiery crimson of fury.

With one final ear-splitting howl, the struggle ceased, and Vulgatypha hung in the sky, whatever private drama she had been fighting at an end. Her long, slender hands rose towards Eryi, nails dripping with her own blood. Overhead, three lightning bolts flashed towards the tower, sizzling out as they struck against Eryi's magic.

The magus's eyes went wide. 'No. *No!*' Orsian struggled, and looked as if he might win free before Eryi's grip tightened upon his neck, the magus-god's ancient magic straining with the effort of holding both his shield and his hostage in place.

Seeing what was about to happen, Tansa raced towards them.

It was now Vulgatypha's turn to laugh. The goddess's dark mirth echoed off the sky, bathing the land in noise and setting the ground shaking again. She raised her fingers. Lightning crackled against her naked form, and her hands sizzled with mastery.

A bolt of purple fire shot from her hands towards Eryi and Orsian, and Tansa threw herself into its path. It struck her in the chest in a hiss of flames and sparks, and she knew an instant of maddening, wordless, paralysing pain before the world went dark.

Before she even hit the ground, Orsian knew she was dead.

Tansa's body flew across the slate and came to a stop against the low merlons at the tower's edge. She lay there, unmoving.

Rage and grief rose in Orsian like a flash flood. His hands grasped Eryi's knife, and the magus's arm came away as Orsian wrenched himself free. Eryi grabbed for him, but Orsian elbowed him in the face, and he raced towards Tansa, coughing against the thick smoke that had blossomed where Vulgatypha's bolt had struck the tower. As Orsian reached Tansa, something sharp struck him in the back just below the heart, and he cried out in pain as it punched through his mail and deep into his flesh. Orsian went down hard as his legs went from under him.

'*NOOOOOOOOO!*'

The scream of agony did not come from Orsian, but from Vulgatypha. Orsian had landed face first against Tansa's body, but he twisted to see, relying on the smoke to hide him from sight.

Before his eyes, Vulgatypha was fading, shrinking, her features softening into those of Orsian's mother as she floated down towards the tower. By the time she landed, there was no trace of the goddess, just Viratia Brithwell, her mouth round with horror, long hair plastered to her skin with rain.

'*Orsian!*'

She ran towards him, but Eryi raised a hand, and Viratia was thrown onto her back as if she had been struck by an invisible fist.

She rushed to her feet, her eyes suddenly once again the hot red of Vulgatypha, and roared her fury towards Eryi. Barely ten yards separated them now. Vulgatypha raised her hands as if she meant to crush Eryi's head between her palms. Eryi flicked a finger, and dozens of broken tiles rose from the battlements below which began swirling in a vortex around Vulgatypha.

The goddess snarled. 'For all your talk and posturing, you still fear to fight me.'

Vulgatypha took a step towards him, but a spinning shard dashed against her head, momentarily stunning her. She grabbed it and made to launch it towards Eryi, but before she could a second piece struck her, and then a third. As Orsian watched, the maelstrom of spinning tiles tightened around her until it was so close that she could not move an inch without one striking her. The goddess forced herself forward, but she had only moved a few yards before her face was a mess of blood, blinding the eyes that cycled rapidly between Vulgatypha's and Viratia's. She flailed wildly, as if at war with herself, and still the tiles kept spinning, tearing at her face.

Eryi watched, his laughing mouth a pitiless black crater. 'Erland is *mine*, Goddess! *Mine!* Your stolen body fails you!'

Orsian tried to rise, but the howling vortex of tiles was swirling so fast that its draught kept him pinned to Tansa's body. He could feel a weak heartbeat through her dress, and he tried to cover her as best he could while chips of spinning tiles peppered them like hailstones.

Eryi was still laughing. Vulgatypha had slipped to her knees. She was failing; the rain had lessened, and the clouds no longer crackled with lightning. The magus walked towards her, his hands cupped before him as he manipulated the twisting storm of masonry that tore at the goddess. He seemed to be pouring more and more power into it; merlons and tiles were breaking away from the tower and adding themselves to the cyclone.

'*It is not enough to be free, Goddess!*' he cried. '*For all your tricks, you are mortal now, and I am the god! Begone! Leave the world to those with the strength to rule!*'

Battling against the gale, Orsian struggled to his feet. Eryi could not be allowed to win either. The knife was still embedded in Orsian's back. Gritting his teeth, he reached behind him and hissed with pain as he withdrew it. When Vulgatypha fell, he would kill Eryi and end this. Whatever remained of his mother, he could not save her now. He gripped the blade in his fist, moving against the wind to stand behind Eryi, ignoring the sharp ache of his wound and the warmth of gushing blood down his back.

Eryi seemed to be struggling now to control his storm. It spun ever faster, and flesh began to slough from his bones, beads of his own blood being drawn into the vortex as the pink lesions that dotted his body split apart.

Orsian watched with his heart threatening to beat out of his chest. *He's going to fail.* For all the power Eryi poured into his magic, Vulgatypha endured, refusing to be cowed even as her body bled from a hundred different wounds. With a piercing smile she pushed herself up onto one foot. Eryi's eyes grew wide.

Vulgatypha stood, and the weakened tower crumbled beneath her. It teetered, and with a roar like the sky breaking apart a whole section of Hessian's solar disintegrated.

She made no sound as she fell, or perhaps it was simply not audible over the noise of tonnes of collapsing stone. Vulgatypha tumbled, taking nearly half the tower with her.

Orsian remained fixed to the spot as Eryi dragged his weeping, waning body to the ragged edge of the tower. He peered over the side, and Orsian heard a deafening explosion of bricks and mortar as Vulgatypha and the tower struck the Piperskeep courtyard. The whole keep rumbled, the tower teetered again, and Orsian for a moment thought the rest of it was going to be dragged down with her.

Eryi watched for a few seconds more, and turned away. 'It is done then.' He was breathing hard. Bones were sticking out beneath his ravaged flesh. 'Finally, I am free of her.'

Orsian raced forward, the blade raised over his head ready to be plunged into Eryi's heart, but the magus flicked a finger, and he was sent spinning away to crash into the merlons next to Tansa's prone body.

'It is over, Orsian.' Eryi was eerily calm now, his voice as still as the sky overhead. 'I am your god, and I will have your obedience.'

Orsian came to his feet, but before he could reply a shining blue light began to blossom at the centre of the tower. It began as a tiny point of colour, but in a few seconds stretched to form a circle several feet across, shimmering like a rolling lake and so bright it burnt to look at. Orsian squinted, and beyond the threshold saw an immense chamber of red clay, and a small, silhouetted figure plummeting towards them.

Eryi's eyes grew wide. '*No. Impossible.*'

The figure burst from the gateway and landed with their feet wide apart, a wild mane of blonde hair whipping in the squalling wind, tiny fists clenched in readiness as they stared at Eryi. After several seconds, Orsian recognised her.

Pherri had returned.

As soon as she crossed the threshold, Pherri felt the magic of her own world rush back to her. It crackled at her fingertips, willing her to reach for it, an endless source of power within her grasp that was all the more potent for its long absence. She breathed deep, holding the magic at bay, almost scared to touch it in case it overwhelmed her.

She found she was smiling. Pherri stared at the shocked expression on Eryi's face, taking in his mangled, bloodied, cadaverous body. 'You look to have suffered, magus.'

Eryi snarled and raised a claw-like hand towards her. Pherri felt him trying to push her back into the closing portal, but his magic was no more than the beat of a fly's wings. With the barest measure of will, she fixed herself in place, letting Eryi tear himself apart as he tried to force her back.

'*BEGONE!*' he shrieked, his face contorting in horror. 'Erland is mine! Mine!'

Pherri kept her silence, letting an eerie calm wash over her. She opened herself up, feeling all of Erland; every blade of grass, every soldier still on his knees staring up at Piperskeep, every drop of water that made the Pale River.

Across that water, West Erlanders looked to the east, staring at the luminous blue dawn too bright to be the rising sun. On the battlements and in the city, men and women rose to their feet, craning their necks for a better view. As far away as Cliffark and in the depths of the Shrouded Sea, merchants and sailors turned their eyes towards Piperskeep.

Let them see. Pherri measured out a thimbleful of will, and focused it upon the towering summit of Eryispek. *Go*. In a burst of light, a new portal grew to devour her and Eryi, and the frosted mountaintop rose up before them, the sky hanging low like a tent canopy. Pherri felt the Mountain's slick ice beneath her feet, and drew strength from it, willing herself to stand upright as Eryi engulfed her in a bone-chilling storm of sleet and snow, letting her own ice-hard will consume her until his magic was no more than the touch of a chilled lake upon her fingertips.

Pherri drew from the Mountain, knowing she could stand here forever. The portal was closing behind her, but with an inch of will she bid it to stay open, letting Eryi tear himself apart as he strived to force her into retreat. She did not take a single step back.

Eryi's skin was almost wholly gone now, torn from his bones with his own mad desire. Pherri watched the last bit of pale flesh slough from his forehead, reminded of the Sorrowseer.

'It is over,' she said, and Eryi's skeletal jaw opened in a silent howl of anguish.

With all the will, focus, and energy she could muster, Pherri tore the bones from their tendons, and clenched her fist in a single burst of power to crush them to powder. White dust hung in the air like mist, but Pherri was not finished. She drew Eryi's remains to her, spinning them into a tight ball. His will still raged against her, but it was of no more concern than the tantrum of an infant.

Pherri threw the remains into the portal, and with a final act of will she slammed it shut.

It disappeared as quickly as it had formed, and Pherri collapsed to her knees, suddenly back atop the ruins of Hessian's tower, feeling its rough slate beneath her palms. Grey clouds marred the sky, and the pounding rain was already beginning to soak her, but in that moment Pherri did not care. She was free, and she had won. She breathed the cool air of home, raising her head to the sky to feel the downpour on her face.

'Pherri!'

Orsian's voice was alive with alarm. He was pointing behind her, and Pherri turned, struggling to her feet.

The sight that met her turned her blood to ice.

Vulgatypha. The goddess hung in the air on an act of will, her immortal power undimmed by the injuries that scarred her body. Before Pherri's eyes, her wounds began to close, skin stretching and knitting, the black blood that stained her flesh receding back inside flawless skin.

'*I thank you, Pherri.*' The goddess's voice rumbled with equal parts glee and malice. '*Now kneel, serve me, and be spared. We shall build a new world together, on the ashes of the old.*'

Pherri almost collapsed back to her knees, too weary to stand. Already drained from escaping Laguthina, she had held nothing back in her struggle against Eryi, and it had sapped her last reserves of strength. Nevertheless, she forced herself to remain standing, even as her legs began to shake.

The goddess bared her teeth. '*KNEEL.*'

At her shoulder, Pherri felt her brother step forward to stand beside her, and Orsian took her hand in his. She looked up into his eyes and smiled at him. 'I'm glad you're alive.' They would die together.

Orsian's lips spread in a sad smile. 'I'm glad you're back.'

Pherri steadied her will, ready to hold back Vulgatypha's power until the last of her energy was spent and her body melted into nothingness. She felt Vulgatypha draw upon an endless well of divine strength. Purple lightning smouldered beneath the grey clouds, and Vulgatypha pulled it to herself, her fingers crackling as the fizzing orange fissures in the sky began to brighten and thicken, splitting the grey heavens into jagged shards of pottery. The earth trembled, then shuddered, on the edge of a void as Viratia wrought the last gasp of existence. Pherri could feel it again, the low hum of the world of the dead rising to a crescendo. Below, screams rose from the battlefield as the light began to fade, and a hot, heavy stillness fell over Erland like the final reprieve of calm before the tempest that would mark the end.

'*VIRATIA.*'

In front of Pherri's eyes, the sky seemed to tear in two, and the vision before her almost made her heart stop.

She remembered the words of Laguthina. *The prophecy.* The shadow of a man formed in the sky, thrice as tall as he had stood in life, with wild hair the shade of midnight and dark penetrating eyes like burning coals. His features sharpened, revealing a heavy jaw and a coarse black beard. Mail and leather covered his body, and in his hand he gripped a sword that rippled with the dusky fires of the afterlife.

Her father, Andrick Barrelbreaker, a man so implacable that not even death could contain him.

'*Viratia, it is time.*' His voice rumbled like thunder, and Vulgatypha's red eyes danced with doubt. '*Come away from there, and let our children live.*'

Her shining, naked body seemed to shrink slightly. Her harsh features thawed, and as the goddess blinked Pherri swore she saw her mother there, her eyes soft with love. The goddess spasmed, and some inexorable force dragged her towards Andrick.

'Viratia. Viratia. You know that is who you are. Come. Be at peace.'

The fiery light left Vulgatypha's eyes. A flourish of tears formed behind a tender gaze of cool blue, and Viratia Brithwell looked down at her children. She smiled once at them, bright with love, and her body began to float towards her husband. He reached out a hand, and she grasped it. The clouds parted, and a door opened beyond the sky, and together Andrick Barrel-breaker and Viratia Brithwell stepped through into the world beyond.

'He came back for her,' Pherri whispered. Her grip on Orsian's hand softened as she sank to her knees, overwhelmed with exhaustion and wonder. The rain had ceased, and the clouds faded before the rising sun as it crested over the city. She buried her face in her hands and wept, for all that she had gained, and all that she had lost.

Her magic was gone. It had disappeared as soon as the spirit of Vulgatypha had passed beyond the threshold into the unknowable land of the dead. She had crossed half another world to retrieve it, and yet she had never been gladder than to see it go.

'I'll be back,' said Orsian. He placed a hand on his sister's shoulder, checked her for injuries and found none, then raced back towards Tansa, the wound Eryi had left in his back still burning.

She had not moved. Orsian turned her body over, and stared down into the dead gaze of the girl he had loved.

He pressed a finger and thumb to her face and closed her eyes, his tears slipping onto her ash-pale skin like warm rain. His head swam with grief, for Tansa, for Errian, for their parents, for everything they had lost, and that he would have to live and remember this day. They had won, and paid a price he could hardly comprehend.

After a while, Pherri came for him, and Orsian allowed himself to be led away. Together, they descended into Piperskeep. On the battlefield below, kneeling warriors lumbered to their feet, staring entranced up at the tower. And all across Erland, the bright light over Merivale faded, and folk returned to their tasks, uncertain what they had just seen.

CHAPTER 42

'It could be worse, Majesty,' the mason told Ciera, as they walked through the deserted corridors of Piperskeep. He was a young man, gaunt and serious, still the only mason Ciera could find brave enough to re-enter Piperskeep. 'But not by much. The roof and battlements are a mess, but it's these hairline cracks that trouble me most; no telling how far down they go.' He wiped his brow and traced a thin line in the wall with his finger. 'Could be nothing to worry about, or with time it might bring the whole castle down around us, but if rain gets into those cracks and freezes this winter...' He tailed off as if the thought was too frightening to contemplate. 'We should patch up the roof and battlements quickly. That'll give me time to take a proper look at the foundations.'

Ciera pursed her lips. Just another worry to add to a long list, she supposed. 'And the rest?'

'The courtyard where the tower fell might take months to clear, there's still rubble in the great hall to remove, and we may never find enough men bold enough to fix the tower – every man I've spoken to says they wouldn't be caught dead up there.'

Ciera's eye twitched with irritation. She could have shown these workmen plenty of people who had already been killed by the tower. Over thirty servants and guardsmen had been crushed by falling masonry, and the same again wounded, with injuries ranging from sprained wrists to broken legs. Of the servants still among the living, only the very bravest of them would dare to set foot inside Piperskeep for the time being.

'Do what you must to secure the roof,' Ciera told him. 'But don't neglect the hall either – I want it cleared. I'll make sure you have the coin you need.'

The mason bowed. 'At once, Majesty.' He turned and with an urgency in his step hurried the other way down the corridor.

The state of the keep was a small concern, weighed against the many thousands of corpses being piled into burn pits outside the city, either mortally wounded in battle against the Prindians or left charred and twisted by the huyar explosion. Burik had somehow survived despite being close to the blast and in the thick of the fighting, but Jerem and Mikol Gurathet were both dead, slain in the rushed counter-attack that might have saved the few *hymerikai* still living.

With her inspection of the castle complete, Ciera headed for the floor where Orsian and Pherri were recuperating, through deserted corridors and up silent staircases. She kept no guard with her; the Prindians were not going anywhere, and every man was needed on the walls.

They had found the Barrelbreaker's children together, collapsed at the bottom of the stairs to Hessian's tower. It had taken all Ciera's threats and cajoling to summon servants to carry them to their beds, and for two days now neither of them had risen.

Pherri was yet to wake. Ciera had been shocked at her condition, so small and fragile she might have been a child only half her age. The healer said though that physically she was fine; whatever ailed Pherri was beyond her skill and understanding. Aimya was tending to the girl herself, spooning fresh water and honey into her mouth every hour in the hope of putting some flesh back on her bones. Ciera did not understand where Pherri had been, or how she had reached them, or what she had done, but there would be time enough to learn and thank her when she woke.

The kingdom needed a magus again. Someone as able as Pherri would be a vital servant to her son's crown. If she could recover her strength swiftly, her magic might turn the tide against the Prindians. Ciera had not forgotten their threat, even if everybody else had in the wake of the gods' appearance. She had sent word that they were to send for her as soon as the girl was up and speaking.

Orsian seemed to have taken the brunt of the gods' fury. The healer said that the wound in his back would have pierced his heart had it been an inch higher or deeper, and that another hour without tending the wound would have left him with too little blood to revive. Unlike his sister, he was awake, but even in his weakness it had taken being restrained by two surviving *hymerikai* to prevent him returning to the tower for Tansa's body. Ciera had sworn to him she would take care of Tansa if he would only allow himself to rest.

Ciera could not help but respect Tansa; when everyone else could only stare, she had climbed towards the gods to save the man she loved. It made Ciera think of Tam, that bold boy she had clung so dearly to, but in the life of a queen there was no room for such sentimentality. It was better that the Cliffark girl was gone. The remaining heads of the nascent Cliffark council – the likes of Abner the veteran sailor and Marrec the grasping merchant – would be more amenable to compromise. And with Tansa dead, Orsian would be more useful to Ciera and Andrick; he was the Lord of Violet Hall now, and a marriageable proposition that would bind a lord somewhere to Andrick's fledgling crown. The repeated failures of the East Erland lords to provide aid to Merivale until Ciera had appeared in their land at the head of an army was a difficulty that would need to be rectified. Alternatively, with Orsian's marriage she might persuade a lord of West Erland to switch their banner.

She made for Pherri's room first, the chamber of the late Theodric, set away from the other bedchambers so as not to give anyone sleepless nights. Such was the awe the girl was held in, it had seemed the best place for her, though the servants had been almost shaking with fear when they carried her inside and had fled at the first opportunity. Only Aimya was brave enough to enter Theodric's rooms, swearing she had seen too much magic to be cowed by a dead man.

Ciera opened the door and slipped inside. For all the fear Theodric had instilled in people, it was a room much like any other in Piperskeep, and she felt no creeping sense of dread nor tickle of the unexplained as she crossed the threshold. Pherri's bed was set beside a window, lit by glancing shards of early afternoon light, and she was tucked under a heap of furs with her head propped up on a pillow. Sister Aimya sat in the window, beside a small table with a pot of honey and flagons of water and wine. She had been dozing but stirred as Ciera entered.

'You look exhausted,' said Ciera, striding to the bed and sitting down in the chair across the bed from Aimya. 'I can send for the servants and have them take over if you prefer.'

Aimya shook her head, pushing herself up in the chair. She had finally changed out of her robes into servant garb. 'It's the least I owe her, for all those years I went along with worshiping that maniac.' She scratched at her forearm as if some horror of Eryi still lurked under her skin. 'She saved the world, and now everyone's afraid to go near her. Some thanks.' Aimya made a face. 'And her own mother... can you even imagine?'

Ciera had locked away her last recollection of her own mother at the back of a mind, where it could not hurt her. *All those years I thought she hated me, and at the end she gave her life for mine.* 'She's very powerful.' It was strange, looking down at Pherri, knowing that such might lurked within such a frail body. 'I'm sure she will recover.'

'She's still just a girl,' said Aimya, frowning. 'I don't see what her power has to do with it.'

Power has everything to do with it. 'When will she be well again?'

Aimya squinted at Ciera as if she had grown a second head. 'She woke briefly an hour ago. We spoke.'

Ciera lurched to her feet. 'Why was I not told? I *commanded* you to send for me!'

Aimya came to her feet also, with more care than Ciera had done. 'If you are hoping to use her against the Prindians, you'll be wasting your breath. Her magic's *gone*, Ciera. Magic left the world when Vulgatypha did. That's what she told me.'

Eryi's balls. Ciera let out a deep breath through her nostrils. She looked down at Pherri, watching the girl's fluttering eyelids. 'Perhaps it will return once she's fully recovered.'

'Or perhaps it won't.' Aimya's tired face was tight with anger, but Ciera did not care; her concern was for Merivale. *Does she not understand the Prindians are still outside our walls?* A magus might make all the difference. 'I suggest you leave, Majesty. Pherri needs rest.'

Ciera gave the sister a glance up and down. Aimya might deny she ever held Eryi in her heart, but still she scrabbled for something new to give her life meaning, like a drowning sailor grasping for driftwood. 'Very well, I will leave. But the next time she wakes, you *will* send for me. I'll be on the walls.' Ciera turned on her heel and made for the door.

As she reached for the handle, Ciera paused. 'Did she say if they would come back?'

'She believes not. But who can know the power of a god?'

Ciera gave a slow nod, without turning to meet Aimya's eye. 'Truer words have never been spoken, Sister.' *And who can know the power of a queen?* With or without Pherri's magic, Ciera's fight against the Prindians was only just beginning.

CHAPTER 43

Beside the Ram's Gate, Helana ascended the stairs to the battlements, her legs protesting with every step. The battle had worked muscles she had not even known she had, but at least she was alive.

Atop the rampart, Gruenla waited for her. The mercenary woman looked as if she could fight again at a moment's notice. Her Cyliriens had likely borne fewer losses than any other force on the field.

'How's the nose?' asked Gruenla as Helana came to stand alongside her. The battlements were lined with spearmen, gazing nervously towards the muddy disorder of the Prindian camp. They had withdrawn west of the battlefield, leaving behind a confusion of churned earth and corpses. To the north and south, two groups of men with shovels were digging burn pits ready to receive the dead.

'Stings like fire,' said Helana, leaning against the parapet to rest her aching legs. She lifted a finger to her face and winced at the tenderness. Gruenla had set Helana's broken nose in the aftermath of the battle of Eryi and Vulgatypha; rare calm when it seemed everyone else had misplaced their senses. The sight of two gods flashing against the heavens and the shade of Andrick Barrelbreaker appearing in the sky had caused both sides to lose their taste for slaughter, and those living had staggered back towards the safety of camp or city. Helana and the Cyliriens had fallen in with the East Erlanders, and in their dazed state the Prindian forces had let the traitors in their midst slip away.

Within the walls, Merivale teetered between fear and violence. Everywhere Helana went, folk seemed unable to resist staring up at the ruins of Hessian's tower, as if at any moment the gods might return. Ciera Istlewick had ordered that every man between the ages of twelve and fifty who could still stand and hold a spear was to report and prepare to defend the walls, but the taverns were heaving with them, revellers spilling into the street and falling over themselves as if this were the end of days. Helana had seen the bodies of two street preachers, battered to death and left to rot. Elsewhere, a furious mob had surrounded the Eryian temple, barricading the priests inside, but the Brides of Eryi had escaped the worst of the retribution against the gods' adherents by immediately announcing their dissolution, its members discarding their robes and slipping away into the city.

She relayed all she had seen to Gruenla. The Cylirien woman's mouth quirked in what might have been a smile. 'Can't really blame them for getting drunk and killing all the true believers after what they've seen this year. After facing down the Imperium and two gods the prospect of a Prindian attack probably seems like a relief.'

Helana knew Gruenla did not feel as nonchalant as she tried to make out. She had not even mentioned the coin Helana owed her, which just went to show how fearful she and her band of mercenaries were now of this land where gods seemed to erupt from the ground like weeds. Based on the views of the other Cyliriens Helana had spoken to, they could not wait to see the back of Erland.

'You been up to the castle?' Gruenla asked.

Helana nodded. 'My cousins still haven't woken; the healers don't seem sure what's wrong with them. Ciera still seems to think there'll be a battle.' She would have liked to stay and watch over Orsian, but not while there were still tasks undone.

'Maybe there will be,' said Gruenla. She pointed to the Prindian camp. 'Does it look like they're going home? They're confused and demoralised now, but don't bet Rymond's mother's given up on taking the city. She didn't let an Imperium invasion hold her back; two gods in the sky is just another day.'

There were whispers that Rymond had taken a severe wound and lingered on the edge of death. If he succumbed, what would that mean? No matter how demoralised and scared the West Erlanders might be, Helana could well imagine Breta Prindian arguing that the walls were riper for conquest than ever, promising the crown to Lord Rostar Darlton and finding some Prindian cousin from a distant and lesser branch for him to wed.

Helana looked along the line of spearmen. A pair of *hymerikai* stood among them – some of the lucky few who had escaped the battlefield whole and hale – but mostly they were young boys. Pale, fearful faces peered out from beneath their helms.

'Princess Helana.'

She turned towards the sound of her name. A bearded man in the red-marked mail of the *Hymeriker* faced her, his left hand gripping a stick to keep the weight off his right leg.

It took Helana a moment to recognise him. 'Burik.' She glanced down at his leg. 'What happened?'

'Dislocated kneecap. Horse fell on me. What happened to your nose?'

'I was somewhere I shouldn't have been and none of you *hymerikai* were there to protect me.'

Burik grinned ruefully. 'Too few of us left standing for that now. You're alive, and that's what counts.' He shifted his posture and winced, but produced a skin from within his mail. 'I came over to thank you both. Reckon I'd be dead if the Cyliriens hadn't turned on the Prindian rear.' He took a swig and held it out to her. 'Wine?'

Wine... Helana knew now why fighting men drank so much. It would take more than a skinful of wine to wash away the blood, the stink, and the screams of battle. More than once she had woken in the night, choking on the sensation of a shield being pressed up against her face, blood and dirt in her eyes, and the iron-tinged reek of gore in her nostrils. She claimed the skin from Burik, and poured a long draught down her throat, then wiped her mouth with the back of her hand and passed it to Gruenla.

'Reckon we'll hold them if they come?' asked Gruenla, raising the skin towards Burik in thanks before taking a drink.

Burik's mouth twitched, and his eyes scanned furtively along the walls. He dropped his voice to a low murmur. 'I have never known morale so low as this.' His speech was heavy with pain, whether from his leg, grief, or regret Ciera could not say. 'Not every *hymerika* believed Eryi waited for us above the clouds, but enough of them did. It's made some of them question what we're fighting for. And seeing the Barrelbreaker...' Burik's voice cracked, and he had to force a swallow to keep going. 'There's barely a hundred of us left who can fight, and we've all seen too many friends die, and glimpsed that what's waiting for us above ain't a feast above the clouds with blessed Eryi. The men are dazed, frightened like I've never seen them.'

Burik stared at the ground, shaking his head from side to side. 'The Wild Brigade are all dead. Half the Cliffarkers are hiding in the city, too frightened to fight. We've still got the Cyliriens and the rest, but it won't be enough. If the Prindians bring all their strength to bear against Merivale, we won't last half a day.'

No, thought Helana. *Never again*. It was time for wiser, calmer heads to prevail in Erland. Perhaps the vision of warring gods would herald a new age of peace. She gave a wry smile at her hopeless optimism.

She only hoped that Rymond still lived. *It will be marriage, if he survives*. He would hold her to that as the price of peace. And she would have to pay it. Whether it was to be one realm or two, Erland needed stability. A fresh blood tie between the Prindians and the Sangreals might save Rymond from East Erland's vengeance in the years to come, and the gods knew there were worse horrors than marriage. She would have position, and she did not believe Rymond was the sort to confine her to Irith Castle. More likely she could rule while her husband drank and smoked himself onto an early pyre, if she could wrest the reins of power from his mother. The hunting in West Erland was good enough – perhaps she could even persuade Creya to join her; the memory of the plain-speaking huntswoman brought a slow smile to Helana's face. And as for any children she and Rymond might have... well, that was what wetnurses and servants were for.

'Burik,' she said. 'I'd be grateful if you could escort me below and order the men to open the gate.'

Rymond stared at the stump of his arm, cut halfway between his elbow and his wrist, wincing as Brant applied a cooling poultice. In his curiosity, he had earlier looked at it uncovered, in all its monstrous glory, and thrown up half his breakfast. The healer said that infection must have set in while Rymond had been left for dead in the dirt. Not badly, but enough to necessitate cutting and burning away more of the mortified flesh. There had been strict instructions not to partake in any wine or smokesticks to aid his recovery, which Rymond was reluctantly taking seriously.

'You've done this before,' he said to Brant, impressed by the youth's practised hand.

'My dad had a ram that lost its leg to a wolf. We only had two, and it fell to me to keep it healthy. Nearly kicked my face off a few times.'

From across the tent, previously the residence of the deceased Lord Clymore, Rymond's mother cackled. As if to taunt him, she was enjoying both a cup of wine and one of Rymond's smokesticks. 'The Sheep King. A fitting title, given the sense you showed trying to fight seven thousand men yourself.' She raised her hand, displaying the stub where a digit had been removed by the Imperium. 'Did you suppose it would impress people, to give an arm where I gave a finger?'

Rymond winced, holding back a cry as Brant applied the poultice to a particularly tender area. 'I'm glad you find the loss of my sword arm so amusing. Could you pretend to show a little sympathy? Do you understand how much this hurts?'

'Your birth took a day and a half. Do not speak to me of pain. Be glad it is only your arm.'

Rymond winced again. *Only the gods know why I brought her with me.* Although, what did the gods know? Rymond's record in battle against the Sangreals was better than theirs.

'But I will admit,' added his mother, 'I am relieved to see you awake.'

Rymond had been so weakened after losing his arm that he only vaguely recalled the battle between the gods. By the time Andrick Barrelbreaker's shade had appeared while Rymond cringed in the dirt he had been sure he was hallucinating. Most of the hours since Brant had found him he had been dosed up to his eyeballs on drowshroom. *Barrelbreaker.* His ruined arm spasmed, drawing another yelp. *Be glad he did not come for you.* Rymond had enough enemies among the living.

'Though I hope you do not think this changes anything,' Breta continued. 'I have counted our living, and the Sangreal dead. We still have the numbers to take Merivale.'

Rymond could only laugh. 'Mother, if you think the men will fight after what happened—'

'You are their *king*. It is for you to make them fight.'

Before Rymond could reply, the tent flap was pulled back, and Millas stuck his head in. 'Princess Helana's here, Majesty.'

Perhaps it was the aftereffects of the drowshroom and his mild yet lingering fever, but Rymond did not think Helana had ever looked more beautiful than standing at the entrance of the too-small tent, silhouetted by cool autumn sunlight. Her dark hair was tied back, she was garbed in hard-wearing leathers and battered mail like a Cylirien, and her nose was bulbous and red, but she smiled slightly, and Rymond felt the pain in his arm melt away like warm butter. 'Did you leave the safety of Merivale just for me? I'm flattered. What happened to your nose?'

'Something much less serious than whatever happened to your hand.'

Breta glanced up at Helana, scowling. 'Did you bring that treacherous Cylirien woman with you? The world should see how this family deals with traitors.' She looked at Rymond, her eyes like daggers. 'Seize her and sound the attack, while they are unprepared. You have waited—'

Rymond felt his temper rising. 'Mother—'

'I swear, if you mention the gods, I will clout you around the ear. Do you think the Sangreals will have regard to the appearance of these so-called gods when their bastard prince is grown and he rides into West Erland at the head of a reborn *Hymeriker*? You will lose more than your hand, I promise you. For once in your life—'

Rymond leapt to his feet. '*Mother*, for once in *your* life, be silent! Do you imagine I do not know what could happen if

Andrick Sangreal reaches manhood? I know! I know *better* than you what I stand to lose!' Rymond's stump throbbed, but he raised it and tore off the poultice for his mother to see, biting his cheek against the pain. 'I have lost my fucking *arm* for the sake of this pointless, centuries-old squabble over who gets to be king of this or that, and I swear if you ever try and tell me what is at stake I will send you to the Brides of Eryi!' Rymond's arm felt as if it were on fire, and with his remaining hand he grasped the back of his chair to stop himself buckling with the pain. He could feel the blood draining from his face as if he might faint. 'Now, get out,' he barely managed to say. 'All of you. I will speak with Helana alone.'

Breta Prindian had paled at the sight of the disfigured stump, and for a brief moment Rymond imagined he saw a tear form on a lower eyelash. 'I speak because I care,' she breathed. She rose, and crossed the tent to kiss Rymond on the cheek and grasp him by his good shoulder. 'I will never defy you, but nor will I stand by and watch your follies without a word. Do what you will, but what I will never be is *silent*, Rymond. Not where your life is concerned.' She swept from the tent, dragging Millas and their cupbearer along in her wake.

Rymond sank into his chair with a sigh. 'You as well, Brant,' he murmured. 'We'll replace the poultice later.'

'I'll do it,' said Helana. She looked at the stump and bravely suppressed a grimace. 'At least I'll try to.'

Rymond gave a weak smile. 'We can learn together.' He supposed he should be angry with her for turning the Cyliriens, but it did not seem to matter terribly now. He had brought that on himself.

Brant departed, and Helana lowered herself into the stool at Rymond's right hand.

'The Brides of Eryi have disbanded,' said Helana, as she began to prepare a second poultice. 'They've cast off their robes and fled, like they want to pretend their order never happened.'

'Their god was real though,' said Rymond. 'In that I give them more credit than nearly every other religion of the world. And better him than Vulgatypha.' Rymond would sooner have lost his other arm than stood before such malevolent power again.

'Better neither of them. Nobody can be trusted with that sort of power.'

'Not even a king?'

'Especially not a king. You've seen the mess kings make of things.'

'I didn't make a mess of everything,' said Rymond, unable to hide his indignance. 'I saved you, didn't I?'

'And you have me to thank for saving you and your mother, but unlike her at least I'm grateful.' Helana leant forward to kiss Rymond's cheek, and it coursed with fire, before immediately he let out a yelp as his stump was stricken with a cool, stinging sensation.

'Thought it might distract you,' said Helana, binding the poultice into place.

'What would distract me is a smokestick and a glass of wine,' said Rymond. He hesitated. *Eryi's balls, she's right that I've made a mess of everything else. I might as well get this part right.* A year earlier, and so much damage and pain would have been avoided. His beating heart was causing his stump to throb again. 'Either that, or your hand in marriage.'

'Bit late for that, isn't it?' Her tone was sharp, but Rymond could see the smirk Helana was trying to hide. 'I practically threw myself at you, you turned me down, and now you're an invalid. Suppose I want a husband with two hands?'

'That is why you're here though, isn't it?' said Rymond. 'I don't believe you crossed the field just to pass the time of day.'

Helana's lip gave a twist. 'Maybe. If I say yes, I want no more than two children. After that, you'll leave me alone if I ask.'

'Am I so hideous? Four, or more if there is only one boy.'

'Do you suppose we get to choose? What if I have nothing but girls? Three.'

'Three, rising to four if two or more of them are girls. Otherwise we'll have to stop my mother murdering you in your sleep.'

Helana nodded, seemingly satisfied. 'I can live with that. And you will supply me with all the hunting gear I require – horses, bows, servants, the lot.'

'Agreed, but no boars, not after last time.'

'It was you who got gored, not me.'

Helana touched his stump a little too firmly, and tears sprang to Rymond's eyes as he fought to silence his cry. 'Fine. And you'll do your utmost to keep your younger brother in check? Gifts, fond memories of your father, and the like?'

A small laugh escaped Helana's lips. 'Are you so afraid of an infant?'

'I am wary of the man he might become.'

Helana shrugged. 'If it's so important to you.'

She seemed to have finally finished with the poultice. Rymond began to pull his stunted arm away, but Helana seized his rolled-up sleeve to hold it in place while she finished, making Rymond wince again. 'We are agreed, then?' he said.

'What if I say no?'

'Then I will be forced to fall upon Merivale with all the strength available to me and bring the city to heel.' He kept his tone light; he did not have the spirit to try and make her believe he was serious. 'Some accident will befall your half-brother, and I will weep genuinely at the misfortune of it all, and claim that I meant for him to be sent into honourable exile with generous terms for his good behaviour. Your cousins and some lords will mutter, but my reign will be secure, until such time as someone has the wherewithal to assassinate me.'

Helana was smiling, shaking her head as she put the

finishing touches to the poultice. 'You'll have to try harder to convince me you're that sort of monster, I'm afraid.'

'I am astonished.' Rymond found he was smiling also. It was possible he needed Helana more than he had imagined – he could not face his mountainous debts and the likes of Rostar Darlton alone. 'Do you suppose I am a good man?'

'Not a good man, but a better man than some.'

Not a good man, but a better man than some. 'On such feeble truths are kingdoms founded.'

'Kingdoms, and marriages.'

'You'll do it then.'

Helana stopped, and for a moment Rymond detected just a hint of regret in the slight drop of her eyelashes. 'Just swear to me that you'll never try to put me in a cage. I will not be merely your blood shield against my brother, nor just a wife and mother. I demand an army of servants, so that I am free to do as I please and am never required to speak to my children until they are old enough to have an original thought.'

'By all the gods, I could not agree more.'

And, believing they had finally run out of things to say, Rymond reached out his hand to Helana's cheek, and bent to kiss her.

CHAPTER 44

Sunlight slanted through the window like spears from the heavens. It was open slightly, and a cool autumn breeze brushed against Pherri's face and tickled at her skin. Her eyelids fluttered reluctantly against the daylight.

She had been dreaming. A true dream, not *prophika*. Da'ri had been there, and Theodric, and Phyrrai, though what they had been doing Pherri could not recall. It had been peaceful though, so peaceful she had not wanted to return.

Her body felt corpse gaunt beneath the mountain of furs they had piled on top of her. Knowing it was a bad idea, Pherri reached for the thinnest sprinkling of magic, drawing on her will and her own life force to try and move one of them, just a fraction of an inch.

Nothing stirred. She felt nothing but a reminiscent hum where the air touched her fingertips. Pherri smiled. She had told Aimya of her suspicions, and while she felt relief there was also a vestige of sadness. It might have been nice, to try and learn again, without the twin threats of Eryi and Vulgatypha polluting the joy of study. For a time, she had been a magus, and now she was only a girl again.

'Are you awake?'

The voice from the end of the bed tugged at Pherri's awareness. Slowly, she shifted, and opened her eyes.

It was Orsian. A little worse for wear, with bandages around his torso and shoulder visible beneath a loose tunic, but unmistakably her brother. Smiling, Pherri pushed herself up into a seated position, struggling against the weight of the furs. 'Orsian.' Her voice came out in a croak, and she reached for the jug of water on the nightstand and drank hungrily from it. 'Should you be up?' The last time she had seen Orsian, they had been collapsed together at the bottom of Hessian's stairs in a pool of Orsian's blood, each of them barely within the bounds of consciousness. It would have been a cruel irony for them to die in one another's arms after being apart for so long.

He moved his lips in a way that was somewhere between a smile and a grimace. 'The healer was reluctant, but Gruenla badgered him into letting me. I'd have gone mad spending another minute wrapped up in furs being poked and prodded like a pincushion.'

'Gruenla?'

'Some Cylirien of Helana's. Said she was sent to look after me, though her idea of care was mostly telling me that there are men with far worse injuries than me and I should stop being so lazy.' He moved to sit, and as he lowered himself into a chair Pherri noted how stiffly he held himself. 'In my defence though, none of them got stabbed by a god.'

The mention of Eryi hung between them like a cloud of smoke. Pherri sighed. 'I suppose you have questions.' She felt anticipatory exhaustion at the thought of answering them again. In her brief hours of wakefulness over the last few days, she had told most of it to Aimya, from beginning to end, from her journey with Theodric to her first encounter with Eryi and from her arrival in the other Erland to the Sorrowseer and then the confrontation between Vulgatypha and Eryi on the tower.

Orsian shrugged, then winced at the tug in this shoulder. 'Aimya's told me most of it. It will keep until you're stronger.'

Pherri hoped she would feel strong enough at some point. She suddenly realised she was starving. 'Is there any food?' she asked. 'I think I'm ready for something other than honey.'

'I'll fetch some,' said Orsian. 'The servants won't come near you; easier if I get it myself.'

'Have someone else do it,' said Pherri. 'Don't pull out your stitches.' But he was already making for the door. 'Orsian, wait.'

Her brother turned back a few feet from the bed. 'Don't you want to talk about—?'

Orsian frowned. 'I told you – it will keep until you're better.'

'I didn't mean about that.' Pherri hesitated. 'Who was that girl—?'

'That will keep as well,' said Orsian brusquely. 'She's gone. That's all there is to say.' He turned to leave again.

'What was her name?'

But Orsian was already at the door. 'I'll be back with food.' He opened it and left as if he were being pursued by fire.

Pherri stared after him. *Perhaps it is not only the servants who are scared of me.* Less than a year ago, she and Orsian had been as close as twins, for all the differences that divided them, yet speaking with him today had been like the awkward encounter of two strangers.

Maybe we are strangers now. Pherri sighed, then threw off her covers and sat at the edge of the bed facing the window. Outside, she could hear the bustle of the keep. It was quieter than before, and also further away, as if Pherri heard it through a veil of fog.

What is left for me here? Pherri asked herself, holding back the tears. She and Orsian ought to have spoken of their family; they had not even seen each other since their father's death – the first one, not the strange shade that made Pherri shiver to think of – and now Errian and their mother were gone as well. He had been the one person she thought might understand. But Orsian had fought his own battles, with his own private losses, and now could not even speak of them.

I am not a magus any more. I am not even a daughter. Barely a sister. In the new world after the gods, it should have been possible to be whatever she wanted to be, but what was that? Who was she?

It made her long for Phyrrai. Her shadowtwin would have understood, perhaps. She wondered if she would make it back from Pipersmont to her own Erland, and what might await her there.

Perhaps Pherri's own journey would be just as arduous. Because after one had slain a god, saved the world, and lost their magic, where was there to go?

Orsian escaped the room before the tears began to fall. He found an alcove and sank to his knees, holding his hands to his face to stifle the great wracking sobs that seemed to emanate from deep in his gut.

After everything, seeing Pherri lying there, his clever sister who he had thought might be lost forever, had been too much, with her sunken eyes that were too old for her and the gaunt cheeks of an invalid and the dry, thinning hair of a corpse.

When she spoke, she seemed fine, almost so detached from the cares of mortals that grief and pain did not touch her. But how could she be fine? Orsian wasn't, and he had not been through half what Pherri had been through.

'Damn you, Errian,' he whispered. He thought of Errian because he could not bring himself to think of Tansa. He could have stayed with her in Cliffark, where he might have been happy, and Tansa would still be alive, but that would have required Orsian resisting the twin lures of family and Erland, loyalties he could not shake, not even for her. Now though, it was as if something within him had cracked with his brother's death, as if the instinctive drive that pushed him to act had crumbled. Had he truly defined himself so profoundly by the brother he had thought he hated?

Errian should have been the Lord of Violet Hall. As a boy, Orsian had been so bitter and jealous that he had strived to be the better son, the dutiful warrior, his own father in miniature.

And now... he saw what that was worth. He did not want Violet Hall, and his father's shade had not even noticed him. If Andrick Barrelbreaker watched Orsian's deeds from the life beyond and cared enough to feel pride or shame, he had hidden it well.

He glanced down at his waist, where for so long a sword had always been buckled. *I am done with war.* Sangreal or Prindian, he no longer cared. He would do his duty to Violet Hall and to Pherri, but otherwise—

'Orsian?'

Orsian hurried to his feet, turning away towards the alcove as he did so to wipe his tears, and when he looked back found himself staring into the green eyes of Helana.

Her hair was thicker than it had been, and her frame thinner, with the bright defiance that had always burnt in her eyes slightly diminished, but she was still as beautiful as the last day he had seen her, when she had fled from Piperskeep and Hessian's threats of marriage. And yet, Orsian's heart beat no faster, and his tongue did not suddenly feel too large for his mouth. It had been only a year before, yet his supposed love for Helana seemed to belong to another time and place, a time of innocence, before loss and defeat and magic and gods. Before Tansa.

'Helana.' He wiped his nose and sniffed. 'You look well.'

His cousin laughed, and the sound was like music to Orsian's ears. 'Is that all you have to say after all this time, after

I've come looking for you? By the accursed gods, Orsian, come here.' She spread her arms, and he almost fell forward into them, and though he now stood several inches taller than her he buried his face against her shoulder, the tears flowing freely once more.

'I'm sorry,' he managed to say through his sobs. He pulled back and wiped his nose again. 'Not sure what's wrong with me.'

Helana smiled and cupped his cheek, staring into his face with soft eyes. 'Aren't you? I'd hope we've all shed a few tears by now.'

'I can't.' Orsian straightened up, feeling foolish but getting his sobbing under control. 'I'll rip my stitches.' He coughed. It was strange to see Helana in Piperskeep again, after all this time. 'Did the Prindians release you?'

'In a sense.' There was a brittle melancholia in Helana's smile. 'I have negotiated a peace with Rymond Prindian.'

'A peace?' A weight seemed to lift in Orsian's gut, and he felt his face brighten with relief. 'At what price?' Though even as he asked, he knew the answer.

'Breta Prindian called it the eternal price of peace – marriage.' She sighed. 'I am not unhappy. You may not want to hear this, but he is a good man, and he swears he had no part in your father's death. For the sake of peace, I will stomach it.'

'For the sake of peace, I will believe you.' *He can be no worse than Hessian.* Hating the Prindians seemed a foolish, childish thing now. 'How do Ciera and Breta Prindian feel about this?'

Helana shrugged. 'They stare at one another from behind their masks and plot. I am not so naïve as to believe peace can last forever, but I will take a lifetime.' She paused. 'Perhaps with your guidance, Andrick Sangreal can grow to be a better man than his father.' She made a face as if she had just imbibed vinegar. 'My brother, the king. It seems strange that I should have a brother who is still at the breast.'

Orsian smiled sadly. 'I fear I am not sure what guidance I can offer him. I don't know how to rule a kingdom; I'll barely manage Violet Hall. Errian—'

Helana pressed a finger to Orsian's lips. 'If I can marry for peace, you can ride to Piperskeep once in a while and teach my little brother how not to turn into his father.' She looked at him sternly, daring him to disagree. 'Because if not you, then who? Peace is worth fighting for, Orsian. A better world for our children is worth fighting for.'

Children. The word sounded foreign in Orsian's head. *I will never have children.* But he could not let Helana down. *Pherri. Violet Hall. Peace.* Those were things worth living for. 'I think I can do that.'

'See that you do.' Helana beamed. 'The wedding will be in two days. If you can get yourself recovered in time I'll save a dance for you.'

CHAPTER 45

'Should I pin the sleeve up, Majesty?'

Rymond glanced down from adjusting his hair in the mirror to where Brant was fussing at his sleeve, already trying different rolling and folding techniques to give his tunic a shape over the stump at Rymond's elbow.

'Or, we could stuff the bottom half with something? Maybe if I—'

'Brant, no amount of fiddling with the sleeve is going to make people forget that half my arm is missing. Just leave it loose.'

Brant dropped his eyes. 'Of course, Majesty.' He turned away to fetch a sword belt, adjusted so that Rymond could draw it with his left hand, in theory if not in practice. His swordwork had finally been beginning to improve as well.

Rymond closed his eyes with a deep breath. 'I'm sorry, Brant. Still getting used to it. Do the rest and I'll think about it.'

He wondered whether Helana would be more pleased to see her husband with a pinned elbow or an empty sleeve. It was a ridiculous question. For all else that might be said of his bride, Helana was not the sort who would care. He was half-tempted to ask Brant to remove the sleeve entirely and let the world gape.

Rymond scratched at his collar. There would have been no harm in it; these were not garments he was likely to wear again. In the feverish appetite to get this wedding over with so West and East Erland could attend to more important matters, green thread had been sourced within Merivale, coarse and uncomfortable. Poor fare for a king, but that was fitting in the circumstances. Cheap thread, for a broken king, in a ruined castle that did not belong to him.

When their deal had been made, he had not wholly appreciated the significance of Ciera's demand that he wed Helana in the ruined hall of Piperskeep. Regardless of his kingship, it sent a message that Sangreal dominance was undisturbed.

He ought to have given more regard to the girl. Might have done, had he not been still wracked with agony from his inflamed stump. West Erland's independence was secure, but after negotiating the full peace treaty with Ciera it had cost him far more than it ought to, cancelling out Helana's bride portion. Gold, stone, masons, grain... All would be diverted from his lands to help the rebuild of Merivale, in addition to a tenth of his yields to be tapered off over the next ten years.

Rymond sighed, as Brant continued to struggle with the adjusted sword belt. All he could do was live with it, and prepare for the next war, whenever that may be. West and East Erland could not remain divided for long. He would need to sire an heir swiftly, before the boy Andrick got too far ahead in age. Rymond did not see himself ever leading an army in the field again. He had time to prepare; Ciera would not move against him before Merivale was rebuilt, and that might take years. The crucial point was that he had Sangreal recognition that West Erland belonged in perpetuity to the Prindians. He could rule as he pleased, with the same rights as his ancestors before him and freedom for his people. The amounts he still owed his lords in recompense for the Imperial occupation was unfortunate, but he hoped to settle with most of them in exchange for land.

He looked down again at Brant. He was a brave and resourceful young man, but he would never make a servant. 'Just leave the sword, Brant. The world knows I can't use it anyway.'

'Do *not* leave it,' came a voice from the door. 'Crippled or not, kings wear swords.'

Rymond sighed. He had not even heard his mother enter. 'As you please, Mother.' He met her eye in the mirror. Imprisonment had diminished her – her hair was beginning to grey, and she was not so sprightly as she had once been – but he could admit she was still an imposing and beautiful woman. 'Enjoying the festivities?'

'What passes for festivities. It's a meagre wedding that girl has laid on for us.'

Rymond could not help but smile at his mother's frankness. 'Generous in the circumstances. They'll be clearing rubble from the hall right up until Helana enters.'

'All the more reason we should have pressed our advantage. East Erland could have been yours. Be sure you remember that when I'm dead and that Sangreal brat crosses the Pale River.'

It was all very typical of his mother. They had almost witnessed the end of the world, and now on her son's wedding day her primary concern was how they might have turned that to their advantage. 'I secured West Erland's full independence, without further bloodshed. I will take that as a victory.'

'For now.' Breta moved towards where Rymond was standing in front of the long mirror, scrutinising him up and down while Brant knelt to polish Rymond's boots. She sniffed. 'And when war comes again, whose side do you suppose your wife will take? I do not trust her.'

'I thought you liked her?'

'That is not the same thing.'

'We have an agreement.' He lifted his hand, marking the points off one by one by raising his fingers. 'Peace, heirs, her freedom, her faithfulness.' Rymond met his mother's eye. 'A fair agreement.'

'A fool's agreement. Your deal with the Istlewick girl and marriage to Helana Sangreal will not settle the future of Erland.'

'I know that.'

But it would do for now.

Most of the rubble had been cleared from the central areas of Piperskeep's hall, but chunks of masonry still littered the edges, and overhead large patches of blue sky were visible past the jagged ruins of the vaulted ceiling. The masons had assured Ciera that the structure was stable, but she could not help glancing anxiously upward at every breath of wind that howled past.

Chairs now filled with guests had been laid out in rows across the useable breadth of the hall, with an aisle left down the middle. Few of the seats matched – Hessian had preferred to make his audiences stand, and they had needed to be sourced from all over the keep – but that was a trifle in the circumstances. Ciera had acquiesced to the Prindian request that the tapestries of great Sangreal deeds be removed – they could do nothing about the vast panes of stained glass displaying the same – but she had lined the hall with the *hymerikai* in their place. The remaining ones at least, plus several young boys who had hastily given their oaths to their swaddled king. It might take years to restore East Erland to its former military strength.

Ciera closed her eyes for a moment. Even on this day, she could not escape the enormity of the task that awaited her. East

Erland would be reformed root-and-branch, with taxes that encouraged hard work and allowed men to prosper, a new generation of *hymerikai*, and a radical system of government where decisions did not rest in the hands of just one man. In a few years, with sufficient strength and support behind her, she could then restore Cliffark's status as a true part of East Erland, and one day perhaps retake West Erland as well. Rymond's kingdom was already drowning in debts, and while he was looking backwards seeking inspiration from his ancestors and preparing to rule like a domineering king of old, Ciera was looking forward, to the country Erland could one day become.

In her arms, Andrick grizzled in his sleep, but settled. Ciera looked down at him and smiled. *I am doing this for you*. By the time her son was ready to rule in his own name, East Erland would be the clear power in the region.

She looked to the dais, where Rymond Prindian awaited his bride, smiling and whispering with his servant and the rakish Lord Darlton. For all his follies, Prindian had a gift for earning men's trust; she could not afford to underestimate him. Her eyes were drawn to where his right sleeve had been pinned. At least he was unlikely to lead men to war again any time soon. She could afford to be patient, to allow Andrick time to grow to manhood. When the time came, he could choose whether and when to retake West Erland.

Ciera felt someone's eyes on her, and turned her head to see Breta Prindian regarding her from across the aisle. It would have been hard to miss her, probably the most richly dressed person in the hall. Ciera flashed her a smile, which the Prindian woman returned.

By the brittleness of it, she could tell that the Prindian matriarch knew that Ciera had got the best of her negotiations with Rymond, with promises of aid and coin extracted in exchange for very little. East Erland lacked the strength to retake West Erland, for now – Breta might even suspect how they would have struggled to hold Merivale had the depleted West Erlanders attacked rather than seeking peace. To Ciera, it was the first proof that she was the right person to rule Erland, the only one with the vision to fulfil the country's potential.

Ciera looked around those seated and felt a moment of shame for the way her mind was whirring. Those she ruled had no interest in fighting the Prindians again; after losing so many and seeing the sky lit up by a conflict between gods, the division of West and East Erland would matter little to them. She scanned the sea of faces: Haisie, seated next to her smiling down at Andrick, who might now have a childhood free from war; bold Burik, standing against the opposite wall, the last of Naeem's brood of warriors, who might now marry a Merivale woman and breed his own strong sons; Sister Aimya, on the dais awaiting her role in the marriage ceremony, free to choose her own path instead of giving her life to a supposed god who cared nothing for her; Orsian and Pherri, sitting together in the row behind Ciera, their drawn expressions revealing nothing except that they had given all they had, and lost everything and everyone they loved. Ciera knew that time would be a healer for them, just as it had been for her. So many young faces, free to forge the path and the country that they desired.

Nevertheless, Ciera would do her duty. *Hope for peace, but prepare for war.*

Helana's chamber seemed smaller now than when she had left almost a year ago. Perhaps everywhere would now, after life among the Thrumb in their open, airy forests, and all those weeks travelling with Rymond and his motley band of insurgents. The walls that had once been her home seemed to close in around her, bricking her in stone by stone.

Enough of that, she scolded herself. It was not the walls she feared, but marriage.

Her eyes flicked to her mother's portrait, a beautiful woman with Helana's long dark hair. A woman Helana would never know.

Were you afraid? It was hard to imagine a woman loving Hessian. The few times Helana had dared to ask her father for his memories of her mother, his rage had been cataclysmic. What were Helana's fears compared to what her mother might have felt? She did not love Rymond, but he understood her in his way. Love might come, in time. They had shared interests in hunting and gaming. And it would bring peace to Erland, exactly what she had set out to do when she had left the previous winter. She had got to where she had hoped to, in a roundabout way, several thousand corpses and two beaten gods later.

'You look like you're chewing a wasp, Princess.' Creya was seated at the table, over a large cup of wine. 'If you don't want to go through with it, I can get us out through the forest.'

Helana smiled. She had missed the plain-speaking huntswoman. It had seemed appropriate to have Creya here with her, since she had been the one to travel with her when Helana had first begun her journey. 'I gave the queen my word unfortunately. And I do want to, or at least I don't *not* want to.'

Creya shrugged and made a face. 'Suit yourself. At least you shouldn't have to worry about a one-armed man striking you.'

Helana laughed. 'He'd regret it.'

'Yarl hit me once. Just the once though, I made sure of that.' With a sigh, Creya took a long sip of wine. 'I still miss him though, lazy, silent sack of shit that he was.'

Creya's husband Yarl and two of her sons had died during the Imperial assault on Merivale. Her eldest son, Yarl the Younger, had followed not long after when a wound had putrefied. Helana had got all four of them places in the Merivale

Watch to save them from war, but in Erland it seemed war had a way of finding a man anyway. Creya had batted away Helana's attempts to commiserate with her – '*I said goodbye when I burnt them – what's done is done.*'

Helana felt suddenly morose. Would things have been different if she had married Rymond a year ago? Andrick might still be alive, and Creya's husband and sons. But then, her uncle would never have returned from death to save them from Vulgatypha. A person could drive themselves to madness thinking about such possibilities. If Pherri told it true, there would be many worlds where Yarl and his sons were still alive, perhaps even the one she had seen in a casheef vision, with Andrick, Viratia, Errian, Jarhick, Theodric, and all the rest. She might even have liked to see Hessian one last time.

She steeled herself, focusing on the here and now. 'It will be fine,' she said, to herself as much as to Creya. 'We'll hunt and drink and laugh, and I'll pop out some babies. Once Rymond's got a few heirs maybe I'll travel, see the world, cut my hair and stow away on a ship.' She might even take casheef again, see if any magic at all lingered in the world since Vulgatypha's death. Pherri seemed sure it was all gone, but who knew really?

'The world's overrated, Princess. Give me the forest over the world any day.'

Helana smiled. As a queen she might make her kingdom as she wanted it to be, as Ciera seemed to be preparing herself to do. Rymond would never manage it himself. He needed her.

She finished her cup of wine in one. 'I'm ready.'

Helana rose, gathered up the many skirts of her lavish crimson dress, and headed for the hall.

From his chair on the aisle, Orsian kept his eyes forward, fixed on a point somewhere above Rymond's head. The young king stood waiting patiently for his bride. Facing Rymond was Sister Aimya – just Aimya now, he supposed; an Eryian ceremony had been quite out of the question, but Ciera had said that *someone* had to administer matters, and a former sister of the Brides of Eryi seemed as good a candidate as any. Women, even brides, had never been allowed to marry couples before; to allow a former sister to do it had been thought a compromise between the old ways and the new. And of course, had one of the old Eryian priests shown their face they might not have liked the welcome they received. Ciera had told Orsian privately that she was already drawing up plans to pension them off and seize their churches. Orsian had never seen the point of priests anyway.

If he did not catch anybody's eye, he would not have to speak with them. The curious glances on him and Pherri prickled at his skin; once the feast was brought out and the wine had been served, he was sure people's courage would rise to match their curiosity and compel them to engage him and Pherri in conversation. Orsian meant to be well away by then; he had no interest in their congratulations or their questions, and even less in the condolences of the few who might know what Tansa had been to him.

He had resolved to return her body to Cliffark for burning, until Pherri had pointed out that the old ways were not important; they had glimpsed the secrets of the dead, and there appeared to be no great feast above the clouds waiting for them. Orsian had burnt her all the same, privately in the woods, stopping only to slice away a lock of her hair with his knife. He touched the locket under his tunic, remembering the brief taste of freedom he had known with her, their weeks in Cliffark, all the laughing, teasing, and kissing which not even the jealous presence of Cag could spoil, before Orsian had got it into his head that he had to return to Merivale. He had been true to who he was, and yet he could not shake the regret.

He felt the pressure of Pherri's hand against his, and looked down to his sister. She was still small, but there was a tired wisdom in her blue eyes that aged her far beyond her twelve years. It was hardly a surprise.

'Are you well?' she asked.

'Fine,' said Orsian hoarsely. 'As it goes.'

Pherri gave a weary smile and squeezed his hand again. Orsian returned his gaze to the stained glass above Sister Aimya and Rymond. It felt a long time ago he had regarded the Prindians as his enemy, when all that had occupied him had been proving his worth and winning favour with his father and King Hessian. When he looked at Rymond now he saw a young man a little like himself, struggling against the weight of expectation. He did not believe Rymond lusted for power as Hessian had, nor that he truly wanted to marry Helana, but he would do his duty.

His eyes flickered momentarily from Ciera to Breta Prindian. Hessian's widow was smiling, looking down at her son and speaking quietly with Haisie, the young servant girl at her side, while Breta Prindian chatted amiably with Princess Tarvana, who seemed not to mind in the least that her husband, Lord Balyard, was dead. Both Ciera and Breta were mother to a king, and both were trying to disguise the way their eyes slid to one another, but Orsian saw them. It was as though they each half-suspected the other would try something, on the day of the marriage that was supposed to bring the two kingdoms to peace. Orsian's nose creased in disgust.

At the back of the hall, the band began to play. It had been a struggle to find musicians; they had a piper, a tambourine player, and a fiddler with two strings missing. Their music bore a vague resemblance to a pleasant tune, if one did not listen too carefully, and every eye in the hall turned as Helana entered. Her hair had been coiffed and pinned, and she wore a long dress of Sangreal scarlet, cinched at the waist, with a silver shawl covering her shoulders. Gasps rose from the congregation as Helana made her way down the aisle, smiling in a way that was most unlike herself. Orsian too thought she looked very beautiful, but his palms did not break out in a sweat as they once might have done. He smiled at Helana as she passed, and she gave him a friendly wink.

I did not love her. He touched the locket over his clothes, suddenly cold against his chest. The girl he loved was gone. At his side, Pherri squeezed his hand again.

Orsian barely heard Aimya's address. It had all the rhythms of what a priest might have said, and none of the piety. Regard was given to the strange circumstances, with hope that this day might mark a new chapter in Erland's history, free of the horrors of war, the tyranny of the Imperium, and the madness of gods. Some vague exhortations for Rymond and Helana to love and cherish one another, and to rule West Erland together fairly and justly. Hopes for a new age of peace and prosperity.

And just like that, it was done. Rymond placed a ring garnished with a huge emerald of Prindian green upon Helana's finger, and Orsian jolted upright as the crowd began clapping and Rymond placed a chaste kiss on Helana's lips. The band began to play again, and the couple who represented a new hope for Erland began making their way hand in hand back down the aisle, as six noble girls younger than Pherri bearing baskets followed them, throwing rose petals over the newly-weds. Orsian was surprised to see Esma among them, recently adopted by the family of some lord or other.

Perhaps that is one thing we can be proud of. An East Erland ruled by Ciera might give a chance to children like Esma and Pitt. Or not.

As the couple left the hall – they would re-enter shortly – the servants leapt into action. Anxious stewards ushered guests out of the way as chairs were rearranged and long tables brought forth.

'I liked what Aimya said about the future,' said Pherri as they rose, allowing a servant to pull their chairs away. 'It gave me hope.' His sister seldom smiled any more. After all they had been through, Orsian never felt sure what to say to her. She was not the same girl he had known before their father's death. 'Will you stay in Merivale, or return to Violet Hall?'

Orsian had barely thought of Violet Hall. It was his now, but it did not feel like it. Violet Hall had been meant for Errian. Orsian smiled ruefully at the memory of his brother. If not for Errian, he would be dead. It was one of the few good recollections he had of him, his brother raging against all the power of Eryi and Krupal with no more than the sword in his hand, yet it was the one that mattered the most. The one he would strive to remember him by. 'Are those the only options?'

Pherri chewed at her lip, a familiar gesture that warmed Orsian's heart. 'I just thought it would be one or the other.'

Orsian paused to take two cups of wine from a servant, still resolutely not meeting anyone's gaze. 'Where would you like to go?' he asked, handing Pherri the cup.

Pherri paused thoughtfully. 'I don't know.'

Orsian sighed. That was the problem. Neither of them had any clue how to navigate this new world. He would be expected to be Lord of Violet Hall, or take some other role at Ciera's behest, and Pherri... What did the future hold for Pherri? She could not be a magus any more. He supposed he would be expected to find a husband for her, but he did not see that in Pherri's future. She could stay at Violet Hall for as long as she liked.

Pherri's eyes flicked behind Orsian, and he turned to see Ciera. He dropped into a bow. 'Majesty.'

She smiled, raising a cup of wine. 'To Rymond and Helana.'

Orsian and Pherri repeated the words back to her. They touched their cups together and drank.

'Orsian,' said Ciera, barely after her cup had left her mouth.

'Or Lord Orsian, I suppose. I was hoping we might speak privately.'

Orsian sighed. He had a rather good idea of what was coming. 'Pherri, could you leave us for a while?'

Pherri obediently wandered off, and Orsian smiled to see her being beckoned to join Haisie and the girthy youngest son of the late Lord Gurathet – the older one – perhaps slightly older than the two girls. Somewhere along the way of the war, the invasion, and the battle with the gods, the old social order seemed to have dissolved before their eyes. Or perhaps it was just the wedding.

He looked back to Ciera, who began. 'I wanted to ask you—'

'You want me to be your son's *balhymeri*.'

Ciera smiled knowingly. 'I checked, and you'll be the youngest ever. So, you'll do it?'

Orsian glanced at Breta Prindian over Ciera's left shoulder. She was not watching them, but he felt sure she was aware the two of them were speaking. 'What do you need a *balhymeri* for? I thought today was about bringing peace?'

Ciera's smile faltered slightly. 'Come on, Orsian. We don't know what the future will bring.' She dropped her voice and moved closer. 'We don't know what Rymond and his mother have planned, or if the Imperium might come again, or who knows what else might happen.' She glanced about, seemingly mentally ticking off the West Erlanders and their allies. 'I don't trust them.'

Orsian let out a low sigh. *And so it starts again*. Perhaps paranoia was a natural part of power. Against the wall, he saw Burik laughing with a gaggle of young *hymerikai*. Their eyes met, and Burik raised a cup in Orsian's direction, who returned the gesture with a smile.

He returned his gaze to Ciera, who was looking up at him expectantly. Orsian took a breath. 'Give it to Burik,' he said.

'He's been through a lot for you. He's earnt it. His father should have been *balhymeri* after mine.'

Ciera's eyes narrowed. 'I won't ask again, Orsian. It's now or never.'

Orsian nodded. 'I choose never.'

She left him without another word, and Orsian moved to his place at the table on the dais, glad it was nowhere near Ciera's. The festivities continued, with much toasting and dancing and loud drunkenness, but Orsian was in the mood for none of it. Once he had eaten, he seized a flagon of wine and disappeared.

After the meal, Pherri moved tables to join a peculiar mixture of children her own age. Haisie, Ciera's servant; Elgin Gurathet and Willam Storaut, two boys of around eleven, one fleshy and one skinny; and Pitt and Esma, two orphans her brother had brought from Cliffark.

The boys had snagged a jar of whisky from somewhere, and were passing it back and forth under the table, gagging on their occasional sips. Pherri was content with wine; she had never really been one for the company of other children – other than Phyrrai – but the drink warmed her, and made her feel more at ease with the others.

'What was it like doing magic?' asked Elgin, leaning over the table towards her. 'You know people are scared of you? My brother says—'

'No one gives a pig's fart what your brother thinks,' said Esma, glaring at him. 'Leave her alone. I'm not scared of her, and Pherri doesn't have to talk about it if she doesn't want to.'

Pherri placed a grateful hand on the younger girl's arm. 'It's fine.' It made sense people would fear her. And if they could not understand how she had done magic, they would equally not be able to understand that she could not do it any longer. She paused, thinking. 'Do you like swords?'

'He does, but I'm better,' drawled Willam.

'I'd be better than both of you,' declared Pitt. 'I'll be the first of us to be a *hymerika*. When I—'

'Will not!' said Elgin. 'My father—'

Several shouted interruptions later, the three boys were rolling together under the table, where they were soon joined by a pair of excited hounds eager to join in. Pherri looked around for an adult who might separate them, but nobody seemed terribly troubled. A little way away, Lady Gough was dancing with Chieftain Arka, both swaying drunkenly with cups of wine in their fists. At the next table, Gruenla of Cylirien was playing a drinking game with Rucius the Ulvatian, Burik, and several other *hymerikai*, all laughing away. Further down, Lord Urwen Storaut was snoring with his head on the table.

'Let's just leave them.' Haisie picked up the whisky and sniffed at it, then made a face and put it down. 'They can have that.'

Pherri skipped happily away with Esma and Haisie, feeling joy in their easy camaraderie. She would have gladly explained magic to Elgin, but in truth it was nothing like a sword. Using magic was feeling you could shape the world and everything in it to your whims, with the only limits being your talent, capacity, and conscience. It was the latter of those that Eryi had lacked, the natural bonds that might otherwise have given him an affinity with people eroded over millennia of isolation. Pherri had longed for magic in the other world, needed it, but now with Vulgatypha gone all she felt was relief. Magic was too much for anyone to wield safely, too easy for it to allow you to think of yourself as *different*, or worse *better*. Life was simpler without it.

'The queen says they're bringing dessert out soon,' said Haisie excitedly, as the three of them raced down the benches, sampling food from discarded plates and sniffing unattended drinks before deciding whether to try them.

'Let's go to the kitchens and get the first pieces!' said Esma, thrusting fresh cups of sweet wine into the others' hands.

Pherri was about to reply, but over Esma's shoulder she saw Orsian disappearing through a door and up a set of stairs, grasping a flagon.

She frowned. Her brother was much changed in their time apart. He had always been serious, but now he seemed permanently detached from everything, as if his only desire was for the world to leave him alone. Pherri grieved both Errian and their mother, but she had never been close to her eldest brother, and she had felt the depth of their mother's love for them in the moment before their father dragged her beyond the veil into death. Orsian, Pherri suspected, had never really recovered from their father's death, then had seen Errian die just as it sounded as if her brothers might have been ready to set their differences aside. He had lost their mother as well, without the comforting touch of her soul Pherri had felt through her magic.

And then there was this girl, Tansa, whose name he would not even speak. Perhaps he grieved her most of all, for the future they might have had together.

'I'll come and find you later,' said Pherri to Esma and Haisie. She ran after Orsian, waving goodbye to them both.

She climbed the stairs, seizing a cloak as she passed, and found her brother on a balcony, gazing west. The first snowflakes of winter were beginning to fall, and she shivered and pulled the cloak tighter around herself against the cold.

'I saw you leave,' she said, approaching the balcony to stand beside him. 'Thought you might want to talk.'

Orsian smiled reluctantly, but he did not look at her. His lips were stained with wine, and his hair was dishevelled. 'Probably drunk enough to talk now.' He hiccoughed and covered it with a swig of wine. 'I'll go back to Violet Hall in a few days. Much to put right probably.' He paused. 'Are you coming?'

'I didn't mean about that. Don't you want to...' Pherri fumbled for the right words. 'You've not spoken about any of them – Father, Mother, Errian, or Tansa.'

'I did Father proud.' His voice faltered slightly, and a tear ran from the corner of his eye. 'I think. I... We... Well... *You* saved Erland. I did my bit though. Errian did too. I'm proud he was my brother. He died the way he lived, with a snarl on his face and a sword in his hand. Mother... by Er— by the gods or whoever, I don't even understand what happened; maybe you can tell me. But she's with Father now. That's what she'd have wanted.'

He swallowed another measure of wine. 'Tansa...' He shrugged. 'What's there to say? I loved her, probably always will, but she'd have wanted her death to mean something.' He gestured vaguely in the direction of the hall. 'Then I see Ciera and Breta Prindian down there plotting, wondering when the next war will come, just Rymond and Helana's marriage maybe holding the whole peace together by a thread... makes me wonder what it was all for. Maybe we're all just as capable of killing ourselves as Eryi and Vulgatypha. Maybe none of it mattered.' He sighed heavily, and hung his head. 'Fighting's cost me everything. I don't want to do it any more. Just not sure anyone else has learnt the same lesson.'

Pherri reached out and gripped her brother's hand. 'So stand for peace then. You're a *lord* now, Orsian, and a hero. Maybe you can change things.'

He looked down at her. 'Maybe. But if I'm a hero, what are you? Reckon you've got more sway than I have.'

Pherri smiled, glad to see her brother hopeful, if only for a moment. 'We'll do it together then. Better two peaceful kingdoms than one at war with itself.'

Orsian raised his flagon. 'I'll drink to that.'

Pherri touched her cup to his, and they both drank.

They stood in silence, watching the snow fall over Merivale and the plains that stretched all the way to Violet Hall. To their right, the south-western face of the Mountain was silhouetted against the inky sky. Neither of them spared even a glance for it.

EPILOGUE

SIXTEEN YEARS LATER...

The sky was a cloudless eggshell-blue, as idyllic as only a summer sky can be. In the garden atop Piperskeep's highest tower, crimson flowers shone in bright yellow sunlight. Far below, smoke from the kitchens wafted upward on the breeze, together with snatches of shouting and clashing steel from *hymerikai* training in the yard. Merivale spread out below like a miniature town sculpted in intimate detail, rows of rooftiles, streets paved with new cobbles, and a bustling market.

For King Andrick Sangreal, it was a rare moment of tranquillity. He was seated on the bench at the garden's centre with his eyes closed, letting the wind ruffle his long golden locks while he listened to the flowers and the gentle whispers of their trembling petals. Even up here though, he could not wholly escape the world below. The clamour of warriors was the nearest disturbance, but further afield he could hear the commotion of half a hundred different trades, and shouting from the market that had risen on the site of the old Sanctuary of the Brides of Eryi. The temple had been pulled down, its stone used to build new homes to replace the hovels that had once leant against the city walls. Another one of his mother's many triumphs.

With a sigh, Andrick opened his eyes. He might have been content had it been only the noise of the city, but growing up in Piperskeep the singing steel and manly banter of the *Hymeriker* were as inescapable to him as they were unwelcome.

Ascending footsteps reached him from the stairs. He turned in time to see Haisie, his mother's maid, rising into view. She was a decade older than him, slender with blonde hair cut short and a white scar running down one cheek.

'I knew you'd be up here.'

'It's hardly a secret,' said Andrick. 'Where else would I be?'

'Where you ought to be: in the yard.' She sat down at the other end of the bench. 'Burik came looking for you; I thought you'd rather I found you than him.'

Bloody Burik. The *balhymeri* was the bane of Andrick's life. 'How is he my *balhymeri*? He hates me.'

'I know he works you hard. Probably he wants to prove himself to your mother by moulding you into a warrior; everyone knows he's only *balhymeri* because Lord Orsian's turned Ciera down so many times. When you're eighteen you can dismiss him if that's what you want.'

Andrick laughed, then pulled up his sleeve to reveal his arm. 'Does this look like the arm of a warrior?' It was skinny as a stick. 'It's not fair – he'll make me fight Pitt again. He's ten years older than me!'

'And six inches shorter.' Haisie squeezed his arm at the elbow, and Andrick blushed awkwardly at the feel of her fingers against his skin. 'You're just getting used to your body. You've grown nearly a foot in the last two years – the seamstresses are always complaining about how often they have to let your clothes out.'

Andrick shook his head. 'It's not just my arms.' He looked away from her, embarrassed. 'I'm... scared. I don't like being hit.'

To her credit, Haisie did not laugh. 'Would anyone?' She grinned at him. 'And surely the point is not to get hit.'

'That's not the problem.' Andrick hunched forward and puffed out his cheeks, rubbing his hands through his hair. 'I know it's fine to be scared, but they all expect me to be something I'm not. Being named for the Barrelbreaker is bad enough – I can hardly be expected to live up to the memory of a man who came back from the dead to defeat a god – but everyone else fought in the war. You were only a child, and you've still got the scars to prove you were there! Aunt Pherri was barely older than you! How can I be a king over people who defeated the Imperium and two gods when all I did was piss and cry? Even if I *could* be a warrior, which I can't, it wouldn't change anything. I can't live up to my mother either; the whole country's half in love with her.'

He had blurted out more than he intended, but Andrick decided he might as well keep going. 'Sometimes I think she'd be better off just keeping hold of the crown, or giving it to Rymond Prindian. You know him and Helana have just had their fourth child?'

Haisie nodded. 'Another girl. You'll be able to have your pick.'

Andrick's face twisted in disgust, making Haisie laugh. 'Don't even joke about it. I'm their half-uncle.'

'That's never stopped you nobly borns before.' Haisie raised an eyebrow, smiling wickedly. 'Have you ever looked at your family tree? More of a family bush in places.'

This time Andrick laughed along with Haisie's jest, causing a pair of blackbirds that had been pecking at the flowerbeds to take flight. As anxious as the topic made Andrick, it felt good to make a joke of it, and he had nobody else to laugh about it with.

'I'm serious though,' he said, once their laughter had died down. 'And marriage is another thing, even if my mother promises it doesn't have to be a Prindian, I never asked to be this great hope of a dynasty. It's not fair – nobody else has to get married. Aunt Pherri and Uncle Orsian aren't – how did they get away with it?'

'It's not for want of trying on your mother's part. I doubt there's a noble maid in the country who she's *not* tried to set Lord Orsian up with. And your aunt Pherri...' Haisie lowered her voice. 'You saw her when she last visited. The woman's skin and bone. Your mother sent me to help her dress for dinner and I was almost scared to touch her in case I broke something. At the table she didn't eat a bite. She wastes away a little every year.'

Andrick nodded soberly. 'I know, I know.' He paused, shifting his gaze to contemplate the vast shadow of Eryispek. There had been attempts to rename the Mountain, but none would stick. In the clear summer air, it was easy to make out its features; the steep snow with patches of vegetation on the western side, fading to the arid red clay of the flatter eastern face. 'Is it really true she could do magic? Really?'

'Of course it's true. What, did you think Eryi and Vulgatypha upped and left of their own accord?' Haisie paused, and though there was no danger of being overheard lowered her voice. 'Lady Pherri thinks it's magic disappearing from the world that's caused her illness. She told your mother she doubts she'll be well enough to travel here again.'

Andrick gave a long exhale, resting his elbows on his knees. It was what Haisie had chosen not to say out loud that troubled him: his aunt Pherri was dying. 'I should visit Violet Hall again,' he muttered. Sometimes he thought Pherri was the only one in the family who understood him. He had questions only she could answer, and it might be that he did not have long to ask them.

He rose suddenly. 'You can tell Burik I'm on my way.' He could not hide from his *balhymeri* forever. 'Just give me a moment.'

Haisie rose with him. She looked up at him warningly. 'Promise?'

'Promise.' He took Haisie's hand and squeezed it. 'Thank you.'

Haisie squeezed his hand back. 'You can rely on me, Majesty, for anything. No matter how tall you get, you'll always be the squalling bundle your mother and I carried across East Erland.'

She departed, leaving Andrick alone.

Andrick strode to the north wall of the balcony, staring at Eryispek, fingering the coin in his pocket. He took it out, and held it up to the Mountain, turning it over between the stern profile of the father he could not recall and the crude etching of Eryispek on the other side.

'What does it mean?' he murmured to himself. He could tell no one, at least not until he was sure.

Andrick tossed the coin up and held out his palm, holding both *heads* and *tails* in his mind.

The coin landed on its edge and stayed there, waiting to fall.

A LETTER FROM R.S. MOULE

Dear Reader,

Thank you so much for choosing *The Madness of Gods*. I hope you enjoyed reading it as much as I enjoyed writing it. If so, I would be sincerely grateful if you could leave a rating or review with your retailer. It makes a huge difference, firstly to know that someone enjoyed it, and secondly to encourage interest in the series.

If you have any thoughts you would like to share with me, I would love to hear from you. Please get in touch through any of the links to social media below. These are also a good way to stay notified of my new releases.

If you would like stay informed about my books, just sign up at the following link. Your email address will never be shared, and you can unsubscribe at any time.

www.secondskybooks.com/rs-moule

For the avoidance of doubt, this third volume concludes the Erland Saga, at least for now. I always intended that the Erland Saga would be a three-book series. Yet, as I approached the finishing line of *The Madness of Gods*, I found that I could not quite bear to bring it to a close, hence the slightly open-ended epilogue. Please forgive me. I may one day return to tell the story of what happens next, but for now there are other worlds I want to create and other tales I want to tell. Keep an eye out for those, and some day perhaps we can return to Erland together.

Thank you so much for your support.

Roger Moule, January 2024

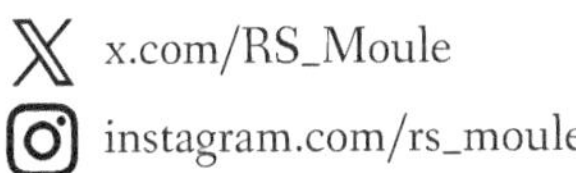

ACKNOWLEDGEMENTS

I wrote the first few hundred awkward words of what eventually became the Erland Saga in August 2015, almost nine years before the publication of this third volume. The journey to finishing and publishing the series would not have been possible without the following people. Thank you.

My wife, Eloise, who tolerates me at my worst and my slightly better. There may be parallel worlds in which we did not meet, but in none of them is there an Erland Saga. I will never stop being grateful.

Our cat, Tinks, who is present for almost every word that goes on the page, whether curled up at my feet or treading over my keyboard.

My sister-in-law, Nina, my second pair of eyes.

My family, who buy too many copies.

My friends, who ask how the next book is going and listen patiently while I complain about lost evenings, deadlines, and the failure of the English language to recognise that the plural of *roof* should be *rooves*.

Aaron Munday, for bringing the series to life with his amazing covers.

Colin Mace, for taking my prose and turning it into audio dynamite.

Rhian McKay and Maureen Cox, for copyediting and proofreading respectively.

Jack Renninson, my editor at Second Sky. If I am a better

writer now than when Jack and I met, and I do hope that I am, that's thanks to Jack.

The whole team at Second Sky. Noelle Holten, Mandy Kullar, Alba Proko, Sarah Hardy, Richard King, Melanie Price, Myrto Kalavrezou, Melissa Tran, Saidah Graham, everyone. There is nobody I would rather trust with my books.

Finally, you, the reader. Sometimes, writing is its own reward, but it's even better when somebody reads it. You make it possible for me to do what I love.

PUBLISHING TEAM

Turning a manuscript into a book requires the efforts of many people. The publishing team at Bookouture would like to acknowledge everyone who contributed to this publication.

Audio
Alba Proko
Sinead O'Connor
Melissa Tran

Commercial
Lauren Morrissette
Jil Thielen
Imogen Allport

Cover design
Aaron Munday

Data and analysis
Mark Alder
Mohamed Bussuri

Editorial
Jack Renninson
Melissa Tran

Copyeditor
Rhian McKay

Proofreader
Maureen Cox

Marketing
Alex Crow
Melanie Price
Occy Carr
Cíara Rosney
Martyna Młynarska

Operations and distribution
Marina Valles
Stephanie Straub

Production
Hannah Snetsinger
Mandy Kullar
Jen Shannon

Publicity
Kim Nash
Noelle Holten
Jess Readett
Sarah Hardy

Rights and contracts
Peta Nightingale
Richard King
Saidah Graham

Milton Keynes UK
Ingram Content Group UK Ltd.
UKHW011958020524
442050UK00004B/146